Thunderclouds in
the Forecast

Thunderclouds in the Forecast

A NOVEL

Clarence Major

TRIQUARTERLY BOOKS / NORTHWESTERN UNIVERSITY PRESS
EVANSTON, ILLINOIS

TriQuarterly Books
Northwestern University Press
www.nupress.northwestern.edu

All names of characters and places and incidents in this novel are fictitious. They are the
invention of the author's imagination. Any resemblance to actual names or factual events or
real persons is entirely coincidental and unintentional.

Printed in the United States of America

10   9   8   7   6   5   4   3   2   1

Library of Congress Cataloging-in-Publication Data

Names: Major, Clarence, author.
Title: Thunderclouds in the forecast : a novel / Clarence Major.
Description: Evanston, Illinois : TriQuarterly Books/Northwestern University Press, 2022.
Identifiers: LCCN 2021019813 | ISBN 9780810144262 (paperback) | ISBN
    9780810144279 (ebook)
Subjects: LCSH: Interracial friendship—Fiction. | Ex–foster children—Fiction. | LCGFT:
    Novels.
Classification: LCC PS3563.A39 T47 2022 | DDC 813/.54—dc23
LC record available at https://lccn.loc.gov/2021019813

Even a blind hog sometimes can find an acorn.

—FOLK SAYING

CONTENTS

Acknowledgments

ix

THUNDERCLOUDS IN THE FORECAST

Part 1. The Instrument of Providence

3

Part 2. Extemporizing Procedure

37

Part 3. A High C Accurately Struck

81

Part 4. The Orgastic Future

135

Part 5. A World Not Yet Born

169

ACKNOWLEDGMENTS

MANY THANKS TO ALL THE skillful people who saw this novel through the publication process and who worked to give it a public presence: Parneshia Jones, Maia Rigas, Erin DeWitt, Anne T. Strother, Olivia Aguilar, Anne Gendler, JD Wilson, Pamela Major, and so many others. To them all I am deeply grateful.

Thunderclouds in
the Forecast

PART 1

The Instrument of Providence

What is called chance is the instrument of Providence and the secret agent that counteracts what men call wisdom, and preserves order and regularity . . .

—HORACE WALPOLE TO THE COUNTESS OF OSSORY, JANUARY 19, 1777

1

IT WAS SATURDAY, THE MIDDLE of April, and it was noon. A local freight boxcar was blocking the tracks. The conductor said, "We'll be here at least an hour, maybe longer. Folks, if you want, get off and do a little sightseeing here in little old Lorena—go ahead, but don't go too far. If you're not back here by one o'clock, we might leave without you. It all depends on how soon they can get that boxcar moved off our tracks."

Ray was thirsty and headed for Main Street in town. There he quickly found Wynn's Old Beer Tavern. The second he entered the place, the yeasty smell overwhelmed him. Coming in from the bright sunny day, he paused for a second just inside the doorway to let his eyes adjust, then he looked around. He saw the bartender behind the long, ancient curving bar. He was a balding guy, maybe thirty-five or forty, in a denim shirt washed so many times the blue had faded to gray.

Then Ray saw there was only one customer, standing at the far end of the bar. He was a tall and straggly man with dirty blond hair and an unkempt blond mustache stained with tobacco juice.

Ray walked over to the bar and stopped at the first stool he came to and sat down. The bartender, frowning, came up the bar to him and stood there looking at him. Finally, he said, "Yeah?"

"I'd like a glass of your house beer."

Slowly and without losing his frown, the bartender picked up a tall glass from the tray on the counter behind the bar and pumped beer into it.

The blond man down the bar was staring at Ray. Finally, he called out: "Say, fella, you from 'round here?"

"No, just passing through."

"Well, make sure you keep going. We don't like your kind in this town." Then he drained his glass.

The bartender said, "Pete, you want another one?"

"No, Bill, thanks, not now."

The blond man slammed his empty glass down and walked toward the front door.

As he was passing Ray, his shoulder bumped Ray's back.

Ray swung around. "Hey! Watch where you're walking."

"What?"

"You heard me," Ray snapped.

The blond guy swung at Ray, but Ray lifted his arm and blocked the blow of the stranger's fist.

The man called Pete then backed up, glaring at him, and continued drunkenly over to and out through the saloon doors with the doors swinging behind him.

Bill the bartender was grinning now and staring at Ray.

"What's with that guy?"

Bill said, "Lorena is a small town. We don't see many strangers coming through here unless they're coming to the university. That's all." He paused, then said, "Can I ask where you from?"

"New York."

"It figures," said Bill, smirking. "How happen you turn up here in Lorena, California?"

Ray hesitated, not sure how to answer or even if he should answer. Then he said, "I'm headed for San Francisco."

"You're better off in San Francisco than here. In a little town like Lorena, a lot of folks are set in their ways, if you know what I mean; but that fella Bill actually lives over in Godwin. There are a lot of good old boys like him over there. They don't mean no harm." He paused, chuckling. "Just visiting San Francisco?"

Ray decided not to mention Scotty. He said, "Yeah."

"Well, good luck."

Ray put money on the bar.

"Keep your money," said Bill. "Consider that one on the house."

A half hour later Ray was eating a taco in nearby Jo Jo's Café when he heard the Amtrak train start up and pull out of Lorena. He looked at his Timex watch. It was ten to one. *Dammit*, his watch was slow!

"Dammit," he said out loud, "I missed my train." He turned to the woman sitting two stools over and said, "Excuse me, miss, what time do you have?"

She looked at her watch. "It's one thirty. I heard you say you missed your train. There's always another train coming through here. Where're you headed?"

"San Francisco."

She laughed. "Another train will be here at four this afternoon. Why not enjoy our little town till then?"

Ray looked at her eyes. They were gray green in a round face with fat cheeks. It was a face full of playful expectation. She had generous unpainted lips and a dimple in her prominent chin. Her red hair had grown out now so far that the blond roots were showing.

Ray said, "Sounds like a good idea."

She said, "My name is Alice, Alice Whitney. I have a middle name, but I use it only when I sign legal documents. It's Lorraine."

"Lorraine! Were you named after Lorena?"

"No, unfortunately, I was not. Lorraine was my grandmother's first name. Alice was my great-grandmother's name."

She looked to be thirty-nine or forty, about ten years older than he was.

"I'm Ray, Ray Jansen, nice to meet you, Alice. You're a Lorena native?"

"Sure am."

"You got any recommendations for how I might spend my time here in Lorena while waiting for the train?"

"I got a lot of recommendations, Ray, but I'd better tell you only the polite ones." She laughed again.

He was thinking maybe he should just buy a paperback novel and sit on a bench in the waiting room or out on the station platform and read and wait for the train. He'd always loved reading mysteries and detective

7

and science fiction novels. That's how he got through lonely and often miserable adolescent years in the shelter. No, why do that now? That's something he could do anytime.

Ray felt attracted to Alice. He liked her laughter; it was done with her whole body. She was relaxed and easygoing. He wasn't surprised at his attraction. He'd always been attracted to older women, especially motherly types. Alice struck him as motherly. He said, "You can tell me the nice ones and the not-so-nice ones too. I don't mind."

She chuckled. "No, it wouldn't do any good. You'd have to stay here at least a few days."

He was beginning to like her even more. He said, "Well, maybe I could stay here a few days."

"Did you have luggage?"

"Yes, just a suitcase with a tennis racket and balls and some clothes in it. I figure Amtrak will somehow get my suitcase back to me. If not, it was just stuff I can replace easily: shirts, pants, underwear, socks, and stuff like that."

Ray looked out the window and saw a man walking along the sidewalk. He was wearing a ten-gallon cowboy hat and expensive cowboy boots. Ray said, "What kind of town is this?"

"It's a good town," the woman said. "The town was named in 1895 in memory of Madame Lorena. In the 1840s she ran a brothel here for miners. They were men from all over who'd caught the gold rush fever. From the 1850s through the 1870s, they called it No Name Town. Hotel Lorena now stands where her brothel once stood. When she became respectable and rich, she tore down the brothel and built Hotel Lorena in its place. When the bank wouldn't do business with her, she bought the bank. She also got the city to okay card club gambling at the Casino Lorena on the first floor of the hotel. The ballroom is where the casino used to be back in the nineteenth century; but gambling now is illegal throughout the state except on reservations."

"Madame Lorena sounds like quite a character."

"She was. Very few ever knew her last name, which was Borrego. To everybody back then, she was always just Madame Lorena or Lady Lorena."

"A good name: Lorena."

"Yes, and also in 1895 they had a sculptor from Seattle make a ten-foot statue of her out of stone, and they put it up in the little downtown park. I can show it to you later if you'd like to see it."

"You've done your research."

"I work at the university, Lorena State University. I'm CAO in the Ag Department. During my lunch break I sometimes sit in the campus library and read while eating my sandwich. Today being Saturday I felt like getting away from home for lunch."

He smiled and nodded.

"Shortly after Lorena's statue went up, the city council voted to start a college where people could study mining and farming. The mining department didn't last long because the gold rush fever ended in disillusionment around 1855."

"Suddenly it was over?"

"Yes. The only people besides Lorena who got rich were the merchants in towns serving the miners and that guy named Levi down in San Francisco making trousers for the men."

"What about farming?"

"For several decades the farming department evolved into the heartbeat of the town and the school, and by the end of World War One LSU, then known as Lorena State College, had evolved into one of California's best-known agriculture colleges, and later it became a university when we started offering a graduate degree. The farmers around here depend on us for a lot of know-how."

Ray didn't know what else to say.

She continued, "We also have a low crime rate in this town. We're a town of conservatives and liberals and some in-between people."

"You should maybe run for office."

She laughed. "I've thought about it. But seriously, ours is a friendly little college town. We've got a lively farmers market and a greenbelt and manicured parks, and a stream named Tranquilo Creek that runs through town. It's very pretty and peaceful down by the creek. I go there sometimes just to relax and stop thinking about things."

"Population?"

She said, "About sixty-eight thousand."

"Small, huh? What are the demographics here?"

9

"According to the last US Census report there were forty-two thousand white people and six hundred African Americans and three hundred Native Americans and fourteen thousand Asians and several thousand people identified as other."

"So, if I stay overnight or a couple of days, I won't be the only African American in town?"

"Not by a long shot. Unlike Godwin, Lorena has always welcomed people of color of all types. Godwin used to have a policy of no blacks after dark. It was that kind of town. If a black person was caught there after dark, he or she was likely to be beaten up or even arrested. The police and yahoos worked together."

"You must have a great memory to retain such information."

"I do have a great memory."

"I'll need a hotel room."

Alice smiled. "Sure. Hotel Lorena is the best in town."

2

ALICE PARKED HER WHITE 1975 Plymouth Fury in front of her house. It was a white house with shiplap walls. To the left of the entrance there was a swing on the front porch. It was painted red and suspended from the porch roof. The paint was peeling, and the chains looked rusty.

Ray got out and followed Alice up onto the squeaky front porch.

At that moment the screen door flew open and a chubby girl, about fifteen, came running out. She was blond with gray-green eyes and a rosy-pink complexion.

She clearly was distressed. She shouted, "Mom, Hope is acting like a bitch again! I'm so *sick* of her. I want her to move and stay with Dad. Why can't she live with Dad?"

Alice glanced at Ray apologetically. "Margo, now is not the time to discuss this kind of nonsense."

The girl was now looking critically at Ray.

Alice said, "Margo, this is Ray," and to him: "Ray, this is my oldest daughter, Margo."

As Margo and Ray exchanged greetings, she said, "Ray what? What's your last name?"

He said, "Jansen, Raymond Jansen."

"How do you know my mom? Who *are* you?"

He liked Margo's straightforwardness. He said, "I met Alice downtown at Jo Jo's Café during lunch. I'm from Brooklyn, New York, on my way to San Francisco. I liked her and the town so much, I decided to stay a little while. She showed me to a hotel. Your mom had to stop at her office to pick up something, then she came back to my hotel and invited me to dinner and here we are."

"You're having *dinner* with us?"

"I think that's the idea. Is that okay with you?"

"It's okay with me. I don't eat at the same time Mom eats. I don't like the way she chews."

At that moment another girl, younger, maybe twelve years old, burst out onto the porch. She was darker and skinny with dark brown hair and big black eyes in seemingly a permanent state of anger and alarm.

Margo said to the girl, "Hope, this is Raymond Jansen, somebody Mom picked up downtown. Apparently, he's having dinner with her tonight."

Alice said, "Margo, you don't have to sneer when you talk."

"I wasn't *sneering*."

Hope said, "I'm not eating dinner tonight so it's no concern of mine." She turned, opened the screen door, and flew back into the house, slamming the screen door behind her.

Alice looked at Ray and said, "Teenagers. See what I have to put up with?"

After Alice and Ray ate a dinner of burgers and green beans at her dining room table, she took the plates into the kitchen, where Hope was standing at the counter eating cornflakes out of a soup bowl.

Ray got up and stood in the kitchen doorway. "That's your dinner?"

In a resentful voice, Hope said, "Yeah." She kept her sight lowered on her cornflakes.

Alice said, "Where's Margo?"

"In her room."

They could hear rock-and-roll music coming from Margo's room just off the kitchen.

"Margo!" shouted Alice.

Margo opened the door and stuck her head out. "What d'you want? I'm busy!"

"Listen, I'm taking Mr. Jansen back to his hotel. After that I'm going to look in on Rita. She's been sick in bed for a few days now. I want you and Hope to clean the bathroom and wash the dishes. I mean it! When I come back, I *don't* want to see dishes in the sink!"

Margo rolled her eyes, looking toward the ceiling, and mumbled something under her breath.

Hope said, "It's Margo's turn. I washed them this morning."

"I don't care," said Alice. "You work it out between the two of you. I want it done, and for God's sake, clean up that filthy bathroom too!"

3

HOTEL LORENA WAS A BIG red-stone three-story building stretching a full block. You knew on sight that the hotel was a relic of the previous century.

As Ray and Alice approached the front desk, Ray saw that the desk clerk who'd checked him in earlier had been replaced by the night clerk.

"Welcome to Hotel Lorena, I'm Tom Hobson," said the clerk. Pinned to his shirt was an insignia with his name. He was a healthy-looking, tall, red-headed young man with a red beard and mustache; he carried himself in an erect self-important manner. His hair was parted on the side and neatly cut and combed, and his blue eyes dared you to challenge him in any way.

Ray said, "I checked in earlier. I'm in room two thirty-three."

Hobson turned to the mailboxes and took a key out of box 233. "Here you are, sir."

Alice stood silently beside Ray.

Standing there, Ray looked around. Earlier he hadn't had a chance to really see this amazing hotel lobby. Off to the left, down the hallway with its marble floor from Italy, was the gift shop and the bar, and to the right was the Lorena Restaurant.

"If you need anything," said Hobson, "just call down to the front desk. I'll be here or Marie Valdez, the other night clerk, will be here."

The hotel radiated quaint charm. On the way in, he'd noticed that some of the upper rooms had fancy iron balconies. He had also noticed that those rooms had windows rounded at the top. Ray assumed they were the expensive suites. He could well afford one, but he felt no need for such a room.

Ray and Alice stepped away from the desk and stopped at the stairway.

He said, "Well, Alice, I guess this is goodbye, at least for now."

Alice said, "Actually, I've never seen the rooms here. They're supposed to be really quaint and interesting. They say Lorena herself designed the layout for the rooms, the whole place, really. In any case, she told the architect how she wanted everything done. She was in her eighties when she built this place."

"You want to come up and take a look?"

She said, "I'd love to."

There was no elevator. As they were walking up the steps, Ray said, "I feel like we're back in another time."

"I know what you mean."

With the big iron key, Ray unlocked the door and invited Alice to walk in first. Hesitantly, she stepped inside and quickly looked around. She said, "Wow! This *is* quaint."

The door opened into a little sitting room with a fancy coat rack and a gold and red ornate bench. The walls of the sitting area and the room had light blue wallpaper with a rose design. Across from the bench was the closet.

Alice went to the bathroom and he followed her.

"Look at that *sink*!" she said.

It was a brass bowl with a faucet.

"And the toilet!" she cried.

The toilet bowl was gray, and the base was in the shape of a bent knee.

They returned to the bedroom. Alice sat down on the side of the bed and with a fixed smile of amazement continued to look around. She said, "I think you'll be comfortable here. Don't you?"

"Yes," he said, and walked over and stood in front of her. He reached down for her hand, and she gave it to him. He kissed it. "Thank you," he said in a gentle whisper.

15

She was staring up at him with a look of unmistakable longing or more specifically desire.

Ray knew what was about to happen. He leaned down and their lips met in a soft kiss, then he sat down beside her, and they continued to kiss. Five minutes later they were undressed and under the cool covers and locked in a warm embrace.

Afterward, they sat up side by side in the bed against stacks of pillows covered with pillowcases designed with a nineteenth-century woman dressed in white carrying a blue and pink parasol. Alice asked, "So, why are you going to San Francisco?"

He smiled. "I'm going to try to locate an old friend, a guy I grew up with. We were in a shelter in Brooklyn."

"A shelter? You grew up in a shelter?" Alice's eyes widened.

"Sure did; eighteen years. I was born a ward of the state of New York. I lived for a brief time with three different families. It was on a trial basis. It was always on a trial basis. The Jansen family was the first. They gave me the name Jansen. I never understood why because they didn't really adopt me. They wanted to, but the state said no to them. At the shelter they were already calling me Raymond, because of a street in Brooklyn."

"Wow!" she said. "Why were you named after a street in Brooklyn?"

"The church was on that street. As an infant I was found in one of those boxes that cornflakes are shipped to stores in. The box was left on the doorstep of Holy Angels Church on Raymond Street in Bedford-Stuyvesant, Brooklyn."

Again she said, "Wow!"

"Later, at Dorchester Supermarket whenever I saw one of those boxes the boys were unpacking to restock the shelves with cornflakes, something happened in me. I wanted to cry but I couldn't, then I felt angry. It was strange."

"I understand that," she said.

"It wasn't so bad. I learned early on how to take care of myself. At least I wasn't a baby found in a dumpster the way my friend Scott O'Brien was."

"Is he the friend in San Francisco?"

"That's right. We were so close, a couple of times we were chosen together for foster care. One time they kept him and sent me back. The other times they kept me and sent him back." Ray laughed.

16

"How'd you two get to be so close?"

"I think it started when we were eight and nine or even earlier. Scotty was nine and I was eight when one Saturday afternoon he and another boy named Cole and I were tossing a ball back and forth on the sidewalk in front of the shelter. Suddenly, just horsing around, Cole pushed me out into the street in front of an oncoming car. He thought it was a fun thing to do. Just a thoughtless moment on his part. I was lying in the street dazed because my head had hit the pavement. But Scotty acted quickly: he grabbed my legs and pulled me out of the way of the oncoming car just in time. The car just missed my head by a couple of inches."

"Oh, my God, that's terrible," said Alice. "Kids can do some dumb things, but you were lucky, and I see why you value his friendship. He saved your life."

"Ironically, Scotty usually was the one in trouble. Before he was fifteen, he was arrested several times for stealing. At fifteen they took him out of the shelter and sent him to reform school. Six months there and they sent him back to the shelter. Again, when he was seventeen, he was sent back to reform school, this time for fighting. One time he stole a car to go for a joyride. He left it parked somewhere. That one he got away with."

"Some friend you have! That must have been a crazy time for you."

"Yeah, but I tried to focus on positive things. Scotty wasn't all bad. He had a lot of bad luck. When he was sixteen, one of the girls in the girls' shelter accused him of getting her pregnant, but Scotty insisted that the baby wasn't his. He got married when he was twenty-one. That marriage lasted a year and half. Then he got married again when he was twenty-five. That marriage also ended quickly. All his life he's worked all kinds of jobs, mostly low-income jobs: construction work and tree trimming and handyman work, then he finally learned the art of bartending. He's now a good bartender and has no trouble finding work. Scotty is a hopeless romantic and a wanderer; but like I said, when I think of Scotty, I try to focus on the positive things. He actually attended CUNY for almost a year. At that point I thought he was turning his life around. At CUNY, he was great at math and his grades were excellent. He's an intelligent guy. With more focus, Scotty could become somebody, maybe a mathematician, even a professor of mathematics. Who knows? For someone left in a dumpster to die when he was an infant, he could have done worse. That was not a promising start in life, but I like to think that Scotty *still* has potential to do something other than tending bar, not that there is anything wrong with tending bar. It's a worthy skill and it has served him well. Thinking positive is my motto!"

"Yes, he saved your life. That was positive. That was heroic!"

"From an early age we shared an interest in sports, especially football and basketball. We were both Giants fans, but I had a great admiration for any amazing player, like quarterback Terry Bradshaw of the Pittsburgh Steelers and running back Walter Payton of the Chicago Bears and cornerback Willie Brown of the Oakland Raiders; there were so many great players Scotty and I used to watch on TV. We couldn't afford to go to games, but most of all we admired the great players of the New York Giants, guys like running back Frank Gifford, and fullback Franco Harris and linebacker Jack Ham of the Pittsburgh Steelers."

"I've heard some of those names, but I'm no big football fan, sorry."

"You might think kids living in a shelter wouldn't be members of the Boy Scouts, but Scotty and I were."

"I'm not surprised you were in the Boy Scouts. So, you knew nothing about your parents?"

"Nothing! I was just three or four days old when the janitor of the church found me in a cardboard box on the doorstep. Like I said, it was Holy Angels in Bedford-Stuyvesant. They estimated my birth date as August seventeenth."

"That's really sad, Ray."

"It's a weird way to start out, but I've done pretty well."

"You mind if I ask what kind of work you do?"

"I was manager in a supermarket, Dorchester Supermarket, in Bedford-Stuyvesant."

"Is that what you plan to do in San Francisco, work in a supermarket?"

"No! I have enough to hold me for a while. I won the lottery last year. I was one of the winners. There were three of us. I was the big winner. So, I won a lot of money, but I'm not wealthy, not filthy rich."

"Was this the New York State Lottery?"

"That's right."

"And what were the numbers?"

"Eighty-two, twenty-two, ninety-seven, seventy-two, sixty-six, and ninety-nine."

"You're the first person I've ever met to win a lottery; sounds like you are sitting pretty."

"Not even close, but I have enough to last a while." He was not going to tell her how much he'd won, although he knew if she wanted to, she could easily find out.

"How long is a while?"

"Maybe a couple of years. I've invested most of it and maybe it will grow."

"Does your friend Scott know you won the lottery?"

"No. He's going to be shocked." He laughed. "On second thought, maybe he won't be shocked. He's had so many shocks in his life by now, he's probably shock-proof."

"Is Scotty African American?"

"No, he's white."

She nodded, smiling.

"With his good looks, Scotty broke a lot of hearts and he's apparently not done. Sure, when he went to jail, he got a lighter sentence than the black boy next to him for the same crime."

"Can't blame him for the court's racism," she said.

"I know. Despite the tension that was always there between us, we were brothers; and we're *still* brothers."

"What kind of tension?"

"You know, the stuff the world forced on us." He paused. "Circumstances forced Scotty and me together. Scotty and I lived once with a family, the Coopers. It was on a trial basis—it was usually on a trial basis. Often it didn't go beyond that. They were a family of four: Dale and Natalie and their two kids, an eleven-year-old girl called Honey and the boy, William, otherwise known as Billy-Boy. At the dinner table, Dale and Natalie, Honey and Billy, got the best cuts and the largest portions. Mrs. Cooper doled out the food with the strictness of a drill sergeant. Scotty and I, in a sense, got the leftovers. We did all the housework and yard work such as cleaning and carrying out the garbage and mowing the lawn and cleaning gutters. Like so many families that took us in on a trial basis, they simply wanted two strong teenage boys as workhorses."

Alice said, "Well, that's unfortunate; but I would like to think that human beings are better than that, at least most of the time."

"I would too." He paused. "A black family applied for me once, but in the end, they were unqualified and rejected. One of the white families Scotty and I were chosen by was the Halberstam family. They treated us well. I mean, they didn't treat Scotty better than they treated me. We both had to work but they weren't working us like slaves the way the Coopers did."

"By the way, you came on the train—why didn't you *fly* out here?" she asked.

"I've never been on an airplane, and I'm not sure I want to fly."

"Oh, you're afraid of flying?"

"Yes. I'm afraid to try it, but I'm going to have to one day because I'd like to travel to other countries."

She clicked her tongue against the roof of her mouth then said, "What d'you plan to do when your money runs out?"

"The next time I work it will be for myself. What about you? You know everything about me now and I know nothing about you."

"Well, you know I have two kids. I was married. My ex-husband, Don, is CEO of a spring water bottling company down in Atlanta; company's called Sky Blue. A division of Sky Blue is also in Godwin, a little town near here. Don was working there as a manager during the years of our marriage, then they decided to give him a promotion, which meant moving him to Atlanta."

"Yeah, I've heard of Sky Blue. We had it at Dorchester."

"Dorchester?"

"The supermarket in Brooklyn where I worked."

"Oh. Don and I are on friendly terms. At first, we weren't, but for the kids' sake now we've worked it out. We've declared a truce. He comes up to visit the kids about twice a year. I sometimes let them go down there for a couple of weeks in the summer. This summer they don't want to go, so I guess he'll be coming up here in the summer. Their going down there gives me a break from all the teenage craziness." She chuckled. "Where'd you go to school, Ray?"

"Clarkson University in Potsdam. I majored in business management. How about you?"

"Clarkson is Ivy League. Lucky you! I also majored in business. I guess I stuck with it and ended up with a BSBA from Berkeley, which turned out to be a good thing because I managed to get a good-paying job. Originally, I wanted to go into one of the sciences, something like biochemistry or physics, but my abilities at abstract stuff and higher math were not good enough. I switched to business. My folks were happy as a hog in slop."

"A scientist, huh?"

"Yes," Alice said. "When was the last time you saw your friend Scott?"

"Six months ago. I saw him the day before he left the city. We were drinking beer and sharing a pizza in Anna's Pizza Parlor on the boardwalk at Coney Island, Scotty said, 'I've never felt at home anywhere, not in the shelter, not in the foster homes,' and he looked at me and he knew I felt the same way. I guess you can see we both are still searching for a place to call home."

Ray didn't tell Alice that for years while growing up, he lay awake in bed at night wondering who his birth parents were and why they gave him up. He fantasized that his mother was a teenage girl who had gotten knocked up by a teenage boy. Probably both were high school kids and in no position to raise a child.

Or maybe his parents were married adults and the wife, his mother, had gotten pregnant by her lover and her husband forced her to give up the child.

Or even worse, his mother was a prostitute who got pregnant and left the child in a cardboard box that had originally held boxes of cornflakes.

4

Two hours later alice got dressed. While she was looking in the mirror in the sitting area and combing her hair, she asked, "Are you still planning to leave for San Francisco tomorrow?"

He hesitated. He thought about the question. Except for his now-delayed quest to track down Scotty, he certainly had no pressing business to tend to in San Francisco.

Scotty wasn't expecting him tomorrow. Ray hadn't told his friend exactly when he would arrive. All he'd said on a postcard was "Coming out there soon." He wanted to surprise Scotty.

What was there to prevent him from staying here in Lorena for a few days? He could catch a train to San Francisco, an hour and a half from here, any day of the week.

Ray said, "I ran into a little bit of a problem in a bar before I met you."

"What happened?"

Ray told her exactly what happened, and she said, "Sure, there are people like that here, but they don't represent the spirit of Lorena. This is primarily a liberal college town. Guys like that are usually from Godwin. It's a little hick town northwest of us."

Well, he thought, *sure. There are people like that guy anywhere and everywhere, even in a liberal college town.*

22

Later she said, "I wish you'd stay at least a few days. We could have fun, do things together. Tomorrow is Sunday; we could go on a picnic up in the mountains."

He thought about the word "fun." Wasn't that also what he was after? He hadn't planned to find it in Lorena, California.

"Let's talk about it tomorrow," he said. "Can you come have breakfast with me?"

"Let's make it lunch. Noon?"

"Sure."

She came over and kissed him on the lips. "See you tomorrow."

5

RAY WAS STANDING OUTSIDE Hotel Lorena's front entrance Sunday at noon when Alice drove up in her Plymouth. Behind the wheel she looked ten years younger and happy as all get-out.

The minute he climbed into the passenger's seat, she said, "You're looking spiffy. I made some sandwiches and got a couple of bottles of white wine. Should we go up into the hills and find a nice secluded spot to have our picnic?"

He thought it sounded fine and said, "Yes. Perfect."

The drive up the narrow road into the foothills and beyond was unlike anything Ray had experienced since he was twelve, when a group of kids from the shelter were taken by bus up into the Adirondacks, where they spent a couple of days camping. It was his first time out of the city.

The guide had been a plump, kindly woman with a square face and light brown hair turning white in random places. They had several sessions with her. She explained the plants and the wildlife to the kids. Ray was surprised to discover how interested he was in nature: the flowers, such as trout lilies, pink lady slippers, sorrels, spotted touch-me-nots, dewdrops; pine and larch and spruce trees; and the hobblebush, steeplebush, and wild raisin shrubbery.

The guide talked about the Adirondacks' native wolves, bull moose, and brown and black bears; she also talked about the cougars, eagles, foxes, bobcats, owls, hawks, and their habitats. Ray and the other kids had seen some of these animals in picture books and at the Bronx Zoo, but to be told that they were running freely in this very area excited his imagination.

This was a whole new world to Ray. It was during those days in the Adirondacks that he discovered how limited his world had been. That trip excited his imagination about the rest of the world beyond Brooklyn.

He never forgot that trip, but the outing was never repeated. He memorized many of the names of plants and animals he had seen and even looked them up in the *Encyclopaedia Britannica* at the shelter's library.

The clearing he and Alice found was a spot surrounded by summer red paintbrush flowers and yellow poppies and young pine with a pungent aroma. They spread Alice's colorful blanket across a bed of young grass growing in the clearing and sat down facing each other. You could see that this was an area recovering from a devastating fire.

As they were setting up, Alice said, "Tonight I have to go to a faculty gathering at Phil Crosby's house; he's the chair. It's just a social gathering. He likes to do things like this to give faculty and staff a chance to get to know each other on a friendly basis. They are all pretty much couples, and I hate arriving single all the time. Would you be interested in going with me as my escort?"

Ray hesitated, then said, "Sure," but he was wondering how he was going to talk with those people about farming or methods for improving vegetables. He knew nothing about the subject. Maybe they would talk about day-to-day things. He would wing it and finesse it. Those were things he was good at.

During his college years, Ray played poker. He got to be pretty good. At the poker table, he learned a lot about how to get along in a group and how to keep afloat and how to read people, but he was still working on his empathy. At the party he figured he should have no problem.

Alice opened the basket and took out a bottle of white wine and a corkscrew. "Would you do the honors?"

"Sure." He took the corkscrew and the bottle and expertly uncorked it with a tiny pop, something he'd learned to do at college parties.

Alice already had two paper cups ready. Ray carefully poured wine into the cups till they were two-thirds full.

"Perfecto!" said Alice, taking a sip. "Tell me what it was like at the shelter."

He recorked the bottle and propped it against the basket. Looking up at the sky, he said, "Sometimes I want to weep when I think about all those boys and girls Scotty and I grew up with at the Brooklyn children's shelter."

"That was the name?"

"The nickname. Formally it was called the John Paul Christopher Children's Shelter, established in 1895. It's in a landmark building."

"What a place to grow up in."

"Yes, and even today to think of those kids makes me feel sad. There were orphans, runways, bullies, broken kids, kids with broken hearts, some with mental illness, and they would be sent to juvenile hall, military academies, boot camps, and reform schools. Many of them had mothers who were prostitutes or junkies or just unfortunate people with serious mental illnesses barely holding on to life, and maybe their fathers were criminals or drunks or just unfortunate broken people. Scotty and I were among a lot of angry, lonely kids, many of them fighting back as bullies, many caving in to the overwhelming conditions they were living under. And maybe we were a bit broken ourselves. Some of those kids turned to crime or drugs; some killed themselves—they couldn't take it."

"Sounds awful, Ray." She sighed. "What do you plan to do when you find your friend Scott in San Francisco?"

He hesitated. "We'll probably get caught up, drink beer and talk, go out for dinner. When Scotty and I get together, we solve the problems of the world. *I* tend to solve the problems of the world. He dismisses any kind of attempt at such a thing. He's more cynical than I am. I think Scotty has given up on finding any goodness in humanity, but I hope I'm wrong about that."

"Huh," uttered Alice. "What kind of guy is Scott, anyway? I find it's pretty rare for two men to be close friends unless they have something special in common, a profession, a passion for shooting guns or sports or art or music or philosophy or politics."

"I told you how he saved my life; but later as teenagers, Scotty and I were into one thing after another. We agreed on a lot of things. At one point we were into karate and jiujitsu, kickboxing and judo, that kind of stuff. We went through phases. We got passionate about music. He had a trumpet at one point that Mrs. Kohler, the shelter director, made him get rid of. He got Mr. Willis, one of the janitors, to pawn it for him and ended up with about a tenth of what it was worth."

Ray sipped his wine. "Scotty and I enjoy each other's company. Or, at least we used to when we were kids. Later he was at City and I was at Clarkson, but we got together a lot and even double-dated a few times. Scotty dropped out of CUNY during his first year. He'd majored in mathematics. It's just like Scotty to pick something like mathematics, a subject he knew nothing about, just grabbed it out of thin air, and said, 'Wow, this is something I want to learn more about.' Scotty has a good mind, but he avoids using it. He's scattered. He was always mocking serious discussion and in so doing actually *involving* himself in serious discussion, perhaps unwittingly."

"How do you mean?" Alice frowned and took a sip of wine.

"In trying to discuss, say, the merits of democracy versus fascism, the role of the individual in society. Scotty was lighthearted about every-thing. I'd say something serious like how easy it is for societies to fall under authoritarianism or fascism, and he'd laugh and make a joke; and he'd say something like, 'They get what they deserve.' I guess the fact that I was the serious one and he was the joker made us a good match. You know what I mean?"

"I think so," she said. "Like a comedy team?"

"Well, not exactly, but touché."

"No offense. You guys reversed the traditional comedy act."

"How so?"

She laughed. "The black guy used to be the clown and the white guy the straight and serious one—but that was back in the fifties when the Rat Pack were using Sammy Davis as the butt of their jokes." She laughed again.

Ray didn't laugh. "I see your point."

Alice said, "In college at UC Berkeley I took a course called Culture of American Humor. We spent a whole week on blackface comedy. I'm talking about the blackface comedy routines of vaudeville. There were a *few* Negro comedy teams like the minstrel team of Williams and Walker. They were billed as 'two real coons.' If a black man was light-skinned like Bert Williams, he'd have to black-up with charcoal and paint his lips to make them appear bigger just to keep the howling audience happy."

"That was back in the 1890s?" Ray said.

"Yes," Alice said. "Ray, you must have been a beautiful kid because you're almost too handsome for any woman."

"That's not how I see myself."

"The way you see yourself and the way the world sees you are two different things." She paused. "When you got out of the shelter, what did you do, where did you go? Did you find work and a girlfriend?"

"When I turned eighteen, I left the shelter. I had forty dollars in my wallet when I moved into a cheap hotel on the edge of the East Village. The owner knew I was looking for a job. I got lucky. Mr. Swartz was his name. One day he said, 'Why don't you run the front desk for me?' and I did."

"That was luck," she said.

"Yep! Sure was." He smiled. "I enrolled that same month at Clarkson for business administration."

"Did you find a girlfriend?"

"Yes, but not in college. A month before my nineteenth birthday, I met a beautiful woman named Joanne Davis. She owned and ran a little pet shop next door to the hotel called Joanna's Bow-Wows and Meows Pet Shop. I noticed she would smile at me when I passed by. One day she was out on the sidewalk where she kept some pets in cages trying to attract customers. She asked me my name and one thing led to another. A couple of weeks later we were in a serious relationship."

"She must have been a good bit older than you, huh?"

"Yes. She *said* she was thirty-five, but I suspect she was older, maybe forty or so. She and I were together for about six months, then she was charged by the government with income tax evasion; and that led to her almost having a nervous breakdown. She thought they were picking on her because she was African American. She worried so much that her personality changed. She was caught up in lawyers and government threats. She feared she was going to jail. She had white friends who had the same kind of tax problems who were not harassed as she was. The government tried to also charge her with tax fraud, but that case fell through. Our relationship suffered during that time. Eventually she had to pay so much in back taxes that she lost her business. She ended up a broken person. Her troubles ended our relationship. Eventually she moved back to Columbus, Ohio, to live with her sister."

"That's sounds pretty awful," said Alice, shaking her head.

"It changed me. I loved Joanne, and the things that happened to her broke my heart."

After a period of awkward silence, Alice said, "You must have had girlfriends before and after Joanne?"

He looked at her expectant expression. "I was very shy around girls. Later on, in college during my second and third year, I dated but nothing serious came of any of it. Sure, when I went to work at the supermarket, I had a crush on a divorced woman. Her name was Lee. She was also African American."

"Wow! You *do* like them older, don't you?"

He said, "As I said before, Scotty and I double-dated a few times; just platonic stuff. With him being at City and me at Clarkson, it wasn't an everyday thing, but we got together for football games and beer parties and just hanging out and catching games on TV with other guys and sometimes girls. Once we even took two girls to a football game that they weren't interested in. They got there and fell in love with football."

"How were you paying the bills?"

"I was still the desk clerk at the hotel, working nights and going to school during the day."

"And Scotty?"

"By the time he dropped out of City, he was tending bar in Manhattan and making a pretty good living. He had a small apartment and he was doing pretty well."

She took out more sandwiches and handed Ray one; as he was unwrapping it, she looked at his and said, "Ham and cheese on rye with mayo."

"My favorite." He bit into it and began to chew. It was good. The bread had the right amount of crunch contrasted with the smooth Gouda cheese and the creamy mayo and salty ham.

29

Alice said, "What was the first thing you did once you realized you'd won the lottery?"

"I was in shock. I walked around in a daze."

"When you got access to actual cash, what did you do?"

"I invested some; I put some in the bank as ready cash. Then I sat down with my lawyer and figured out which charities I wanted to donate to. I set up at my bank regular monthly donations to go to several organizations that fight injustice and bigotry of all kinds."

"To reduce your taxes?"

"No, to help in the struggle."

"What struggle?"

"The struggle against injustice and bigotry."

"Oh."

Around seven, Alice and Ray arrived at the chair's home; it was up a hill and in a row of similar rather plain wood-framed houses. This was an older, well-to-do neighborhood. The houses were built during a period of American prosperity just after World War Two.

A large man with a receding hairline and deep-set eyes opened the door with a big smile. "Hey, Alice! How you doing? Come on in! Who's your friend?"

"Philip, this is Ray Jansen. Ray, Philip Crosby."

As Ray and Philip shook hands, Ray felt the chair squeeze his hand unnecessarily hard. Ray guessed Philip was trying to send him some kind of message.

They were standing just inside the doorway. Philip closed the front door. Ray could hear the buzz of the party back somewhere in the house: excited chatter and glasses clinking and the Bee Gees singing "Jive Talking."

Right behind big Philip was a skinny woman with a hard face, a face that reflected much heartache. Her lips were thin, and her hair was thinning. She would have a bald spot in a few years. Philip said, "Ray, this is my wife, Hazel, Hazel Godfrey. When we got married, she was wise not to take my name. After all she has *God* in her name." He burst into a booming laugh that rocked his sizable stomach.

"Nice to meet you, Hazel," Ray said, smiling.

"You too," she said. "Don't listen to Phil. I kept my family name because I saw no reason not to. Come on, guys, come on back and join the party."

Alice and Ray followed Hazel and Philip down the short hall and made a brief turn where the music grew louder, and they entered a living room full of electric lights and people in various small groups, some sitting and some standing, many already on their second or third drink, talking rapidly and excitedly and sometimes learnedly.

Hazel said, "Alice, we need to introduce your new friend to everybody." Leaving Alice to talk with a group of people already engaged in some sort of discussion about the department budget, Hazel guided Ray over to a stuffy-looking gray-haired man about five feet eight, Ray's height, with a pot-gut, wearing a suit but no necktie. "Ray Jansen, meet Gilbert Walker. Ray, Gilbert specializes in perfecting horseshit for greater crops."

They laughed, so Ray laughed.

The introductions continued. Hazel introduced him to Cheryl Seltz, Gilbert's wife, an unusually short woman with a big head and short graying hair; then he met David Grant, a man with dull gray eyes, with a military demeanor, chin out and shoulders back. They shook hands.

Hazel led Ray from group to group introducing him to various Ag people he had no interest in knowing. Yet he was over a barrel and he didn't want to be rude.

Hazel seemed in her element. He was introduced to Christine Blair, a stuffy woman about forty with a Dutch accent; Andrew Vaughn, a little brown-skinned white man with graying hair; Laura Waterman, a blond woman in her late thirties who had a drunken smile; and John Hogg, a man with a German accent and a liquid smile. Hogg was tall and awkward and walked as though his knees were in bad shape.

There were others. Ray also met Dean de Marco, a short guy who might as well have had academic ambition stamped across his forehead. He met Merlin Smith, a wily little fellow with wild hair and a bright smile. And Cynthia Rudder, a flirt with red hair and green eyes, married with two teenage boys. He met Robert Diggs, a plump and lively fellow in need of a shave who said although he was in agriculture his secret love was tai chi and meditation.

He met Giovanni Granucci, probably thirty-nine or forty, a tall solemn man with a long John Carradine face. Standing alongside Granucci was

Angela Croft, nondescript and serious as a life sentence. She was working with him on a fertilizer research project.

Angela looked at Ray with distant curiosity. "What do you do, Ray?"

"I was in retail management." That was something he told people rude enough to ask the no-no question. It was true, but it also concealed the mundane nature of what he actually did on a daily basis.

Part of his supermarket job was to troubleshoot all day up and down aisles and in the front checkout section. If a customer had a gripe about something and voiced it to one of the clerks, Ray had to step in and resolve the problem as peacefully as possible, hopefully without losing the customer's loyalty to the store.

If an employee was slacking on the job, that was an issue he had to confront. If one was chronically late or found to have stolen money from the cash register or lied on his or her application, Ray dealt with such issues.

It was the kind of job he never took home with him; and certainly, he didn't want to take it to a party, especially now that he was no longer doing that work.

Hazel disappeared and Angela took up the mission, introducing him to Keith Brock, a big intense man with a barrel chest and a bald head with a halo of hair around his ears.

Then there was Eliot Bernstein. He too was large, but also fat, with a big round face. His voice was loud and high-pitched.

Among the guests the only African Americans there were a couple: Darren McIntosh and his wife, Anne McIntosh. Darren was a dark-skinned and distinguished-looking man who had won more international scientific awards than anybody in his department. He was the oldest professor in the Agriculture Department. He had also served as chair for many years.

Darren said, "Mr. Jansen, I hope we get a chance to chat a bit before the evening's over."

"It would be a pleasure."

His wife, Anne, with a light complexion, was gracious and plump. Ray noticed that she was watching him carefully to see if she was eventually going to approve or disapprove of him as a person.

At this point Alice reappeared and whisked him away to the food and drinks table in the adjoining dining room. He was thinking: *This is not what I left New York to do, yet it is turning out to be an interesting digression in more ways than one.*

By the time Ray had a little paper plate of olives, a few wedges of Gouda, Gorgonzola, and cheddar cheeses and Ritz Crackers in hand, Hazel was once again at his side. "Come, come, Ray, I got somebody *special* I want you to meet."

Alice raised her eyebrows in a kind of fake surprise as Hazel pulled him away. He nearly dropped his plate. She steered him back into the living room and over to a woman sitting at one end of the couch.

"Ray, this is Lucille Copley, she's not in the Ag Department. She works at the Lorena Science Research Center. Lucille, this is Ray Jansen, from New York."

While faintly smiling as if she were the queen holding court, Lucille lifted a hand toward Ray, and he shook it. "Nice to meet you, Ray. Won't you sit down?" Speaking with friendly authority, she patted the empty cushion next to her while still holding a faint smile.

Ray was guessing that Lucille was about thirty-eight or thirty-nine, maybe younger, maybe older. She had a kind face, but she was not beautiful, not even pretty; she was good-looking in an intelligent and handsome way.

Hazel said, "I'll leave you two to get to know each other," and she walked away back toward the dining room.

Lucille said, "What kind of work did you do in New York, Ray?"

"Retail management."

Lucille said, "It's refreshing to meet somebody from somewhere else. This town and its people get pretty boring at times. When I heard that you'd just arrived in town from New York—Alice told me—I wanted to talk with you. Is that okay?"

Ray said, "Would you put this over on the end table for me?"

Lucille took the paper plate and placed it on the end table. "So, tell me about yourself," she said.

Ray panicked as he always did when asked by a stranger about his past. That was a subject he considered off-limits. He hesitated. He didn't want anybody's pity. He'd talked recently with Alice about everything in his past, but a short time earlier Alice and he had quickly become intimate, and he somehow felt comfortable telling her about his life.

Lucille said, "Never mind, I ask too many personal questions."

"It's okay," he said.

"Alice says you're going to be staying in town a few days. Is that true?"

"Well, I was headed for San Francisco when the train got waylaid here in Lorena, and when it left, it left without me; so here I am." He showed her both palms.

"If I may ask: Why were you going to San Francisco? You have relatives there? A new job, perhaps?"

"No, no new job. I got a postcard from my best friend telling me a lot of wonderful things about California, especially about San Francisco. I've always heard good things about the state and especially San Francisco. Why do you ask?"

"Well, if you've lived there as I have, it's not so great. Sure, it has a fine reputation, but it's expensive as hell and the intensity can be draining; but you have a friend there, so you won't have to start from scratch."

Suddenly Alice appeared and said, "Oh, there you are. Are you about ready to go?" She looked at her wristwatch. They'd been there about an hour.

Ray caught on quickly. "Oh, sure." He stood up and shook hands again with Lucille. "Nice talking with you, Lucille."

"You too," she said. "We'll meet again, Ray, I hope." Then to Alice: "Don't worry, Alice, I'm not going to steal him."

Alice smirked and turned away.

Ray didn't respond to that and Alice took his arm and they walked toward the hallway leading to the front door.

On the way they found Philip and Hazel and thanked them for their hospitality. Alice said, "I have to get home to make sure my kids haven't burned down the house." In a whimsical voice, she said, "Remember, I did put in an appearance."

Hazel laughed. "Those girls of yours are far too well behaved to ever do such a thing."

"Ha! You have no idea!"

In the car on the way back, Alice said, "What was Lucille talking to you about?"

Ray hesitated. "Oh, just introductory kinds of things. She asked how long I'd be in town."

34

"I *bet* she did. She's a notorious bitch for trying to grab any good-looking man she can get her hands on, especially someone new in town. Was she flirting with you?"

"I didn't think so."

Rather than dropping Ray off at Hotel Lorena and going home, Alice parked the car at the curb in front of the hotel and got out with him. She didn't say anything, and he didn't say anything. She walked right into the lobby with him. The two desk clerks never once looked up.

Inside the room Ray took her in his arms and kissed her alcohol-tasting lips.

She smiled and said, "You taste good."

He smiled and kissed her again.

"Was that my goodbye kiss?" she said tauntingly.

PART 2

Extemporizing Procedure

It is safer to accept any chance that offers itself, and extemporize a procedure to fit it, than to get a good plan matured, and wait for a chance to use it.

—THOMAS HARDY, *FAR FROM THE MADDING CROWD*

6

TUESDAY MORNING RAY WOKE UP in a room on the fifth floor of Union Square's Hilton Hotel in San Francisco, and for a moment he thought he was still in Hotel Lorena.

Then he remembered Scotty. He'd start with the address Scotty gave him. He got out of bed and picked up his trousers lying across the back of the armchair. He fished in the pockets till he found the folded post-card Scotty had sent him.

He sat on the side of the bed and unfolded it and reread it: *Hey, Ray, it's great out here in California, man. I'm tending bar and making big bucks. My new girlfriend's name is Connie. She is a bright star in my life. San Francisco is great! It's nothing like New York. After what you and I went through growing up, if anybody deserves a better life it's you and me. Come on out! You'll like it out here. Your friend for life, Scotty.*

Scotty had squeezed in his address at the bottom of the card. The writing was so tiny, Ray had a hard time making it out. Was it 3345 Valencia or 8846 Yalencia?

Ray was hoping that Scotty was beginning to live a more conventional life, no longer womanizing or boozing.

When Scotty moved back to Manhattan after staying in Queens for a brief time, he had been working as a waiter at a bar and restaurant called Walker's Place down on Bleecker Street.

The bartenders there were good to him. They taught him more about mixology and how to serve drinks in an attractive manner. Walker's Place was also where Scotty stole money from the cash register. He was never caught, but he felt guilty about it. One day, he said, "Ray, that's something I'll never do again. It wasn't worth it."

Outside in front of his hotel, Ray found a few taxis waiting for passengers. As he approached the first one, the driver quickly put up his "occupied" sign, though clearly there was nobody in the taxi. In fact, the driver had been sitting there looking through a magazine.

Ray went to the second taxi, opened the back door, and got in.

He said, "I'm not sure about the address but let's first try 8846 Yalencia."

The taxi driver, a young Mexican American with an angelic face, said, "There's no such address in San Francisco."

"Okay. How about 3345 Valencia Street?"

The driver said, "That one's in the Mission District."

As the taxi climbed the narrow streets up into the Mission District, Ray sat back and quietly watched the passing scenery. All the mostly wood-frame houses seemed crammed together up the hillside. The area was quaint and countrified, yet pleasant and charming.

The taxi pulled to a stop in front of a tall and narrow three-story gray house with ornate purple window frames and lattices.

Ray said, "Would you wait here for me?" as he paid the cabby and gave him a generous tip.

The driver hesitated, then said, "Okay."

"I'll wave to you if it's all right to leave. Okay?"

"Okay," he said. "I'll wait but I won't wait long; otherwise, I have to turn on the meter."

"Of course." Ray climbed out and strolled up to the front door. It was a window door, and Ray could see dimly through the frosted window. Just as he was about to press the door buzzer, he noticed a handwritten note pinned above the buzzer: *Doorbell out of order, please knock hard.* The name above the buzzer was Hans Adolf Bauer.

Inside, a dog started barking and a man shouted, "Calm down, calm down, Benji!"

40

A big man with a long face and droopy eyes opened the door. A friendly-looking light brown Labrador retriever stood beside the man. Ray was glad to see that the dog was wagging his tail. The dog and the man were looking at Ray expectantly.

"Hello, I'm not sure I have the right house, but I'm looking for Scott O'Brien? He gave me this address."

The man smiled faintly. "Are you Mr. Jansen?"

"That's right."

"Come on in, Mr. Jansen. Don't mind Benji. He won't harm a flea, and come to think of it, maybe he *should* harm a flea: he certainly has had to endure them from time to time. But no, I assure you, he's flea-free; so, not to worry." He laughed at his own joke. "By the way, my name is Hans Adolf Bauer."

Ray stepped inside. "Sounds like you already know I'm a friend of Scott's."

Hans had not yet closed the door. He was looking out at the taxi parked at the curb.

"Are you keeping the taxi waiting?"

"Yes."

"Oh, you don't have to do that. I'd be happy to call a taxi for you when you're ready to go."

"Oh, okay. I'll be right back."

Ray stepped out on the porch and waved to the driver, signaling that he was now free to leave. The cabby gave him a salute, started the motor, and pulled away from the curb, turning around in the middle of the narrow road and heading back downhill.

Hans closed the door. "Please come in and have a seat, Mr. Jansen," he said, leading Ray from the dark, narrow, short hallway directly into the living room. Two armchairs faced the fireplace.

Ray said, "Call me Ray."

"Very well; Ray it will be." As he spoke, Hans eased himself down into the chair on the right by the unlit fireplace. He gestured for Ray to sit in the other armchair. "Sorry to say, Scotty isn't here. You just missed him."

"Where is he? Do you know how I can contact him?"

"No, not exactly. You see, while he was living here, Scotty got himself into a bit of a jam."

41

"What happened?"

Hans grinned and shook his head. "He got involved with a married woman. I guess she fell for his good looks: that curly red hair and those freckles." He chuckled.

Benji stretched on the floor beside Hans's chair.

Smiling, Ray said, "Yeah, that's Scotty. A lot of women like his devil-may-care style."

"Problem was," said Hans, "she is supposedly happily married. She and her husband have the apartment on the top floor."

"Maybe she knows where he went?"

"I'm sure she does. She left here with him. Took all her stuff, even took the little pistol her husband, Theo, lent her for protection. Theo is upstairs, but I don't think you want to talk with him; introducing yourself as a friend of Scotty's would not sit well."

"What else can you tell me that might help me find Scotty?"

"Not a lot, Ray. The woman he's with is Constance Goddard if that helps. Her husband is Theodore Goddard. Theo is heartbroken."

Benji looked up, wagged his tail a couple of times, then laid his head back on the floor between his paws.

"Would you like to see Scotty's room?"

"Sure, I'd like to see it."

Hans stood and said, "Follow me. It's up on the second floor in the rear."

Ray climbed the steps behind Hans's slow climb.

Hans was talking as he ascended the steps slowly toward the second floor: "He left here so quickly, he left a few things here and told me to throw them out. I haven't yet done so, but not because I expect him to return."

They reached the second-floor landing and Hans said, "Here we are." He turned the doorknob and opened the door to a dark room. Hans stepped inside and switched on the light. "It's no grand affair but he was comfortable here. He was saving his money and doing well till he met Connie."

There was a queen-sized bed with the headboard against the right wall. On it was a green blanket and no bedspread. One large window was on the left wall. A small dresser was along the wall nearest the door where Ray was standing. Ray saw no personal items.

"What sort of things did he leave?" said Ray.

"Step over here. They're in the top dresser drawer."

Ray followed him to the dresser and pulled open the drawer.

There were three or four *Playboy* magazines, a pack of condoms, a comb, cigarette papers, and a broken pair of sunglasses. As Ray gazed at these items, he wondered why Hans wanted to show them to him. He said, "This is all that he left?"

Hans chucked. "Yes. He's clearly not coming back for *these* items."

"No, not likely," said Ray.

"Please pardon my indiscretion, Ray. Let's go back downstairs."

Ray went down first, and once they were settled in the living room, Hans said, "Do you mind if I ask a personal question?"

"What's on your mind?"

"You're a black man, Scott is white. Do you fellows have trouble maintaining friendship in this society?"

"Interesting question."

"If it's too personal, please don't answer. My interest is purely impersonal, empirical, and social. My background is in psychology and sociology, and my own personal history is behind my question: my grandfather on my mother's side was in Hitler's Nazi army. Schmidt was his name. He was in charge of gassing thousands of Jews in Poland. That personal history has given me cause to fight all racism and all kinds of hatred. Lately, I've been reading a lot about America's social history. It is pretty bloody and cruel."

"I don't mind answering the question, Hans. Scotty and I have been friends since we were small kids. For the most part we haven't had to put up with intolerance, but there have been incidents, unpleasant incidents."

"Care to give me an example?"

"We were in our early twenties, maybe twenty-two and twenty-three; and this one time we went to a karate studio up in Harlem. We both wanted to join. The guy at the desk gave me a card to fill out but told Scotty they didn't have any more available spaces. I gave the card to Scotty and told the guy at the desk, 'My friend needs the slot more than I do.' He said, 'Sorry, we don't have any more slots available, period.'"

"Oh my God," muttered Hans.

"A few times, Scotty and I were together, and *I* was shunned or outright rejected. You wouldn't think that in this day and age, in New York City, there are still bars and restaurants that don't want to serve black people. They know they can't openly discriminate, so they find other ways around the law. One time, Scotty and I went into a pretty upscale restaurant in Midtown. The host rushed up to us just as we entered and, looking directly at me, said, 'What do *you* want?' I was taken aback. I looked at Scotty; he was baffled, then I looked back at the host and said, 'We'd like a seat by that window over there,' which confused her. It was clear she had been told to confront black people in this way to make them feel unwelcome, in the hope they might go away. Anyway, she had no choice but to seat us. For an hour we sat there, and no one came to take our order. We knew now what management was up to. They were trying to make us leave. We didn't leave. Scotty went and found the server and politely told her we'd like to order, and she finally came over and took our order. We ate, and on the way out the busboy, a Puerto Rican kid, caught up with us as we were leaving and said, 'The cook and the owner don't like Negroes; the cook put something in your food. They don't want you here. They think it ruins their business.' Sure enough, an hour later I was sick as a dog, throwing up in the toilet bowl; and Scotty was fine."

Hans muttered, "Die Schande der Menschen; ah, the shame, the shame of people." He paused. "I like Scotty. He's kind of wild but not at heart a bad sort. We used to sit here in this very room and talk. He is quite a talker, you know."

"Yes, I know."

"He used to tell me about all of his adventures and misadventures. Once when he was a little boy at the shelter, the older boys crushed his spirt by telling him there was no Santa Claus. He said that was the beginning of his disillusionment. He said soon after that he went through a period when he stole things from stores—candy bars, toys, little things; then he suddenly stopped. He said he never got caught. No doubt about it, Ray, your friend Scotty is a scoundrel, but a lovable scoundrel!" Hans laughed.

Ray laughed too. His was free, unrestrained laughter; then he said, "I'd forgotten about the stealing. He must have been six or seven at that time, but I remember the Santa Claus story. He and I got thrown in together

44

around the ages of eight and nine. We learned we had been abandoned as infants; and we were the only two in the shelter at that time with similar histories, that is to say, no known parents."

Benji got up and walked over to Ray. As he stood there slowly wagging his tail, Ray patted him on his head and massaged his ears.

Finally, Ray said, "And you don't know where Scotty and the woman are now?"

"No, not the slightest idea, but I suspect they're still in California." Hans paused. "Connie's a California girl from a respected family up in Lorena. Her maiden name is Mann, and she says she's descended from an old aristocratic German family. Mann *is* a very respected name in Germany. Anyway, she was born in Lorena. It's a little ag college town up near Sacramento."

"You've got to be kidding! I got stranded there on my way out here."

"You don't say! What a coincidence!" said Hans. "How did that happen?"

"The train got stalled there because a boxcar was on the track."

"Oh, that kind of poor-planning nonsense."

"Yes. You think they might be in Lorena?"

"It's a possibility. I know her folks are still there."

"This is amazing. I was planning to go back there anyway just to visit, but if Scotty is there that changes everything."

"Connie is a good girl and she is well educated. I think she has a master's degree from UC Berkeley in something or other, but she hasn't done anything with it. Theo also comes from a well-to-do family. They lost their fortune through bad investments and risky real estate, but they built it up again. Back in '68 Theo dodged the draft. He hid out, even thought of escaping to Canada, to avoid going to Vietnam. He was involved in antiwar demonstrations. He still carries himself like he's well-to-do. Theo's a bit older than Connie. My guess is she married him to get away from the tight hold her family had and may still have on her up there in Lorena. If you ask me, she was in love with Theo but that didn't last. I think she got bored and restless; and Scotty came along; and she saw her chance to again escape."

"Thanks for the information, Hans." Ray thought about Scotty and women. The guy had always attracted women. Ray remembered Scotty

45

was involved for about three months with a young woman named Nina; then for some reason Nina soured toward him, and Scotty then took up with Nina's younger sister, Lana, but that turned out to be an even briefer relationship. After that, Scotty had sex with their mother, Debbie, who was going through a divorce.

He later told Ray that after sex with Debbie, she and he stayed awake all night lying side by side in bed that first night talking. Debbie needed to vent.

She complained about her husband's kindness and gentleness. The complaint struck Scotty as odd. People didn't normally complain about kindness or gentleness, but Debbie found her husband too passive and too dull.

She said she needed excitement and adventure, and that was why she'd always had affairs to keep her life exciting.

Hans said, "I don't know; maybe I've talked too much."

"Theo sounds like a nice person."

"He is. He was an only child. Grew up in L.A. His family's estate is in Los Angeles County."

"Too bad he lost his wife."

"Yes, but he'll recover. Theo comes downstairs and drinks a glass of wine with me once in a while; but he has an outside-stairway entrance, so I don't see much of him. We share an interest in history, especially the American Revolution and the Civil War."

"Well, thanks again. I won't take up any more of your time." Ray stood up.

"Oh, no problem, I enjoy visitors."

"I think I'll run along and see if I can figure out how to locate Scotty."

"Scotty told me about you, obviously. He said you might come out here from New York, but he never said it was definite. That's how I knew who you were."

"And he didn't leave any word for me?"

"No, he got out of here so fast with Connie that he didn't have time to say 'goodbye.' Theo was angry enough to shoot him. And I'm pretty sure Theo has a .38 automatic up there in his apartment."

"Do you know bars or restaurants Scotty frequented? Maybe I can track him down that way?" Ray was thinking Scotty and Connie might still be here in San Francisco. It would be easier to hide in a big city than in a small town like Lorena.

"Scotty used to tend bar at a tavern down on Mission Street near San Jose Avenue. I've passed there many times. I think it's called McCabe's or McBride's. I think he was fired for some reason."

Ray stored the name in his memory. "Thanks. I'll check it out."

Hans said, "I'll call you a taxi." And he stood and walked over to the phone on the end table by the couch.

On the way there, the taxi driver said, "There is no McCabe's at that location. You must mean McBride's Tavern on Mission Street."

"That's the one," said Ray.

The taxi stopped and double-parked in front of McBride's. Ray paid and thanked the cabby and climbed out, then the taxi sped off.

Ray walked across the sidewalk and went into McBride's.

The usual barroom darkness greeted him and so did the usual beer smells. "I Shot the Sheriff" by Bob Marley and the Wailers was coming from the jukebox. Three men and one woman sat on barstools, each with a drink on the bar in front of them. It was clear they were not together, but two of the men had struck up a conversation about baseball. Ray looked at the woman's face reflected in the mirror behind the bar. She was brooding about something.

Ray eased up onto a seat near the door. The bartender was a young guy, tall and heavyset with an obvious lower back problem He was already aware of Ray, and he came up the bar limping and stood before Ray. "Hi, there! May I help you?"

"I'll have a Bud Light."

"One Bud Light coming up."

While sipping his beer, Ray watched for a chance to talk with the bartender when he seemed idle. The chance came quickly. "Say, my name is Ray. I'm looking for a friend of mine, Scotty, who works here or used to work here. You know how I can get in touch with him?"

"Black or white guy?"

"White."

"You mean Scotty O'Brien?"

"He's the one," said Ray.

The bartender frowned. "How do I know you're a friend of his? For all I know you might be a cop looking to arrest the guy."

"I'm not a cop. Scotty and I grew up together in New York."

The bartender's face changed. A broad smile spread across his face. "You must be Raymond Jansen. Scotty talked about you a lot; said you were coming out to California."

"Yes, I am, and here I am."

The bartender stuck out his hand. "I'm Steven Biggs."

Ray shook hands with Steven. "Pleased to meet you, Steven."

"Call me Steve." He kept smiling. "I haven't seen Scotty in a while. I think he may have left town but, yeah, he used to work here and even after he was fired, he'd stop by to shoot the breeze with me. We became pretty good friends. Hung out together a bit. Caught a few games. On our night off, we'd go barhopping to pick up chicks. That kind of stuff."

"Double-dated?"

"Yeah, Scotty is quite the lady's man." At this point Steven lowered his voice. "You must know that when Scotty was about eighteen or nineteen, for a brief time, he was a pimp."

"A pimp?"

"Yeah, a pimp, in Queens, he said. He said he'd just gotten out of the shelter and moved over to Queens and was staying in a seedy hotel where he met these whores—excuse me, I mean prostitutes—who were working the streets. He fell in with this one woman from New Jersey, I forget her name, maybe it was Sandy, who had left her husband and was hustling on the streets, mostly giving head, you know, not undressing, to make ends meet. She had a twelve-year-old son."

"No," said Ray, "I didn't know Scotty was pimping. I knew he moved to Queens and for a time he and I lost contact."

"Did you know that he used to drink heavily?"

Ray said, "Heavily? Yeah, I guess so. I saw him drunk a few times."

"Scotty told me he was embarrassed to remember the time when he went and knocked on the door of an apartment where he used to live. He had no idea who lived there. A young guy and two girls opened the door. Guess what Scotty said to them?"

"What?"

"He said, 'My name is Scotty. I need love.'"

"Wow! What happened then?"

"They slammed the door in his face. He woke up the next morning in his own bed with no memory of how he got there; but he remembered the door slamming in his face."

"This is all news to me."

"I thought you already knew all this stuff." Steve laughed. "Last time I saw Scotty he was with a girl named Connie. They didn't stay long. She had a glass of wine and he had a Bud and they left."

"You know any of the other women he dated? I might be able to track him down if I can talk to them."

"Sure, there was a married woman named Libby. She lived over in Berkeley; but she came over here often. She had to sneak around to see him. One time she was screwing Scotty while her husband was in the hospital for a gallbladder operation. She got a big kick out of cheating. Many times, she told her old man she was visiting a girlfriend here in the city. She would have the girlfriend cover for her. She and Scotty would be in a hotel in bed screwing while she called her husband just to say good night. They both almost died laughing."

Ray thought that sounded like something Scotty would do. Yeah, that was Scotty.

"He also hooked up with a young woman named Leta Sanchez in Oakland. It may be over; it may not be over. She is a schoolteacher and there are rumors that she's married. She is a nice girl, but I'd bet it won't take her long to figure out that Scotty isn't interested in commitment; but then maybe she isn't either."

"Sounds like Scotty has been very busy." Ray sighed. "And you don't know how I can get in touch with her?"

"Can't help you, pal. Scotty used to live near here, a couple of blocks away, then he moved somewhere else. He still came around but, like I said, the last time I saw him was maybe two weeks ago when he brought that gal named Connie in here."

Ray stood up and drained his glass, then put money on the bar and said, "Well, thanks, Steve. May I come back and talk with you again if I need to?"

"Anytime, pal."

Before going to bed that night, Ray watched the late news. He figured there was no point in checking the room's copy of the San Francisco phone directory for the name Scott O'Brien. If he found one, it wasn't likely to be Scotty. Even if Scotty was still in the Bay Area, it was unlikely he had a phone listed in his name. He'd never been in one place long enough to have done such a thing.

Ray turned off the TV with the remote and lay down and replayed his actions. Sunday night after Alice left him to go home to her two daughters, he had made up his mind he would catch the commuter train to San Francisco on Monday and try to figure out how to locate Scotty.

That morning he had also called Alice at home before she left for work and told her he'd be at the Hilton in Union Square and that he'd call her as soon as he could.

He would try to locate his luggage at Amtrak in San Francisco; then he'd get on with his life as he'd originally planned. Ray intended to make a new life for himself, and California was beginning to look like an excellent place to begin.

Now it was Wednesday. Ray knew he needed structure in his life. He had a work ethic he could not ignore, but he was in no hurry. At some point he planned to go into business for himself; but he had not yet decided on what kind of business he wanted to pursue.

It would not be the kind of retail work he had been doing in New York. No, the work had to be pleasing, and happiness was the goal. He had enough money to start his own business. He could open a restaurant. But no, he'd seen too many start-up restaurants in Brooklyn fail within the first year. He knew nothing about running a restaurant or any kind of brick-and-mortar business.

Lying there, with the sunlight showing at the edges of the curtain hinting at another beautiful San Francisco day, he thought of Alice. In retrospect the weekend interlude seemed unreal, like something that had happened in a dream. With eyes closed he saw Alice's face. Already he missed her.

How quickly he had begun to feel comfortable with her! It was a kind of comfort he had not often had before. They'd parted with the understanding that they would continue to see each other. Either she'd come to San Francisco or he'd return to Lorena. She'd said, "Call me as soon as you can, okay?" He'd assured her he would call.

After a shower and breakfast downstairs in the hotel restaurant at ten o'clock, Ray walked outside onto Mason Street and stopped and looked around. It was sunny and warm, and he felt refreshed. From where he stood, he could see that Union Square was already busy.

The square was crowded with people, many of them probably tourists. At one corner a violinist was playing to a crowd standing around him. At another end there was a trio of guitar, trumpet, and drums; and an even bigger crowd stood listening to them. A few couples were dancing to the music.

What a way to begin the day! A couple of boys on skateboards were skating around and between the crowds. A juggler was juggling about six balls all at once; and in the distance, there was the department store Saks Fifth Avenue across the Square. To the left stood a line of double-decker tourist buses along the curb. People were lined up waiting to board them.

Ray walked over and went up the steps onto the square. He stood for a while listening to the violinist. He was playing one of the Italian concertos by Bach.

It was one of Ray's favorites. In high school he'd taken a music course and became interested in classical European music. At home in his apartment in New York, he often listened to the classical music station on the radio. The same station also played jazz.

Hearing Bach, he felt carefree and happy; but he couldn't spend all day here. He exited the square and walked along Geary to Stockton, turned and continued on Post, and turned onto Powell. He needed to exercise. In New York he'd always been a walker; and this was the first time he'd had a chance to walk some distance.

He waited there on the corner of Powell, waving to taxis. Two or three with passengers went by. One without a passenger also went by. Then after about five or six minutes one stopped, and Ray opened the back door and climbed in. "Amtrak Station, please."

Without saying anything, the cabby gunned the car and took off. They arrived in a short amount of time.

At baggage claim, Ray stood in line. There were three people ahead of him, two women and a man. When his turn came, he explained what had happened in Lorena, how he'd missed getting back on the train and his luggage went on to San Francisco without him.

The clerk asked him to describe the suitcase. "It's brown leather with a strap around it. My name, Raymond Jansen, is on a tag affixed to the handle." The clerk quickly found the suitcase and asked Ray for ID, which he produced, and his suitcase was handed over.

Back in the hotel room, he placed his suitcase on the luggage stand and undressed down to his underwear. He turned on the TV, then got on the bed to watch the news. In men's singles Guillermo Vilas had won the Monte Carlo Open tennis tournament. Then the newsman started talking about Monday's Boston Marathon and Jack Fultz's victory.

At five thirty Ray picked up the telephone and got an outside line and dialed Alice's home number. "Hello, Alice?"

"This is Margo, who is this?"

"Ray. Sorry, Margo, may I speak with your mother?"

"You can't tell *my* voice from her voice?"

He laughed.

She shouted, "It's not funny. I don't sound *anything* like her. Hold on."

"Thank you," he said, but she was gone.

Then the phone went dead.

Ray dialed the number again. This time Alice answered.

"Alice, it's Ray. How are you?"

"I'm fine. I'm even better now that you've called. Did you just call a minute ago?"

"I did."

"I thought so. Margo said some man wanted to talk with me. She knows your name. I don't know what I'm going to do with that girl."

"I didn't locate my friend Scotty. I went to the address he gave me and met the owner of the building, a very nice man, but Scotty moved. He might be up there in Lorena."

"What a surprise!"

"I got my luggage back today."

"Good. So, what are you going to do in San Francisco?"

"Good question. I'm not sure."

"I miss you. When will I see you? I was thinking about coming there this weekend, but I can't leave the girls alone and I don't have anybody to stay here with them. My sister is out of town."

"I'll come to see you. I told you I would, and I meant it. I can't afford to stay here at the Hilton indefinitely. It's too expensive."

"Your savings would go a lot further here in Lorena, and if Scotty is here, all the better."

"That's true." He paused. "Is there a town newspaper?"

"Yes, two: the *Lorena Sentinel* and *Lorena Star-Dispatch*."

"First I'll try to locate the parents of that woman Connie he's with. If they're not listed . . ."

"Constance Mann?"

"Yes."

"Your friend Scotty is with *Connie Mann*? I'm shocked!"

"Yes. They may or may not be living at her parents' house. They may not even be in Lorena. The landlord said they *might* be in Lorena."

"Connie was younger than me, but we went to the same high school." Alice paused. "I want you to come back to me. I miss you. You could get a place here."

"That's true. I'm considering renting an apartment, and maybe I'd be better off renting it there. Eventually I want to buy a car and a house. I've got to make my money last. I like California, I like Lorena."

"You're better off here than in San Francisco. San Francisco is a very expensive city. You'd pay three times more there than you would here."

He considered Alice's point. "Besides seeing and being with you, that's a damn good reason for coming back there. It's definitely something to consider."

"Your money really would go a lot further here. It's the truth, Ray. I'm not just saying that because I'd love to have you here, although that also is the truth."

"Yes, I know. I miss you too."

Over the next three or four days, Ray wandered around the city. He jumped on and off several trolley cars, riding the Powell-Hyde line down to Fisherman's Wharf, where he ate lunch. There was a wild chance that he might run into Scotty.

The next day he rode the Powell-Mason line to the Market Street turntable. He wandered around in that area. Later the same day he explored Chinatown and ate lunch in an upstairs restaurant there.

The day after that he took a taxi out to Golden Gate Park and walked around in the Japanese Tea Garden and through the Conservatory of Flowers and the Botanical Garden and around the windmills and the Beach Chalet Brewery and Strawberry Hill. He felt relaxed and peaceful, but he was beginning to feel lonesome. Families with happy children and couples holding hands all around him, obviously happy, deepened his loneliness. He loved the city, but San Francisco could not be the all-purpose panacea to his problems.

He took a taxi back to Union Square. In the square he stopped and listened to an old black man sitting on a stool with an upside-down hat on the ground in front of him. The handwritten sign alongside the hat said *I'm Washboard Joe*. On the ground resting against the stool was a washboard he was using as a musical instrument. In a gravelly voice, Washboard Joe was singing a deeply moving rendition of "Sitting on the Dock of the Bay." Ray dropped a few dollars in the hat.

After a couple more days of aimlessly wandering around in the city and feeling lonely and lost, Ray made up his mind to return to Lorena and to Alice.

She was not the woman in New York he had fantasized about eventually meeting in California, but she was a good woman. That alone was a good reason to return to Lorena. There was also the prospect of Scotty in Lorena.

7

That Monday at three, seven days after he left Lorena, Ray walked into the lobby of Hotel Lorena carrying his suitcase.

The desk clerk Tom Hobson smiled and said, "Welcome back!"

"Thanks!"

After Ray was signed in and upstairs in the same room he'd had before, he thought about calling Alice to let her know he'd come back. For how long? He didn't know. Alice was still at work and wouldn't be home till five thirty. Calling her at the department was a no-no. Not that she'd ever told him not to.

Right now, he was feeling comfortable just being back in a small town. Oddly enough, it was what he was used to. In its way his neighborhood in Brooklyn was a small town. It was provincial in its own citified way and small-town life was what he was comfortable with.

Ray knew Alice was the larger part of the reason for returning. He missed the comfort he felt with her, a kind of motherly comfort that he had rarely felt before. So what if she was thirty-nine and he was only twenty-nine?

At six o'clock he dialed Alice's number. Margo said, "Hello?"

"Margo, may I speak with your mom?"

He heard her shout, "Mom! Some man on the phone for you!"

Alice came to the phone. She was chewing something. "Hello?"

"It's me, Ray. I'm back at Hotel Lorena."

"Excuse me, I was eating a peanut butter and jelly sandwich. I didn't get lunch today. Meetings all day! Crazy, crazy! What do you mean you're at Hotel Lorena?"

"I'm back and I missed you. I got tired of the city."

"That's wonderful news, Ray! I'm delighted! Can you come over tonight?"

"Yes, I want to. We have a lot to talk about. I've got a lot of planning to do. I'm thinking of finding an apartment and maybe eventually buying a house either here in Lorena or somewhere else in northern California."

After he hung up Ray left his room and walked down the carpeted steps to the lobby and bought the two local newspapers, the *Lorena Sentinel* and *Lorena Star-Dispatch*, from the machine and took them back to his room.

During the day Alice's front door was always open. He knocked lightly on the screen door. Alice opened it and he stepped inside. Right off they hugged and kissed like hugging and kissing might soon be banned.

Margo was sitting on the couch just a few feet away watching TV. She groaned loudly, showing her disgust.

Over Alice's shoulder Ray could see Hope with her hands covering her eyes. She said, "Tell me when you guys stop that smooching. I'm keeping my eyes closed till then."

While Alice was cooking cheese omelets with toast for their dinner, Ray stood in the kitchen doorway watching her.

The girls were still up in the front room watching TV.

At the dining room table while eating, Ray said, "This afternoon I checked the classified ads in the two local newspapers for apartments to rent. I found three potential apartments I'm going to look at tomorrow."

The first apartment Ray looked at was in an old building near campus. Years as a student rental had left the place trashed.

Despite the smell of fresh paint, urine-stink was deep in the woodwork and floor. Had some guy at a drunken all-night party who couldn't find the toilet let loose right against the wall of the living room? Or had a tenant come home so drunk he couldn't find his own toilet? There were also patched holes in the walls. Had an angry fist caused them?

The second one was about a mile from campus out on McNeil Street. It was in a house originally intended for one family but was now broken up into apartments. Ray was shown the apartment on the first floor to the left, which included the living room. The place was clean, but he would have to share the kitchen with the other downstairs tenant. The listing hadn't made that clear.

The third apartment was in a newly built redwood apartment complex, the Van Brandt Apartments out on Van Brandt Avenue, a street that led up into the nearby hills. Two stories, four apartments per building; and there was a total of six units. It was a big place, and only about half of the apartments were rented so far.

The manager Andrew Copley said, "So, what do you think?"

Copley was a tall, weathered-looking guy, maybe thirty-five or so, with bushy eyebrows and dry reddish hair and big hands that looked like they'd lifted a lot of heavy weights.

Ray was coming up the little hallway back to the living room where Copley waited for him. "I like it. I'll take it."

"Okay, let's go over to the office and do the paperwork."

As they walked across the parking lot to the office, Ray said, "You said three hundred a month? Can we make it a month-to-month lease?"

"Yes. It's a month-to-month lease. We keep it that way because students tend to want short-term leases."

Inside, Ray sat facing Copley, who was behind his desk typing up the agreement, and Ray felt pleased with this step he was taking to return to Lorena.

He'd started out in New York loaded with a fat bank account and two good credit cards, determined somehow to try to change his life for the better, but he'd never imagined he'd settle in a little-known town in northern California called Lorena.

Copley finished the contract in triplicate and pushed it across the desk for Ray to sign. Ray spent a few minutes scanning the contract; then he took the pen the manager was holding out to him and signed on the dotted line. He then handed the document back to Copley. Copley tore off the bottom copy and handed it to Ray.

57

"On the back," Copley said, "you'll see that we have tenant rules. No storing anything on your terrace. No loud parties. No nails in the walls. If any appliance such as your dishwasher breaks down, let me know. Don't call a handyman or try to fix it yourself. Let me know if you have any problems at all in the apartment."

"Okay."

"We have a lot of students from the university staying here in the complex. They can at times be quite problematic: loud parties, destruction of property. We're trying to make a quiet transition from being just a housing development for college students to getting more adults like you in here. We'll always have them here, but we don't want to be solely a place for one social group. We want to diversify. That was our intention in building this complex in the first place, but when the students started coming, we couldn't in good conscience turn them away, and it would have been illegal anyway."

Ray said, "Thanks for the heads-up."

"By the way, Mr. Jansen, what kind of work do you do?"

"I was in retail management in New York. I'm living on my savings right now till I find a new job."

"You may have a hard time finding a retail management position in this town. There just isn't much here: just a few stores, two or three doctors, a hospital, a drugstore, a post office, a hardware store, and a pet shop. Kids born in Lorena leave as soon as they're old enough. May I ask why you came from New York to Lorena?"

"It was an accident. The train got stalled here and I missed getting back on. I was on my way to San Francisco."

"So, if I'm not being too nosy, why not live in San Francisco? There are many more job opportunities there than you'll ever find here—especially in retail management."

Ray didn't want to tell Copley about Alice or that he didn't need to find work right away. He said, "I tried San Francisco. I didn't like it. So, I came back here."

Copley smiled, his eyes twinkling. "Well, I hope you find what you're looking for here."

Ray stood up. "Thanks."

Copley stuck his hand across the desk, and they shook hands.

After finding a place to live, Ray walked from the Van Brandt Apartments complex to downtown in ten minutes. At First National Bank on Leahy Street, he stepped up to the information counter and said to the clerk, "I'd like to open an account."

He was escorted to a cubicle where a young man directed him through the process of opening a new account.

Then Ray decided to transfer about a third of his New York checking and savings account. To make the transfer he needed to see a different clerk in the next cubicle over. The clerk here was a thin blond woman in her forties.

When he told her how much he wanted to transfer, her eyes widened and she said, "I can't transfer that much money without my supervisor's approval. Wait a moment, please."

She went away and returned with an older woman in a navy-blue business suit. She had a blank expression and dark brown hair and gray eyes.

Ray explained what he wanted to do and gave her the information she needed to access his account at Chase Manhattan Bank in Brooklyn.

"Okay," said the supervisor, and she went away for about ten minutes, then returned and said, "It's done. I had to do it on a different machine." Her smile was stiff. She asked, "Anything else, Mr. Jansen?"

"No, thank you."

With his new checking and savings account set up, he thanked them both and left the bank, feeling better than he'd felt in several days. Now that he had an apartment and a bank account, he was beginning to feel a sense of place, a sense of belonging; and if Scotty was somewhere in Lorena, Ray was sure he'd eventually find him.

He also liked the sense of comfort he was beginning to feel in his relationship with Alice. He wasn't ready to call it love, but whatever it was, it was making him feel better. He worried though that he might be projecting his *ideal Alice* onto an Alice who was entirely somebody else. Time would tell.

He felt he also needed a lot more to begin to feel completely at home in this new place. He needed a good car; he needed to meet more people and develop a circle of friends. He wanted to learn the streets and the stores.

It would all take time. Even finding Scotty might take time. After all, Scotty might be hiding. If so, he certainly was justified. But Ray was excited. Staying here in Lorena might give him a new start in life, and somehow Lorena felt more manageable than San Francisco.

He also wanted to win the friendship of Alice's girls. But he knew it wouldn't be easy. It was clear they didn't trust him. They had good reason. Probably they had seen their mother go through one relationship after another only to end up hurt each time. To them he was just another potential disaster for their mother.

Before, while traveling on the train all the way from New York and for that brief time in San Francisco, he'd felt unmoored, rootless, homeless really. Here in Lorena he felt different, more secure.

Ray was beginning to realize that this new beginning in Lorena, in an unexpected place, might lead to the happiness and contentment he had left New York to find. Reconnecting with Scotty he now suspected was turning out to be just a catalyst to get here.

Lorena though was the last place on earth he would have thought he'd begin to embrace this elusive thing called happiness, yet here he was and somehow it felt like the right place to be.

It was four thirty. Hotel Lorena was only a seven-minute walk from the bank. It felt good to leave the hot streets and enter the cool lobby of the hotel.

Smooth and calm music was coming from the bar, so rather than going upstairs to his room, Ray decided to get a drink at the bar and relax.

He eased up on a stool in the middle of the line of stools and smiled at the bartender.

Only the bartender was in the bar. She was a woman in her mid-thirties with blond hair and a face that was once pretty, but it belonged to a woman who had suffered too many defeats and they now claimed a place on that pretty face.

"What would you like, honey?" she said.

"Whatever beer is on tap, thank you."

"You got it." She drew the beer into a glass and sat it in front of him. "You're the new guy from New York who checked in yesterday?"

"That's right. How'd you know?"

60

"Tom, the daytime clerk on the front desk, told me."

"I don't remember telling him I was from New York."

"Your credit card is from a New York bank," she said, smiling. She stuck out her hand. "Hi, my name is Laura."

Ray shook her hand. "I'm Ray. Nice to meet you, Laura. You like working here?"

She wrinkled her nose. "Yeah, kind of. Except it gets to be a drag when there are no customers coming in. I like to keep busy and I'm a talker. If I don't have anybody to talk to, I get bored just sitting here wiping the bar down."

"Isn't it happy hour right now?"

"Yeah, and where *is* everybody? Lately guys have been going straight home rather than stopping in for a beer or a shot before heading home to the family. I don't know why, but they still come on Friday—Friday happy hour is plenty busy, and weekends too."

"So, Friday should be jumping?"

"I wouldn't say jumping but busy enough to keep me from being bored; and I don't have to rush home after work to relieve the babysitter anymore. My daughter is now thirteen. She's a good girl and a beauty. I'm just glad she doesn't know it yet. Lord knows, I've put that girl through a lot, and she's been nothing but sweet about it. Her dad and me separated seven years ago. He's back east now so she doesn't get to see him like she used to when he was living in San Francisco."

Ray sipped his beer and since he couldn't get a word in edgewise, he just relaxed and listened until she started asking him questions.

"You have kids, Ray?"

"No, I don't; I've never been married."

"Your family back east?"

That was the question he dreaded. As usual he lied; he said yes. In a way he told himself it wasn't a lie: the shelter manager, Jan Kohler, and the kids he grew up with and the Jansen family and the Cooper family and the Halberstam family were all his one big family.

Laura said, "I'm originally from Denver. I don't have much contact with my mom and dad. They still live there. Actually, my dad kicked me out when I was seventeen; and he and I haven't gotten along since. He found a diaphragm in my purse and went berserk. And why was he looking in my purse? Rather than praising me for using a contraceptive like a sensible parent would have done, he said, 'I don't want no whore living in my house, you're no longer my daughter, so get out now.'"

"Wow! That's pretty cold-blooded."

"He is a cold-blooded son of a gun. I would never do that to my daughter, Sara, even if she came home pregnant. I'd do everything I could to help her. For God's sake, we're all just human and we make mistakes. Have you ever made a mistake, Ray?"

"Too many to count." He brought the glass up to his mouth and drank the beer to keep from saying any more.

"I myself sure have made my share. I was tending bar in Denver six years ago when I met this guy named Oscar—Oscar Young. Business was slow, like it is here today; so rather than going back to my stool and reading my copy of *Readers' Digest* magazine, I stood there and talked with him. He seemed kind of lonely. He was a middle-aged fellow in his mid-forties. I was in my late twenties. He told me all about his business. He said he had over a hundred employees; he came off as this big-time successful contractor with an estate in Folly Beach, South Carolina; he said he was in Colorado on business."

"Folly Beach?"

"Yes, isn't that a hoot? The people who named that place had a sense of humor. He asked me about myself, and I told him how I'd wanted to start my own business making doilies. I was always good at decorating things; any kind of decorating, such as interior decorating. I was making these cute little ornamental doilies with elaborate designs, but I didn't have enough money to get set up in business. Oscar got all excited and said he would invest in my doilies business; but he said it would be easier to work with me if I moved down to Folly Beach with him where he could help me manage the business."

Ray knew what was coming.

"Well, foolishly, I moved to Folly Beach, taking my little girl, disrupting her schooling, getting her started in a new school down there. It was crazy. We moved in with Oscar in this little house he had on the beach and I got busy making the doilies. The first week went fine. I didn't think much of the fact that Oscar was gone a lot because he had convinced me he was a very successful businessman. To make a long story short, a lady in a house a couple of doors down stopped me one day and said, 'Honey, don't do this to yourself and your child. Leave that man. He's a married man with a family in Myrtle Beach, and he comes over here to be with you when he can get away. He's done this for years, bringing women like you here. Don't lower yourself like this.' Well, at first, I had trouble believing her. For days I brooded on it and when Oscar showed up, I gingerly asked questions which he skillfully dodged. Then one day I asked the telephone operator for Oscar Young's number in Myrtle Beach, and when a woman answered the phone, I said, 'Hello, may I speak to Mrs. Young?' and she said, 'I'm Mrs. Young.' I said, 'Please tell your husband I'm leaving him,' and she said, 'Well, dear, you have my blessing, but I can assure you that some unsuspecting woman will replace you in no time.' So, that is an example of the kind of dumb mistakes I have made in my life, and I don't like being tricked and made to feel stupid because I'm not stupid."

"Yeah," Ray said, "but it's hard keeping your guard up all the time and not trusting anybody. You don't want to live like that."

"No, I don't, but I've always been too trusting and not sensitive enough to what people are really about. Now, take you. I can't tell anything about you. You seem to me to be a perfectly nice guy; and I guess you are, but how can I know for sure?"

"You can't." He took a sip of beer.

"If you were a bad guy, you would have said, 'You can trust me.'" She sighed. "Before Sara was born, I did have a brief relationship in Los Angeles with a guy who was mean as a rattlesnake. After a few months, I was scared of him. I thought he might eventually kill me. He used to grab me and shake me and shout in my face. He was very violent. He almost broke my spirit, but I got out just in time."

Ray looked at his watch. It was almost six. Alice was probably home by now. He finished his beer and set the empty glass down on the doily. He picked up the little embroidered mat. It was very intricate.

Laura was watching him.

"Is this one of yours?"

"It certainly is."

"Beautiful work."

"Thank you."

63

Ray stood up. "Nice talking with you, Laura. I'll see you again soon, I'm sure. Take care." He left a five-dollar bill on the bar: enough to cover the cost of the beer and a large tip for Laura.

Upstairs in the room Ray dialed Alice's number. She said, "I was wondering when you'd call. I was just about ready to call you."

8

THURSDAY MORNING RAY FINISHED BREAKFAST in the hotel restaurant and set out walking toward nearby Walter Hale Greer Fine Furniture store on Boyle Street. It took him ten minutes to get there. Everything in town was in walking distance. That's how small the town was, and Ray liked it. He had to stop and wait for only one traffic light to change. Had he been in Brooklyn walking the same distance, he'd have had to wait for at least three or four traffic lights.

The façade of the store was impressive, with large window displays of the newest and most fashionable furniture. Ray stood on the sidewalk and took in the displays with recliners, end tables, rockers, footstools, sectionals, beds, dressers, and kitchen tables and chairs.

Then, with a brisk determined stride, he walked inside. A young man with thinning hair and a rosy smile and in a cheap suit and tie came immediately toward him. "May I help you?"

"Yes, I'd like to consider some furniture for my apartment."

"Certainly." The young man's name tag said he was Nichols McNeal. McNeal said, "You live here in town?"

"Yes, I do."

The young man's rosy smile had become a plastic fixture on his face. "Oh, interesting. I thought I knew everybody in town."

"I'm new in town."

"Do you work here in town?"

"No, I'm between jobs but my credit is excellent. I'm from New York and I was in retail management."

"Retail management?"

"Yes, and I have an apartment here in town at the Van Brandt Apartments over on Van Brandt Avenue."

The plastic smile fell apart. McNeal said, "I don't think my boss would approve selling furniture to someone who is new in town and doesn't have a job or any prospects for a job."

"If you won't accept my credit, I can pay cash."

McNeal hesitated then said, "I'm still not sure I can sell you furniture."

"Let me speak to your boss."

"He's not here right now."

"When will he return?"

"He's gone for the day."

"Will he be here tomorrow, and what's his name?"

"Yes, he should be here tomorrow. Name's Hugh Greer."

"Would you ask your boss to call me at Hotel Lorena?"

He hesitated. "Uh, you can leave your phone number, sure."

"Ask him to call me. My name is Raymond Jansen. Thank you."

Then Ray turned and walked out.

When Ray entered the lobby of the hotel, he stopped at the front desk to see if Alice had called. The clerk Tom Hobson, looking very stern and standing upright in a very business-like manner and without a smile to accent what he no doubt believed to be the seriousness of his position in life, said, "Yes, you do have a message. You can take it here or over there on the lobby phone or upstairs in your room."

"Thank you, Tom. I'll take it here in the lobby."

"Very well, just pick up and I'll connect you."

Ray stepped over to the phone on the wall and in a second or two Hobson transferred the message: "Mr. Jansen, this is Hugh Greer. Please let me extend to you my apology for my clerk Nick McNeal. I was in the back when you came in. Nick should have called me out. He's new here and is still in training. You are welcome to pay by cash or to use your excellent credit. I ran a credit check on your name. Just as you told Nick, you have excellent credit. We would have no trouble selling you furniture. Again, I apologize and hope to see you soon."

9

FRIDAY NIGHT FOR THE FIRST time Ray spent the night with Alice. Trying to sleep beside her, his sleep was restless. He got up twice to go to the toilet to pee.

After breakfast he said, "I want to see if I can contact Constance Mann to see if she can tell me anything about Scotty's whereabouts."

"Have you checked the phone book?"

"Not yet, do you have one?"

"I *had* one, but my friend Annette borrowed it and never brought it back. Now I won't get one till they come out next year." She paused. "Call the operator. The operator will give you the number. There's the phone right over there."

Ray picked up the phone and dialed the operator. "The Mann family's number, please."

The operator said, "There are three by that name. Two are unlisted, so I can't give you those numbers."

Then she gave him the one that was listed. He dialed it and let it ring for a long time. There was no answer. He'd have to try later.

Spending the night at Alice's house was so that they could go together in her car Saturday morning out to Snellings Automobile Panorama on Greenspan Avenue, a road leading out of town to Highway 80.

Ray wanted to buy a car and Alice said Snellings was the best dealership. Snellings had a high rating and got more new cars monthly than did Snellings' two competing dealerships, Copeland Auto Mall and Nash Auto Sales.

Alice woke first, then gently tugged at Ray till he woke. He opened his eyes and for a second didn't know where he was or who she was, then he clicked back into reality and said, "Okay, okay." He groaned and turned over.

"I'm going to wake the girls, then I'm taking a shower. You want to take a shower with me or later?"

"I'll take mine after you finish." Taking a shower made sense, but he hadn't thought about it. Had he been in his hotel room, it would have been a natural thing to do, but here in Alice's house he felt uneasy about taking a shower.

Alice sat up on the side of the bed. Ray expected her to put on a robe, but she stood up and left the room completely naked.

He could hear her back there waking up her daughters. She opened Margo's door first and said, "Time to get up, Margo! Rise and shine!" then she opened Hope's door and said, "Come on, Hope, get up!"

Ray lay there wondering if Alice often walked around naked in her house. If so, apparently her daughters were used to seeing her like that. He both liked it and disliked it. *She's a free spirit*, he thought, *without hang-ups or puritan ideas about the body.*

After Ray and Alice showered, she made scrambled eggs, bacon, and toast for Ray and herself. Then they sat together at the dining room table eating.

After breakfast he said, "Here's some money." He gave her a stack of twenties. "I don't want you feeding me. If I'm going to be eating here, I want to contribute my part."

She smiled and took the money and tucked it into her purse on the chair beside her.

In the nearby bathroom they could hear Margo taking her shower, hear the water splashing and hear her singing. Hope didn't believe in showers. She took baths, sitting in the tub for an hour or two. But this morning she told Alice she wasn't going to take a bath. "I'm not dirty."

The four of them were now in the living room. Hope was sitting on the floor in front of the TV watching cartoons, and Margo was on the couch methodically painting her fingernails red. Both girls were dressed in T-shirts and shorts and both were barefoot.

Ray and Alice were ready to leave. He was dressed in his clothes from the day before, a blue dress shirt and chino slacks. She was wearing a yellow summer dress with vertical purple stripes that made her look thinner than she was.

"You guys know what your Saturday morning chores are," said Alice. "When I get back, I want to find them done. Okay?"

Neither one responded.

Alice drove onto the Snellings lot and parked in the visitors section. They got out and walked toward the showroom.

Even before they reached the glass door, a middle-aged man with a big head that had a bald spot on top rushed out to meet them. A big smile spread across his rosy cheeks when he said, "Hi, folks! Beautiful day, huh? Come out to look at some cars?"

"Yes," Ray said with a guarded smile.

"I can show you around if you like?"

"No thanks," said Ray, "we'll just look around on our own."

"Sure, but if you need me, just put your lips together and whistle." His laughter was an exaggerated cackle.

Alice said, "Thank you."

"Certainly," said the salesman, and then he walked back toward the showroom, but he didn't go inside. He stood just outside the glass door watching them.

Together they started along the row of new cars, stopping first at a red Pontiac Firebird.

Ray said, "No, not for me."

Then they stopped at a Triumph TR6 convertible.

Alice said, "This is a nice one, very sporty, a head turner."

"Yeah, but too much of a head turner. I want something less flashy."

Next was a blue Porsche 912. Ray looked at the sticker price on the window. *Too expensive*, he thought. He was thinking he could afford it, but why blow that much money on four wheels?

70

Then came a blue Jeep CJ.

Alice said, "This would be great for the hills around here. You could go up into the mountains with no trouble."

"That's true, but I don't want a Jeep."

A white convertible Cadillac Eldorado was next.

"Now, here's your baby," said Alice, laughing.

He grunted, shaking his head.

They checked out a Dodge Dart, a 1976 AMC Pacer, a Ford Thunderbird, a Pontiac Grand Prix, a Ford Bronco; then they came to a little silver Volkswagen Scirocco.

Ray looked it over carefully. "I like this Scirocco. It's named after the Mediterranean wind."

"I didn't know that. But it's small, Ray. What if I wanted you to take the girls and me somewhere?"

"It'll easily seat four people, even five if you had to."

Ray kept looking it over. It was a three-door, four-passenger deal with the engine in front rather than the traditional rear as in the VW Bug; and it was front-wheel drive and hatchback; this one was made in Germany. He'd heard that some VWs were now being manufactured in countries other than Germany. "This one might be perfect for me."

"You made up your mind that quickly, huh?"

"Well, I want to drive it and see how it handles. If I like the way it drives, I'm going to just pay cash and not haggle with them."

Alice raised her eyebrows in mock surprise.

Already the same salesman was walking toward them. He'd been watching them all along. Even before he reached them, he called out, "Found something you'd like to try out?"

71

10

IT WAS EARLY TUESDAY MORNING. Ray was in Stanley's Café, a joint that boasted in neon lights BREAKFAST AND LUNCH. It was on Coker Street just off Main, a couple of blocks from Ray's apartment. There were only a few tables and a long counter. At the moment there were ten customers. Ray was sitting in a booth by the window. A plate of bacon and eggs and toast was in front of him.

Stanley brought a cup of coffee over to Ray and set it down beside his plate.

"You have a telephone directory?" said Ray, looking up.

"Sure, take the one back there in the telephone booth. Just be sure to put it back when you're done with it," said Stanley. He was a big guy with a headful of iron-gray hair and bushy gray eyebrows over gray eyes.

Ray got up and walked back to the booth and returned with the directory.

Looking through the Lorena telephone directory, he quickly found a listing for Mann. He remembered the operator telling him there was more than one Mann family in town. Here in the directory he saw the one Mann number the operator had mentioned. There was also an address. He took out his notepad and a pen and jotted down the address and phone number.

After breakfast he went back to the phone booth, stepped inside, and dialed the number. A woman answered, saying, "Hello? This is Mildred Mann."

"Mrs. Mann, my name is Raymond Jansen. I'm trying to locate Constance. Is she available to speak to me?"

"Yes, hold on a moment."

He waited about five seconds, then heard her voice. "Hello, this is Connie."

"Constance, I'm Ray, a friend of Scott's. Can you tell me how I can get in touch with him?"

"You're Ray Jansen, Scott's friend in New York?"

"That's right, but I'm here in Lorena."

"You're in Lorena! Wow! Scott told me you might be coming out to California. I know he would like to see you."

"Do you know how I can get in touch with him?"

"I think so. Scott talked so much about you. Can you meet me for lunch tomorrow?"

"Sure."

"Great! By then I will have some information about how you can contact Scott."

"That would be fine. Where do you want to meet?"

"How about Sally's Diner on Boyle Street? They make a great grilled cheese sandwich."

"Noon?"

"Noon is fine," she said.

Ray got there the next day at a quarter to twelve. The diner was old and seedy. The counters and tabletops were cracked and fading. The plastic-covered seats in the booths were sagging from years of use.

The hostess approached him at the entryway. She was a fat young woman with black hair, wearing a lemon-yellow apron. There were several old men at the counter probably eating a late breakfast. They looked like retired workers and were talking politics and bemoaning the condition of the country.

The waitress came toward him and said, "How many?"

"Two."

She picked up two menus from the stack on the counter by the cash register. "Have a seat anywhere," she said, following him.

Ray walked along the line of fifteen empty booths and sat in one in the middle. The seat sank under his weight.

The waitress plopped down the two menus, one in front of Ray and the other across from him. Then she walked away.

He was sitting by a window. Outside on a paved area between the diner and the nightclub next door, carpenters were sawing wood. They were doing repair work inside the nightclub called Mona Lisa's Smile. Ray watched and listened to the electric saw cut through the wood. The sound was sharp and brittle.

He picked up the greasy menu, a big plastic thing with colorful pictures of the various dishes available. The breakfast items—eggs, grits, hash browns, toast, home fries, sausage, ham, Spam, corned beef hash, chicken-fried steak, and sirloin—looked good, and Ray felt sure the picture looked a lot better than the actual food would.

He hadn't had any breakfast, but it was now lunchtime. He considered the traditional breakfast, then the day-starter skillet specials. It was too late for the early bird special. Maybe a breakfast scramble was the way to go.

The pancakes and waffle selections looked scrumptious: a stack of pancakes served with sausage links and lots of syrup, Belgian waffles, buckwheat cakes, or potato pancakes topped with strawberries and pecans. Yummy!

The omelets too looked appealing and savory: spinach or ham and cheese or a southwestern or peppers and mushrooms or avocado and bacon or black olives and cheddar cheese.

Then there were the tasty-looking breakfast burritos. They also were a possibility. They came filled with scrambled eggs and cheese.

Just as he was thinking it might be smart to settle for a good old-fashioned eggs Benedict and hash browns, the waitress came over and said, "Would you like a cup of coffee while you're waiting?"

"Sure, I'd like a cup of coffee. Thanks."

While Ray waited for the coffee, he turned to the lunch menu. Topping the list of sandwiches was Connie's grilled cheese. It looked mouthwateringly good. For an additional cost, you could add ham or bacon to it; but the club, the tuna melt, the turkey, and the BLT also looked inviting and tasty.

The waitress brought the coffee and Ray took a sip. He didn't use cream and sugar. It was good coffee but too hot to drink. He set it aside to let it cool a bit.

A variety of burgers was also pictured: western, mushroom, chili, and traditional, no frills.

He looked at his watch. It was fifteen after twelve. Where was Connie? Was she going to stand him up? The booths were beginning to fill up with people coming in for lunch. The old men at the counter were starting to leave.

Then he saw a woman coming through the doorway who was probably Connie. She was smiling as she made eye contact with him. Approaching, she waved to him. How did she know he was the one? *Sure*, he told himself, *that's an easy question*: he was the only black person in the diner. He was easy to spot.

Still smiling, she sat down in the booth facing Ray and nervously picked up the menu without looking at it. She said, "So, you're Ray! You look nothing like I imagined you would."

"How did you imagine I'd look?"

"Heavier, I guess, and darker, with shorter hair. Instead, you're slender, very fair-complected, with long curly hair. You look like that movie star—I can't think of his name. You know which one I mean?"

He laughed. "No, but I can assure you I'm no movie star."

She took a deep breath and let it out. "Sorry I'm late," she said, now finally looking down at the menu.

He waved away her comment. "No problem."

"I had to drop my mother off at the doctor's office on the way here, and it took longer than we thought. I had to detour around that road construction at Main and Gibson, and traffic was backed up."

He gave her what he hoped was a sympathetic smile. At the same time, he studied her face.

She was pretty, with an oval face framed by straight light brown hair that fell to her shoulders. Her mouth was full and shapely, and her nose was small and neat; there was a friendly twinkle in her gray-blue eyes. She reminded him of someone he'd seen before. It was just a feeling.

The waitress returned and they placed their orders. Connie ordered a grilled cheese sandwich on rye bread with deli pickles on the side. Ray ordered scrambled eggs and whole wheat toast.

After the waitress left, Ray said, "Where is Scotty?"

"I don't know," she said with a frown.

"Yesterday you said you might have some information today."

"That's true and again I made a few calls to San Francisco, thinking he'd turned up back there, but none of the people we knew there have seen him lately."

"I thought you two were together?"

"Yes, we were, but how did you know that?"

"I talked with your former landlord, Hans."

"Oh, yeah, I should have known. So, you know everything?"

"No, I don't know *everything*. I know you were or *are* married to a man named Goddard." He paused. "What happened?"

The waitress returned with a pitcher of water and filled their glasses. After she left, Connie said, "Scotty and I had a big fight, an argument, I mean. When we left San Francisco, we came up here and were staying in my parents' guest room. My parents didn't approve of him. Dad told him he had to leave. They almost came to blows. Dad become very angry. Mom and I tried to stop them, but they ignored us. Bottom line, Dad told Scotty to get the hell out of his house right now, and Scotty packed up his suitcase and left."

"Pretty abrupt, huh?"

"Yes, and I didn't get a chance to say anything to him, to find out where he was going. He and I earlier that day were arguing about something I no longer remember what it was about. It was ridiculous."

"Wow! Pretty intense day."

"Yes. The problem started when I left my parents to marry Theo. He and I had met down in San Francisco at a dinner party given by one of my college friends at UC Berkeley, Kelly Marie. She was friends with Theo's daughter, Lindsey, who is only three years younger than I am. Theo has a son too, Georgie, who's a year older than Lindsey. Mom and Dad thought Theo was too old for me. He's seven years younger than Dad. I brought Theo up here a week before we got married, and the meeting was a disaster. They begged me not to marry him. Obviously, that didn't work. Theo and I got married in San Francisco a week later. So, you see the resentment was deeper than just Scotty. I mistakenly thought they would like Scotty because he and I are closer in age and I knew how much they disliked Theo; but I was wrong again. They disliked

Scotty even more than they did Theo. Dad said Scotty had no *direction* in life."

"Wow! What was Scotty doing to make money up here in Lorena?"

She looked embarrassed and looked down at her lap. "He wasn't here long enough to find work. He and Dad got into it the second day we were here. So, the answer is nothing. He left after three or four days. In San Francisco he was tending bar. Other than that, I don't know. My parents thought he was selling drugs, but I saw no evidence of that nor did they. I don't see how he could have established himself as a drug dealer. It was a silly idea my parents had. They just wanted him gone from my life. It was just their crazy suspicion but, like I said, Scotty was working as a bartender when we were living up on Valencia. He was tending bar at a place down at Fisherman's Wharf. I think he might be doing that again somewhere in the city."

"Yeah, I can see that. He tended bar in New York too."

"He made good money when he was working. He paid our way everywhere we went."

Ray watched her eyes closely.

"Listen, Ray, I love Scotty and I know in my heart that we are going to be together again." She smiled sadly. "I know he'll eventually get in touch with me. I think he just doesn't want to call me at my parents' house. If I could afford to move somewhere else, I would."

"Where else besides San Francisco do you think he might be?"

"I can't think of anyplace else. Like I said, I suspect he returned to San Francisco. I called Hans again last night and some other people we know in San Francisco but nobody's seen him."

"Scotty is pretty resilient," Ray said.

Connie smiled sadly. "Yes, he is. Do you know that once when he was about fifteen, he was used as a pawn in a scam?"

"No, tell me."

"He was on the bus from school going back to the shelter when an old car hit the bus so that it couldn't go forward. The bus door opened and an ambulance-chasing con artist rushed onto the bus taking names and asking people if they were injured. He said he was a lawyer—if he was a lawyer, he was probably a disbarred lawyer. He whispered to Scotty, 'I can get you a lot of money for your injury,' but Scotty wasn't injured. The man said, 'Come with me, kid,' and Scotty went with him to a crooked doctor's office; the doctor wrote up a false complaint to the municipal transportation company's insurance company in Scotty's name. The ambulance-chaser guy gave Scotty fifty dollars, saying, 'This is your part of the settlement'; and he later figured the doctor and the crooked-lawyer guy ripped off the insurance company for a ton of money. Poor kid, he was so poor and hungry, he fell for the scheme. He later realized he shouldn't have gone with the con artist in the first place; but after that he was determined never to be used again. He is resilient *now* and more ethical than he was then as a hungry kid."

"He never told me that story," said Ray. "He was resilient and he also had his antennae up for danger. One night he was coming from karate at the gym. He was about fifteen. He was the only one standing at a bus stop on Bushwick Avenue, or maybe it was Lafayette Avenue—I don't remember which one it was. Anyway, he was at the corner of a cross street waiting for the bus to come so he could get back to the shelter. It was dark and it was winter and very cold. A man in a car stopped and opened the passenger door and said, 'Come on, kid, I'll give you a ride to where you're going,' and Scotty, by now having sharp antennae for trouble, turned and ran halfway up a dark side street, then ducked down steps to a basement entryway and hid there in the pitch-dark with his heart beating so loud he said he could hear it. He heard the man's car tires screeching as he came shooting up the dark street trying to catch him. It had taken the man time to get his passenger door closed, which gave Scotty time to run and hide in that basement doorway. The car shot right by where he was hiding, and Scotty came back up to the street and ran back to Lafayette and kept running up Lafayette till he came to the next bus stop on the same route where there were a lot of people waiting in a well-lighted area."

Connie said, "That's terrifying." She shuddered. "He never told me about that incident. Did he tell anybody at the shelter?"

"He told me, but he didn't tell anybody else for fear they would stop him from going to karate."

The waitress brought their food, and they stopped talking and started eating. She said, "Gosh, I didn't know how hungry I was. This grilled cheese sandwich is to die for."

He spread scrambled eggs onto a piece of toast and started eating. After a couple of minutes, he said, "Do you believe Scotty loves you?"

"He *said* he does." Her face showed she was considering the question and her answer. Now more firmly she said, "Yes, I believe he loves me. We're good together. We're soulmates. I'm in the process of divorcing Theo; and as soon I get my divorce, Scotty and I will get married."

"But you don't even know where he is."

She flushed red and stuttered, "That's true but . . . but that doesn't matter. I know where his heart is; and, like I said, he's very likely in San Francisco tending bar. He's not at the Fisherman's Wharf place. I called there. They haven't seen him."

"If he loves you, why hasn't he contacted you?"

"I told you he was mad at me."

"No, you said you fought. Why was he mad at you?"

"About a week or so after Scotty and I got up here, Theo sent me a letter telling me how much he loved me and wanted me back, that all would be forgiven. He's older than I am. I loved him; he was fatherly to me. I saw in him some things that I liked that I never saw in my own father. So, I wrote him a kind letter saying no, I would not come back, but that I would always have a kind of love for him. Absentmindedly, I left the letter on the dresser. I wasn't trying to hide it or deceive Scotty. I didn't have a stamp and an envelope at that moment. Scotty saw it and read it, and that is what pissed him off. That fight led to another fight the next day about something minor, something stupid."

"From Scotty's point of view, you are still in love with your husband?"

"Yes, but that is a different kind of love than what I feel for Scotty. I don't want to *be* with Theodore Goddard."

Ray was listening carefully.

"The Goddard family has money, and his father has a big estate in Los Angeles County. Theo is on a very limited income from the estate right now, but he will inherit his father's business. Theo's father made his money in high-end real estate; he's an engineer. He's building and selling million-dollar furnished homes to movie stars and millionaires. He built a lot of the mansions in Beverly Hills and in Hollywood Hills. The old man is getting up in years. Someday, like I said, Theo will inherit all that wealth, but I didn't marry him for that reason." She paused. "I follow my heart. My heart is with Scotty, and as soon as he realizes it, he'll contact me, I'm sure of it because I know he loves me."

"After Scotty discovered the letter and you fought that next day and your dad got mad at him and told him to get out, he just walked out, not telling you where he was going?"

"Not exactly."

"What happened?"

"I told you, Dad *put* him out; Dad told him to get out and not to come back. I didn't have time to talk with him."

"You haven't heard a word from him?"

"No, like I said, I've called just about every bar in San Francisco, but no luck."

"Yet you are sure he still loves you?"

"Absolutely sure. He just needs time to cool off. It's not the first time we had an argument. If you only knew what Scotty and I have, you would understand."

Ray said, "I know Scotty. I think I understand."

"When I first met Scotty, he told me his parents were rich and that both his mother and father were educated at Yale and that they expected him to go there too; but he refused and went to CUNY, where he at first studied premed. Giving that up, he switched to fine arts, but he said he soon realized it wasn't for him. He said he needed time to think about his future so, with a stipend from his parents, he traveled to Europe and knocked around London, Paris, Nice, Copenhagen, and Rome for a year and a half, mulling over his future. He said it was his coming-of-age trip, not the Grand Tour. Then, after telling me this, one night when he was drunk he broke down and cried like a baby, and he told me it was all a lie and that he grew up in a shelter and that he'd never been to Europe. And he told me the horrible truth: as an infant he was left in a dumpster."

Connie and Ray finished lunch and he paid, and they walked out together. He walked her to her car. "My dad's car," she said, getting in.

"If you hear from Scotty, let me know," he said, while writing down his address on a piece of paper.

PART 3

A High C
Accurately Struck

Every high C accurately struck demolishes the theory that
we are the irresponsible puppets of fate or chance.

—W. H. AUDEN

11

Ray's furniture was delivered early in May, just a week after he signed the paperwork, but it didn't come from Walter Hale Greer's store. Instead of returning to them after being rebuffed, he went to Erickson's Home Furnishings on Greenspan Avenue.

The store was gigantic, stretching a full city block. In addition to a plush supply of living room, bedroom, dining room, sitting room, and kitchen furniture and accessories, there was a massive room of original sculpture, paintings, and prints. Many were framed and hanging, and many others unframed and in stacks. There was also a room full of bookcases of all types and tables and benches.

At Erickson's, Ray bought everything he needed for his small apartment: bed, couch, kitchen table and chairs, armchair, a couple of framed prints for the living room, the works, on credit just to build up his already good credit.

In New York Ray had lived in apartments that were mostly furnished. For the first time he was now buying furniture and it was an adventure.

At Sears he bought dishes, silverware, pots and pans, and glasses. He also went shopping and stocked the refrigerator and kitchen cabinets with food. This was important because as a child he was always hungry. Stocking up on canned goods and dry produce such as rice and pasta and beans now was visceral insurance against hunger.

No matter where he was, whether in the state shelter or temporarily in a private home, he felt he was rarely given enough food. Portions were usually small. Also, if he was given chicken, it was always the wing or the back, never the breast or thigh. Fatty hamburger and a little spaghetti were usual.

Just knowing that his shelves were well stocked was enough to quiet his fear of hunger.

He was feeling elated and didn't mind that there were so many things to arrange. He made stops in town to get a telephone installed; he had the gas and electricity turned on.

Getting set up here in Lorena, he felt like he was on an exciting adventure and at the same time it was a kind of rebirth. In New York he had also lived in rented apartments. Embarking on living in a new apartment back then always felt like a struggle—not an adventure, not a metaphor of rebirth. There were always landlord and landlady rules and regulations to follow, dos and don'ts to obey.

Here in Lorena his daily routine quickly evolved. He was up by seven and after a shower he dressed and walked down to the Gibson Street Café at the corner of Gibson and Leahy or to Stanley's Café on Coker and Main. He alternated between the two diners. He normally lingered over a breakfast of orange juice and sunny-side-up eggs with two strips of bacon and a toasted English muffin.

While eating he read the *Lorena Sentinel* and the *New York Times*, both of which he picked up out front from the vending machines. Because of his investments, Ray kept an eye on the stock market on a daily basis. He called his broker, Beth Schuller, in New York about once or twice a month, but he resisted reacting to the whims of the market.

Occasionally he also heard from his lawyer, John V. Deering. The "V" was for Victor. Deering handled the initial processing of Ray's lottery win into money and safely into the bank.

In the afternoon twice a week, he intended to spend an hour or two at Halter & McCarty's Fitness Center on Main Street one block down from the Culver Bar. So far, he'd gone only twice.

One morning Beth called. She said, "Ray, I grew your money big-time this morning by investing heavily in Kellogg's Corn Flakes." He smiled to himself, thinking, *How ironic.*

Late afternoons were so far a toss-up. He might watch TV till it was time to go to Alice's place, or he might read a detective novel or a mystery or a thriller. At Bob Smith's Bookstore, which sold both used and new books, he'd recently bought a stack of books: *Ragtime*, *Breakfast of Champions*, *Carrie*, *The Bluest Eye*, *Gravity's Rainbow*, and other recently published books, mostly novels.

He also pondered ways to get in touch with Scotty, who might be in San Francisco or even somewhere here in Lorena. Finding Scotty in a town this small was not as easy as it might seem; yet he was still on the lookout for a flash of red hair in some passing car or along the sidewalk.

Finding Scotty, though, was becoming less important than making a life for himself now that he was here. Scotty's postcard had gotten Ray to California. He had to start thinking of it as a catalyst.

Maybe that was the point; but Ray was worried about his longtime friend and was anxious to contact him to see how he was doing. In the back of his mind, Ray had the idea that he might be able to help Scotty, yet offering Scotty money would be a delicate situation. Scotty was extremely proud and stubborn.

Ray was now spending more nights with Alice at her house than at his own apartment. It was a bit disorienting, but he was managing okay. Doing so threw off the routine he was establishing, but the chaos of his early life had prepared him for the disruption.

Wednesday night Alice went with her friend Annette Newberry to see the newly released movie *All the President's Men*. Alice had an adolescent-like crush on one of the actors in the movie, Robert Redford. She never missed a Redford movie. She said everybody was talking about the movie, and she'd heard that it was really good.

It was already six o'clock. Ray walked downtown to the Culver Bar on Main Street. Unlike the cowboy bar, Wynn's Old Beer Tavern, the Culver was known as a watering hole for liberals and intellectuals. Many people from campus tended to gather there.

Ray entered for the first time and sat at the bar. Six people were already at the bar: two women and four men were solemnly drinking, and they were gazing at the TV mounted on the wall behind the bar. The music was easy rock. When Ray's eyes adjusted to the dark, he looked down the bar and saw Cynthia Rudder, one of the people he'd met at the party.

He walked over to her and said, "Hello! Cynthia, right?"

She smiled. "That's right. You have a good memory. How have you been? Still getting settled?"

"Yes. May I join you?"

She patted the empty seat beside her. "By all means."

The bartender, a heavyset woman about thirty, came and stood before Ray; she was wearing a dumpy muddy-colored dress and had a fixed squinty smile. "Hi there! Can I fix you a drink?" She placed a napkin on the bar in front of him.

Ray ordered tap beer. She drew the beer and placed the full mug in front of him.

Cynthia said, "Ray, have you met Susie?"

"No."

"Hi, Ray, I'm Susie Boyle, your friendly local barmaid." She cackled and stuck her hand out across the bar for him to shake.

Ray shook hands with her. "Glad to meet you, Susie. Any relation to Boyle Street?"

"Yes. The street was named after my great-grandfather, who was a mayor here in town back in the olden days." Her smile stretched into a grin. The grin was so wide, her eyes closed to a squint and her cheeks puffed up.

He had not expected such a response. He had tossed the question to her as a light conversation piece. "You're descended from town royalty," he said. "I'm impressed."

She grinned widely again and curtsied while holding the hem of her dress out from her legs. She bowed her head slightly.

Another customer came and sat at the far end of the bar. Susie sauntered down to place a cocktail napkin on the bar in front of him and to take his order.

Turning to Cynthia, Ray said, "So, how have you been?"

"Oh, crazy. Our chair, Phil Crosby, is disgusted with the whole situation. Gilbert Walker is too. One of our professors, David Nelson, is guilty of fraud. He's lied about everything on his vita. He lied to get hired and he's lied to get promoted. The chair, in cahoots with the dean, had tried to keep a lid on this violation of ethics, this criminal act, so that the scandal does not bring disgrace to the department and the whole campus, but as always happens the word got leaked and now everybody knows about it."

"Now what happens?"

"Well, they'll probably quietly fire the guy with a year's pay."

"Why would they do that? Why not just fire him? Why give him money for a whole year?"

"Because he has tenure and, though he's committed a crime, the university would rather quietly pay him off to keep it out of the newspapers. When it comes to something like this, they always take the cowardly way out."

It was still early in May. Saturday evening Ray and Alice had finished dinner and were on her backyard patio sitting in her wooden yard chairs. The girls were in the house watching TV.

Alice said, "I have an offer to go with an ag research team to Japan. I have to make up my mind quickly because the team is leaving in two weeks. The chair of the department is going. I would go as his assistant, to take notes. I'm seriously considering the offer. It would be an opportunity. Japan is a place I will never visit otherwise, and all my expenses would be paid."

"How long would you be gone?"

"Two weeks. That's not a long time." She reached over and touched the back of Ray's hand. "You can go with me if you want, but you would have to pay your own way."

Ray considered the offer and quickly rejected it. "No, I would just be in the way. I don't like that tagalong feeling."

Later, in the evening, Ray and Alice were in the living room watching *The Carol Burnett Show*. During a commercial, Alice said, "Do you ever think about who your parents were?"

"Yes, but not as much as I did when I was younger."

"I imagine not knowing is pretty painful?"

"I don't know if 'painful' is the right word. I've long been curious about my origins and from time to time when I was younger, I made stabs at trying to find out; I even searched for my parents, but I always ran into a wall. Eventually, I made peace with the fact that I probably will never know. There were no clues, nothing to go on."

"So, you and your friend Scotty were in the same boat?"

"Yes. People, especially adults, thought it odd that he and I were like family."

"Was it because he was white, and you were black?"

"Yes, I assumed that was the reason. By the time we were adults, we were each other's only link to a similar past." He paused. "We've gone over all of this before. Why bring it up again?"

Alice was about to respond but her phone rang. It was on the side table in arm's reach of where she was sitting on the couch. Ray was in the armchair across from her.

Alice picked up the receiver. "Hello? Oh, hi, Annette! Yeah, I'm seriously considering going. What? Just watching *The Carol Burnett Show*. Sure, if you want to. That will be fun! Come on over."

Ray remembered hearing about Alice's friend Annette Newberry and immediately thought of leaving. "You're having company?"

"It's just Annette. She's coming over to help me select clothes for my trip to Japan."

"So, you've made up your mind?"

"Not completely, but in case I go, I'll know what I'm going to take. It's just girl play. Annette likes to do stuff like that. It'll be fun."

He stood up. "I think I'll go. I have so much I still need to do to get my apartment in some kind of living order."

"Oh, don't go, please. I was hoping you'd spend the night. Don't you want to spend the night?"

He thought about it. It was not a bad idea. "Okay." He sat back down and refocused on the TV show.

Ten minutes later, he heard Annette coming up onto the front porch. The front door was opened. She opened the screen door and stepped into the living room. This was Ray's first time seeing her.

She was a very tall, thin woman with an emaciated-looking body; her skin looked damaged by smoking, and she had an alcoholic-looking face. Ray suspected she was neither emaciated nor alcoholic but was suffering from some sort of serious medical condition.

She gave Ray a startled look. Alice quickly introduced her to Ray. Annette said, "I've heard so much about you; you look nothing like I expected." She smirked.

Having heard the screen door close, both girls came from their rooms to see who had arrived.

Annette asked, "Alice, who's going to stay here with the kids?"

"My sister, Karen."

"We don't need a babysitter, Mom!" shouted Margo.

"Did Karen's divorce become final yet?" said Annette.

"It'll be final next month," said Alice. Then to Margo: "It's not a matter of babysitting. I can't legally leave you girls here alone. You want me to go to jail?"

"We're not little kids anymore," said Hope.

"Looks who's talking," said Margo. "Hope, you're only twelve. It's because of you we have to have a babysitter."

Hope said, "No, it's not! Is it because of me, Mom?"

"No, sweetie. You both are too young to be here alone, so if I go to Japan, Karen will be here with you. She'll come here every day after work and stay overnight; and I want you both to not give her a hard time. If you do, I will hear about it."

Hope sat down and tucked her skinny legs under her on the couch. She started watching TV and absentmindedly started picking at a pimple on her chin.

Margo abruptly left the room. She would soon be back there in her room probably daydreaming about her current male teen idol, maybe Bobby Sherman or Davy Jones or Donny Osmond. Ray had no idea, but Alice once said that Margo spent a lot of time in her room with her door closed playing sentimental pop songs and daydreaming about her latest crush.

"Have a seat, Annette," said Alice.

Annette smirked. "I didn't come to sit down, Alice. Let's go through your dresses, girl, and see what you need to take with you on your trip. I'm excited!"

Alice stood up. "Okay, I see you mean business."

The door to Alice's bedroom was only a few feet from where Ray was sitting. The bedroom door was opened, and Alice led Annette into the room.

Although the TV was fairly loud with canned laughter and Carol Burnett's jokes, Ray could hear the two women discussing the clothes. They were not more than a few feet away. Annette said, "You simply must take this red dress, Alice!"

"Oh, I don't know if that's a good idea, Annette."

"Don't you know you *have* to take a red dress on a trip like this? A little red dress is an absolute necessity." She lowered her voice: "Don't forget your diaphragm, either!"

Alice whispered, "Hush, not so loud!"

"Oh, I forgot. I didn't know I was talking loud."

"Here, just pile the dresses on the bed. I'll go through them and see what I *really* want to take with me. I can't take *all* of these."

"Alice, you know you have got to take this little *red* dress. You must!"

12

Sunday afternoon, ray was sitting in Alice's backyard reading the *Lorena Sentinel*.

Hope came down the back steps and over to Ray. "Stand up, Ray, I want you to help me do something, stand up."

"What do you want to do?"

"Just stand up, I'll show you."

Ray put the newspaper down and stood up. "Now what?"

Suddenly Hope leaped up on him, locking her thin legs around his hips. She then threw her upper torso away from him with her arms reaching down till her hands touched the concrete of the patio.

When she did this, Ray heard something in his lower back snap. He knew something had broken, probably a disk or vertebra; and he knew it was going to be with him the rest of his life.

The girl had taken him by surprise, leaping on him without warning, not even telling him what she was trying to do. Now, from her upside-down face, she said, "I'm trying to do a handstand. When I release my legs, take my ankles and hold them up straight. Okay? I want to show you I can walk on my hands."

Then she released her leg grip, and he held her by her ankles. "Now what?"

"Don't let go till I tell you to."

"Okay."

"Now! Let go!"

Ray released the grip he had on her ankles, and Hope walked on her hands away from him across the concrete patio for a few feet before she lost her balance and tumbled down, red in the face and laughing.

The next day at five thirty, Ray picked up Alice at the college. While driving toward her house, he said, "Do you know of a good back doctor in town?"

"You're having *back* problems?" She was alarmed.

"Yes. It's my lower back." He was not going to tell her about Hope causing it. No way.

"Sure, Dr. Roger Dees is said to be one of the best in northern California, and he lives right here in Lorena. I've seen him a couple of times about lower back problems. I think I still have his card right here in my purse." She started digging in her purse for the business card. "Here, I found it," she said, handing the card to him.

He released one hand from the steering wheel and took the card and slipped it in the chest pocket of his shirt. "Thanks. I'll make an appointment."

"He's very honest and outspoken. If he recommends an operation, he tells you the benefits and the risks; but don't let him scare you with the risks."

It was Sunday near the end of May. Ray drove Alice to the airport for her trip to Japan. Before she went through security, she put down her carry-on, turned to him, and said, "Karen will call you. She wants to meet you. She'll be coming to the house every day after work to keep an eye on the girls. You should stop by the house at least once in a while. The girls are very fond of you. You like them?"

"Yes, of course I do."

"Margo wants you to teach her to drive. She's got her learner's permit. She's almost sixteen, too young for a license; but maybe she's not too young to start learning. She's so determined to learn; I've tried teaching her from time to time, but it didn't work out. She gets mad at me and we end up arguing."

"I'll see what I can do." Ray kissed her lightly on the lips. "Have a great trip," he said, already feeling in this moment that Alice's leaving for Japan troubled him for a reason he was not able to articulate. He knew it had something to do with the fact that their relationship was just starting.

He watched her get in line; then he left.

Now it was Monday, five thirty in the afternoon. Ray's phone rang. "Hello?"

"Hello, Ray, this is Karen, Alice's sister. I'm at Alice's house. I guess she told you I'd be keeping an eye on the girls?"

"Yes, she did."

"We've never met, so I thought you might like to stop by for a cup of coffee with me or even have dinner with me and the girls?"

"Sure."

"Great! I just drove from Sacramento; that's where I work. The traffic this afternoon was unusually hectic. I don't know why. Usually it's a thirty-minute drive for me, but today it took almost an hour—and I drive fast."

"What kind of work do you do?"

"I'm a salesperson at Brockway & Moyle, Inc.; it's a midsize department store chain. I stand behind a counter and show women jewelry. It's not so bad. We also get a lot of teenage girls in there looking for costume jewelry. The variety makes the day go faster."

"I know about retail sales. You're smart to make it fun rather than a drag."

A short time later, Ray drove up and parked behind a green VW Bug in front of the white shiplap house. He saw a tall, skinny woman with dark hair and a complexion considerably darker than Alice's. She was standing on the front porch, leaning against the banister and eating a vanilla ice cream cone. Margo was in the swing. They were obviously in conversation. Both turned and looked at him as he drove up and switched off the motor.

Even before he climbed the steps to the porch, he said, "You must be Karen?"

"I am, and you must be Ray." She had a quizzical expression.

"I am," he said with a smile. He saw right away that Karen was wired differently than her older sister, Alice. She was all nerves and energy, in contrast to Alice's calculating and calm nature. Karen was also prettier, with tons of long, dark silky-black curly hair. He wondered if she and Alice had the same father.

Margo said, "Ray, would you teach me to drive?"

Before Ray could respond, Karen said, "This girl has been after everybody to teach her to drive—me, Alice, her dad, everybody; and she's only fifteen!"

"Almost sixteen!" shouted Margo.

"You won't be sixteen till July sixteenth."

"Will you, Ray?" said Margo. "Mom says it's okay for me to ask you. So, will you, pretty please, please, please?"

"Alice mentioned it to me, so okay. We can start with some simple instructions."

Ray called Dr. Dees's office the next day and was surprised that he was able to get an appointment for that afternoon. He had no trouble finding the doctor's office on Coker Street in the middle of the block in a little family home converted into an office with a sign planted out on the lawn: DR. ROGER DEES, MD.

Ray walked toward the receptionist behind the desk. A nameplate on the desk read BARBARA AUSTIN. She was thin and blond and about twenty-five. Barbara was smiling as Ray approached her.

He explained why he was there. She checked her schedule and said, "Yes, Mr. Jansen, I have you down for two. The doctor will be with you shortly. He's presently with another patient."

"Thank you." He sat down and gazed out the window at a great oak tree waving gently in the breeze.

Five minutes later a heavyset woman with auburn hair and fat cheeks and a no-nonsense frown came out and approached him. "Mr. Jansen, I'm Dr. Dees's nurse, Sally Keys. If you'll follow me, I'll get you started."

"Okay." He stood up and followed her down a hallway and into a small side room. It was obvious that bedrooms were partitioned off to make small units along this hallway.

"Have a seat, and I'll take your blood pressure," she said. She stood in front of him with the blood pressure apparatus and wrapped the sleeve around his arm and tightened it. Ray listened to the air releasing from the apparatus. When it was done, Sally Keys said, "Your blood pressure is normal, one-eighteen over sixty." She paused. "He wants me to X-ray your back. Is that okay?"

"Sure."

"Come over to this machine," she said.

He followed her across the room to the X-ray machine.

"Stand with you back against this plate."

He did as he was told.

She went behind a partition and he heard a clicking sound from there, then she said, "It's done. Have a seat. It'll be just a minute. I have to develop this."

She left the room holding an object about the size of a large square platter.

He sat down and noticed a rack of magazines on the wall alongside the doorway. He got up and walked over to the rack to take a closer look: *Newsweek*, *Seventeen*, *Time*, *Rolling Stone*. He sat back down without taking one.

A half hour later, a middle-aged man of about average height with graying hair suddenly came into the room looking very concerned. He entered in a rush. His hand was extended. "Hello, Mr. Jansen, I'm Dr. Dees. Good to meet you. I hear you're having back problems."

"Yes."

The doctor sat down in a chair facing Ray. "I've seen your X-ray and it looks like a bulging disk. It's going to get worse over time if you don't have an operation. If you decide on an operation, remember the success rate is only about fifty percent; and even with a successful operation, it might not prevent the pain that you are now feeling. The pain could stay with you for years to follow and it might never go away entirely. Also operating on the lower back successfully is not likely to prevent your spine from eventually curving. By the time you are sixty, if you live to be that old, your spine probably will be so curved that it will interfere with your ability to walk in a natural way. I've seen it happen over and over in older patients. Any questions?"

"No."

"Now for the bad news: There are thousands of intricate nerves in the back, and if during an operation any of those nerves are damaged, you might end up paralyzed and have to spend the rest of your life in a wheelchair. Any number of things can go wrong during a back operation. You might even die. If I do the operation or if any doctor does the operation, you'd have to sign a document that exonerates the doctor from blame for anything that might go wrong. So, you have a lot to consider."

"Sounds pretty awful, Doctor."

"Well, there are other options. I can give you a prescription for pain medication. You can also exercise in a way not to prevent any further injury; and I think over time you will learn how to protect your back. My nurse will give you an exercise chart on your way out. Any questions?"

"I guess not."

"Then I'll write you a prescription with codeine, but be careful." Dr. Dees stood up and smiled. "Are we done?"

"Yes, Doctor. Thank you."

The doctor reached out for Ray's hand and they shook. Ray left the office dismayed and depressed.

Once Ray had the bottle of pain pills from the drugstore, he was hesitant to start taking them.

He was worried that he might want to continue for the sedative effect, and if he did, he might eventually become addicted to codeine; but he started anyway.

Dr. Dees had prescribed four per day. Ray took three that first day. The next day he took only two, all the time monitoring his body's response to the drug.

The sign on the office door read SID ELLISON, CHIROPRACTOR. Ray opened the door and entered. He was immediately facing a pretty young woman behind a small desk that looked like it'd been kicked and banged around for many years in used furniture stores. The waiting room, if this was a waiting room, was about the size of a large walk-in closet. The nameplate on her desk said PENNY HALL.

"Hello, I have an appointment; my name is Raymond—"

"Raymond Jansen. Let me see, yes, Raymond, I have you down for today at ten thirty. You're early, about ten minutes early. That's good. Please have a seat, and Mr. Ellison will see you shortly."

A few minutes later the inner door opened, and Mr. Ellison came out. He was a tall, well-built man with black hair, and he was wearing eyeglasses with thick black frames. He reminded Ray of the comic book character Clark Kent, also known as Superman. "Mr. Jansen? I'll see you now. Please come in," he said.

Ray followed him into the examination room, where there was a long chiropractic table with a hole at one end for the patient's face. In the corner there was a small table and two chairs arranged around it.

"Have a seat, please." The chiropractor sat down. He crossed his legs and rested one arm on the table.

Ray sat down facing him.

"I understand that you are having back problems?"

Ray told him what happened.

"Well, to find out what's going on, we'll have to X-ray your back first. Then we'll decide the best steps to take to correct the problem."

After the chiropractor developed the X-ray, he came back in the room holding a black plastic sheet about twelve-by-twelve inches. He sat down and leaned forward with the X-ray so that Ray could see it up close.

"You see here in this area, it shows that one of your disks is rubbing against the vertebra. I recommend acupuncture. I can give you some relief with the acupuncture, then you can come back for back adjustments. Okay?"

"Yes, okay. The pain is pretty intense. If acupuncture relieves the pain, that's what I want." Even as he spoke, Ray was thinking he probably needed surgery; and he was sure that the chiropractor was not going to say so.

"First, I'll do an adjustment," the chiropractor said in a matter-of-fact manner.

When Ray was stripped down to his waist, the chiropractor worked with strong hands from Ray's shoulders down to his feet, poking, pushing, and pressing.

"Now for the needles," the chiropractor said in a self-satisfied tone.

Still lying facedown on the table, Ray felt the chiropractor touching his lower back; then he felt one tiny needle piercing after another across the area. It was not painful, certainly no more painful than a flu shot. In ten or fifteen minutes, the doctor was done, and Ray walked out feeling better.

Ray was almost home and ready to turn into the Van Brandt parking lot when suddenly the rear end of the Scirocco jolted and lifted up, then flopped down with a thud. Ray's head bounced up and down as the seat belt snapped tighter against his chest. He'd been hit from behind.

What the . . . ? He sat there trying to recover from the shock. In the rearview mirror, he saw the young man who'd hit him getting out of his car. Ray watched him inspect the front end of his own car before checking Ray's car. He sat there trying to calm down and trying to determine if he was hurt physically.

At the moment he felt okay, then he opened the door and stepped out and walked back to the young man, who now was looking both angry and nervous. Ray could see that the young Hispanic man was half drunk. He could also smell the alcohol on the guy's breath.

Ray looked at his car. The damage was minor. Only the fender was slightly bent. In a situation like this, he knew it was best to let the offender speak first.

The young man said, "I didn't know you were going to stop so suddenly like that." He paused. "Please don't call the police or report this to your insurance company. I'll pay for the damage." He reached into his back pocket and pulled out his wallet. "I'm on probation. If the police get involved, I'll lose my license."

Ray looked again at the damaged fender. "Well, I can't tell how much it's going to cost to get this fender fixed or replaced."

The young man pulled out a fistful of twenties from his wallet and counted out three hundred dollars in twenties. "Is this enough?"

"I don't know," Ray said while writing down the license plate number of the young man's car.

"Well, here is another hundred; no, I'll make it eight hundred. This should do it, don't you think?"

The young man counted out eight hundred dollars and held the money out to Ray, but he hesitated to take it.

"Please take it. I can't afford to lose my license. I drive a truck for a living. Like I said, I'm already on probation."

"Okay," Ray said, and he took the eight hundred and stuck the money in his pocket.

13

Karen was in the swing watching. Ray and Margo were in Alice's car. It was automatic, unlike Ray's manual standard shift. Standard would have been too difficult. Margo wanted to learn on an automatic. She was sitting in the driver's seat, and Ray was in the passenger seat. He said, "Okay, simply turn the key, just turn the key so that the motor kicks in. Don't do anything else."

Margo turned the key and the car started.

"Okay, now release the emergency brake."

She did as she was told.

"Now put the car in drive."

She put it in drive.

"Keep your foot on the brake. Now lift your foot off the brake and gently press the accelerator; and keep both hands on the steering wheel; yes, like that up at the top."

The car rolled forward for about ten yards.

"Foot on the brake again and slowly stop the car."

The car stopped.

"Now, put it in reverse while still holding the brake down. Okay, release the brake and slowly back up just a few feet, no more."

Margo did as she was told.

"Now, just keep doing that and going forward a few feet and stopping, then backing up a few feet; that's all I want you to do today."

She did it five or six more times. "Wow!" she said. "This is so much better than what Mom had me doing. She just told me to drive around the block, and I got scared and confused, and we ended up yelling at each other."

That following Thursday evening, Ray was home in his apartment watching the news when his phone rang. "Hello?"

"Hi, Ray, it's Margo. My dad is here. He would like to meet you. Can you come over? Karen is sending out for pizza."

"Sure."

Ray felt a sinking feeling in his stomach. Was this going to be an occasion for the ex-husband to inspect the ex-wife's boyfriend?

Ray walked into the living room. Margo and Hope were sitting on the couch at opposite ends watching TV. He heard Karen in the kitchen call out, "Is that Ray?"

Margo answered, "Yes!"

The ex-husband was sitting in the armchair facing the front door. Ray noticed that the ex-husband's head turned slightly to the side the way a dog turns his head when he's trying to understand what he's looking at.

Although Ray's back was hurting from the injury Hope caused, he smiled. He was no longer taking the pills.

The ex-husband stood up and extended a hand to Ray. "Hello, Ray, I'm Donald, Donald Whitney."

"Hello, I'm Raymond Jansen."

"Nice to meet you, and by the way just call me Don. May I call you Ray?"

"Yes, of course."

"I hope this isn't too awkward for you, Ray. I just came up to visit my daughters. I don't get up this way nearly often enough."

"Where do you live?" The question was like a reflex. Ray already knew the answer.

"Atlanta, Georgia. I'm with the Sky Blue Water Bottling Company."

Hope said, "Dad is the CEO, chief executive officer! He has three hundred people under him."

"Not *under* him, you idiot!" said Margo. "*Working* for him!"

"Means the same thing," said Hope, pushing her bottom lip out in a pout.

Don said, "Now, girls, I just got here. I don't want to hear bickering. Please try to be civil toward each other."

"She started it," said Hope.

The pungent aroma of pizza with sausage, peppers, and mozzarella was floating in from the kitchen through the dining room to the living room.

Margo said, "Ray, Mom called this morning! She's having fun. The conference hours are in the morning and her afternoons are free. She's doing a lot of sightseeing. She has some dinner parties she has to go to in the evenings, but she's loving all of it."

Karen called out from the dining room. "Come and get it, you guys!"

They gathered around the dining room table. Karen got busy cutting the pizza and placing slices on paper plates. Margo helped with the distribution.

With a mouth full of pizza, she said, "Guess what, Dad?"

"What, Margo?"

"Ray is teaching me how to drive and unlike Mom he takes his time and I'm feeling so much more confident."

"That's nice, sweetie. Just be careful. You're only fifteen."

"You forget, Dad, you told me you learned to drive when you were ten years old," said Margo with a "got you" look. "Your dad started teaching you early."

Karen said, "I didn't learn to drive a car till I was eighteen, but Alice learned young. I think she was about fifteen or sixteen."

"I don't want to drive a car," said Hope. "When I grow up, I'll have my own private chauffeur."

"Then you'd better be sure to marry a millionaire," said Karen.

"I won't need to marry a millionaire," Hope said, "because I'll *be* a millionaire."

"And just how do you plan to make so much money?" said Margo with a sneer.

"I don't have to tell you," Hope said, sneering back at her.

Don said, "Girls, let's enjoy this delicious pizza and not fight at the table. Are you guys carrying on like this because your mom is away?"

Laughing, Karen said, "Don, are you kidding? These two carry on like this all the time. It's how they express their love for each other."

Without looking up from his plate, Don said, "Ray, what sort of work do you do?"

"I'm between jobs right now. I was manager in a Dorchester Supermarket in Brooklyn, a small chain back east."

"I've heard of it. We have shipments that go there. Why'd you quit?"

"I wanted to relocate to California and here I am."

"I see. You plan to return to retail management?"

"It's a possibility," Ray said. "I majored in business administration. It's where I'm comfortable."

"He's independently wealthy, Dad," said Margo.

"Hardly," Ray said, giving her a surprised look.

"Mom said you were," said Hope.

"Well," Ray said, "let's just say I can take my time in finding work in California."

"Sounds like a nice place to be," said Don. "Why California?"

"A friend of mine from childhood moved out here and he wrote to me about how great life was out here, but I was ready for a change anyway. I wasn't happy in New York, so when I had the means to do so, I made the move."

Slowly the conversations around the table dried up, and when they finished talking, only one slice of pizza was left. Margo was the first to depart. She took that last slice with her to her room and slammed the door.

The first Sunday in June at four in the afternoon, Ray was at the airport waiting for Alice to arrive from Japan. He stood in the crowd, focused on the arrival gate. Word had just been announced that the plane had touched down and it was taxiing to the gate.

Although knowing he should be feeling joyous anticipation, instead he felt anxiety and even a sense of dread. When he saw her emerge, he made eye contact immediately. He watched her face. In that moment there was panic in her eyes. Rather than smiling and waving happily to him, she quickly looked down. It was a telling moment.

Yet driving her home, he tried to be cheerful. "How was your trip? Did you enjoy Japan?"

"Yes," she said in a dry voice, "it was fun; but I had a lot of work to do and I'm tired. It was a long flight. I'm exhausted. I just want to crawl into bed and sleep for thirty hours."

He affectionately touched the back of her left hand resting on her lap. Traffic was light, and the sun was still high, causing a blinding glare in his eyes. He squinted all the way till the turnoff for Lorena.

When Alice and Ray walked in, Hope and Margo were waiting in the living room watching a game show. Ray was surprised that the girls did not jump up and embrace their mother. They acted as though she was just coming home from work. They said, "Hey, how was it?" the way one might say, "How was your day?"

Ray sat down and focused on the TV screen.

Alice dropped her luggage by the front door, and she started stripping out of her clothes. She kicked off her shoes. "I'm going to bed. I'm exhausted."

Ray stood up. "I'm going home," he said.

Standing there naked, Alice gave him an alarmed look. "Why? I was hoping you'd spend the night. I just got back and you're leaving me already?"

"Well, you're tired. You need to sleep."

"But I want to sleep with your arms around me."

"Mom, we don't want to hear any mushy talk," said Hope.

"Yeah," said Margo, "keep it for the bedroom."

Alice said, "Do you guys know what you're going to eat for dinner?"

"Yeah, we got stuff: there's leftover pork roast that Aunt Karen cooked yesterday," said Margo. "By the way, Karen had a hot date tonight. She couldn't be here to greet you."

"I don't want any pork roast," said Hope. "Yuck!"

Margo said, "Ray, why don't you buy us a pizza?"

"You just had pizza a few days ago," he said.

"We can eat pizza every day," said Hope. She leaped up. "I'll call for a pepperoni pizza."

She picked up the telephone on the end table by the chair Ray was sitting in. She dialed and ordered the pizza.

Alice said, "I'm going to bed." Without an ounce of self-consciousness about her nakedness, she walked into her bedroom and closed the door behind her.

Then she opened the door and stuck her head out and said, "Ray, I'll be waiting."

Margo shouted, "You'll be asleep!"

Then Alice shut the door again.

Ray ate pizza with the girls, then watched TV with them till ten o'clock. When he left the living room, Margo had fallen asleep on the couch, and Hope was still watching TV.

When Ray climbed into Alice's bed in his T-shirt and boxer shorts, she was sleeping so deeply, she was not snoring as usual. He spooned himself against her naked backside and embraced her. She snuggled against him.

As she mumbled unclear words in her sleep, she reached back and gripped him in her fist, all the while still mumbling something with slurred words, but it wasn't clear who she was talking to as she guided him in.

Ray dreamed he and Alice were at the top of the Statue of Liberty, a place he last visited when he was eleven, but the Statue of Liberty was in downtown Lorena and there was nothing odd about the dislocation.

In the morning while eating breakfast with Alice at her dining room table, Ray said, "I'm going to buy a house here in town. This town is beginning to feel like home to me."

"That's a great idea, Ray! Why don't *we* buy the house together?"

"Together?"

"Sure, we can take out a loan together."

He didn't want to tell her that he was thinking of paying cash and the thought of co-owning a house with Alice did not appeal to him. It gave him an uneasy feeling.

"I plan to pay cash for the house," he said.

"It's okay if you don't want to buy it with me. I understand, but cash is not a good idea, Ray. It's better to get a bank loan so you'll have the credit established here in town. I know you have great credit, but this would make it even stronger."

"That's not a bad idea."

"Let's just go to the bank to see what they say. Do you mind?"

"Why do that if we're not buying together?"

"Just do it for me, okay? I want to see if we would have been able to get a loan together. I'm curious about *my own* credit status."

It seemed like a crazy idea and it didn't seem quite ethical, but he saw no harm in going through with it if initiating the process would give her the credit information she was looking for.

"We can go to the bank tomorrow," she said.

He hesitated, then said, "Okay."

This proposal to buy a house together and her trip to Japan and meeting her ex-husband all had caused a seismic shift in his hopeful attitude toward the relationship. Alice was moving a lot faster than he in cementing it.

He was thinking what he needed most was to see the chiropractor again. His back was killing him. He was comfortable only when lying down flat on his back. Sitting was difficult. So was standing, and even walking caused discomfort. Something back there was definitely broken.

14

R<small>AY WAS LUCKY ENOUGH TO</small> park outside on busy Leahy Street on a one-hour meter right in front of the bank. It was Tuesday in the morning before Alice had to be at work. She and Ray walked into the First National Bank of Lorena together. The bank had to check his and Alice's credit scores. She would then have the information she wanted.

They walked in and took a number and waited to see a loan officer. Three customers were ahead of them. Concerned about the time, Alice kept looking at her watch.

She normally got to work at eight. It was already nine o'clock. She'd phoned in to say she would be late. If she walked in late, the world would not fall apart; but since she insisted on her staff getting there on time, she herself needed to set a good example.

They finally got called over to speak with the loan officer, a big man with a jutting jaw and a receding hairline. Ray explained to him what they wanted.

The officer said, "Where are you employed, Mr. Jansen?"

"I'm currently unemployed."

The officer asked both for social security numbers, then quickly checked their credit histories. Ray was surprised that the officer was able to check their credit so quickly.

Finally, the loan officer said, "Sorry, folks, no can do. Mrs. Whitney, it's not that your credit is bad, it's just that you already own two houses

106

and neither one is fully paid for; and, Mr. Jansen, your credit is good too, but you are unemployed. That is not a good risk. Your credit score, Mr. Jansen, is eight seventeen and yours, Mrs. Whitney, is six fifty-two, but no, I can't help you folks. Anything else?"

"No," said Ray, relieved; and he stood up, ready to leave.

Alice sighed deeply. "But . . . ," she said, then, "Never mind." And she also stood up.

"Again," the loan officer said, "I'm sorry."

Outside on the way to the parking lot, Alice said, "Why didn't you tell him you won the lottery?"

"It wouldn't have done any good; besides, you got the information you wanted. Didn't you?"

She didn't respond. She looked crestfallen.

Ray drove her to work. On the way he wondered why Alice had never mentioned the other house, probably a rental.

That evening when Ray went to Alice's house, he took with him a present. He'd bought two backrest pillows for reading in bed. One was green with flowers and the other was blue with an abstract sequence of yellow squares and red circles.

The girls were sacked out in the living room watching *Match Game*. The host, Gene Rayburn, was doing an imitation of an old man, Mr. Periwinkle. Brett Somers, a regular, responded with a full-throated laugh. Charles Nelson Reilly, another regular, blew pipe smoke toward the ceiling, and Richard Dawson leaned over and kissed Fannie Flagg on the cheek.

Hope giggled.

Alice was standing in the living room kicking off her high heels one at a time when Ray walked in and excitedly said, "Look what I bought for us so we can read in bed together!"

The pillows were in a big see-through plastic bag.

He could see that Alice had just gotten in from campus and that she was not in a good mood. Through squinting eyes, she glared at the pillows as though they were something hideous.

He handed the bag to her, but she refused to take it. She said, "I don't want these. *We* don't need these." She shook her head and sneered. "I don't see myself like that: old in bed reading. That's not *who* I am. Why'd *you* want these damn things, anyway? Are you trying to get old before your time?"

He felt crushed and speechless. At that moment he resolved not to spend the night. He'd come up with a good reason.

After dinner with Alice, driving home that night, Ray saw a red light flashing in his rearview mirror. He pulled over immediately and parked.

He watched the police cruiser pull up behind his car and stop with the top red light still flashing. The officer in uniform got out and, carrying his ticket book, slowly approached Ray's car. Ray was watching him in the rearview mirror.

Ray felt relief seeing that the guy was actually a cop. In recent days he had heard news stories of men dressed as cops in various cities in several states with flashing lights on their cars stopping drivers to rob them or in the case of women sometimes to rape and rob them.

At the same time Ray felt nervous. The slightest move on his part might be misunderstood, and Ray knew he could end up dead. Many cops were nervous and afraid and quick to shoot. Ray also knew that many cops feared black men, even black cops. They believed them to be dangerous. That fear had a long history going back hundreds of years. Being black and being stopped was not promising.

When the cop came up alongside Ray's car, Ray had already rolled down his window; and in a pleasant and polite voice, he said, "Hello, Officer," and waited with both hands visible on the steering wheel.

Ray saw that the cop was young, probably in his mid-twenties, with rosy cheeks and pudgy all over with baby fat and that he was nervous. The cop said, "Driver's license and registration."

Ray said, "The registration is up here on the visor. May I reach for it?"

"Are you trying to be a wise guy?"

"Not at all, Officer."

"Okay, okay, just show me your registration and driver's license."

"My license is in my wallet, Officer. I'd have to reach into my back pocket to get it. Is that okay?"

"Just take it easy," said the young cop, whose nervousness was now turning to anger.

108

Ray got the registration and the license together and finally into the hands of the officer, then he quietly waited with both hands resting in plain sight on the steering wheel.

He was wondering why he was stopped, but out of fear of further antagonizing the cop or fear of being seen as disrespectful, Ray kept his lips sealed and waited to speak only if spoken to. He'd heard of so many instances of black men being shot for the slightest offense, real or imaginary, in situations like this.

The cop carefully examined the documents, then handed them back to Ray. "Okay," he said, "just slow down. You were over the speed limit."

The cop walked back to his car where the red light was still flashing. Ray waited till the cop drove away before pulling back onto the road.

Over the speed limit? Ray knew he was no more than five miles over the speed limit and not consistently even that much. Wasn't five miles over the speed limit acceptable? If not, why was everybody doing it and more?

15

On a Friday afternoon in the middle of June, Alice and Ray were in her backyard on the patio. She said, "The best real estate agency in the town is Duran & Duncan. John Duran is a crackerjack realtor; and so is Gigi."

The following Monday morning, Ray easily found Duran & Duncan Real Estate, Inc., on Gibson Street.

His appointment was at ten A.M. He arrived ten minutes early.

The agency was in a family home converted into real estate offices. He parked in their lot, which was a backyard that had been converted to a parking lot.

The receptionist, Erin, was a thin blond girl who looked like she'd had a rough week. She gave Ray a weak smile and said, "Please have a seat, Mr. Jansen. Gigi will be with you in a moment."

He sat down in one of the chairs against the wall in what obviously was once somebody's living room.

Five minutes later a short, heavyset woman entered the waiting room from one of the offices. This was Gigi Angelico-Hurley. As she approached, Ray saw her sizing him up. She had a peaceful gaze. Her hair was iron gray; it matched her unblinking eyes. Everything about her said experience and self-confidence.

He stood up as she approached. They shook hands.

"Mr. Jansen, it's so good to meet you. It was nice of Alice to recommend us. Would you like to go for coffee or perhaps breakfast?"

"Breakfast would be fine."

"Lovely. My treat."

They took a booth in Stanley's on Coker. After they placed their orders, Gigi said, "Would the house be for you alone?"

"Yes."

"What's your price range?"

"Fifty to eighty thousand."

While she was eating crepes and he waffles, Gigi said, "Since I'm going to guide you through this process, you have a right to know who I am. I was born in Rome. I married an American ag professor many years ago. We met in Rome when I was just in my early twenties. He was twenty years my senior. He passed away two years ago from a heart attack. Albert Hurley was his name. I loved him dearly. We had three daughters; and I thank God for them. They are wonderful girls. Denise, the oldest, is at Harvard Medical School; she's going to be a wonderful doctor. She cares about people. She wants to save the world, especially the poor of the world. Harriet is a senior at George Washington High, and Stacy is in her last year at Ben Franklin Elementary. Both are still living at home with me. I know I won't have their company for long, so I'm enjoying every minute they're still with me. They're growing up to be wonderful girls. Tell me about yourself, if you don't mind?"

He told her only the basic facts, that he was born in New York, got a degree in business, and worked in retail management. He could tell by her expression that she was not pleased with what he'd said. She obviously wanted to hear about more personal things—things he at the moment was too sensitive to talk about with Gigi despite the fact that he instantly liked her and she had been so completely open with him.

He'd opened up to Alice only after they'd been intimate, but Ray knew he was inconsistent in this regard. He couldn't bring himself now to say he had no parents and that he was left in a cardboard box on a church doorstep and that he grew up helter-skelter in a shelter and in occasional foster homes.

Finished with breakfast and back at the office, Gigi gave Ray some pamphlets of houses to consider. He flipped through them. Most of the houses were located in nearby Sacramento or Godwin.

As he was leaving, Gigi walked with him outside onto the porch. Shaking his hand, she said, "It's a buyer's market right now. You chose a good time. Tomorrow, I'll pick you up at nine A.M., and we'll go look at some beautiful houses in your price range. Okay?"

After looking at and considering six houses, Ray chose a two-story Cape Cod gray stucco in Lorena with four bedrooms, a living room with a high ceiling, a family room that was open to a large kitchen with lots of daylight coming in. The dining room with a bay window was to the right of the front door. Three of the bedrooms were upstairs and one downstairs off the hallway.

The house had a two-car garage.

"A physics professor and his family lived here," Gigi said. "They had the house built and they're the only family that has lived in this house. He got a job offer back east. That's why the house is now vacant. They want to sell fast and that's to your advantage."

The front lawn was already well developed. The front entrance was flanked by two large oak trees on either side of a long concrete walkway leading up to the covered front entryway, where there were double doors with decorated windows above.

The backyard was also large. Oleanders grew along the left fence. Four tall mature cypresses were clustered in the left corner. They seemed to reach up to the sky.

The patio surrounded the house from the entrance to the kitchen all the way around, connecting from the side driveway to the garage. In the back it was flanked by a stretch of well-kept lawn bordered by a bed of sea pebbles and shrubbery growing along the fence.

The house was listed at $80,000. Gigi talked the seller down to $75,000. Since Ray was paying cash, the amount of paperwork was far less than the usual mountain involved in such a transaction.

The Duran office manager said, "Cash?" He obviously didn't trust Ray or cash. The manager was more comfortable with people paying a mortgage and lots of interest over many years.

Ray knew that the manager's hesitation was not due to any other kind of bias. Lorena had a strict policy of nondiscrimination in housing, and expensive houses existed alongside modestly priced houses.

Ray said, "I won the New York State Lottery."

After three weeks the sale was final, and Ray owned the house; he stopped in the Duran office to thank Gigi for guiding him through the process. He sat across from her desk, and she leaned back in her swivel chair and, smiling, said, "Now that you have a big house, you need a family: a wife and some children." She chuckled.

He blushed with embarrassment. "It *is* a big house."

"What are you going to do with all that space?"

"Well, Gigi, it's more than a home; it's also an investment. I'm tired of living in apartments. I've lived in apartments since I, uh . . ."

"Since you what?"

He decided to tell her. By now, he felt close enough to her and he liked her and considered her a friend. "When I was a kid, I never had a home." He paused and considered what he was about to say.

"I grew up in a shelter. I lived mostly there till I was eighteen. I never knew my parents." His voice was unemotional. "I was left in a cardboard box on the doorstep of a church."

He did not want anybody's pity—understanding, yes, but not pity.

She got up and came around the desk and placed an arm around his shoulders. "From the moment I met you, Ray, there was something in your eyes that told me. I *felt* it! I knew!"

"Thank you."

"In a way, I know what it feels like to feel homeless, to want stability. For years I was torn between Rome and California. I felt I didn't belong in either place. I would go back to Rome, visit my uncle the musician. After my parents died, he was my only contact with the city where I was born. I'd walk around Rome and not feel the sense of ease I'd felt there growing up. It was no longer my city. Then I'd come back to Lorena and, in a similar way, I would not feel the easy comfort I believe my friends here felt and had always felt; and after Albert died, I've continued in that limbo. When my oldest daughter went off to college, a great loneliness overtook me. The kids are my only salvation and my anchor. I was living for them and I know that when the younger two leave, I will have only a big empty house; but it will be my last refuge. So, Ray, in my own way, I understand why you need that big house; even if you continue to live in it by yourself."

He thought he should say, *I hope to someday find the right woman and marry and maybe have children*, but he said nothing.

16

It was early July. He was now moved out of his apartment and into his big house. A gas stove was already in the house. Ray went to Sears and bought a refrigerator, a hot water heater, and a water softener to replace the ones there, and he bought a washer and dryer. The refrigerator, the hot water heater, and the water softener were all delivered within a week.

Alice was over and was walking from room to room. She came back to the living room and said, "Well, at least it's a good investment. If we're going to live together after the girls are gone, I wouldn't want to live here. At that point you could sell it or rent it out, but the best thing about it is that it's on the Upper North Side; this is the best neighborhood in town, with great old mansions and a variety of styles. I'm sure you've noticed."

"Couldn't miss them," he said simply. Her plan for his and her future together continued to baffle him, yet he was still hoping that the comfort he felt in her presence would evolve into something deeper.

Ray felt that the fact she was ten years older than he was behind her tendency to dictate their future without consulting him, and he silently resented it. There were times when he wanted to give voice to that resentment but resisted because of his lifelong habit of avoiding conflict as much as possible.

The avoidance of conflict and the absence of trust he reckoned had to do with his upbringing because as a child he'd felt on guard against dangers everywhere.

At times he wondered if he was capable of love. He knew all the theories and serious and funny ways people talked about love: a euphoric feeling or tenderness or intimacy or fondness or endearment or unconditional affection or deep feelings of passion and compassion or sexual attraction or to be smitten or besotted or obsessed or have a weakness for someone and so on. He sensed all such definitions somehow missed the mark, leaving him still unsure.

Ray had felt degrees of all of these emotions but still was not sure what so-called true love was. Could it be that the comfort he felt with Alice was already true love? He knew that love was a social construct, not something driven by nature; but maybe over time it had become second nature to humans. People definitely *felt* something they were calling true love.

But wait a minute. That comfort he felt with Alice and her daughters had raggedy edges. It was surrounded by a persistent anxiety and doubt. Yeah, that sounded right. Such was his dilemma.

On a Wednesday in July, Ray went to see Vicki Jankowski, a masseuse on Leahy Street. He'd found her in the telephone book. She worked out of her home, with one of her bedrooms set up as a massage room with a professional massage table placed in the center of the small room.

Vicki was an unusually large woman. She was also fat. Ray guessed she weighed at least three hundred pounds. She was very pink with lots of curly blond hair. Her small eyes were constantly saying to the world: *I know I'm not up to your standards, but please consider what I've had to endure.* Ray could tell she was friendly and gentle and honest.

He said, "My back is killing me."

"What happened?"

"I picked up something heavy," he lied. He thought the lie was more acceptable than the truth. It wasn't entirely a lie: something heavy did break something in his back. The lie was that he picked it up. *No,* his inner voice said, *no, it jumped unannounced upon you.*

Vicki said, "I'll leave the room so you can undress."

When she returned, he was down to his green and blue boxer shorts with little figures of guys playing golf. He was facedown staring through the hole in the table.

Vicki worked firmly at his back for a half hour, then she had him turn over. She worked his feet and his neck and shoulder muscles. "All of these parts are connected," Vicki said. "The more they relax, the less of a problem you'll have in the lower back."

She finished and he felt more relaxed. That feeling lasted for about an hour.

The following Wednesday, Ray and Alice finished a dinner of rigatoni and green peas and steak. They remained seated at her dining room table. The girls were in the living room. They'd eaten earlier and were now having ice cream and cake and watching sitcoms.

Alice said, "Have you met any of your neighbors yet?"

"Yes. I was outside watering the shrubbery in front. One of my neighbors, an old man, was walking his dog. The dog stopped to sniff at my grass. The dog looked like he was looking for a place to poop on my grass. While the man waited for the dog, I said, 'Hello, beautiful day, isn't it?' The old man glared at me, sneered, and rather than returning the greeting, he spat on the sidewalk."

"Oh, dear."

"Another time I was on the porch getting my mail out of the mailbox. Another elderly man was passing by. I said, 'Hello,' and he too glared and refused to return my greeting; but otherwise, everybody else has been very friendly. I've met a doctor, a retired businessman, a nurse . . ."

"A nurse?"

"A *male* nurse."

"Oh."

"It's clear I'm the only African American in the neighborhood. Some of them don't like it, but I think most of them are fine with my presence."

"Give them time. Everybody's a racist. It's a racist country. We're steeped in racism. Give your neighbors time, and they'll eventually adjust to your presence."

"I don't think everybody is a racist. When you say everybody is a racist, you risk normalizing racism, and I don't think that's your intention." He paused. "Most of my neighbors are already very friendly, and some have even reached out to me."

"Good," she said.

"It's better than good."

Alice just shrugged. "Well, on another subject, today at work all hell broke loose. I had to deal with a big cheating scandal in the department, and it may be that the cheating is more widespread than we in the Ag Department thought. It may be campus-wide."

"Who's cheating?"

"Students and maybe their parents too. We found three cases where parents paid big money to have somebody else take their child's SAT test, and that's not all: one of our grad students, a girl named Gloria, paid a postdoc to write her dissertation. The cheating at the undergrad level is rampant. This came to light last year and supposedly the problem was fixed and the guilty were punished; but I'm not so sure it's over at the undergrad level. The people in Student Legal Services are so lenient on students that they're allowed to get away with all kinds of cheating: from copying things out of books to paying professionals or smarter students to write their papers. The smart students are hustling to make money by writing term papers for lazy students. It's all unethical and in violation of academic standards. The offenses go on and on."

This was Ray's third massage. He knew by now that Vicki loved to talk while she worked. She'd asked him about himself, and he'd opened up to her, surprising himself by telling her the truth about his life. It gave her an avenue for talking about herself. "I grew up scared," Vicki said, "scared to go to school because the other kids laughed at me for being a big person. They called me fat and stuff like that. So, rather than going to school, I'd leave home and go to the public library and hang out all day and read books. I read a lot of books—mostly silly stuff, I confess. I certainly can't say I was educating myself. I was avoiding the bullies at school. Then I messed around and got pregnant. It happened with the first boy who was nice to me. My parents helped me raise my daughter. I knew girls back then who got pregnant and their parents kicked them out. I was lucky. Virginia is sixteen now. She's not doing all that great in school, but at least she hasn't gotten pregnant."

"Does Virginia see her father?"

"She saw him only about three or four times during all the years she was growing up." She sighed. "He's almost as much of a basket case as I am." She laughed. "I think for a time he was an alcoholic, and I suspect he was on drugs too. He lives in Godwin. When Virginia was little, I tried to keep in touch with him for her sake so she would know her father, but he showed no interest in her. Now that she's older she wants to know him, but she's also angry at him for never having made any effort to be a father to her. Poor girl, she cries herself to sleep and I try to comfort her, but it doesn't seem to help."

Saturday morning, the first week of August, around ten in the morning, Ray and Alice were on the floor in an empty bedroom in his new house. They were naked and lying on their backs side by side.

"Did you like that?" she said.

"Yes. How come you never did that before?"

"I didn't know you wanted me to." She sighed. "Besides, I wouldn't want to do it in my house with the girls all over the place. I never know when they're going to pop in and see something they shouldn't see."

"What's on your agenda for today?"

"There's a new guy running for city council, Josh Cordova; he's a good Republican and I'm going to spend some time this afternoon looking at the material about him that came in the mail. He's going to be interviewed tonight on our local Channel Five news. He predicts that Ronald Reagan will become president. I'm interested in what Cordova has to say. I know he stands for fewer taxes and he's against abortion. That's a good start."

"Are you a *Republican*?"

"I like to think of myself as an Independent, but I always vote Republican. Why?"

Ray said, "I'm a Democrat. I always vote Democrat. I had no idea you were a Republican."

"Is there anything wrong with my being a Republican? You just enjoyed a Republican blowjob. You weren't complaining then."

"Touché! I'm not complaining now. I'm just surprised."

"I'm not talking about you personally, but I know what Democrats say about Republicans: that we're racist, and that we're for big banks and

119

big business, and that we're for the rich making more money; and that we're against regulations of any kind and that we're against civil rights and that we find ways to keep minorities from voting and that we don't support the little guy and the working class; and that we're the party of white men and white women; and that we're against social services, such as welfare and social security and public health care for all; but none of those things are true. We're a party that stands for promoting the welfare of the country and the economy and the betterment of all people. We don't like welfare queens. They rip off the system. There's more money in circulation when Republicans are in power and that helps everybody; and taxes are lower, too, when Republicans are in power. I like lower taxes. That's why I'm a Republican."

"Welfare queens? Welfare queens is a myth pushed by newspapers and used by politicians to cut social benefits for the desperately poor." He smiled cynically. "You can't seriously believe there are thousands of black women ripping off the system?"

"I don't know about thousands, but there must be some."

"Let's change the subject," he said angrily. "Why are you so sold on Cordova?"

"I like Cordova because he's *for* the death penalty. Maybe he'll be able to curb so much of the talk about abolishing the death penalty altogether. I expect to see him move up quickly to a state position and then maybe run for Congress or the Senate. The Supreme Court did the right thing to reinstate the death penalty. A man like Gary Gilmore deserves the death penalty. Don't you think so?"

"Putting him to death simply ends his suffering. Locking him up for life is punishment. Death is not punishment."

"I don't agree," she said flatly.

"I suppose you're also against that Supreme Court decision three years ago, *Roe v. Wade*?"

"As a matter of fact I am against it, and I'll tell you why: it's murder, it's taking an innocent life before it has a chance."

"But you're also for the death penalty. We know now that a lot of innocent people have died in the electric chair."

"Two different things. Innocent life in the womb hasn't committed any crime such as rape or murder. Those seven judges that voted to uphold what they called a woman's right to choose, citing the Fourteenth Amendment's right to privacy, were ignoring the sanctity of the unborn life."

Ray sighed. "Looks like we're on opposite sides of the fence when it comes to just about everything. I'm against the death penalty. It's barbaric. I'm for a woman's right to make decisions about her own body. Unwanted pregnancy has harnessed women for centuries. It's time for it to stop. I believe this country should have health care for all and free colleges for all."

"*My goodness*, you are not just a Democrat—you are a *socialist*." She laughed.

"Maybe I am," he said firmly. "It's an honorable thing to be."

Alice raised up on her elbows and looked at him. "I don't care if we have different opinions about things; that should not make any difference in how we *feel* about each other. Should it?"

"Having different opinions about *everything* doesn't make it easier," he said with a bright smile that he hoped was not ironic.

17

I⏉ WAS ELEVEN A.M. THAT following Monday. Ray drove up and parked his Scirocco in front of Connie's parents' house and turned off the motor and waited. His Wilson bag of tennis rackets and balls was in the back seat.

Within five minutes he saw Connie bounding down the front steps. She was dressed in a white jersey and white shorts and white tennis shoes. She ran the distance of the long walkway to the car.

She opened the door to the passenger seat and hopped in and turned to him. "Look at *you*, mister, all cool in your tennis outfit and shoes."

He smiled and started the motor and pulled away from the curb. "You'll have to direct me," he said.

"Just drive over to Main; stay on Main till you come to the end, then turn left onto County Road 106. It's just past the Norwood turnoff."

As he pulled up to the first stoplight, he said, "Have you heard from Scotty?"

"Yes, I have. He's tending bar in Oakland at a place called Adam and Eve's Apple. It's a restaurant and bar. I went down to see him. I just got back a couple of days ago."

"How's he doing?"

"Not too well. He's got a room in a rooming house on Ninety-Third Avenue. He has to share the toilet and the kitchen with three or four other tenants. He sleeps on a cot he bought at the Salvation Army. His room is about the size of a closet, but he's saving his money so he can get an apartment so we can be together again. While I was visiting, he stayed with me in my hotel room. He says he wants to get out of Oakland as soon as he can because he says there's too much crime and drug dealing."

"Is he drinking heavily?"

"Not too heavily: just white wine, and I didn't see him using any drugs, not even marijuana."

"Maybe I should send him some money."

"That's not a good idea. He's far too proud to accept money from you. He would think that would make him obligated to you and corrupt your friendship. Scotty wouldn't like that. He's too proud for that, Ray. No, he has to succeed on his own. He refused help from me. I offered him money and he turned me down. That's the kind of person he is."

"I know, I know."

"I'm sure you know," she said.

"Did you tell him I was in California looking for him?"

"I certainly did. I also gave him your telephone number. I told him you'd just bought a house."

"What did he say then?"

"He wondered where you got the money."

"You tell him I won the lottery?"

"No, I didn't because I didn't know you'd won the lottery. This is the first I'm hearing anything about you winning the lottery."

"Thought I'd told you."

"He said now that you're doing well, you might be too high-and-mighty to be friends with a lowly bartender. I urged him to call you, and I told him that you wanted to hear from him."

"He hasn't called."

She said, "I sensed that he's feeling disappointed in himself and ashamed to contact you because now you're doing so well, and he obviously is not."

"That doesn't sound like Scotty." Even as Ray said this, he had second thoughts. They'd always been in competition in a friendly way with each other.

That competition was part of the cement of their friendship, but Ray was trying to break the old childhood habit because he wanted to learn how to compete only with himself and not with his best friend or for that matter with anybody, but it was hard.

"I know. I told him he wasn't being himself. I said that Ray is your best friend. You must contact him, and he promised he would." She laughed. "Guys competing with each other is a novelty compared to women. Gosh! Some of my girlfriends are outright cutthroat when it comes to competition—competition over anything, but especially over guys."

"Give me his number and I'll call him and dispel this nonsense, if there is any in his mind."

She took a notepad from her purse and scribbled down the number, then handed the sheet of paper to Ray. "Here," she said. "I'm glad you're going to call him. He's working nights. Best to call him around noon after he's awake."

They reached the tennis courts and parked and walked out to the courts. Connie said, "I want to tell you something, something I haven't told Scotty, but I will tell him."

Ray tensed. "What is it?"

"I've become a stronger person now, stronger because I've turned to Buddhism. There is a medicant monk who lives here in Lorena. His name is Erik Lynch. I've become a student of his. I want to work my way up to becoming a lay Buddhist in the Soto Zen tradition and, who knows, one day I too may become a medicant and teach others the way of freedom from cravings that lead to suffering."

"I don't know much about Buddhism."

She said, "You should look into it. You learn that all human life is subject to suffering and that the cause of suffering is desire and attachment to things. I'm learning to give up a lot, maybe even Scotty, in the sense of wanting him to do what I want him to do. I'm learning to let him be himself and to take him as he is. I'm putting brakes on my desire to change him. My experience with my husband, and now with Scotty, actually drove me to Buddhism."

"I'm not a religious person," Ray said without apology.

She laughed. "You don't have to be religious to be a Buddhist. It's more a philosophy of life than a religion. You learn to overcome your desire for things and especially the things that cause you to suffer. In my own case,

124

as I said, that's trying to change Scotty. I turned to Buddhism to try to give up desire. I'm almost there."

"I'm not inclined to take on a formal philosophy of life," Ray said. "I went through a lot of bitter unhappiness as a child and as a teenager. As a young man, college was an anxiety-ridden struggle, but I stuck with it. Later I worked unhappily in a supermarket. I guess I cannot turn to religion or philosophy because I don't believe there is any divine force guiding us. I believe we're existentially on our own. I'm convinced that we, probably unlike the rest of life on earth as we know it, evolved into what we are accidentally and not because some moral and ethical God chose us." He stopped talking for a moment and took a deep breath, then said, "I'm entirely secular, but I try to be always ethical and uphold good moral values. I don't need religion or philosophy to be a good person. I do believe that through persistence we can perfect ourselves in every way possible. None of this has anything to do with the good luck I had in winning the lottery. That is not what I'm talking about. That was just random luck. I would be on this same ethical and moral path had I not won the lottery."

She was silent for a moment, then said, "Ray, you've just described a philosophy; you are the kind of person who *should* turn to Buddhism."

"Let's go play tennis," he said.

The courts were surrounded by plush lawns and mature pine, maple, and alder trees. The grounds were wet, either from rain in the night or from a nearby sprinkler system. There were two courts. Court number two was occupied by an elderly couple lazily hitting a tennis ball back and forth.

Ray and Connie started slowly warming up by hitting the balls back and forth. He ignored the pain in his back. Ray knew Connie had a lot more experience, having grown up playing tennis.

He said, "You know I'm not very good at this, but I'm glad you asked me to come out and play with you today. At Clarkson I got pretty good, but I haven't kept it up. I'd have to get back in shape and practice more to get my skill level up."

"I'm glad you had the rackets and balls," she said cheerfully.

"I need to develop a better backhand."

"Yes, but you make good contact with the ball. Your eye-hand coordination is excellent. All you need is more practice."

They played gentle tennis for about an hour, then she said, "Should we stop and go get some lunch?"

"Excellent idea."

Technically she won.

After lunch he dropped Connie off at home and drove to Hotel Lorena. It was one thirty. He wanted to get a drink before going home. He would call Scotty around three o'clock. That would be soon enough. It would give him time to wake up, and it would be several hours before he'd have to go to work.

There were two guys already at the Hotel Lorena bar. It was a typical slow afternoon. Both guys looked like construction workers maybe between jobs.

Just as he expected, Laura Borg was tending bar. She looked tired, but when he sat down at the bar, she perked up and gave him a friendly smile. "Hey, stranger," she said, placing a mug of tap beer in front of him.

"Hey there, Laura. How are you?" he said, picking up the mug and taking that first cool sip and hearing the suds whisper.

"Aside from nursing Sara through her growing pains and losing sleep and being underpaid, I'm okay, I guess. What's up with you?"

"I'm puzzling over calling my oldest friend. I hear that he's depressed and unhappy with life. I'm trying to figure out what to say to him. I guess I'm feeling a little guilty since I'm doing all right and I know he's not."

"You need to ask yourself why you feel guilty for doing all right. That's an odd thing to be feeling, wouldn't you say?"

"I guess it's because he and I came up together; we started from zero and now he's still at zero and I'm not. It's kind of like what those guys on the battlefield feel when a buddy is shot and dies—they start feeling guilty. They wonder why him and not me. They feel like they should have gone down too."

"That's the crabs-in-a-bucket syndrome stuff. Pull yourself out of it. To hell with what's trying to pull you back to the bottom."

He drank his beer. "Okay, okay," he said, "I'll try. I guess the best thing to do is call him and hear what he's thinking." Ray put the mug down. "Let's not talk about me."

"You started it," she said, smiling.

"What's going on in *your* life?" Ray said with an equal smile.

126

"The usual chaos," said Laura, as she wiped the bar. "I just broke up with my latest boyfriend. I've got to stop choosing losers. How come I can't meet anybody but out-of-work construction workers? How come I can't meet a brain surgeon or a high-class lawyer? One loser after another is just not cutting it, and the older I get, the younger they seem to be. They're babies! I have to teach them *everything*. They know nothing about a woman's body. It's depressing! I overeat and I'm not sleeping well. I see my life ten years from now and it scares me. I'll be alone and living in a little two-room apartment and still working afternoons tending bar. Sara will have two brats and will want me to babysit them all the time while she goes out dancing."

When Ray got home, he sat down by the telephone in the kitchen and dialed the number for Scotty that Connie gave him. It rang four times before he heard the voice of an elderly woman: "Hullo?"

"Hello, is Scott O'Brien there?"

"Hold on, I'll knock on his door and see."

"Thank you."

Five minutes later the elderly woman said, "Hold the phone. He's coming. He wasn't dressed. I think he might have been asleep."

Ray waited with the phone to his ear. About five or six minutes later, he heard Scotty's "Hello?"

"Hey, Scotty, it's Ray."

"Ray! Great to hear your voice, man! I know you got out here some time ago. I apologize for making getting together so difficult, but my life's just been hectic. How the hell have you been, guy?"

"I've been okay, Scotty. How are *you*? I've met your girlfriend, Connie, up here in Lorena. She told me how to get in touch with you, said you're tending bar and working in Oakland."

"That's right. She told me she'd met you. Listen, man, like I said, I'm sorry to have put you through a cat-and-mouse game trying to catch up with me, but life has been kicking my ass."

"Sorry to hear that, Scotty."

"Listen," Scotty said, "I'm planning to break it off with Connie. I just haven't gotten around to it yet. She's a nice girl. I still think she did the right thing leaving her husband. She wasn't happy with him."

"She's a good woman."

"I know, I know, but I just can't deal with her family, especially her father. There's no way she and I are going to be able to have a successful relationship with him hating me the way he does."

"Take her away from her parents, far away."

"She wouldn't stand for that. She's deeply attached to them. She's living with them now. A few years ago, she moved to San Francisco and got married trying to get away but was not able to really make the break. She kept going back, and while she was down here, she talked with her mother by phone every day, sometimes two or three times a day. I mean she had long, long conversations with her mother, and the talk was just random talk about things like what she ate or what she wore yesterday, that kind of stuff. Her parents run her life."

"So, what are you up to now?" said Ray while gazing through his patio door at his backyard and feeling guilty about the luxury that now surrounded him.

"Leta and I are back together. Man, I love this woman! She lives here in Oakland. She's a sixth-grade teacher. She's married but she and her husband have nothing to do with each other. They still live in the same house but go their separate ways. She's in the process of divorcing him, and she's planning on getting her own apartment. She's twenty-five—five years younger than I am. She's got lots of class, and she's the smartest woman I've ever met. She grew up bilingual, speaking Spanish and English, and she speaks French too. She's quiet and poised. I love her, Ray, and she loves me!"

"That's great, Scotty, but you'd better level with Connie."

"I know. I'm going to call her today, maybe tonight."

"Why don't you tell her in person? You shouldn't break it off with her on the phone."

"You're right. I'll get it done. Don't sweat it."

"I've been thinking of coming down there."

"Absolutely! I hear you bought a big house and you're driving a new car! What did you do, rob a bank?"

"I won the New York State Lottery."

"You did not!"

"Yes, I did. I really did!"

"Wow! You *really* did. Do you know how lucky you are? Do you know what the chances of that happening are?"

"Yes, one in about thirteen million and some; and it was the first ticket I ever bought."

"Wow!" Scotty said again. "I can't believe you're rich! Think where we came from! Now you're rich! Was your name in the newspapers?"

"No, I got a lawyer, made copies of the winning ticket, and kept the original under lock and key, and I never went public."

"Probably a smart move," Scotty said.

"Funny thing, I don't think of myself as rich. I drive a Volkswagen and I wear a Timex wristwatch."

"Man, if I won the lottery, I'd buy the most expensive Rolex I could buy, and I'd drive a Bugatti or a Lamborghini or maybe I'd buy both and a Bentley and a Porsche."

"You can drive only one at a time, Scotty. My little Volkswagen gets me where I want to go. I don't need a fancy car."

"Yeah, you've always been that way. I know what it is. You and me both were always scared we weren't going to get enough to eat so we held on to every penny we got for fear that tomorrow we might starve."

"Those were rough times."

"I wonder what the folks back at the shelter would say?" Scotty laughed out loud. "I can just see the shock on their faces, especially old lady Jan Kohler. Did you tell your foster mom and dad, Eve and Paul Jansen, and the Coopers and old lady Halberstam?"

"I did and they wished me well."

"They didn't want any money?" He laughed.

"Nope; didn't ask for a penny." Ray paused. "Listen, Scotty, I'm going to drive down there to Oakland to see you. If you need any help, let me know."

"I'm doing okay, like I said, I got a good woman, and I'm not drinking, at least not much, and I'm planning to move into a bigger place as soon as I can."

"If you change your mind, let me know and I can wire you some cash to help out."

"Thanks, Ray, you've always been there for me. I appreciate it. Listen, rather than your coming down here, I'm going to take the train up there to Lorena. It's a short ride, and it'll do me good to get away on Monday, my day off. I can break it off with Connie then. So, I'll come up this coming Monday; I'll take the three forty-five; it arrives there at five fifteen."

"Great! Yeah, it's a good idea to level with Connie while you're here, and I will pick you up at the station. You can stay with me. That will be August sixteenth."

"Looking forward to it, Ray; it's been a while. We've got a lot of catching up to do."

That next Monday, Ray was on the train platform at four thirty. There were three sets of tracks running by the station. The commuter train would come in on the one closest to the platform.

It was a hot day, ninety degrees in the shade. He stood in the shade under the overhanging shelter of the awning waiting.

Across the tracks two boys were walking along picking up rocks and throwing them ahead. A man and woman and two small children, a boy and a girl, were also on the platform waiting. They were seated in the sun on the bench farther down.

There were occasional sounds of cars starting in the nearby parking lot to the left. The smell of mint was in the air. On the way in, he'd noticed a lot of mint vines growing along the side of the station.

He checked his Timex. It was now five fifteen. He looked down the track. No train in sight.

At quarter to six, Ray saw the train approaching. Now all he had to do was stand back and wait for Scotty.

The train pulled into the station, huffing and puffing before coming to a complete stop. Immediately the doors were opened. Men, women, and children stepped down from each of the five cars. In total, Ray counted eight adults and four children. Scotty was not among them. The doors closed and the train moved on, slowly picking up speed.

18

Ray stepped inside the station and waited for the phone booth to be available. A man in there was talking and gesturing wildly and angrily. He finally came out and got in line to buy a ticket. There were three people ahead of him.

Inside the booth Ray stood and dialed Scotty's number. The phone rang six or seven times before a voice said, "Hullo?" It was the same woman who'd answered before.

"Would you please call Mr. O'Brien to the phone."

"Hold on, please."

Ray waited five minutes, then the woman said, "I knocked on his door and there was no answer. May I take a message? I can pin it to his door if you like."

"Yes, please ask him to call Ray." He gave her his number.

"I'll pin it to his door."

"Thank you."

There was nothing to do now but wait to hear from Scotty. Surely, he must have an explanation.

That following Thursday the phone woke him at six in the morning. Half asleep, clumsily he picked up the receiver. "Hello?"

"It's Alice. Ray, sorry to wake you so early in the morning, but would you be able to pick up Hope at eight this morning and drive her to school? She has to be there by eight thirty. Normally, I take her, but this morning I had to get to the office early for an urgent meeting the chair is calling regarding cheating and other legal issues."

"It's summer, why does Hope have to go to school?"

"Summer school is in session, so a lot of kids are still there, but Hope is not in summer school. It's her indoor soccer team practice. They meet throughout July and August on Thursday mornings; they're getting ready for the fall games."

"Okay, okay," he said, while pulling himself up to a sitting position on the side of the bed. "I'll get dressed and take her."

"Thanks, sweetheart, you're a lifesaver!"

When Ray drove up and stopped in front of Alice's house, he saw Hope standing on the front porch. She was already dressed in her soccer outfit, and she was standing with her arms crossed, looking angry and impatient. Seeing her reminded him of the pain in his lower back. It was now constant.

With her backpack on her back, she ran down the steps. Ray opened the passenger door for her. She opened the back door instead and climbed in. She slid down in the seat so that her head was below the window level.

He turned around and said, "Why are you sitting back there?"

"Because I want to."

"Okay," he said, and started the motor and pulled away from the curb and headed to Jessie Redmon Fauset Middle School on Main Street.

Still some distance from the school as they approached the redbrick building with its green window frames, Ray saw up ahead lots of moms and dads double-parked and letting girls about Hope's age off at the curb in front of the school. Other kids were milling about. Some were sitting on the lawn in groups talking. There were children walking along the sidewalks toward the school, probably summer school students.

Hope shouted, "Stop! Let me off here!"

Ray slowed down. "Here? We're two blocks away. I don't mind taking you up to the entrance."

"No! *No!*" she shouted. "I don't want you to take me up there. I want to get out here, *right now.*"

He pulled over to the curb and stopped.

Hope opened the door and jumped out and slammed the door and ran up the sidewalk. He sat there watching her run.

It was ten A.M. on a Friday morning. Ray was watching the news on TV. Gerald Ford was nominated by the Republicans to run for president.

Ray was not thinking about the news. His focus was on other matters. Lately he had not been spending the night with Alice. He was seriously feeling distant from her, and he was worried about Scotty, who still had not called back. His phone rang and he got up and picked up the receiver. "Hello?"

"Ray, it's Connie. How are you?"

"Fine, Connie. I meant to call you. I talked with Scotty. He was supposed to come up here to visit, but . . ."

"I know, I know. He told me all about it. He called me a couple of days ago to tell me he's in love with another woman, the same woman he was involved with before I met him. I've been crying for days. I'm practicing yoga to keep from thinking about him. Still I feel like such a fool, but I shouldn't be surprised or even hurt. If I were more advanced in my Buddhist practice, I would be handling this much better."

"I'm sorry, Connie."

"I'm hurt for investing so much of myself and my emotions in him. He's your friend, and I'm sorry to have to say it, but I believe Scotty can't love, not really; he thinks he can, but he has had such a difficult life, I don't believe he knows *how* to respond to love when it's given to him. I gave up everything for him, and I was ready to spend the rest of my life trying to make him happy."

"He broke up with you by *telephone?*"

"Yes. He said he couldn't come up because he quit his job at Adam and Eve's. He has just started a new job and couldn't take any time off. He's now working at the bar in Restaurant Blanton. That's a hoity-toity place in Berkeley; it's on North Shattuck."

"Well, he could have at least called me."

"I know," she said. "He's sometimes thoughtless, even rude."

"It was pretty rotten of him to break up with you on the telephone."

"It was rotten, period. Listen, I just wanted to tell you what happened. Let's get together soon, okay?"

"Sure."

"I've got to go. I have to take my dad for his physical therapy. He has arthritis in his arms and legs; it's bilateral, they're giving him exercises. I'll talk with you later."

PART 4

The Orgastic Future

Gatsby believed in . . . the orgastic future that year by year recedes before us . . .

—F. SCOTT FITZGERALD, *THE GREAT GATSBY*

19

Ray said, "Alice, I don't think our relationship is working."

"What do you mean?" she said in suppressed alarm.

He didn't respond; instead, he looked off toward the traffic on Main Street. His gaze was reflective.

They were sitting in his car in the parking lot of Stanley's Café. It was one o'clock and eighty degrees on Sunday, August 22, and the forecast was for a hundred today. He gazed at the droopy line of trees across the street, trees suffering from lack of water. Northern California was at the beginning stages of what promised to be a prolonged drought.

Alice said, "I think we have a strong relationship. Why are you saying this? What's the problem?" There was desperation in her voice.

"I just don't think we're right for each other." Even as he said these words, he realized this was going to be more difficult than he had thought.

"Who is she? Is it that Constance Mann woman?" Now her voice was full of anger.

"No. There is no other woman."

"Is it that you don't want a woman with children?" Her anger was growing, and it showed in her raised voice.

"No, I like Margo and Hope. They're fine girls."

"Ray, I don't see that we have any problems. I know I'm ten years older than you, but what difference does age make? Is there a problem with our lovemaking? Is it that now that you have a big fine house and lots of money, you want a younger woman?"

"I had lots of money before I came to Lorena, and I'm not looking for a younger woman." He realized that he was not handling this well, but maybe there was no easy way to end this relationship.

"Then let's talk about *how* you feel. I'm sure we can work it out. Whatever the problem is, I'm sure there is a solution. We've made a commitment to each other to work through our problems."

"We've never talked about any such thing."

"But our actions spoke. We are a couple, a committed couple. We have a relationship, Ray. Now you want to throw it all away. Why?"

"Alice, I've been slow to admit it to myself that there are many things wrong with our relationship. One example: You use being older to dictate to me. You assume you know what's best for us. There are other issues . . ."

"Then why don't you write down what you're feeling. Maybe that is a way to start? Would you do that? If I don't know what annoys you, how can I fix it? I *can* change."

"I don't want to write on a piece of paper a list of complaints about you because you don't deserve that. I *thought* I was comfortable in our relationship, but I was fooling myself. I told myself I was comfortable because I *wanted* to be. I want to feel comfortable, but somehow it's just not happening."

"Comfort? There will be problems, but we have to deal with them as they come, Ray. That's how you get to comfort. You overcome your problems. Every relationship has problems. It's about getting along and companionship and sticking together through the hard times and trying to have a good life. You can call it comfort or love if you want, but that's not what it's about. Don't be so romantic!"

Ray said, "Alice, we're just not compatible."

"That's nonsense! Is it that you don't like the fact that I'm a Republican? I have no problem with you being a Democrat. I can't see why political beliefs have to be an issue."

"It's not an issue."

"I'll tell you, Ray, as handsome as you are, what attracted me to you in the first place was not your good looks. I saw in your face a sorrow and a sadness that I related to and that I understood; I saw suffering, and I understood that suffering. I instantly felt that we could be together and happy for the rest of our lives. That's what I felt. Long after the girls are grown and with children of their own, you and I would still be together and happy, but now you tell me you don't think our relationship is working. I had no idea you were thinking such a thing. How long have you felt this way?"

"It's been evolving."

She sat there silent for a moment, then said, "Drive me home, please."

Monday morning Alice called him, "I didn't go to the office today. I called in sick. I stayed up all night writing a letter to you, trying to clear my thoughts. Would you come over and read my letter?"

"Sure."

When he got there, Margo opened the door for him. He said, "Hey, Margo, how's it going?"

Without responding, she sneered at him, and he watched her scornfully walk away back to her room.

Alice's bedroom door was closed, and Hope wasn't anywhere in sight.

Now Alice opened her bedroom door and looked at him. Her eyes were swollen red. "Come on in," she said.

He followed her in, and she closed the door once he was in the dark bedroom with her, where she apparently had been lying fully dressed on the bed in the dark and crying.

Alice sat on the side of the bed and reached over and turned on the lamp and a dull yellowish light illuminated the room. This was a familiar room where he and Alice had slept together, a room where their bodies joined in the most intimate way possible, and yet he now felt uncomfortable here.

Ray thought it best to let her speak first. Finally, she said, "I tore up the letter I wrote to you. Reading it back to myself made me sick. I realized I wrote the letter not to you but to myself; but I'm glad I wrote it because it made me consider everything from a different perspective." She paused.

He said nothing, choosing to let her continue to talk.

She cleared her throat and said, "When my marriage ended, I told myself I'm not going to commit myself fully to another man till I am absolutely sure he is the right one." She took a deep breath and let it out. "Don was such a prick. The thing that ended our marriage was his involvement with a young woman up in Toronto. Her name was Julia Epstein. Although she was only twenty-one, she was in line to receive a lot of family money. Her family manufactures mattresses up in Vancouver, and she happened to be in Toronto that summer checking out the University of Toronto as a potential school. Don met her secretly while he and I were up there on vacation. She was staying in the same hotel. She became a student at the University of Toronto, but during the summers she'd come down here to California to see Don. I had no idea any of this was going on. Julia had a boyfriend in Toronto she was living with, but she couldn't give up Don. At first, they were seeing each other only once a year. When Julia found out her boyfriend Sid Hein was cheating on her, she started coming down here even more often to see Don. It was her way of getting back at her boyfriend. Many years later, after she was married, not to Sid, but to a British drummer in a rock band, Don and I ran into her in London. She had read in the newspaper that Don along with a bunch of other businessmen from around the world were in London for a big important conference on business and manufacturing and the international economy. Don said she was the daughter of one of his business associates. It was the first time I saw her. She came to our hotel and we had dinner with her at the hotel restaurant. It wasn't till that dinner that I began to sense intimacy between the two of them. I could *smell* it. Something in her eyes and the way she wet her lips between sentences and the way she looked at Don and the way Don was acting, so shy and guarded, told me what had been going on. He eventually confessed the whole affair, told me everything. I was deeply hurt."

"I don't know what to say, Alice."

"Don't say anything. The hurt I felt then was like what I feel now; but never mind! Tell me how are *you* feeling?" she said.

"I'm okay. I just don't want you to take this as a rejection of you."

"What else can it be?"

"It's simply a recognition that two perfectly fine people are not compatible."

"That's what *you* say. I happen not to agree."

"That means we are at loggerheads. We agree to disagree."

140

For a moment she didn't respond, then she said, "You're standing there so cold and distant; it's like you've suddenly become a different person, not the person I shared my bed with, my home, my food. Sure, you contributed to the expenses. We'd become a family. My girls are crazy about you, and I thought you liked them."

"I do and they know it."

"They are heartbroken, you know. This hurts them too."

He didn't respond.

"Last night Margo and I cried together. She's very fond of you. She's very grateful that you taught her to drive. Now she feels betrayed."

He still said nothing.

"After you left yesterday, I called my friend Annette and she was very sweet. She kept saying this too will pass, just like the dirt Don did to you. She said, 'Alice, just go ahead and have a good cry and just know that you are going to be just fine; it's not the end of the world.' In a way, I know she is right, but that doesn't ease the heartache and the feeling of rejection. When you and I first met, my sister Karen said that this was likely to happen. She said that you were too young for me. She thinks you have a lot of growing to do. I just dismissed her comment as typical Karen cynicism. My friend Rita called this morning. She wants to take me out to dinner. She also wants to comfort me. I have good friends who care about me. If you insist on going through with this, I'm not going to let it kill me. My friends are there for moral support. I can always turn to them."

He felt awful and unaccountably guilty.

"Ray, I've put so much into trying to make this relationship work. It's hard to say how disappointed I am."

Was Alice trying to make him feel guilty and through that effort to keep him from leaving her?

Ray had the feeling that one or both of the girls were outside the door listening.

"I'm sorry it has to be this way, Alice." He stepped toward her, intending to try to comfort her.

She put up a hand like a traffic cop signaling for traffic to stop. "Don't touch me. I don't want your sympathy. If you can't return my love, I don't need your sympathy."

"Then I guess I should go. We're getting nowhere with this conversation."

"By the way," she said, "you owe me thirty dollars."

He didn't question it, although he knew he had given her the usual agreed-upon amount every week, whether or not he ate dinner with her. He pulled his wallet from his back pocket and lifted three twenty-dollar bills from it and handed them to her. "This should cover it."

He turned and walked to the door and stopped and looked back at her sitting there in a dejected manner, and she was staring at him with eyes of despair and anger. Her face was swollen from crying.

Then he opened the door.

Margo was standing there in the living room. Her cheeks were flushed red, and her eyes were blazing with anger. She walked to the front door and yanked it open and stood there waiting for him to walk past her.

He did just that and opened the screen door to let himself out. Then she slammed the door so hard the house shook.

20

H<small>E FELT BAD ABOUT HURTING</small> Alice. To try to take his mind off his sorrow, he got ready to buy furniture and other things to fill his house. So far, it was largely empty except for the kitchen and the room he slept in. That room contained most of the things he'd moved from his apartment to the house.

In college he'd read a novel called *The Great Gatsby* in which the protagonist was a wealthy man who lived alone with servants in a big fancy Gothic mansion. Gatsby was unlucky in love.

Ray was not going that route. This was 1976, not 1922. Ray was black and Gatsby was white in a country that took those factors very seriously, and Scotty was no Nick Carraway with a Yale education and the "right" social connections. There was no cute Daisy or racist Tom or Jordan Baker in Ray's world.

In both the book and in Ray's life it was summer, but one takes place on the East Coast and the other on the West Coast. Ray's house was big and expensive, but it was not a Gothic mansion. He would have no live-in servants. He was going to cook for himself and take out his own garbage; and he was not planning on lots of big parties, just one housewarming. There was so far no Daisy in his life to impress. Ray came from the bottom of society and Gatsby, though not born rich, started considerably further up the social ladder.

There were some inescapable similarities: Ray and Gatsby were both newly rich and they both were new to the communities in which they lived, and, like Gatsby, Ray didn't know the so-called "right people"; in Ray's case, known as the upper class of Lorena—unless Connie and her family counted as such.

Upper was upper and middle was middle. Alice and her family didn't qualify as upper. They were middle and the same went for all those folk Ray met at the university: they too were middle, not upper. In Ray's mind upper meant inherited old money.

The minute Ray stepped into Erickson's Home Furnishings, Mr. George Erickson himself rushed to meet him at the door. He was a slender and dapper man of about fifty with thinning black hair and thin lips. He eagerly shook Ray's hand and said, "Mr. Jansen, pleased to see you again. How might I help you, sir?"

"Mr. Erickson . . ."

"Call me George, please."

"Yes, George. I've bought an eight-room house with three bathrooms; and I need to furnish it."

"Phew! That's a tall order, but we can handle it, I'm sure, and congratulations. Let's first go over here to the living room furniture."

Ray walked with George across the way to the living room furniture. They stopped and stood there. That section seemed to stretch for miles to the left, and it was packed with furniture.

"Would you like for me to show you around, or do you want to look around on your own?"

"I'll look around on my own, thank you."

"Look around, Mr. Jansen, take your time. I'll be nearby, just call me when you need me."

Ray took out his pen and pad to make notes of his selections. Then he started.

After twenty-five minutes of looking, he'd selected a traditional antique-like gold love seat with two cushions, a traditional antique-like sofa, and two matching armchairs; he chose a traditional classical dark walnut coffee table with scalloped top; it also had elaborate apron carvings and curbed feet like those of a lion. The sofa and chairs were to be arranged around this impressive thing.

He was paying only passing attention to prices.

To fill out the room, he selected two more armchairs and four end tables to flank them and four regal-like lamps to sit on the end tables.

At this point he wondered if he was being too decadent, but it was just a passing thought. *What the hell*, he thought.

He noticed George off in the distance with his arms folded, watching. They made eye contact and George smiled. Ray gave him the victory sign.

Ray continued, moving on to the dining room section. Here he spent less time. After only ten minutes he selected a traditional cherrywood cabinet with rounded corners and elaborate ornamental designs along the top and in the trim; six gilded cherrywood chairs to go with the gilded dining room table; and a cherrywood buffet. He also selected a gilded console for the dining room.

He wrote down the names, with the item identification numbers, so there wouldn't be any misunderstanding in the delivery.

In the bedroom section, Ray selected two bed frames of cherrywood and cherrywood dressers. He already had one bed.

He was keeping one of the bedrooms for his study. He selected a large cherrywood desk and a big brown leather office chair for that room.

In the store's fine art section, he selected about thirty oil paintings of abstract expressionist landscapes and impressionist figures and a variety of wood and clay tribal sculptures. They were not by well-known artists. Some were copies of masterpieces. These were to be placed throughout the house.

Then he moved to the accessories section. Here he selected a variety of freestanding Victorian-style table lamps to go throughout the whole house and six freestanding floor-to-ceiling bookcases. He also selected five or six classical wall mirrors for the upstairs and downstairs hallways and for the bedrooms.

As he was making these selections, he was thinking he should soon have a housewarming party. Yes! It would be great! He'd invite everybody: Alice, Scotty, Connie, Karen, Laura Borg, his chiropractor Sid Ellison, his real estate broker Gigi, his masseuse Vicki; all the people he'd met at the university; even the people down in San Francisco: Hans and the bartender Steven Biggs. Whether or not they would come was another matter.

Then he stepped into the carpet room. He was overwhelmed by the array of Persian and Afghan designs. All the floors in the house were polished hardwood. He wanted rugs to go in the living room and the dining room and the hallways and in the bedrooms. He selected and noted on his notepad enough of the Persian and Afghan wool rugs to go throughout the house.

When he looked at his watch, he realized he'd been in the store nearly three hours. George had gone away and returned twice. He was now back but still keeping his distance.

With the notes to selections in hand, Ray signaled for George by raising his hand; and the store owner came at a trot.

George said, "Looks like you found a few items to your liking." He laughed.

Ray said, "Perhaps you would make a copy of these pages?"

"Absolutely, Mr. Jansen. You want all these items?" He was looking at the pages.

"Yes. It's a large empty house, George. When can they be delivered?"

"Right away, Mr. Jansen. Let's go and do the paperwork. How do you wish to pay?"

"As soon as you have a total figure, I'll write you a check."

"Absolutely! Absolutely!"

That afternoon Ray checked the classifieds in the *Lorena Star-Dispatch*. He wrote down on his notepad by the phone three names of housecleaning services: Probst Janitorial Services, Juan Lopez House Cleaning, and Maria Pollack Housekeeping, Inc.

Ray called the Probst number and got an answering machine, then he left his number; same with the Lopez number; but with the Maria Pollack number, Maria herself answered. She spoke English with a midwestern accent. Ray said, "I'm looking for a housekeeper, someone to come in once a week."

"That is what we're here for," said Maria cheerfully.

Ray made arrangements for Maria to come see the house the next day. He opened the door. She was a pleasant and plump woman with very pink skin. She was short and energetic. He instantly liked her, and he hired her on the spot. She looked throughout the house and told him what the service would cost.

She said, "Most of the time I will be the one cleaning your house, along with another woman, her name is Rosa Hernandez; but I also have four other women besides Rosa who work for me, and when Rosa and I can't come, two of them will come and do the job. Is that okay?"

"Fine."

In a very businesslike manner and voice she said, "If you are here, there's no need to give me a key. If you let me in at the front door, I can always discreetly leave through the side door or the back door. No one has to know. My helper and I will arrive here at ten thirty on Monday mornings unless you instruct otherwise."

"I'll always be here to let you in."

"If you're to be out of town, you must let me know in advance. Okay?"

"Absolutely. You will know in advance."

"Thanks!"

"You got it," he said. He liked her.

The next morning Ray heard a lawn mower in the neighborhood. He went outside and waited till he saw who was pushing it. A man, about forty, was cutting grass across the street. Ray saw the man's old red pickup truck parked at the curb. Printed on the door was PORTER LANDSCAPING.

Ray waited till the man was finished and the motor was off, then he waved to him. "Hello!" he called as he started walking across the street toward the man.

The man met him halfway.

"I'm looking for someone to cut my grass," Ray said, "and generally take care of the front and backyard."

"I'd be interested in doing it," the man said. His blond hair was long, and he wore it in a ponytail tied at the nape of his neck with a rubber band. He had a hook nose and there was blond stubble on his chin and cheeks and his eyebrows were extremely bushy. He was sturdy with broad shoulders, his skin weathered and sunburned, and his hands were rough and callused from work. His fingernails were broken and dirty.

He was wearing a sweaty-looking dirty blue shirt and jeans and heavily scuffed boots.

"My name's Ray, by the way. What's your name?"

"Chester, Chester Porter."

Ray shook hands with Chester Porter.

"Sure," he said, "I come to this street every Monday morning. I do three houses down there and two up the street. I can do yours at that time."

21

Ray called Connie. She said, "The Judy Clark-Johnson Catering Service has a fine reputation. My parents have used them several times. I also recommend the Walter Holloway Trio, if you want musicians." She paused, then continued, "I went to high school with the people in the trio: Walter, vocal and guitar; Stephanie Clipper, vocal and saxophone; Clifford Melcher, drums. They're all excellent musicians."

Ray responded, "If I can get them, you bet I'll hire them!"

Judy Clark-Johnson was an honest, ethical, hardworking woman of about forty with seven part-time employees. Elizabeth and Janet would be coming with her to the party to serve the guests.

Connie said Judy maintained a small office on Leahy above Ormsby's Pet Shop. Business was not great, but Judy was doing okay. Her workers had other jobs and helped her mostly on weekends when the catering service was most often booked.

Connie told him about Judy and her food. Judy did most of her own cooking. The offerings were eclectic: a bit of East Indian, a bit of Chinese, a bit of Mexican, a bit of Italian, and a bit of French. There were plenty of meat dishes, but she also offered something for vegetarians and even vegans. She got her baked breads and cakes from the Munson Bakery on Coker.

"If you want me to ask Judy for you, I will," said Connie.

"Thank you, Connie! That would be wonderful!"

Ray's handwritten invitations went out on the last day in August. Some of the addresses he was able to find in phone books. Connie helped with others.

He called Scotty, and Scotty said, "Sorry I didn't get back to you, Ray. Things have been crazy here, but I'll come to your party, for sure. I feel horrible. I urged you to come out here to California, and I've done nothing but disappoint you since you got here. I feel like I've let you down. Anyway, I plan to make it up to you, man. I'll bring Leta. I'm looking forward to having a beer with you and for you to meet Leta. I think I'm going to marry this girl as soon as her divorce is granted."

"Okay, Scotty, see you at the party."

Next, Ray called Hans, who said, "I'll try to come."

He called Steven Biggs, who said, "I'll bring my girlfriend."

He called Connie and asked her to continue to spread the word.

He called Alice. She said, "I'm surprised to hear from you. I'm even more surprised that you're giving a party and want me to come."

He sent an invitation to Darren McIntosh, the only black person in the Ag Department. Maybe Darren and his wife, Anne, would come. Alice had told Ray that Darren was born in Baltimore. His father was from the Bahamas, where he'd grown up on a plantation where they grew okra and onions. Darren spent summers in the Bahamas with his father's relatives, and while growing up he learned a lot about farming. He later did research on those crops and went on to become an expert in their growth, care, and development. He was an adviser to the US Department of Agriculture.

It would be good to have a chance to talk with a black man for a change. Ray had lived mainly in a white world. The Jansens were white. While Ray was still an infant, Mr. and Mrs. Jansen attempted to adopt him and even gave him the name Jansen. In the final stages, the adoption was denied by the family court. Mr. Jansen had a criminal record. At age fifteen he had been convicted of stealing a car for a joy ride that ended with the car wrecked beyond repair.

Saturday around six thirty, Ray walked through the rooms of his new home, taking it all in. The overall impression was one of faux imperial splendor. A chill went through his body. Was this amazing house with its fine furniture really his to keep? The reality hit him suddenly. How did a poor shelter kid from Brooklyn with limited prospects get all of this? Gatsby never questioned his right to wealth.

People started coming a short time later. Ray stayed at the front door greeting them; most of them came in groups of twos and threes and fours and even five at a time.

A bunch of people he'd met at the university came all at once. Some of the names he remembered: Philip Crosby, Hazel Godfrey, Gilbert Walker, Cheryl Seltz, Keith Brock, Angela Croft, Giovanni Granucci, Robert Diggs, Merlin Smith, and David Grant; Christine Blair arrived with another woman. There were others whose names he didn't remember. They'd come along with those who were formally invited. That was all right with Ray. There were people at Gatsby's parties he didn't know, and even while they were there, Gatsby never met them.

Walter and Stephanie were singing "Tonight's the Night."

Ray shook hands with Darren McIntosh and his wife, Anne, at the door. Ray said, "Hope we get a chance to chat later."

"Sure thing," said the professor as his wife smiled at Ray.

Professor McIntosh was a stocky elderly man with grayish-brown skin and shortly cropped hair that was beginning to gray at the edges. Ray could tell that the professor's eyes were bloodshot from poor health and not from drink.

His wife was also stocky and had a lighter brown complexion with shoulder-length hair. She was a kindly-looking matronly woman.

The professor said, "Beautiful home you have here!"

"Thank you, Professor."

"Call me Darren."

At the door he kept greeting each and every person warmly and said, "Hello! Come in and enjoy yourself. There's food and plenty of wine and beer and music." They could hear the music the minute they entered. Gatsby never stood at the entrance greeting his guests. Often while the party was in progress, he would leave the room for long periods of time.

Stephanie was an attractive and tall blond young woman with a small mouth and an engaging smile. She was dressed in bright lime-green culottes. She was now singing "Fool to Cry." She sang with emotion and even passion. You could tell she was feeling it.

Server Elizabeth was walking around with a tray of ham-and-cheese baked snacks, sausage on sticks, and crabmeat-stuffed mushrooms. People were grabbing the stuff left and right. Elizabeth had to keep refilling the tray and start her rounds all over again. She kept a pleasant smile all the while.

They kept coming: Connie came alone at seven, and Alice arrived with her sister Karen soon after Connie. Alice looked at Ray with bewilderment and anger. For Ray it was an awkward moment. He wondered why he'd invited her. To show that he had no ill feelings? Who knew? Maybe it would turn out to be a bad idea.

Walter was singing "If You Leave Me Now." He was a skinny fellow with big teeth in a wide mouth. He was wearing a blue summer suit and white tennis shoes.

The three of them—Connie, Alice, and Karen—right away got into a discussion. They'd all gone to the same Lorena high school.

As Ray continued to monitor the door, he glanced back repeatedly at the living room. He saw many groups gathered and holding wineglasses and chatting. The party had taken on a life of its own.

Elizabeth and Janet were still walking around with trays of snacks, and fingers kept reaching for the goodies till the trays were empty. Then the servers reloaded and again started the rounds.

The big bright living room was buzzing with chatter against music that was mellow enough to remain in the background.

Ray was pleased with the harmony between the talk and the background music. It was turning out just as he hoped. He wanted people to enjoy themselves. As long as they were enjoying each other's company, all the better.

He was relieved that he did not have to entertain them. He could be among them as a participant and let his role as host relax. He too could now stand talking with a glass of wine in hand and as a tray approached occasionally reach for a snack.

Elizabeth was reloading. Server Janet was still walking around with a tray full of party snacks: pigs in a blanket and croquettes and little meat pies. The guests were eagerly taking her offerings.

152

Cheryl Seltz said to Hazel Godfrey, "Hazel, I love your hair." Hazel had her hair done up in a new way. Janet offered them bite-sized baked snacks. Hazel took one but Cheryl said no thanks.

People were energized. Gilbert Walker was in conversation with David Grant and Eliot Bernstein. Eliot was excited. His loose heavy jowls shook as he gestured wildly. Keith Brock, Giovanni Granucci, and Cynthia Rudder were also talking and gesturing in a very excited manner. Robert Diggs was wandering around with a bottle of beer in his right hand. Dean de Marco and Hazel were now dancing to the music. Others soon joined them.

Ray was on his way to get another glass of white wine when Darren McIntosh stopped him and said, "I've just heard that you won the New York State Lottery. Is that true?"

"Yes, it's true."

Darren laughed, showing big, slightly yellowed teeth. "Was the win simply an addition to your wealth, or did the win take you from rags to riches?"

Ray resented the question but graciously answered. "I was working as a manager in a supermarket."

"So, you were always pretty well-off?"

"No, I was born dirt poor, homeless, and without parents."

Darren's eyes stretched, and he stared at Ray with disbelief with his mouth open. Ray could tell Darren felt insulted.

"Is that true?"

"It's true."

"No one's born without parents," said Darren.

"I never knew who my parents were. As an infant I was found in a cardboard box on the doorstep of a church."

Ray could see that Darren now believed him. "Then you did come from rags to riches. Please excuse my tasteless attempt at humor, Mr. Jansen. How unlucky for you, but it appears that fate or providence came to your service in the end."

"Call me Ray. Tell me, Darren, how has it been for *you* in this town and in this department?"

Darren straightened his shoulders, took a deep breath and let it out, then said, "I was born to a black mother and a black father and grew up in an all-black neighborhood in Baltimore. My father was a farmer from the Bahamas. He taught me a lot about farming. My contact with people other than black folk was minimal. Now, I'm the first and only black man in this department. It's taught me a valuable lesson: race is folly."

"What do you mean?"

"Race is a smoke screen. We know that there is no marker for race in the entire genetic code. The relationship between race and facts is kind of like paper money's relationship to gold. We know that the paper itself is worthless, it only *represents* value, that it in itself has no *real* value like gold or diamonds. That is how superficial race is. Used to be that US paper money represented the gold at Fort Knox but no more. The paper has value because we *say* it does. Same with race. Its reality begins and ends in our imaginations. Think about it."

"I'm thinking," said Ray, smiling. "You've given me a lot to digest. Thank you." Ray continued to smile. "Excuse me, Darren, I'm going to get another glass of wine and mull over what you've just said. Please continue to enjoy yourself, sir."

As he walked away, Ray remembered as a kid sometimes wondering what his own personality and outlook would have been like had he too been raised in an all-black family in an all-black neighborhood.

He would never know, and he couldn't change the past. He had to keep moving forward and to keep focused on the present and the future and on future prospects, and to be just and fair in dealing with others. He sensed that it was the only healthy way for him to live in his own skin and in the world in which he found himself.

Everything seemed to be going splendidly. Stephanie, backed up by the Walter Holloway Trio, was now singing "Don't Go Breaking My Heart."

It was now eight thirty, and Scotty and Leta still had not arrived. Ray was about ready to give up on them. He'd always been reluctant to give up on Scotty, but it was so in character for Scotty to say he'd be there and not show up. He always had a convincing excuse. Ray knew his friend to be a smooth liar. It was one of Scotty's most skillful defenses.

Over the years Ray kept hoping Scotty would change, but lately Ray had not forgotten how unreliable Scotty could be. Even as a teenager,

Scotty's word had been capricious; yet there were the surprising times when he acted honorably and did what he said he was going to do. Scotty was erratic and unpredictable. He always left you guessing.

Alice came over and asked, "Is your friend Scotty here?"

"I invited him but so far he hasn't come."

After a derisive chuckle, she said, "Your friend sounds like a trickster figure straight out of folk culture. He's everywhere and nowhere. He says one thing but means another. Go figure!"

"That's Scotty," said Ray, ignoring her pessimism.

"I see you've made a lot of new Democrat friends." Her smile was cynical.

"No, really, they are mostly *your* friends."

She laughed from the gut. "Well, maybe in time they will become *yours* too. After all, you're new in town. People have to get to know you. I hope they will get to know you better than *I* did." She grinned maliciously. "Remember, whether you're dealing with Democrats or Republicans, you'll never be just a token nigger in this town. We're *good* people here." She then turned and walked away.

By nine o'clock, Ray was able to move permanently away from the door and spend more time chatting with his many guests. He got another glass of wine and again circulated. He felt hurt by Alice's last remarks. She was trying to hurt him as much as she could. It seemed to him that kind of hostility and bitterness was unnecessary. At the same time he knew he had hurt her deeply and he felt bad about it.

Christine Blair was standing talking with the woman who arrived with her. Ray walked over to say hello to them both.

Christine said, "Ray, this is Kay Bishop, a friend of mine; she teaches French at Godwin Community College. Hope it's okay that I brought her along."

"Absolutely!" Ray shook hands with Kay and gazed into her eyes. She gazed back unblinkingly into his eyes. He realized something was going on between the two of them. He wasn't yet sure of what, but it made his heart beat faster.

There was something about some older women that instantly attracted him. He felt a quickened heartbeat and a sense of expectation for something not immediately clear to him. Intellectually he often explained it as latent mother-longing, but that explanation never pleased him.

He preferred to believe that his attraction to certain older women for whatever reason was driven simply by his preference for mature women. No deeper analysis was necessary. For him, Kay had that certain something he responded to.

A couple of times Ray noticed that Alice was watching him even when she was in conversation with other people.

Christine said, "School is starting soon. Good thing you're having your housewarming party now. If you'd waited two more weeks, most of us would be too busy getting ready for classes, Xeroxing syllabi and typing quizzes, getting rosters lined up and memorizing student names."

"I didn't know," Ray said. "I guess I got lucky."

David Grant walked over to Ray and said, "Gee, this is a big expensive house. It must have cost a fortune. You live here alone?"

"Yes, I do."

"Do you *deserve* all this?" David was grinning.

"Yes, this and more."

"Then I guess you drive a Bentley or a Lamborghini?"

With a smile, Ray said, "No, I drive a Volkswagen."

David turned his head sideways and looked at Ray from the corners of his eyes. His expression said, *Are you sure?*

Ray knew David was mocking him. He felt unhappy about this conversation, but he was determined to not feel anger. Not tonight, not at his own party.

Ray smiled at David. He said, "Excuse me, David." He turned and walked away. David stood there with a drunken fixed grin watching Ray gravitate back toward Kay and Christine, but they both were presently engaged in conversation with two other women.

From a distance Ray couldn't take his eyes off Kay. He sipped his wine and tried not to be obvious. Kay was attractive, with a round head set on a long graceful neck. Her face was stern and long and her nose was also long, and her lips were very thin, almost nonexistent. She had short light brown hair and friendly gray eyes.

Along with the friendliness he saw a sign of resignation or perhaps doubt of some kind or perhaps permanent sadness. Whatever it was, it touched something in him. Bags were beginning to form below her eyes, perhaps a sign that she was not sleeping well. He figured she was probably more than a few years older than he, maybe thirty-five or even older—older than she looked.

She was still talking with the other women. Waiting for an opportunity to speak to her, Ray kept trying to make eye contact with her. He told himself that his attraction to her needed no explanation. Attraction was too subjective to explain.

After about ten or fifteen minutes, he finally made eye contact with her and smiled. He walked over to her and she returned his smile. Ray said, "I'm delighted Christine brought you to the party."

"So am I," she said. "You have a lovely home."

"Thank you, Kay. Listen, I was wondering if you'd be interested in having breakfast or lunch or dinner with me sometime?"

Out of the corner of his eye, he noticed Alice watching.

Kay said, "Sure, I'd love to. When do you want to get together?"

"How about dinner tomorrow night?"

"Sure," she said. "I live in Godwin. You want to come out there?"

"That would be fine. What time?"

"Around five thirty or six?"

He nodded. "Yes."

She opened her purse and took out a notepad and jotted down her address. "Here's my address and phone number. Just take the road out of town going north. It turns into the county road to Godwin. You drive through Godwin till you come to Jeff's Country Store on the left at the stop sign. There, you make a left turn and just keep driving till you see a group of mailboxes; then turn right. You'll see my house. It's a little white house out in the middle of nowhere. You won't see an address, but it's the only house there. If you get lost, go back to Jeff's and give me a call, and I'll come and lead you."

The trio was between songs.

Alice was still watching.

Ray's telephone rang and he said, "Excuse me, Kay."

He weaved his way through the thicket of guests and entered his bedroom and closed the door, and then picked up the receiver. He glanced at the clock. It was ten o'clock. "Hello?"

"Ray, I'm so sorry, man, Leta and I got in her car, ready to come up there, and the car wouldn't start."

"That's okay, Scotty. No apology necessary."

"How's the party going?"

"It's still going and there are a lot of wonderful people here, but people are beginning to leave. It's getting late. It's not like when we were younger going to all-night parties."

"Those were the days! Those Soho and East Village parties!"

"Listen, Scotty, I've got to get back to my guests. Let's talk tomorrow afternoon."

"I have to work tomorrow. I'll be home till five thirty."

"Okay, okay, we'll talk soon," Ray said hastily. "Bye!"

He returned to the living room. As his guests were leaving, most of them thanked him for his hospitality. He was feeling good about the way the party had gone. Even despite Alice's obvious discomfort and insult, he felt that the evening had been a success.

When Kay and Christine were ready to leave, Ray walked them to the door and said good night to them both. Ray didn't know if Christine knew about his plan to see Kay again, so he was careful to say nothing, but it was Kay herself who said, "See you tomorrow!"

The caterers and musicians were packing up and also getting ready to leave. There were beer bottles and dirty wineglasses all over the place. The caterers collected those and stray paper plates and plastic glasses and dumped them all into a large black plastic trash bag, the kind used for tree leaves.

By eleven all the guests were gone. Ray walked back to the kitchen and sat down at the table and wrote a check for Judy Clark-Johnson for the catering. Then he wrote one for Walter Holloway for the entertainment.

That done, he went back to the living room, where Walter, Stephanie, and Clifford were all packed up and ready to go.

He handed Walter the check. "Thank you, Walter, and you too, Stephanie, for the beautiful music. The songs were fabulous. You guys were great!"

Walter took the check. "Thank you," he said with a tired smile. "Anytime you need us, just let us know."

158

Clifford Melcher, the drummer, had already taken the instruments out to their Volkswagen bus.

Then Ray turned to Judy and went through the same ritual with her. She took the check and said, "Anytime, anytime. It was a great party. I love cooking for people, love seeing people enjoying my food, it makes me happy."

Judy's helpers, Elizabeth and Janet, were already taking boxes and bags out to the van.

22

Sunday morning ray was up by nine. He had never been able to sleep late. As soon as daylight appeared, his eyes popped opened and he was soon up and about. This morning was no exception; and he was surprised he had no hangover from the white wine.

Judy and her helpers had cleaned up well after the party.

Ray was hungry. He realized he had not eaten much since lunchtime the day before. He put on his robe and went to the kitchen and made a pot of coffee and fried bacon and eggs and with whole wheat toast he sat at the kitchen table and ate breakfast. He was sipping coffee and trying to imagine what his upcoming date with Kay would be like. Pondering it, he felt a sense of anticipation and anxiety.

At noon he went for a walk down along the creek toward the downtown area but turned back before he got downtown. He crossed the little wooden bridge and came back up on the other side of the creek that the locals called Tranquilo Creek. Above, the sky was clearing of clouds and the morning air was fresh and he was feeling refreshed. The trees along the creek were still wet from a brief shower in the night.

He sat down on a rock near the creek. He picked up a purple and pink pebble and tossed it into the bubbling creek. Just then a couple of brown and white ducks came along downstream. The splash of the pebble attracted their attention, but when they realized the splash wasn't made by something edible, they kept swimming.

Ray was thinking about Alice as she was last night. He felt annoyed by how she kept watching his every move. There was anxiety if not anger in her face as she watched him talk to people, especially women.

How long would it take her to get beyond this anger and grief and feeling of rejection? After all, he intended to live in her town for the foreseeable future. In a small town like Lorena, they were bound to come in contact with each other.

Then he thought of Kay Bishop and again felt a rush of anticipation. He told himself he wasn't expecting more than conversation and possible friendship. She certainly hadn't shown any sign of being interested in him in any other way.

At five o'clock he got in the Scirocco and headed for Godwin. The drive on the two-lane road out there was peaceful. Autumn was in the air. September leaves were turning purple and brown and yellow and red and falling from trees alongside the road. The road was in good condition. Beyond the trees was fertile farmland with fields of yellow wheat stretched out on both sides.

He passed only one car, a yellow 1930 Roadster, coming along on the other lane. He drove within the thirty-miles-per-hour speed limit. No impatient car was behind him. It took him twenty minutes to get to the outskirts of Godwin.

He passed a neat group of redbrick buildings far off to the right and wondered if that was the site of Godwin Community College. It looked like a little country college surrounded by mature trees.

In town he slowed down to the speed limit of fifteen miles per hour and drove slowly through the main street of the downtown area of wooden storefronts. It was Sunday quiet. On the other side of town, he soon saw on the left a big sign looming over a store: JEFF'S COUNTRY STORE.

He made the left turn there just as Kay had instructed. Along this road, farmland stretched out on both sides of the two-lane country road.

A few minutes later when he saw the cluster of mailboxes, he knew he was near. There he turned right and saw her little white shiplap house with green shutters; it was like a modest shrine to the afternoon sunlight. The nearest other house was down the road about a quarter of a mile.

Ray pulled into the little dirt road leading out to Kay's house and parked alongside her car, a lime-green Ford Elite. He sat there for a moment reflecting.

He thought of the two recent relationships he'd had in New York. It was depressing to remember how they'd each ended in disappointment. Lee, the divorced woman, he discovered was also still involved with her ex-husband. Chi, the older of the two, was diagnosed with breast cancer. She moved to Minnesota for treatments. She was cured but never returned to New York.

Lee and Chi were before he won the New York State Lottery. Would it have made a difference in the relationship with either of them? He thought not, but money had changed his status. People were looking at him differently.

In matters of love, he wondered if wealth now had made him a prisoner over an abyss into which he was hoping not to fall; but the abyss remained below him as a continuous threat. He was also beginning to mistrust his judgment of the women he was drawn to.

He got out and walked up the four steps to the wooden front porch and pressed the button alongside the door. Inside he heard the doorbell chime musically three times. Through the glass and its inside white lace curtain, he could see Kay coming toward the door.

She opened it and, smiling, said, "Right on time! Come in!"

He returned her smile as he stepped inside the living room. "Thank you. How are you?"

"Splendid!" she said. "I thought we'd go to Arnett's Steak House. It's very popular here in Godwin."

"Sure, sounds good."

She was wearing a white cotton dress with green and blue dots all over it and a little white cotton jacket and black low-heel shoes.

From where he stood just inside the front door, Ray saw that hers was a hyper-neat home filled with traditional rustic furniture. He could see all the way through the house back to a hallway ending with a parlor.

In one corner of the living room was a great old grandfather rocking chair with a cushion that looked like it had never been sat on and in another corner was a classic green love seat with a woven and colorful

Indian blanket thrown across the back. Beside the excessively clean fireplace was a stack of firewood stacked in perfect uniformity.

An old armchair and an equally old couch rounded out the room.

It was a peaceful spotless place. On the wall opposite the fireplace were several large black-and-white photographs in modest frames of very old men and women in nineteenth-century attire, no doubt Kay's ancestors. Covering the floorboards and in the center of the room was an unusually large Navajo rug, once colorful now faded.

Kay said, "Welcome to my humble abode." She now seemed to him a bit spiritless and stouter than he remembered. It made him wonder about his initial perception of her; and she walked with a slight limp. He hadn't noticed it at the housewarming.

She led him out of the living room through the dining room into the kitchen, an old-fashioned country kitchen with an ancient sink and equally old refrigerator that hummed loudly, and a gas stove placed alongside a wood-burning stove.

"I pulled a muscle in my leg," she said, looking back at him with an expectant smile.

The dining room table with no tablecloth was of heavy rustic wood. A vase with bright yellow goldenrods sat in the center of the table. The table and its six heavy wooden chairs sat on a heavy wool rug with designs of a buffalo pattern in brown and red.

Now in the kitchen he stopped and stood awkwardly. She was at the sink for a moment washing her hands, then she turned to him. She looked at her watch.

"I made reservations for seven," she said.

"Perfect!"

"We have time. Would you like something to drink? I have orange juice, grape juice, beer, and red wine."

Her smile was stiff and guarded as though she hoped he'd pick orange juice or grape juice.

"I'll have orange juice."

"Good choice," she said, and sprinted to the refrigerator. "Sit down, sit down."

He sat down, still feeling uncomfortable. The house seemed so neatly arranged and spotless that it made him nervous to touch anything, even the seat of a chair with his bottom. The kitchen sink was sparkling white and the surface of the butcher's block serving as a kitchen island looked unused. The new-looking red-and-white dishcloths were folded and hung uniformly on their rack by the sink.

She handed Ray a small glass of orange juice.

"Thank you," he said softly.

"Est-ce que tu parles français?"

"No," he said. "I took Spanish in college, but I never took French."

"Too bad, I was hoping you spoke some French. You should learn."

"Yes, I should," he said, thinking he should also do a lot of things he was not doing. He said, "C'est la vie!"

"So, you *do* speak French!" She was excited.

"Not a bit," he said. "Everybody knows 'c'est la vie.'"

He took a sip and sat it on the kitchen island.

"Wait, wait," she said, "I'll get you a coaster. I don't want water marks on that surface."

He quickly picked up the glass and awkwardly held it till she returned with the coaster.

He finished drinking the juice and nervously set the glass on the coaster.

A little while later she said, "I guess we should get started, so we can get there before the rush; then we can get a good table."

"Sure." He stood up. "May I use your restroom before we leave?"

She hesitated, then said, "Sure. It's right down the hallway there. First door on the left."

When he came out, she was standing outside the door. He'd flushed the toilet and the tank was now noisily refilling. He'd washed his hands and used one of her neatly hanging towels to wipe his hands.

Without saying anything, she left him standing outside the toilet as she entered it. From where he stood, he could see her. She peeled off a sheet of paper towel and wiped out the sink; then she took the hand towel he'd used and carefully refolded it and hung it back the way she'd originally had it.

When she came out, he noticed that her cheeks and ears were flushed from a sudden surge of emotion. She said, "I like to keep things neat."

"Sure," he said, following her out onto the front porch. "Aren't you going to lock your door?"

"Oh, no, I never lock the door. There's no need. Ours is a very safe community. Years ago, it was a town where black people could not come after dark. It never was the blacks breaking the law. Our roustabouts used that custom to cover their own nighttime dirt. Those were awful times. We still have some old-timers who persist in thinking that way, but Godwin is a good town full of good law-abiding people. There hasn't been a crime in this town in ten years; and then that one ten years ago involved a domestic fight where a woman ended up shooting an abusive husband."

"Did he die?"

"Later in the hospital he died."

Arnett's Steak House was on the corner of Main and Green out on the eastern edge of town. The parking lot was nearly full of cars, but Ray managed to find one space available down at the end of the lot.

The restaurant was abuzz with excited chatter. Though this was a place sporting starched white tablecloths and white napkins and fine silverware, the diners were dressed casually. It was full of middle-aged and elderly people eating an early dinner. It was a typical American steak house with lots of bottles of steak sauce and catsup and hot sauce on the tables. The tables had their own little cozy lamps with beige shades with tassels.

Ray and Kay were escorted to a table in the center of the room. He'd always resented sitting in the center of a busy restaurant. He preferred to be by the wall or by a window. Normally he would have asked for a different seat, but in this situation he decided not to bother.

As they ate rare steak and tiny new potatoes in butter and green peas and drank red wine, Ray noticed that Kay seemed less spiritless. The wine seemed to have gone immediately to her head. He was becoming more curious about her. "Tell me, Kay, what's your passion?"

"French, of course, the French language and French culture and French literature."

"I assume you've been to France."

"I try to go every summer. I first went there fresh out of graduate school, my first year here at Godwin. I went on a Fulbright-Hays Inter-University Exchange Award: the Franco-American Commission for

Educational Exchange. I exchanged with a junior professor like myself at Paris Diderot University on rue Thomas Mann. For a young woman raised in a small Colorado town as I was, the first taste of France was an elixir. Do you know Paris?"

"Never been there, but I will go someday, maybe sooner than later."

"Oh, you *must*!" She beamed.

"Yes, I've known for a long time that my life has been too limited. I look back on who I was in New York and I realize I was provincial, a Brooklyn provincial. I'm glad I came out here. Even in the short time I've been here, I've started to see how having done so was a healthy move."

"That's wonderful, Ray. Have you ever been married?"

"No," he said, a bit surprised by the question.

"What kind of work do you do?"

He looked her in the eyes. "I was the manager in a supermarket in Brooklyn before I came out here."

"That sounds interesting. What was *that* like?"

He smiled. "It was a stressful job. We had at least two armed robberies a year, and there were thefts to deal with all the time. They were done mostly by kids out to steal stuff like candy bars or anything small like lipstick, hairbrushes, Band-Aids, you name it. One girl had stuffed a fashion magazine in her jeans, and it fell out before she could get out of the store. She ran. I always called the cops when we had an armed robbery, but I never called them in to deal with the kids. I handled those myself. I had three assistant managers, one overseeing the checkout people at the cash registers. They had the hardest jobs. Then we had the boys and girls, high school kids mostly, who bagged groceries and rounded up shopping carts in the parking lot. They also helped people carry their groceries out to their cars. They weren't allowed to accept tips. The day-to-day chores were easy enough. There were peak shopping hours and there were slow hours. During the slow hours, I had the clerks restock the shelves. One of my assistant managers was in charge of dealing with distributors and reordering. I also had two regular people whose job it was to keep the shelves organized and restocked. The people in produce were a separate team. Their manager also answered to me. Managing the store was a job that kept me on my toes."

"It does sound *very* stressful!"

"It was and I was always under pressure to turn a monthly profit."

"I'm impressed," Kay said.

He now wanted to ask her more about herself. She lived alone. He wondered how long she had lived alone and if she preferred it. He wanted to start her talking again. He said, "Tell me about your experiences in France."

"When I go I usually stay in an apartment I rent from a longtime friend, a real estate agent, Françoise. And when I can, I stay in my favorite arrondissement, Montparnasse. Over the years, I've stayed in apartments in Bercy, the twelfth; in Opéra, the ninth; in Montmartre, the eighteenth. I also like it up there because of the wonderful old basilica, Sacré-Cœur. From up there in front of the basilica, you can see the whole glorious city. When you go to Paris, you will *love* it!"

"Maybe you will go with me and show me around."

She blushed and looked at her plate. She'd finished eating and she'd done a good job of finishing her food. "Anything is possible," she finally said with a weak smile, looking up into his eyes.

Three hours later in her living room, he stood up from the couch and said, "Well, I've had a wonderful time with you, Kay. I hope we can do this again."

Surprised, she leaped up from the couch. "Aren't you spending the night? I just assumed you would. Besides, it's dangerous driving at night on that unlit two-lane road between here and Lorena. There've been horrible nighttime crashes. People have died. Didn't you notice the little memorial symbols planted at turns in the road?"

"No, I didn't."

"You're welcome to spend the night here if you like. You can sleep on the couch or . . ."

He turned and looked at her, surprised by her offer. She was earnest. "Sure, if you want me to."

"Of course I want you to," she said, gently touching his arm.

"Okay."

She went to her bedroom and came back with two clean folded sheets and a light purple knit blanket and handed them to him. "You know where the bathroom is," she said, smiling.

After Kay was gone and her bedroom door was closed, he spread one sheet on the couch and placed the other one and the blanket on the back of the couch ready to be used for cover.

He figured he probably didn't need the blanket. Then he took off his shoes and stripped down to his T-shirt and boxer shorts and lay down and pulled the sheet over himself up to his neck. He lay there waiting for sleep to take him.

He could see from the light at the bottom of her bedroom door that Kay was probably not yet asleep. She was probably reading. A good habit, he thought, and a good way to get sleepy enough to fall asleep. He had nothing to read.

About an hour later Kay's door eased open, and in her nightgown she came out on tiptoes and over to him and whispered, "Are you asleep, Ray?"

"No," he whispered back.

"If the couch is uncomfortable, you can come join me if you want. The bed is so much more comfortable than this couch."

"Okay," he said, unsure of what lay ahead.

He got up and walked alongside her into her bedroom.

"Just go ahead and get in bed on the right side. I like the left side. I'm going to the bathroom for a minute."

Twenty minutes later he heard Kay coming out of the bathroom. She was still wearing the long flannel nightgown, and she had cold cream all over her face. She got into bed on the left side, then she switched off the light and he felt the weight of her body land as she slid under the covers with him. He lay there with his eyes closed trying to summon sleep, then he felt her arm against his arm.

He lay beside her in the darkness and listened to her breathing and wondered if she was listening to his. He felt there was nothing to do but sleep, and he soon fell asleep.

PART 5

A World Not Yet Born

Each friend represents a world in us, a world possibly not born until they arrive, and it is only by this meeting that a new world is born.

—ANAÏS NIN

23

Monday morning ray stood at his front bay window watching Chester Porter out front planting fall flowers in his front yard. It was only September, but it was beginning to look and feel like October. There were thunderclouds in the distance. He saw that the trees in his yard were already turning fall colors of red and yellow and purple.

Chester had already cut the oleanders along the left side of the backyard fence to keep them from hanging over onto the next-door neighbors' roof. Ray didn't want any complaints from his neighbors, people who were so far friendly. Having already seen the danger of those oleanders getting out of control, he'd asked Chester to keep an eye on them.

The week before, Chester had taken up all the grass and replaced it with rich top soil and fertilizer. Now he was putting down blue flax, brambles, buckwheat, blackberry, virgin's bower, mariposa lily, sticky phacelia, old man's beard, and miner's lettuce. Chester said these plants would bring back butterflies, hummingbirds, and bees; all of which, lately, seemed to be vanishing.

The phone rang. His first thought: *It's Kay;* second thought: *It's Scotty.* By the time he reached the phone, he suspected it was a wrong number or a bogus call. "Hello?"

"How are you, Ray?" It was Alice. She didn't wait for him to respond. She continued: "I'd like to talk with you. I think we have some unsettled issues that we need to talk about."

He was dreading the idea of meeting with her, but he said, "What d'you want to talk about?"

"I'm at work, let's not talk on the phone. This is private. Can you meet me at Sally's Diner on Boyle for coffee at five thirty?"

"All right."

It was the lull period between lunch and dinner. Alice was sitting alone at one of the three tables for two by the wall. A cup of coffee was at her elbow. She was watching him approach. He sat down in the empty chair facing her.

The waitress came over from behind the counter carrying the coffee container and an empty cup. She refilled Alice's cup and asked Ray what he wanted.

"Just coffee," he said. "No cream, no sugar."

She filled the empty cup with black coffee and placed it in front of him and left.

Alice was still gazing at him, now with unblinking sadness. Finally, she said, "I apologize for the hurtful things I said."

"Thanks."

"I see you got a new girlfriend," she said with a sneer.

"What?"

"Didn't you and Kay get together?"

He didn't respond.

"You don't have to answer that question. I shouldn't have said that anyway. That's not why I asked you to meet me."

"What's on your mind, Alice?"

"I want to tell you why I was attracted to you." She took a deep breath, held it, then slowly released it. "There is a deep core of sadness in you that I was attracted to because I have that same deep core of sadness in myself. It was our *link*."

"Alice, you've talked about this sorrow and sadness before."

"Yes, but I don't think you understand how important this is. I felt that you and I were *meant* to be together. The girls would grow up and leave, and you and I would have a life together. We'd be able to travel a lot and enjoy life, but obviously you weren't thinking the same way."

He said nothing in response.

Tears rolled down her cheeks. "You don't know how difficult it has been, Ray. I'm a single woman trying to raise two girls. You were the first man I truly believed I had a chance with for a lasting relationship; and I was wrong. You don't know how hard that is."

He still said nothing in response.

"The girls are angry with you for hurting me."

"I know and I'm sorry you are hurt, Alice."

"You know but you don't care enough to—"

"I do care, but I have to do what's best for both of us. If I'm not happy in the relationship, you won't be happy."

"Is Kay best for you?"

How ironic, he thought. He knew he could easily say, *No, Kay's not best for me*, but he didn't want to open that can of worms. He said, "Alice, we're not getting anywhere with this conversation. We've been through all of this already."

"Then just leave," she said angrily, banging her coffee cup on the table. People turned and looked at them.

He took out his wallet, placed five dollars on the table, got up and said, "Take care, Alice, be well," and walked out.

Not knowing Scotty's hours because they changed so often, Ray got home and immediately dialed the number for Restaurant Blanton in Berkeley, hoping to catch Scotty there. A woman answered and Ray asked for Scotty. She said, "Is that the new bartender?"

"He started there a short time ago, yes, as a bartender."

"Oh, honey, I think he's on the night shift, from nine to midnight, something like that."

The minute he hung up, the phone rang. He thought of letting the answering machine get it, fearing it might be Kay or even Alice, but thinking it might be Scotty, he picked up. "Hello?"

"Ray, it's Kay."

"Hi, Kay. We had a lovely time, didn't we?"

"Well, that's one of the reasons I'm calling you."

"Oh?"

"I should've told you last night that I had a hysterectomy three years ago. It was because of cancer growing in that area, cancer of the cervix. They found it before it reached stage four. I was lucky. The doctor said the safe thing was to go ahead with a hysterectomy. Maybe I should have told you that was the reason I didn't want to do anything. I've had female problems a long time. The radiation caused problems, and it has made activity with a man extremely unpleasant. I've tried and it just doesn't work anymore."

"Good thing they caught the cancer in time."

"Yes, before it reached stage four."

He thought of her going to France every summer; it sounded like a good life. That activity told one story, and living alone out in the middle of nowhere told another. Maybe she didn't need a man. She seemed to have a good life without one.

"Were you ever married, Kay?"

"Heavens no!" She laughed. "Oh, years ago when I was a youngster in my early twenties, there was a Swiss boy—he was only twenty-one; that's still a boy. I thought I was in love with him, but after that affair went nowhere, I took my little broken heart back home and for a long time I gave up on men, then the cancer sort of finalized that."

"What happened to the relationship with the boy?"

"He was involved with a girl from Belgium at the same time he was leading me on, making me think we were in an exclusive relationship."

"Were you in school there?"

"Yes, we were all just youngsters, foreigners studying French and literature at the Sorbonne, the University of Paris."

"How'd you find out about the girl from Belgium?"

"One Sunday when he told me he had to stay in and study, I went for a walk along the Seine just to enjoy the beautiful spring weather; and I just happened to come upon Michel and the Belgian girl. Her name was Elise and they were walking along ahead of me happily holding hands."

"Oh my!"

"I confronted them right there on the spot. He turned red as a beet with embarrassment. Elise got belligerent and told me off, saying that they were engaged and planning to marry. She called me a 'crazy American girl with delusional ideas.'"

"Then what happened?"

"That was the end of it. From then on, I avoided them till the term ended. When I returned the next year, they both were gone."

He thought it time to change the subject, so he said, "What do you enjoy doing now?"

"Studying and reading and teaching. I've devoted my life to my students. They have so much wonderful potential. Over time some of my colleagues become cynical about teaching and they give up on students, but I have never felt that way. They are my life."

"That is a worthy commitment," he said sincerely.

"When will I see you again?" she said with hesitation.

"Kay, I think you are a wonderful person . . ."

"Uh-oh," she cried, "I know what's coming: 'Let's just be friends.' Right?"

"Well, Kay, that's not a bad idea. I think we are *already* friends."

"Yes, I know. You don't have to say any more." She paused. "It always ends this way."

"I thought you hadn't had any relationships."

"I haven't because after the first date they end like this."

"How often has that happened?"

"Oh, not more than three or four times."

"I know it sounds like a cliché, but I consider it an honor to have you as a friend, Kay."

"Thank you. I'm going to cry now."

"Don't cry."

"Listen, Ray, I'm hanging up now. Goodbye, Ray."

"Goodbye, Kay." He hung up feeling awful.

24

EARLY MORNING AROUND SIX A.M. on the last Wednesday in September, Ray's phone rang, waking him. Groggily, he reached over to the bedside table and picked up and said, "Hello?"

"Ray! Ray! Something awful might have happened to Scotty. They said a man named Scott O'Brien was murdered three days ago. I just heard it on the early news that Scott O'Brien was killed in a Berkeley motel called the Mead Motel. I'm praying to God that it wasn't Scotty. Scott O'Brien is a common name. It is, isn't it?"

"Calm down, Connie. Why is it just being reported if it happened three days ago?"

"When they first reported it three days ago, they did not release the victim's name, so I wasn't paying much attention, since there are so many murders in the Bay Area all the time. We don't get much news about the Bay Area up here in Lorena."

"Slow down, Connie, please slow down. It could be somebody else. There must be thousands and thousands of men named Scott O'Brien. Exactly what did you hear?"

"They said as soon as they learn more details, they would update the report. The police did not release the name of the killer, but apparently they caught him."

Ray sat up on the side of the bed. "Listen, I'm going out to the walkway and get my morning newspaper and see if there's anything in the *Sentinel*."

"Can you meet me for breakfast, say, around nine this morning?"

"Sure, Connie. Where do you want to meet?"

"Stanley's on Coker. Okay?"

"Sure, see you there at nine."

Ray put on his robe and house shoes and went out to the walkway. The morning air was refreshing and helped to wake him fully.

Back in the house he made a pot of coffee, and when it was done, he sat at the kitchen table and opened the *Sentinel*. He turned the pages slowly, careful not to miss even the smallest item, but he saw nothing about a Scott O'Brien killed in Berkeley.

He rubbed his eyes and folded the newspaper and finished his coffee. He told himself he was not worried, but he was and he knew he was.

After he showered and shaved, it was eight thirty. He got dressed and was ready to meet Connie. It would take only ten minutes to get to Stanley's.

As Ray walked into Stanley's, he saw Connie dressed in a dark blue exercise outfit and walking shoes. She was seated in a booth by one of the windows, and she waved to him as he approached.

He sat down facing her. Sighing, he said, "There was nothing in the morning newspaper. On the way here, I had the car radio turned to a San Francisco news station. They didn't say anything about a motel killing."

"I haven't heard any more," she said. She looked tired and worried.

The waitress came. Her name tag said she was Lisa. Lisa was in her fifties and tall, wearing a clean starched yellow uniform; she had her hair permed and tinted purple, and her fingernails were excessively long and also painted purple. "What can I get for you fine folks this morning?" Her smile showed her teeth to be too white to be the ones she was born with.

They ordered breakfast—Connie had pancakes, syrup, and coffee, and he ordered sunny-side-up eggs, two strips of bacon, whole wheat toast, and coffee.

They both ate too quickly.

Sipping coffee, Ray said, "I'm going to Berkeley tomorrow to see what I can find out. Mead Motel, right?"

"That's right. I hope to God it wasn't Scotty," she said with fear in her eyes. "For God's sake, let me know as soon as you find out anything."

At home that evening at five o'clock on the local news, Ray heard: "Scott O'Brien, the young man killed at the Mead Motel, was from New York. Apparently, he grew up in a shelter there and has worked as a bartender here in the Bay Area for at least a year or so."

For Ray, that news report confirmed that it was Scotty. Tomorrow Ray would head for Berkeley.

25

It was late thursday after dark when Ray got there. The motel was on a side street off University Avenue just before you get to the marina. Ray drove till he saw the motel sign, then he turned into the driveway and drove across the parking lot and stopped under the Mead Motel carport.

The door to his right had the word OFFICE printed on the glass. He turned off the motor and sat there looking in at the old woman behind the little check-in counter. She had white hair and extremely pale skin that was illuminated under electric lights.

He got out and walked over to the glass door and opened it. A little bell over the door rang three times.

"Good evening," he said in his best friendly voice, hoping to put the old woman at ease. He smiled.

She looked up startled and said, "H-hello . . . can I help you?"

At the moment an elderly man came from a back room. Ray guessed they both were in their early eighties. Seeing Ray, his eyes widened. "Can I help you? Are you looking for a room?" the man asked.

"No," Ray said. "I was hoping you'd be able to give me some information about Scott O'Brien." Ray continued to hold his frozen smile.

"You're a reporter?"

"No, sir, Scott O'Brien was a close friend of mine. We grew up together in a New York shelter. I was hoping you could tell me what happened."

"I understand," said the woman.

The man stood beside the woman. Like her, he was tall and heavyset. He was bald on the top and had a halo of white hair around his ears. He said, "We've told the police and the newspapers everything we know."

"Like I said, Scotty and I were kids together," Ray said. "I haven't seen much or heard much about what happened."

The woman said, "What do you want to know?"

Ray could tell she was softening. He said, "I'd just like to know about my friend's last hours."

"You plan to talk to newspaper people?" the man said.

"No, it'd be just for me, just to try to get some kind of closure for our friendship."

The man came around the counter and said, "Have a seat over here, Mr. . . . uh . . ."

"Jansen, Raymond Jansen."

The man walked over and sat down in the little waiting area right off the entrance where there were four chairs arranged around a low coffee table. In the corner was a red machine with the word COCA-COLA in white letters at the top. Beside it was a cigarette machine sporting a picture of a pack of Marlboro cigarettes and the Marlboro Man, and on the wall beside the cigarette machine was a pay phone.

"I'm Hilton Mead," the man said. "I'm sorry about your friend. It's been an awful mess for us, having a murder take place here; it's hurt our business. The murder happened only four days ago. They just took down the police tape yesterday. We're still in shock."

The woman came over and sat down beside her husband.

Hilton Mead said, "This is my wife, Emma. We've been in business here for thirty years; and we've never had anything like this happen before. We run a decent and respectable place of business. It's just been heartbreaking for us."

Emma said, "Hilton, Mr. Jansen doesn't want to hear about our heartache. He's here about his friend, Mr. O'Brien."

Hilton said, "Well, I guess you know everything that was in the newspapers and on the TV and radio news?"

"I've heard very little."

"Our night clerk, Eddy, signed in Mr. O'Brien and Mrs. Leta O'Brien around ten thirty. It was after midnight when he was murdered; they were here about two hours before it happened. I found out later from the newspaper that her real name is Leta Sanchez and that she is twenty-five and married to a man named Bradford Joe Blevins, owner of Blevins' Heating & Air Conditioning over in Oakland. He's the one they're holding as a suspect. Mr. O'Brien signed in with his real name. That was unusual. You wouldn't believe how many people we get in here who use fake names."

Emma said, "It's because they're sneaking around with somebody who's not their wife or husband. That gal is married; she should have known better. She is a teacher. They had her students on TV saying how shocked they were, and the principal of the school was interviewed. They all said what a fine person she is and how surprised they were that she would step out on her husband like that."

Hilton said, "They were having a threesome with our maid, Pat, when Bradford arrived with a gun. You see, unknown to us, our nighttime maid Patricia Ramsey had all along been turning tricks in the rooms at night. When Mr. O'Brien and Leta Sanchez checked in, Eddy must have propositioned them and they bought it. Pat was lucky she was not shot too; so was Leta Sanchez. Leta had gone in that little Jeep wagon of hers, leaving Mr. O'Brien and Pat in the room. The police said she went out to get more booze. While she was gone, Bradford knocked on the door and Mr. O'Brien apparently got up and opened it, thinking it was Sanchez returning. That's when Bradford shot him, six times in the chest and neck. He died on the spot. Leta got back and found Mr. O'Brien dead and blood all over our brand-new carpet and Pat hysterical. By the time the cops and the coroner got here, Mr. O'Brien was already dead. The day before the murder, Bradford had taken most of his money out of the bank and that showed premeditation, and when he was caught that night on the highway, he was headed north, probably on his way to Canada. None of the newspapers reported the threesome. Leta was gone for maybe an hour before she came back with the booze and found police and lights flashing. Our place of business was turned into a crime scene. One of the police officers called us at home, and we got down here as fast as we could. There were so many cops here, I couldn't count them all."

Ray was speechless.

Emma said, "Patricia worked for us as our maid for about six months, and she worked the nightshift. She kept the place clean, and she made the beds and emptied the trash in the rooms. We have a daytime person, Virgil, who's been with us for years. Pat's parents sounded like nice people on the phone, and Pat seemed like a nice country girl. She's not from the Bay Area. She moved here from a little town in Kansas called Great Bend. We hired her so Hilton and I could get some time off from trying to keep this place clean and running. The night clerk Eddy was in on her hustle. He'd set himself up as her pimp. She was paying him to keep quiet and to protect her if one of the men got rough with her. We're getting on in years. I'll be eighty in two weeks, and Hilton is already eighty-two. Like Hilton said, she was turning tricks every night in the rooms. Got so bad, men would go away and tell their friends about her and they'd come check in. We didn't know she had a heavy heroin habit and she needed the money to support her habit, and I guess she was also buying heroin for that no-good young man she was living with—they called him Butch."

"None of this about Pat was in the newspapers," said Hilton. "We found out what she was doing on our own."

"How'd you find out?" Ray was curious.

Emma said, "After we started suspecting this was going on, we had one of my cousins check in just to see if he would be propositioned, but Eddy must have gotten suspicious and nothing happened. Eddy probably thought Gregory was a cop. Pat never approached him. He spent the night in room six and left the next morning. At that point we thought, 'Well, maybe we were mistaken in our suspicions.'"

Hilton said, "Eddy and Pat were a clever team. Sometimes they would lock the front door to keep new legitimate customers from coming in. He'd put our sign on the door that says 'Back in Ten Minutes,' but he never got back in ten minutes. We were told just yesterday by potential customers that they came here and the door was locked. We had that sign made up for legitimate purposes such as going to the toilet or having to respond to a customer in a room when somebody needed more pillows or the TV was not working and other reasons, but Eddy and Pat used it for their own purposes."

Emma said, "Pat confessed a lot to the police. She said that even men who checked in with their wives or girlfriends would come back up here to the office while their wives or girlfriends were down there in the room, and she'd take them back in the office. Eddy stood guard. We fired both of them three days ago on the spot. Like I said, Pat broke down and told the police everything. We'd already seen the evidence on the daybed. At first, we thought Eddy and Pat were leaving those stains; but the stains on the daybed were what first caused us two weeks ago to get suspicious of both Eddy and Pat."

Hilton said, "I put that daybed in there so I could take a nap from time to time while Emma was manning the daytime desk and vice versa."

"But usually Pat would go to the room after the man had already paid Eddy when he checked in," Emma said. "Eddy would later give Pat her share. They had a cozy little enterprise going at our expense."

"So, Bradford just shot Scotty in the doorway?" said Ray.

"Yes," said Hilton, "and with Pat in bed. It's a wonder one of the bullets didn't hit her."

Ray was in shock.

Emma said, "I'd not too long ago talked with Pat's mother by phone. She was grateful we'd given her daughter a job, even a minimum-wage job. Her mother said otherwise Pat might have been homeless. She said they tried their best with that girl. We thought she was a nice girl and we hired her because she came from good folks in Kansas, but we didn't know she was mixed up in drugs till one of the police officers told us; and we certainly didn't know Pat was living with a drug dealer who had just gotten out of prison. People call him Butch, but his real name is Jimmy LaCroix Jr."

Hilton said, "This morning we heard on the news that Butch was arrested for beating Pat's baby boy, Daniel, to death. Pat and Butch said the baby fell down the steps; but after the police investigation, the police concluded that the bruises were consistent with a beating and not a fall. The two of them, Pat and Butch, are now facing murder charges. Like I said, they tried to cover it up by saying the baby fell down those steps in that house they were renting in Oakland, but the police said there were bruises all over that boy's body. It must have been horrible for the child."

"Unspeakable!" said Emma, shaking her head in disgust.

"It is all just too hellish for words," said Hilton with a deep sigh. "It's taken a lot out of us, and we don't have that much time left."

"What happened to Scotty's body?"

Hilton gave Ray a sad smile. "We don't know. They couldn't find anybody to claim the body."

"I thought I might try to give him a burial. I'm probably the only person who knew he was out here in California." Ray shrugged.

Emma said, "You can check at the morgue. His body might still be there. It's on Shattuck Avenue next door to the police station."

"Thanks." Ray looked away. "Well, thank you both. I guess I'd better not bother you folks with any more questions." He stood up.

"I should have known something horrible was going to happen that night," Emma said. "That very day the weatherman Mike Johnson on KWTV said there were thunderclouds in the forecast. It wasn't raining here, but when we left that afternoon to go home, the sky was so black you would have thought it was nighttime. It was on a night like that that my mother and father were killed in a six-car crash out on the highway back fifteen years ago this coming Thursday."

Hilton slowly rose to his feet and he was followed by Emma. She pulled at the seat of her dress.

Hilton said, "You look like a respectable upstanding young man, Mr. Jansen. How did your friend Mr. O'Brien end up like this?"

Ray shrugged. "Luck, I guess. I've had good luck. He had bad luck."

"It's ironic," said Hilton, "that a person with all the advantages that come with being white and being male that this country affords such a person would end up like Mr. O'Brien did and that you a person of color with all the disadvantages that that brings apparently had good luck. When you first walked in here, I confess I wasn't sure about you. You know how it is. Colored people are so often depicted on TV as bad people that it makes us nervous when we come in contact with them. It's unfortunate that we've been conditioned to think that way about colored people. I know it's silly on my part, and I also know that there are a lot of good colored folks out there."

"Scotty and I started off in the same place," said Ray.

"That makes it all the more to my point." Hilton shook his head in bewilderment. "I guess you're right: it's just luck. Right here in the Bay

Area, we've got thousands of young white men who are homeless and on drugs, or they're mentally ill and living on the streets, sleeping in doorways or alleys with no future prospects."

Ray wondered if he should try to shake hands with Hilton. He wasn't ever sure if such a gesture on his part was going to get a positive response, so, he waited to see if Hilton would extend his hand, but he didn't. Ray turned and walked toward the exit.

He stopped and turned and faced them. "Thank you again for all your help."

He drove across the Golden Gate Bridge into San Francisco and checked into the Union Square Hilton, where he'd stayed back in April.

Before going to bed, he checked the Berkeley phone book and found the address of the Berkeley City Morgue on Shattuck Avenue, right at the edge of downtown Berkeley, next to the Berkeley City Police Station.

26

The next day around eleven, Ray drove back over into Berkeley to try to find the morgue. It was a sunny but cool morning.

Numbed from shock, he was feeling sad. He had not slept well. Images of Scotty's bullet-riddled naked body on the motel floor crowded his sleep.

The Berkeley City Morgue looked like a nineteenth-century country bank repurposed as a morgue. No Parking signs lined both sides of the street.

So Ray drove to the next block and parked in a vacant space in a row of cars parked at an angle in front of Wong & Wing Asian Supermarket Fine Imported Foods. An old man in coveralls was sitting on a crate in front of the store gazing off into the middle distance.

Ray got out and locked his car and walked back to the morgue. He stepped inside the revolving door and entered the lobby.

Standing just inside the doorway, a uniformed guard stopped him. "May I help you?" He was a very authoritative-looking black man with a good-looking face and a strong jawline. A gun was on his hip and his hands were huge.

"Yes, I'm here to see if my friend's body might be here."

"Are you a close relative?"

"No," Ray said.

"You need to be a relative. If you're not a relative, you can't claim or see a body."

Ahead across the lobby, Ray saw the receptionist counter. In big letters above the counter was the word INFORMATION. To the right of the counter on the wall was the word MORGUE with an arrow pointing down the hallway.

Ray smiled, trying to be pleasant. "May I at least speak to the receptionist?"

While keeping an untrusting gaze on Ray, with his tongue the guard sucked his teeth. "He's going to tell you the same thing I just told you. You got to be a relative." He paused. "But go ahead."

Ray walked down the lobby to the receptionist counter. Up close, Ray saw the man's name tag: JOE FLAHERTY. "Hello. My name is Raymond Jansen. I was told by Mr. and Mrs. Mead, over at the Mead Motel, that Scott O'Brien's body might still be here."

Joe Flaherty smiled. "I assume you're not a relative?" He was a little guy with a quick tongue and darting eyes.

"Scott had no relatives. He and I grew up together in a shelter for children."

Ray watched Flaherty consider that information, his eyes darting about. "Only a relative can inquire about a body, but it doesn't matter. You're too late. Mr. O'Brien's remains were buried in a pauper's grave yesterday."

This didn't surprise Ray. "Can you tell me where? I'd like to go out and pay my respects to an old friend."

"It's an unmarked grave out at Sweet Dreams."

"That's the name of the cemetery?"

"You got it! It's over in Emeryville. Just keep driving till you reach the Emeryville Golf Course. It's to the left. You can't miss it; but like I said, he's in an unmarked grave. I don't see how you're going to pay respects to an unmarked grave."

"I'll find a way. Thank you." Ray took a deep breath and let it out, then he turned and walked back up the lobby past the guard, and in passing he nodded and thanked him, then walked out through the revolving door.

Driving out on San Pablo Avenue, Ray finally saw the Emeryville Golf Course. He had the car window down, and he could smell the nearby ocean. After that he easily found Sweet Dreams. Fog hadn't yet lifted completely from the area. The gate for auto traffic was closed.

Ray parked on the side of the road and got out and walked in through the open pedestrian iron gateway. There had to be a pauper section somewhere. He figured he might spot the right grave if he looked for freshly turned earth. He walked around, stopping to read headstones, some grand and others small and modest. DENIS EASTMAN, 1936–1974, *My love gone too soon from this earth*; PAULA DUFFY, 1923–1969, *In loving memory of my wife of twenty years*. Name after name: ADDISON, FULTON, KESSLER, POE, BERMAN, CASTRO, POHL, THOMPSON. Death was a thriving business.

Ray was looking for the unmarked graves and for signs of fresh-looking dirt. Ten minutes later he came to that area at the back of the cemetery, but there were three plots of freshly turned earth. He walked to the first one and stood for a moment.

He told himself he didn't believe in magical thinking, but at a time like this, he forgave himself for giving in to it; yet so far, he felt nothing. Then he stepped over to the second one and stood there and waited. He felt nothing here, either.

At the third one Ray stopped, and he told himself this was the one. He tried to whisper goodbye words but couldn't bring his voice up to that level. He felt choked and sad and angry.

Finally, he managed to say, "Ah, Scotty! Here you go again!"

He stood there a while as clouds gathered above, then he turned away and walked back across the cemetery and out to his car and got in and headed back to San Francisco, where the sky was clearing.

W9-DAV-091

INTRODUCTION TO

NURSING RESEARCH

INCORPORATING EVIDENCE-BASED PRACTICE

FIFTH EDITION

JONES & BARTLETT
LEARNING

Multiple-Choice Questions

1. Which of these examples characterizes a successful application of safe and competent nursing care delivery?
   A. The nurse investigates the latest online information in deciding how the care is to be provided.
   B. The nurse examines peer-reviewed nursing research articles to determine the best care to be provided.
   C. The nurse asks a clinical instructor from the university how the care for a client should be given.
   D. The nurse provides care following the instructions provided when attending school.

2. The ACA and the IOM/RWJF and Carnegie Foundation reports are national movements to:
   A. reaffirm current nursing practice.
   B. ignore current nursing practice.
   C. transform current nursing practice.
   D. eliminate current nursing practice.

3. A nurse is seeking a research article to use as the underpinning for an adjustment in the manner in which care is given. An example of a research article is a manuscript that provides a(n):
   A. overview of how to provide care.
   B. discussion of the method used for the research along with recommendations.
   C. discussion of a case study without any recommendations.
   D. overview of guidelines for a particular type of case.

4. Which of these forms of evidence carries the highest degree of credibility?
   A. Research study using a nonexperimental study
   B. Intuition
   C. Research study using a random control sample
   D. Research study providing a case study approach

5. A problem-focused trigger would generate which of the following PICOT statements?
   A. Registered nurses have less work stress than other healthcare providers.
   B. Adult cardiac patients involved in bedside rounding compared to multidisciplinary rounding have an increased understanding of their treatment plan.
   C. Palliative care patients enjoy music therapy more than pet therapy when provided by their family members.
   D. Registered nurses can use any nursing theorist to provide sound care.

6. Which of these PICOT questions or statements demonstrates effective development?
   A. What type of care is best used for pediatric patients?
   B. Nurses prefer 12-hour shifts to 8-hour shifts to allow more time with family.
   C. Individuals using saline for hep-lock flushes have fewer complications.

Multiple-Choice Questions

Review key concepts with these questions at the end of each chapter.

   D. Hospitalized children have less stress and heal more quickly when allowed to use play therapy in comparison to pet therapy while recovering from surgery.

7. You are a BSN-prepared nurse who wants to initiate a research project on your unit. To get the other nurses to participate, you would:
   A. ask the doctors what they think.
   B. check the educational level of other nurses on the unit.
   C. ignore your desire to learn more at this time.
   D. give a presentation to your peers on the benefits of research.

8. Research is often not valued because:
   A. it costs too much.
   B. administrators want it.
   C. search engines are easy to access.
   D. staffing is not an obstacle.

Discussion Questions

1. You are a public health nurse working in an outpatient community health facility. You are responsible for clients and their families in a six-county area. During the course of a week, you have from 6 to 10 clients or their families who experience stressful situations related to their diagnosis of diabetes mellitus type 1. These families and their loved ones experience confusion and frustration as they confront and deal with the complex nature of the healthcare situation. You have been asked to explore the following question: How do others in this type of situation deal with the numerous stressful challenges? Which type of searchable question could you develop to drive the data search related to this request?

2. As a BSN staff nurse, you are excited that your hospital wants you to participate in an evidence-based project. You have been chosen to chair a task force. How would you approach this task?

3. You are an ADN-prepared staff nurse at an acute care facility who has enrolled in an RN-BSN program. One of the key messages presented by the RN-BSN program is the importance of evidence-based nursing practice. In your first course in the program, you are asked to identify an evidence-based topic for development. The faculty members instruct you to select a topic that will be functional in your workplace. Which types of activities would you carry out to aid in the selection of this topic?

Suggested Readings

Bovino, L. R., Aquila, A. M., Bartos, S., McCurry, T., Cunningham, C. E., Lane, T., Rogacki, N., DosSantos, J., Moody, D., Mealia-Ospina, K., Pust-Marcone, J., & Quiles, J. (2017). A cross-sectional study on evidence-based nursing practice in the contemporary hospital setting: Implications for nurses in professional development. *Journal for Nurses in Professional Development, 33*(2), 64–69. doi:10/1097/NND.0000000000000339

Briggs, P. Hawrylack, H., Mooney, R., Papanicolas, D., & Taylor, P. (2017). Engaging nurses in clinical research. *Nursing2017, 47*(2), 14–16. doi:10.1097/01.NURS.0000510757.23703.43

Carter, E. J., Mastro, K., Vose, C., Rivera, R., & Larson, E. L. (2017). Clarifying the conundrum: Evidence-based practice, quality improvement, or research? *JONA, 47*(5), 266–270. doi:10.1097/NNA.0000000000000477

Discussion Questions

Students can use these assignments to apply information in the text to everyday practice.

INTRODUCTION TO
NURSING RESEARCH

INCORPORATING EVIDENCE-BASED PRACTICE

FIFTH EDITION

EDITED BY

Carol Boswell, EdD, RN, CNE, ANEF, FAAN
Professor
Texas Tech University Health Sciences Center
Odessa, Texas

Sharon Cannon, EdD, RN, ANEF
Regional Dean and Professor
Texas Tech University Health Sciences Center
Odessa, Texas

JONES & BARTLETT
LEARNING

World Headquarters
Jones & Bartlett Learning
5 Wall Street
Burlington, MA 01803
978-443-5000
info@jblearning.com
www.jblearning.com

Jones & Bartlett Learning books and products are available through most bookstores and online booksellers. To contact Jones & Bartlett Learning directly, call 800-832-0034, fax 978-443-8000, or visit our website, www.jblearning.com.

Substantial discounts on bulk quantities of Jones & Bartlett Learning publications are available to corporations, professional associations, and other qualified organizations. For details and specific discount information, contact the special sales department at Jones & Bartlett Learning via the above contact information or send an email to specialsales@jblearning.com.

16816-7

Production Credits

VP, Product Management: Amanda Martin
Product Manager: Tina Chen
Product Assistant: Anna-Maria Forger
Director, Relationship Management: Carolyn Rogers Pershouse
Senior Project Specialist: Leah Corrigan
Senior Marketing Manager: Jennifer Scherzay
Product Fulfillment Manager: Wendy Kilborn
Composition and Project Management: S4Carlisle Publishing Services

Cover Design: Kristin E. Parker
Rights & Media Specialist: John Rusk
Media Development Editor: Troy Liston
Cover Image (Title Page, Chapter Opener):
  © MATJAZ SLANIC/iStock/Getty Images Plus
Printing and Binding: LSC Communications
Cover Printing: LSC Communications

Library of Congress Cataloging-in-Publication Data
Names: Boswell, Carol, editor. | Cannon, Sharon, editor.
Title: Introduction to nursing research : incorporating evidence-based
  practice / edited by Carol Boswell, Sharon Cannon.
Description: Fifth edition. | Burlington, Massachusetts : Jones & Bartlett
  Learning, [2020] | Includes bibliographical references and index.
Identifiers: LCCN 2018032810 | ISBN 9781284149791 (pbk. : alk. paper)
Subjects: | MESH: Nursing Research--methods | Evidence-Based Nursing
Classification: LCC RT81.5 | NLM WY 20.5 | DDC 610.72--dc23 LC record available at
  https://lccn.loc.gov/2018032810

6048

Printed in the United States of America
22 21 20 19 18   10 9 8 7 6 5 4 3 2 1

Brief Contents

Preface   xiii

Acknowledgments   xv

Contributors   xvii

Chapter 1   Connection Between Research
             and Evidence-Based Practice 1

Chapter 2   Overview of Evidence 31

Chapter 3   Overview of Research 61

Chapter 4   Overview of Quality 79

Chapter 5   Ethics for Nursing Research
             and Evidence-Based Practice 91

Chapter 6   Asking the Right Question 121

Chapter 7   Literature Review: Searching
             and Writing the Evidence 141

Chapter 8   Quantitative Research Design. 171

Chapter 9   Qualitative and Mixed Research
             Methods 189

Chapter 10   Population Management 223

Chapter 11   Data Collection 243

Chapter 12   Reliability, Validity,
             and Trustworthiness 271

Chapter 13   Data Analysis 301

Chapter 14   The Research Critique Process
             and the Evidence-Based Appraisal
             Process. 323

Chapter 15   Translational Research, Improvement
              Science, and Evaluation Research
              with Practical Applications...........347
Chapter 16   Application of Evidence-Based
              Nursing Practice with Research 365

Glossary   387
Index   397

Contents

Preface xiii

Acknowledgments xv

Contributors xvii

Chapter 1 **Connection Between Research and Evidence-Based Practice 1**

Carol Boswell and Sharon Cannon

Introduction 1

Providing a Line of Reasoning for EBP and Evidence-Based Research 3

Assessing the Need for Research in the Practice Arena 7

The Importance of Generating Evidence . . . 19

Obstacles to Using Research 21

Responsibility for Using Research 24

Summary Points 25

Chapter 2 **Overview of Evidence 31**

Pam Di Vito-Thomas and Carol Boswell

Introduction 31

Foundations for EBP 35

Qualities of Evidence 41

Evidence Grading Methods 47

Conclusion 52

Summary Points 53

Chapter 3 **Overview of Research 61**

Sharon Cannon and Margaret Robinson

Introduction 61

Historical Perspective 61

Theory, Research, and Practice 67

Sources for Nursing Research 70

Summary Points 71

Chapter 4 **Overview of Quality 79**

Sharon Cannon and Carol Boswell

Introduction 79

History of Quality Improvement 80

Purpose of Quality Improvement 81

Sources of Quality Improvement 81

Settings 84

Application of QI 85

Summary Points 87

Chapter 5 **Ethics for Nursing Research and Evidence-Based Practice 91**

Sharon Cannon and Theresa Delahoyde

Introduction 92

Ethical Theories 92

Historical Overview 95

Research Ethics: Progress in the 21st Century 97

Environment for Ethical Research 98

Developing Researchable Questions 102

Participant Recruitment and Informed Consent 103

Data Collection and Data Analysis 105

Issues in Quantitative and Qualitative Research 106

External Pressures 106

EBP and Ethical Implications 107

Emerging Ethical Issues in Research,
EBP, and QI............................110

Conclusion 112

Summary Points........................112

Chapter 6 Asking the Right Question..........121

Julie A. Baker-Townsend,
Kathaleen C. Bloom, and Lucy B. Trice

Introduction...........................122

Identifying Researchable Problems......122

Determining the Significance of the
Problem 124

Examining the Feasibility
of the Problem......................125

Addressing Nursing Research
Priorities 126

Problem Statement....................127

Research Question.....................127

Hypotheses 132

Defining Variables for the Study........134

Evidence-Based Practice
Considerations......................135

Summary Points.......................135

Chapter 7 Literature Review: Searching and Writing the Evidence 141

Travis Real, C. Erik Wilkinson,
and Carol Boswell

Introduction...........................142

Definition and Purpose of the
Literature Review 142

The Literature Review Within the EBP
and/or Research Process.............144

Differentiating a Research Article
from a Nonresearch Article..........146

Conducting a Literature Review
Search..............................147

The Importance of Librarians in the
Literature Review Process 148

The Research Idea: First Step...........148

The Research Question: Second Step ...149

Definition of Database.................150

Databases Useful in Nursing 150

Basics of Searching 153

Other Key Information.................157

Evaluating the Literature...............157

Writing the Literature Review 162

Linking the Literature Review to
Evidence-Based Nursing Practice.....165

Summary Points.......................165

Chapter 8 Quantitative Research Design ...171

Sharon Cannon

Introduction...........................172

Characteristics of Quantitative
Research Design 172

Descriptive Design 174

Experimental Design 175

Nonexperimental Design 176

Time-Dimensional Design 177

Quasi-Experimental Design 178

Control...............................180

Research Design, Quality
Improvement Projects, and
Root Cause Analysis.................180

Evidence-Based Considerations........181

Summary Points.......................182

Chapter 9 Qualitative and Mixed Research Methods..........189

JoAnn Long, Samara Silva, and Carol Boswell

Introduction...........................190

Qualitative Research 190

A Brief History of Qualitative Methods...191

Comparing Qualitative, Quantitative,
and Mixed Methods.................191

Approaches to Qualitative Research.....192

Sampling Strategies in Qualitative
Research............................196

Approaches to Qualitative Data
Collection...........................197

Approaches to Qualitative Data
Analysis.............................198

Methodological Rigor in Qualitative Research...........................199

Understanding and Using Qualitative Study Results............200

Mixed Methods Research...............201

Types of Mixed Method Strategies......205

Data Collection Procedures.............206

Data Analysis and Validation Procedures..........................208

EBP Considerations.....................209

Conclusion............................209

Summary Points........................211

Chapter 10 Population Management..... 223

Kathaleen C. Bloom, Julie A. Baker-Townsend, and Lucy B. Trice

Introduction...........................224

Why Sample?..........................225

Whom to Sample?.....................226

How to Sample?.......................227

How Many to Sample?.................231

Specific EBP Considerations............234

Conclusion............................236

Summary Points........................236

Chapter 11 Data Collection ... 243

Carol Boswell

Overview of Data Collection Methods and Sources................243

Accessible Data Versus New Data.......245

Key Categories of Data for Nursing Studies......................246

Significant Facets of Data Collection Schemes............................247

Test Methods..........................248

Questionnaire Methods.................249

Interview Methods 253

Focus Group Methods 254

Observation Methods 256

Secondary (Existing) Data Methods.....258

Biophysiological Methods 260

Systematic Analysis....................261

Achievement of the Data Collection Strategy...................263

EBP Considerations 263

Summary Points........................264

Chapter 12 Reliability, Validity, and Trustworthiness .. 271

James Eldridge

Introduction...........................272

Reliability as a Concept 274

Forms of Reliability 275

Validity 288

Conclusion 293

Summary Points.......................294

Chapter 13 Data Analysis 301

James Eldridge

Introduction...........................301

Quantitative Analysis 303

Qualitative Analysis....................315

Quality Assurance 317

Conclusion 318

Summary Points........................319

Chapter 14 The Research Critique Process and the Evidence-Based Appraisal Process 323

Carol Boswell and Sharon Cannon

Rationale for Doing a Research Critique..............................323

Elements of a Research Critique.........325

Process for Conducting a Research Critique..............................330

Critically Assessing Knowledge for Clinical Decision Making.........337

Employing EBP Guidelines: Instruments for Holistic Practice...................340

The Evidence-Based Appraisal 340

Summary Points........................342

Chapter 15 **Translational Research, Improvement Science, and Evaluation Research with Practical Applications...... 347**

Carol Boswell

Introduction............................348
Translational Research 348
Improvement Science 351
Logic Modeling.........................352
Action Plans...........................356
Conclusion 358
Summary Points........................359

Chapter 16 **Application of Evidence-Based Nursing Practice with Research 365**

Sharon Cannon and Carol Boswell

Introduction............................365
Process for EBP 367
Conclusion 373
Summary Points........................375

Glossary 387
Index............................. 397

Preface

Research, quality improvement, and evidence-based practice (EBP) go hand-in-hand as nursing comprehension flourishes and increases. Healthcare transformations stemming from the Patient Protection and Affordable Care Act; the Institute of Medicine's 2010 report *The Future of Nursing: Leading Change, Advancing Health*; and other challenges compel nurses to embrace and evolve nursing knowledge through these diverse evidence-development designs. EBP has evolved into a significant component for authenticating quality health care. The concept of EBP entails the integration of clinical expertise with investigational corroboration from evidence, which includes research. Nurses must assimilate reliable and astute evidence into policies and procedures. These EBP-based policies and procedures are utilized for the delivery of holistic health care. The public anticipates that each skill or task needs to be achieved using a specific technique that is justified by evidence.

Introduction to Nursing Research: Incorporating Evidence-Based Practice, Fifth Edition presents deep-seated research information employing evidence-based research examples. Every concept connected with the research process is covered. In addition, the information concerning the interconnectedness of research, EBP, and quality improvement is examined. Alternative facets encompassed in this text are the growth and development of comprehension about what makes up the range of evidence. This undertaking attempts to make the information significant and appropriate to nurses working in healthcare settings and who are encouraged to participate in EBP. Research should be FUN (functional, understandable, and nonthreatening).

This text characterizes the challenge to convey practical quality improvement, EBP, and research probabilities to the frontline nurse who is responsible for the ongoing management of health care. The contemporary healthcare arena requires that care be instituted using an authentic, evidence-based foundation. Therefore, the nurse must be knowledgeable and qualified to evaluate and instigate care grounded in evidence, which embraces research conclusions and quality improvement outcomes. The motivation for this edition focuses on supplying an understanding of preparatory research developments along with an EBP mindset. The decisive and fundamental practices of planning, conducting, and reporting research data are illustrated utilizing a perspective of EBP. Every attribute in the delivery of nursing care demands meticulous consideration and documentation of EBP, quality improvement, and research outcomes for the care provided.

To anticipate these challenges, this edition of *Introduction to Nursing Research: Incorporating Evidence-Based Practice* was structured to assist the nurse in scrutinizing the strengths and challenges evident in research projects, quality improvement reports, published reports, and unpublished manuscripts. By acquiring knowledge about which features signify convincing evidence, nurses can utilize appropriate research findings and quality improvement outcomes with additional evidence while disregarding inappropriate conclusions.

Four articles, listed below, are predominantly used throughout this text as exemplars to demonstrate chapter concepts. Chapters use these articles to showcase the components being examined within the materials.

Continuous Quality Improvement:

Brennan, C., & Parsons, G. (2017). Enhanced recovery in orthopedics: A prospective audit of an enhanced recovery program for patients undergoing hip or knee arthroplasty. *MEDSURG Nursing, 26*(2), 99–104.

Systematic Review:

Kwan, T. M., & Sullivan, M. (2017). The use of intravenous ibuprofen and intravenous acetaminophen in surgical patients and the effect on opioid reduction. *MEDSURG Nursing, 26*(2), 124–131.

Qualitative:

Woolston, W., & Connelly, L. M. (2017). Felty's syndrome: A qualitative case study. *MEDSURG Nursing, 26*(2), 105–109.

Quantitative:

Cortez-Gann, J., Gilmore, K. D., Foley, K. Q., Kennedy, M. B., McGee, T., & Kring, D. (2017). Blood transfusion vital sign frequency: What does the evidence say? *MEDSURG Nursing, 26*(2), 89–92.

Acknowledgments

We would like to convey our appreciation and esteem for our exceptional colleagues who wholeheartedly agreed to the management of modernizing specific chapters. The impact and practicality of this text stems from the proficiency and adeptness of the contributing authors, to whom we are extremely indebted. Numerous contemporary colleagues have affiliated with us in this edition of *Introduction to Nursing Research: Incorporating Evidence-Based Practice* to provide remarkable and pertinent information correlated to the distinctive subjects.

We again acknowledge those reviewers who provided analysis for the first and subsequent chapters, which furnished real-life examples in clinical settings and supported the emphasis of the chapter content. From their reflections, we were able to conserve the scholarly balance of the text. Critiques and recommendations offered by the various users of the text offered insights for insertion into future editions. The ideas and recommendations delivered by the end users have been beneficial in facilitating the unique objective of this text. In the fifth edition, we accentuate the understanding that evidence is crucial to enhance the fields of evidence-based practice (EBP), quality improvement, and nursing research. We again acknowledge Mary E. Nunnally, who imparted her valuable editorial perspective to the initial edition. We greatly appreciate the work provided by prior contributors to this textbook: Dr. Jane Sumner, Dr. Dorothy Jackson, and Dr. Donna Scott Tilley.

Dr. Carol Boswell and Dr. Sharon Cannon

Every once in a while, our lives are enhanced by very special people. One such person is my friend and colleague, Dr. Carol Boswell, who continues to seek new opportunities and especially explore creative innovations to promote evidence-based practice (EBP). Many wonderful colleagues and friends have enriched my life through their loyal support, especially our colleagues who have joined us on this evidence-based journey. I have truly been blessed to know them and try each day to pay forward their many kindnesses.

My family has played a significant part in the shaping of my life, so I wish to say a special thank you to my parents G. E. and Laurine Cannon (who are always with me in spirit); my family, especially Joe and Lynn Tischner, and Ryan Ganey; my grandchildren, Kelly Tischner, Andrew Ganey, Shelby Ganey, and Shannon Ganey; and my brother and sister-in-law, Gene and Cathi Cannon.

Dr. Sharon Cannon

The people who have continued through all five editions of this text to allow me to advance, blossom, and stretch for the highest levels possible are Marc E. Boswell; Dwight and Wanda Miller; Michael and Casey Boswell, Jeremy Boswell, and Stephanie Boswell; and Matthew Boswell, Kobe Boswell, Kayia Howard, and Caleb

Boswell. Each of these individuals keeps me firm to my values while affording me several occasions to laugh and enjoy life. They are my genuine cheering section, thus affording me reinforcement and support. Another key individual who has been regularly and actively involved during the development of my career and this textbook is Dr. Sharon Cannon. In addition to these marvelous and amazing individuals, I want to acknowledge the remarkable colleagues who augment my professional and personal life. These individuals provide encouragement and fervor to persist on a trek to amplify and enhance the expertise associated with evidence-based practice (EBP), quality improvement, and nursing research. To be challenged to strive for the mountaintops is an appreciated and astonishing opportunity. With the creativity and confidence of my family and friends, I have been able to tackle and overcome the craziness of the world while welcoming the authenticity of a person's humanity.

Dr. Carol Boswell

Contributors

Julie A. Baker-Townsend, DNP, RN, WHNP-BC, FNP-BC
Assistant Professor
School of Nursing
College of Health
University of North Florida
Jacksonville, Florida

Kathaleen C. Bloom, PhD, CNM
Professor
School of Nursing
College of Health
University of North Florida
Jacksonville, Florida

Theresa Delahoyde, EdD, RN
Dean of Undergraduate Nursing
Bryan College of Health Sciences
Lincoln, Nebraska

Pam Di Vito-Thomas, PhD, RN, CNE
Division Chair and Professor of Nursing
MacMurray College
Jacksonville, Illinois

James Eldridge, EdD
Associate Professor
University of Texas of the Permian Basin
Odessa, Texas

JoAnn Long, PhD, RN, NEA-BC
Professor of Nursing and Director of Research & Development
Department of Nursing
Lubbock Christian University
Lubbock, Texas

Travis Real, MLIS
Unit Assistant Director
Library of the Health Sciences at the Permian Basin
Texas Tech University Health Sciences Center
Odessa, Texas

Margaret Robinson, MSN, RN
Retired
Midland, Texas

Samara Silva, MSN, RN, CLC
Lubbock Christian University
Lubbock, Texas

Lucy B. Trice, PhD, RN, ARNP, FNP-BC
Professor, Director Emeritus
School of Nursing
College of Health
University of North Florida
Jacksonville, Florida

C. Erik Wilkinson, MLS
Unit Associate Director/Faculty Associate
Library of the Health Sciences at the Permian Basin
Texas Tech University Health Sciences Center
Odessa, Texas

CHAPTER 1

Connection Between Research and Evidence-Based Practice

Carol Boswell and Sharon Cannon

CHAPTER OBJECTIVES

At the conclusion of this chapter, the learner will be able to:
1. Translate the essentials for research to ratify evidence-based practice.
2. Define evidence-based practice.
3. Indicate impediments to evidence-based research.
4. Distinguish the nurse's role in evidence-based practice.
5. Interpret how evidence-based practice affects nursing practice.

KEY TERMS

Evidence-based practice (EBP)
Obstacle
PICOT

Research
Research process
Research utilization

▶ Introduction

The overarching principle for healthcare practice is the provision of quality nursing care to all clients without consideration of social, financial, cultural, or other individual characteristics. As the nurse initiates contact with the client, the client should be confident that the care provided by that nurse is based on the most current, up-to-date health information available. Having established the currency of the health information to be utilized, the nurse and client must also agree that individualized application of this information is necessary. (Although the healthcare field defines "client" and "patient" differently, for the purposes of this text, these terms are used interchangeably.) Thus, the need for **evidence-based practice (EBP)** is confirmed by our expectations related to nursing care.

The nurse who receives the assignment to care for an elderly male, a young child, or a critically ill adult female must come to the nursing practice arena with more than the latest information. The majority of the information must be tested and confirmed. To see how this works, let's consider the idea of cardiac information, although any disease process could be utilized for this purpose. Within nursing practice, certain health information concerning the management of cardiac complications, such as a myocardial infarction, is accepted. The initial question that should be asked by a nurse would be: Is this disease management information corroborated by research results? The answer to this question is frequently an unsure response by the nurse. Too often, the healthcare provider delivers the care because it is the known process or because it has been ordered instead of providing care based on the evidence found within the profession. Yoder and colleagues (2014) found that "staff nurses perceive finding and using research evidence as an esoteric activity that lies beyond their immediate responsibilities" (p. 35). However, the informational basis for each aspect of the nursing care to be provided should be analyzed to determine its sources and the strength of the information. Does the information come from general usage, or is it information that has been established through research or other critical analyses to be accurate?

Having determined the basis for the care to be provided, the nurse must then determine the application of the information based on the individuality of the client situation. The application of the information for each client situation depends on the specifics of the client's needs, the client's expectations concerning health, and many other aspects requiring modification of the confirmed knowledge application. The foundation of nursing care delivery must be research tested, research confirmed, and/or analytically investigated knowledge tempered by an awareness of the unique characteristics of the client and the situation.

The process of EBP includes assessing and delineating a problem through communication of an identifiable problem, pursuing and appraising the obtainable details, implementing a practice intervention as a product of the evidence, and evaluating the accomplished process for effectiveness. Initially, EBP requires the identification of the practice problem, followed by the utilization of tested research and other evidential results to improve the care provided to the clients. According to Conner (2014), the essential assessment questions are interchangeable—whether the clinical question involves treatment, diagnosis, outcomes, or causation:

- Are the conclusions of the study compelling and expected?
- Which outcomes were understood?
- Will the results smooth the progress toward the management of the patient's care?

The requirement to integrate sustained practices into the delivery of health care that cultivated the opportunities and development of EBP in the current healthcare arena is paramount. Bucknall (2012) notes that cognitive approaches, intuition, and analysis of information play key roles in how evidence is acknowledged, evaluated, and incorporated into the clinical decision-making process that affects patient outcomes. Clinical decisions are frequently not corroborated by unambiguous, persuasive evidence. Nurses are asked to make real-world decisions with limited information in a fast-paced environment. Time is valuable to the nurse at the bedside, so any course of action has to be both practical and rational (Cannon & Boswell, 2010). This responsibility to make knowledgeable, well-supported decisions based on sound facts emphasizes the need to become effective and efficient at EBP, quality improvement (QI), and research utilization.

The purpose of QI is to furnish a methodical, data-driven project concerning attitudes to enrich procedures and/or outcomes (Conner, 2014). The idea of QI is directed toward the improvement of patient outcomes. QI does tend to be site specific, which is one of the key aspects where it differs from research. The goal of the results obtained from a QI project is not to have information that is generalizable to another site, nor is it to set up the results as best practices. However, when multiple sites discover the same outcomes from consistent QI projects, the data then move toward best practices.

▶ Providing a Line of Reasoning for EBP and Evidence-Based Research

Health care is a complex system addressing multiple health-related aspects in an attempt to accomplish the anticipated outcome for the client. Throughout the healthcare arena, nursing care is provided to individuals in need of assistance related to their health status. This attention requires nurses to identify a core foundation of information that reflects quality care. Thus, the need for EBP to be developed around a research-centered foundation was envisioned.

Malloch and Porter-O'Grady (2015) suggested that the management of EBP requires the use of unique clinical applications based on accessible, up-to-date research. In the quest for quality nursing care, the nurse must use both reliable clinical knowledge and high-quality clinical information. This process of establishing a core foundation of knowledge has been called many things over the years, such as best practices, evidence-based practice, and quality of care. No matter what the practice is called, the basis for the care to be provided must be grounded in evidence. According to Melnyk and Fineout-Overholt (2015), healthcare providers must be able to locate, analyze, evaluate, and use the significant evidence to ensure that patients are certain and convinced that their providers are basing care on evidence for optimal outcomes. This assurance that the care being provided is confirmed from a tested research/evidence foundation inspires patient confidence in the nurses' commitment to quality health care. Nurses should not rely on unsubstantiated treatment plans but rather must endeavor to critically analyze aspects of the care to be provided to be sure that quality, tested practices are utilized in the provision of nursing care for each individual.

Three new developments in health care and nursing have had an impact on the understanding of the importance of EBP and research in nursing in the United States. First, in 2010, the Patient Protection and Affordable Care Act (PPACA), also known as the Affordable Care Act (ACA), was passed by Congress and signed by President Barack Obama (Mason, Leavitt, & Chaffee, 2012). Catalano (2015) suggests that the ACA will result in nursing responding to societal needs with increased attention while still maintaining the previous nursing focus. The ACA has a primary focus on affordable, accessible care with an emphasis on supporting research effecting safe, quality patient care. According to Young, Bakewell-Sachs, and Sarna (2017), the ACA "drove changes in care around readmissions and hospital-acquired conditions, and introduced payment models that fostered innovation in care models that emphasize population health- and community-based and primary care" (p. 263). Nurses are being asked to step into the lead roles for community health, along with preventive health management. While the implementation of the ACA is ever changing, the current direction for nursing seems to be toward preventive healthcare management. As a result, nurses are being called on to consider and implement best practices in outpatient settings with increasing regularity. Another area that has been affected by the ACA relates to funding issues. According to Logsdon and colleagues (2017), "the economic downturn, in conjunction with CMS (Center for Medicare and Medicaid Services) changes, has negatively impacted hospital budgets" (p. 273). Value-based purchasing is the current trend related to the funding of healthcare activities. Each and every intervention is carefully scrutinized for functionality and effectiveness. As institutions are working to implement value-based purchasing concerns, 30-day readmissions, and healthcare-associated infections, the changes influence the care provided by nurses. Along with value-based purchasing, the thrust has moved to value-based care affected by value-based nursing. The Health Resources and Services Administration (HRSA, 2014) confirms this perception by stating that within the new models of health care, innovative roles for nurses with new opportunities for advancement will be realized. As nurses provide patient-centered, nurses will increasingly find themselves actively engaged in EBP and research projects. According to Welton and Harper (2016), "the cost of nursing care is difficult or impossible to measure on a per patient basis" (p. 7) in terms of dollar values. With the focus on the electronic medical record (EMR), the expectation for innovative methods for assessing the actual impact of individual nurses on best practices and quality care is being strongly investigated. Nurses must embrace the idea of best practices and quality care that is founded on EBP to reflect the value and functionality of nursing within the healthcare arena.

The second development in 2010 came from the Carnegie Foundation recommendation in a report by Benner, Sutphen, Leonard, and Day (2010) calling for radical transformations of nursing education. Two of their recommendations support the need for nurses to have an education grounded in inquiry and research to provide evidence-based care. For the educational community, attention must be given to ensuring that nurses coming out of nursing programs understand and incorporate EBP into the essence of the practice of providing holistic nursing care.

The third development came from the Institute of Medicine (IOM; 2011) and the Robert Wood Johnson Foundation (RWJF) report regarding the future of nursing. This report urged support for interdisciplinary nursing projects so research can involve the development of models of care and solutions to improve health and health care. Stavor, Zedreck-Gonzalez, and Hoffmann (2017) stressed that the IOM established the expectation that 90% of all clinical decisions would be based on accurate, suitable, and state-of-the-art evidence by the year 2020. They identified eight research priorities for nursing practice and nursing education. The priorities for research included areas such as delivery models, reimbursement, care trends, nurse residencies, and funding for nurses' training. Herlehy (2011) authenticates the ideas set forth by the report to "underscore nurses' unique contributions and capacity to enhance the quality of care through practice, education, and leadership" (p. 519). Nursing brings to the table aptitudes and competences that reinforce and advocate for safe and quality health care for all generations and cultures. The incorporation of EBP, research, and QI provides the fortification and reinforcement of the evidence needed to provide effective and efficient health care in multiple settings. Welton and Harper (2016) champion the idea that the costing of nursing is difficult on a per-patient basis due to the challenge of measuring quality. This process of identifying means to showcase the quality efforts of nursing on a per-patient basis is imperative to advancing the profession of nursing within the current healthcare arena.

These three new developments (ACA, the Carnegie Foundation recommendation, and the IOM report) require nurses to examine their knowledge; skills; and, most important, their values about EBP and research. Each of these three developments has provided further clarification of the expectations for safe, effective care to every individual encountering healthcare issues. Looking at how to best address the burdensome aspects of health care through effective utilization of key providers allows for the successful management of health challenges.

🔾 THINK OUTSIDE THE BOX

Consider the following four routine activities done by nurses during a typical clinical day: bowel sounds, turning every 2 hours, nothing by mouth for 8 hours prior to surgery, and normal oral temperature levels. Carefully consider what evidence was used in your institution as the foundation for these tasks. Are the skills for the tasks in your practice setting based on research, personal preferences, clinical guidelines, or traditions?

The practicing nurse has to value the ideas of the EBP process, research, and QI to facilitate its complete incorporation and implementation. Nurses must understand the value of integrating carefully analyzed results from research, QI, and other sources with personal experiences and client values when determining the treatment plan that best addresses a situation's identified challenges. Even when healthcare providers utilize the most advantageous evidence accessible, each engagement with an individual continues to be distinctive. The treatments and outcomes will change based on the uniqueness of the client's values, preferences, interests, and/or diagnoses. According to Fonteyn (2005), nurses who are involved with EBP tend to demonstrate increased critical thinking skills along with implementation of research outcomes. Saunders and Vehviläinen-Julkunen (2016) ascertained that "nurses worldwide state they are familiar with, have positive attitudes toward, and believe in the value of EBP in improving care quality and patient outcomes, nurses perceive their own EBP knowledge and skills insufficient for employing EBP, and do not use best evidence in practice" (p. 129). Nurses are taught, encouraged, and expected to think critically. This process of critical thinking corresponds to the use of EBP on clinical units and in primary care settings. Critical thinking embraces the need for health care to be based on a foundation of proven research and other tested data while including the client's perspective. The use of unconfirmed reports, hearsay, and unfounded information, combined with a lack of client input, does not fit with the provision of sound, quality nursing care at this point in time. The evolution of EBP has moved the focus of client-centered care to the forefront of nursing care.

Fineout-Overholt and Melnyk (2005) state that continuous opportunities for learning EBP must be given to providers to enhance and sharpen EBP skills for posing searchable, answerable questions, locating the optimal evidence that can be accessed, while competently and proficiently evaluating research and evidence reports for establishing significant evidence vital for encouraging an evidence-based environment in which to practice. A key element within the effective provision of EBP is the nurse's expertise. Each nurse brings serviceable knowledge to the practice arena. During the process of providing nursing care to a group of individuals, nurses build an underpinning of knowledge on which they draw when delivering future care. This underpinning knowledge base intensifies and expands with each client encounter that the nurse has. Thus, the knowledge base is not stagnant but rather increases throughout an individual's nursing career. A competent nurse uses each healthcare encounter to augment and strengthen his or her knowledge base.

Mick (2017) maintained that, on a consistent basis, nurses are obligated to iden-tify questions and challenges related to patient needs and quality practice issues so that appropriate interventions can be recognized and addressed. Even if nurses are not actively involved in an actual research project, they must understand the method for accessing published information and assessing it for applicability. Bator, Taylor, and Catalano (2015) propose that nursing research is essential. Nurses educated at all levels must use research and EBP to improve the care of patients. According to Mick (2017), healthcare instructions, ritual and tradition, and personal choice must be used by the nurse to determine the optimal best practices to use with various patient and management encounters during the performance of nursing care. We all know that individuals rise to the level to which we expect them to rise: If we set low expectations, they will rise to meet the expected level of performance. If we establish challenging expectations, they will strive to attain them. Nurses seem to manage the nursing care provided without directly acknowledging the underlying foundation. This process or intuition grows as the nurse gains experience and expertise (Benner et al., 2010). Intuitive management of health care is an example of working at an expert level, but nurses do need to investigate regularly the foundations they are using to make the decisions regarding quality health care.

Research is a methodical examination that uses regimented techniques to resolve questions or decipher dilemmas. The conclusions resulting from this focused chain of examination provide a base on which to build a practice of care that is centered on tested solutions. Research is a scientific process using fundamen-tal expertise to clarify and visualize key aspects as it enhances a discipline's ability to anticipate outcomes. This anticipation and guidance are related to a discipline's ability to incorporate into practice the sound evidence derived from valid research endeavors. Although EBP goes beyond research results, the foundation for the practice is the grounded knowledge that comes from the research process and QI. This underpinning allows for the safe and effective provision of quality health care. According to Melnyk and Fineout-Overholt (2015), the publishing of research and other evidence along with the translation into practice to advance patient care takes too long and is a source of anxiety in healthcare organizations and federal agencies. Moving the use of researched evidence into the actual patient care setting requires that nurses become increasingly familiar and comfortable with the process of critiquing and applying the evidence to the practice arena.

Each of these aspects—thought process (decision-making process), client preferences (holistic patient care), research (nursing confirmation), and nursing expertise—is included in the EBP definition used in this text (**FIGURE 1-1**). Although all of these aspects are required, the actual situation directs the weighting of the

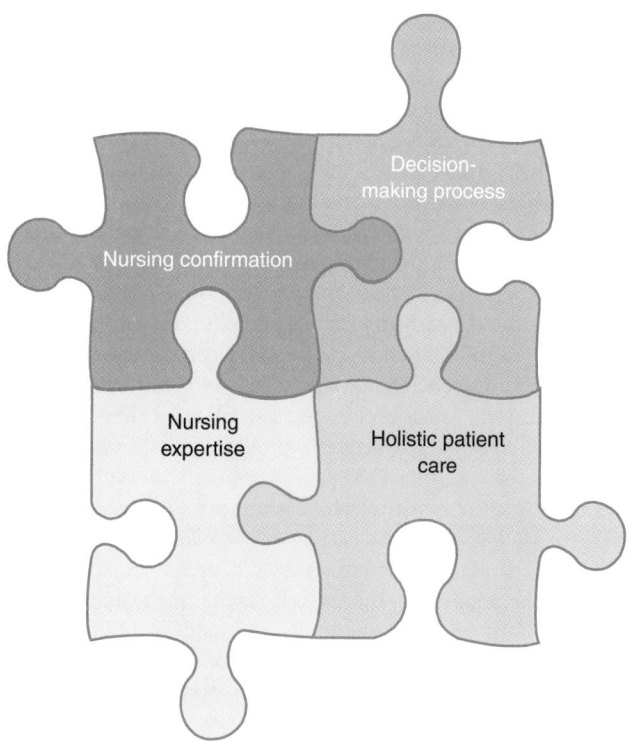

FIGURE 1-1 Evidence-based practice representation.

aspects because each situation is unique. A reliable consideration of the distinctive characteristics—evidence, patient values, and clinician's expertise—included in EBP requires a decision-making process to address each situation. In this text, EBP is defined as a process of using confirmed evidence (research and quality improvement), decision making, and nursing expertise to guide the delivery of holistic patient care by nurses. Holistic nursing care encompasses the clinical expertise of the nurse, patient preferences, cultural aspects, psychosocial facets, ethical considerations, and biological components. The research process and scientific data generated serve as the foundation on which the decision-making process for nursing care is based.

▶ Assessing the Need for Research in the Practice Arena

Benefiting from research evidence in conjunction with other types of evidence in the practice arena is a multifaceted process that entails altering provider performance. This process is challenging even when the comparative rewards are compelling and robust. The nurse is essential to the success of the EBP process. Each nurse, whether in the acute care, home health, community health, or other healthcare setting, regularly identifies nursing aspects of care. Those aspects of care may seem to (1) address the care needs of the client appropriately, (2) not fit the current accepted provision of care, or (3) be better addressed via some other method of care. According to Laskowski-Jones (2015), "if nurses don't read and evaluate whether or not research findings have relevance to this work, they run the risk of practicing in a way that's either ineffective or possibly even deleterious to patient care" (p. 6). Most nurses have at some point in their practice identified a situation that needs to be reevaluated. Within the day-to-day provision of nursing care, the question arises about why nurses perform a procedure a certain way when something else seems to work better. It could also be a question of how the care can be better provided to meet the client's needs and expectations. The healthcare community is also encouraging this line of questioning in an effort to identify the best methods for the provision of care. The expectation behind EBP is that everyone will become involved in the identification, examination, and implementation of research-founded, evidence-tested health care that can result in the provision of effective, validated client care. Nurses must accept the responsibility of being active in providing quality care to their clients. To do so effectively, they must base the provision of care on results that support the care being administered in a wide variety of healthcare settings.

According to Mick (2017), "evidence has shown that up to 2 decades (20 years) may pass before the findings of original research become part of routine clinical practice" (p. 33). The application of research results in the everyday provision of nursing care takes both time and energy by each and every nurse to ensure that the quality of care is appropriate. All nurses have the responsibility of ensuring that the care they provide to their clients is based on sound nursing knowledge, not just "the way we have always done it."

Ryan and colleagues (2017) ventured that excellence in nursing care is based on nurses' attitudes; values; behavior; and associations with patients, peers, and administrators resulting in improved health outcomes. Practicing nurses must become actively engaged at multiple levels of the different phases of the research endeavor. At each phase, the nurse's clinical expertise should be readily valued as the process moves forward to establish the evidence for use in the clinical setting.

Outcomes research is a growing expectation within health care. The specification of quality health procedures involves individuals striving to distinguish and acknowledge the outcomes from identifiable and distinctive healthcare patterns and interventions (Agency for Healthcare Research and Quality, 2000). Outcomes research is viewed as a mechanism for determining which quality care is possible and how to get to that point of significance and usefulness for the patient. The linkage of outcomes experienced with the care expected empowers research to cultivate improved channels for monitoring and improving the quality of care provided within the healthcare arena. Translational research is an endeavor that seeks to move the evidence that has been collected by effective research projects into the actual provision of health care. Nurses at the bedside must become champions for the inclusion of timely, documented, substantiated results into the active provision of health care to benefit clients confronted with the relevant health issues.

Titler, Everett, and Adams (2007) discuss the notion of implementation science as "the investigation of methods, interventions, and variables that influence adoption of evidence-based healthcare practices by individuals and organizations to improve clinical and operational decision making and including testing the effectiveness of interventions to promote and sustain use of evidence-based healthcare practices" (p. S53). Through the use of concepts such as implementation science,

research (conducting of research), **research utilization** (application of research), QI, and EBP are coming together for the improvement of healthcare delivery. As nurses develop confidence in investigating the diverse routines, interventions, and obstacles within the provision of quality care, advanced and tested systems of health-care delivery will become progressively more obtainable and acknowledged. The idea behind clarifying the process of research is to enable practicing nurses to utilize the scientific thought process to validate and augment the nursing care provided to clients. The entire process of critiquing research articles and conducting research projects is designed to strengthen the nursing professional's critical thinking abilities, thereby allowing for the delivery of the most holistic care possible in the work environment. An essential skill required for authentic EBP is the capability of professionals to ana-lyze methodically each type of result and evidence to justify the best data to utilize in the provision of holistic health care on a daily basis. Without this foundation, which enables them to examine the evidence methodically, nurses are left to vacillate among varying interpretations of healthcare information. As mentioned earlier, the ACA and the IOM/RWJF and Carnegie Foundation reports of 2010 leave no room for nurses to ignore the need for research in the practice arena. Having defined research and established the need for research, an examination of EBP is in order.

⏏ THINK OUTSIDE THE BOX

Look at the different definitions for evidence-based practice. How do you see patient preferences being utilized with research? How can nurses' expertise be integrated productively into sensible nursing care management?

Exploring EBP in Light of Research
Definitions of EBP

Many different definitions of EBP exist. Each definition tends to add another dimen-sion to the concept of EBP. Each different dimension should be considered carefully and thoroughly as EBP is implemented to ensure that actual nursing practice is com-prehensive. Within each definition, however, certain aspects are consistently iden-tified. The consistent and unique aspects can be visualized as shown in **TABLE 1-1**.

Melnyk and Fineout-Overholt (2015) conceptualize EBP as a method that allows healthcare providers to deliver the maximum quality of care when addressing the multifaceted requests of their patients and families. EBP is defined as "a problem solving approach to clinical decision making that incorporates a search for the best and latest evidence, clinical expertise and assessment, and patient preference and values within a context of caring" (Melnyk, 2004, p. 149). Both of these definitions reflect the use of problem solving with clinical involvement and patient contribution.

Rutledge and Grant (2002) define EBP as "care that integrates best scientific evidence with clinical expertise, knowledge of pathophysiology, knowledge of psy-chosocial issues, and decision making preferences of patients" (p. 1). This definition incorporates the ideas of pathophysiology and psychosocial components into the mix.

According to Porter-O'Grady (2006), "Evidence-based practice is simply the integration of the best possible research evidence with clinical expertise and with patient needs. Patient needs in this case refer specifically to the expectations, concerns, and requirements that patients bring to their clinical experience" (p. 1). This definition tends to further emphasize the importance of the patient within the entire process.

Gray, Grove, and Sutherland (2017) define EBP as "conscientious integration of best research evidence with clinical expertise and patient values and needs in the delivery of quality, cost-effective health care" (p. 18). Consequently, these authors integrate the idea of cost-effectiveness as an additional consideration when determining the appropriate EBP components.

Magee (2005) defines evidence-based medicine as "the conscientious, explicit, and judicious use of current best evidence in making decisions about the care of individual patients" (p. 73). The entire focus of this definition is evidence-based medicine. It is directed toward physician care, not nursing care.

While definitions from other disciplines can be helpful, nursing needs to take the components presented and apply the concepts to the practice of nursing care. As can be seen, each of these definitions includes a decision-making process with the

TABLE 1-1 Comparison of Qualities Included in Evidence-Based Practice Definitions

Author (Year)	Quality of Care	Multi-Faceted	Decision-Making Process
Newhouse, Dearholt, Poe, Pugh, and White (2007)			X
Melnyk and Fineout-Overholt (2015)	X	X	
Melnyk (2004)			X
Rutledge and Grant (2002)			X
Porter-O'Grady (2006)			
Gray, Grove, and Sutherland (2017)	X		
Magee (2005)			X
Pravikoff, Tanner, and Pierce (2005)			X
Omery and Williams (1999)			X
DiCenso, Cullum, and Ciliska (1998)			X

use of evidence balanced by patient and provider interactions. Another definition that includes this balance submitted by Pravikoff and colleagues (2005) for EBP is "a systematic approach to problem solving for healthcare providers, including registered nurses (RNs) characterized by the use of the best evidence currently available for clinical decision making in order to provide the most consistent and best possible care to patients" (p. 40). For their part, Omery and Williams (1999) define EBP as "a scientific process [that], with its inherent ability to explain and predict, enhances a practice discipline's ability to anticipate and guide interventions" (p. 50). Both of these definitions consolidate the idea of systematic processing with that of anticipatory consideration when providing nursing care.

As early as 1998, DiCenso, Cullum, and Ciliska (1998) offered a model for evidence-based decision making that integrates research evidence, clinical proficiency, patient choices, and accessible assets. Within this model, each element is weighted differently based on the particular client circumstances. The evidence desired for an EBP process can be accessed via sources as diverse as

Clinical Focus	Foundation of Practice	Client Involvement	Other Aspects
X		X	
X	Evidence, expertise, assessment	X	
X	Evidence, expertise, pathophysiology, psychosocial		
X	Evidence, expertise	X	
	Research	X	Cost
	Evidence	X	
X	Evidence	X	
	Expertise		
X	Evidence, proficiency	X	Assets

bibliographical databases or a QI department located within a healthcare agency. The evidence used within this process can include research, integrative reviews, practice guidelines, quality improvement data, "big data sets," clinical experience, expert opinion, collegial relationships, pathophysiology, common sense, community standards, published materials, and case studies. According to Ferguson and Day (2005), the forms of evidence, in descending order of credibility, include the following:

- Randomized, controlled trials
- Single randomized, controlled trials
- Controlled trials without randomization
- Quasi-experimental studies
- Nonexperimental studies
- Descriptive studies
- Expert consensus
- Quality improvement data
- Program evaluation data

Multiple formats of evidence are necessary and purposeful; the credibility of the evidence must be measured conscientiously when determining a plan of action. Each evidence design supplies information to incorporate into the decision-making process. The support for the information (evidence) is better in those designs that are based on research rather than those based on opinion.

Each of the proposed definitions supports the definition identified for this text, in which EBP is viewed as a process of using confirmed evidence (research and quality improvement), decision making, and nursing expertise to guide the delivery of holistic patient care. The four consistent aspects found within all of these definitions are (1) a decision-making process; (2) confirmed evidence from research, QI, or other sources; (3) nursing expertise; and (4) client involvement (holistic patient care) (see Figure 1-1). The evidence that can have an impact on the care provided to clients can come from either a personal direction or visual focus. According to Mick (2017), personal evidence takes on the aspects that the individual nurse brings to the process from unique experiences based on the interpersonal relationships occurring within the nursing process. The second focus of evidence can be seen as an aesthetic process that allows the nurse to incorporate intuition, interpretation, and values into the delivery of both the art and practice of nursing (Mick, 2017). Each of these facets of evidence plays a strong part in allowing the nurse and patient to develop an individualized process for managing the healthcare challenges. Thus, provision of care does not become a cookie-cutter type of health care but rather allows for the unique needs of the parties involved in the health environment

As EBP has evolved within the field of health care, the idea of what constitutes appropriate evidence has also matured (**FIGURE 1-2**).

While research results constitute the strongest category of evidence, other evidence—such as quality improvement results, policy/procedure confirmation, and protocol guideline confirmation—is nevertheless beneficial to the provision of safe and effective health care. Within the realm of EBP, each component of the evidence must be assessed carefully in terms of the strength and applicability of the information to the unique client setting. Each agency and nurse must consider critically the results and evidence available concerning an identified healthcare problem.

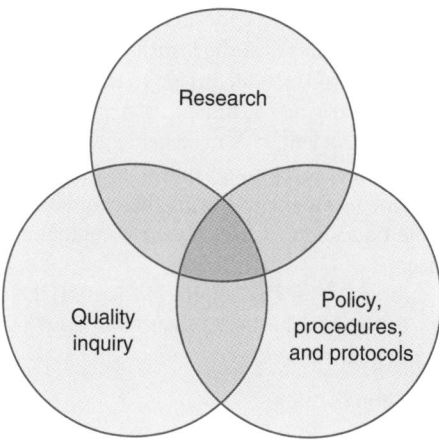

FIGURE 1-2 EBP evidence confirmation.

As the results and evidence are thoroughly examined for practicality and efficiency, nursing care practices can be modified to manage the various aspects of care.

Posing Forceful Clinical Questions

Melnyk and Fineout-Overholt (2015) declared that a key aspect within the process is asking the "right" question. The clarification of the question focuses the search for valid evidence so that it speaks to the issue under examination. Developing a searchable question involves focusing on the key aspects to avert a complicated and time-consuming search that uncovers primarily unrelated resources. As the issue under examination is carefully considered to determine the principal focus for the investigation, two components need to be considered. First, the initial attention should be directed to answering the "who," "what," "why," "when," "where," "how," and "how much" questions for the issue. Second, the scrutiny should then turn to the outcome of interest, which reflects the nursing diagnosis and/or research project.

Melnyk and Fineout-Overholt (2015) describe the two types of initial questions as background questions and foreground questions. Background questions address the core knowledge within the healthcare field. Conner (2014) calls this type of question a "knowledge-focused trigger" (p. 3). Knowledge comes from literature, new philosophies, or new regulations. This type of information provides a strong foundation of knowledge related to biological, psychological, and sociological facets of care that can be located in any textbook. Background questions are viewed as broad searches that can frequently be answered by information obtained from textbooks (Echevarria & Walker, 2014). These questions generally begin with the word *what* or *when*. These types of questions serve as the underpinnings for other questions. Obtaining answers to these questions does not require access to research databases because the information is preparatory to the provision of basic holistic care. In contrast, foreground questions address the scientific evidence about diagnosing, treating, or assisting patients as they work to comprehend their healthcare challenges (Melnyk & Fineout-Overholt, 2015). This type of question can be classified as a "problem-focused trigger" (Conner, 2014, p. 3). The problems can come from an identified clinical problem, risk management, finances, or QI. Echevarria and Walker (2014) clarify that foreground questions are used to answer a precise and distinctive clinical issue. At this point in the process of EBP, the search for answers to the identified question focuses on the combination of core knowledge and scientific evidence.

The use of the acronym **PICOT** is helpful in focusing the development of the foreground questions (**BOX 1-1**). The PICOT acronym has the following meaning (Melnyk & Fineout-Overholt, 2015):

P   Patient population of interest

I   Intervention of interest

C   Comparison of interest

O   Outcome of interest

T   Time

🔁 THINK OUTSIDE THE BOX

Within every organization, obstacles affecting the incorporation of changes such as EBP exist. Examine your institution. Which obstacles do you see? What can you do to challenge and conquer these obstacles?

BOX 1-1 Examples of Searchable Questions for Research in EBP

Example 1: Labor and Delivery

You are a staff nurse in a rural hospital that performs 120 to 150 vaginal deliveries each year. Within the past 6 months, the institution has hired a certified registered nurse anesthetist (CRNA) to help with anesthesia for the facility. The CRNA and physicians have decided to begin offering epidural anesthesia for routine vaginal deliveries. You offer to seek out studies that address the use of epidural anesthesia in the labor and delivery process.

Preliminary Question: Is epidural anesthesia appropriate for all laboring patients?

Clarification of Question: This question identifies the population and time as all laboring patients and the intervention as the use of epidural anesthesia. It fails to document any comparison with other anesthesia methods or the outcome that the hospital is interested in achieving. Here is the PICOT analysis:

Population: All laboring patients
Intervention: Use of epidural anesthesia
Comparison: Use of narcotic pain management
Outcome: Reduction in labor complications
Time: Individuals in labor

Revised Searchable Question: For all laboring patients, will the administration of epidural anesthesia be more effective in reducing labor complications than other forms of anesthesia administered during the labor process?

Example 2: Readmission Rates

Due to value-based funding, acute care facilities are carefully considering ways to decrease the number of 30-day readmissions resulting from a wide variety of illnesses. One of those illnesses is congestive heart failure (CHF).

Preliminary Question: What follow-up activities can be used to affect 30-day readmission rates for patients being dismissed from the hospital with a diagnosis of CHF?

Clarification of Question: The limitations of this question include the failure to stipulate clearly the population and to supply adequate particulars about the situation. Here is the PICOT analysis:

Population: Patients being discharged from a hospital following treatment for CHF symptoms

Intervention: Phone calls by registered nurses within 48 hours of discharge to check on transition to home care

Comparison: Mailing a reminder to complete all follow-up care

Outcome: Effective management of CHF symptoms from home along with decreased number of readmissions for CHF symptoms.

Time: Within 30 days from discharge

Revised Searchable Question: During the 30 days following discharge from the acute care setting, will patients who had a diagnosis of CHF have effective management of their CHF symptoms at home and decreased need for readmission for the same symptoms following the use of a phone call to discuss home care by registered nurses within 36 hours of discharge compared to receiving a mailed reminder of complete follow-up care expectations?

Example 3: Pediatrics

You work for the pediatric unit at the local hospital. The same children are readmitted for earaches, injuries, and respiratory diseases. You have been assigned to prepare and deliver parenting classes for young parents who have had their children admitted to the hospital. As you are thinking about the classes to be prepared, you question whether the adolescent parents are at greater risk and if they need different information than the general community of parents. You want to provide the most recent and best practices for child rearing. An additional concern that you have is the manner in which to provide the classes to meet the needs of the parents.

Preliminary Question: Which type of information must be included, and how should the parenting class be provided for parents?

Clarification of Question: Although the population has been somewhat specified, additional clarification is needed. Another limitation within the preliminary question is the lack of clarification about the interventions, comparisons, outcomes, and time component of the PICOT. Here is the PICOT analysis:

Population: Parents who have had children admitted to the hospital for recurring health problems

Intervention: Online parenting classes addressing symptoms that need to be reported to the healthcare provider

Comparison: Face-to-face parenting classes

Outcome: Reduction in the number of admissions for recurring health problems

Time: Not needed for this question

(continues)

Revised Searchable Question: Do online parenting classes compared to face-to-face classes improve the knowledge level for parents who have had children admitted to the hospital for recurring health problems and reduce the number of readmissions for the same disease process?

Example 4: Cancer-Related Illness

A 75-year-old woman who had been admitted to the hospital for cervical cancer treatment asks to talk with you about general cancer-related issues. She has three children between the ages of 40 and 55 years. She is worried about their potential for developing cancer and wants to know what she should tell them about getting routine checkups. She does tell you that her father died of colon cancer at the age of 71 years.

Preliminary Question: Which type of routine screening examinations should be performed for middle-aged adults who have a family history of cancer?

Clarification of Question: Within this question, the population is briefly delineated. The question does not clearly denote the intervention, the outcome, or the time aspects of a PICOT question. Here is the PICOT analysis:

Population: Individuals with a family history of cancer
Intervention: Scheduling of aggressive cancer screening examinations
Comparison: Scheduling of routine cancer screening examinations
Outcome: Early diagnosis of cancer
Time: Not needed for this question

Revised Searchable Question: For individuals with a family history of cancer, what effect does aggressive versus routine cancer screening examinations have on the early diagnosis of cancer?

Example 5: Staffing

As a new nurse manager on a medical–surgical unit in a large acute care setting, the unit has had a turnover rate of 25% during the last 6 months. The patient satisfaction scores do not reflect good nursing care being provided. The unit is staffed with four BSN-prepared nurses, four AD-prepared nurses, three LVNs, and eight CNAs.

Preliminary Question: What type of nursing shift timing should be used to improve the staff retention on this unit?

Clarification of Question: The question does not adequately define the population or the intervention for addressing the concerns. It is voiced more as a global type of question. The PICOT analysis could be:

Population: Full-time nursing staff employees
Intervention: Use of 12-hour shifts with primary care model
Comparison: Use of 8-hour shift with team nursing care model
Outcome: Improved staff retention rate and improved patient satisfaction findings
Time: Not needed for this question

Revised Searchable Question: For full-time nursing staff employees, will the use of 12-hour shifts with a primary care nursing model improve the staff retention rate and patient satisfaction findings when compared to 8-hour shifts using a team nursing approach?

Note: AD = associate degree; BSN = bachelor of science in nursing; CNA = certified nursing assistant; LVN = licensed vocational nurse.

In considering the population (first component) within the question, thought is needed to determine specific information about the characteristics of the group under investigation. This description could relate to age, gender, diagnosis, medical unit, and/or ethnicity. The process needs to be specific enough to provide direction while not restricting the search too much. According to Dawes and colleagues (2005), "there is a balance to be struck between getting evidence about exactly your group of patients and getting all the evidence about all groups of patients" (p. 13). Care must be given to providing enough specificity to ensure that the search addresses the appropriate population while not excluding relevant information. As the PICOT is developed, care must be given to the purpose for the PICOT. The PICOT (thus each component) is used to help clarify the evidence that is being sought to address the triggers/problems identified.

The assertion of the intervention (second feature) for the question is a crucial aspect that requires thorough reflection and attention. This facet stipulates the topic under consideration. It does not have to be an action step (and therefore an activity) but rather is the key topic for clarification. This facet of the query should seek to include the contact, treatment, patient insight, diagnostic test, and/or predictive aspect that is thought to produce the best outcome (Melnyk & Fineout-Overholt, 2015). Clarification of this portion within the questioning process diminishes the potential for having to backtrack later when the results are not as clearly delineated as anticipated.

The third part of the question formation—the comparison of interest—is an optional facet within the questioning process. The comparison is an alternative action that can be used for the identified populations to gain the outcome that is being sought. A comparison intervention is a secondary treatment, insight, test, or predictive aspect that can be used as an alternative process to reach the outcome being pursued for this population. A PICOT question does not need to state that a comparison is the lack of the identified intervention. The lack of the identified intervention is not a comparison intervention and may be unethical at times. The only time that a comparison of interest is used in the PICOT format is when a different intervention is available that could result in the same outcomes. Within this component, the comparison of different treatment options would be analyzed to reach the desired outcome as identified in the PICOT. In many situations, alternative treatment decisions may not be available. The lack of supplementary preferences does not restrict the development of EBP guidelines.

The fourth feature for consideration in PICOT questions is the outcome of interest. According to Schmidt and Brown (2019), it is extremely essential to deliberate this piece sensibly to ascertain correctly the outcome that is anticipated. Care must be given to the outcomes that are anticipated by using the identified intervention compared to the alternate "comparison" intervention. According to Ryan and colleagues (2017), outcomes tend to address the themes of processes, environment, and/or behaviors. The outcome should be those one or two results that are expected as a consequence of using the intervention treatment. Why is the intervention treatment better for obtaining the results than the other alternative treatments for the population?

The final part to consider is time. Timing for the outcome of interest is a principal characteristic to scrutinize. While time is not included in all PICOT questions, it is valuable for inclusion on the questions that can be affected directly by the passage of time.

Having presented these considerations for preparing the question(s) for concentrating the evidence-based search, it must be acknowledged that too specific a question can also be a major problem. No single approach exists to ask a searchable question; thus, care must be given to clarifying the questions prior to moving forward to the investigation of the evidence. The PICOT format cultivates clarification of the heart of the area for investigation. The predominant rationale must be the narrowing of the investigation to allow for the effective determination of evidence to strengthen the delivery of holistic nursing care for the client population.

It is interesting that as EBP evolves, PICOT has also evolved. Initially, PICOT was restricted to the four facets of population, intervention, comparison, and outcome (PICO). As one searches for information about how to develop an EBP question, PICOT can be viewed as PICOTS, which adds *setting* to the questions, or as PICOT-SD, which incorporates the *study design* into the statement of the problem (Delfini Group, 2012). These modifications to the question format come from the field of medicine to provide directions for ensuring that the best question can be developed for driving the different types of inquiries. The majority of EBP questions tend to take the format of PICO because time and other aspects are not used consistently within the formation. The other aspects can be used to clarify and amplify the question when needed to allow for an improved acquisition of evidential documents to consider.

As our thoughts move to the **research process**, the use of different types of questions for various research types must be clarified. Questions focusing on "how many" or "how much" are frequently answered through the use of quantitative studies. According to DiCenso and colleagues (2005), a quantitative question involves three components—population, intervention/exposure, and outcomes. Questions that are directed toward discovering how people feel or experience a specific state of affairs or environments are answered through the use of qualitative research designs. Qualitative questions are worded to include only two parts—population and situation (DiCenso et al., 2005). These questions focus on characteristics that provide a foundation for composing EBP questions and analyzing research results to confirm EBP practices. By using the PICOT format to determine the current level of evidence related to a topic, the transition to a research project becomes increasingly focused. The evidence found aids in the determination of the contemplation and essence of the research or quality improvement process. The body of knowledge will be advanced as the next steps in knowledge confirmation are taken by the research or quality improvement project being based on the evidence available to this point in time.

Research Utilization

In the past, lip service has been given to the need for nurses to apply research to practice. More recently, with the emergence and acceptance of EBP, the literature regarding research utilization in the clinical arena has proliferated. The need for improved patient outcomes, decreased healthcare costs, greater patient safety, and higher patient satisfaction are driving forces for the use of scientific data in the decision-making process of nursing care provision (**BOX 1-2**).

As a result of the promotion of the use of research as a basic component in nursing practice, one might ask, "Is nursing research being applied to nursing practice?" Surprisingly, the answer is both yes and no. Logic seems to dictate that if EBP can improve patient care, EBP should be implemented. Most healthcare organizations are attempting to incorporate EBP in their institutions. Unfortunately, obstacles to the use of EBP often focus primarily on research utilization and understanding EBP.

BOX 1-2 Suggested Resources to Support the Retrieval and Appraisal of Evidence

Agency for Healthcare Research and Quality (www.ahrq.gov)
Cochrane Database of Systematic Reviews (www.cochranelibrary.com/cochrane
-database-of-systematic-reviews/index.html)
Institute of Medicine of the National Academies (holds the documents produced by the
IOM related to patient safety; http://www.nationalacademies.org/hmd/)
Joanna Briggs Institute (www.joannabriggs.org)
The Joint Commission (http://jointcommission.org)
Medscape (integrated information and educational tools; www.medscape.com
/nurseshome)
Morrisey, L. J., & DeBourgh, G. A. (2001). Finding evidence: Refining literature searching
skills for the advance practice nurse. *AACN Clinical Issues, 12*(4), 560–577.
National Comprehensive Cancer Network (www.nccn.org)
National Guidelines Clearinghouse (www.guideline.gov)
National Library of Medicine (allows free searches of MEDLINE through PubMed; www
.ncbi.nlm.nih.gov/pubmed)
Oncology Nursing Society (ONS)—"Putting Evidence into Practice (PEP)" section (www
.ons.org/practice-resources/pep)
Registered Nurses' Association of Ontario (RNAO), Nursing Best Practice Guidelines
(http://rnao.ca/bpg)
Sarah Cole Hirsh Institute for Best Nursing Practices Based on Evidence (https://nursing
.case.edu/hirsh/)
School of Health and Related Research (ScHARR), University of Sheffield—Information
Resources (www.shef.ac.uk/scharr/sections/ir)
Sigma Theta Tau Virginia Henderson Library (www.nursinglibrary.org/vhl/)
University of Alberta—Evidence-Based Medicine Tool Kit (www.ebm.med.ualberta.ca
/ebm.html)
University of North Carolina at Chapel Hill Health Sciences Library, Nursing (http://
guides.lib.unc.edu/nursing)

Note: Access verified December 8, 2017.

▶ The Importance of Generating Evidence

Discovering Significant Evidence

As stated earlier, to practice nursing based on "how we are taught" assumes that no further need to produce evidence is acknowledged. That dangerous assumption was investigated as early as 1975, when Ketefian's (1975) study revealed that nurses did not use research for making decisions about nursing care (Polit & Beck, 2008). Carter and associates (2017) confirm that "the timely and effective translation of research findings into practice and the organization of nurses' contributions to this process remain a challenge" (p. 266). Moving research and nursing contribution to evidence into the practice arena requires time and energy from the members of the profession. Nurses must embrace the idea that practice in every setting requires evidence to be successful. Carter and associates (2017) demand that clinical scholarship assimilate the nurses' dynamic involvement to advance patient care, enhance the nursing profession, and generate new knowledge for health care. Embracing the idea of practice based on evidence is paramount for the advancement of the profession.

Lack of innovation and failure to develop a rationale for nursing care results in decreased respect for nursing as a profession. According to the American Nurses Association (ANA; 2016), 84% of Americans rated nurses as honest and ethical. Nurses have held the number one position of most trusted professions for 16 years in a row according to the Gallup poll (Brenan, 2017). Consequently, generating and using scientific evidence can only improve the image of nursing and provide better outcomes from nursing care.

Another force underlying the need for generating evidence, and its incorporation into practice, is the increasing cost of health care. Healthcare costs are spiraling upward at an uncontrollable rate that demands nurses perform their work in the most cost-effective way. As Bucknall (2012) notes, a thorough assessment of the relevancy of the facts along with the anticipated contributions to a particular conclusion is needed for materials to move from simply being facts to serving as evidence. Each and every fact must be carefully gauged to ensure that the cost of delivering the care remains within an acceptable level while still leading to high-quality, high-safety health care. In fact, the nursing profession cannot afford to ignore innovative approaches in nursing care that will reduce costs while simultaneously improving outcomes.

Impact on Practice

The potential impact of using research in evidence-based nursing practice is enormous. No longer can nurses rely on "how I was taught" or a "gut feeling." Research provides tangible scientific data to promote optimal patient outcomes. The nurse at the bedside must be an integral participant in the development of EBP. Nurses are the individuals who observe what works and what does not work in the real world of health care. The expertise that this hands-on practice brings to the research process is of paramount importance to the effective development of a body of nursing knowledge.

Patients interact with nurses and, as Gallup poll surveys (ANA, 2016) indicate, patients trust them with their care. As a result, nursing practice that incorporates research also increases patient satisfaction. In turn, assisting a patient to recover health brings satisfaction to the nurse and helps keep the cost of health care at an acceptable level.

Within the current healthcare environment, nurses are expected to embrace continuous performance improvement (CPI) processes such as Six Sigma and the plan–do–check–act (PDCA) cycle. These continuous improvement processes are being driven by the IOM's (2003) "Health Professions Education: A Bridge to Quality," which identified five core areas of concern: providing patient-centered care, working in interdisciplinary teams, employing evidence-based practice, applying quality improvement, and utilizing informatics. According to Finkelman and Kenner (2007), "The [IOM] report recommends (1) adopting transformational leadership and evidence-based management, (2) maximizing the capability of the workforce, and (3) creating and sustaining cultures of safety" (p. 8). As a result, nurses are confronted with the challenges of transforming care at the bedside (TCAB); situation, background, assessment, recommendation (SBAR) communication strategies; readmission criteria; EMRs; and the Triple Aim/Quadruple Aim in Healthcare. The

Triple Aim has a fundamental purpose of improving the health of the population through the process of refining patient experiences and reducing healthcare costs (Bodenheimer & Sinsky, 2014). CipherHealth (2017) articulated the fourth aim, which addresses the importance of staff satisfaction. According to CipherHealth (2017), "working towards quadruple aim goals can help hospitals see financial and organization improvement from enhanced staff engagement, cost efficiencies, and higher levels of patient satisfaction" (para. 9). Change is imperative for each of us working within the healthcare field. It is our responsibility to become knowledgeable about the evidence that is available as we select mechanisms to address core areas and national imperatives to change and transform care provided by nurses and healthcare providers.

Nurses must ask targeted, concise questions about the nursing care that is being provided. Rolston-Blenman (2009) suggests that success in embracing a culture of change and innovation entails recruiting nurses to advocate for the objectives, resulting in a culture that empowers them to conceive the tools they require for success on the frontline. Settling for the status quo is no longer acceptable. Instead, nurses must take the lead in querying the healthcare delivery venue in relation to the appropriateness and safety of the care being provided. Evidence-based nursing practice requires that each nurse develop an "inquiring mind" to ensure that the resulting patient outcomes are high quality, safe, cost effective, and appropriate in the current healthcare arena.

Nursing is truly both an art and a science. EBP not only provides elements of each aspect but also contributes to the profession's overall development. As a result, EBP improves everyday practice by providing empirical data to guide nursing interventions. Prompted by national developments, nurses need to collaborate with physicians and other healthcare providers to improve patient outcomes. Nurses should not work in silos but rather as crucial members of the healthcare team. Generating evidence for use by all professionals requires teamwork and collaboration because silos of research are no longer the standard approach. As a result, partnerships of individuals and agencies allow for more efficient use of resources and decreased costs.

▶ Obstacles to Using Research

Much of the literature discusses barriers to using research for the guidance of practice. Merriam-Webster (2017a) defines *barrier* as "an object that impedes the way." A barrier inhibits success. Perhaps another word better defines the challenge of utilization of research in nursing practice— **obstacle** An obstacle is "something that impedes progress or achievement" (Merriam-Webster Dictionary, 2017b, para. 1). An obstacle can be conquered. As a result, the term *obstacle* will be used instead of *barrier* when talking about motivations for not employing research utilization in evidence-based nursing care.

The nurse must strive to recognize approaches to overcome each impediment to the path to success; thus, it becomes a challenge to rise above the obstacle and be successful. The use of theories can be viewed as a barrier within the application of research, for example. The complexity of theories and functionality of using theories within the field of research can be perceived as a challenge by the nurse providing care at the bedside. An in-depth discussion of theories is beyond the scope of this text, although it is useful to generate a general dialogue about the use of theories within the research process. Nurses at the bedside do need to understand the connection between theory, research, and practice.

While it may seem easy to employ research in practice, it is essentially a complex problem. Three major categories of obstacles deter nurses from readily incorporating research into their practice—education, beliefs/attitudes, and support/resources. Mick (2017) confirms that strategic obstacles encountered by nurses when adopting the EBP and research processes as a component of their daily practice are the excessive burden of providing quality patient attention affected by restrictions resulting from existing time, resources, and organization. These aspects overwhelm nurses as they strive to incorporate scholarship into the work environment.

🔲 THINK OUTSIDE THE BOX

Discuss the integration of clinical proficiency in the implementation of evidence-based nursing care.

Education

Educational preparation ranks high on the list of obstacles to using research for the guidance of practice. Omery and Williams (1999) suggest that the more education a nurse has, the greater the chance the nurse will use research in providing patient care. The National Council of State Boards of Nursing (NCSBN; 2017) has found that in 2015, 65% of respondents to the NCSBN's survey signified that they had achieved a baccalaureate or higher degree. For the 2015 survey, 39% of the individuals stated that their initial nursing degree was the BSN compared to 36% during the 2013 survey (NCSBN, 2017). The NCSBN's executive summary states that the percentage of nurses from all educational levels working in acute care facilities is currently 54%, which reflects a decrease of nurses working in acute care settings by approximately 2% from prior surveys (NCSBN, 2017). Associate Degree in Nursing (ADN) and diploma programs usually do not focus on research. It is important that care be given to providing further education directed toward EBP and research. If nurses practice as they were taught, then nurses need additional knowledge about research. It is common to hear, "That's the way I was taught." Considering that the average age of nurses is 48.8 (NCSBN, 2017), the fallacy of that line of thinking becomes apparent; such a nurse may have been taught 20 to 25 years ago. Research may have seemed too "mystical" and to have no relevance to nurses educated during that time period.

Another aspect of educational preparation that influences a nurse's use of research is the way in which research is taught. Even though baccalaureate and graduate programs include research courses in their curricula, many graduates continue to resist engaging in or exploring research. Learning research can be likened to learning a foreign language. Researchers continue to organize their conclusions in scientific and technological verbiage that is intricate and arduous to comprehend. A frequent misperception is only an academician at a state-of-the-art university can conduct research. The thought that research is feasible and beneficial when linked to clinical practice appears to be inadequately explained to novice nurses. Thus, it is no wonder nurses do not understand research, much less want to use it in their practice. Without adequate motivation to use all aspects of an educational program, nurses are unwilling to translate research to practice.

Beliefs/Attitudes

A major portion of the literature attributes the lack of research use by nursing professionals to beliefs and attitudes regarding research. Several authors (Carroll et al., 1997; Cronenwett, 2002; Jolley, 2002; Omery & Williams, 1999; Pravikoff et al., 2005) suggest that negative attitudes concerning the use of research represent obstacles to incorporating EBP into nursing care. This negativity is true of both healthcare organizations and individual nurses. The administrators in each organization must acknowledge the value of research within their operations. If nurses feel supported and confident in their capability to employ research, they will willingly assimilate research findings into their practice.

Support/Resources

The third major category of obstacles to the incorporation of EBP is support and resource availability. With one of the focuses of the quadruple aims being cost, administrators list finances as a rationale for limiting or hindering the use of EBP and research. When a nursing shortage exists, staffing becomes a major issue. Allowing staff members adequate time to do the essential reading and analysis to update their clinical or EBP knowledge or to attend continuing nursing education offerings is not always possible in such circumstances.

Another problem relates to the lack of access and availability of research materials. Many organizations do not have a library, librarian, or personnel familiar with accessing current research findings. Agencies tend to provide access to web platforms to be used by the nurses when investigating different topics instead of using actual librarians. Nurses who lack computer skills may not know how to conduct online searches. Without the assistance of a library, librarian, or information technology personnel, nurses may not seek out EBP data. Both new and older generations of nurses have little, if any, expertise in using search engines for obtaining evidence to enhance their practice. Even when a nurse has the requisite knowledge and skills to be able to conduct EBP database searches, state and federal policies may prevent the searches from being conducted within the healthcare organization. For example, privacy issues relating to Health Insurance Portability and Accountability Act (HIPAA) guidelines inhibit access to the World Wide Web from agency computer systems.

One can easily understand why EBP has a steep learning curve as practitioners struggle to overcome these obstacles. Lack of nursing educational preparation, lack of value assigned to research by organizations and individual nurses, and lack of support/resources must be critically examined. Solutions to these problems must be found if nursing is to promote widespread use of EBP. According to Vratny and Shriver (2007), guidance, eagerness, mentorship, clinical investigation, and insightful practice are what really increase evidence-based practice and help it flourish. An aspect that intensifies thoughts about support relates to mentoring. Kelly, Turner, Speroni, McLaughlin, and Guzzetta (2013) found that empowering staff in the components of inquisitive thinking allows for the development of the skills needed. Terms such as "culture of inquiry," "culture for excellence in nursing research," and "discipline thinking" are now being used and are viewed as a way to clarify and define the idea of mentoring and supporting individuals in a quest for evidence. The formalizing of programs showcases the support and resources available for individuals willing to make the journey. Yoder and colleagues (2014) support the idea of incorporating champions for both research utilization and EBP at all levels within an organization to ensure that EBP is embraced. The use of champions allows for the effective implementation of the concepts of EBP within the daily workings of the unit/agency.

In the future, as agencies support nurses in recognizing the extent of improvement possible in clinical care and patient outcomes through the use of EBP, nurses will seize the opportunity to move nursing care forward and seek empowerment as part of their professional growth. Of course, expecting all organizations and every nurse to conduct research is unrealistic. Nevertheless, use of research in EBP provides the opportunity for research utilization by all.

▶ Responsibility for Using Research

Given the formidable obstacles to research, why do research at all? Few would argue with the premise that having evidence to improve patient outcomes is desirable. As Brockopp and Hastings-Tolsma (2003) say, "Professional nurses have the responsibility to participate in the promotion of evidence-based practice. Such expectations are both societal and professional" (p. 459). A better-informed consumer will inevitably demand higher-quality care. Thus, given their greater accessibility to healthcare information, today's healthcare consumers expect nurses to use current data to provide quality care. To do so, nurses must continuously explore new evidence and incorporate that evidence into nursing practice. Nurses must take an active role in developing a body of knowledge. Nursing has the responsibility to generate scientific data and to use that data to achieve optimal outcomes. EBP uses the best clinical data available in making decisions about nursing care. Thus, the profession demands that nurses not only be responsible for the use of research but also participate in research to add to the body of nursing knowledge through EBP.

According to Kitson (2007), health organizations globally are examining ways to better comprehend how to enhance the quality, effectiveness, and safety of the health care they deliver, which are the components of the Institute for Healthcare Improvement (IHI) Triple Aim. Two key movements in health care have led to this quest for excellence: quality/safety initiatives and the evidence-based practice innovation. By striving to acquire a foundation of knowledge while holding fast to honesty, integrity, and respect for the wide variety of perspectives and experiences within the healthcare delivery system, nursing can establish a firm base on which to build the practice of health care for each individual patient encountered.

Overcoming obstacles to the use of research in practice can improve patient outcomes, decrease costs, and increase the body of knowledge for the nursing profession as a whole. Nursing practice leads to research questions, and vice versa. Practice and research as evidence confirmation are inseparable pieces of the puzzle of EBP, as depicted in Figure 1-1. Posing questions about nursing care frequently generates scientific data, which in turn often generate further questions to be explored.

Summary Points

1.   Current national legislation and reports continue to have an impact on the importance of EBP and research utilization.
2.   A core body of nursing knowledge stems from the process in which research is incorporated into practice; this strategy has been called best practice, quality of care, and EBP.
3.   EBP is a process of utilizing confirmed evidence (research and quality improvement), decision making, and nursing expertise to guide the delivery of holistic patient care.
4.   The PICOT acronym offers a structure for rendering dynamic, clinical questions to construct scientific questions.
5.   Obstacles to research utilization are education, beliefs/attitudes, support/resources, lack of time, and lack of mentoring.
6.   Generating evidence augments the core of nursing knowledge, which advances nursing as a profession.
7.   The combination of nursing practice and research is central to advancing EBP.
8.   Safe, effective patient care is not an extravagance but rather an obligation.

⚑ RED FLAGS

- Within the documentation of a research project, specific decisions concerning the planning and implementation of the process must be defended by rationales. In EBP, randomized controlled trials are viewed as one of the most powerful types of evidence. As a result, some research characteristics are viewed as stronger designs (quantitative, experimental, and randomized sampling) than other facets of the process. In this text, the categorization of a red flag will reflect features of the research project that need to be examined carefully to determine the quality of the process employed. These areas are not strictly forbidden within research but rather are points that need to be taken into consideration. Within the documentation, these aspects should be corroborated by rationales reflecting the thought process utilized for those pieces.
- When an individual is appraising an article for inclusion in an EBP situation and/or policy and procedure rationale, the presence of red flags should be seen as a gateway to consider the justification for the decisions made by the research team. If the research team has provided sufficient justification for each of the research decisions, a study characterized by red flags can still be a strong study. The documentation of the research report by a researcher is a process of validation and justification of the various judgments made during the planning, implementation, and analysis processes. The researcher has the responsibility to document the validation for the decisions incorporated into the study such as ethics, sampling, design, and data collection.
- Red flags are areas within the documentation of the study that raise concerns. These areas are not items that should never be done but rather are items that should be supported by sound, clear rationales as to why the researcher used the research components.

Multiple-Choice Questions

1. Which of these examples characterizes a successful application of safe and competent nursing care delivery?
    A. The nurse investigates the latest online information in deciding how the care is to be provided.
    B. The nurse examines peer-reviewed nursing research articles to determine the best care to be provided.
    C. The nurse asks a clinical instructor from the university how the care for a client should be given.
    D. The nurse provides care following the instructions provided when attending school.

2. The ACA and the IOM/RWJF and Carnegie Foundation reports are national movements to:
    A. reaffirm current nursing practice.
    B. ignore current nursing practice.
    C. transform current nursing practice.
    D. eliminate current nursing practice.

3. A nurse is seeking a research article to use as the underpinning for an adjustment in the manner in which care is given. An example of a research article is a manuscript that provides a(n):
    A. overview of how to provide care.
    B. discussion of the method used for the research along with recommendations.
    C. discussion of a case study without any recommendations.
    D. overview of guidelines for a particular type of case.

4. Which of these forms of evidence carries the highest degree of credibility?
    A. Research study using a nonexperimental study
    B. Intuition
    C. Research study using a random control sample
    D. Research study providing a case study approach

5. A problem-focused trigger would generate which of the following PICOT statements?
    A. Registered nurses have less work stress than other healthcare providers.
    B. Adult cardiac patients involved in bedside rounding compared to multidisciplinary rounding have an increased understanding of their treatment plan.
    C. Palliative care patients enjoy music therapy more than pet therapy when provided by their family members.
    D. Registered nurses can use any nursing theorist to provide sound care.

6. Which of these PICOT questions or statements demonstrates effective development?
    A. What type of care is best used for pediatric patients?
    B. Nurses prefer 12-hour shifts to 8-hour shifts to allow more time with family.
    C. Individuals using saline for hep-lock flushes have fewer complications.

    D. Hospitalized children have less stress and heal more quickly when allowed to use play therapy in comparison to pet therapy while recovering from surgery.

7. You are a BSN-prepared nurse who wants to initiate a research project on your unit. To get the other nurses to participate, you would:
    A. ask the doctors what they think.
    B. check the educational level of other nurses on the unit.
    C. ignore your desire to learn more at this time.
    D. give a presentation to your peers on the benefits of research.

8. Research is often not valued because:
    A. it costs too much.
    B. administrators want it.
    C. search engines are easy to access.
    D. staffing is not an obstacle.

Discussion Questions

1. You are a public health nurse working in an outpatient community health facility. You are responsible for clients and their families in a six-county area. During the course of a week, you have from 6 to 10 clients or their families who experience stressful situations related to their diagnosis of diabetes mellitus type 1. These families and their loved ones experience confusion and frustration as they confront and deal with the complex nature of the healthcare situation. You have been asked to explore the following question: How do others in this type of situation deal with the numerous stressful challenges? Which type of searchable question could you develop to drive the data search related to this request?
2. As a BSN staff nurse, you are excited that your hospital wants you to participate in an evidence-based project. You have been chosen to chair a task force. How would you approach this task?
3. You are an ADN-prepared staff nurse at an acute care facility who has enrolled in an RN-BSN program. One of the key messages presented by the RN-BSN program is the importance of evidence-based nursing practice. In your first course in the program, you are asked to identify an evidence-based topic for development. The faculty members instruct you to select a topic that will be functional in your workplace. Which types of activities would you carry out to aid in the selection of this topic?

Suggested Readings

Bovino, L. R., Aquila, A. M., Bartos, S., McCurry, T., Cunningham, C. E., Lane, T., Rogucki, N., DosSantos, J., Moody, D., Mealia-Ospina, K., Pust-Marcone, J., & Quiles, J. (2017). A cross-sectional study on evidence-based nursing practice in the contemporary hospital setting: Implications for nurses in professional development. *Journal for Nurses in Professional Development, 33*(2), 64–69. doi:10/1097/NND.0000000000000339

Briggs, P. Hawrylack, H., Mooney, R., Papanicolas, D., & Taylor, P. (2017). Engaging nurses in clinical research. *Nursing2017, 47*(2), 14–16. doi:10.1097/01.NURS.0000510757.23703.43

Carter, E. J., Mastro, K., Vose, C., Rivera, R., & Larson, E. L. (2017). Clarifying the conundrum: Evidence-based practice, quality improvement, or research? *JONA, 47*(5), 266–270. doi:10.1097/NNA.0000000000000477

Chipps., E., Nash, M., Buck, J., & Vermillion, B. (2017, April). Demystifying nursing research at the bedside. *Nursing Management, 48*(4), pp 29–35. doi:10.1097/01.NUMA.0000514063.45819.c1

Kowalski, M. O. (2017, February). Strategies to heighten EBP engagement. *Nursing Management, 48*(2), pp. 13–15. doi:10.1097/01.NUMA.0000511928.43882.55

Logdon, M. C., Kleiner, C., Oster, C. A., DiSabatino Smith, C., Bergman-Evans, B., Kempnich, J. M., & Hogan, F. (2017). Description of nurse scientist in a large health care system. *Nurse Administration Quarterly, 41*(3), 266–274. doi:10.1097/NAQ.0000000000000237

Newhouse, R. P. (2006, July/August). Examining the support for evidence-based nursing practice. *Journal of Nursing Administration, 36*(7–8), 337–340.

Ryan, C., Powlesland, J., Phillips, C., Raszewski, R., Johnson, A., Banks-Enorense, K., Agoo, V. C., Nacorda-Beltran, R., Halloway, S., Martin, K., Smith, L. D., Walczak, D., Warda, J., Washington, B. J., & Welsh, J. (2017). Nurses' perceptions of quality care. *Journal of Nursing Care Quarterly, 32*(2), 180–185. doi:10.1097/NCQ.0000000000000211

Rycroft-Malone, J. (2003, July). Consider the evidence. *Nursing Standard, 17*(45), 21.

Shingler-Nace, A., & Gonzalez, J. Z. (2017). A pathway to EBP evidence-based nursing management. *Nursing2017, 47*(2), 43–46. doi:10.1097/01.NURS.0000510744.55090.9a

Stavor, D. C., Zedreck-Gonzalez, J., & Hoffmann, R. L. (2017). Improving the use of evidence-based practice and research utilization through the identification of barriers to implementation in a critical access hospital. *JONA, 47*(1), 56–61. doi:10.1097/NNA.0000000000000437

Young, H. M., Bakewell-Sachs S., & Sarna, L. (2017). Nursing practice, research, and education in the west: The best is yet to come. *Nursing Research, 66*(3), 262–270. doi:10.1097/NNR.0000000000000218

References

Agency for Healthcare Research and Quality (AHRQ). (2000). *Outcomes research fact sheet*, AHRQ Publication No. 00-P011. Retrieved from http://archive.ahrq.gov/research/findings/factsheets/outcomes/outfact/outcomes-and-research.html

American Nurses Association. (2016). Nurses rank #1 most trusted profession for 15th year in a row. Retrieved from http://www.nursingworld.org/FunctionalMenuCategories/MediaResources/PressReleases/2016-News-Releases/Nurses-Rank-1-Most-Trusted-Profession-2.pdf

Bator, S., Taylor S., & Catalano, J. T. (2015). Nursing research and evidence-based practice. In J. T. Catalano (Ed.), *Nursing now!: Today's issues, tomorrow's trends* (7th ed., pp. 581–610). Philadelphia, PA: F. A. Davis.

Benner, P., Sutphen, M., Leonard, V., & Day, L. (2010). *Educating nurses: A call for radical transformation*. San Francisco, CA: Jossey-Bass.

Bodenheimer, T., & Sinsky, C. (2014). From triple to quadruple aim: Care of the patient requires care of the provider. *Annals of Family Medicine, 12*(6), 573–576. doi:10.1370/afm.1713gh

Brenan, M. (2017). Nurses keep healthy lead as most honest, ethical profession. Retrieved from http://news.gallup.com/poll/224639/nurses-keep-healthy-lead-honest-ethical-profession.aspx

Brockopp, D. Y., & Hastings-Tolsma, M. T. (2003). *Fundamentals of nursing research* (3rd ed.). Sudbury, MA: Jones and Bartlett Publishers.

Bucknall, T. (2012). Bridging the know-do gap in health care through integrated knowledge translation. *Worldviews on Evidence-Based Nursing, 9*(4), 193–194.

Cannon, S., & Boswell, C. (2010). Challenges and opportunities for teaching research. In L. Caputi (Ed.), *Teaching nursing: The art and science* (2nd ed.). Glen Ellyn, IL: College of DuPage Press.

Carroll, D. L., Greenwood, R., Lynch, K. E., Sullivan, J. K., Ready, C. H., & Fitzmaurice, J. B. (1997). Barriers and facilitators to the utilization of nursing research. *Clinical Nurse Specialist, 11*(5), 207–212.

Carter, E. J., Mastro, K., Vose, C., Rivera, R., & Larson, E. L. (2017). Clarifying the conundrum: Evidence-based practice, quality improvement, or research? *JONA, 47*(5), 266–270. doi:10.1097/NNA.0000000000000477

Catalano, J. T. (2015). *Nursing now!: Today's issues, tomorrow's trends* (7th ed.). Philadelphia: F. A. Davis.

CipherHealth. (2017). The quadruple aim in healthcare. Retrieved from https://cipherhealth.com/the-quadruple-aim-in-healthcare/

Conner, B. T. (2014). Differentiating research, evidence-based practice, and quality improvement, *American Nurse Today, 9*(6). Retrieved from http://www.americannursetoday.com/differentiating -research-evidence-based-practice-and-quality-improvement/

Cronenwett, L. R. (2002, February 19). *Research, practice and policy: Issues in evidence-based care.* Online Journal of Issues in Nursing [Online serial], *7*(2). Retrieved from http://www .nursingworld.org/MainMenuCategories/ANAMarketplace/ANAPeriodicals/OJIN/Columns /KeynotesofNote/EvidenceBasedCare.aspx

Dawes, M., Davies, P., Gray, A., Mant, J., Seers, K., & Snowball, R. (2005). *Evidence-based practice: A primer for health care professionals* (2nd ed.). Edinburgh, Scotland: Elsevier Churchill Livingstone.

Delfini Group. (2012). 5 "A"s of evidence-based medicine & PICOTS: Using "population, intervention, comparison, outcomes, timing, setting" (PICOTS) in evidence-based quality improvement work. Retrieved from http://delfini.org/blog/?p=416

DiCenso, A., Cullum, N., & Ciliska, D. (1998). Implementing evidence-based nursing: Some misconceptions. *Evidence-Based Nursing, 1*(1), 38–40.

DiCenso, A., Guyatt, G., & Ciliska, D. (2005). *Evidence-based nursing: A guide to clinical practice.* St. Louis, MO: Elsevier Mosby.

Echevarria, I. M., & Walker, S. (2014, February). To make your case, start with a PICOT question. *Nursing, 44*(2), 18–19.

Ferguson, L., & Day, R. A. (2005). Evidence-based nursing education: Myth or reality? *Journal of Nursing Education, 44*(3), 107–115.

Fineout-Overholt, E., & Melnyk, B. (2005). Building a culture of best practice. *Nurse Leader, 3*(6), 26–30.

Finkelman, A., & Kenner, C. (2007). *Teaching IOM: Implications of the Institute of Medicine reports for nursing education.* Silver Springs, MD: American Nurses Association.

Fonteyn, M. (2005). The interrelationship among thinking skills, research knowledge, and evidence-based practice. *Journal of Nursing Education, 44*(10), 439.

Gray, J. R., Grove, S. K., & Sutherland, S. (2017). *Burns and Grove's The practice of nursing research: Appraisal, synthesis, and generation of evidence.* (8th ed.). St. Louis, MO: Elsevier.

Health Resources and Services Administration. (2014). *The future of the nursing workforce: National- and state-level projections, 2012–2025.* Retrieved from http://bhpr.hrsa.gov/healthworkforce /supplydemand/nursing/workforceprojections/nursingprojections.pdf

Herlehy, A. M (2011). Nursing's role in the transformation of health care. *AORN, 93*(5), 519–523.

Institute of Medicine (IOM). (2003). *Health professions education: A bridge to quality.* Washington, DC: National Academies Press.

Institute of Medicine (IOM). (2011). *The future of nursing: Leading change, advancing health.* Washington, DC: National Academies Press.

Jolley, S. (2002). Raising research awareness: A strategy for nurses. *Nursing Standard, 16*(33), 33–39.

Kelly, K. P., Turner, A., Speroni, K. G., McLaughlin, M. K., & Guzzetta, C. E. (2013). National survey of hospital nursing research, part 2: Facilitators and hindrances. *JONA, 43*(1), 18–23. doi:10.1097/NNA.0b013e3182786029

Ketefian, S. (1975). Application of selected nursing research finding into nursing practice. *Nursing Research, 24*, 89–92.

Kitson, A. L. (2007). What influences the use of research in clinical practice? *Nursing Research, 56*(4S), S1–S3.

Laskowski-Jones, L. (2015). Research: The path to enlightenment. *Nursing 2015 45*(1), 6.

Logsdon, M. C., Kleiner, C., Oster, C. A., DiSabatino Smith, C., Bergman-Evans, B., Kempnich, J. M., & Hogan, F., (2017). Description of nurse scientist in a large health care system. *Nurse Administration Quarterly, 41*(3), 266–274. doi:10.1097/NAQ.0000000000000237

Magee, M. (2005). *Health politics: Power, population, and health.* Bronxville, NY: Spencer Books.

Malloch, K., & Porter-O'Grady, T. (2015). Innovation and evidence: A partnership in advancing best practice and high quality care. In B. M. Melnyk & E. Fineout-Overholt (Eds.), *Evidence-based practice in nursing & healthcare: A guide to best practice* (3rd ed., pp. 255–273). Philadelphia, PA: Wolters Kluwer.

Mason, D. J., Leavitt, J. K., & Chaffee, M. W. (2012). *Policy & politics in nursing and health care* (6th ed.). St. Louis, MO: Elsevier Saunders.

Melnyk, B. M. (2004). Integrating levels of evidence into clinical decision making. *Journal of Pediatric Nursing, 30*(4), 323–325.

Melnyk, B. M., & Fineout-Overholt, E. (2015). *Evidence-based practice in nursing and healthcare: A guide to best practice* (3rd ed.). Philadelphia, PA: Lippincott Williams & Wilkins.

Merriam-Webster Dictionary. (2017a). Barrier. Retrieved from https://www.merriam-webster.com /dictionary/barrier

Merriam-Webster Dictionary. (2017b). Obstacle. Retrieved from http://www.merriam-webster .com/dictionary/obstacle

Mick, J. (2017). Funneling evidence into practice. *Nurse Management,* 27–34. doi:10.1097 /NUMA.0000520719/70926.79

National Council of State Boards of Nursing. (2017), The 2017 national nursing workforce survey: Executive summary. Retrieved from https://www.ncsbn.org/2015ExecutiveSummary.pdf

Newhouse, R. P., Dearholt, S. L., Poe, S. S., Pugh, L. C., & White, K. M. (2007). *Johns Hopkins Nursing evidence-based practice: Model and guidelines.* Indianapolis, IN: Sigma Theta Tau International.

Omery, A., & Williams, R. P. (1999). An appraisal of research utilization across the United States. *Journal of Nursing Administration, 29*(12), 50–56.

Polit, D. F., & Beck, C. T. (2008). *Nursing research: Generating and assessing evidence for nursing practice* (8th ed.). Philadelphia, PA: Lippincott Williams & Wilkins.

Porter-O'Grady, T. (2006). A new age for practice: Creating the framework for evidence. In K. Malloch & T. Porter-O'Grady (Eds.), *Introduction to evidence-based practice in nursing and health care* (pp. 1–29). Sudbury, MA: Jones and Bartlett.

Pravikoff, D. S., Tanner, A. B., & Pierce, S. T. (2005). Readiness of U.S. nurses for evidence-based practice. *American Journal of Nursing, 105*(9), 40–51.

Rolston-Blenman, B. (2009). Nurses roll up their sleeves at the bedside to improve patient care. *Nurse Leader, 7*(1), 20–25.

Rutledge, D. N., & Grant, M. (2002). Introduction. *Seminars in Oncology Nursing, 18*(1), 1–2.

Ryan, C., Powlesland, J., Phillips, C., Raszewski, R., Johnson, A., Banks-Enorense, K., Agoo, V. C., Nacorda-Beltran, R., Halloway, S., Martin, K., Smith, L. D., Walczak, D., Warda, J., Washington, B. J., & Welsh, J. (2017). Nurses' perceptions of quality care. *Journal of Nursing Care Quarterly, 32*(2), 180–185. doi:10.1097/NCQ.0000000000000211

Saunders, H., & Vehviläinen-Julkunen, K. (2016). The state of readiness for evidence-based practice among nurses: An integrative review. *International Journal of Nursing Studies, 56*, 128–140. doi. org/10.1016/j.ijnurstu.2015.10.018

Schmidt, N. A. & Brown, J. M. (2019). *Evidence-based practice for nurses: Appraisal and application of research* (4th ed). Burlington, MA: Jones and Bartlett Learning.

Stavor, D. C., Zedreck-Gonzalez, J., & Hoffmann, R. L. (2017). Improving the use of evidence-based practice and research utilization through the identification of barriers to implementation in a critical access hospital. *JONA, 47*(1), 56–61. doi:10.1097/NNA.0000000000000437

Titler, M. G., Everett, L. Q., & Adams, S. (2007). Implications for implementation science. *Nursing Research, 56*(4S), S53–S59.

Vratny, A., & Shriver, D. (2007). A conceptual model for growing evidence-based practice. *Nursing Administration Quarterly, 31*(2), 162–170.

Welton, J. M. & Harper, E. M., (2016). Measuring nursing care value. *Nursing Economic$, 34*(1), 7–14.

Yoder, L. H., Kirkley, D., McFall, D. C., Kirksey, K. M., StalBaum, A. L., & Sellers, D. (2014). Staff nurses' use of research to facilitate evidence-based practice. *American Journal of Nursing, 114*(9), 26–37.

Young, H. M., Bakewell-Sachs S., & Sarna, L., (2017). Nursing practice, research, and education in the west: The best is yet to come. *Nursing Research, 66*(3), 262–270. doi:10.1097/NNR. 0000000000000218

CHAPTER 2

Overview of Evidence

Pam Di Vito-Thomas and Carol Boswell

CHAPTER OBJECTIVES

At the conclusion of this chapter, the learner will be able to:
1. Explain the importance of EBP as key to the provision of quality nursing care.
2. Identify different qualities for classification of information as evidence.
3. Discuss various methods for grading evidence.

KEY TERMS

Case-controlled	Forensic science
Case report	Ideas
Case series	Observation
Clinical decision making	Opinions
Consensus	Qualitative research
Editorials	Quality improvement
Evidence	Quantitative research
Evidence-based practice (EBP)	Research
Expert opinion	

▶ Introduction

Evidence-based practice (EBP) has established itself as the foremost process for addressing clinical problems to improve the quality of health care. The impact of EBP continues to echo across nursing practice, education, and research. Clinical expertise and the patient's unique circumstances with respect to patient values integrated with research evidence provide high-quality, cost-effective point-of-care to patients. Nurses are strengthening coalitions with stakeholders both within and outside nursing to launch evidence-based quality initiatives for redesigning care that involves multiple direction-setting recommendations from the Robert Wood Johnson

Foundation (Institute of Medicine [IOM], 2010) to the American Nurses Association (2018) and the Nursing Alliance for Quality Care (2016) (Loversidge, 2016; Stevens, 2013). Healthcare system leaders and individual nurses are challenged to integrate standardized EBP that support continuous performance improvement (Warren et al., 2016). As nurses engage in the process of examining the existing evidence on a topic of concern with direct relevance to their practice, they engage in the requisite skills and knowledge of critiquing research studies and determining the level of empirical evidence on a topic. Nurses are investigating multiple levels of research related to individual nurses, organizations, and systems. They are engaging in professional development to overcome knowledge deficits on new and expanding topics regarding EBP. Nurses are incorporating patient preferences into nursing care to make appropriate and immediate application to clinical practice. Patients and family members soon realize that the care provided by the healthcare professional is established on trustworthy, responsible, and reliable information in compliance with the plan of care can that is supported and embraced (Harper et al., 2017; Mick, 2015). Nurses must be leaders in moving EBP forward in the current healthcare environment.

Previously, the Institute of Medicine's (IOM, 2002) Health Professions Education Summit prescribed the future for health professions' education, regulation, policy, advocacy, quality, and industry and developed strategies for restructuring clinical education to be consistent with the principles of the 21st-century health system. The goals set the national agenda that educators, accreditation and licensing agencies, and certification organizations should ensure that students and working professionals develop and maintain proficiency in five core areas: delivering patient-centered care, working as part of interdisciplinary teams, practicing evidence-based medicine, focusing on quality improvement, and using information technology.

These core competencies continue to be translated and integrated into healthcare policies and governmental funding initiatives directed toward expanding healthcare accessibility and provision of care in expanding acute care and diverse community settings. The following is a statement from the CEO of the Robert Wood Johnson Foundation (Lavizzo-Mourey, 2015):

> While nurses are a known and integral player in meeting America's primary and acute care needs, there's growing recognition that nurses are a critical lynchpin in building bridges among health care, the community, and the social supports needed to create a Culture of Health—so that everyone in America lives the healthiest life possible. Today's report underscores the importance of a diverse workforce of nurses who work to their full potential. While we are making progress toward that goal, there is more to do, and we look forward to collaborating with the business, education, nonprofit, and other sectors to position nurses to maximize their impact. (para. 2)

Nurses, along with other healthcare providers, must embrace the idea of a culture of health. Health care appears to be moving toward the concepts of preventive health. Evidence to support this movement is gaining in strength and importance.

These interrelated competencies "should be applied in most clinical interactions and lead to improved quality to gather data about outcomes that could be associated with better patient care, the desired goal" (Finkelman & Kenner, 2016,

p. 269). Energy and effort must be invested to secure an understanding of these interrelated competencies to move toward evidence-based patient care outcomes. Nurses have the collective numbers through professional associations, technology, education, and other professional colleagues to advance health care with a renewed focus on prevention of disease/disability and health promotion because research on outcomes is essential (Milstead, 2016). Building nursing coalitions and networking among nursing organizations yields a combined effect to support the best patient outcomes. The diversity of national, state, and international nursing organizations can be accessed at the following website: https://nurse.org/orgs .shtml. Here, practitioners can explore nursing's synergized impact via the collective numbers.

Currently, evidence-based quality improvement and healthcare transformation are driven by the Affordable Care Act (ACA) of 2010 (Public Law 111-148), which is changing horizons in today's healthcare environment based on the supposition that every citizen deserves the right to a healthy and productive life (Nickitas, Middaugh, & Aries, 2016). The ACA has set the stage for the changes anticipated in health care over the next several years. An important provision within EBP emphasizes patient preferences in order to provide the best healthcare outcome for the unique patient-centered situation. Four critical elements have been identified for integrating patient preferences into EBP: (1) healthcare redesign, (2) decision support, (3) empowered organizational culture, and (4) informed and empowered nurses (Burman, Robinson, & Hart, 2013).

The ACA was once conceived as a mix of publicly funded health care and privately purchased insurance, but more recently, a shift in the balance, giving the government a larger role, has occurred. Advocates of the Children's Health Insurance Program (CHIP), Maternal Infant and Early Childhood Home Visiting (MIECHV), Elder Justice Act of 2010 (Public Law 111-148), immigrants, and community health centers (CHCs) look to the new era of quality healthcare outcomes and reform. Nurses have more positive attitudes as they perceive their own EBP affecting and improving outcomes (Savage, Kub, & Groves, 2016).

Hannele and Vehviläinen-Julkunen (2016) identified four main themes of nurses in a thematic analysis that "voiced" the value of EBP in improving the quality of care and patient outcomes: (1) nurses' familiarity with EBP, (2) nurses' attitudes toward and beliefs about EBP, (3) nurses' EBP knowledge and skills, and (4) nurses' use of research in practice. The availability of EBP mentors and champions are needed to support trends and affirm the EBP process for a more collaborative approach to EBP implementation. When tasks related to the steps of the EBP process are divided between clinical nurses and EBP mentors based on their EBP competencies, clinical nurses can be supported in the integration of best evidence into daily practice settings. Administrators, mentors, and educators continue to encourage all nurses to perceive EBP as a consistent approach to providing patient care rather than an "extra" duty or project. This type of collaboration between EBP mentors and clinical nurses forms a more pragmatic approach to EBP implementation in clinical practice with diverse environments and with limited resources as clinical nurses strive to integrate and translate the best evidence into their daily practice. These actions make healthcare delivery more effective and cost-efficient because nurses will be freed to focus on their primary roles and job functions (Harper et al., 2017; Mick, 2015). Whether nurses are accessing external evidence from rigorous research or internal evidence from practice initiatives, consistently implemented EBP leads to optimal quality of care and patient-centered outcomes. The steps of the EBP process, as provided by Melnyk and Fineout-Overholt (2015), are:

1. Cultivate a spirit of inquiry within an EBP culture and environment.
2. Ask the burning critical question in PICOT format.
3. Search for and collect the most relevant best evidence.
4. Critically appraise the evidence (i.e., rapid critical appraisal, evaluation, and synthesis).
5. Evaluate outcomes of practice decisions or change-based evidence.
6. Disseminate the outcomes of the EBP decision or change. (pp. 10–16)

Hannele and Vehviläinen-Julkunen (2016), along with Burman, Robinson, and Hart (2013), promote these initiatives and found that, in the acute care setting, incorporating EBP outcomes into the strategic plan is essential to creating accountability at the nursing unit level and improving the quality of patient-centered care. Strategies that include the practical implementation of EBP goals include:

- Facilitating all levels of nursing professionals to engage in shared government to empower the provision of health care
- Providing educational opportunities to facilitate the use of EBP principles by frontline healthcare providers
- Growing mentors to aid in the development of an energized culture committed to EBP
- Utilizing all the educational resources to devise and furnish EBP programs of learning
- Seeking online EBP resources such as project databases to support new projects while ensuring trust and established foundations for EBP
- Allowing healthcare providers to use dedicated time for advancing EBP
- Ensuring that all job descriptions and annual evaluations include components of EBP to demonstrate the importance of this aspect to safe patient care
- Authenticating baseline measures for use in clinical setting related to EBP activities with a consideration of cost-effectiveness and timely management (Burman, Robinson, & Hart, 2013).

EBP is well documented as an integral part of all local, regional, national, and global healthcare environments. Farokhzadian, Khajouei, and Ahmadian (2015) maintained that nursing care needs to move toward quality improvement in EBP and indicate that it is necessary to equip nurses with knowledge and skills required for EBP. A majority of nurses do not attend any formal training on EBP and thus are not as familiar with the concept of EBP, thus engendering unfavorable attitudes and self-efficacy toward EBP. "The most important supporting factor was mentoring by nurses who have adequate EBP experience" (Farokhzadian, Khajouei, & Ahmadian, 2015, p. 1113). Dogherty, Harrison, Graham, Vandyk, and Keeping-Burke (2013) found both positive and negative themes related to factors at the individual, environmental, organizational, and cultural levels. Positive themes that emerged included importance of the issue, development of partnerships and a project team, engagement of key stakeholders, and characteristics of a facilitator—clinical and process expert, broker of knowledge, good communicator, and possession of political savvy. Negative themes included lack of engagement and ownership, dissonance and conflict, and lack of evaluation and sustainability. Organizations and practitioners planning for change in facilitating the implementation of an evidence-based practice can emphasize these positive themes and address the negative barriers that may be encountered. Although the process of translating evidence into clinical practice can be challenging, Irwin, Berkman, and Richards (2013) affirm that "evidence-based practice implementation can be a rewarding and inspirational experience for nurses that fosters teamwork and collaboration to improve patient care" (p. 549). Nurses from all areas of practice must embrace the different aspects for turning evidence into action throughout the healthcare environment. In addition, Johnston et al. (2016) reveal key personal, professional, and organizational barriers that undermine efforts to encourage the implementation of research in nursing practice. The barriers revolved around uncertainty over how to keep up with evidence, lack of clarity over using clinical tools, insufficient training, and lack of structured supervision. Although evidence-based health care results in improved patient outcomes and reduced costs, nurses do not consistently implement evidence-based best practices. Nurses believe in evidence-based care, but barriers remain prevalent, including resistance from colleagues, nurse leaders, and managers. Turning barriers around and building innovative strategies to facilitate and support better implementation of EBP include research-focused appraised goals, organization policies, and procedures that promote autonomy among nurses while ensuring that trainers are credible and using real-life examples in their sessions. Additional strategies are having dedicated supervision sessions, the assignment of a local champion to oversee, and supporting changes to nursing practice.

▶ Foundations for EBP

As nurses begin the work of understanding EBP, a firm appreciation for the interconnectedness of the different aspects within EBP, research, and quality improvement becomes essential. Each of these aspects has unique characteristics, but all serve to advance the quality of care provided within the healthcare setting. An appreciation for the consistencies and differences among these concepts is important to establish a foundation to use the best evidence to improve healthcare delivery. In answering the question, "What is evidence?" it is important that we differentiate external evidence that is generated through rigorous **research** methodologies and is intended to be used in other settings from internal evidence generated through practice initiatives such as outcomes management of **quality improvement** projects generated from data within organizations to improve clinical care.

The distinction between **quantitative research**, which uses the positivist paradigm, and **qualitative research**, which uses the constructivist paradigm, needs to be established. Quantitative researchers use a deductive process, a scientific method that moves in a systematic series of steps according to a prescribed plan beginning with the definition of a problem to the solution of the problem. By gathering empirical evidence (data) that is rooted in objective reality, control of the research situation in minimizing bias, maximizing validity, and generalizing the research findings beyond the study are possible. Using an inductive process, qualitative researchers emphasize the dynamic, holistic, and individual aspects of human life within the context of those who are experiencing them to integrate information to develop a theory or a description of the phenomenon under observation. Nursing's evolving culture involves using rigorous research studies for the best evidence so that actions taken are clinically appropriate and lead to optimal patient outcomes (Polit & Beck, 2017). Inquisitive thinking is required for each aspect of both research paradigms to lay the foundations for an EBP. Also, Chilcote (2017) concurs and supports the use of intuition in nursing during clinical decision making and encourages nurse educators to promote the use of intuition. By taking the time and energy to consider research findings, quality improvement outcomes, and EBP activities effectively, nurses can integrate the critical components to allow for the provision of safe and high-quality health care. EBP has emerged as the preferred mechanism to integrate the best available evidence to guide nursing care and improve patient outcomes through the use of the best evidence (Visovsky, Maguire, Zambroski, & Palacios, 2017).

According to Melnyk and Fineout-Overholt (2015), evidence-based **clinical decision making** includes critical components of "the external evidence from research, evidence-based theories, opinion leaders, and expert panels; clinical expertise, and internal evidence generated from outcomes management of quality improvement projects, a thorough patient assessment, evaluation and use of available resources; and patient preferences and values" (p. 4). EBP takes on the concept of clinical decision making and processing information rather than conclusions used to guide the process for implementing practice change that leads to improved practice. By 2020, 90% of clinical decisions are expected to be supported by accurate, timely, and up-to-date clinical information and will reflect the best available evidence (IOM, 2009). EBP is many sided and involves more than critical appraisals of research because clinicians need to apply the findings from all evidence pertaining to individual circumstances as part of their clinical decision-making process.

Finney, Johnson, Duffy, & Krysia (2016) support the notion that nurses recognize the need to integrate the best **evidence** into busy clinical practice settings. Healthcare professionals, nurse advocates, leaders, educators, clinicians, and stakeholders must collaborate to create policies. These policies need to be integrated into nursing and interprofessional education (IPE) to provide learning opportunities that facilitate supportive academic and clinical practice environments to achieve the IOM (2015) proclamation to create a "culture of health." As EBP resonates across nursing practice, education, and research, the need for redesigning care that includes multiple decision-making efforts for the optimal provision of safe and effective health care in any practice venue is magnified (Loversidge, 2016; Stevens, 2013). In line with multiple direction-setting recommendations for safe, effective, and efficient health care, both national experts and nurses have responded to launch initiatives that maximize the valuable contributions that nurses have made, can make, and will make to deliver fully on the promise of an EBP. Rapidly changing initiatives include practice adoption, education and curricular realignment, model and theory development, scientific engagement in new fields of research, policy change, and development of a national research network to study improvements that will lead in change and advance health.

Nursing, as an evidence-based profession, requires nurses to be able to understand, synthesize, and critique research (Fothergill & Lipp, 2014). The development of EBP competencies and the incorporation of the competencies into healthcare systems will promote the provision of high-quality, safe, and cost-effective care. EBP competencies must be embedded through a variety of mechanisms such as mission statements, job descriptions, development of EBP mentors, ladder programs, and policy and procedure committees that affect every practicing nurse in healthcare organizations. Nurses will flourish in an environment that promotes EPB, clinical inquiry, clinical expertise, and the patients' voice (Melnyk, Gallagher-Ford, & Fine-out-Overholt, 2017). Setting EBP goals throughout healthcare services is a challenging and doable goal wherein implementing up-to-date research, research utilization, and quality improvements is a pivotal cornerstone for the future of nursing practice. To better understand the interconnectedness of EBP and research, review**FIGURE 2-1**. It provides a visualization of the flow for research as it relates to EBP.

Clinical inquiry generated in the work environment leads to pertinent clinical questions because what works for one patient may not work for other patients, even within the same setting (Melnyk & Fineout-Overholt, 2015). Whether research or quality improvement activities are needed, the initial step is always the identification of the clinical question and the problem to be addressed. The clinical question is generated from practice and focuses on a specific population (P), an independent variable or intervention (I), comparison intervention to current practice (C), and dependent variable or outcome (O), within a projected time frame (T) (if applicable). As a problem is identified, a PICOT (population, intervention, comparison, outcome, time) statement is formed. The PICOT statement is an organized, effective framework for structuring the problem into a manageable format. This PICOT statement drives

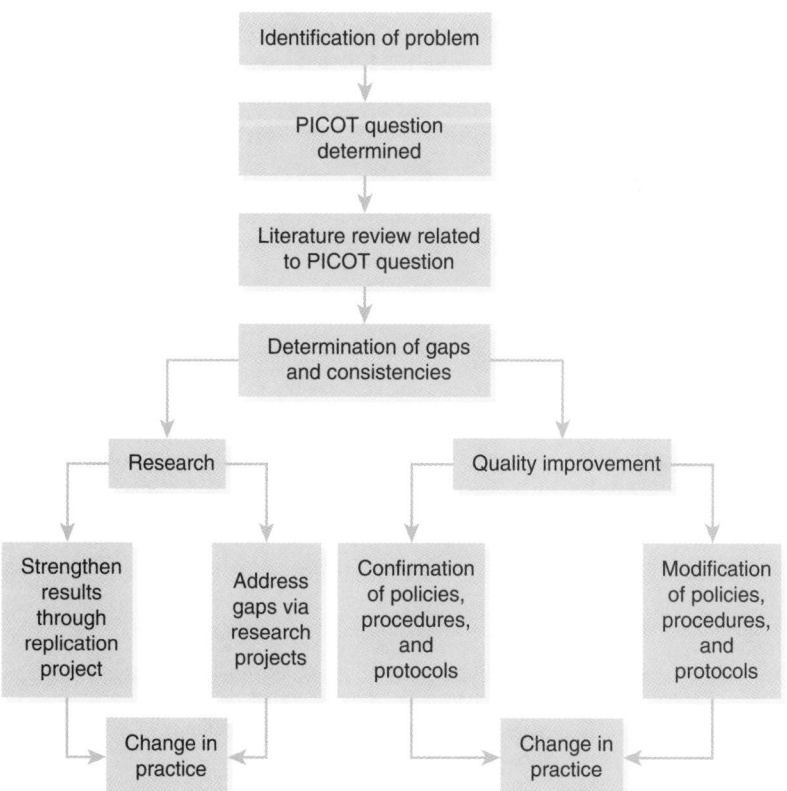

FIGURE 2-1 Flowchart for research related to evidence-based practice.

the review of the literature, with each part of the PICOT statement providing key words and subject headings to narrow the search for relevant articles during the literature review. This attention to the statement allows for a truly in-depth evaluation of the accessible evidence relevant to the problem topic under investigation. While most of the evidence will be available through the literature, other forms of evidence can be accessed and included in this part of the process. All evidence pertinent to the problem topic should be included within the review. Once the literature has been collected and reviewed, gaps and inconsistencies within the literature can be determined.

Based on these gaps or consistencies, the next step can be taken toward establishing a thorough foundation constructed on the *best* evidence. These gaps and consistencies can either lead to a research study (quantitative or qualitative design) or a quality improvement project. Brennan and Parsons (2017) conducted a quality improvement project to validate the evidence for enhanced recovery programs (ERPs) to help reduce length of stay for hip and knee arthroplasty patients. Modifying current protocols currently in place is projected with the quality improvement (QI) project that leads to good patient outcomes. "The review of practice is ongoing to facilitate provision of high-quality patient care. The success of ERPs requires continuous strong leadership, an organized program framework, and standardized procedures" (p. 104). (See **FIGURE 2-2**.)

Quality improvement is the process of bringing standards of practice to the actual bedside or expanding practice arena. Within this process, the functionality of the standard within a variety of settings is addressed. In bringing forth the quality improvement change resulting from the EBP analysis, new standards are developed for the bedside setting. When the evidence found in a literature review and the

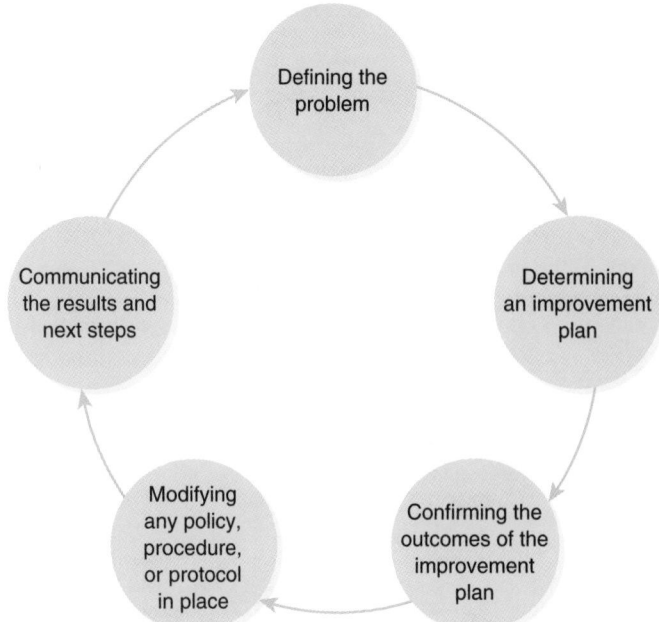

FIGURE 2-2 Quality improvement flowchart.

evidence analysis reflect that a problem exists, the application of a standard of practice at the bedside setting is the quality improvement action required. In Figure 2-1, the quality improvement can either confirm a policy, procedure, and/or protocol already in place, or it can drive their modification. Either way, the change resulting from the EBP analysis is a local change and/or modification rather than a more global alteration.

Hain and Kear (2015) assert:

> In the quest for the Triple Aim of health care—improving the experience of care, improving the health of populations, and reducing per capita costs of health care—nephrology nurses can no longer afford to practice the way we have always done. Instead, it is critical to consider the best available evidence, personal expertise, and patient/family preference when engaging in clinical decision-making. (p. 11)

Quality improvement works to validate the current practices while ensuring that continuity of health care is provided. The process of quality improvement can be visualized within Figure 2-2. Many quality improvement plans are available in the literature. The basic process is for the question to be asked, current structures examined, changes made accordingly, and those changes within the local venue evaluated, followed by communication of the next steps related to the process.

The implementation of healthcare standards must be considered carefully to validate the best practices within the uniqueness of the expanding practice venues. As the ACA has launched the development and dissemination of evidence-based standards throughout the United States, the practice roles and responsibilities of nursing are expanding: "Every day, healthcare professionals will need to exercise their clinical judgment, political acumen, and leadership skills to make important and much needed changes that further increase access to and improve the quality and affordability of health care" (Nickitas et al., 2016, p. xv). Questions persist in understanding how Medicare and Medicaid reimbursements will affect the outcome of care for a multitude of patient-related expenses, including nursing services. Some Medicare questions include the following: "What are the different parts and options for Medicare coverage?" "What are my Medicare rights?" "What if I need help paying Medicare healthcare costs?" "How does Medicare determine payment levels?" "What will be the current guidelines for payment levels of healthcare professionals?" "Will payment be related to productivity and quality outcomes?" Answers to these and other pertinent questions may be found at the following website: https://www.medicare.gov/. Prior to the ACA, Medicare served all eligible beneficiaries through Medicare Part A (Hospital Insurance Programs), Medicare Part B (Supplementary Medical Insurance), Medicare Part C (Medicare Advantage), and Medicare Part D (a voluntary program for outpatient prescriptions drugs). The scope of government involvement in collaboration with healthcare professionals is yet to be determined because multiple factors are difficult to identify and control in order to procure quality improvement activities and ensure continuity of health care within the complex issues of healthcare reform (Milstead, 2016). Today, the ACA affects Medicare beneficiaries and requires that all Americans have health insurance, including minimum essential coverage standards. Nurses and other healthcare professionals will join together to advocate for public policy based on the evidence to enforce healthcare management that is responsible and accountable as Medicare enrollment grows and expenditures rise. The relevance of evidence-based management requires current healthcare principals to look outside standard resources for existing information and investigate deeper into the most recent peer-reviewed research articles on healthcare administration (Buchbinder & Shanks, 2017; U.S. Department of Health and Human Services, 2017). Pulling the most up-to-date evidence is critical for ensuring that the care provided represents the best practices currently known.

On the other side of the flowchart in Figure 2-1, the gaps and consistencies may identify the need for further evidence to provide a foundation for the clinical question and the problem to be addressed. If the gaps and consistencies suggest that further research is required to arrive at an answer for the identified problem, a full research project should be planned and implemented. When the evidence is not strong enough to denote the best practice for a problem topic under investigation, additional research projects are required to provide that foundation for the management of the identified challenge. Both aspects of the process are focused on changing and/or improving the practice provided at the bedside or other similar community healthcare settings. If research is the direction in which the nurse should proceed, the best process for arriving at a sound conclusion should be determined (see **FIGURE 2-3**). As a research endeavor is planned, the methodology for best

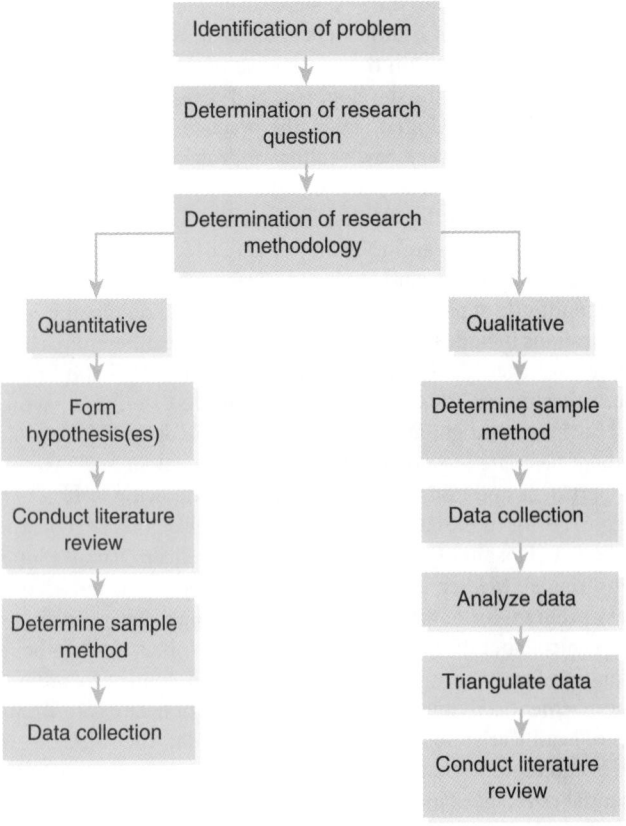

FIGURE 2-3 Research methods flowchart.

addressing the problem must be selected. The flowchart in Figure 2-3 identifies the steps commonly followed when conducting quantitative or qualitative research. The steps are similar for both types of research, but they do reflect the uniqueness of the research approaches. At this point, the general flow within the process is strategic for understanding how and why the levels and strengths of evidence are assigned to these types of decision-making processes. Due to the systematic decision-making activities incorporated into the different research methodologies, the assignment of degrees of strength for the resulting evidence and/or findings has been made through evidence grading methods.

Whether a project is research or quality improvement, the beginning component is assessing the current state of the evidence. Schreiber (2013) poses the following:

> EBP is an integral part of all healthcare domains: clinical, academic, and research. As with any new thought paradigm, information is produced in significant volume, leading to decision points or crossroads that necessitate a time to reflect and process the current body of knowledge before moving forward. (p. 210)

Individuals directly responsible for the safety and quality care of the patient must embrace the entire process of EBP for it to become a common tradition within the provision of health care. "What evidence is available?" "How valid and reliable is the evidence?" and "What is the level of the evidence?" are key questions in this context. Understanding what evidence is and determining how to evaluate the evidence are necessary for the process. The querying of evidence to support the different procedures used in the advancement of health care, along with the questioning of the validity and reliability of that evidence, must be foremost and fundamental for each and every interdisciplinary healthcare provider.

Since the beginning discussion concerning EBP, many different models have been suggested within various professional disciplines. The nursing profession has numerous EBP models available to help nurses understand and implement effective EBP within the practical delivery of health care (see **TABLE 2-1**). When considering any EBP model, nurses should consider the foundational principles and steps used within the EBP process. These principles and steps help to reflect the process and ensure that the EBP is practical and functional within the designated work environment.

▶ Qualities of Evidence

The Agency for Healthcare Research and Quality (AHRQ; 2014) notes that a goal for effective primary care can improve health and cost outcomes and patients', clinicians', and staff members' experience. Evaluations can help determine how best to improve primary care delivery. For example, Nickitas and Mensik (2015) note that integrated staffing models that build the metrics of safety, quality, and patient and nurse engagement will add value to health care, resulting in "better care for individuals, better health for populations, and outcomes at lower per capita costs" (p. 40). Each piece of information being considered for care delivery must be evaluated carefully and critically due to the many varying forms and strengths of the levels of evidence. Nurses are uniquely positioned to evaluate and apply the best evidence

TABLE 2-1 Comparison of Six EBP Models

	ARCC (Advancing Research and Clinical Practice Through Close Collaboration) Model	Clinical Scholar Model	IOWA Model	Johns Hopkins EBP Model (PET Process)	Larrabee's Model for EBP Change	Promotion Action on Research Implementation in Health Services (PARiHS) Framework
Foundational focus	Unify research and clinical practice to advance EBP within an academic medical center	Promote the spirit of inquiry, education for direct care providers, and guide a mentorship program	Pragmatic multiphase change process with feedback loops; applicable and easy to use by multidisciplinary healthcare teams	Strategic goal to build a culture of nursing practice based on evidence	Integrated principles of quality improvement, team work tools, and EBP strategies	Untested conceptual framework; useful for research implementation
Date of original planning	Conceptualized in 1999	Published in 1999	Originated in 1994; updated in 2015	Originated in 2002	Revised version of Rosswurm and Larrabee (1999)	Developed over time
Theoretical bases	Cognitive behavioral theory	Diffusion of innovation theory; four central goals	Problem-solving steps in the scientific process	Mentored linear process	One-time philosophical decision to pursue EBP	Four different types of evidence (research, clinical experience, and patients' and caregivers' experiences) and local context information. Successful implementation (SI) used in context of culture, leadership, and evaluation

Steps/stages used in EBP					
0 = Cultivate spirit of inquiry 1 = Ask the burning question using PICOT format 2 = Search/collect most relevant evidence 3 = Critically appraise the evidence 4 = Integrate best evidence with clinical expertise and patient preferences 5 = Evaluate outcomes 6 = Disseminate outcomes	Assess Ask Acquire Appraise Apply Audit	1 = Select a priority topic based on triggers 2 = Form a team 3 = Assemble evidence 4 = Critique and synthesize evidence 5 = Set forth the EBP recommendations 6 = Decide if findings support a practice change 7 = Develop and pilot the practice change 8 = Determine if the change is appropriate for adoption 9 = Monitor structure, processes, and outcomes 10 = Disseminate findings	Phase 1 Practice question Recruit team Develop/refine EBP question Define question scope Assign responsibility Schedule meetings Phase 2 Evidence Conduct search Appraise level and quality of individual evidence Summarize individual evidence Synthesis body of evidence Develop practice recommendations Phase 3 Translation Determine fit, feasibility, appropriateness Create action plan Secure support Implement plan Evaluate outcomes Report outcomes to stakeholders Identify future steps Disseminate findings	Step 1: Assess the need for change in practice Step 2: Locate the best evidence Step 3: Critically analyze the evidence Step 4: Design practice changes Step 5: Implement and evaluate change in practice Step 6: Integrate and maintain change in practice	Uses elements and sub-elements on a continuum from high to low

Data from Kitson, A. L., Rycroft-Malone, J., Harvey, G., McCormack, B., Seers, K., & Titchen, A. (2008). Evaluating the successful implementation of evidence into practice using the PARIHS framework: Theoretical and practical challenges. *Implement Sci, 3*(1). doi: 10.0086 /1748-5908-3-1; Melnyk, B. M. & Fineout-Overholt, E. (2015). *Evidence-based practice in nursing & healthcare: A guide to best practice.* (3rd ed.). Philadelphia, Wolters Kluwer; Thompson, C. J. (2017). Use the 6A's to remember the evidence-based practice process, Retrieved from https://nursingeducationexpert.com/evidence-based-practice-process/

within their daily practice to improve patient outcomes (Makic, Rauen, Watson, & Poteet, 2014). Nurses must assume the responsibility that is placed on them to provide health care based on the best evidence available. Within the field of **forensic science**, the idea of evidence is dominant. Evidence is viewed as the data on which judgments and decisions are made. To be beneficial, evidence has to be established by scrutiny and contemplation of the materials from multiple vantage points. Many accrediting bodies have increased their attention on the use of evidence to make decisions (Lee, Johnson, Newhouse, & Warren, 2013), and regulatory agencies are renowned for using supporting information and benchmarking as evidence of compliance with standards.

Consequently, sound evidence is more than just the simple decisions set forth by one or two individuals. Sound evidence is based on hard and fast particulars, details, and specifics that can be confirmed from different views of the same materials. Within the forensic science discussion of evidence, it is classified as having class and individual characteristics. Class characteristics are established on the physical qualities that are shared by a group of like items. Individual characteristics are those qualities that are unique to the specialized entity. By using the factors and concepts from forensic science concerning evidence, greater latitude in regard to accepting and utilizing other beneficial forms can be exercised.

Within the discussion of evidence, several factors need to be carefully considered. Finkelman and Kenner (2016) support that an EBP review and nursing research are not the same thing and that an EBP review includes evidence from research results; clinical expertise; other sources; and patient's assessment, preferences, and values. In essence, research cannot and will not answer all the questions concerning health care; however, Eaton, Meins, Mitchell, Voss, and Doorenbos (2015) affirm that "evidence-based pain management can be considered an innovation because it requires shifting an existing idea or practice and developing a new opinion toward a new idea or practice (p. 166). Evidence must be considered carefully and thoughtfully for each aspect of health care to ensure that the optimal level of health care is being provided.

Nursing care topics must be investigated using the most relevant information for an EBP review. Finney et al. (2016) propose the use of critically appraised topics (CATs) that provide a summary of the best available evidence to answer a clinical question for general practice nursing. The CAT topics combine nursing clinical experience and clinical academics that provides a cross-linking of skills and knowledge. Once the information is collected, the distinctiveness of the results should be focused on that identified topic. The data under consideration must represent the wholeness of what is known about a topic. Distinguishing traits of the methodological and statistical results along with the topic also need to be understood, evaluated, and contemplated (Cumulative Index of Nursing and Allied Health [CINAHL] library database, 2018).

Another important aspect to consider is the frequency that the results are seen. When the same results are observed without regard to person, place, or situation, the results are viewed with increased confidence. When multiple sources in various venues are found to come to the same conclusions about a topic, the reliability of the findings is strengthened. This aspect can also be viewed as the persistence in the result. *Persistence* and *consistency* within the results add support and strength to the quality of the evidence.

A final aspect to consider carefully when contemplating evidence is the likelihood of any alternative explanations for the results obtained. Alternative styles of evidence must be considered carefully so that the justification for the findings yields more power and influence. Improved patient outcomes will follow from the valid results from critical appraisals of the best evidence (Peterson et al., 2014). Within the consideration of all evidence, critical thought must be applied to the definitive evidence when working in health care.

Other relevant sources of evidential material are case studies, which may provide information that is not reported in the results of clinical trials or survey research (Melnyk & Fineout-Overholt, 2015). The consideration of case studies can have several different dimensions. A case scrutinizes the lives of individuals, dealings, resolutions, episodes, phases, projects, and/or other systems to determine the uniqueness of the situation. Case studies do not follow rigid sets of rules, and the greatest strength of case studies is the depth of the investigation that is possible when using small numbers (Polit & Beck, 2017). The case or situation drives the consideration of specific aspects identified in the case. Case series and case reports can be intermeshed with case studies. Each type of case scenario adds additional depth to the evidence. A **case series** incorporates several case studies that have resulted in similar outcomes. Thus, the findings can be combined to provide additional strength to the results documented. A **case report** is the documentation of the aspects identified within a situation. The strength of this evidence is based on the clarity of the report provided. In addition to the outcomes, the situation and environment where the case occurred lend depth and influence to the resulting materials. A useful resource for case reports on some of the most common medical diagnoses is available through the "Evidence-Based Care Sheets" at the Cumulative Index of Nursing and Allied Health (CINAHL) library database. These care sheets organize "what we know" and "what we can do" using a coding matrix of the references listed in order of strength.

Another form of evidence that can be considered is **expert opinion**. Expert opinion is the furnishing and/or contributing of applicable and significant information by an individual who is viewed as an authority based on a set of criteria. Different rules can be utilized to identify the expert based on the materials being sought. While biases are possible due to the nature of the evidence provided by the expert, the expectation is for the expert to qualify any opinion based on what is known about the topic under investigation.

In conjunction with the topic of expert opinion, the definitions of ideas, editorials, and opinions must be clarified. An idea encompasses thoughts, convictions, and/or principles. An idea can be based on potentially or actually existing foundations. **Ideas** are considered to be individual work; thus their influence can be minimal. Brainstorming ideas and critically thinking about those ideas have merit because they may lead to innovations for patient-centered care initiatives.

Editorials are the statements of the opinions of an owner, manager, or similar individual. Again, the weight of this type of evidence is based on the perceived biases associated with the thoughts and statements. Finally, **opinions** represent a person's beliefs, judgments, and/or values about a designated subject. Opinions can be viewed as evidence, but these have the same caveats as noted with ideas and editorials. Opinions are attitudes and viewpoints that do not rest on adequate foundations to be viewed as completely unbiased because they reflect an individual's worldview.

A third type of evidence that can be considered is **observation**. Observations begin with the individual striving to attentively perceive and/or scrutinize a situation. Following the inspection and surveillance, the observer documents those aspects pertinent to the topic or activity being observed. This process can have biases associated with the observations. To minimize this concern, the context, including when, where, and how the observations were gathered, is often part of the evidence. Documentation of the observation requires the clear determination of what constitutes an observed activity. For example, multiple nonverbal behaviors can be recorded as evidence of noncompliance when in fact they can be attributed to lack of understanding or a mental health issue. By designating which behaviors will be counted and which will not, the quality of the evidence can be increased.

A final example of alternate forms of evidence is a **consensus**. A consensus occurs when individuals involved in the process come to a mutual understanding. A consensus usually is understood to mean that the majority has reached an agreed resolution. Because the evidence (consensus) is based on a majority and not the complete agreement, the strength of the results can be questionable. As with the other forms of evidence, attention to factors and types of evidence must be integrated into the classification of the data. Each and every type and piece of evidence, whether provided by research or via some other avenue, must be scrutinized thoroughly and unconditionally to ensure the validity of the claims being made.

Melnyk and Fineout-Overholt (2015) affirm that the "critical appraisal of evidence is the hallmark of EBP" (p. 80), and the quality of the journey toward that evidence is important. Dogherty and colleagues (2013) support this idea, because "efforts have shifted from focusing on methods for rigorously synthesizing study results into practice recommendations and improving guideline quality toward implementation" (p. 129). The quality of the evidence is becoming increasingly critical, and best practices in health care include diffusing evidence into practice (Makic et al., 2014). The use of evidence, which has a strong foundation to move nursing care forward, is imperative and expected by the public.

In providing care, a nurse may use four generally accepted patterns of knowledge—empirical, aesthetic, ethical, and personal—and synthesize, or mesh, the four types of knowledge together. These types of knowledge provide various vantage points by which to consider the material put forth as evidence to better understand patients for higher quality care.

Empirical knowledge relates to quantitative explanations, predicting, and explaining (Finkelman & Kenner, 2016). Using the levels of evidence to help guide the use of the information discovered is vital for effective and competent management of patient-centered care and/or management of patient care and resources. *Aesthetic* knowledge embraces those facts and information that reflect emotion and awareness of the beauty and art around us. This term includes the idea that data must be interpreted within the environment in which it was formed or discovered. Removing the information from that setting can and does modify the application of the findings.

The third form of knowing is *ethical*. The incorporation of ethical knowledge within the venue of evidence brings in the ideas of right and wrong. Finkelman and Kenner (2016) connect ethical knowing with the focus on a person's moral values— what *should* be done. Nursing can relate this knowing to the professional Code of Ethics for Nurses (American Nurses Association, 2015). Ethical considerations must always be considered when selecting and moving evidence toward safe healthcare practices. This ethical aspect incorporates the patient's desires into the utilization of the evidence.

The final type of knowing is *personal* knowledge. Personal knowledge and clinical expertise are critical components within EBP. Personal knowing allows participants in the process of healthy living to be actively engaged and involved. These individuals are not passive members but enthusiastic contributors to the consideration of the evidence and the plan of care. The clinical question becomes the key within this process of accessing the evidence. Background questions (asking about general information) are foundational and broader in scope than foreground questions (asking about specific knowledge) (Melnyk & Fineout-Overholt, 2015). A well-prepared question with clinical relevance focuses the search for evidence on these types of questions. Notably, the type of question facilitates the types of evidence to be sought. It also promotes the evaluation of that evidence using these different forms of understanding the knowledge bases. For some questions, empiric knowing would be important. For other queries, the ethical and/or aesthetic component could be the driving force toward the level of evidence needed.

As the concept of evidence becomes understandable and transparent, attention must be directed toward classifying the different levels of evidence to allow for consistency within the discussion. Without a uniform means of evaluating the evidence, communication of the nature of the evidence will be confusing and disoriented.

Nurses must become increasingly aware of their current practice—what is and is not known through evidence—and support it with research conclusions appropriate to the distinctive interventions that can be utilized. Nurses need to embrace a standardized objective approach for use when evaluating evidence of all types—research, quality improvement, expert opinion, or case studies—to ensure that nursing care is delivered with the best evidence available.

▶ Evidence Grading Methods

The World Health Organization (WHO) and a growing number of other organizations have adopted the Grading of Recommendations, Assessment, Development and Evaluation (GRADE) system in order to both assess the quality of research evidence and develop clinical practice guidelines. The GRADE approach aims to separate the quality of evidence from the strength of the recommendations. GRADE provides explicit criteria for rating the quality of evidence (including study design), risk of bias, inconsistency of the evidence across studies, potential indirectness of the evidence, imprecision and magnitude of the intervention effect, probability of publication bias, dose–response in relation to intervention and outcome, and potential for residual confounding (Davoli et al., 2014). Levels of evidence are highly considered when critiquing a research study to ensure that the evidence is credible (e.g., reliable and valid) and appropriate for inclusion into practice. Resources for clinicians, including practice alerts and a hierarchal rating system for levels of evidence, serve to determine the strength of research studies, assess the findings, and evaluate the evidence for potential implementation into best practice (Peterson et al., 2014). Commonly, the highest to the lower ranges of levels of evidence have a spectrum of publications from meta-analysis, systematic or integrative literature reviews, randomized controlled trial (RCT), not randomized controlled trial, qualitative study, histories, case studies, guidelines, review of the literature, research utilization report, quality improvement report, legislation, policies, procedures, protocols, practice exemplars, and expert opinions. Clinical questions, diagnoses, prevention strategies, and quality improvement designs use a combination of levels of evidence from systematic review, meta-analysis, RCTs to qualitative studies, and cohort and case-control studies. Nurses and healthcare practitioners are developing rationales for selecting scales to establish the quality and level of evidence EBP for optimal patient outcomes until standardization occurs. Currently, numerous scales for levels of evidence are available for consideration with some using three levels and some as many as seven. Different criteria are used to determine the quality of the evidence. ANA has selected these key resources as examples of different scales and grading criteria: Johns Hopkins Nursing Evidence-Based Practice, University of Illinois at Chicago University Library, Centre for Evidence-Based Medicine; University of Virginia Health Sciences Library (Information Mastery: Navigating the Maze: The Pyramid), University of Illinois at Chicago University Library, Centre for Evidence-Based Medicine; University of Washington Health Sciences Library, U.S. Preventive Services Task Force Levels of Certainty Regarding Net Benefit, Cochrane Consumer Network Levels of Evidence, The Joanna Briggs Institute, and the University of Minnesota Bio-Medical Library.

The Association of periOperative Registered Nurses (AORN) board decided to evaluate the different methods using the AHRQ's three domains of evidence—quality, quantity, and consistency. Within this scoring of the different methods, the AORN group identified only one method that addressed the five criteria that were evaluated: the Oncology Nursing Society (ONS) Putting Evidence into Practice (PEP) schema. Peterson and colleagues (2014) affirm that "the purpose of determining the level of evidence and then critiquing the study is to ensure that the evidence is credible and appropriate for inclusion into practice" (p. 59). After the critique of an article is completed, the information assessed is awarded a specific grade based on the strength of the evidence presented in the publication. For the most part, the "levels of evidence" categories developed by the various organizations are compatible, with only minor differences. Each of the formats used to score and/or grade evidence categorizes the evidence from strongest to least supported evidential materials, but the rating hierarchies are not established to allow for a value judgment about the quality of any study or to provide clinicians with information about the significance to practice. Attention must be given to the use of these tools to gain a better understanding of the evidence and be able to defend the rationales used for providing care through varying interventions based on the individual setting. When comparing and contrasting Kwan and Sullivan's (2017) systematic review; Cortez-Gann and colleagues' (2017) quantitative research; and Woolston and Connelly's (2017) qualitative study the methodologies demonstrate the varying levels of evidence that range from level 1 to level 3 to a level 4. (See **FIGURE 2-4**.) The higher a methodology ranks, the more "the results accurately represent the actual situation and the more confidence clinicians can have that the intervention will produce the same health outcomes in similar patients from whom they care" (Melnyk & Fineout-Overholt, 2015, p. 92).

To score/grade the article by Hanna, Weaver, Slaven, Fortenberry, and DiMeglio (2014), for example, the research methodology would need to be established. The study states that it is part of a larger longitudinal study. No control group was used along with no evidence of randomization within the sample and no intervention resulting in the research methodology being a nonexperimental design. According to Figure 2-4, a nonexperimental design would be a level 4 on this hierarchy tool. In contrast, the article written by Iverson and colleagues (2014) states that

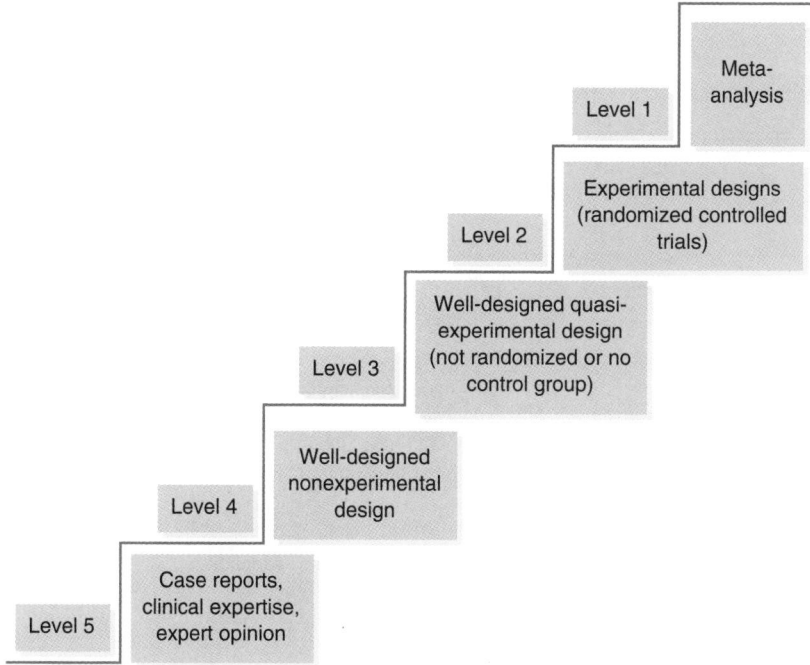

FIGURE 2-4 Hierarchy of levels of evidence.

Modified from United States Prevention Service Task Force (USPSTF). (2009). Slide presentation from the AHRQ 2008 annual conference. Retrieved from http://www.ahrq .gov/about/annualmtg08/090808slides/Lin2.htm

it is a qualitative research design. Thus, it would classify as a level 5 using the tool in Figure 2-4. To determine the strength of the evidence in both of the articles using **FIGURE 2-5**, each could be placed at either level A or B depending on the health care provided in the local area.

Each grouping has unique characteristics based on the agency or organization responsible for the determination of the categories. Numerous organizations, such as the AHRQ, Joanna Briggs Institute, and Cochrane Collaboration, among others, have developed "levels of evidence" hierarchies in an effort to help reviewers categorize the strengths and weaknesses of various studies. One such hierarchy developed by the U.S. Preventive Services Task Force (USPSTF) is shown in Figure 2-4. Within this ladder, quantitative and qualitative types of research design are designated as a specific level within the hierarchy of research study designs. One drawback with this ranking is the lack of classification of mixed method studies. Reviewers must make their own decisions about classifying such studies as quantitative or qualitative because no level for mixed method studies has been established. Another concern raised with this hierarchy relates to the four levels given to research results and the classifying of all other types of evidence as level 5. The message from the ordinal ranking of this hierarchy is that research is the only valid evidence mechanism.

The ONS PEP schema was identified as meeting specific criteria for evaluating the evidence; it can serve as an effective foundation for use within the clinical

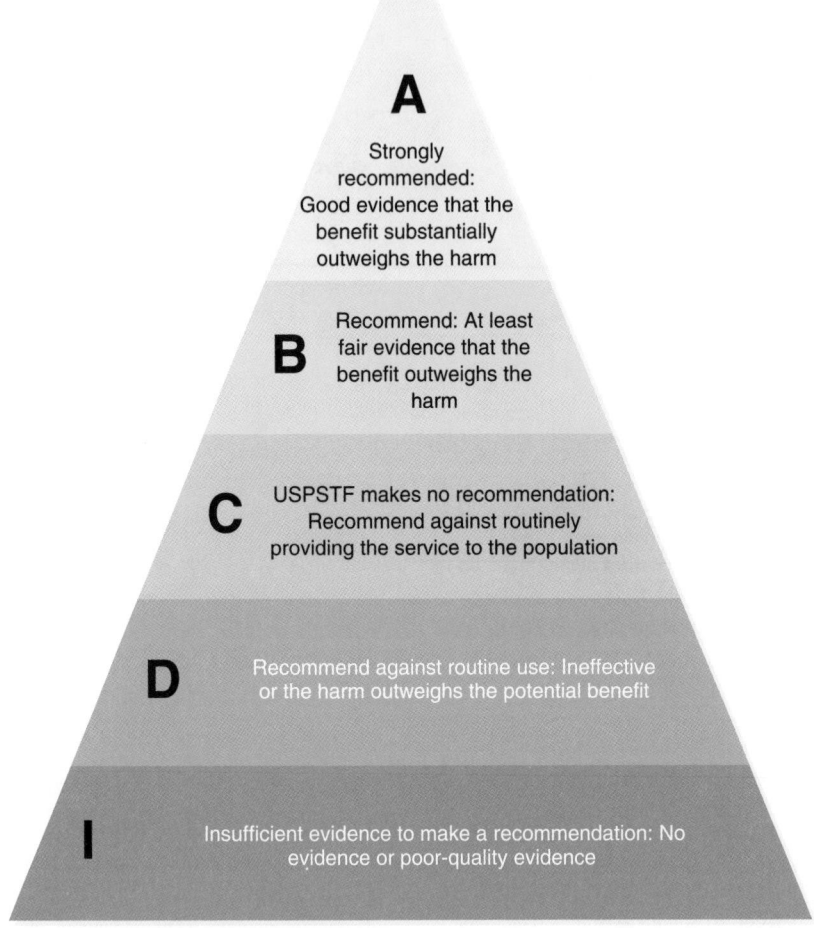

FIGURE 2-5 Tools for evaluating evidence.

Modified from U.S. Prevention Service Task Force (USPSTF). (2007). Slide presentation from the AHRQ 2007 annual conference. Retrieved from http://archive.ahrq.gov
/about/annualmtg07/0927slides/finch/Finch-28.html

arena. This tool is used after the selection of articles and evidence is determined.
The use of this tool is to aid in the determination of whether the practice should
be included in the day-to-day performance of health care (Steelman, Pape, King,
Graling, & Gaberson, 2011). Within the schema, specific decision rules for summa-
tive evaluation of a body of evidence have been established to guide the reviewers
in making the designations of recommended for practice, likely to be effective, ben-
efits balanced with harms, effectiveness not established, effectiveness unlikely, and
not recommended for practice. Each rating tool should be carefully and thoroughly
evaluated to determine which one works best in the designated clinical setting.

The American Association of Critical-Care Nurses (AACN) Evidence Rat-
ing System updated change clarifies the distinction between experimental and

nonexperimental studies in the hierarchy and makes the AACN system consistent with other published hierarchies used to rate evidence. Within the leveling of evidence, the schematic discussed by Peterson and colleagues (2014) used the first two levels to reflect experimental research designs. The third level continues to be quantitative research at the level of either experimental or non-experimental. The final three levels presented by Peterson and colleagues (2014) reflect lower levels of evidence such as opinion articles, theory discussion, and/or manufacturer's recommendations. Nurses can use these levels of evidence to determine the strength of the studies being considered while evaluating the findings. Once a study is determined to be at a designated level of evidence, the nurse can consider what steps need to be taken to implement the evidence into practice. "Evidence-based nursing care is a lifelong approach to clinical decision making and excellence in practice" (Peterson et al., 2014, p. 61).

Each type of scoring tool for evidence has its strengths and challenges. Each agency and/or nurse must carefully consider which format works best in which setting. Another type of classification for evidence comes from the Trip (formerly Turning Research Into Practice) database. This leveling of evidence provides three basic divisions. Evidence falls into one of three global categories—filtered information, unfiltered information, or background information/expert opinion (Harvey Cushing/John Hay Whitney Medical Library, n.d.). While this process appears to address different levels, the hierarchy shows that six out of the seven levels speak to research endeavors. Again, all other types of evidence are placed into the one lowest level within the structure. This hierarchy does provide an additional designation for the levels of filtered information, which addresses the critical analysis and meta-analysis levels. The Joanna Briggs Institute (JBI; 2012a, 2012b) has moved toward the use of the Feasibility, Appropriateness, Meaningfulness, Effectiveness (FAME) level of evidence and the Appraisal of Guidelines Research and Evaluation (AGREE) collaboration. Within the JBI approach to levels of evidence, evidence documents are scored based on four criteria: feasibility, appropriateness, meaningfulness, and effectiveness. Effectiveness relates to whether an intervention performs as expected. Appropriateness considers the psychosocial aspects of the intervention. It is concerned with the impact that the activity will have on the consumer and whether it will be accepted by the individual. Meaningfulness considers the effect of the intervention on the individual. Within each of these areas, a document would be scored from 1 to 4. Level 1 is the strongest level of evidence. In addition to these four components, each document is also assessed for economic evidence. The majority of this ranking focuses on meta-synthesis of research. As the AGREE tool and FAME grid are examined, aspects such as **case-controlled**, observations, expert opinion, and consensus can be found only in the lowest levels of the document. In conjunction with the level of evidence ranking, JBI developed a practice focus ranking document that accompanies the AGREE collaboration. This document grades the evidence used within the guideline from level A to level C based on the appropriateness of application to a practice setting. By having this document alongside the levels of evidence (FAME) document, individuals can look toward the application within the practice setting.

AHRQ has also developed a "tool for evaluating the strength of the evidence" (USPSTF, 2009); see Figure 2-5. With this tool, the evidence is assigned a level of strength based on the anticipated benefit and/or harm to the patient. The process used with this rating schedule looks at the application of any evidence into the practice arena. None of the five levels speak to the idea of research. Each level clarifies a different amount of benefit or harm for the patient from the use of the service. Differences in classifications using this tool continue to be a problem because individual opinions have to be used to rank or assign the levels.

SUNY Downstate Medical Center (2014) provides an evidence pyramid as a means of classifying and/or ranking evidence. This pyramid has nine levels. Within these levels, the ranking progresses from systematic reviews and meta-analyses at the top to *in vitro* ("test tube") research at the base. Within the middle range on the pyramid, the levels of case series; case reports; and ideas, editorials, and opinions are listed. While the framework is interesting, the placement of research at both the top and bottom of the pyramid is confusing. Animal research and *in vitro* research tend to be quantitative research, which is held to be strong evidence by other ranking groups. No rationale was provided as to why the pyramid develops from quantitative research to expert sources and finally ending back with quantitative research designs.

With the integration of evidence-based practice into the research critique process, the classification of research projects in terms of the "level of evidence" and the strength of the evidence using instruments such as the AHRQ tool seeks to improve the clarity of the information available for making clinical decisions about the modification of policies, procedures, and clinical guidelines.

⬛ THINK OUTSIDE THE BOX

- Look at the different types of evidence. List the strengths and weaknesses for each type of evidence. Can you identify any other types of evidence that should be considered when establishing healthcare practice?
- Select one or two research articles. Use at least two of the different rating tools to evaluate the evidence and classify it based on each tool. Which tool was easiest to use? Which provided the best review of the evidence? Which tool was difficult to use and why?
- Debate the use of a rating tool. Do healthcare professionals need to rate all of the evidence they use? Is the rating of evidence just added work that does not meet the needs of the clinical workplace?

▶ Conclusion

EBP has established itself as the foremost process for addressing clinical problems to improve the quality of health care as the impact of an EBP continues to be echoed across nursing practice, education, and research. Currently, evidence-based quality improvement and healthcare transformation are driven by the Affordable Care Act (ACA) of 2010 (Public Law 111-148), which is changing horizons in today's healthcare environment based on the supposition that every citizen deserves the right to a healthy and productive life (Nickitas, Middaugh, & Aries, 2016). Whether nurses are accessing external evidence from rigorous research or internal evidence from practice EBP leads to optimal quality of care and patient-centered outcomes. Nurses believe in evidence-based care, but barriers remain prevalent, including resistance from colleagues, nurse leaders, and managers. Turning barriers around and building innovative strategies to facilitate and support better implementation of EBP are a challenging and doable goal. Up-to-date research, research utilization, and quality improvements are a pivotal cornerstone for the future of nursing practice. Quality improvement brings standards of practice to the actual bedside, and new policy and standards are developed for the bedside setting. Quality improvement works to validate the current practices while ensuring that continuity of health care is provided. Although a lack of standardization of the definitions of levels of evidence and quality exists, numerous scales or levels of evidence are available to use when scoring/grading the evidence. Levels of evidence are highly considered when critiquing a research study to ensure that the evidence is credible (e.g., reliable and valid) and appropriate for inclusion into practice and research, and they magnify the need for redesigning care that includes multiple decision-making efforts for the optimal provision of safe and effective health care in any venue (Loversidge, 2016; Peterson et al., 2014).

In providing care, a nurse may use some of these methods of knowing from four generally accepted patterns of knowledge—empirical, ethical, personal, and aesthetic, plus synthesizing (pulling the four types of knowledge together)—to provide an EBP. Nurses use evidence of levels schema to determine the strength of research studies, assess the findings, and evaluate the evidence for potential implementation into the best practices. Each nurse must accept the challenge of investigating the evidence that is available to support and advance the practice of nursing care and health care in the local setting. Health care can no longer be provided based on the "way we have always done it." Each nurse must recognize and acknowledge the responsibility for advancing the evidence of how and why the interventions are done. Only when this process is done will health care be able to provide quality health management. The careful consideration of evidence quality is based on logical steps and criteria. Agencies must consider the different formats available to determine which one works best in each setting. The primary responsibility is to question the evidence and not just accept it because it is there. Nurses must be willing to evaluate and confront the data to ensure that the care provided does rise to the appropriate level to advance the quality of the health care provided.

Summary Points

1. Evidence includes that which can be proven and/or disproven. It is an indication or sign related to a topic.
2. Taking the time and energy to consider the evidence effectively is imperative.
3. The proof and/or indications that can be pulled together to determine the best line of action, instead of the amount of research that may have been done, become the driving force.
4. A grading process allows one to carefully and cautiously consider the evidence presented in light of a unique clinical environment.
5. A firm appreciation for the interconnectedness of the different aspects within EBP, research, and quality improvement is paramount.
6. A critical appraisal of EBP must consider more than just the available research.
7. Whether an individual is considering research activities or quality improvement efforts, the initial step is always the identification of the problem to be addressed.

8. Each piece of information must be carefully and thoroughly considered concerning the foundation on which the outcome is established.
9. Persistence and consistency of results add support and strength to the quality of the evidence.

🏳 RED FLAGS

- All evidence must be carefully and thoroughly questioned prior to the acceptance of the validity of the information.
- Sources of evidence should provide enough information concerning the development of the materials along with the outcomes for others to be able to evaluate the quality of the evidence.

Multiple-Choice Questions

1. What does an evidence-based practice lead to in the expanding healthcare environment?
    A. Defragmented healthcare provision in acute care settings
    B. Sound foundation for patient-centered care management
    C. Compliance with the medical plan of care
    D. Optimal quality of care and patient-centered outcomes

2. What is currently driven by the Affordable Care Act of 2010 to ensure every citizen deserves the right to a healthy and productive life?
    A. Coding new resources for patient-centered care
    B. Evidence-based healthcare transformation
    C. Working in interdisciplinary healthcare teams
    D. Practitioners providing evidence-based medicine

3. What critical element most likely affects the day-to-day positive health outcomes for integrating patient preferences?
    A. Healthcare redesign and funding from national health initiatives
    B. Empowered organizational outcomes emphasizing health
    C. Continuity of care provided by point-of-care empowered nurses
    D. Strong administration that promotes interdisciplinary practice

4. What nursing practice goal supports better implementation of an evidence-based practice?
    A. Building innovation strategies to provide patient-centered care
    B. Updating standards of practice and policy through institutional projects
    C. Redesigning care through more diverse delegation practices
    D. Validating care based on levels of evidence and professional guidelines

5. What type of methodology best serves a nurse within a limited time frame who desires to conduct an evidence-based investigation related to patient preferences for medication administration in a cardiac rehabilitation unit?
    A. Mixed-methodology study
    B. Quantitative study
    C. Qualitative study
    D. Quality improvement project

6. Which action best supports the healthcare team rounding together to provide patient-centered care?
   A. New electronic data entry programs and pocket devices
   B. Quality improvement projects and initiatives
   C. Actively engaging in interdisciplinary teams
   D. Computers at the bedside for immediate charting

7. When the nurse strives to facilitate the implementation of evidence-based practice within an institution to change to a "culture of health," what theme may emerge during the process?
   A. Changes for shorter shifts within employee and ancillary health services
   B. Nurses emerge as the critical lynchpin in interdisciplinary practice.
   C. Marginal sustainability, evaluation, and sound quality outcomes
   D. Imbedded accountability and responsibility for staff members

8. What is the nurse's best response to a peer that states, "We have always done our dressing changes this way!"
   A. "We do seem to get about the same results with these dressings but use more staff time."
   B. "The quality indicators are unclear about the outcomes on current dressing changes."
   C. "Each nurse must recognize the evidence for how interventions are done."
   D. "Let's add this topic to our next staff meeting with the sales representative."

9. What is a primary concern related to scoring or grading the level of evidence for inclusion into practice?
   A. The tools used lack classification for levels of mixed method studies.
   B. Clinicians level their discipline-specific theories to developed tools.
   C. There are too many tools, which makes finding one that is an appropriate level for the diverse clinical settings too difficult.
   D. Levels of evidence are to be highly considered when critiquing a research study to ensure that the evidence is credible.

10. Why are persistency and consistency important considerations when assessing the evidence?
    A. Support and strength are added to the quality of the study results.
    B. Expectancy shows whether an intervention performs as expected.
    C. Psychological aspects of the intervention are included in tool development.
    D. The impact on the consumer is easy to determine.

Discussion Questions

1. The Institute of Medicine's *Future of Nursing* report identified four central recommendations to advance the nursing profession and health care: (1) Nurses function at their full extent of knowledge and education, (2) nurses become active at the decision-making table, (3) there must be seamless academic progression for nurses to advance within the educational system, and (4) adequate and reliable data are required to advance health care. Carefully and thoughtfully consider these four recommendations in light of the use of EBP. How can the nursing profession best address these four central

recommendations related to EBP? How does implementing tools to grade/score evidence provide strength and rationales for using the evidence in daily healthcare practice?

2. Steelman and colleagues (2011) listed the task force recommendations for implementing the use of a rating scale within a site. The recommendations included determining the steps for completing an evidence review, establishing a consensus minimum for those involved in the review, developing educational materials to be used to update staff and committee members on the process, and allocating resources for the process. Based on these recommendations, what guidelines would you develop to be used in your setting to select and incorporate a rating system for evidence review?

Suggested Readings

Akbashev, M. Y., Pittman, J. R., & Dressler, D. D. (2017). Efficiently finding and using evidence to guide clinical practice and improve care. *Journal of the American Academy of Physician Assistants, 30*(11), 31–38. doi: 10.1097/01.JAA.0000525915.05473.01

Goodman, S. N. (2013). Bayesian methods for evidence evaluation: Are we there yet? *Circulation, 127*, 2367–2369.

Gray, M., Bliss, D., & Klem, M. L. (2015). Methods, levels of evidence, strength of recommendations for treatment statements for evidence-based report cards: A new beginning. *Journal of Wounds, Ostomy, and Continence Nursing, 42*(1), 16–18. doi: 10.1097/WON.0000000000000104

Matos, E. A. (2017, September/October). From best evidence to best practice. *Nursing Made Incredibly Easy*, 11–14. doi: 10.1097/01.NME.0000521817.82214.d9

Mick, J. (2017a). Call to action: How to implement evidence-based nursing practice. *Nursing2017. 47*(4), 36–43. doi: 10.1097/01.NURSE.000051603.0303.5c

Mick, J. (2017b). Funneling evidence into practice. *Nursing Management. 47*(4), 36–43. doi: 10.1097/01.NUMA.0000520719.70926.79

Oermann, M. H. (2012). Building evidence for practice: Not without dissemination. *MCN: The American Journal of Maternal Child Nursing, 37*(2), 77.

Porritt, K., Gomersall, J., & Lockwood, C. (2014). Study selection and critical appraisal: The steps following the literature search in a systematic review. *AJN, 144*(6), 47–52.

Riley, J. K., Hill, A. N., Krause, L. B., Leach, L. B., & Lowe, T. J. (2011). Examining nurses' attitudes regarding the value, role, interest, and experience in research in an acute care hospital. *Journal for Nurses in Staff Development, 27*(6), 272–279.

Robertson-Malt, S. (2014). Presenting and interpreting findings: The steps following data synthesis in a systematic review. *AJN, 114*(8), 49–54.

References

Agency for Healthcare Research and Quality. (2014). Improving primary care practice. Retrieved from http://www.ahrq.gov/professionals/prevention-chronic-care/improve/index.html

American Nurses Association. (2015). Code of ethics for nurses. Retrieved from http://www.nursingworld.org/codeofethics

American Nurses Association. (2018). Health system reform. Retrieved from http://www.nursingworld.org/healthcarereform

Brennan, C., & Parsons, G. (2017). Enhanced recovery in orthopedics: A prospective audit of an enhanced recovery program for patients undergoing hip or knee arthroplasty. *MEDSURG Nursing, 26*(2), 99–104.

Buchbinder, S. B. & Shanks, N.H. (2017). *Introduction to healthcare management* (3rd ed.). Burlington, MA: Jones and Bartlett.

Burman, M. E., Robinson, B., & Hart, A. M. (2013). Linking evidence-based nursing practice and patient-centered care through patient preferences. *Nursing Administration Quarterly, 37*(3), 231–241. doi: 10.1097/NAQ.0b013e318295ed6b

Chilcote, D. (2017). Intuition: A concept analysis. *Nursing Forum, 52*(1), 62–66.

Cortez-Gann, J., Gilmore, K. D., Foley, K. Q., Kennedy, M. B., McGee, T., & Kring, D. (2017). Blood transfusion vital sign frequency: What does the evidence say? *MEDSURG Nursing, 26*(2), 89–92.

Cumulative Index of Nursing and Allied Health library database. (2018). Evidence-Based Care Sheets. Retrieved from http://research.library.gsu.edu/c.php?g=115819&p=753890

Davoli, M., Amato, L., Clark, N., Farrell, M., Hickman, S. Hill, Magrini, N., Poznyak, V., & Holger, J. S. (2014). The role of Cochrane reviews in informing international guidelines: A case study of using the grading of recommendations, assessment, development, and evaluation system to develop World Health Organization guidelines for the psychosocially assisted pharmacological treatment of opioid dependence. *Society for the Study of Addiction, 110,* 891–898.

Dogherty, E. J., Harrison, M. B., Graham, I. D., Vandyk, A. D., & Keeping-Burke, L. (2013). Turning knowledge into action at the point-of-care: The collective experience of nurses facilitating the implementation of evidence-based practice. *Worldviews on Evidence-Based Nursing, 10*(3), 129–135.

Eaton, L. H., Meins, A. R., Mitchell, P. H., Voss, J., & Doorenbos, A. Z. (2015). Evidence-based practice beliefs and behaviors of nurses providing cancer pain management: A mixed-methods approach. *Oncology Nursing Forum, 42*(2), 165–172.

Farokhzadian, J., Khajouei, R., & Ahmadian, L. (2015). Evaluating factors associated with implementing evidence-based practice in nursing. *Journal of Evaluation in Clinical Practice: International Journal of Public Health Policy and Health Services Research, 21,* 1107–1113.

Finkelman, A., & Kenner, C. (2016). *Professional nursing concepts: Competencies for quality leadership* (3rd ed.). Burlington, MA: Jones & Bartlett Learning.

Finney, A., Johnson, K., Duffy, H., & Krysia, D. (2016). Critically appraised topics (CATs): A method of integrating best evidence into general practice nursing. *Practice Nurse, 46*(3), 32–34.

Fothergill, A., & Lipp, A. (2014). A guide to critiquing a research paper on clinical supervision: Enhancing skills for practice. *Journal of Psychiatric and Mental Health Nursing, 21*(9), 834–840.

Hain, D. J., & Kear, T. M. (2015). Using evidence-based practice to move beyond doing things the way we have always done them. *Nephrology Nursing Journal, 42*(1), 11–21.

Hanna, K. M., Weaver, M. T., Slaven, J. F., Fortenberry, J. D., & DiMeglio, L. A. (2014). Diabetes-related quality of life and the demands and burdens of diabetes care among emerging adults with type 1 diabetes in the year after high school graduation. *Research Nursing & Health, 37,* 399–408. doi: 10.1002/nur.21620

Hannele S., & Vehviläinen-Julkunen, K. (2016). The state of readiness for evidence-based practice among nurses: An integrative review. *The International Journal of Nursing Studies, 56,* 128–140.

Harper, M. G., Gallagher-Ford, L., Warren, J. I., Troseth, M., Sinnott, L. T., Thomas, B. K. (2017). Evidence-based practice and U.S. healthcare outcomes. *Journal for Nurses in Professional Development, 33*(4), 170–179.

Harvey Cushing/John Hay Whitney Medical Library. (n.d.). Evidence-based practice (EBP) resources. Retrieved from http://guides.library.yale.edu/EBP

Hauk, S., Winsett, R. P., & Kuric, J. (2012). Leadership facilitation strategies to establish evidence-based practice in an acute care hospital. *Journal of Advanced Nursing, 69*(3), 664–674. doi: 10.1111/j.1365-2648.2012.06053.x

Institute of Medicine. (2002). Health Professions Education Summit: Report of activity. Retrieved from http://www.iom.edu/Activities/Workforce/HealthProfessionsED/2002-Jun-17.aspx

Institute of Medicine. (2009). Roundtable on Evidence-Based Medicine: Charter and mission statement. Retrieved from http://www.ncbi.nlm.nih.gov/books/NBK52847/

Institute of Medicine. (2010). The future of nursing: Leading change, advancing health. Retrieved from http://www.nationalacademies.org/hmd/Reports/2010/The-Future-of-Nursing-Leading-Change-Advancing-Health.aspx

Institute of Medicine. (2015). Assessing the Progress on the IOM Report. Retrieved from http://www.nationalacademies.org/hmd/Reports/2015/Assessing-Progress-on-the-IOM-Report-The-Future-of-Nursing.aspx

Irwin, M., Berkman, R., & Richards, R. (2013). The experience of implementing evidence-based practice change: A qualitative analysis. *Clinical Journal of Oncology Nursing, 17*(5), 544–549.

Iverson, K. N., Huang, K., Wells, S. Y., Wright, J. D., Gerber, M. R., & Wiltsey-Stirman, S. (2014). Women veterans' preferences for intimate partner violence screening and response procedures within the Veterans Health Administration. *Research Nursing & Health, 37,* 302–311. doi: 10.1002 /nur.21602

Joanna Briggs Institute. (2012a). Grades of recommendation. Retrieved from http://joannabriggs .org/jbi-approach.html#tabbed-nav=Grades-of-Recommendation

Joanna Briggs Institute. (2012b). Levels of evidence FAME. Retrieved from http://joannabriggs.org /jbi-approach.html#tabbed-nav=Levels-of-Evidence

Johnston B., Coole, C., Narayansamy, M., Feakes, R. Whitworth, G., Tyrrell, T. & Hardy, B. (2016). Exploring the barriers to and facilitators of implementing research into practice. *British Journal of Community Nursing, 21*(9), 392–399.

Kander, M. (2014). How medical reimbursement works in skilled nursing facilities. *The ASHA LEADER, 19,* 26–27.

Kwan, T. M., & Sullivan, M. (2017). The use of intravenous ibuprofen and intravenous acetaminophen in surgical patients and the effect on opioid reduction. *MEDSURG Nursing, 26*(2), 124–131.

Lavizzo-Mourey, R. (2015). Joint statement on the Institute of Medicine's progress report on *The Future of Nursing.* Retrieved from https://www.rwjf.org/en/library/articles-and-news/2015/12 /statement-on-nursing-report.html

Lee, M. C., Johnson, K. L., Newhouse, R. P., & Warren, J. I. (2013). Evidence-based practice process quality assessment: EPQA guidelines. *Worldviews on Evidence-Based Nursing 10*(3), 140–149.

Loversidge, J. (2016). A call for extending the utility of evidence-based practice: Adapting EBP for health policy impact. *Worldviews on Evidence-Based Nursing, 13*(6), 399–401.

Makic, M. B. F., Rauen, C., Watson, R., & Poteet, A. W. (2014). Examining the evidence to guide practice: Challenging practice habits. *Critical Care Nurse, 34*(2), 28–44.

Melnyk, B. M., & Fineout-Overholt, E. (2015). *Evidence-based practice in nursing & healthcare: A guide to best practice* (3rd ed.). Philadelphia, PA: Wolters Kluwer.

Melnyk, B. M., Gallagher-Ford, L., & Fineout-Overholt, E. (2017). *Implementing the evidence-based practice (EBP) competencies in healthcare: A practical guide for improving quality, safety, & outcomes.* Sigma Theta Tau International.

Mick, J. (2015). Addition of a decision point in evidence-based practice process steps to distinguish EBP, research and quality improvement methodologies. *Worldviews on Evidence-Based Nursing, 12*(3), 179–181.

Milstead, J. A. (2016). *Health policy and politics* (5th ed.). Burlington, MA: Jones & Bartlett Learning.

Nickitas, D. M., & Mensik, J. (2015). Exploring nurse staffing through excellence: A data-driven model. *Nurse Leader, 13*(1), 40–47. doi: 10.1016/j.mni.2014.1.1.006

Nickitas, D. M., Middaugh, D. J., & Aries, N. (2016). *Policy and politics for nurses and other health professionals* (2nd ed.). Burlington, MA: Jones & Bartlett Learning.

Nursing Alliance for Quality Care. (2016). Retrieved from http://www.naqc.org

Peterson, M. H., Barnason, S., Donnelly, B., Hill, K., Miley, H., & Whiteman, K. (2014). Choosing the best evidence to guide clinical practice: Application of AACN levels of evidence. *Critical Care Nurse, 34*(2), 58–68.

Polit, D. F., & Beck, C. T (2017). *Nursing research: Generating and assessing evidence for nursing practice* (10th ed.). Philadelphia, PA: Wolters Kluwer/Lippincott Williams & Wilkins.

Rosswurm, M. A., & Larrabee, J. H. (2007). A model for change to evidence-based practice. *Image: The Journal of Nursing Scholarship, 31*(4). Retrieved from https://doi.org/10.1111/j.1547-5369 .1999.tb00510.x

Savage, C. L., Kub, J. E., & Groves, S. L. (2016). *Public health science and nursing practice: Caring for populations.* Philadelphia, PA: F.A. Davis Company.

Schreiber, J. A. (2013). Beyond evidence-based practice-achieving fundamental changes in research and practice. *Oncology Nursing Forum, 40*(3), 208–210.

Steelman, V. M., Pape, T., King, C. A., Graling, P., & Gaberson, K. B. (2011). Selection of a method to rate the strength of scientific evidence for AORN recommendations. *AORN Journal, 93*(4), 433–444.

Stevens, K. (2013). The impact of evidence-based practice in nursing and the next big ideas. *OJIN: The Online Journal of Issues in Nursing, 18*(2), 4.

SUNY Downstate Medical Center. (2014). *Guide to research methods.* Retrieved from http://library .downstate.edu/EBM2/2100.htm

U.S. Department of Health and Human Services. (2017, November 23). Centers for Medicare and Medicaid Services. *Medicare & You.* CMS product number 10050.

U.S. Preventive Service Task Force. (2007). Slide presentation from the AHRQ 2007 annual conference. Retrieved from http://archive.ahrq.gov/about/annualmtg07/0927slides/finch/Finch-28.html

U.S. Preventive Services Task Force. (2009). Slide presentation from the AHRQ 2008 annual conference. Retrieved from http://www.ahrq.gov/about/annualmtg08/090808slides/Lin2.htm

Visovsky, C., Maguire, D., Zambroski, J., & Palacios, L. (2017). Bringing evidence-based practice to Latin America: Transforming nursing education and practice. *The Journal of Continuing Education in Nursing; Thorofare, 48*(11), 512–516.

Warren, J. I., McLaughlin, M., Bardsley, J., Eich, J., Esche, C. A., Kropkowski, L., & Risch, S. (2016). The strengths and challenges of implementing EBP in healthcare systems, *Worldviews on Evidence-Based Nursing, 13*(1), 15–24.

Woolston, W., & Connelly, L. M. (2017). Felty's syndrome: A qualitative case study. *MEDSURG Nursing, 26*(2), 105–109.

CHAPTER 3
Overview of Research

Sharon Cannon and Margaret Robinson

CHAPTER OBJECTIVES

At the conclusion of this chapter, the learner will be able to:
1. Discuss the evolution of evidence-based practice (EBP), nursing research, and current healthcare trends.
2. Identify the value of using models and frameworks in nursing research.
3. Differentiate between basic and applied research.
4. Delineate sources for nursing research.

KEY TERMS

Applied research
Basic research
Best practice
Bundling

National Center for Nursing Research (NCNR)
National Institute of Nursing Research (NINR)
National Institutes of Health (NIH)

▶ Introduction

The roots of research utilization can be traced back to the time of Florence Nightingale in the mid-1800s. Over the past 160 years, nursing research has encompassed a variety of models, settings, and foci. The following historical perspective illustrates the trajectory of nursing research.

▶ Historical Perspective

Evolution from Nightingale to the Present

Florence Nightingale's work on sanitation in the 1800s was one of the early efforts at linking environmental variables to clinical outcomes. In the early 1900s, the focal point of nursing research was on nursing education. In the 1940s, the concentration shifted to the availability of and demand for nurses in time of war. A major milestone occurred in 1952 when the first edition of the journal *Nursing Research* was published. In the 1970s, clinical outcomes again reemerged as a focus for nursing research, and the *Nursing Studies Index* by Virginia Henderson was produced. Today, through evidence-based practice (EBP), the focus is on the application of research findings to clinical decision making in an effort to improve individual patient outcomes.

Florence Nightingale's (1858) *Notes on Matters Affecting the Health, Efficiency and Hospital Administration of the British Army* was one of the first published works that outlined the clinical application of nursing research (Florence Nightingale Museum Trust, 2003; Riddle, 2005). Florence Nightingale created a polar-area diagram (or coxcomb) to display data related to the causes of mortality in the British Army during the Crimean War (**FIGURE 3-1**). This early pie chart used color graphics to depict deaths secondary to preventable disease, war injuries, and all other causes. Using these data, Nightingale calculated the mortality rate for contagious diseases such as cholera and typhus. Her statistical analysis demonstrated the need for sanitary reform in military hospitals.

🔲 THINK OUTSIDE THE BOX

Explore the various approaches used to generate knowledge in your practice area. For example, which information has been used to determine the method of catheterizing a laboring mother? Which information serves as the basis for the range of blood sugars used in elderly patients who are newly diagnosed with diabetes?

🔲 THINK OUTSIDE THE BOX

What would Florence Nightingale say about nursing research and EBP today?

Federal support for nursing research began in 1946, with the creation of the Division of Nursing within the Office of the Surgeon General. In 1955, the **National Institutes of Health (NIH)** established the Nursing Research Study Section. At the same time in 1955, the American Nursing Foundation was established to promote nursing research (American Nurses Foundation, 2018). A 1983 study entitled *Nursing and Nursing Education: Public Policy and Private Actions*, published by the Institute of Medicine (IOM) (1983), recommended that nursing research be included in the mainstream of health-related research. With growing public support, the Health Research Extension Act of 1985 authorized the development of the **National Center for Nursing Research (NCNR)** at the NIH. The NIH Revitalization Act of 1993 elevated NCNR to an NIH Institute and established the **National Institute of Nursing Research (NINR)** (n.d.).

> The National Institute of Nursing Research supports basic and clinical research to establish a scientific basis for the care of individuals across the lifespan—from the management of the patient during illness and recovery to the reduction of risks for disease and disability, and the promotion of healthy lifestyles. (NINR, 2013)

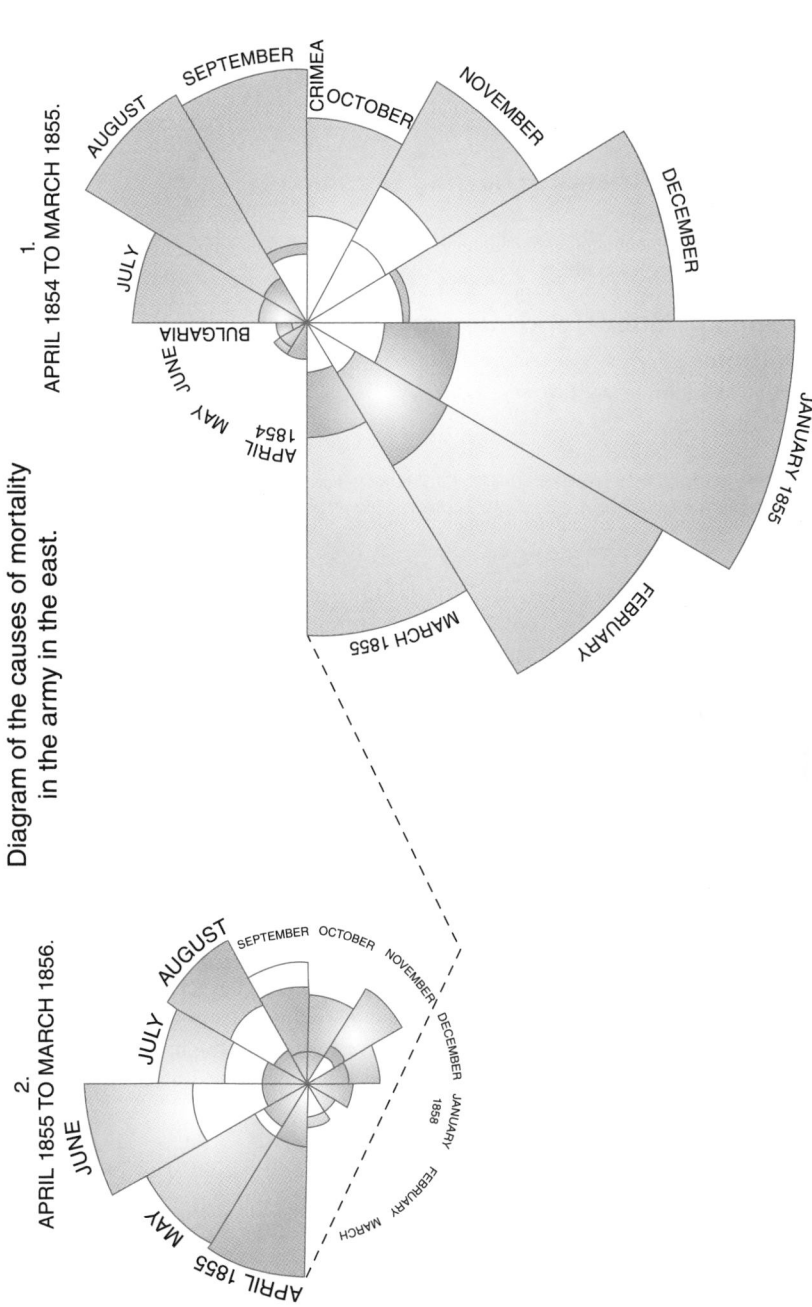

Diagram of the causes of mortality in the army in the east.

1. APRIL 1854 TO MARCH 1855.

2. APRIL 1855 TO MARCH 1856.

FIGURE 3-1 Polar-area diagram.

Nightingale, F. (1858). *Notes on matters affecting the health, efficiency and hospital administration of the British Army*. London, UK: Harrison and Sons. As cited in Riddle, L. (2005). Polar-area diagram: Biographies of women mathematicians. Retrieved from http://www.agnesscott.edu/lriddle/women /nightpiechart.htm

---

BOX 3-1 Areas of Focus for Nursing Research

Leading Reform in Nursing Education
Education-Practice Linkage
Domain-Specific Knowledge
Technology in Nursing Education

Advancing the Science of Nursing Education
Robust Research Designs
Educational Measurement and Evaluation
Research Scholar Development

Developing National and International Leaders in Nursing Education
Nursing Education Workforce Diversity
Building Capacity

Reproduced from National Institute of Nursing Research (NINR). (2015). NLN research priorities in nursing education 2012-2015. Retrieved from http://www.nln.org/docs/default-source/default-document-library/researchpriorities.pdf?sfvrsn=2

The strategic planning process at NINR identified areas of focus for prospective nursing research (**BOX 3-1**). In April 1993, the board of directors of the American Nurses Association (ANA, 1993) adopted a position statement that acknowledged the following: "Research based practice is essential if the nursing profession is to meet its mandate to society for effective and efficient patient care" (p. 1). It went on to identify the role of nursing research for the associate degree in nursing (ADN), bachelor of science in nursing (BSN), master of science in nursing (MSN), and the doctoral-prepared practitioner. The position statement outlined a process whereby clinicians identify relevant clinical problems for investigation and researchers design studies to address these problems (**BOX 3-2**).

Early nursing research focused on the development of the profession of nursing, not the clinical practice of nursing. In 1970, a study conducted by Lysaught

> revealed that little nursing research has been conducted on the actual effect of nursing interventions and that nursing had few definitive guidelines for its practice. The study recommended that investigation of the impact of nursing care on the quality, effectiveness and economy of health care be conducted. (Polit & Hungler, 1978, p. 11)

Thus, began a new era in which clinical practice emerged as a priority for nursing research.

⏻ THINK OUTSIDE THE BOX

Discuss the barriers you might encounter when trying to implement EBP and research utilization in your area.

BOX 3-2 Research Roles at Various Levels of Nursing Education

Associate Degree
Helping to identify clinical problems in nursing practice
Assisting with the collection of data within a structured format
Using nursing research findings appropriately in clinical practice in conjunction with nurses holding more advanced credentials

Baccalaureate Degree
Identifying clinical problems requiring investigation
Assisting experienced investigators to gain access to clinical sites
Influencing the selection of appropriate methods of data collection
Collecting data and implementing nursing research findings

Master's Degree
Collaborating with experienced investigators in proposal development, data collection, data analysis, and interpretation
Appraising the clinical relevance of research findings
Creating a climate in the practice setting that promotes scholarly inquiry, scientific integrity, and scientific investigation of clinical nursing problems
Providing leadership for integrating findings into clinical practice

Reproduced from American Nurses Association (ANA). (1993). Position statement: Education for participation in nursing research. Retrieved from http://nursingworld.org/MainMenuCategories/Policy-Advocacy/Positions-and-Resolutions/ANAPositionStatements/Archives/rseducat14484.html. Courtesy of American Nurses Association. This is a retired position statement and is no longer ANA's official position on the issue.

In the 1980s, clinical pathways were introduced into nursing practice. A clinical pathway is a plan of care developed by a multidisciplinary team that outlines the sequential care that should be provided to a predictable group of patients. Early clinical pathways focused on high-volume admissions in the acute care setting, such as elective surgeries and routine obstetrical care. Clinical pathways should incorporate the applicable research. However, the intent of a clinical pathway is to manage the progression of an individual patient through a clinical event. These pathways emerged in response to shifting payment methods for health care and focused on the critical path, whose steps must be accomplished for the patient to have a cost-effective and timely discharge. Measures of success generally were a reduction in the total cost to provide care and a reduction in the average length of stay for each patient. In the late 1990s, a growing concern arose that many hospitals had adopted clinical pathways without strong evidence that they were clinically or economically effective.

The emergence of EBP takes the application of research one step further to focus on outcomes-based practices. The emphasis is now on the assessment and evaluation of clinical practices that have demonstrated their ability to improve morbidity and mortality for patients. Frequently, multiple interventions have been identified that together enhance the clinical outcome; this practice has come to be known as **bundling**. A bundle is a group of interventions related to a disease or care process that, when executed together, result in better outcomes than when the interventions are implemented individually. Evidence suggests that consistently implementing these practices with all patients who have a specific disease or procedure can improve patient outcomes (Institute for Healthcare Improvement, 2006). In 2005, the Institute for Healthcare Improvement introduced care bundles for the prevention of central-line infection and ventilator-acquired pneumonia as part of the 100,000 Lives Campaign. In this case, the outcomes-based practices focus on a single aspect of care that is known to have serious complications.

Blending evidence-based research and applying it to clinical practice and patient outcomes were goals of the work of the IOM (1999) in its landmark publication *To Err Is Human: Building a Safer Health System*. In the preparation of this report, research in human factors was applied to health care in an attempt to understand where and why systems or processes break down. Specifically, the report's authors looked at how practices in healthcare settings could be made safer to prevent adverse outcomes for patients.

In 2004, the IOM expanded its original work to look at the work environment of nurses in its publication *Keeping Patients Safe: Transforming the Work Environment of Nurses* (IOM, 2004). This report further described the need for bundles of mutually reinforcing patient safety defenses as part of the effort to reduce errors and increase patient safety. It described "bundles of changes" that are needed within four aspects of care to strengthen patient safety: (1) leadership and management, (2) the workforce, (3) the work process, and (4) organizational culture. The IOM in 2010 suggested major challenges in providing health care with an emphasis on primary care versus specialty care in the community instead of acute care facilities (IOM, 2010).

As EBP emerged, a major shift occurred beginning in 2010. National trends began to emphasize patient outcomes, cost containment, and reimbursement related to hospital readmissions. In addition, demand for patient involvement in healthcare decision making has been emphasized even more: No longer would health care be "doing for" the patient; rather, it would be "doing with" the patient. The importance of EBP and research is currently focused on patient-centered care. The recent establishment of the Patient-Centered Outcomes Research Institute (PCORI) is a result of the Affordable Care Act (ACA), which is a prime example of efforts to make the patient the center of care and to make the provision of outcomes specific to the patient (National Pharmaceutical Council, 2012). In addition, the IOM established 10 priorities for research that include specific diagnostic criteria and treatments for current and future health issues.

Along with recommendations of the IOM, the Agency for Healthcare Research and Quality (AHRQ) continues to provide extensive review of evidence for patient care (Bator, Taylor, & Catalano, 2015; Ciliska, DiCenso, Milnyk, & Stetler, 2005). AHRQ focuses on the quality and safety of patient care and designs processes to speed up the usage of EBP in practice (Bator et al., 2015).

Recent changes in Medicare/Medicaid reimbursement have also forced healthcare organizations to reexamine how services are provided. Gold (2014) indicates the ACA is also the impetus for the provision of accountable care organizations (ACOs), which are regulated by the Centers for Medicare and Medicaid Services (CMS). A major area of concern for CMS is quality reporting and performance of ACOs, which include: "(1) patient experience of care; (2) care coordination; (3) patient safety; (4) preventive health; and (5) at-risk population/frail elderly health" (Gordon, 2011, p. 2).

Obviously, research and EBP will play a significant role in patient-centered care and ACOs in the future. Quality assurance/quality improvement (QA/QI) initiatives will provide the necessary evidence for generating knowledge about what does and does not work. Nursing EBP and research will be heavily involved in the years to come.

The major rationale for conducting research is to build a body of nursing knowledge, thereby promoting improvement in patient outcomes. This building of knowledge is accomplished by using results of research in the provision of nursing care that is based on scientific data rather than on a hunch, a gut feeling, or "the way I was taught." As a profession, nursing must hold its members accountable for providing safe, cost-effective, and efficient care. EBP that incorporates research findings is a model for nurses to use in their practice.

▶ Theory, Research, and Practice

Parker and Smith (2010) define theories as "organizing structures of our reflections, observations, projections and inferences" (p. 7). Fain (2009) defines research as "a systematic inquiry into a subject that uses various approaches (quantitative and qualitative methods) to answer questions and solves problems" (p. 5). Polit and Beck (2008) define research as "a systematic inquiry that uses disciplined methods to answer question or solve problems" (p. 3). Research can be more readily considered a specific explanation. Fawcett and Garity (2009) have an interesting approach to theories and EBP. They suggest, "theories can be thought of as evidence" (p. 6). The theory becomes evidence to guide practice. Research is therefore equal to theory development.

When considering the relationship between theory and research, one could conclude that theory gives direction to research, which in turn guides practice. As a result, many nursing research projects include a nursing theory/theoretical framework and concepts to guide the research and provide implications for nursing practice.

The evolution of the relationship of theory to research to practice has been ongoing since the days of Florence Nightingale. The current emphasis in research is on translational research and implementation science. These changes move theory into a new dimension for application to practice. If translational research is seen as a method to move a theory into another dimension, and if implementation science is perceived as supporting EBP and research utilization, then the relationship to practice is further enhanced and becomes stronger. Thus, implementing research (evidence) and theory into practice (translation) optimizes EBP.

It is beyond the scope of this text to examine theory in depth. Sometimes a theory is not identified for a research or evidence-based project; however, a theory is still important. The researcher or nurse using evidence to guide nursing care must, at the very least, incorporate a model, framework, plan, or system that gives direction to the project. Van Achterberg, Schoonhoven, and Grol (2008) connect models to research and theories for implementation of EBP.

⟳ THINK OUTSIDE THE BOX

Which model and/or theoretical frameworks do you think can be most appropriate for a medical/surgical unit?

Models and Frameworks

Nursing research is a way to explain and predict the care that nurses provide, including the underlying rationale. As a result, models of nursing care and their frameworks provide ample opportunities for the generation of new nursing knowledge. As Malloch and Porter-O'Grady (2006) indicate, "Professional Care Models give nurses responsibility and authority to provide patient care. In addition, nurses are accountable for coordinating care and ensuring that continuity of care is provided across the continuum. Patients' unique needs are addressed to achieve outcomes" (p. 236).

Merriam-Webster (2018b) defines a model as "a pattern that suggests a clear and detailed prototype" (p. 2 of 10). Many nursing care models and research models are prototypes of problem-solving processes that begin with a question. Nurses ask clinical questions on a daily basis and often conduct research on an informal basis. When a nurse observes the same phenomenon occurring with multiple patients having the same diagnosis, a pattern emerges. The nurse has validated, through experience, his or her observations, just not in a formal, structured research model. As Burns and Grove (2009) state, "A framework is an abstract, logical structure of meaning. It guides the development of the study and enables you to link the findings to the body of knowledge used in nursing" (p. 126). When a theory is not used, a care model, plan, or system is needed in EBP and research. A model, plan, or system then functions as a framework.

Validation of Best Practices

Best practice is a term used by many different types of professionals in many different settings. The definition of *best practices* varies depending on the meanings assigned to the words *best* and *practices*. Bator and colleagues (2015) suggest "best practice is defined as clinical nursing actions that are based on 'best evidence' available from nursing research" (p. 593). According to the College of Nursing Iowa (2018), best practice incorporates "core concepts, interventions and techniques that are grounded in research and know to promote higher quality care and living for older people" (p. 1 of 5). Merriam-Webster (2018a) defines *best practice* as "a procedure that has been shown by research and experience to produce optimal results and that is established or proposed as a standard suitable for widespread adoption" (p. 1). In this text, *best practices* is defined as those nursing actions that produce the most desirable patient outcomes through scientific data and are a standard for widespread adoption.

🔁 THINK OUTSIDE THE BOX

Most of the research projects associated with EBP tend to be examples of applied research. Brainstorm some possible projects that would be classified as basic research.

For best practices, research utilization supports decision making for nursing practice through a problem-solving process. Reaffirmation through scientific data validates the desired outcomes and reinforces best practices. This reaffirmation is an excellent example for reality testing. While a wealth of information is available, nurses have little time to look for information and therefore often practice as they were taught. At times, a nurse thinks or feels that the result of an action is accurate when it actually is not. Burns and Grove (2001) cite an example related to patient consumption of oxygen. The nurse's sense might be that getting a patient up to the bedside commode results in more oxygen consumption than when the patient uses a bedpan. However, research has shown this is not accurate. Thus, reality can be tested through scientific inquiry, which leads to validated best practice.

Fineout-Overholt and Melnyk (2005) suggest that *best practice* is a term used by others, not just healthcare providers. According to these authors, "without well-designed research, best practices cannot claim universal application" (p. 27); consensus builds best practices that are achieved through evidence.

Simpson (2005) suggests that, through EBP, nurses could overlook the truth about nursing practice. Nurses need to look at what practice is and what is really done. Perhaps, research and practice need to merge to have a major impact on practice. Through this merger, practice and research would combine to become a validated best practice. Hopp and Rittenmeyer (2012) promote the term "best available research evidence" for making decisions based on the best evidence (p. 13).

Nelson (2014) conducted a concept analysis and postulates that best practice "represents quality care which is deemed optimal based on a prevailing standard or point of view" (p. 1).

Basic Versus Applied Research

Basic research can be defined as research to gain knowledge for knowledge's sake (Brockopp & Hastings-Tolsma, 2003; Burns & Grove, 2009; Fain, 2009). Another way to look at basic research is that it tests theories (Fawcett & Garity, 2009). Sometimes basic research is also called bench research, such as laboratory experiments intended to elucidate cell structure. Simply stated, basic research is often useful later when, for example, a researcher addresses how a new drug being tested affects a cell's structure. Fain (2009) indicates that basic research is conducted with little concern for how it might ultimately be applied to practice.

⚙ THINK OUTSIDE THE BOX

Apply Florence Nightingale's ideas about preventable diseases to research and EBP.

In contrast, **applied research** has a direct impact on practice and modifies current practice. Cherry (2018) suggests applied research solves practical problems. Most nursing research is applied research that assists in decision making related to nursing care. Applied research occurs in multiple settings and with diverse populations. This type of research can also include the development of new approaches for care. Modification, development, and evaluation of nursing care through best practice form the heart of EBP. Applied research builds a body of knowledge for nursing practice and guides the nurse in providing patient care. An example of applied research in nursing would be a study that generates new information about the use of soap and water versus hand-cleansing gels in preparation for a sterile dressing change. An applied research project might indicate that soap and water are more effective in preventing potential wound infections. The nurse would then use the applied research results in preparation for doing a sterile dressing change.

Basic research differs from applied research primarily in terms of its focus and intent. Basic science (also known as bench science) is conducted in a laboratory and seeks to add to the knowledge base. Applied research is grounded in the practice area and its application to practice. Fain (2009) suggests that, while basic research and applied research are quite different, they can be considered on a continuum where basic research is required for interpretation of findings of applied studies. One might say that basic research in nursing is building a body of knowledge (theory) and that applied research is the application of the theory to the clinical arena (practice).

▶ Sources for Nursing Research

Most nursing research comes from two primary sources: academia and healthcare settings. One might expect that nurses doing research in academic settings would focus only on educational research and that those conducting research in health care would focus only on practice settings. Although that distinction may hold true in some cases, most often both areas produce research for both education and practice because they are closely aligned with each other.

Academia

A major thrust of research in education is the evaluation of programs, technologies, and instructional design. Research in education flourished from the mid-1980s until about 2001, when funding for nursing education withered. An act of Congress specified that no funding from the NCNR could be distributed for research in nursing education (Diekelmann, 2001). As a result, nurse educators had to seek funding outside the discipline, where the competition was intense. Consequently, little nursing education research was conducted. Nurse-educator researchers turned to research in clinical practice. Although that effort translated into some positive gains for clinical practice, it drastically affected the research needed to support innovative programs, teaching/learning activities, and other aspects of nursing education.

Since 2000, when the National League for Nursing (NLN) was reorganized, increased emphasis and financial support have been directed toward research in nursing education. In its reorganization, the NLN (n.d.) recognized the need for a "quality nursing education that prepares the nursing workforce to meet the needs of diverse populations in an ever changing healthcare environment . . . and to change the landscape related to funding for nursing education research . . . to lead in promoting evidence-based teaching in nursing" (p. 1). This commitment to nursing education research is also expressed in the NLN's mission and goal statements. Nurse educators have recognized the need to continue seeking external funds from outside the discipline. Grants have also come from several government agencies and foundations. The current impetus for obtaining funding from outside sources is a direct result of the nursing shortage and reports on health care generated by agencies such as the IOM. Due to the nursing shortage (which appears destined to last for years), research in nursing education has a promising future. The relationship with EBP will likely remain in the forefront when such research in nursing education is carried out.

Healthcare Settings

For healthcare settings to serve as a source for nursing practice, a process for research is necessary. In Chapter 2, Figure 2-3 is a flowchart detailing the steps to commonly follow when conducting quantitative or qualitative research in healthcare settings. The flowchart assists the nurse in identifying the best process for obtaining a sound conclusion for the best method to address the problem. Using the flowchart, the nurse can identify the problem and determine the research question and the research methodology (either quantitative or qualitative). It is important to note that outcomes of research and EBP determine what works and what doesn't work. In many ways, the research process is similar to the nursing process of assess, plan, implement, and evaluate. According to Cronenwett (2002), in 1999 Marita Titler observed that outcomes achieved in a research study might not be replicated with multiple caregivers in the natural clinical setting. The variable demands on the bedside nurse and multiple comorbidities that exist in the hospitalized patient can make it difficult to replicate findings. Cronenwett (2002) has noted, "evidence for practice mounts slowly over time, as scientists discover first what works in controlled environments and second what works in daily clinical practice" (p. 3).

Today, it is our challenge to move from a focus solely on research development to the use of valid and reliable evidence in clinical practice. Nurses have been identified as champions in the adoption of EBP. It is equally important that healthcare institutions implement mechanisms that diffuse available evidence into the practice environment.

▧ THINK OUTSIDE THE BOX

Many nursing theories can be found in the literature. Conduct a search to find evidence of nursing research utilization of a selected theory.

Summary Points

1. Florence Nightingale's work emphasized clinical applications of nursing research through the creation of a polar-area diagram.
2. From 1900 to 1940, nursing research focused on nursing education.
3. The first issue of *Nursing Research* was published in the 1950s with the notion to share research information with colleagues. The American Nursing Foundation was also established in the 1950s to promote nursing research.
4. The 1960s focused on models and frameworks of nursing practice.
5. In the 1970s, Virginia Henderson introduced the *Nursing Studies Index*.
6. In the 1980s, the Institute of Medicine recommended that nursing research be included in health-related research. In addition, the National Center for Nursing Research was established.
7. In the 1990s and 2000, both the National League for Nursing and American Nurses Association developed position papers on research-based practice.
8. In 2004, the Institute of Medicine published *Keeping Patients Safe: Transforming the Work Environment for Nurses*, which focused on the need for

bundles of mutually reinforcing patient safety defenses as part of the effort to reduce errors and increase patient safety.

9. Recent national trends such as the ACA have had a major impact on the way care is delivered and emphasize the importance of QA/QI.
10. Models and frameworks of professional practice are validated through research.
11. EBP incorporates research as a professional care model.
12. Basic research is gaining knowledge for knowledge's sake.
13. Applied research has a direct impact on practice.
14. Sources for research in nursing can be found in academic and healthcare settings.
15. The research process can be defined by a series of detailed steps.

⚑ RED FLAGS

- Research projects should be grounded by a model or theoretical framework to anchor the concepts identified within the project.
- Assumptions about best practices must be based on scientific evidence rather than just on everyday consensus of opinion or intuition.

Case Scenario

Incorporation of EBP into bedside nursing generally requires a change in nursing practice. Change theory models point out that each change process inevitably has potential barriers to effective implementation of the desired change. To implement EBP more effectively, one must identify these barriers to implementation of change. Fink, Thompson, and Bonnes (2005) conducted a nursing research project in an attempt to better understand barriers to implementation of nursing research among inpatient nursing units at a large, university-affiliated Magnet hospital:

> The purpose of this study was to examine the effect of multifaceted organizational strategies on registered nurses' (RNs') use of research findings to change practice in an academic hospital. The specific aims were to (1) identify nurses' attitudes and perceptions about organizational culture and research utilization, (2) identify perceived barriers and facilitators to nurses' use of research in practice, and (3) determine which factors are correlated with research utilization. (Fink et al., 2005, p. 121)

Survey tools, including the BARRIERS to Research Utilization Scale and the Research Factor Questionnaire, were used to gather data. The majority of respondents (83%) were registered nurses who held a baccalaureate or advanced degree in nursing. The results demonstrated an improvement in nurses' perception after implementation of multifaceted interventions. The authors also identified journal club participation as a major strategy to facilitate the use of research in clinical nursing practice.

Case Scenario Questions

1. How might the findings vary in a(n):
   - academic teaching facility that was not a Magnet hospital?
   - community-based hospital setting?
   - outpatient or procedural-based nursing practice?
   - hospital setting that has primarily ADN graduates?
2. What do you anticipate would be the findings in your own clinical practice environment?
3. If you implemented a journal club, do you believe that it would increase the use of research findings in your clinical practice area? Why or why not?

Multiple-Choice Questions

1. The research role of the BSN nurse includes:
   A. identifying clinical problems that require investigation, assisting experienced investigators to gain access to clinical sites, and collecting data.
   B. creating a climate in the practice setting that promotes scholarly inquiry, scientific integrity, and scientific investigation of clinical nursing problems.
   C. collaborating with experienced investigators in proposal development, data collection, data analysis, and interpretation of results.
   D. providing leadership in integrating research into practice.

2. Potential areas of nursing research identified by the National Institute of Nursing Research include:
   A. stem cell research.
   B. application of pharmaceuticals in clinical practice.
   C. chronic illness, health promotion, disease prevention, and end-of-life care.
   D. healthcare literacy.

3. What year was the first issue of *Nursing Research* published?
   A. 1858
   B. 1952
   C. 1985
   D. 1992

4. The *Nursing Studies Index*, the first annotated index of nursing research, was the work of:
   A. Florence Nightingale.
   B. Virginia Henderson.
   C. Marita Titler.
   D. Dorothea Orem.

5. The American Nurses Association position statement acknowledges that:
   A. researchers identify clinical problems and study them.
   B. faculty members identify clinical problems and study them.
   C. clinicians identify clinical problems and researchers design them.
   D. faculty members and researchers identify clinical problems and study them.

6. Clinical pathways are developed by:
    A. nursing teams.
    B. physician teams.
    C. educator teams.
    D. multidisciplinary teams.

7. A bundle is a group of interventions related to a disease or care process that:
    A. results in better outcomes than when the interventions are implemented together.
    B. results in diverse outcomes when the interventions are implemented individually.
    C. results in confusing information about a single disease or care process.
    D. provides insufficient evidence to alter clinical practice related to individualized interventions.

8. Professional care models give nurses:
    A. accountability.
    B. authority.
    C. responsibility.
    D. all of these.

9. Best practice is an excellent example of which kind of testing?
    A. Cognitive
    B. Reality
    C. Didactic
    D. Evaluation

10. Basic research is also known as bench research and is defined as research to gain knowledge for:
    A. use in academia.
    B. use in clinical practice.
    C. knowledge's sake.
    D. use in biochemistry.

11. Applied research builds a body of knowledge for nursing practice because it is the basis of:
    A. EBP.
    B. clinical pathways.
    C. nursing processes.
    D. nursing diagnoses.

12. Sources for nursing research come primarily from two sources:
    A. business and occupational settings.
    B. academic and healthcare settings.
    C. urban and rural settings.
    D. pharmaceutical and business settings.

13. Best practices in nursing can be defined as:
    A. a well-written plan of nursing care.
    B. a systems approach to nursing care.
    C. nursing actions that produce desirable patient outcomes.
    D. a way for nurses to justify their care.

14. The Institute of Medicine's publication *Keeping Patients Safe* focuses on:
    A. building a safer health system.
    B. processes to report medication errors.
    C. transforming the work environment for nurses.
    D. healthcare reform.

15. Theories are:
    A. a guide for research and practice.
    B. considered to be a specific explanation of an idea.
    C. not essential to research or EBP.
    D. static and do not change over time.

16. QA/QI data are now considered:
    A. valid research to guide practice.
    B. valid evidence to guide practice.
    C. generalizable to all practice.
    D. unlimited to any practice.

17. The research process allows for:
    A. the best method to address the problems.
    B. little comparison of outcomes.
    C. limited measures of evaluation.
    D. extra time for the nurse at the bedside.

Discussion Questions

1. Identify potential opportunities for you to use EBP in your current clinical setting.
2. Identify barriers to implementing EBP in your clinical setting.
3. Identify three clinical problems requiring investigation in your nursing practice. What steps might you take to begin to explore these identified problem areas?
4. Compare your QA/QI data to national standards.

Suggested Readings

Booth, W. C., Colomb, G. G., & Williams, J. M. (2003). *The craft of research* (2nd ed.). Chicago, IL: University of Chicago.

Dimsdale, K., & Kutner, M. (2004). Becoming an educated consumer of research: A quick look at the basic methodologies of research design. Retrieved from http://www.air.org/files/Becoming_an_Educated_Consumer_of_Research.pdf

Gerrish, K., & Lacey, A. (2006). *The research process in nursing* (5th ed.). Oxford, UK: Blackwell.

Gold, J. (2014). FAQs on ACOs: Accountable care organizations explained. Retrieved from http://khn.org/news/aco-accountable-care-organization-faq/

Johnson, B., & Webber, P. (2005). *An introduction to theory and reasoning in nursing* (2nd ed.). Philadelphia, PA: Lippincott Williams & Wilkins.

Kilbom, J., & Cogdill, S. (2004). Writing abstracts. St. Cloud State University and LEO: Literacy Education Online. Retrieved from http://leo.stcloudstate.edu/bizwrite/abstracts.html

Shirey, M. R. (2006, July/September). Evidence-based practice: How nurse leaders can facilitate innovation. *Nursing Administration Quarterly, 30*(3), 252–265.

van Meijel, B., Gamel, C., van Swieten-Duijfjes, B., & Grypdonck, M. H. F. (2004). The development of evidence-based nursing interventions: Methodological considerations. *Journal of Advanced Nursing, 48*(1), 84–92.

References

American Nurses Association (ANA). (1993). Position statement: Education for participation in nursing research. Retrieved from http://nursingworld.org/MainMenuCategories/Policy-Advocacy/Positions-and-Resolutions/ANAPositionStatements/Archives/rseducat14484.html

American Nurses Foundation (2018). History. Retrieved from https://americannusresassociation

Bator, S., Taylor, S., & Catalano, J. T. (2015). Nursing research and evidence based practice. In J. Catalano (Ed.), *Nursing now!: Today's issues, tomorrow's trends* (7th ed., pp. 581–674). Philadelphia, PA: F.A. Davis.

Brockopp, D. Y., & Hastings-Tolsma, M. T. (2003). *Fundamentals of nursing research* (3rd ed.). Sudbury, MA: Jones and Bartlett.

Burns, N., & Grove, S. K. (2001). *The practice of nursing research: Conduct, critique, and utilization* (4th ed.). Philadelphia, PA: W. B. Saunders.

Burns, N., & Grove, S. K. (2009). *The practice of nursing research: Appraisal, synthesis, and generation of evidence* (6th ed.). St. Louis, MO: Saunders Elsevier.

Cherry, K. (2018). What is applied research? Retrieved from https://www.verywellmind.com/What-is-applied-research-2794820

Ciliska, D., DiCenso, A., Melnyk, B. M., & Stetler, C. B. (2005). Using models or strategies for evidence-based practice. In B. M. Melnyk & E. Fineout-Overholt (Eds.), *Evidence-based practice in nursing and health care* (pp. 39–70). Philadelphia, PA: Lippincott Williams & Wilkins.

College of Nursing Iowa. (2018). Csomay Center—Best practices for health care professionals. Retrieved from https://nursing.uiowa.edu/hartford/best-practices-for-healthcare-professionals

Cronenwett, L. R. (2002, February 19). Research, practice, and policy: Issues in evidence-based care. *Online Journal of Issues in Nursing, 7*(2). Retrieved from http://www.nursingworld.org/MainMenuCategories/ANAMarketplace/ANAPeriodicals/OJIN/Columns/KeynotesofNote/EvidenceBasedCare.aspx

Diekelmann, N. (2001). Funding for research in nursing education. *Journal of Nursing Education, 40*(8), 339–341.

Fain, J. A. (2009). *Reading, understanding, and applying nursing research* (3rd ed.). Philadelphia, PA: F.A. Davis.

Fawcett, J., & Garity, J. (2009). *Evaluating research for evidence-based nursing practice.* Philadelphia, PA: F.A. Davis.

Fineout-Overholt, E., & Melnyk, B. (2005). Building a culture of best practice. *Nurse Leader, 3*(6), 26–30.

Fink, R., Thompson, C., & Bonnes, D. (2005). Overcoming barriers and promoting the use of nursing research in practice. *Journal of Nursing Administration, 35*(3), 121–129.

Florence Nightingale Museum Trust. (2003). The passionate statistician. Retrieved from http://www.florence-nightingale.co.uk/cms/index.php/florence-royal-commission

Gold, J. (2014). FAQs on ACOs: Accountable care organizations explained. Retrieved from http://khn.org/news/aco-accountable-care-organization-faq/

Gordon, J. H. (2011, April). Overview, issues raised, and probable controversies. *Accountable Care News*, pp. 2, 4. Retrieved from http://www.communityoncology.org/UserFiles/pdfs/accountable-care-news-review.pdf

Hopp, L., & Rittenmeyer, L. (2012). *Introduction to evidence-based practice: A practical guide for nursing.* Philadelphia, PA: F.A. Davis.

Institute for Healthcare Improvement (IHI). (2006). 100K lives campaign. Retrieved from http://www.ihi.org/engage/initiatives/completed/5millionlivescampaign/documents/overview%20of%20the%20100k%20campaign.pdf

Institute of Medicine (IOM). (1983). *Nursing and nursing education: Public policies and private actions.* Washington, DC: National Academies Press. Retrieved from http://www.nap.edu/openbook.php?isbn=0309033462

Institute of Medicine (IOM). (1999). *To err is human: Building a safer health system.* Washington, DC: National Academies Press.

Institute of Medicine (IOM). (2004). *Keeping patients safe: Transforming the work environment of nurses.* Washington, DC: National Academies Press.

Institute of Medicine (IOM). (2010). The future of nursing: Leading change, advancing health: Health and Medicine Division. Retrieved from http://www.nationalacademics.org/hmd/Reports /2010/The-Future-of-nursing-leading-change

Malloch, K., & Porter-O'Grady T. (2006). *Introduction to evidence-based practice in nursing and health care.* Sudbury, MA: Jones and Bartlett.

Merriam-Webster. (2018a). Best practice. Retrieved from https://www.merriam-webster.com /dictionary/bestpractice

Merriam-Webster. (2018b). Model. Retrieved from https://www.meriam-webster.com/dictionary /model

National Institute of Nursing Research (NINR). (n.d.). Important events in the National Institute of Nursing Research history. Retrieved from http://www.ninr.nih.gov/aboutninr/history# .VgMEVo9VhBd

National Institute of Nursing Research (NINR). (2013). Mission statement. Retrieved from http:// www.ninr.nih.gov/AboutNINR/NINRMissionandStrategicPlan

National Institute of Nursing Research (NINR). (2015). NLN research priorities in nursing education 2012–2015. Retrieved from http://www.nln.org/docs/default-source/default-document-library /researchpriorities.pdf?sfvrsn=2

National League for Nursing (NLN). (n.d.). NLN mission statement. Retrieved from http://www .nln.org/about/mission-goals

National Pharmaceutical Council. (2012). *The patient-centered outcomes research institute resource guide.* Retrieved from http://www.npcnow.org/Public/Research___Publications/Publications /pub_cer/The_Patient_Centered_Outcomes_Research_Institute_Resource_Guide.aspx

Nelson, A.M. (2014). Best practice in nursing: A concept analysis. Retrieved from http://www .journalofnursingstudies.com/article/S0020-7489(14)00128-X/abstract

Nightingale, F. (1858). *Notes on matters affecting the health, efficiency and hospital administration of the British Army.* London, UK: Harrison and Sons.

Parker, M. E., & Smith, M. C. (2010). *Nursing theories and nursing practice* (3rd ed.). Philadelphia, PA: F.A. Davis.

Polit, D. F., & Beck, C. T. (2008). *Nursing research: generating and assessing evidence for nursing practice.* Philadelphia, PA: Lippincott Williams & Wilkins.

Polit, D. F., & Hungler, B. P. (1978). *Nursing research: Principles and methods.* Philadelphia, PA: J. B. Lippincott.

Riddle, L. (2005). Polar-area diagram: Biographies of women mathematicians. Retrieved from http://www.agnesscott.edu/lriddle/women/nightpiechart.htm

Simpson, R. L. (2005). Leader to watch. *Nurse Leader, 3*(6), 10–14.

van Achterberg, T., Schoonhoven, L., & Grol, R. (2008). Nursing implementation science: How evidence-based nursing requires evidence-based implementation. *Journal of Nursing Scholarship, 40*(4), 302–310.

CHAPTER 4

Overview of Quality

Sharon Cannon and Carol Boswell

CHAPTER OBJECTIVES

At the conclusion of this chapter, the learner will be able to:
1. Define quality improvement and quality assurance.
2. Review the history of quality improvement.
3. Describe the purpose of quality improvement.
4. List sources of quality improvement.
5. Identify settings for quality improvement.
6. Apply principles for guiding improvement to nursing practice in relation to research and evidence-based practice.

KEY TERMS

Hospital Care Quality Information from the Consumer Perspective (HCAHPS)

Quality assurance (QA)

Quality improvement (QI)

Research

▶ Introduction

Quality assurance (QA) and quality improvement (QI) are terms used every day in all types of healthcare facilities. In fact, the terms are often used interchangeably, although the terms are defined differently. According to Boswell and Cannon (2017), who reaffirmed their 2014 definition, QA is "an orderly practice of examining a product or service to determine if it meets precise requirements" (p. 94). Merriam-Webster (n.d.) defines QA as a program to monitor and evaluate projects, services, or a facility to ensure standards are met. Boswell and Cannon (2017) state that QI is "a process utilized to investigate a policy, procedure, or protocol to determine if it addresses an aspect identified through an evidence-based practice process and works to validate current practice" (p. 94). Obviously, the definitions have some overlap, but keep in mind that both emphasize the necessity of meeting standards through a process that ensures benchmark standards are met while continuously trying to make the standards even better by analyzing the evidence (data). An example of a QI initiative is the **Hospital Care Quality Information from the Consumer Perspective (HCAHPS)**, which measures high-quality service via patient satisfaction.

▶ History of Quality Improvement

The history of quality improvement goes back to medieval Europe, when guilds were used by craftsmen (American Society for Quality, n.d.). Over the years, many notable names have been connected with the ideas and concepts of quality assurance, quality improvement, and continuous improvement. These include Ignaz Semmelweis, Florence Nightingale, Ernest Codman, and W. Edwards Deming, well-known individuals who sought to lay the foundation for quality care at all levels of engagement. Much of the work currently housed within QI in the healthcare arena has been taken from the work done within other fields, such as the automobile industry, aeronautics, and computer technology. The efforts and/or principles related to improvement in one unrelated area can segue into other areas such as health care to advance the work within that discipline. This smooth uninterrupted transition from one discipline to another has benefited the public as a whole.

Within health care, Parry (2014) noted evidence finding that only 54.9% of patients within healthcare settings in the United States received the recommended care for the health problems identified. QI was noted to be a major concern within the United States due to this finding. The Institute of Medicine (IOM, 2001) defines quality as "the degree to which health services for individuals and populations increase the likelihood of desired health outcomes and are consistent with current professional knowledge" (para. 3). In 1965, the push for quality improvement efforts was emphasized more within health care. That year, Congress embarked on the formation of the Medicare and the Medicaid programs using Title XVIII and Title XIX of the Social Security Act (Marjoua & Bozic, 2012). While neither of these programs directly discussed QI, they did set out conditions of participation within the different programs that set the benchmark for the quality expected. Although the initial efforts resulting from legislative efforts did move the focus forward, the process was slow.

In 1966, Dr. Avedis Donabedian established a framework for quality that was based on "the elements of structure, process, and outcomes to examine the quality of care delivered" (Marjoua & Bozic, 2012, p. 267). The Donabedian model provided the foundation for care processes that undertake to move patient outcomes to the forefront of health care. As a result of this advancement in the field, the IOM was established in 1970, followed by the establishment in 1989 of the Agency for Health Care Policy and Research (currently called the Agency for Healthcare Research and Quality [AHRQ]; Marjoua & Bozic, 2012). Both agencies have been strong advocates for healthcare quality. Between 1995 and 2000, multiple initiatives and task forces embraced the sentinel reports published at the time.

As a result of these efforts, the Leapfrog Group was formed by the Joint Commission. Based on this group and on the efforts during this time, the National Quality Forum (NQF) was created in 1999; its mission is to advance and upgrade health care within the United States. The NQF has been successful in launching national goals and priorities for healthcare quality. An endorsement by the NQF has "become the 'gold standard' for healthcare performance measures" (Marjoua & Bozic, 2012, p. 268). The forum's members include stakeholders, hospitals, healthcare providers, consumer groups, purchasers, accrediting bodies, research organizations, and healthcare QI organizations. All of these groups are focused toward the goal of improving the health care of all individuals.

▶ Purpose of Quality Improvement

As evident in the review of the history of QI, efforts to improve health care have lagged behind other industries. However, with the Joint Commission and other accreditation agencies' requirements to implement QI strategies and the push from a 1999 IOM report, the purpose of QI in health care and nursing specifically has been clearly delineated. The major thrusts of QI are to:

- Eliminate errors
- Decrease sentinel events
- Improve patient care and patient safety
- Decrease the financial costs of health care
- Promote health
- Focus on patient-centered care

To understand the purpose of QI as listed here, let's examine an initiative that demonstrated the purpose of QI. Saidleman (2015) discussed the 2000 founding of the Leapfrog Group, which is supported by the Robert Wood Johnson Foundation. According to Saidleman (2015), "the Leapfrog Group's mission is to promote giant leaps forward in the safety, quality, and affordability of health care by:

- Supporting informed healthcare decisions by those who use and pay for health care, and
- Promoting high-valued health care through incentives and rewards" (p. 380).

▶ Sources of Quality Improvement

Marjoua and Bozic (2012) stated, "The ubiquity of health care challenges in the United States is often attributed to the problems of underuse, overuse, and misuse of resources" (p. 3). The lack of accountability related to inadequate management of care along with the challenges of rising healthcare costs has resulted in incomplete and inadequate information on healthcare outcomes. Another critical area related to the management of quality health care lies in the area of "incentivized payment systems that encourage volume without regard to value" (Marjoua & Bozic, 2012, p. 267). The healthcare community has embraced the changes currently being proposed. These productive steps have united the healthcare community, stakeholders, patients, and consumers to demand advancement toward an improved healthcare delivery environment. Each group has accepted the challenge to ascertain their role to distinguish quality care, resulting in the expectation that quality is the foundation for health, not a byproduct.

Two key publications have been the foundation for the recent advancements in QI: *To Err Is Human: Building a Safer Health System* (IOM, 1999) and *Crossing the Quality Chasm: A New Health System for the 21st Century* (IOM, 2001). Both publications were instrumental in bringing the challenges and inconsistencies within quality improvement of health care to the attention of the public. These publications, along with subsequent reports, have shaped the strategic directions for QI toward redesigning care-delivery opportunities, ensuring that patients are cared for in a safe environment, furthering measurement and informed purchasing aspects, and reforming the health professional education processes.

As resources related to QI are reviewed and considered, a clear understanding of the differences and similarities between research, evidence-based practice (EBP), and quality improvement becomes essential. TABLE 4-1 provides a comparison grid for these three processes. Each of the processes is contrasted in regard to

TABLE 4-1 Research, EBP, and QI: Comparison Grid

Category	Research	EBP	QI
Definition	Prescribed, methodical, and meticulous technique of investigation	A process of using confirmed evidence (research and QI), decision making, and nursing expertise to guide the delivery of holistic patient care	Appraise the efficiency of clinical interventions and furnish guidance for achieving quality outcomes, productivity, and cost containment
Purpose	Confirms and filters accessible knowledge while generating new knowledge	Supplies an underpinning for optimal patient care by assimilating the strongest evidence accessible, transforms research into practice, advances stability and reliability within practice	Champions pressing workflow enhancement in the practice setting, equates organizational standards with benchmarks and guidelines, contemplates cost efficacy, transforms processes for efficient management of care
Commonalities and differences	Systematic problem-solving method driven by inquiry	Systematic problem-solving method driven by evidence	Systematic problem-solving method driven by data

Category	Research	EBP	QI
IRB approval needed	IRB required before implementation of engagement with participants	IRB not usually required unless dissemination of results is anticipated that could expose participants	IRB not usually required unless dissemination of results is anticipated that could expose participants
Supervision	Compliance with local, state, and federal law required, usually through IRB approval	Institutional	Institutional
Limitations	Theoretically based; dependent on statistical analysis; time consuming; some topics are not researchable	Begins with clinical/practice question; outcome dependent on "best" evidence located	Not theoretically based; cause-and-effect outside the scope; numerous internal validity threats possible; rapid cycle; integrated into practice in a timely manner
Generalizability	Yes, based on research design used	Probable, depending on organizational context	No, results are specific to unit and/or agency
Opportunities for knowledge dissemination	Expected following completion of research	Increasingly common	Expected within the agency but not usually beyond it
Influence on practice	Generation of new knowledge for practice	Seeks to improve practice through translation of evidence	Seeks to improve practice on unit and within organization, incorporates knowledge
Methods	Quantitative Qualitative Mixed method Systematic reviews Meta-analysis	PICO, PICOT, PICOTS, PICOT-DM Iowa Model of EBP ACE Star Model of Knowledge	Plan–do–check–act (PDCA) Plan–do–study–act (PDSA) Six Sigma Lean Six Sigma

Data from North Dakota Center for Nursing, (2014). *Comparison of quality improvement, evidence-based practice, and nursing research*. Retrieved from http://www.ndcenterfornursing.org/wp-content/uploads/2013/02/; Shirey, M. R., Hauck, S. K., Embree, J. L., Kinner, T. J., Schaar, G. L., . . . McCool, I. A. (2011). Showcasing differences between quality improvement, evidence-based practice, and research. *The Journal of Continuing Education in Nursing, 42*(2), 57–70.

the definition, purpose, commonalities and differences, internal review board (IRB) approval needed, supervision, limitations, generalizability, opportunities for knowledge dissemination, influence on practice, and methods. By viewing the processes in a grid format, a comparison of the concepts and values assumed under each process can be carefully and systematically contemplated.

Weston and Roberts (2013) provided the goals addressing the quality initiatives established by the National Quality Strategy. These three aims encompass the current expectations for quality and performance improvement and include better care for all members of society, healthy people living in healthy communities, and affordable care for everyone. Each of the aims provides a clear vision of the expectations for health care both in the United States and globally. These aspirations are achievable through "improvements in nursing care efficiency, patient engagement, and access to knowledge" (Weston & Roberts, 2013, p. 7 of 10). Within the contemporary healthcare landscape, excellence and performance strategies will be foundational for advancing the healthcare agenda. Each member within the healthcare profession will be expected to endorse and strengthen the progression toward the appropriate level of quality improvement at all levels of health.

Melynk and Fineout-Overholt (2015) sum up the ideas of QA as involving "planned, systematic processes which should have been established using evidence, that is, the *how* of practice" (p. 521). By using a systematic process in the investigation of the evidence and the healthcare setting, the resulting outcome will demonstrate quality and appropriate management of the health encounters. QA and QI are the attempts by the healthcare community to pledge to provide competent, effective healthcare management while certifying that the care provided has been based on best practices. QI efforts are best accomplished by multiple groups evaluating the same phenomenon and arriving at the same unambiguous results.

New tools are being used to evaluate the quality of care provided. Nursing has taken the challenge to evaluate the quality of nursing care: "The American Nurses Association (ANA) has developed nursing-sensitive indicators including nursing staffing information and patient care outcomes such as pressure ulcers, patient falls, and nosocomial infections" (Izumi, 2012, p. 2). These indicators are called the National Database of Nursing Quality Indicators (NDNQI). Hospital administrators, along with accreditation organizations, are using these indicator results to provide a thorough picture related to the nursing care provided within the participating agencies. The NDNQI results are used in conjunction with the core indicators developed by other agencies to provide a transparent view of the quality of care provided in health care throughout the country.

▶ Settings

QI in health care takes place in multiple settings, which include but are not limited to the following:

- Long-term care
- Schools
- Clinics
- Outpatient surgery centers
- Pharmacies

- Medical equipment companies
- Home healthcare agencies
- Industrial sites
- Correctional facilities
- Acute care facilities

As described earlier, QI is a primary concern for all healthcare venues. Nursing is an essential component in all of them. Interaction through interdisciplinary QI activities is an expectation. The nurse plays a central role in all aspects of QI, whether on a single unit or for the organization as a whole. In particular, nurses are positioned well to have an impact on and improve services provided to the client regardless of the setting, healthcare system, or the processes used to improve the quality of care.

▶ Application of QI

Acute Settings

Draper, Felland, Liebhaber, and Melichar (2008) acknowledge "nurses are pivotal in hospital efforts to improve quality" (p. 2). For the American Association of Colleges of Nursing (AACN), Rosseter (2010) gave a press release applauding the 2010 Carnegie Report that indicates quality care depends on a qualified nursing workforce. Nurses are key to the activities and engagement at the bedside. They are ready to assist and implement measures with patients. As the Affordable Care Act (ACA) has been implemented, a variety of entities, "such as accreditation and regulatory bodies, quality improvement organizations, medical specialty societies, state hospital associations, and health plans" (Draper et al., 2008, p. 2), have all become increasingly interested in the quality of care provided within healthcare settings.

Health care has embraced the ideas laid out within the ACA, and core quality measures have been determined and established. Hospitals must utilize the core quality measures as they strive to maximize their revenue streams. Medicare, Medicaid, and insurance groups are utilizing the core quality measures to determine the reimbursement rates to be used for different hospitals and healthcare agencies. The public has become more aware of these core measures as they select healthcare providers. Hospitals with sound core quality measure levels are viewed as safer and better healthcare agencies to use, thus improving the reimbursement levels for those institutions. These "report cards" gain in importance as agencies are feeling the impact from the ACA implementations. Nurses are called upon to step up and assist with these quality measures. According to Draper and colleagues (2008), the following five key strategies are needed to foster quality improvement within this healthcare setting:

- Accommodating hospital leadership that takes an active role in the process
- Establishing expectations for all staff members to seek quality as a shared responsibility
- Requiring staff members to be accountable within the process
- Employing the idea of champions within the ranks of the staff members
- Furnishing appropriate, valid, and ongoing resources to utilize the staff successfully

To be effective within this process, the majority of the staff members must accept individual ownership for the development and management of patient safety and quality efforts. Without each member realizing the role that he or she plays within the process, holes within the quality will develop and expand.

According to the Health Resources and Services Administration (HRSA, 2011), QI must be viewed as a team process. Each member of the team within the acute care setting has a role to play within the process to ensure patient safety and effective management of healthcare interventions. Because the process of QI is understood to be a complex, multidisciplinary activity, a team approach to the process is imperative. Each discipline has a responsibility during the process to advance the management of effective and safe health care for each individual within the acute care setting.

In addition to the work done within the acute care setting, the idea of QI is rapidly moving toward continuous quality improvement that moves from home care to acute care back to home care. All aspects across the continuum must be included within the plan for quality. Health care is no longer only in one segment but is a comprehensive and extensive management of the healthcare needs of the individual in a holistic manner. Healthcare providers cannot look at only the physical aspects within the current environment. The total picture that has an impact on the patient must be considered as the treatment options are investigated.

Community Settings

Just as nurses in acute care, nurses in community settings such as clinics, schools, outpatient centers, or home health must be prepared to work as team members with other professionals. Every level and every department must be involved, regardless of the size or type of organization. In many instances, team members may not all be in the healthcare profession. Those who work in health care comprehend the healthcare system. Those who are not healthcare providers will need to be informed about QI and health care to provide appropriate feedback and processes necessary in QI activities. Frequently, this evolution becomes an essential component in the nurses' role in QI in community settings.

In 2011, the HRSA published guidelines for QI that are composed of modules for a QI process/system. The modules discuss the importance of QI, roles in QI, improvements for sustainability of the QI program, references, and additional resources, including tips and a tool kit. The program is designed for and can be used in all healthcare settings.

🔖 THINK OUTSIDE THE BOX

1. Visit Medicare's Hospital Comparison website at www.medicare.gov/hospitalcompare/. Select three hospitals at the site to compare. Discuss how a patient and/or the patient's family might use this information. How might you use this information to select the agency that you want to work in or do not want to work in?
2. Go to the HRSA website's QI page at www.hrsa.gov/quality/toolbox/methodology/qualityimprovement/. How could you use the information at this website in your setting?

Summary Points

1. The history of quality improvement goes back to the medieval Europe, when guilds were used by craftsmen (American Society for Quality, n.d.).
2. Ignaz Semmelweis, Florence Nightingale, Ernest Codman, and W. Edwards Deming are examples of well-known individuals who sought to lay the foundation for quality care at all levels of engagement.
3. Two key publications that have formed the foundation for the recent advancements in QI are *To Err Is Human: Building a Safer Health System* (IOM, 1999) and *Crossing the Quality Chasm: A New Health System for the 21st Century* (IOM, 2001).
4. Medicare, Medicaid, and insurance groups are utilizing the core quality measures to determine the reimbursement rates to be used for different hospitals and healthcare agencies.
5. Each member of the team within the acute care setting has a role to play within the process to ensure patient safety and effective management of healthcare interventions.
6. QI is conducted in multiple healthcare settings.
7. The nurse plays a pivotal role in QI, regardless of the setting.
8. All levels and departments of an organization must be involved.
9. HRSA has published a guide for QI programs in health care.

⚑ RED FLAGS

- Quality improvement is a must. All members of the healthcare team must take an active role in the determination and management of quality improvement within health care.

Multiple-Choice Questions

1. The management of quality care is known by several different names. Which of the following names is *not* used when discussing quality improvement?
    A. Quality assurance
    B. Continuous improvement
    C. Managed care
    D. Quality improvement

2. What two federal funding sources helped to advance the efforts of quality improvement in 1965?
    A. Title XVIII and Title XIX
    B. Affordable Care Act and Medicaid
    C. Title XIX and Title XX
    D. Advancement in insurance and Title XVIII

3. What agency was successful in launching national goals and priorities for healthcare quality, resulting in having their endorsement viewed as the "gold standard" for healthcare performance measures?

A. Leapfrog Group
B. National Quality Forum (NQF)
C. Agency for Healthcare Research and Quality (AHRQ)
D. American Nurses Association (ANA)

4. What are the three aims encompassed within the current expectations for quality and performance improvement as established by the National Quality Strategy?
    A. Better care for all members of society, healthy people living in healthy communities, and affordable care for all
    B. Continuing care for selected members, healthy people living in rural communities, and prohibitive care for the upper levels of the population
    C. Management of costs for health care, adequate nursing staff to care for the population, and equality for rural and urban communities
    D. Appropriate care for selected members, individualized care for rural communities, and inexpensive outpatient care

5. Which of these groups is not directly interested in advancing quality improvement efforts for the nation?
    A. Accreditation and regulatory bodies
    B. Medical specialty societies
    C. State hospital associations
    D. National academic regulatory bodies

6. What strategy could be used to foster quality improvement within the acute healthcare setting?
    A. Accommodating hospital leadership that takes an active role in the process
    B. Establishing expectations for nursing staff only to seek quality as a shared responsibility
    C. Requiring physicians and administration only to be accountable
    D. Furnishing inapt and null resources to force the staff to take responsibility

Discussion Questions

1. As health care becomes more involved with core measurements, the report cards for agencies will be available to compare the work done by the different agencies. Visit www.medicare.gov/hospitalcompare/ and identify which of the different aspects could be most valuable to patients and their families. Develop a tool to use with a patient or a family to make them aware of the materials provided from this site and others like it.
2. Carefully consider Draper and colleagues' (2008) five key strategies that are needed to foster quality improvement within the healthcare setting. What type of resources and programs would need to be in place to incorporate some or all of these strategies successfully? Prioritize the five strategies according to how they would facilitate the development of a high level of quality within the health agencies in your area.
3. You are a school nurse in your local school district and have been asked to develop a QI program. How would you begin? What resources would you need? Who should be on the QI team?

Suggested Readings

Centers for Medicare and Medicaid Services. (2015). Hospital compare. Retrieved from http://www
.cms.gov/Medicare/Quality-Initiatives-Patient-Assessment-Instruments/HospitalQualityInits
/HospitalCompare.html

Kovner, C. T., Brewer, C. S., Yingrengreung, S., & Fairchild, S., (2010). New nurses' views of quality
improvement education. *The Joint Commission Journal on Quality and Patient Safety, 36*(1),
29–35.

Warshaw, G. (2013). Quality improvement. *Annals of Long-Term Care, 21*(7). Retrieved from http://
www.annalsoflongtermcare.com/article/quality-improvement

References

American Society for Quality. (n.d.). History of quality. Retrieved from http://asq.org/learn-about
-quality/history-of-quality/overview/overview.html

Boswell, C., & Cannon, S. (2017). *Introduction to nursing research: Incorporating evidence-based
practice* (4th ed.). Burlington, MA: Jones & Bartlett Learning.

Draper, D. A., Felland, L. E., Liebhaber, A., & Melichar, L. (2008). The role of nurses in hospital
quality improvement. *Center for Studying Health System Change Research Brief, 3*, 1–8.

Health Resources and Services Administration. (2011). Quality improvement. Retrieved from
http://www.hrsa.gov/quality/toolbox/methodology/qualityimprovement/index.html

Institute of Medicine (IOM). (1999). *To err is human: Building a safer health system*. Washington,
DC: National Academies Press.

Institute of Medicine (IOM). (2001). *Crossing the quality chasm: The IOM health care quality initiative*.
Washington, DC: National Academies Press. Retrieved from http://iom.nationalacademies
.org/Global/News%20Announcements/Crossing-the-Quality-Chasm-The-IOM-Health-Care
-Quality-Initiative.aspx

Izumi, S. (2012). Quality improvement in nursing: Administrative mandate or professional
responsibility. *Nurse Forum, 47*(4), 260–267. doi:10.1111/j.1744-6198 .2012.00283x

Marjoua, Y., & Bozic, K. J. (2012). Brief history of quality movement in US healthcare. *Current
Reviews in Musculoskeletal Medicine, 5*(4), 265–273. doi:10.1007/s12178-012-9137-8

Melnyk, B. M., & Fineout-Overholt, E. (2015). *Evidence-based practice in nursing & healthcare:
A guide to best practice* (3th ed.). Philadelphia, PA: Wolters Kluwer.

Merriam-Webster. (n.d.). Quality assurance. Retrieved from http://www.merriam-webster.com
/dictionary/quality%20assurance

North Dakota Center for Nursing. (2014). *Comparison of quality improvement, evidence-based
practice, and nursing research*. Retrieved from http://www.ndcenterfornursing.org/wp-content
/uploads/2013/02/Comparison-of-QI-EBP-and-Nursing-Research-Final-Document.pdf

Parry, G. J. (2014). A brief history of quality improvement. *Journal of Oncology Practice, 10*(3),
196–199. doi:10.1200/JOP.2014.00436

Rosseter, R. (2010). Press release. AACN applauds the new Carnegie Foundation report calling for
a more highly educated nursing workforce. Retrieved from http://www.aacn.nche.edu/news
/articles/2010/carnegie

Saidleman, V. (2015). Ensuring quality care. In J. T. Catalano, *Nursing now!: Today's issues, tomorrow's
trends* (7th ed., pp. 376–410). Philadelphia, PA: F.A. Davis.

Shirey, M. R., Hauck, S. K., Embree, J. L., Kinner, T. J., Schaar, G. L., Phillips, L. A., . . . McCool,
I. A. (2011). Showcasing differences between quality improvement, evidence-based practice,
and research. *The Journal of Continuing Education in Nursing, 42*(2), 57–70.

Weston, M., & Roberts, D. W. (2013). The influence of quality improvement efforts on patient
outcomes and nursing work: A perspective from chief nursing officers at three large health
systems. *Online Journal of Issues in Nursing, 18*(3), 1–10. Manuscript 2. doi:10.3912/OJIN
.Vol18No03Man02

CHAPTER 5
Ethics for Nursing Research and Evidence-Based Practice

Sharon Cannon and Theresa Delahoyde

CHAPTER OBJECTIVES

At the conclusion of this chapter, the learner will be able to:
1. Explain why ethical theories used in nursing practice are important for nursing research.
2. Acknowledge how international and national ethical principles have influenced ethical nursing research.
3. Discuss the impact of the history of human experimentation on nursing research today.
4. Delineate the ethical implications in each step of the research process.
5. Identify specific ethical issues when various research methodologies are utilized.

KEY TERMS

Autonomy	Justice
Beneficence	Morality
Code of ethics	Nonmaleficence
Ethical theories	Respect
Ethics	Scientific misconduct
Fidelity	Trustworthiness
Human experimentation	Veracity
Informed consent	Vulnerable subjects
Institutional review board (IRB)	

▶ Introduction

This chapter focuses on ethics in two areas: research and evidence-based practice (EBP). The literature for ethics in research is plentiful. However, literature regarding ethics in EBP is just emerging. Similarities and differences in ethics exist in both research and EBP. Because ethics in research is abundantly found in the literature, ethics in research is examined first.

Nurses practice within a unique social world with norms, controls, rules, and regulations. Nurses embody the art of caring and are required to do no harm to patients. Nurse researchers, acting as social scientists, examine the human condition in relation to health and illness. They, too, are governed by all the ethical principles encompassed within biomedical research. The International Council of Nurses (ICN) and the American Nurses Association (ANA) have developed ethical codes to control the practice of the nursing profession. Whether providing nursing care or doing EBP projects or research, nurses must engage in moral, ethical activities. Each ethical code specifies that a nurse researcher needs to be qualified to conduct research, regardless of the particular role (e.g., principal investigator, clinical research coordinator, or member of an institutional review board [IRB; known as a "research ethics board" in Canada]). This clarification means the researcher must understand all the elements required to maintain the highest ethical standards. The nurse researcher must understand what is morally and ethically appropriate to study and disseminate to be able to protect the vulnerable—a group that includes everyone who participates as a subject and who trusts the nurse researcher will be ethical. "Without an ethical practice environment, the patient is unprotected, as is the nurse who must meet moral obligations" (Cipriano, 2015, p. 3).

Nursing research, which lies within the domain of social science, is critical for the development of nursing knowledge. As a social science, nursing research is concerned with the human condition and, as such, is directed and controlled by all international ethical codes. The pursuit of nursing research requires participants to respect the specific ethical constraints and standards that are discussed in the sections that follow. This chapter discusses the ethical issues in each step of the research process. Universal ethical theories and their relevance to nursing research are presented, as well as theories that underpin all the health disciplines. A brief review of the history of human experimentation and the need for ethical practice is provided. The chapter also discusses the emerging ethical issues not only with research but also with EBP and quality improvement (QI).

▶ Ethical Theories

To appreciate **ethical theories**, it is important first to understand the definitions of morality and ethics. **Morality** refers to "traditions or beliefs about right and wrong conduct" and is influenced by social and cultural practices, whereas **ethics** is "the study of social morality" (Burkhardt & Nathaniel, 2014, p. 35). Morality is what a person believes to be right and wrong and is shaped by what a person has been taught within society and her or his own culture. Cipriano (2015) suggests a moral person possesses integrity, respect, moderation, and industry, which are characteristics expected of nurses. Ethics is how a person makes judgments between right and wrong. Not infrequently, little distinction is made between the two; however, both morality and ethics are important in making decisions.

Ethical theories provide society with general guidelines for making decisions, but it is a person's moral philosophy that ultimately factors into the decision. According to Burkhardt and Nathaniel (2014), moral philosophy is "the philosophical discussion of what is considered good or bad, right or wrong, in terms of moral issues" (p. 35). Individuals have their own personal moral philosophies that guide ethical decision making. Tschudin (1992) points out that ethics are identified as either normative or descriptive. Normative ethics are prescriptive ethics; they relate to the standards that have been laid down and are generally accepted in any society as the guidelines for what one should do. From normative ethics emerges the code by which a profession lives, which is particularly true in nursing. In contrast, descriptive (or scientific) ethics arise from what people do.

Most occupations have a professional **code of ethics** to provide a more formal process for applying moral philosophy and to "govern professional behavior" (Burkhardt & Nathaniel, 2014, p. 35). In nursing, the ANA has a "Code of Ethics for Nurses," which was revised in 2015. This code of ethics guides the practice of nursing and is "the promise that nurses are doing their best to provide care for their patients and their communities and are supporting each other in the process so that all nurses can fulfill their ethical and professional obligations" (ANA, 2015). In recognizing the importance of ethics to nursing practice, the ANA declared the 2015 National Nurses' Week theme to be "Ethical practice, Quality care" (*The American Nurse*, 2015, p. 1). In addition, the ANA promoted 2015 as the year of ethics. In health care, professional codes of ethics incorporate several basic principles to help guide healthcare professionals in determining right from wrong and in making ethical decisions. These basic principles include **autonomy**, **beneficence**, nonmaleficence, **veracity**, **justice**, and **fidelity**.

🔁 THINK OUTSIDE THE BOX

Consider the basic principles of ethics and morality. What basic principle shapes your decisions? How will your morals shape ethical decisions related to your nursing practice?

Embedded in an ethical theory is the freedom of the individual but also consideration for the common good: "A right action is only right if it is done out of a sense of duty, and the only good thing without any qualification is a person's goodwill: the will to do what one knows to be right" (Tschudin, 1992, p. 51). Nursing has the obligation to protect the vulnerable patient—and therein lies the cause for justice. For the nurse researcher, the obligation is to protect the human subject.

Values Theories

Principles of ethics not uncommonly used in health care include (1) respect, (2) autonomy, (3) beneficence (or nonmaleficence), and (4) justice. All ethics codes related to **human experimentation** stress **respect** for persons, both from the perspective of individual autonomy and by emphasizing the rights of those with diminished autonomy to the same protections. Autonomy refers to the ability to make careful choices. In relation to research, a potential subject should receive all the information required to make an informed decision. It is important to note here that there is a distinct difference between assent and consent. For clarification, giving assent to a study means the subject(s) want to participate in the study. Consent means the subject(s) give their permission to be a participant in the study. This is of particular importance for intervention projects involving children (*IRB Advisor*, 2017). O'Mathúna (2015) emphasizes the importance of the ethics and integrity of anyone conducting research.

Beneficence refers to the practice of maximizing benefits while minimizing risks. In relation to research, as stated by the Council for International Organizations of Medical Sciences (CIOMS, 2002),

> this principle gives rise to norms requiring that the risks of research be reasonable in light of the expected benefits . . . the research design be sound . . . investigators competent to perform the research and to safeguard the welfare of the research subjects.

Another term for *beneficence* is nonmaleficence, or the doing of no harm to the individual. Beneficence is identified as an obligation, and every effort must be made to ensure the well-being of the research subject. The Belmont Report (National Institutes of Health [NIH], 1979) indicated that the principle of beneficence applies to society at large as well as to specific investigators. Thus, obligations are inherent in all human research projects that have implications measured in terms of long-term effects for society at large.

Finally, the principle of justice is particularly applicable to the "vulnerable" but is more widely viewed as the "ethical obligation to treat each person in accordance with what is morally right and proper, to give each person what is due to him or her" (CIOMS, 2002, p. 11). The Belmont Report (NIH, 1979) describes what is due as "(a) to each person an equal share, (b) to each person according to individual need, (c) to each person according to individual efforts, (d) to each person according to societal contribution, and (e) to each person according to merit." *Equal* in this instance implies equity, although clearly at times not everyone will be equal. Nevertheless, there should be equity or justice in distribution of whatever is distributed. The implication of "distributive justice," to which both CIOMS and the Belmont Report refer, is that the issue of vulnerability of human subjects must be addressed as the same for everyone.

In human studies, nursing and medical practitioners are tending to vulnerable subjects simply by virtue of the illnesses that brought patients to the attention of healthcare providers. CIOMS (2002) describes vulnerable as:

> substantial incapacity to protect one's own interests owing to such impediments as lack of capability to give informed consent, lack of alternative means of obtaining medical care or other expensive necessities, or being a junior or subordinate member in a hierarchical group. (p. 11)

Human subjects are therefore vulnerable before they are invited to participate in research projects, and this imposes further ethical obligations on the researcher to protect them. One example of a vulnerable population is research involving children. In an article in the *IRB Advisor*, Dr. Victoria Miller (2017) suggests that the notion of children as "little adults" should be eliminated. She promotes including children in the adult model of consent to participate where appropriate such as asking questions or expressing an opinion about the research.

▶ Historical Overview

The 20th century saw an explosive increase in human subject research, with significant medical breakthroughs as a result of this type of experimentation. Although guidelines and standards for ethical research were not established until later in the early 20th century, ethical oversight and control were desperately needed to protect all human subjects. Several famous research studies have provided a framework for this historical overview. Some had excellent outcomes, while others did not. In all cases, it became evident that more stringent ethical standards were needed to protect the public.

For example, in 1789, in England, Edward Jenner first inoculated his son at 1 year of age with swinepox against smallpox, a lethal disease. This vaccination method proved to be ineffective, and later Jenner used cowpox on other human subjects. This approach was successful and led the way for effective inoculation against smallpox (Reich, 1995). Despite his undoubted achievement, Jenner's work raises a number of key ethical issues:

- No consent was obtained from the subject.
- No understanding was established as to whether the agents used (i.e., swinepox and cowpox) were safe for human use.
- Research was performed on a minor who would have had no understanding of what was happening, although the argument could be made that because the researcher was the father of the child, it was a nonissue. However, this practice would be deemed unacceptable today.

Nevertheless, throughout Western European history, there is evidence of the relevance of ethical behaviors in human research. Moses Maimonides (1135–1204), a physician and philosopher, "instructed colleagues always to treat patients as ends in themselves, not as means for learning new truths" (Reich, 1995, p. 2248). Claude Bernard, writing in France in 1865, stated

> Morals do not forbid making experiments on one's neighbor or one's self . . . the principle of medical and surgical morality consists in never performing on man an experiment which might be harmful to him to any extent, even though the result might be highly advantageous to science, i.e., to the health of others. (Reich, 1995, p. 2249)

However, recognition of the need for regulated ethical constraints emerged as a result of horrific episodes during the 20th century. The worst documented atrocities were probably the Nazi experiments that were conducted mainly on prisoners during World War II. These experiments included "putting subjects to death by long immersion in subfreezing water, deprivation of oxygen to learn the limits of bodily endurance, or deliberate infection by lethal organisms in order to study the effect of drugs and vaccines" (Reich, 1995, p. 2253). In addition, "Nazi experimental atrocities included investigation of quicker and more effective means of inducing sexual sterilization (including clandestine radiation dosing and unanesthetized male and female castration and death)" (Reich, 1995, p. 2258).

In addition to these appalling events, highly unethical human research studies were performed in the United States. The most infamous was the Tuskegee Syphilis Study (Centers for Disease Control and Prevention [CDC], 2011), which involved African American males suffering from secondary syphilis; the treatment of penicillin (the recommended and available medication) was deliberately withheld from these patients so that the progression of the disease could be studied. The Tuskegee study, which was initiated in the mid-1930s, was not halted until 1972, when a newspaper published an account of it. At no time were the human subjects fully informed about the study, and in some instances they appear to have been deliberately misinformed. Among the many sad aspects of the study was the fact that subjects more than likely, in all innocence, infected others because their syphilis was not being treated. Therefore, maleficence was directed not only toward the study subjects but also toward their families, which compounded the researchers' ethical lapses.

Instances of human drug testing or usage with inadequate ethical oversight have also occurred. Thalidomide, a widely used sedative in the 1950s (though not in the United States), was given to some pregnant women to control morning sickness. When the tragic malformations of the fetuses were made public, thalidomide was removed from the market for this particular use. Thalidomide was one of a group of drugs for which it is evident that there was already knowledge about the potential for teratogenicity (malformation of fetuses). Yet because this drug had been "widely praised, advertised, and prescribed on the grounds that it was unusually safe" (Dally, 1998, p. 1197), it was never properly tested for safety before human use. Instead, because of the highly effective advertising campaign conducted by the drug's manufacturer, the medical community ignored the evidence and went on using thalidomide. This case highlights another aspect of the relevance of stringent ethical controls in human research studies.

More recently, the inadequate design of a medical research study at Johns Hopkins School of Medicine led to the death of one of the subjects. In this instance, prior to the initiation of the study on the inhalation of the drug hexamethonium, a limited and sketchy review of the literature was performed using only a medical index website. Such reviews are limited in terms of how far back they can search. The failure to explore the full history of the drug resulted in a healthy 24-year-old female losing her life. A review of the literature from an earlier period would have revealed potential hazards in association with this drug and its proposed route of administration. This case points to the importance of the careful design and organization of a study before it is initiated. Fault lay at many levels, not the least of which was the researcher but also perhaps with Johns Hopkins' research review board (Perkins, 2001).

⬛ THINK OUTSIDE THE BOX

Consider several examples of human experimentation that have occurred during the history of medical research. Have these projects resulted in beneficial outcomes for society? Can human experimentation be justified when the greater good of society is at stake? Defend your thoughts.

As technology evolves in an ever-changing healthcare field, nursing researchers need to continue to be vigilant about ethical oversight and control. Good ethical nursing research should adhere to ethical principles, be scientifically sound, and be subject to independent review boards (Doody & Noonan, 2016).

▶ Research Ethics: Progress in the 21st Century

The core ethical issue in medical research is the need for voluntary consent of the potential research subject so that a fully informed individual participates. Many efforts have been made to address this issue, but perhaps the most significant progress came from the Nuremberg Trials, in which the Nazi war crimes were investigated. The result was the Nuremberg Code of 1946, in which it is stated, "The voluntary consent of the human subject is absolutely essential . . . This means that the person involved should have legal capacity to give consent . . . the research subject should be so situated as to be able to exercise free power of choice" and human subjects "should have sufficient knowledge and comprehension of the elements of the subject matter involved as to make an understanding and enlightened decision" (Reich, 1995, p. 2253).

In the United States during the 1960s, different agencies within the federal government began more stringently regulating funded research on human subjects. On July 1, 1966, the NIH, through the Public Health Service, assigned "responsibility to the institution receiving the grant for obtaining and keeping documentary evidence of informed patient consent" (Reich, 1995, p. 2254). It also mandated "review of the judgment of the investigator by a committee of institutional associates not directly associated with the project" (Reich, 1995, p. 2254). Finally, the "review must address itself to the rights and welfare of the individual, the methods used to obtain informed consent, and risks and potential benefits of the investigation" (Reich, 1995, p. 2254).

In 1973, Congress formally recognized the importance of ethical standards in human research when it created the National Commission for the Protection of Human Subjects of Biomedical and Behavioral Research, whose mission was to protect the rights and welfare of research human subjects. Research oversight by the federal government continues with a constant updating of regulations, which can be found in the Code of Federal Regulations, Title 45 and 21—specifically in the Protection of Human Subjects Rule (U.S. Department of Health and Human Services [HHS], 2007). Federal efforts to improve the safeguards to human subjects in research continue, culminating most recently with Health Insurance Portability and Accountability Act of 1996 (HIPAA).

ICN (2012) has followed suit, making the need for protection of human rights very clear in its own code of ethics, which focuses on four principal elements: (1) nurses and people, (2) nurses and practice, (3) nurses and the profession, and (4) nurses and coworkers. Ethical behaviors within these relationships are expected at all times, not just in areas of research. The second statement in the "nurses and people" element of the "ICN Code of Ethics for Nurses" (ICN, 2012) reads as follows: "In providing care, the nurse promotes an environment in which the human rights, values, customs and spiritual beliefs of the individual, family and community are respected" (p. 2). As a social science, nursing research must demonstrate ethical values that reflect the values of the profession at any one time (Jeffers, 2005). Human rights, equity, and justice are stressed specifically in relation to educators and researchers. The "nurses and the profession" element of the ICN's code of ethics states that the researcher must "conduct, disseminate and utilize research to advance the nursing profession" (p. 8). Although ethics is not named directly here, its importance is inherent in the entire document.

As mentioned earlier, the ANA (2015) also has a "Code of Ethics for Nurses," in which specific vulnerable populations are identified. These populations include children, the elderly, prisoners, students, and the poor. The code was published in 1994, copyrighted in 1997, updated and republished in 2001, and revised in 2015. It also indicates that the nurse clinician identifies clinical problems that need examining, and the researcher designs the study in association with the clinician. What is clear in this statement is that research topics in nursing should be focused on practice, which in itself should provide an ethical underpinning for nursing research. In 2017, ANA and the International Association for Clinical Research Nursing published a document focusing on nursing research and the scope and standards of practice for clinical nursing research practice.

▶ Environment for Ethical Research

When the unethical treatment in the Tuskegee Syphilis Study was revealed, the National Commission for the Protection of Human Subjects of Biomedical and Behavioral Research, in 1974, adopted the Belmont Report, which provided a code of ethics to guide all research (Chappy & Gaberson, 2012). The Belmont Report provided the formation of the 45 Code of Federal Regulations (CFR) part 46. This was developed by the Office for Human Research Protection.

Most nurse researchers are associated with institutions that already have ethical regulations in place that the researcher is required to follow. This offers protection to the institution, the researcher, and the human subjects. The research institution housing the project typically has an office for reviewing all research proposals, usually called the **institutional review board (IRB)**. The main purpose of an IRB is to protect human subjects, especially vulnerable populations such as children, prisoners, pregnant women, handicapped or mentally disabled persons, or economically and/or educationally disadvantaged persons. The IRB is charged with reviewing a proposal in advance as well as with periodic monitoring of the research while it is being conducted, all in an effort to protect the rights and welfare of the human subjects (Westlake & Taha, 2012). The IRB serves to

- promote fully informed and voluntary participation by prospective subjects who are capable of making such choices be a suitable proxy and
- maximize the safety of subjects once they are enrolled in the project (Westlake & Taha, 2012, pp. 66–67).

The issues that receive the most intense IRB scrutiny relate to thorough evaluation by the research team of the risks and benefits of the project, the provision of sufficient protection for human subjects, and the implementation of sufficient monitoring of the project once approval is given to proceed (Rothstein & Phuong, 2007). In addition, this office is most helpful in ensuring that the researcher submits all the required paperwork, including the proposal for the study, the consent form that study participants will sign, the budget, and whatever tools the researcher will be using in data gathering (e.g., surveys or instruments or interview guides in the case of qualitative studies).

The HHS CFR controls the IRB offices of various types of healthcare organizations. The membership of the IRB must include at least five members of different backgrounds who also have the competence to review research proposals. It is expected that each member will be culturally and gender diverse and be aware of local community mores. Thus, not only will there be healthcare professionals on the board but there will also be members who are "unaffiliated" with the institution; at least one member must have scientific interests, and one may not (Rothstein & Phuong, 2007). The members are expected to be knowledgeable about all federal guidelines and regulations. When reviewing a proposal, an IRB member may not have involvement with the project (HHS, 2009). Unfortunately, there have been instances when IRB members have had some sort of conflict of interest or lack of objectivity that renders the board less capable of being just, fair, and protective of human subjects (Rothstein & Phuong, 2007).

The IRB members meet once a month to review all proposals, which they have already carefully scrutinized, and they may request further information to make informed decisions. When the IRB is satisfied that the researcher will provide full protection of the human subjects, the researcher is given permission to proceed, and the project is given an identifying number. The researcher must report progress back to the IRB every 12 months. The IRB members expect the researcher to follow the protocol exactly as laid out in the proposal. If the project has more than one researcher, all must be listed on the protocol and, if requested by the institution, the curriculum vitae (CV) of each must also be attached. The issues of specific concern for ensuring ethical research are that the risks to the subjects are minimized (or are at least reasonable, providing the expected outcomes or benefits can be attained); subject selection is equitable; informed consent is sought from participants; and issues relating to data collection and storage, privacy, and confidentiality are managed according to regulations (HHS, 2017).

The approval of IRB studies falls under one of the following categories: exempt, expedited review, or full board review. An exempt review is for "low risk, nonvunerable, nonsensitive, and short-duration studies," whereas an expedited review is for "minimal risk to non-vulnerable subjects and nonsensitive topics" (Kawar, Pugh, & Scruth, 2016, p. 139). A full board review is one in which the research study involves "more than a minimal risk or vulnerable subjects and/or studies that do not qualify for exempt or expedited review" (Kawar, Pugh, & Scruth, 2016, p. 139).

The CFR Title 21 on the U.S. Department of Health and Human Services website (HHS, 2017) outlines regulations specific to the IRB and the subjects being researched; the current version of the regulations includes five subparts:

- Subpart A is the basic set of protections for all human subjects of research conducted or supported by HHS, and was revised in 1981 and 1991, with technical amendments made in 2005. Three of the other subparts provide added protections for specific vulnerable groups of subjects.
- Subpart B, issued in 1975 and most recently revised in 2001, provides additional protections for pregnant women, human fetuses, and neonates involved in research.
- Subpart C, issued in 1978, provides additional protections pertaining to biomedical and behavioral research involving prisoners as subjects.

- Subpart D, issued in 1983, provides additional protections for children involved as subjects in research.
- Subpart E, issued in 2009, requires registration of IRBs that conduct review of human research studies conducted or supported by HHS.

The researcher is expected to be competent to perform the research. Lenz and Ketefian (1995) indicate that in 1989, the Institute of Medicine's (IOM's) Committee on the Responsible Conduct of Research was concerned that there was "a lack of formal training in scientific ethics and the responsible conduct of science as a deficit in the training of scientists and clinicians" (p. 217). Although baccalaureate degree programs and higher levels of nursing education include courses on research, it is often not until a student is writing either a master's thesis or a doctoral dissertation that he or she begins to understand the process that ensures that the research is ethical and legal.

According to Ketefian and Lenz (1995), "scientists have traditionally valued their independence in the conduct of their research. Although independence in research is desired, an institution does not want its reputation sullied by unprofessional, illegal, or unethical research." Research **trustworthiness**, reliability, and usefulness are utterly dependent on the credibility of the researcher, the work, and the institution. The rules and regulations are generally the most rigorous when an institution receives federal funding. In such cases, the IRB office is insistent on all requirements being met. Ultimately, the research has to be honest.

Although multiple brakes are now applied in an attempt to prevent unethical research from occurring, some continue to be concerned that there is still the potential for inadequate protection of human subjects. Wood, Grady, and Emanuel (2002) believe that the review process is "bureaucratic and inefficient" (p. 2) and suggest that IRB members are overworked, frightened by the possibility of federal audits, and do not always understand "ambiguous regulations" (p. 2). They continue: "Federal regulators are aggravated by the limited scope of their authority and variable adherence to regulations" (p. 2), and their concerns are not limited to these particulars. For the nurse researcher, however, adherence to the ethical standards for human subject protection applied by the organization for which the researcher works and the codes of ethics developed by ICN and ANA is crucial, regardless of external concerns. Although the IRB process can be long and tedious, its function is to protect the research participants.

Developing a Researchable Topic

Although nurse researchers may be curious and interested in many topics they believe have the potential for expanding the body of nursing knowledge, some topics may not be realistically researchable for a number of reasons. The critical factor relates to protection of the vulnerable subject. As nurses, we are deeply and intimately involved with human beings at their most vulnerable, and the research topic may well pose a further increase to those individuals' vulnerability. When developing a researchable topic, the nurse researcher is called on to utilize "ethical sensitivity" to decide what is appropriate, to have the "ability to perceive rightness and wrongness" (Weaver, 2007, p. 142), and to know what one is doing affects the welfare of another person either directly or indirectly.

Allmark (2015) discusses ethical concerns related to EBP and reviews the literature with an emphasis on critics who examined the ethics of using EBP. Allmark refers to four ethical concerns regarding EBP: (1) some types of knowledge are not in EBP, (2) EBP runs counter to patient-centered care, (3) testing done by randomized controlled trials (RCTs) is not the same as "most effective," and (4) decisions based on EBP can be unjust. Allmark especially proposes that strength of evidence used to prioritize health care is unethical.

Issues related to the researcher also determine whether a topic is researchable. Volker (2004) indicates that attempting to research certain topics could put the researcher at risk "for loss of professional license, legal actions, imprisonment and peer ostracism" (p. 119). The types of topics that pose a threat to the researcher, according to Volker (2004), include those examining "social deviance, [those impinging] on powerful social interests, or [those examining] a deeply personal sacred value held by study participants" (p. 117). Nurses should not be studying illegal activities as a general rule, of course. Volker uses the example of a patient requesting assistance with suicide—an issue that nurses confront in their practice. A topic such as this presents problems when considering a research project: According to the ANA's (1994) statement on assisted suicide, "Nursing has a social contract with society that is based on trust, and therefore patients must be able to trust that nurses will not actively take human life" (p. 4). Volker does not state that the topic of assisted suicide cannot be examined in a research project; rather, careful vigilance must be exercised to ensure the study design is meticulously developed to protect both the researcher and the research subject. Cipriano (2015) indicates nurses must speak up regarding decisions and actions that are questionable.

In legally sensitive research projects, further measures can be sought that protect the researcher against "compelled disclosure" (Anderson & Hatton, 2000, p. 249) or breaking confidentiality covenants (Volker, 2004) and that offer additional protection for the study subjects. In particular, a Certificate of Confidentiality may be issued by the HHS in such cases. Federal law states that a Certificate of Confidentiality:

> may authorize persons engaged in biomedical, behavioral, clinical, or other research (including research on the use and effect of alcohol and other psychotic drugs) to protect the privacy of individuals who are the subject of such research by withholding from all persons not connected with the conduct of such research the names or other identifying characteristics of such individuals. Persons so authorized to protect the privacy of such individuals may not be compelled in any Federal, State, or local civil, criminal, administrative, legislative, or other proceedings that identify such individuals. (Public Health Service Act, 42 USC 163, 1988)

Volker (2004) makes it clear that "researchers who engage in socially sensitive research must be prepared for scrutiny by diverse professional and lay parties who have varying agendas and interests" (p. 123). Research projects are usually undertaken in institutions that have a well-developed ethical structure and that are highly conscientious in following federal guidelines and regulations to protect the vulnerable patients under their care. As a consequence, the researcher, while developing the project, has resources immediately available for advice and consultation, including the IRB, professional colleagues, attorneys, and an ethics committee.

> **⬛ THINK OUTSIDE THE BOX**
>
> Can you think of some additional vulnerable populations that are emerging in the current healthcare environment? Explain why you see these groups as vulnerable. Which issues need to be considered when determining the vulnerability of a group of people? Of the following two articles, one regarding Felty's syndrome (Woolston & Connelly, 2017) and one regarding blood transfusion vital sign frequency (Cortez-Gann, Gilmore, Foley, Kennedy, & Kring, 2017), which involves a vulnerable population? Give a rationale for your choice.

The topic that the nurse researcher chooses should be one of real interest to him or her. The researcher should be willing to allocate the preparatory time and effort to ensure that the project meets all of the institution's ethical guidelines. Ethical behavior requires intellectual honesty of the researcher—giving credit due to others, not using ideas from others without acknowledgment, and not initiating data collection before institutional approval has been given. Plans for seeking funding for the study, the study design, methodology, data collection, and the dissemination of results (even if insignificant) at the conclusion of the study are also critical parts of developing the topic for research.

Pilkington (2002) makes it clear that if a research project is not scientifically valid, then it is unethical to involve human subjects. It is the responsibility of the IRB to ensure that a study is scientifically valid. In defining whether a research project is scientifically valid, Pilkington (2002) states bluntly, "If a study does not hold substantial promise of answering a significant question(s), thereby generating valuable knowledge, then there is no justification for exposing persons to the actual or potential risks and inconvenience of participation" (p. 197). Scientific validity, therefore, influences how a researchable topic is developed to be an ethical research study. *IRB Advisor* (2017) discusses oversight of QI projects. QI projects in a healthcare system are designed to improve practice within that system. QI activities are not considered research, which would protect human subjects. The issue of randomization of which individuals are to receive treatments may deviate from routine clinical care. Rather than submitting to an IRB, the article recommends a QI-IRB or a clinical decision support committee (CDSC).

▶ Developing Researchable Questions

Although the nurse researcher may have a burning interest in a particular topic, developing the question(s) appropriately is most important when gearing up for a formal study. This development is necessary to narrow the topic to a specific focus, clarify the methodology, determine whether the topic has embedded in it useful questions that will give shape to the study, and ensure that significant research results will emerge and add to the body of nursing knowledge. The questions should be broad enough to obtain results yet not so broad as to yield diffuse and possibly meaningless results.

Thorough reading on the subject can assist in developing questions that meet these criteria. This preliminary investigation can help identify the gaps in the literature and hone the researcher's thinking about what it is specifically that he or she wants to investigate. Communication with both clinician colleagues and fellow nurse researchers can also assist in refining the questions.

The ethical component of this endeavor derives from ANA's demand for effective and efficient care of the patient. If the research design is faulty at any level—and specifically the question development level—then one must ask if the results will improve the efficiency and effectiveness of patient care.

▶ Participant Recruitment and Informed Consent

Vulnerable populations are always a concern for all research regulatory bodies, but some populations are particularly vulnerable—the very young, the frail elderly, prisoners, the mentally incompetent, and women. In addition, issues related to socioeconomic status, education, and language may contribute to a specific population's vulnerability (Anderson & Hatton, 2000; Rogers, 2005). The researcher must be sensitive to these issues and to the points specifically outlined in federal regulations. This can make recruitment more difficult and the need for true **informed consent** crucial. Very specific regulations can be found in the Belmont Report (NIH, 1979), the International Ethics Guidelines for Biomedical Research Involving Human Subjects (CIOMS, 2002), and the HHS's Protection of Human Subjects document (HHS, 2009), including sections relating to the protections needed for specific vulnerable populations.

The key ethical issue embedded in informed consent is that the individual always has the freedom of choice to participate or not participate, and the individual may withdraw from the study at any time. Another term used in conjunction with informed consent is valid consent. Valid consent is thought to involve more information about the process. This freedom of choice is built on a series of components:

- The language is simple enough to be clearly understood.
- The potential subject adequately comprehends the project.
- The subject has had time to think about the study and its potential risks and benefits and to discuss it with family members.
- The consent is not coerced.
- The written consent is documented.

CIOMS (2002) discusses "inducements" to participation, which can be identified as coercion and therefore are not appropriate. Several authors have expressed concern over how to achieve consent and indicate that obtaining consent should in fact be a continuous process throughout a research project. In other words, the researcher should regularly check with the subject to ensure that he or she is still a willing and informed participant (Edwards & Mauthner, 2002; Miller & Bell, 2002). The only payment or compensation allowed includes the costs of transportation or loss of earnings due to participation in the research project. It is unethical to offer more financial incentives because they may encourage a potential subject to consent against his or her better judgment. It is also unethical for the researcher to receive compensation from a pharmaceutical company to conduct a study.

Research using child participants encompasses all the usual ethical issues relating to informed consent, privacy, and confidentiality, but it includes several other factors that may compound these issues. Children exist in a natural power hierarchy with adults, but they are able to communicate and understand according to their interpretation of the world around them (Kirk, 2007). Children must believe they are part of the project, but researchers must be alert to the specific child's "agenda" and continually check with the child to ensure that he or she wants to continue to participate. Parents are also involved with providing informed consent, but researchers must ensure that children do understand what they are getting into and that their consent is given freely. Hanna, Weaver, Slaven, Fortenberry, and DiMeglio (2014) obtained informed consent of parents and youths 18 years old or older. In some instances, only one parent's consent is required, although two parents' consent is preferable. On occasion, a child and parents may not agree on continued participation; in general, it is the child's decision that is accepted in such cases.

IRB Advisor (2017) suggests children be allowed the opportunity to have a voice in the research activity. Miller (2017) discusses the process of assent (wanting to do) versus consent (giving permission) where ethical and legal concerns need to be addressed. She does propose that the process of assent can benefit children through the decision-making model.

The success of the study may depend on the warmth, interest in the child, and rapport established by the researcher so that the child trusts the researcher. These characteristics have been demonstrated to be critical in longitudinal studies with children (Ely & Coleman, 2007), particularly when ill children are subjected to discomforting treatments. A slightly different issue arises with teenagers who, while still legally minors, have the right to give informed consent without parental consent (Roberson, 2007). Parents still have legal responsibility "to ensure the child [receives] appropriate medical care, [but] there is also the ethical need to 'respect the rights and autonomy of every individual, regardless of age'" (Kunin, 1997, cited by Roberson, 2007, p. 191).

Recruiting the desired composition and number of participants may require establishing multiple research sites, which can create some problems for the researcher, even as it confers some distinct advantages to the study. Such studies are "likely to produce generalizable, high quality results . . . [increase the] likelihood of attracting funding . . . [provide access to] a broader range of practice settings and patients with a wider range of diagnoses . . . [and] expedite data collection" (Twycross & Corlett, 2007, p. 35). Multisite research enables experts to work together and perhaps close the theory–practice gap. Of course, some notable difficulties in conducting multisite studies are noted, including those related to establishing and maintaining collaborative, trusting relationships with one's colleagues; meeting face to face; overcoming organizational cultural differences; and having to gain IRB approval at each site.

Young (2017) suggests that IRBs should examine whether risks and benefits are appropriate. She emphasized the importance of ethics in regard to data sharing. The use of data sharing needs to be transparent so that specific outcomes are delineated, in particular with clinical trials for new drugs.

▶ Data Collection and Data Analysis

Protection of vulnerable human subjects remains the critical ethical issue with data collection and analysis. First and foremost, the privacy and confidentiality of the subjects must be protected, which means that the data must be locked securely in a safe place at all times. Data may include audio, video, podcasts, surveys, or other types of digital recordings and media.

Digital recordings, whether audio, video, or both, are increasingly popular. Additional ethical issues—namely, privacy; participant burden and safety; storage, location, and condition of storage of recordings; maintenance of the recordings in storage; access to recordings; use of the recordings as part of a presentation; and whether the actual taping will interfere with clinical care—must be addressed when such data collection methods are used. The IRB will make decisions on all these issues and may require stipulations, such as that faces be blurred and/or eyes are covered with a black box in the final recording.

Each institution has specific guidelines about how long data files must be kept. Lutz (1999) has raised the issue of premature destruction of original data, predominantly in studies on particularly vulnerable populations (e.g., battered women). According to this author, such destruction could occur if the researcher were concerned about court subpoenas that could compromise the participants' safety. However, premature destruction could lead to institutional accusations of scientific misconduct, which suggests that the researcher has a fine line to walk between ethical and unethical actions.

Ethical analysis and interpretation depend on the honesty and trustworthiness of the researchers. Although healthcare organizations make every effort to ensure ethical behavior within their research environments, ultimately it rests with the researchers to ensure that the project is indeed conducted ethically in all areas, including analysis, interpretation, and dissemination of results. The opposite of ethical behavior is scientific misconduct, which brings dishonor to both the individual and the institution and renders the research project meaningless. In addition, concern for the welfare of the vulnerable human subjects is negated when misconduct occurs. **Scientific misconduct**, an extremely serious issue, is defined by HHS as follows:

⬛ THINK OUTSIDE THE BOX

Determine if your school or hospital has an IRB. Which criteria do the board members use when approving a research project?

Fabrication, falsification, plagiarism or other practices that seriously deviate from those that are commonly accepted within the scientific community for proposing, conducting or reporting research. It does not include an honest error or honest differences in interpretations or judgments of data. (Commission on Research Integrity, 1995, p. 1.)

Lutz (1999) has cited Macrina (1995), who states that falsification involves results being manipulated or tampered with, fabrication refers to "totally unfounded results" (Lutz, 1999, p. 90) being produced, and plagiarism is "theft of another person's ideas" (p. 90). History makes evident that falsification, fabrication, and plagiarism are unconscionable and utterly unethical.

▶ Issues in Quantitative and Qualitative Research

There is concern in qualitative research about the increased risk for ethical lapses inherent with this research methodology. As Birch and Miller (2002) state, "this type of research relationship may involve acts of self-disclosure, where personal, private experiences are revealed" (p. 92) and is never value free or "value neutral" (Christians, 2003, p. 213). The researcher must be aware of this potential and approach this type of research by making every attempt to acknowledge any personal biases.

In qualitative research, interviews are commonly used to gather data, resulting in face-to-face exposure for both the researcher and the researched, as was the case in the study of Felty's syndrome (Woolston & Connelly, 2017). The dialogue serves as the research data that are then analyzed and interpreted. The vulnerable patient immediately becomes more vulnerable as the researcher delves into his or her lived experience. Anonymity and confidentiality are inevitably compromised in the interaction between researcher and human subject, which means there is an even greater need for data security and constant awareness on the part of the researcher of these issues. Honesty and trustworthiness of the research and researcher are even more important in such cases. Firby (1995) has stated, in relation to an IRB giving permission for a qualitative research project, "We should not simply assume that because research has been accepted by a committee it is morally justifiable in its methods" (p. 41). The moral obligation of nursing is to do good and to do no harm. Therefore, qualitative nursing research must meet that obligation.

In contrast to qualitative research, quantitative research, which initially arose from the objective methodology of the Enlightenment's scientific paradigm, is more apt to be value neutral. The quantitative researcher is less likely to engage in face-to-face self-disclosure, which protects him or her and the subject. The facts should speak for themselves. However, the researcher must be alert to the potential for his or her biases to influence the interpretation of data. Nevertheless, there remains the ethical principle of justice and the need for informed consent for human participants in such studies. Allmark (2015) cautions that EBP decisions may not be fair or just. Examples given are those in which rare conditions eliminate RCTs, expense for treatments, and removal of patient choice. Those issues impact the design, implementation, and evaluation of research projects. Obviously, regardless of the type of research, researchers should closely examine issues before embarking on projects.

▶ External Pressures

Conducting research studies is never easy, but various pressures making it more difficult may push the researcher toward unethical behaviors. According to Lutz

(1999), these pressures include limited funding, the competition for achieving tenure for faculty, and "increasing emphasis on producing research reports" (p. 92). New technology and seeking cures also place pressure on healthcare providers (Cipriano, 2015).

HIPAA is designed to protect patients against unauthorized disclosure of their health and medical records. At the same time, it adds another source of pressure for nurse researchers because passage of HIPAA has led to some new concerns related to health research. According to Erlen (2005), these regulations were written for healthcare delivery organizations and not for universities per se; nevertheless, the latter organizations have had to develop their own policies and procedures that meet the requirements of HIPAA. At times it has proven difficult to draw "clear boundaries," and universities have tended to err on the side of caution by providing for additional protection of human subjects, privacy, confidentiality, and informed consent. HIPAA compliance has meant additional training for anyone who wishes to engage in research. The institution's IRB office sets the policy for how the researchers of that institution can proceed while adhering to HIPAA regulations.

HIPAA and its ramifications are key ethical considerations for the nurse researcher. With the drive for evidence-based research to underpin practice, the nurse researcher needs to be aware that study data and their interpretation must be shared, but within the constraints of HIPAA. To meet these criteria, data must contain no identifiers of an individual in a sample. Thus, subjects may be given a code number or letter. Only the researcher maintains a list linking the sample identifiers with their associated codes, and this document must be kept secure at all times.

▶ EBP and Ethical Implications

Now that we have explored ethics in the research process, let's examine ethics and EBP. In the clinical environment, considerable effort is being made to implement evidence-based nursing practice. However, the terms *EBP* and *research* are often used interchangeably. EBP is defined as "the combination of scientific evidence, patient preferences, and clinician expertise when making decisions for patient care," and it leads to the "development of best practices to meet the need of clients efficiently and effectively" (Carter, Mastro, Vose, Rivera, & Larson, 2017, p. 267). Such practice is derived from several elements, including experiential knowledge on the part of the nurse (i.e., knowing what works in practice and why), having clinical judgment and skills of critical inquiry, knowing the individual patient both as a human being and in terms of his or her pattern of responses to what is occurring, and knowledge of current scientific research findings (Borsay, 2009; Redman, 2007; Tanner, 2006). EBP is designed to reduce unthinking, ritualistic practices in nursing care (Siedlecki, 2008). Nurses are uniquely placed to establish an ethical practice environment that protects the patient (Cipriano, 2015).

QI, on the other hand, is a data-driven effort that seeks to "improve processes specific to an organization" (Carter et al., 2017, p. 267). It is constantly performed in healthcare organizations. Data are gathered in order to improve patient outcomes through "local innovations in and assessment of the processes and systems of care delivery" (Redman, 2007, p. 217). This process is designed for rapid implementation of change. It is different from the slower, rigorous, empirical research approach, which is more deliberative and follows a "fixed protocol with a clearly defined method and . . . a period of analysis after completed data collection" (Lynn et al., 2007, p. 668). QI is not empirical research. There is some concern, however, related to the ethics of human subject protection in QI practices (Grady, 2007; Lynn et al., 2007). To date, there has been no standard established regarding whether there should be a separate IRB process for QI. According to Hockenberry (2014), "in general, a QI project does not require IRB review and approval because it is not research that is subject to the federal human subjects' protection regulations" (p. 217).

Changes that are derived from QI are not regarded as the strongest evidence in EBP. Rather, EBP depends on generalizable scientific evidence (Batalden & Davidoff, 2007). The research utilized in evidence-based nursing practice uses well-tested scientific study data from studies that have undergone the required ethical scrutiny.

Developing an Evidence-Based Project

Similar to some nurses interested in researchable topics, other nurses may want to pursue EBP projects. Much interest has been generated in QI, patient autonomy, quality of life, and end-of-life issues. The specific process of developing an EBP project is discussed elsewhere; however, ethical issues need to be addressed prior to, during, and after the completion of EBP projects that parallel ethical issues in research projects.

EBP is a broad area that encompasses more than scientific research. In fact, research is considered to be one aspect of EBP. Not all nurses have the knowledge and skill to conduct research, but that does not mean they don't encounter clinical situations that pique their curiosity. As a result, they may wish to pursue information to improve nursing care. Developing an EBP topic also requires sensitivity to vulnerable populations, confidentiality, and existing federal and state guidelines, as well as professional regulations to practice nursing. Keeping all this in mind, the nurse should choose an EBP topic that is of specific interest to him or her to improve nursing practice. EBP projects also require the nurse to meet the institution's ethical guidelines.

The PICOT (population, intervention, comparison, outcome, time) format can be used as a starting point for developing an EBP question. Nurses must consider the ethics of asking an EBP question. The topic selected must be narrow enough to produce results that will improve patient care. At the same time, the design must be carefully planned to eliminate the potential of harm to participants. Stephens (2017) suggests that ethical issues require nurses to think through a situation by using the situational analysis (SA) process. The process has three phases: stop, think, act, which can help to improve performance and outcomes. Protection of human subjects is as important to EBP projects as it is to research. Thus, vulnerable populations are a concern for EBP projects. For example, if you want to collect data about fall rates in your institution, the population might include the elderly and/or children. Ethically, you must ensure that patient privacy and confidentiality are protected. Even if you are only conducting a retrospective chart review of patients who have fallen, you must still keep all patient information in confidence and not reveal any patient identification information. It is also necessary to ensure that participants in an EBP project will be honest in their responses. If a nurse is investigating nurses' medication errors in his or her institution, nurses in the institution must report that a medication error is made. If the nurses making the errors do not report them for fear of reprisal, the information about the number, type, or reasons for the error(s) will not be accurate, and recommendations to decrease medication errors will not be effective. The EBP project must also be ethical in all areas, including design, implementation, and evaluation. EBP projects require the same ethical rigor required in research.

Data collection for EBP generally focuses on institutional benchmarks to improve patient outcomes, patient satisfaction, communication techniques, hospital readmissions, and staff/physician satisfaction, to name just a few potential areas of investigation. An example might be a hospital that wants to decrease the occurrence of pressure ulcers. To accomplish this, the hospital wound care nurse obtains permission to adapt the Braden Scale as part of the nursing assessment of skill. The wound care nurse then educates the staff regarding the use of the Braden Scale and how it is mandatory to chart this assessment so that pressure ulcers can be prevented by early detection. After 1 month, the wound care nurse performs a chart review to determine if nurses used the Braden Scale, if they charted the skin assessment results, and if the number of new pressure ulcers decreased. The wound care nurse may also compare the results with other hospitals in the same geographic area or with other hospitals of the same size and same general population. Thus, data analysis does not necessarily involve statistical tests or methods as seen in research projects.

Data collection and data analysis for EBP projects, such as the wound care example, require the same ethical considerations for protection of human subjects. Many hospitals ask patients if they will allow their information to be used to promote better outcomes and/or for teaching purposes. To be ethical in the example given, the wound care nurse must protect patient confidentiality, remove patient identifying information, and report results in the aggregate (group) and not individually.

Issues in Evidence-Based Projects

As in research projects, anonymity and confidentiality in EBP projects are paramount. The person(s) responsible for EBP projects must protect the human subjects and must do no harm. In addition, they must be alert to any bias that may influence how the data are interpreted. Training regarding issues such as HIPAA is necessary to ensure no violations occur.

Because EBP projects are often specific to an institution, care must be taken to avoid pressure from individuals within the organization who want to show positive results. The EBP project must ensure that policies and procedures are followed and that data are accurately represented.

An additional ethical dimension is encountered when, at the end of the research or EBP project, it is time to publish the results: Journals accept only peer-reviewed manuscripts (Ketefian & Lenz, 1995). Peer referees are required to evaluate the scientific merit of the research study as well as the manuscript's acceptability for a particular journal. To warrant publication, the findings are expected to contribute new knowledge to the practice of nursing (Driever & Pranulis, 2003). Without that expectation, the research is inappropriate, if not unethical. Those who review manuscripts for publication must have the knowledge and expertise to evaluate the work appropriately (Pilkington, 2002). According to Chappy and Gaberson (2012), the "necessity for IRB approval cannot be overlooked . . . most journals will not publish results of projects for which IRB approval was not obtained initially . . . experts advocate for making IRB approval a requirement for all projects . . . because publication may be a goal any time that results are worth sharing" (p. 683).

> ⬆ **THINK OUTSIDE THE BOX**
>
> Should approval by an IRB be a requirement for EBP projects? List the reasons why or why not IRB approval is necessary.

An emerging segment of the literature is focusing on issues related to publication. Conn (2008) discusses how pressure may be put on the author to change results because the manuscript reviewers resist "unexpected outcomes" (p. 161) and want revisions that are not consistent with the results. The authors may need to make changes, but those changes should not come at the expense of reliable data results. Freda and Kearney (2005) discuss how editors can face ethical issues when articles have been published in more than one journal; when data are published in more than one journal with no changes; or when there is evidence of author misconduct, demand for credit for someone "undeserving" of credit, lack of IRB approval, or misconduct related to lack of informed consent or an undeclared conflict of interest.

A study by Henley and Dougherty (2009) revealed another potential problem related to publication of research results: discrepancies in the quality of the reviews submitted by many persons who serve as peer reviewers. According to these authors, "Peer review is the mainstay of the editorial process" (p. 18). The key issues of concern within a paper were poor reviews related to the study's theoretical framework (47.2%), literature review (35.15%), discussion and interpretation of results (22%), and data analysis/presentation (21.9%). In terms of usefulness of the written comments to the author, 14.4% of peer reviews were deemed poor (Henley & Dougherty, 2009). Finally, in terms of usefulness to the editor, 12.2% of peer reviews were poor or inadequate (Henley & Dougherty, 2009). These authors recommended formal training and a probationary period for all potential reviewers.

An additional ethical issue relates to who should be listed as first author when multiple researchers participated in the study. Generally, the principal investigator is listed as first author. In the case of multiple authors, however, negotiation determines the first author named on various publications. Ketefian and Lenz (1995) point out that listing authors in order of the extent of effort they made is the most ethical way of recognizing authorship. These authors also suggest that it is unethical to publish the same manuscript or article in multiple journals. It is appropriate to publish several articles on the same study, provided that each manuscript is written with a different focus. In addition, all contributions and funding sources for an article must be acknowledged.

▶ Emerging Ethical Issues in Research, EBP, and QI

The prevalence of EBP projects has caused much controversy about whether EBP and research are separate. One school of thought is that research is not a component of EBP; the other side, of course, is that research is one aspect of EBP.

Much depends on the definition of each. Proponents of research argue that EBP is specific to an institution, has no theoretical framework, and data are not able to be statistically tested and analyzed. Proponents of EBP state that EBP is broader, includes research where appropriate, and that data collected from specific institutions can be compiled and added to national data banks providing information that has broad implications. Ethical considerations for both will continue to be required regarding protection of human subjects, regardless of the prevailing school of thought.

Although nurses generally have not been involved in animal, genetic, or biological material research in the past, this situation is changing and is likely to continue to do so as more transdisciplinary, translational research occurs. The issues of concern with animals include ensuring that the least harm and suffering are inflicted; using animals only when absolutely necessary; using the fewest animals possible; and, when seeking IRB permission, ensuring someone on the board understands the implications of animal research. In relation to genetic and biological materials research, the same moral and ethical obligations apply as when dealing with any human subjects (Cipriano Silva, 2006).

Stephens (2017), the American Nurses Association and International Association of Clinical Research Nurses (2017), Young (2017), and Allmark (2015) all advocate for nurses to carefully examine ethical issues whether the projects are research EBP or QI. As technology improves and emphasis is placed on outcomes, nurses must be vigilant in conducting projects.

The community-based care facility (i.e., nursing home) is an environment that has been neglected as a site for study in the past but is likely to draw increasing attention from researchers in the future because of the aging of the U.S. population. All of the usual ethical research issues apply in this setting, but some additional concerns may arise relating to ensuring the quality of life, safety, and satisfaction of those residing in nursing homes and to ensuring that the study will not impose an undue burden on the participants. Proxies may be required to give consent for resident participation if the resident is mentally incompetent or extremely frail; however, use of proxies requires that the proxy holder have the authority to give this type of consent, and he or she must be adequately informed of the study's focus. In a study by Cartwright and Hickman (2007), it was discovered that community-based facility administrators had limited understanding of the protections established by an IRB that gives consent to a study, although most seemed aware of federal and state statutory requirements in terms of informed consent. In an attempt to overcome these deficits, Cartwright and Hickman developed what they call a Bill of Rights for Community-Based Research Partners, which could prove valuable for similar institutions.

Another issue emerging is the global aspect of research, especially with low- and middle-income countries (Schroeder, 2017). Schroeder cites studies in China and India as examples of "ethic dumping," in which designs were conducted that provided no intervention when treatments actually exist. Two additional issues that will certainly generate research involve the opioid crisis and mental health issues. There were successful drug trials relating to opioid usage to control pain, but financial gain, easy access and lack of adequate protection, and ethical issues relating to opioid use have emerged. Lack of adequate mental health resources resulting in multiple deaths is an additional issue with ethical aspects for research.

▶ Conclusion

The lessons learned from the history of human experimentation have led to the development of ethical codes, both nationally and internationally. These controls are crucial for the protection of vulnerable human subjects. Indeed, ensuring adequate protection of human subjects requires that particular care be taken in each step of the research or EBP process. The obligations inherent within nursing demand the "moral deliberation, choice and accountability" (Edwards & Mauthner, 2002, p. 14) of the nurse researcher. Nurses in their practice are tending to humans at their most vulnerable, and this level of understanding adds to the responsibility of the nurse as researcher or EBP project director. For years, nursing has topped the list as the most trusted profession. Thus, achieving valid research and EBP that enhances nursing knowledge depends on adherence to the highest ethical standards. The key components necessary to ensure that these ethical standards are met, as described in this chapter, should provide a useful guide for all nurses embarking on a research-based, EBP or QI project.

Summary Points

1. History provides many lessons on the importance of protection of vulnerable human subjects. These history lessons have led to the development of national and international ethical codes of conduct.
2. Both the International Council of Nurses (ICN) and the American Nurses Association (ANA) acknowledge the obligations of the nursing profession to the vulnerable human and, as such, stress ethical standards in nursing research.
3. Ethical theories guide the standards of nursing research.
4. Some populations (e.g., children) are more vulnerable than others, and they must be provided with the utmost protection during the research or EBP project.
5. Each step of the research process involves meeting ethical standards.
6. The privacy and confidentiality of the human subject must always be guaranteed.
7. Informed consent must be given by a human subject participant who truly understands to what he or she is consenting.
8. The honesty and trustworthiness of the nurse researcher or EBP project director are crucial in ensuring valid—and valuable—results are derived from any study.

⚑ RED FLAGS

- Every study must address the ethical aspects of that study. Documentation of this focus may be demonstrated through a statement reflecting IRB approval of the study.
- Every study must speak to how the subjects will be protected from harm—physical and/or psychological—during the research process.

Critical Discussion: Ethical Issues in Nursing Research and EBP Projects

1. A research study of incarcerated women who are human immunodeficiency virus (HIV) positive or have acquired immunodeficiency syndrome (AIDS) is being conducted. You are not the principal investigator, but you are one of the researchers who has received permission to interview some of the women who volunteered to participate. One woman gives you inappropriate information about another prisoner, whom she states propositioned her for sex; the interviewee claims this prisoner has AIDS. As you leave the prison, the warden asks you to relate what happened during this interview. Discuss your responsibilities as a researcher in this sensitive study. A number of critical elements must be taken into account: the interviewee divulging information about another prisoner's possible HIV/AIDS status and behaviors, confidentiality and protection of human subjects, the warden's request, and your ethical responsibility to the study and to your institution.

2. You are the principal investigator studying young teenagers (10–14 years old) who are receiving aggressive treatment for life-threatening cancers. One 11-year-old boy has had many bouts of chemotherapy, which have made him acutely ill. His parents would like the child to participate in the study, but he refuses. What he shares could potentially be of use in treating other young teenagers. Clearly, there are some issues of consent here. Discuss what you should do.

3. You are one of a group of nurse researchers who is participating in a multinational study. The sample will include people of many different ethnic groups, all of whom speak different languages, and will include women and children. You understand the process of IRB review in your own institution, but many other issues arise when one is participating in international studies. Among the issues of concern here are the need for an interpreter, confidentiality, local permission requirements, management of the study in the foreign country, recruitment of persons into the study, and protection of human subjects in a different country. How can these issues be resolved so that the study may be conducted?

4. Your hospital wants to decrease the rate of falls in patients older than 65 years of age. You have been asked to conduct an EBP project regarding these patient outcomes. What are some ethical considerations you must incorporate into this project?

5. Catheter-associated urinary tract infections (CAUTIs) are on the rise. The nurses in a long-term care facility want to eliminate CAUTIs. List at least two ethical issues associated with this project.

Multiple-Choice Questions

1. When developing a nursing research project, why is it important to remember the ethical constraints?
    A. The study will not be approved by the IRB without these constraints.
    B. The protection of human subjects underlies all human research projects.

C. The results will not be trustworthy and replicable.

D. The nurse researcher will not be able to get funding for the project and therefore will not be able to complete the project.

2. The atrocities performed on prisoners in Nazi Germany violated which ethical principles?

   A. Value of life, justice, and respect

   B. Beneficence, nonmaleficence, and value of life

   C. Autonomy, nonmaleficence, and respect

   D. Justice, autonomy, and nonmaleficence

3. Protection of vulnerable individuals is a critical ethical component in human research studies. How did Edward Jenner fail to meet this standard when he tested swinepox on his 1-year-old son?

   A. He thought the new knowledge overrode any concern he should have for the rights of his son.

   B. He did not know any better.

   C. He ignored the point that he could not get informed consent from his son, who was particularly vulnerable.

   D. He did not fail: Given that smallpox was such a lethal disease at that time, it was better for Jenner to ignore his son's vulnerability in order to gain new knowledge.

4. The Tuskegee Syphilis Study lasted many years, and none of the human subjects were properly informed about the study's conduct. Which ethical principle was egregiously ignored in this study?

   A. Autonomy

   B. Respect

   C. Nonmaleficence

   D. Justice

5. Why does an ethical research environment assist with ensuring scientific integrity?

   A. Within this environment, expectations for scientific integrity are laid out.

   B. Federal regulations related to ethical standards are adhered to, increasing the likelihood of integrity.

   C. The researcher always works within an ethical environment, which encourages the practice of ethical research behaviors.

   D. Scientific integrity ensures funding, which means that the study will be completed.

6. Why do federal regulations specify that the makeup of the IRB should reflect cultural and gender diversity and an awareness of local mores?

   A. This practice ensures that all research projects presented to the IRB will receive fair examination and will not be denied without discussion.

   B. Gender studies have not been common until recently, and females react differently to different treatments.

   C. Awareness of local customs and culture means that both IRB members and researchers understand issues of concern in a non-American population.

   D. There is now great interest in researching healthcare issues in persons of different cultures.

7. Why is it important that the researcher be competent to conduct research?
   A. It is not ethically appropriate for an incompetent person to conduct research.
   B. An incompetent researcher will not be able to get informed consent from the vulnerable subject, which is unethical.
   C. An incompetent researcher should always work with someone who is competent so that he or she can learn the process.
   D. Research is a complicated process that has to be learned.

8. What is the issue of greatest concern when developing a research project?
   A. The competence of the researcher to do the research
   B. The availability of funding
   C. The protection of the vulnerable subject
   D. Informed consent

9. A certificate of confidentiality may be required to protect both the researched and the researcher. Why?
   A. The nurse researcher will not thus lose his or her license to practice and do research because of the sensitive topic being researched.
   B. If the research topic is particularly sensitive, this certificate protects patients from divulging issues uncomfortable to them.
   C. The certificate protects the researcher and the researched from being coerced by governmental authorities to reveal sensitive information.
   D. The certificate means that no information is shared with those who should not be informed.

10. Why do research questions have to be developed carefully?
    A. The wrong question for the study means the wrong answer.
    B. Carefully developed and refined questions focus the research project.
    C. Without careful development of the questions, the research results will be meaningless.
    D. It is unethical not to develop questions carefully.

11. Why is informed consent a crucial issue in research projects?
    A. Research results will be more meaningful.
    B. The researcher will be adhering to international codes of ethics from which federal regulations are drawn.
    C. The project will be rejected by the IRB because the subject is not informed about the study.
    D. The consenting subject will understand what the research is about and will have the choice to participate or not.

12. Scientific misconduct on the part of the researcher is very serious. What constitutes scientific misconduct?
    A. Lying about the project to subjects when seeking informed consent
    B. Fabrication, falsification of data, and plagiarism
    C. Attributing only partial authorship to other contributors when they have done most of the work
    D. Making false claims about a project being funded when the researcher is talking about his or her work

13. HIPAA, which was designed to protect all humans and their medical records in this era of electronic paperless records, has imposed another restraint on conducting research. Why?

     A. It is more difficult to obtain IRB permission to conduct a research project.
     B. With paperless medical records, there are no data to analyze, even when interview data and surveys are involved.
     C. The regulations protect against unauthorized disclosure; although IRB permission includes this protection, additional care is taken under HIPAA.
     D. HIPAA ensures that highly sensitive data (e.g., HIV/AIDS status) are not disclosed.

14. Privacy and confidentiality are always issues in human subject research. What are the important steps to ensure that they are protected?

     A. The researcher does not talk about what the subject shares until the project's results are published in a peer-reviewed journal.
     B. All data are kept securely locked in a safe place and destroyed when the study is completed.
     C. Care with replication studies must be taken so that original data are not shared in the second study.
     D. All data are kept securely locked in a safe place and may be destroyed only according to IRB instructions.

15. Both the International Council of Nurses and the American Nurses Association make it clear that the ethical standards of the profession require the same obligations from the nurse researcher. Why?

     A. For the protection of vulnerable clients and patients
     B. For the protection of the nurse researcher
     C. Because of an obligation inherent within the nursing profession
     D. Because practice on which these ethical standards are built focuses nursing research

16. A nurse is developing a question for an EBP project involving the fall rate of patients 65 years of age and older. What should the initial ethical consideration be?

     A. The age of the researcher
     B. The number of falls
     C. The age of the population
     D. The sample size of the population

17. EBP projects in your institution are not required to obtain IRB approval. What must the nurse in charge of the EBP project still do?

     A. Maintain anonymity and confidentiality of patient information
     B. Maintain professionalism in gathering patient information
     C. Provide all staff access to the patient information
     D. Provide patient information obtained to the hospital board of directors

Discussion Questions

1. Several nurses are working together to develop a research project. Only one is doctorally prepared; the others have either a master's degree or a baccalaureate degree. The preparatory work is to be shared equally among all the nurses. As the project evolves, it turns out that those who do not have a doctorate do all the work. At a meeting, the doctorally prepared nurse insists that she be listed as the principal investigator for the grant to be submitted and as the first author on all publications. She bases her request on a belief that the reviewers of the grant would "pay more attention to the application" if the principal investigator has a doctoral degree. Discuss the ethical issues embedded in this situation.

2. The protection of human subjects lies at the heart of any research project. Part of this protection entails the need to obtain informed consent. A female nurse wants to do a qualitative study investigating what it means for males to live with diabetes mellitus and the resultant impotence. Qualitative research usually involves interviewing the human subject, and sexual impotence is a particularly sensitive subject. How should the nurse explain the study to her potential sample to ensure that the consent is truly informed and that the subjects will not drop out of the study because of extreme discomfort during the interview? What are the ethical issues involved?

3. Codes of ethics in human research, developed partly as a result of the atrocities of the mid-20th century, continue to be refined. The dictionary definitions of *moral* and *ethics* suggest that the meanings of these terms can and will change, and the evolving codes support this idea. Yet codes of ethics are based on some universal theories and values theories. Discuss why, despite the universality of these theories, the codes continue to evolve.

4. You have an idea for an EBP project that your hospital has approved regarding the fall rates of pediatric patients on your unit. Discuss the ethics involved with this particular population. How would you incorporate ethics in the data collection, analysis, and report of the project?

Suggested Readings

American Association of Critical-Care Nurses (AACN). (2015). Ethics in critical care nursing research. Retrieved from http://www.aacn.org/wd/practice/content/research/ethics-in-critical -care-nursing-research.pcms

Im, E.-O., & Chee, W. (2002, July/August). Issues in protection of human subjects in Internet research. *Nursing Research, 51*(4), 266–269.

International Council of Nurses (ICN). (2012). *The ICN code of ethics for nurses.* Retrieved from http://www.icn.ch/images/stories/documents/about/icncode_english.pdf

Lanter, J. (2006). Clinical research with cognitively impaired subjects. *Dimensions of Critical Care Nursing, 25*(2), 89–92.

Levine, C., Faden, R., Grady, C., Hammerschmidt, D., Eckenwiler, L., & Sugarman, J. (2004). The limitations of "vulnerability" as a protection for human research participants. *American Journal of Bioethics, 4*(3), 44–49.

National Institutes of Health (NIH). (1979). The Belmont report: Ethical principles and guidelines for the protection of human subjects of research. Retrieved from http://www.hhs.gov/ohrp /humansubjects/guidance/belmont.html

Rogers, B. (2005). Research with protected populations: Vulnerable participants. *AAOHN Journal, 53*(4), 156–157.

Smith, L. (2001, May/June). Ethics and the research realist. *Nurse Educator, 26*(3), 108–110.

United Nations. (2002). International covenant on civil and political rights, article 7. Universal declaration of human rights. Retrieved from https://treaties.un.org/doc/Publication/UNTS /Volume%20999/volume-999-I-14668-English.pdf

U.S. Department of Health and Human Services. (1998). Sponsor–investigator–IRB interrelationship—information sheet. Retrieved from http://www.fda.gov/RegulatoryInformation /Guidances/ucm126425.htm

U.S. Department of Health and Human Services. (2005). Protection of human subjects rule, 45 C.F.R. 46. Retrieved from http://www.hhs.gov/ohrp/humansubjects/guidance/45cfr46.html

References

Allmark, P. (2015). Ethics and evidence-based practice. In M. Lipscomb (Ed.), *Exploring evidence-based practice: Debates and challenges in nursing. Routledge key themes in health and society* (pp. 180–194). London, UK: Routledge. Retrieved from Sheffield Hallam University Research Archive, http://shura.shu.ac.uk

American Nurse, The. (2015). Welcoming in the "year of ethics." *The American Nurse, 47*(1), 1.

American Nurses Association (ANA). (1994). *Position statement: Assisted suicide.* Washington, DC: Author.

American Nurses Association (ANA). (2015). *Code of ethics for nurses.* Retrieved from http://www .nursingworld.org/codeofethics

American Nurses Association and International Association of Clinical Research Nurses. (2017). *Clinic research nursing: Scope and standards of practice.* Silver Spring, MD: American Nurses Association.

Anderson, D. G., & Hatton, D. C. (2000). Accessing vulnerable populations for research. *Western Journal of Nursing Research, 22*(2), 244–251.

Batalden, P. B., & Davidoff, F. (2007). What is "quality improvement" and how can it transform healthcare? *Quality and Safety in Health Care, 16*(1), 2–3.

Birch, M., & Miller, T. (2002). Encouraging participation: Ethics and responsibilities. In M. Mauthner, M. Burch, J. Jessop, & T. Miller (Eds.), *Ethics in qualitative research* (pp. 91–106). London, UK: Sage.

Borsay, A. (2009). Nursing history: An irrelevance for nursing practice? *Nursing History Review, 17*(1), 14–27.

Burkhardt, M. A., & Nathaniel, A. K. (2014). *Ethics and issues in contemporary nursing* (4th ed.). Stanford, CT: Cengage Learning.

Carter, E. J., Mastro, K., Vose, C., Rivera, R., & Larson, E. L. (2017) Clarifying the conundrum: Evidence-based practice, quality, improvement, or research? *The Journal of Nursing Administration, 47*(5), 266–270.

Cartwright, J. C., & Hickman, S. E. (2007, October). Conducting research in community-based care facilities: Ethical and regulatory implications. *Journal of Gerontological Nursing, 33*(10), 5–11.

Centers for Disease Control and Prevention (CDC). (2011). The Tuskegee timeline. Retrieved from http://www.cdc.gov/tuskegee/timeline.htm

Chappy, S., & Gaberson, K. B. (2012). To IRB or not to IRB: That is the question. *AORN Journal, 95*(6), 682–683.

Christians, C. G. (2003). Ethics and politics in qualitative research. In N. K. Denzin & Y. S. Lincoln (Eds.), *The landscape of qualitative research: Theories and issues* (2nd ed., pp. 208–244). Thousand Oaks, CA: Sage.

Cipriano, P. F. (2015). Ethical practice environments, empowered nurses. *The American Nurse, 47*(2), 3.

Cipriano Silva, M. (2006). Ethics of research. In J. Fitzpatrick & M. Wallace (Eds.), *Encyclopedia of nursing research* (2nd ed., pp. 177–180). New York, NY: Springer.

Commission on Research Integrity. (1995). *Integrity and misconduct in research* (U.S. Department of Health and Human Services, Publication No. 1996-746-425). Washington, DC: U.S. Government Printing Office.

Conn, V. S. (2008). Staying true to the results. *Western Journal of Nursing Research, 30*(2), 161–162.

Cortez-Gann, J. Gilmore, K. D., Foley, K. W., Kennedy, M. B. & Kring, T. M. (2017). Blood transfusion vital sign frequency: What does the evidence say? *Medsurg Nursing, 26*(2) 89–92.

Council for International Organizations of Medical Sciences (CIOMS). (2002). International ethics guidelines for biomedical research involving human subjects. Retrieved from http://www.cioms.ch/publications/guidelines/guidelines_nov_2002_blurb.htm

Dally, A. (1998). Thalidomide: Was the tragedy preventable? *Lancet, 351*(9110), 1197–1199.

Doody, O., & Noonan, M. (2016) Nursing research ethics, guidance and application in practice. *British Journal of Nursing, 25*(14), 803–807.

Driever, M. J., & Pranulis, M. F. (2003). New challenges for issues in clinical nursing research. *Western Journal of Nursing Research, 25*(8), 937–947.

Edwards, R., & Mauthner, M. (2002). Ethics and feminist research: Theory and practice. In M. Mauthner, M. Burch, J. Jessop, & T. Miller (Eds.), *Ethics in qualitative research* (pp. 14–31). London, UK: Sage.

Ely, B., & Coleman, C. (2007). Recruitment and retention of children in longitudinal research. *Journal for Specialists in Pediatric Nursing, 12*(3), 199–202.

Erlen, J. A. (2005). HIPAA: Implications for research. *Orthopedic Nursing, 23*(2), 139–142.

Firby, P. (1995). Critiquing the ethical aspects of a study. *Nurse Researcher, 3*(1), 35–41.

Freda, M. C., & Kearney, M. H. (2005). Ethical issues faced by nursing editors. *Western Journal of Nursing Research, 27*(4), 487–499.

Grady, C. (2007). Quality improvement and ethical oversight. *Annals of Internal Medicine, 146*(9), 680–681.

Hanna, K. M., Weaver, M. T., Slaven, J. E., Fortenberry, J. D., & DiMeglio, L. A. (2014). Diabetes-related quality of life and the demands and burdens of diabetes care among emerging adults with Type I diabetes in the year after high school graduation. *Research in Nursing & Health, 37*(5), 399–408.

Henley, S. J., & Dougherty, M. C. (2009). Quality of manuscript reviews in nursing research. *Nursing Outlook, 57*(1), 18–26.

Hockenberry, M. (2014). Quality improvement and evidence-based practice change projects and the institutional review board: Is approval necessary? *Sigma Theta Tau International, 11*(4), 217–218.

International Council of Nurses (ICN). (2012). *The ICN code of ethics for nurses.* Retrieved from http://www.icn.ch/images/stories/documents/about/icncode_english.pdf

IRB Advisor. (2017, August). Gray zone remains between clinical research and quality improvement efforts. *IRB Advisor, 17*(8), 93–94.

Jeffers, B. R. (2005). Research environments that promote integrity. *Nursing Research, 54*(91), 63–70.

Kawar, L. N., Pugh, D. M., Scruth, E. A. (2016). Understanding the role and legal requirements of the institutional review board. *Clinical Nurse Specialist, 30*(3), 137–140, doi:10.1097/NUR.0000000000000197

Ketefian, S., & Lenz, E. R. (1995). Promoting scientific integrity in nursing research. Part II: Strategies. *Journal of Professional Nursing, 11*(5), 263–269.

Kirk, S. (2007). Methodological and ethical issues in conducting qualitative research with children and young people: A literature review. *International Journal of Nursing Studies, 44*(7), 1250–1260.

Kunin, T. F. (1997). Ethical issues in longitudinal research with at-risk children and adolescents. Cited in A. J. Roberson (2007). Adolescent informed consent: Ethics, law, and theory to guide policy and nursing research. *Journal of Nursing Law, 11*(4), 191–196.

Lenz, E. R., & Ketefian, S. (1995). Promoting scientific integrity in nursing research. Part I: Current approaches in doctoral programs. *Journal of Professional Nursing, 11*(5), 213–219.

Lutz, K. F. (1999). Maintaining client safety and scientific integrity in research with battered women. *Image: Journal of Nursing Scholarship, 31*(1), 89–93.

Lynn, J., Baily, M. A., Bottrell, M., Jennings, B., Levine, R., Davidoff, F., . . . James, B. (2007). The ethics of using quality improvement methods in health care. *Annals of Internal Medicine, 146*(9), 666–673.

Macrina, F. L. (1995). *Scientific integrity: An introductory text with cases.* Washington, DC: ASM Press.

Miller, T., & Bell, L. (2002). Consenting to what? Issues of access, gate-keeping and informed consent. In M. Mauthner, M. Burch, J. Jessop, & T. Miller (Eds.), *Ethics in qualitative research* (pp. 53–69). London, UK: Sage.

Miller, V. A. (2017, August). Assent is not consent: Children in clinical trials are not little adults. *IRB Advisor, 17*(8), 3–5.

National Institutes of Health (NIH). (1979). The Belmont report: Ethical principles and guidelines for the protection of human subjects of research. Retrieved from http://www.hhs.gov/ohrp /humansubjects/guidance/belmont.html

O'Mathúna, D. P. (2015). Ethical consideration for evidence implementation and evidence generation. In B. M. Melnyk & E. Finout-Overholt (Eds.), *Evidence-based practice in nursing and healthcare: A guide to best practice* (3rd ed). Philadelphia, PA: Lippincott, Williams & Wilkins.

Perkins, E. (2001). Johns Hopkins tragedy: Could librarians have prevented a death? *Information Today, 18*(8), 51, 54. Retrieved http://newsbreaks.infotoday.com/nbreader.asp?ArticleID=17534

Pilkington, F. B. (2002). Scientific merit and research ethics. *Nursing Science Quarterly, 15*(3), 196–200.

Public Health Service Act, 42 USC 163. (1988). Cited in D. L. Volker (2004). Methodological issues associated with studying an illegal act: Assisted dying. *Advances in Nursing Science, 27*(2), 117–128.

Redman, R. W. (2007). Knowledge development, quality improvement, and research ethics. *Research and Theory for Nursing Practice: An International Journal, 21*(4), 217–219.

Reich, W. T. (Ed.). (1995). *Encyclopedia of bioethics* (pp. 2248–2259). New York, NY: Simon & Schuster Macmillan.

Roberson, A. J. (2007). Adolescent informed consent: Ethics, law, and theory to guide policy and nursing research. *Journal of Nursing Law, 11*(4), 191–196.

Rogers, B. (2005). Research with protected populations: Vulnerable participants. *AAOHN Journal, 53*(4), 156–157.

Rothstein, W. G., & Phuong, L. H. (2007). Ethical attitudes of nurse, physician and unaffiliated members of institutional review boards. *Journal of Nursing Scholarship, 39*(1), 75–811.

Schroeder (2017). Ethics dumping—the dark side of international research. Retrieved from https://theconversation.com/ethics-dumping-the-dark-side-of-international-research. December 12, 2017.

Siedlecki, S. L. (2008). Making a difference through research. *AORN Journal, 88*(5), 716–729.

Stephens, T. M. (2017). Situational awareness and the nursing code of ethics. *American Nurse Today, 12*(11), 56–58.

Tanner, C. A. (2006). Thinking like a nurse: A research-based model of clinical judgment in nursing. *Journal of Nursing Education, 45*(6), 204–211.

Tschudin, V. (1992). *Ethics in nursing: The caring relationship*. Oxford, UK: Butterworth Heinemann.

Twycross, A., & Corlett, J. (2007). Challenges of setting up a multi-centered research study. *Nursing Standard, 21*(49), 35–38.

U.S. Department of Health and Human Services. (2009). Protection of human subjects, title 45, code of regulations, part 46. Retrieved from http://www.hhs.gov/ohrp/humansubjects/regbook2013 .pdf.pdf

U.S. Department of Health and Human Services. (2017). Code of Federal Regulations, 21 U.S.C.A.§56.101 *et. Seq*. US. Food and Drug Administration, 2017.

Volker, D. L. (2004). Methodological issues associated with studying an illegal act: Assisted dying. *Advances in Nursing Science, 27*(2), 117–128.

Weaver, K. (2007). Ethical sensitivity: State of knowledge and needs for further research. *Nursing Ethics, 2*(4), 141–155.

Westlake, C., & Taha, A. A. (2012). The institutional review board: Purpose and process. *Clinical Nurse Specialist, 26*(2), 66–70.

Wood, A., Grady, C., & Emanuel, E. J. (2002). The crisis in human participants research: Identifying the problems and proposing solutions. Retrieved from http://bioethics.georgetown.edu/pcbe /background/emanuelpaper.html

Woolston, W., & Connelly, L. M. (2017). Felty's syndrome: A qualitative case study. *MedSurg Nursing, 26*(2) 105–109, 118.

Young, M. (2017, August). ICMJE underlines ethics on importance of data sharing. *IRB Advisor, 17*(8) 85–86.

CHAPTER 6
Asking the Right Question

Julie A. Baker-Townsend, Kathaleen C. Bloom, and Lucy B. Trice

CHAPTER OBJECTIVES

At the conclusion of this chapter, the learner will be able to:
1. Discuss processes involved in identifying a researchable problem in nursing practice.
2. Write an effective problem statement.
3. Discuss essential characteristics needed to pose a research question.
4. Identify the criteria for establishing research variables.
5. Contrast the various types of hypotheses.
6. Explain the differences between conceptual and operational definitions.
7. Critically evaluate research questions and hypotheses found in research reports for their contribution to the strength of evidence for nursing practice.

KEY TERMS

Associative hypothesis
Categorical variable
Causal hypothesis
Complex hypothesis
Confounding variable
Continuous variable
Demographic variable
Dependent variable
Dichotomous variable
Directional hypothesis
Discrete variable

Extraneous variable
Hypothesis
Independent variable
Nondirectional hypothesis
Null hypothesis
Problem statement
Research hypothesis
Research question
Simple hypothesis
Variable

▶ Introduction

Every research study begins with a problem the researcher would like to solve. For such a problem to be researchable, it must be one that can be studied through collecting and analyzing data. Some problems, although interesting, are by their nature not appropriate research problems because they are not researchable. Problems involving moral or ethical issues are not researchable because the solutions to these problems are based on an individual's values. For example, one could not research a question such as, "Should physician-assisted suicide be legalized?" because the answer to the question depends on one's values rather than on a clearly right or wrong answer. This restriction is not to say that physician-assisted suicide cannot be studied. One could study people's opinions regarding physician-assisted suicide. For example, one might ask the question, "Do cancer patients hold more favorable opinions regarding legalization of physician-assisted suicide than the general public?" The need to avoid moral/ethical questions as a research topic applies to both quantitative and qualitative studies.

Additional factors influence whether a problem is considered researchable when using quantitative research methods. For a problem to be considered researchable by quantitative methods, the **variable** to be studied must be clearly defined and measurable. This clarity is necessary to apply statistical measures that will identify relationships among the variables. Qualitative studies are not subject to the same restriction because the purpose of these studies is to describe in detail the phenomenon of interest as it is perceived by the study subjects. In other words, qualitative studies are descriptive in nature and are not concerned with relationships among variables.

▶ Identifying Researchable Problems

A number of sources from which researchable problems can arise are available. Personal experience, whether as a healthcare professional or as a consumer of health care, is a rich source. For example, reviewing procedure manuals might raise the question, "Does one procedure for giving mouth care apply to all patients?" In considering diverse groups of patients such as those with endotracheal or nasogastric tubes in place; those with acquired immunodeficiency syndrome (AIDS), often accompanied by buccal mucosal lesions; and cancer patients on chemotherapy, one might ask, "Does one size fit all, or should separate procedures be established for each case?" Thus, as many authors point out (Gray, Grove, & Sutherland, 2017; Polit & Beck, 2017; Schmidt & Brown, 2019), practice experience is a major source for identifying gaps in knowledge that would benefit from research.

The nursing literature can also be a valuable source for researchable problems, particularly for the novice researcher (Grove, Gray, & Burns, 2015; Polit & Beck, 2017). For example, the researcher might identify a topic of interest and then review the nursing research literature to determine which kinds of studies have been done in that area. Seeing how other researchers have approached a problem can often spark new ideas or perhaps point to studies that would benefit from replication. In addition to offering such indirect assistance in the development of a problem statement, the research literature, including unpublished dissertations and theses as well as published research articles, provides direct assistance through specific suggestions for future research in the area. These suggestions may be offered under a special heading for future research, or they may be part of the discussion of the findings.

The opioid crisis is one of the key issues in health care today. According to the Centers for Disease Control and Prevention (CDC), the number of opioid prescription deaths has increased by more than fivefold since 1999; greater than 600,000 people have died from drug overdoses from 1999 to 2016 (Seth, Scholl, Rudd, & Bacon, 2018; Warner, Trinidad, Bastian, & Minino, 2016). This preventable cause of mortality has prompted nurse researchers to investigate the use of intravenous (IV) analgesics for pain management in the intraoperative and postoperative period (Kwan & Sullivan, 2017). This research is aimed at decreasing the use of opioids to improve the overall health of our communities.

Social issues often give rise to topics relevant to healthcare research (Polit & Beck, 2016). For example, the feminist movement raised questions about gender equity in health care and in healthcare research. The civil rights movement led to research on minority health problems in general and to explorations of the differences in effectiveness of medical treatment in different ethnic groups.

Shifts in the U.S. population, including increasing numbers of elderly and increasing numbers of individuals with one or more chronic diseases or conditions, also provide impetus for healthcare research. One example topic is the use of diagnostic and corrective joint procedures. While these minimally invasive techniques are popular, the extended wait times for the procedures are not. The long wait times prompted nurse researchers to create a quality improvement plan. This plan included a literature review and ended with a well-developed action plan to improve access to care (Brennan & Parsons, 2017). Other uncommon conditions that affect the aging population have also inspired nursing researchers. While Felty's syndrome is rare, this autoimmune condition is most commonly seen in the elderly population. Nursing researchers have disseminated education on this age-related syndrome by creating a case study to increase awareness and treatment of the condition (Woolston & Connelly, 2017).

⏏ THINK OUTSIDE THE BOX

Develop problem statements, research questions, and/or hypotheses for each of the following examples:
- Which information has been used to determine the method of catheterizing a laboring mother?
- Which information serves as the basis for the range of blood sugars used within newly diagnosed elderly diabetics?
- Which items need to be included into the formation of a problem statement, research question, and hypothesis?

The research priorities of the profession, and particularly of the funding bodies interested in healthcare research, are also a primary source for generating researchable problems (Grove et al., 2015). For example, the National Institute of Nursing Research (NINR, n.d.) is the largest federal funding body dedicated specifically to nursing research. The NINR has as its mission "to promote and improve the health of individuals, families, communities, and populations" (p. 4). The NINR supports

---

BOX 6-1 Funding Priorities of NINR

- Health Promotion and Disease Prevention
- Advancing the Quality of Life: Symptom Management and Self-Management
- End-of-Life and Palliative Care
- Innovation
- Developing Nurse Scientists

Key Themes:
- Symptom Science: Promoting Personalized Health Strategies
- Wellness: Promoting Health and Preventing Illness
- Self-Management: Improving Quality of Life for Individuals with Chronic Illness
- End-of-Life and Palliative Care: The Science of Compassion

Reproduced from National Institute of Nursing Research (NINR). (n.d.). Implementing NINR's Strategic Plan: Key Themes. Retrieved from http://www.ninr.nih.gov/aboutninr/keythemes. Further elaboration within each priority is provided at this source.

---

clinical and basic research and also provides funding for researcher training. The ongoing funding priorities of the NINR are listed in **BOX 6-1**.

▶ Determining the Significance of the Problem

Once the problem of interest has been identified, and before going any further, the researcher must determine the significance of the problem to nursing and the feasibility of studying the problem. Significance refers to whether a problem is worth studying. A number of authors agree on the criteria that can be used to determine the significance of a problem to nursing (Grove et al., 2015; LoBiondo-Wood & Haber, 2018; Polit & Beck, 2016):

- Will nursing's stakeholders (patients, nurses, healthcare community) benefit from the findings of the study?
- Will the findings be applicable to practice, education, or administration?
- Will the findings extend or support current theory or generate new theory?
- Will the findings support current nursing practice or provide evidence for changing current practice and/or policies?

Some authorities (Grove et al., 2015; Polit & Beck, 2017) recommend that two additional criteria be considered when determining the significance of a problem:

- Will the findings address nursing research priorities?
- Will the results of the proposed study build on previous findings?

If the research problem does not meet the majority of these criteria, it should be reworked or, if that is not possible, simply abandoned. The single most important of these criteria is perhaps the first one: Will nursing's stakeholders (patients, nurses, healthcare community) benefit from the findings of the study? If this question cannot be answered with a resounding yes, then the problem is probably not worth studying. Nursing is a discipline that takes pride in research aimed at benefiting patients and changing practice for the better. In the move to evidence-based practice (EBP), benefit to patients and applicability to practice—and especially support for current practice or evidence for changing current practice—are paramount in assessing the significance of a research problem.

▶ Examining the Feasibility of the Problem

Feasibility refers to whether the study can be done. It includes considerations such as cost of the study, availability of study subjects, time constraints, availability of facilities and equipment, cooperation of others, interest of the researcher, and expertise of the researcher (Gray et al., 2017; LoBiondo-Wood & Haber, 2018; Polit & Beck, 2016).

Cost

EBP has emerged from the desire of the majority of healthcare providers (both institutions and individuals) to do what is right for the patient and what will result in more good than harm. The evidence for EBP is gathered through research (Melnyk & Fineout-Overholt, 2015; Schmidt & Brown, 2019), and all research studies cost money to some degree. It is the researcher's task to obtain support for the research from the institution in which it will be conducted as well as from potential funding bodies, both within the institution itself and outside agencies. When seeking this support, the researcher must present a clear picture of the value of the research in terms of patient outcomes versus the costs involved. The current economic climate, which emphasizes the link between outcomes value and resources expenditure, demands nothing less (Malloch & Porter-O'Grady, 2010). The deciding factor with regard to feasibility of a particular study may be how much the study will cost versus the funds and other necessary support that are available to the researcher.

Availability of Subjects

The type and number of study subjects vary depending on the purpose and design of the study. Larger numbers of participants are generally needed for quantitative studies if the findings are to be considered significant, whereas smaller numbers of subjects are appropriate for studies using a qualitative design. Clearly, a sufficient number of subjects must be available for the study to be feasible.

Time Constraints

Studies done in connection with the pursuit of academic degrees (e.g., research projects, theses, dissertations), of necessity, have a time frame for their completion. The same is true for studies supported by grant monies, as well as studies for which grant monies are being sought. For a study to be considered feasible, it must have the possibility of being completed within the applicable time constraints.

Availability of Facilities and Equipment

The need for special facilities and equipment can add greatly to the cost of a study. Not all studies require specialized equipment or facilities, but for those that do, both the cost and the availability of these items must be taken into consideration when determining the feasibility of the study.

Cooperation of Others

All studies require a certain amount of cooperation from others. The researcher may need referrals from others to obtain research subjects, for example, or to arrange for use of laboratories or other kinds of facilities. Student researchers in particular often need assistance with data entry in quantitative studies, data transcription in qualitative studies, and statistical analysis. These types of assistance are frequently offered to student researchers without a fee; however, obtaining the assistance requires cooperation from those providing these services. The study subjects themselves must also cooperate in a sense if the data are to be collected in a timely manner. Thus, the cooperation of these important others is an essential ingredient of a feasible study. Securing that cooperation falls squarely on the shoulders of the researcher. In their discussion of obtaining cooperation from various others, Gray et al. (2017) contend that researchers need to maintain objectivity throughout the course of the study and avoid a tendency to take themselves too seriously.

Interest of the Researcher

Conducting research, although often rewarding when the final results are in, is nevertheless hard work. To embark on a study that is not of fairly profound interest to the researcher is foolhardy at best, and at worst it can lead to failure to complete the study. If the researcher is not interested in doing the research, then carrying out the study is not generally feasible.

Expertise of the Researcher

Ideally, the researcher should have prior knowledge and experience in the field of study in question. This doesn't mean that a study would be considered not possible solely because it is a new area of study for the researcher. Certainly, seasoned researchers frequently "branch out" into new areas of study. When less experienced researchers are involved, however, Polit and Beck (2016) caution that difficulties may arise in developing and carrying out a study on a topic that is totally new and/or unfamiliar.

▶ Addressing Nursing Research Priorities

If the body of knowledge that deals with the practice of nursing is to be expanded, the major focus of nursing research should be on issues that influence patient outcomes. Through this type of research, we will gather the evidence to document the quality and effectiveness of nursing care (Melnyk & Fineout-Overholt, 2015). The specific areas of focus, in terms of patient outcomes, vary widely. As noted earlier, doing research can be costly, so it behooves the researcher to attempt to match his or her research interests not only with those of the institution where the individual works but also with the priorities established by funding agencies. The major federal funding agency dedicated to nursing is NINR. Other funding bodies with research priorities relevant to nursing include the Agency for Healthcare Research and Quality, private organizations such as the W.K. Kellogg Foundation and the Helene Fuld Health Trust, professional organizations such as the American Nurses Foundation and Sigma Theta Tau International, and nursing specialty organizations such as the Association of periOperative Registered Nurses and the American Association of Critical-Care Nurses, to name a few. Taking care to address the funding priorities of a particular organization enhances the possibility of obtaining from that organization the funding needed to complete the research project.

▶ Problem Statement

The **problem statement** presents the idea, issue, or situation that the researcher intends to examine in the study. The statement should be broad enough to cover the concern prompting the study yet narrow enough to provide direction for designing the study. It can be conceptualized in the form of a declarative sentence or a question. In some cases, the term *research question* is used interchangeably with *problem statement*.

The problem statement is the foundation of the study and, as such, is usually preceded by several paragraphs of background information that set the stage for the proposed study. These paragraphs identify the significance of the problem, present justification that the problem is researchable, and provide supporting documentation from the literature. This general discussion of the problem culminates in the problem statement. The problem statement is often further clarified by including the purpose and goal(s) of the study, which are derived from the problem statement.

▶ Research Question

Although the terms **research question** and *problem statement* are sometimes used interchangeably, the research question is often more specific than the problem statement. In addition, research questions (rather than hypotheses) are frequently used to guide studies that are exploratory in nature and aimed at describing variables or perhaps identifying differences between groups in relation to these variables. Research questions also guide studies that examine relationships among the variables being studied but do not test the nature of these relationships. Studies designed to test the nature of the relationships among variables are generally guided by hypotheses rather than research questions (Gray et al., 2017).

🔄 THINK OUTSIDE THE BOX

Formulate conceptual and operational definitions for *catheterization, laboring mother, blood sugar*, and *newly diagnosed elderly diabetic*.

Research questions can be used to guide both quantitative and qualitative studies. Quantitative studies are often initiated to answer several questions derived from the problem of interest, each focused on a specific variable to be measured in the population. For example, West and colleagues (2011) were interested in obesity prevention—specifically, how to prevent regaining weight initially lost during a weight-loss regimen. Most weight-loss methods focus on behavioral skills, that is, changing food choice and/or eating patterns. These same methods are used in maintenance programs but with disappointing results (Wing et al., 2008). West and colleagues (2011) devised a study to compare the efficacy of a motivation-focused treatment versus a skill-based treatment in maintaining weight loss. The following research questions might be used to guide this study:

- Does a motivation-focused intervention affect weight maintenance in individuals who have recently lost weight?
- Does a skill-based intervention affect weight maintenance in individuals who have recently lost weight?
- Do individuals who follow a motivation-focused intervention maintain their weight loss for a longer time period than those who follow a skill-based intervention?

The first two questions above are narrowly focused, dealing with one **independent variable** (participation in a motivation-focused intervention and participation in a skill-based intervention, respectively) and the **dependent variable** (weight maintenance). The third question, while more complex, gets at the heart of the matter: Does one intervention work better than the other?

In another example, Hanna, Weaver, Slaven, Fortenberry, and DiMeglio (2014) were interested in diabetes-related quality of life (DQOL) experienced by young adults. They were specifically concerned with the effect of the demands and burdens of diabetes on quality of life during the year following high school graduation. This is a time of fairly dramatic change for young adults as they move toward independent living, physically, psychologically, and emotionally. Those with type 1 diabetes must also assume independence in managing their diabetes during this time. The authors wished to study the effect that assuming responsibility for their own diabetes management had on DQOL among these young adults. They designed a study to examine the association of DQOL and, among others, various aspects of diabetes care, including glycemic control and assuming primary responsibility for diabetes. The following research questions might be among the list of questions used to guide this study:

- Does glycemic control affect DQOL?
- Does assuming primary responsibility for diabetes care affect glycemic control?
- Do those with consistent glycemic control have a higher perceived DQOL than those who do not have consistent glycemic control?

The first two questions above are again fairly narrow and contain one independent variable (glycemic control and assuming responsibility for diabetes care, respectively) and one dependent variable (DQOL and glycemic control, respectively). The third question, while seemingly more complex, still contains one independent variable (consistent glycemic control) and one dependent variable (perceived DQOL).

Qualitative studies, by their nature, explore phenomena about which little is known (Polit & Beck, 2017). The research questions guiding these types of studies are limited in number and generally broad in scope, and they include variables or concepts that are more complex than those guiding quantitative studies (Gray et al., 2017).

For example, Woolston and Connelly (2017) searched the literature to evaluate published nursing care guidelines for patients with Felty's syndrome. The authors found only two published articles. These two articles were only related to one aspect of Felty's syndrome: rheumatoid arthritis, which is one small part of a multifaceted and complex diagnosis (Nelson, 2011; Primdahl, Clausen, & Horslev-Petersen, 2013). The investigators wanted a greater understanding of the disease. The authors used a qualitative approach and interviewed a patient on three separate occasions to better understand her physical and emotional experience with the disease. The research question guiding this study might be stated as follows: What are the essential themes common to the experience of patients with Felty's syndrome? The qualitative concepts are broad and may include physical, emotional, and spiritual components.

In a third example, Iverson and colleagues (2014) explored women veterans' preferences for intimate partner violence (IPV) screening and response procedures within the Veterans Health Administration. While all women are at risk for IPV, research suggests that women veterans are at a higher risk than other women (Dichter, Cerulli, & Bossarte, 2011). Data were gathered through focus groups, with separate groups for women who had experienced IPV during their lifetime and those who had not. A total of five focus groups were conducted over a 1-year period. The data obtained were analyzed using conventional content analysis, and common themes were identified. A research question guiding this study might be stated in this manner: What are women veterans' preferences for IPV screening and response procedures within the Veterans Health Administration? Again, the concepts in this question are broad and more complex than those for the earlier examples of questions guiding quantitative studies. Because they are designed to get at understanding behavior and the values/perceptions that underlie it, qualitative studies are particularly important as a starting point for designing and implementing nursing interventions (Ketefian & Redman, 2013).

Components of the Problem Statement

A well-written problem statement for a quantitative study, whether written as a declarative statement or a question, has, at a minimum, two components: the population of concern and the variable(s) to be studied. The PICOT format (population, intervention, comparison, outcome, time) described in Chapter 1 has the advantage of clarifying more fully the population of the study, the intervention/comparison of interest, the outcome desired, and the time frame involved.

For example, Kwan and Sullivan (2017) studied IV acetaminophen and IV ibuprofen to decrease pain as an adjunct to opioids in hospitalized patients. As stated, the population (hospitalized patients) is fairly broad and does not provide a lot of direction for the literature search or for the study design. The authors narrowed the literature search to identify literature assessing efficacy of IV ibuprofen and IV acetaminophen in reducing opioid use in surgical patients. The variables of interest would be decreased opioid use and IV ibuprofen and IV acetaminophen. Following the PICOT format, the population of interest (P) would be hospitalized surgical patients, the intervention of interest (I) would be IV acetaminophen and IV ibuprofen, the comparison of interest (C) would be no IV acetaminophen and IV ibuprofen, the outcome of interest (O) would be decreased opioid use, and the time (T) would refer to time of hospitalization.

Strictly speaking, the term *variable* refers to measurable qualities or characteristics of people, things, or situations that can change or fluctuate. For example, blood pressure, pulse rate, anxiety level, and degree of pain are all characteristics of people that can vary from one person to another. A child's reaction to the presence (or absence) of a parent in the hospitalized child's room during painful procedures can vary from one hospitalized child to another. Variables are the foundation of quantitative studies; they constitute what is being studied in the designated population.

Researchers often want to know what causes or influences a particular phenomenon or, in some cases, what alleviates or diminishes that phenomenon. For example, one might want to know if a hospitalized child's anxiety level during a painful procedure would be lessened if a parent were present during the procedure. In this case, there are two variables of interest: the child's anxiety level and the presence of a parent during the painful procedure. The researcher is investigating the effect that the presence of a parent has on the child's anxiety level during a painful procedure. Because the variable "presence of a parent" is having an effect on the variable "child's anxiety level," it is termed the independent variable. By the same token, the variable being affected (i.e., child's anxiety level) is termed the dependent variable. In a study investigating more than one variable, the variable(s) that is (are) acting on, influencing, or causing an effect on the other variable(s) is (are) called the independent variable(s), and the variable(s) being acted on is (are) called the dependent variable(s) (Grove et al., 2015; LoBiondo-Wood & Haber, 2018; Polit & Beck, 2017).

Another type of variable that can affect the outcome of the study but is not the variable the researcher is investigating is referred to as an **extraneous variable**. In the example cited in the preceding paragraph, the age of the child could affect his or her anxiety level, regardless of whether a parent is present in the room, and therefore would be considered an extraneous variable. The researcher could control for the variable of age by limiting the study population to a particular age group. Another variable that might affect the child's anxiety level, regardless of whether a parent is present in the room, is the nature of the painful procedure. The procedure could be specified to control for this variable. With any study, it is important to identify and control for extraneous variables; otherwise, the study results may be confusing and inaccurate. Most studies have extraneous variables of one sort or another. It is important for the researcher to recognize and control for these variables, either in the study design or through statistical procedures, to preserve the validity of the study results. If a study cannot control for an extraneous variable, the variable is then termed a **confounding variable**.

The term **demographic variable** refers to characteristics of the subjects in the study. Data on these characteristics are usually collected during the study and are then used to describe the study group. Many different kinds of demographic information can be collected, including details about age, gender, ethnicity, educational

⬆ THINK OUTSIDE THE BOX

Why is it necessary to have a problem statement, research question, or hypothesis? What benefit does it provide? Is one better than the others? What restrictions are related to the use of the problem statement, research question, or hypothesis?

level, marital status, and number of children. The types of demographic data collected depend on the purpose of the study; however, at a minimum, data on age, gender, and ethnicity should be gathered.

If a variable can take on a wide range of values (from 0 to 100 or larger), it is often referred to as a **continuous variable**. A continuous variable is not limited to whole-number values. Examples of continuous variables include age, weight, salary, and blood pressure. In contrast, a variable that can take on only a finite number of values, usually restricted to whole numbers, is referred to as a **discrete variable**. For example, respiratory rate would be considered a discrete variable because it can take on only whole-number equivalents; although variation in respiratory rate can occur from person to person, a finite number of these variations are compatible with life.

Categorical and dichotomous variables are similar because they represent characteristics that can be measured only in the sense that they are either present or not present. These kinds of variables are often assigned a number for identification, but the number does not represent a quantity. For example, ethnicity might be divided into white, African American, Hispanic, Native American, Pacific Islander, and Asian American, with each classification assigned an identifying number. The assigned number would have no meaning, however, other than identifying the occurrence of each race, perhaps to facilitate counting the number of occurrences of that particular race in the study. In this case, race would be considered a **categorical variable**, with each race included in the study representing a category. If only two categories are possible for a categorical variable, it may be referred to as a **dichotomous variable**. For example, sex is considered a dichotomous variable because only two categories are possible—male and female.

Writing the Problem Statement

As noted previously, problem statements for quantitative studies may be written in the form of a declarative statement or a question (**TABLE 6-1**). The two components that must be included in every problem statement are the population of interest and the variable(s) to be measured. For example, if we were interested in studying the effect of the presence of a parent on anxiety level in children undergoing painful procedures, we might construct a problem statement in the form of a question: "Does the presence of a parent affect the anxiety level in children ages 3–5 years undergoing initiation of intravenous therapy?" Alternatively, the same problem could be stated as a declarative statement: "The presence of a parent affects the anxiety level in children ages 3–5 years undergoing initiation of intravenous therapy." Both statements contain a population of interest (children ages 3–5 years undergoing initiation of intravenous therapy) and two variables (presence of a parent—independent variable; anxiety level of the child—dependent variable). The only difference between the two is the form of the statement—one is presented as a question and the other as a declarative statement. Note also that the elements of the PICOT format are readily apparent in each of these examples.

⟳ THINK OUTSIDE THE BOX

Identify the elements of the PICOT format for each of the problem statements in Table 6-1.

TABLE 6-1 Examples of Problem Statements	
Declarative Statement Format	**Question Format**
Music therapy decreases the level of maternal anxiety during cesarean section.	Does music therapy decrease the level of maternal anxiety during cesarean section?
Nursing home residents who participate in regular exercise have fewer falls than those who do not.	Do nursing home residents who participate in regular exercise have fewer falls than those who do not?
Participation in a support group improves morale in family caregivers of Alzheimer's patients.	Does participation in a support group improve morale in family caregivers of Alzheimer's patients?
Diabetic patients who perceive themselves as obese will participate in a weight management program.	Will diabetic patients who perceive themselves as obese participate in a weight management program?
The number of medication errors made by nurses increases when the number of medications per patient is greater than three (3).	Does the number of medication errors made by nurses increases when the number of medications per patient is greater than three (3)?

▶ Hypotheses

A research question asks whether a relationship exists between variables in a particular population. In contrast, a **hypothesis** stipulates or predicts the relationship that exists. For example, if the research question is "Does the presence of a parent in the room affect the anxiety level in children ages 3–5 years undergoing initiation of intravenous therapy?" then we might develop several hypotheses:

1. The presence of a parent in the room affects the anxiety level in children ages 3–5 years who undergo initiation of intravenous therapy.
2. The presence of a parent in the room reduces the anxiety level in children ages 3–5 years who undergo initiation of intravenous therapy.
3. The presence of a parent in the room has no effect on the anxiety level in children ages 3–5 years who undergo initiation of intravenous therapy.
4. The presence of a parent in the room increases the anxiety level in children ages 3–5 years who undergo initiation of intravenous therapy.

The advantage of a hypothesis over a research question is that the hypothesis puts the question into a form that can be tested. It is the nature of hypotheses to predict relationships among or between variables. For a hypothesis to be testable, it must stipulate a relationship between at least two variables in a given population.

Within EBP, the research question format incorporates the population of interest, the intervention, a comparison of interest, outcomes, and timing to ensure clarity of the subject (note that these are the components of the PICOT format). This process can also be applied to developing one or more hypotheses for a research study. Each hypothesis should contain the population of interest, the independent variable(s), the dependent variable(s), and the comparison of interest, all of which should lead to the outcome of the study.

Hypotheses and Qualitative Studies

Hypotheses are used in quantitative studies but are not appropriate for qualitative studies. By their nature, they present the researcher's opinion in the form of a prediction about the outcome of the study. In qualitative studies, however, researchers focus on the viewpoints of the subjects participating in the study rather than on their own. Thus, the participants' viewpoints, rather than the researcher's hypothesis, guide the qualitative study. Generally, the purpose of qualitative studies is to explore new concepts and ideas about which little is known or to discover new meanings for concepts. In keeping with this purpose, researchers using qualitative methods take great care to set aside their preconceived notions about the phenomena under investigation. A hypothesis would be a disadvantage in a qualitative study because it would predict the outcome of the study and potentially bias the results. Thus, while qualitative studies may generate hypotheses that can then be tested using quantitative methods, they are not themselves guided by research hypotheses.

Types of Hypotheses

A testable hypothesis, also called the **research hypothesis**, predicts the relationship between two or more variables in a population of interest. All four of the hypotheses in the previous example could be considered testable. Hypotheses may be directional, nondirectional, or null:

- A **directional hypothesis** predicts the path or direction that the relationship will take. In the preceding example, both hypothesis 2 and hypothesis 4 are directional hypotheses. Hypothesis 2 predicts a decrease in anxiety with the presence of a parent, and hypothesis 4 predicts an increase in anxiety with the presence of a parent.
- A **nondirectional hypothesis** predicts a relationship but not the path or direction of the relationship. Hypothesis 1 in the previous example is a nondirectional hypothesis; it states that the presence of a parent affects the anxiety level in children ages 3–5 years but does not stipulate the direction of the effect.
- A **null hypothesis**, also called a statistical hypothesis, predicts that no relationship exists among or between the variables in the study. When inferential statistics are used to analyze data, the assumption is that the null hypothesis is actually being tested. Because this is understood, many researchers do not state the null hypothesis when reporting their findings in the literature. In the previous example, hypothesis 3 is stated in the null form.

⚓ THINK OUTSIDE THE BOX

Describe a problem in which a null hypothesis would be used, and state the null hypothesis.

Hypotheses may also be classified as simple or complex: A **simple hypothesis** specifies the relationship between two variables, whereas a **complex hypothesis** specifies the relationships between and among more than two variables. In the previous example, all four of the hypotheses could be classified as simple hypotheses. In each case, there are only two variables—the presence of a parent and the anxiety level in children ages 3–5 years. An example of a complex hypothesis might be "Religious beliefs, presence of social support, and ethnic background affect the perception of pain in patients who are terminally ill with cancer." Here there are four variables—religious beliefs, the presence of social support, ethnic background, and perception of pain. Complex hypotheses may also be termed *multivariate hypotheses* for the simple reason that they contain more than two variables.

In addition, hypotheses may be categorized as associative or causal. These terms reflect the relationship between or among the variables in the hypothesis. For example, in an **associative hypothesis**, the hypothesis is stated in a way indicating that the variables exist side by side and that a change in one variable is accompanied by a change in another. However, there is no suggestion that a change in one variable causes a change in another—merely that the variables change in association with each other (LoBiondo-Wood & Haber, 2018).

In contrast, a **causal hypothesis** is stated in a way indicating that one variable causes or brings about a change in one or more other variables (Grove et al., 2015). As one might expect, the variable inducing the change is referred to as the independent variable, and the variable being changed is the dependent variable. Causal hypotheses may also be called directional hypotheses. Continuing with the example of the presence of a parent in the room with a child during a painful procedure and its effect on the child's anxiety level, two of the hypotheses can be termed causal—hypothesis 2 and hypothesis 4. Hypothesis 2 predicts a decrease in anxiety (dependent variable) with the presence of a parent in the room (independent variable), and hypothesis 4 predicts an increase in anxiety (dependent variable) with the presence of a parent in the room (independent variable).

▶ Defining Variables for the Study

The variables to be studied in quantitative research projects are generally defined in two ways—conceptually and operationally. The conceptual definition is a broad, more abstract definition that is generally drawn from relevant literature, particularly the theoretical literature; the researcher's clinical experience; or, in some cases, a combination of these sources. The conceptual definition is similar to a dictionary definition in that it provides the general meaning associated with the variable, but it is more in-depth and broader in scope. Although considered the starting point, conceptual definitions rarely give direction regarding how the variable will actually be measured for the study. The operational definition, by contrast, stipulates precisely how the variable will be measured, including which tools will be used, if applicable. If a conceptual definition is abstract, an operational definition is concrete. This concreteness is necessary to allow for precise measurement of the variable(s) of interest in the study.

▶ Evidence-Based Practice Considerations

The ability to apply research findings to practice is an expected competency of advanced practice nurses. However, if we accept that it is the desire of all practitioners of nursing to provide "only that care that makes a positive difference in the lives of those whom they serve" (Porter-O'Grady, 2010, p. 1), then it is clear that all professional nurses—from the new graduate to the seasoned veteran—should have the ability to apply research findings to practice. Inherent in this ability is an understanding of how the research process unfolds and what constitutes good research.

Melnyk and Fineout-Overholt (2015) maintain that "the goal of EBP is to use the highest quality of [research] knowledge in providing care to produce the greatest impact on patients' health status" (p. 75). To accomplish this, practitioners—particularly staff nurses who are at the bedside caring for patients on a daily basis—must have the tools to critically analyze research to make appropriate EBP decisions. To analyze research critically, these staff nurses must possess a working knowledge of the language of research; recognize a researchable problem statement; distinguish between and among variables, identifying independent versus dependent variables; determine the population of interest; and, above all, recognize a well-conducted study, one whose findings are worth consideration for applying to practice. In its purest and best form, EBP happens at the bedside. The burden of implementation rests squarely on the shoulders of the staff nurse.

Summary Points

1. Every study begins with a problem that the researcher would like to solve.
2. There are many sources for researchable problems, including personal experience, the nursing literature, social issues, and the research priorities of funding bodies.
3. The significance of the problem to nursing and the feasibility of studying the problem are important aspects to consider before embarking on any research project.
4. The problem statement presents the issue or situation to be examined and should identify the population of interest as well as the variables that will be studied.
5. Variables may be classified in a variety of ways: (a) independent versus dependent, (b) continuous versus discrete, (c) extraneous, (d) confounding, (e) categorical, and (f) dichotomous.
6. The problem statement may be written as a question or as a declarative sentence.
7. Placing the problem statement in the PICOT format helps to clarify the population, variables, outcome, and time frame involved.
8. Hypotheses predict the relationship between or among variables.
9. Hypotheses may take many forms: (a) directional versus nondirectional, (b) simple versus complex, (c) associative versus causal, and (d) null.

10. Variables to be studied are generally defined both conceptually and operationally.

11. For nurses to pursue evidence-based practice, they must understand the research process and all of its components.

RED FLAGS

- Quantitative studies address research problems, research questions, and/or hypotheses.
- Qualitative studies do not use hypotheses; rather, they explore research problems and research questions. If a qualitative study discusses a hypothesis, thought should be given to its focus and validity.
- A hypothesis must have at least one independent variable and one dependent variable; it is usually stated in a declarative statement format rather than as a question.
- Key variables within a study should have at least the operational definition provided for consideration.

Multiple-Choice Questions

1. Which of the following variables is an example of conceptual variable?
   A. Amount of serum in a blood collection tube
   B. Taste in music or musical preference
   C. Amount of money invested in medical research
   D. Treatment duration

2. Which measure does not represent a clear and appropriate outcome measure for a PICOT question?
   A. Death
   B. Excessive thirst
   C. Elevated blood pressure
   D. Change in pressure ulcers staging

3. Which of the following problems involve moral or ethical issues and are not researchable? Select all that apply.
   A. Use of alcohol during pregnancy
   B. Use of pesticides on football fields
   C. Legalization of physician-assisted suicide
   D. Vaccination rates in Muslim communities

4. Developing a research study to investigate the availability of healthcare resources for transgender equality is an example of a research problem generated primarily from:
   A. practice.
   B. social issues.
   C. healthcare trends in society.
   D. theory.

5. True or False: In some cases, the research question may be used interchangeably with the problem statement.
   A. True
   B. False

6. The research question is: "Does massage therapy decrease pain associated with uterine contractions in laboring women?" Which of the following is the independent variable?
   A. Massage therapy
   B. Decreased pain
   C. Laboring women
   D. Uterine contractions

7. Which of the following is the best example of a problem statement containing all parts of the PICOT format?
   A. Laboring women whose significant others leave them during procedures experience more pain.
   B. Hospitalized laboring patients who have a relative with them experience less pain than those who do not.
   C. Hospitalized laboring women whose significant other stays with them during labor experience less pain than those who do not.
   D. Patients who have a relative with them during an epidural experience less anxiety than those who do not.

8. Which of the following best represents a dichotomous variable?
   A. Hemoglobin A1C
   B. Health insurance coverage
   C. Heart rate
   D. Number of visits to the primary care provider

Short Answer

1. Fill in the blanks for the PICOT questions:
   P ____
   I ____
   C ____
   O ____
   T ____

Discussion Questions

1. You work in a cardiology clinic that treats patients who have coronary artery disease and are recovering from a myocardial infarction. Many of these patients have hypertension and are overweight, and you have noticed that some of them have more difficulty following their medical regimens than others. You want to develop a research study to investigate this problem. How would you go about doing so? What would be a possible problem statement?

2. You are a BSN student enrolled in a research course. The instructor has given you the following problem statement: "Does completion of a mandatory health promotion course affect the incidence of smoking cessation among college students who smoke?" Develop four hypotheses that might be drawn from this problem statement: a null hypothesis, a directional hypothesis, a nondirectional hypothesis, and an associative hypothesis. Can all of these hypotheses be developed? If any of them cannot be developed, explain why not.

3. Read the abstract from Szabo, Grap, Munro, Starkweather, and Merchant (2014) and then provide the following information:
    - Identify the population of interest.
    - Identify the variables.
    - Construct a research question that could have guided this study.
    - Construct a null hypothesis.
    - Construct a directional hypothesis.

Suggested Readings

American Journal of Nursing. (2015). *Evidence-based practice, step by step.* Retrieved from http://journals.lww.com/ajnonline/pages/collectiondetails.aspx?TopicalCollectionId=10

Mayo, N. E., Asano, M., & Barbic, S. P. (2013). When is a research question not a research question? *Journal of Rehabilitation Medicine, 45*(6), 513–518. http://dx.doi.org/10.2340/16501977-1150

University of Washington Libraries. (n.d.). *Research 101* [Archived]. Retrieved from http://guides.lib.washington.edu/content.php?pid=55083&sid=2465031

References

Brennan, C., & Parsons, G. (2017). Enhanced recovery in orthopedics: A prospective audit of an enhanced recovery program for patients undergoing hip or knee arthroplasty. *MedSurg Nursing, 26*(2), 99–104.

Dichter, M. E., Cerulli, C., & Bossarte, R. M. (2011). Intimate partner violence victimization women veterans and associated heart health risks. *Women's Health Issues, 21*(4 Suppl.), 190–194. http://dx.doi.org/10.1016/j.whi.2011.04.008

Gray, J. R., Grove, S. K., & Sutherland, S. (2017). *Burns' & Grove's the practice of nursing research: Appraisal, synthesis, and generation of evidence* (8th ed.). St. Louis, MO: Saunders/Elsevier.

Grove, S. K., Gray, J. R, & Burns, N. (2015). *Understanding nursing research: Building an evidence-based practice* (6th ed.). St. Louis, MO: Saunders/Elsevier.

Hanna, K. M., Weaver, M. T., Slaven, J. E., Fortenberry, J. D., & DeMeglio, L. A. (2014). Diabetes-related quality of life and the demands and burdens of diabetes care among emerging adults with type 1 diabetes in the year after high school graduation. *Research in Nursing and Health, 37*(5), 399–408. http://dx.doi.org/10.1002/nur.21620

Iverson, K. M., Huang, K., Wells, S. Y., Wright, J. D., Gerber, M. R., & Wiltsey-Stirman, S. (2014). Women veterans' preferences for intimate partner violence screening and response procedures within the Veterans Health Administration. *Research in Nursing and Health, 37*(4), 302–311. http://dx.doi.org/10.1002/nur.21602

Ketefian, S., & Redman, R. (2013). Nursing science in the global community. In W. K. Cody (Ed.), *Philosophical and theoretical perspectives for advanced nursing practice* (5th ed., pp. 279–289). Burlington, MA: Jones & Bartlett Learning.

Kwan, T. M., & Sullivan, M. (2017). The use of intravenous ibuprofen and intravenous acetaminophen in surgical patients and the effect on opioid reduction. *MedSurg Nursing, 26*(2), 124-132.

LoBiondo-Wood, G., & Haber, J. (2018). *Nursing research: Methods and critical appraisal for evidence-based practice* (9th ed.). St. Louis, MO: Mosby/Elsevier.

Malloch, K., & Porter-O'Grady, T. (2010). *Introduction to evidence-based practice in nursing and health care* (2nd ed.). Sudbury, MA: Jones and Bartlett.

Melnyk, B. M., & Fineout-Overholt, E. (2015). *Evidence-based practice in nursing & healthcare: A guide to best practice* (3rd ed.). Philadelphia, PA: Lippincott Williams & Wilkins.

National Institute of Nursing Research (NINR). (n.d.). NINR mission. Retrieved from http://www.ninr.nih.gov/aboutninr/ninr-mission-and-strategic-plan

Nelson, D. E. (2011). Perioperative care of the patient with rheumatoid arthritis. *AORN Journal, 94*(3), 290–300.

Polit, D. F., & Beck, C. T. (2016). *Nursing research: Generating and assessing evidence for nursing practice* (10th ed.). Philadelphia, PA: Lippincott Williams & Wilkins.

Polit, D. F., & Beck, C. T. (2017). *Essentials of nursing research: Appraising evidence for nursing practice* (9th ed.). Philadelphia, PA: Wolters Kluwer Health/Lippincott Williams & Wilkins.

Porter-O'Grady, T. (2010). A new age for practice: Creating the framework for evidence. In K. Malloch & T. Porter-O'Grady (Eds.), *Introduction to evidence-based practice in nursing and health care* (2nd ed., pp. 1–29). Sudbury, MA: Jones and Bartlett.

Primdahl, J., Clausen, J., & Horslev-Petersen, K. (2013). Results from systematic screening for cardiovascular risk in outpatient with rheumatoid arthritis in accordance with EULAR recommendations. *Annals of Rheumatic Diseases, 72*(11), 1771–1776. http://dx.doi.org /10.1136/annrheumdis-2013-203682

Schmidt, N. A., & Brown, J. M. (2019). *Evidence-based practice for nurses: Appraisal and application of research* (4th ed.). Burlington, MA: Jones & Bartlett Learning.

Seth P., Scholl L., Rudd R. A, & Bacon S. (2018). Overdose deaths involving opioids, cocaine, and psychostimulants—United States, 2015–2016. *MMWR Morbidly Mortal Weekly Rep, 67*, 349–358. http://dx.doi.org/10.15585/mmwr.mm6712a1

Szabo, C. M., Grap, M. J., Munro, C. L., Starkweather, A., & Merchant, R. E. (2014). The effect of oral care on intracranial pressure in critically ill adults. *Journal of Neuroscience Nursing, 46*(6), 321–329. http://dx.doi.org/10.1097/JNN.0000000000000092

Warner M., Trinidad J. P., Bastian B. A, & Minino, A. M. (2016). Drugs most frequently involved in drug overdose deaths: United States, 2010–2014. *National Vital Statistics Reports 65*(10). Retrieved from https://www.cdc.gov/nchs/data/nvsr/nvsr65/nvsr65_10.pdf

West, D. S., Gorin, A. A., Subak, L. L., Foster, G., Bragg, C., Hecht, J., . . . Wing, R. R. (2011). A motivation-focused weight loss maintenance program is an effective alternative to a skill-based approach. *International Journal of Obesity, 35*, 259–269. http://dx.doi.org/10.1038 /ijo.2010.138

Wing, R. R., Papandonatos, G., Fava, J. L., Gorin, A. A., Phelan, S., McCaffery, J., & Tate, D. F. (2008). Maintaining large weight losses: The role of behavioral and psychological factors. *Journal of Consulting and Clinical Psychology, 76*(6), 1015–1021. http://dx.doi.org/10.1037/a0014159

Woolston, W., & Connelly, L. M. (2017). Felty's syndrome: A qualitative case study. *MedSurg Nursing, 26*(2), 105–118.

CHAPTER 7

Literature Review: Searching and Writing the Evidence

Travis Real, C. Erik Wilkinson, and Carol Boswell

CHAPTER OBJECTIVES

At the conclusion of this chapter, the learner will be able to:
1. Characterize the concepts of a literature review.
2. Discuss the purposes of a research/evidence-based practice (EBP) literature review.
3. Differentiate research articles from nonresearch articles.
4. Recognize the importance of collaborating with a library specialist.
5. Categorize the steps for conducting a literature review using electronic retrieval methods.
6. Identify guidelines for appraising research articles.
7. Organize the steps for writing a literature review.
8. Correlate the use of literature review for evidence-based nursing practice.

KEY TERMS

Annotated bibliography
Cumulative Index to Nursing and Allied
   Health Literature (CINAHL)
Database
Discursive prose
Literature review
Medical Literature Analysis and Retrieval
   System Online (MEDLINE)

Medical Subject Heading (MeSH)
PubMed
Reference librarian
Research articles
Search engine

▶ Introduction

This chapter introduces practical guidelines for conducting and writing a literature review aimed toward a nursing-focused, evidence-based proposal and/or research project. Selection guidelines and tips are given for appropriate databases, along with electronic retrieval of scholarly, peer-reviewed articles. Steps are provided for the process of organizing data and writing based on evidence and issues in nursing practice.

Why is the literature review concept so important to healthcare professionals? Literature reviews provide foundations for advancing the project and/or proposal toward inclusion of evidence and best practices related to the topic under consideration. According to Duncan and Holtslander (2012), skills associated with information acquisition are of paramount importance to healthcare professionals. Klein-Fedyshin (2015) states, "Being able to recognize information needs, locate evidence-based knowledge, critically appraise the retrieval, and apply it in practice is vital to nurses" (p. 24). Yet students and practicing nurses still show insecurity and uncertainty in the process of conducting web-based and library searches for appropriate materials. When the latest computer-literate generations, the so-called Millennials or Generation Y, voice these concerns, more attention must be directed to facilitating the process if EBP is to continue as the benchmark for providing holistic nursing care.

▶ Definition and Purpose of the Literature Review

The literature review is, per the National Library of Medicine's (2008) MeSH database, "published materials providing an examination of recent or current literature. It also . . . covers a wide range of subject matter at various levels of completeness and comprehensiveness based on analyses of literature that may include research findings." The work within the literature review can be characterized as a synthesis of the material, not just a summary. Morgan-Rallis (2014) emphasize that a literature review should not be an **annotated bibliography**. The review is guided by the researcher's curiosity about a particular subject, be it a disease, condition, or clinical occurrence. It can also be an opportunity to fill in gaps about the subject area. The purpose for developing and presenting a review of the literature emerges from a desire to document the knowledge and ideas currently established concerning the identified topic. According to Gray (2017), a literature review is an interpretative synopsis of evidence on a focus of interest. The ensuing document conveys the strengths and weaknesses ascertained from the review of the pertinent literature (Taylor, 2012). Each literature review must be characterized by designated concepts and ideas such as the PICOT approach, a mnemonic that translates this way:

P = Population

I = Intervention

C = Comparison

O = Outcome

T = Time

According to Gray (2017), the literature review supplies the reader with a summary of accessible evidence and facilitates a discussion concerning the need for further study. Taylor (2012) adds that a literature review must not be merely a descriptive inventory of the available information, nor is it to be a collection of synopses. The main purpose of the literature review is to identify what is known and unknown about an area that has not been completely resolved in practice. A second purpose is to determine how an issue is resolvable and managed based on research evidence. The literature review provides the background and the context within which the research is conducted. It lays out the foundation of the study. Specifically, a good review of the literature does the following:

- Identifies a research problem and indicates how it can be studied
- Helps clarify and determine the importance of a research problem
- Identifies what is known about a problem and identifies gaps (what is unknown) in a particular area of knowledge
- Provides examples based on documented studies for resolving a nursing issue
- Provides evidence that a problem is of importance
- Identifies theoretical frameworks and conceptual models for organizing and conducting research studies
- Identifies experts in the field of interest
- Identifies research designs and methodologies for conducting like studies
- Provides a context for interpretation, comparison, and critique of study findings (McGrath & Brandon, 2014; Polit & Beck, 2017)

Taylor (2012) sets out four aspects that need to be identifiable within a literature review. The first is the expectation that it is directed toward an identified topic of interest. The author of a literature review must not ramble in the hope of eventually addressing the needed information concerning a topic. Thought and attention to the flow and appropriateness of each entry within the review are based on a directed process. Second, the review needs to provide both what is known and what continues to be unknown about the topic. It is critical that a literature review provide both aspects on the topic. The unknown about the topic is as important as the known. By understanding both aspects, the ongoing development of knowledge related to the topic can be effectively developed and structured. The final document should balance these two aspects to provide a complete picture of the current state of the topic under consideration. Regarding the third aspect, controversial perceptions within the literature should be delineated. A literature review that does not provide all sides to the question does not effectively consider the entire topic. All subject arguments have at least two sides involved in the process. Finally, the summarization of the complete literature foundation on the topic should facilitate the development of any further needed research or EBP projects.

Literature reviews can be provided in either a **discursive prose** format, specifically writing "characterized by reasoned argument or thought" (Oxford English Dictionary, 2013), or as an annotated bibliography. When provided as discursive prose, the material is provided in sections organized by themes or identified trends, not as a summary of the different research projects identified. The annotated bibliography begins with a succinct discussion of each research report and also includes the themes and concepts embedded within a crucial assessment of the information provided. Bolderston (2008) adds, "A good review can be an invaluable tool to the practitioner, providing a succinct summary and analysis of the pertinent information in a given area. As 'discursive prose,' a review can be enlightening, challenging, and readable. There are many rewards associated with producing a useful piece of work" (p. 91). Literature reviews provide a valuable service to establish the foundation on which the next steps of research, quality improvement, and/or EBP can be linked to as a basis for furthering healthcare knowledge.

▶ The Literature Review Within the EBP and/or Research Process

Within an EBP process, the **literature review** serves to identify the evidence that is currently available related to the challenge identified. For this process, determining the PICOT question drives the literature search (see **FIGURE 7-1**). Using Poe and White's (2010) example question, "What is the best available evidence regarding preventive strategies of sharp and needle-stick injuries (NSIs)?" (p. 106), we can write it out in the PICOT format as follows:

> Nurses working with needles and sharp objects (P) should take active measures to reduce sticks (I) or try another method or do nothing (C) so as to reduce sticks, see if they increase or stay the same (O); there should be controls to test before intervention and after intervention (T).

From the evidence that can be located on the topic, a decision concerning the next steps within the process—either research or quality improvement—can be determined. For this PICOT problem, the authors of this chapter conducted a **PubMed** search, narrowing down the results to systematic reviews written specifically for the nursing profession. One promising article, written by Tarigan, Cifuentes,

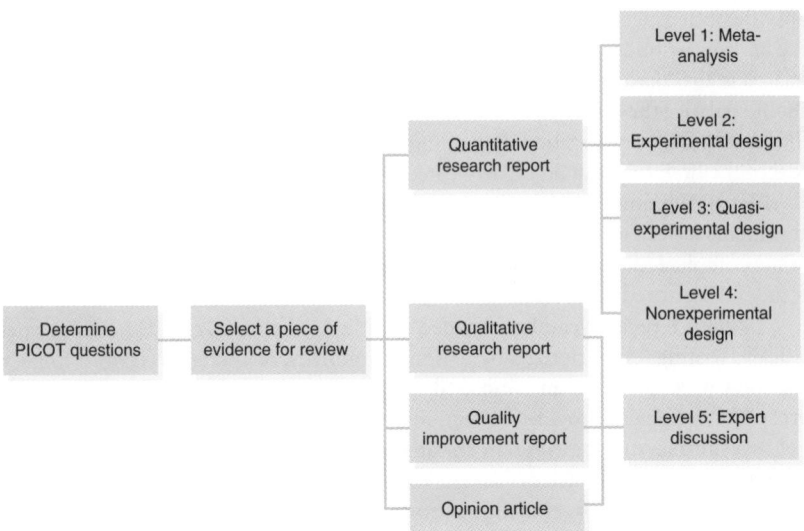

FIGURE 7-1 Flow sheet for ranking evidence.

Quinn, and Kriebel (2015), started with a pool of 250 relevant studies, eventually narrowing down to 17. Based on the review study, the authors concluded that training, combined with safety engineered devices (SEDs), can significantly diminish NSIs.

In terms of its placement in a research article, the review of the literature usually follows the statement of the research problem or the research question. The reason the review comes early in some research projects is because it sets the stage (lays the foundation) for the rest of the study. As mentioned earlier, the review of the literature provides the theoretical framework for how the current study will be structured, helps to frame the research question into a research hypothesis, and identifies what will be studied and measured in the study.

For example, suppose a unit in a local 340-bed hospital has had no nurse resign or otherwise leave in 15 years. This unit exists in a geographical setting where the nursing shortage is rampant. The attrition rate is found to be at an all-time high. A newly hired nursing administrator is curious about this unit. She calls the director of the unit to discuss the reason turnover is so low on this unit. From conversations with several other staff members of this unit, the administrator formulates in her mind the theory that a good manager is the most important link to the low attrition rate on the unit. Although a low attrition rate does not seem to be a problem requiring research, this idea can be adapted into a literature search so that some insight is gained to answer the administrator's question, "Is the staff members' perception of the nurse manager associated with the attrition or retention rate on a unit?" Searching the literature for studies about managers and retention or attrition can further illuminate this research question. The literature review may then describe what has been found to be true from other similar settings by conducting a survey of nurses who have worked in the same facility or unit for at least 15 years. The new administrator could use this survey or questionnaire to conduct a small research study on her hospital's unit. This hypothetical example illustrates the importance of the literature review and demonstrates how it fits within the rest of the research process. The process used in the study came from the review of the literature.

According to Worral, Levin, and Arsenault (2009), the formula for commencing a literature review requires that a problem first be described to drive the selection of materials. Without clearly denoting the problem or challenge, identifying materials for inclusion becomes problematic. The second necessary aspect is the tangible acquisition of materials relevant to the subject being investigated. Ensuring that each document included in the review addresses a component of the subject is imperative. After the materials are assembled for consideration, each document must be evaluated to ascertain the connection between it and the subject matter under investigation. As the review continues to develop, four facets are important to consider. From the outset, the author's credentials and arguments should be carefully considered for relevance and provenance. Second, the author's viewpoints should be evaluated for bias. Another area to consider is the inclusion of contradictory data along with the supportive data. Persuasiveness is another facet that should be carefully weighed during a literature review: Are the themes identified and set forth by the author convincing? Finally, the review should, in the ultimate sense, contribute significantly to the understanding of the identified topic. A closing piece of the formula entails the documentation of findings and conclusions as they pertain to the topic. The dissemination of the findings and conclusions is vital for the next steps within either the EBP process or a research endeavor.

▶ Differentiating a Research Article from a Nonresearch Article

Several valuable resources contributing to nursing practice exist. However, for the purpose of illuminating the value of evidence-based knowledge, this text focuses primarily on data from original research. It is often difficult to locate original research, especially when little has been published in a particular area. If that is the case, the lack of previous studies serves as an opportunity because it can inspire new research on that particular issue.

The importance of research derives from the fact that it has been conducted using a consistently acceptable scientific method known and respected by the scholarly and academic world. It is not just someone's opinion but rather has been examined critically. **Research articles** consistently contain components that are required by scientific decision-making processes. **BOX 7-1** describes components of a research article.

BOX 7-1 Components of a Research Article

- **Title:** The title describes what the study is about.
- **Abstract:** The abstract is a brief summary of the problem of interest to the researcher. It describes, in approximately 120 to 150 words, what took place in the research study and makes a brief statement about the outcome. It helps to determine relevance to the reader who is conducting a search of the literature.
- **Introduction/literature review:** This component gives the background of the research topic and explains why it is important, based on a selective review of relevant literature. It compares and contrasts other research articles while summarizing what is already known and not known about the topic.
- **Purpose of the study/hypothesis/problem statement:** The purpose explains the aim of the study. It is the hypothesis or the research question that the author wants to support or answer.
- **Methodology/procedures/research design:** This component tells what happened. It describes in detail what actions the author took to carry out the study. The method describes the procedure for how the research was conducted and how the information was analyzed or which statistical testing was done. It also describes the population, including how it was selected; the setting where the research took place; the number of participants in the study; the type of study, either qualitative or quantitative; and the tools/methods used to collect the data or simply attain the study information.
- **Major findings/results/analysis/discussion:** This component describes the outcome of the study.
- **Summary/conclusion/ideas for future studies/implications:** This component highlights major findings of the study and identifies gaps. It addresses any areas that need further research. Recommendations for policy or practice should be discussed in this section.
- **Works cited/references/acknowledgments:** The reference list should be organized in a recognized literary format, such as the American Psychological Association (APA) style or other recognized reference format.

It is sometimes tempting to choose nonresearch information or evidence when conducting the review of literature. For example, reports from state agencies, various nursing organizations, or websites may present information that is important to a body of knowledge, yet it has not been critically examined in a research study. Some nationally conducted surveys may provide important information, but they may not be considered true research because not all the people in a particular population were included or not enough people returned the surveys. Unless all of the critical components are incorporated in the research process, the information obtained in the investigation should not be considered research. All evidence offers value, but each has a different level of value based on several aspects, which are addressed elsewhere. As these other forms of evidence are considered within a literature review, the level and/or strength of the evidence becomes increasingly important. As indicated earlier, Figure 7-1 is a flowchart for aiding in the placement of documents toward a level of ranking within the evidence. While this flowchart uses just one example of ranking methodology, the principles found within the flowchart can be applied to other ranking methods as needed.

Individuals often state that they are "going to research" a topic; searching the literature is not considered research but rather a mechanism for providing background information for the research project. The use of the word *research* to describe following a line of investigation does not hold the same meaning as the process of conducting a research study. Whether an individual is conducting an EBP review or research literature review, he or she needs to become very well versed on the evidence available on the topic of interest.

▶ Conducting a Literature Review Search

The guidelines presented in this section are targeted toward the novice researcher. It is highly advised that the student researcher first seek the help of a professional librarian at the beginning of a project and throughout the process when it is necessary to access comprehensive information from relevant sources. Most literature searches can be done by electronic retrieval. Researchers can find most of the material they need from doing their own personal searches; however, the most comprehensive searches are done with the help of a professional librarian. Most librarians are specially trained to search specific databases, like PubMed, or particular aspects of data management and retrieval, in some cases even credentialed.

⬛ THINK OUTSIDE THE BOX

In your current clinical setting, which types of evidence resources are used as the underpinning of policies? Discuss the suitability and usefulness of these types of evidence. What levels of evidence are applied in the process? How much evidence is needed for a policy to be regarded as "based on evidence" at your facility?

Some specialized librarians include research, law, medical, government documents, and consumer health. Many librarians play an essential role in research, providing effective search strategies and approaches for various search engines. Nurses are encouraged to be patient, allowing time for these information professionals to provide strong, evidentiary results. Nurses must also consider their own expertise when starting a research project or conducting literature reviews. They need to embrace the expertise provided by librarians to ensure that the support materials being used are suitable, understandable, and to the point.

▶ The Importance of Librarians in the Literature Review Process

As mentioned above, finding relevant articles that deal with the selected topic is a complex task made easier with the expertise of a research librarian. Librarians are able to assist users with finding information in a timely manner. As a result of their education, training, and experience, they are well versed in searching databases, including the way in which the information is cataloged and organized. They understand the terms and strategies required to retrieve information most relevant to the user. Their specialized knowledge may help the user conduct a more comprehensive search from multiple sources. Librarians' search expertise makes them highly skilled at weeding out irrelevant documents that might otherwise overwhelm the researcher and cost her or him precious time. Leedy and Ormrod (2012) strongly concur, encouraging researchers at all levels to seek out and employ a **reference librarian**.

The pool of library resources is growing exponentially, with new and innovative means for accessing the evidence available for consideration. The reference librarian must become a key player, regularly engaged in accessing the evidence to ensure that the materials compiled deliver the best available confirmation and proof while also providing the other side of the argument. Scholars also need to be sure that they are presenting the full picture related to the topic under investigation. All views of the topic need to be supported, thus allowing a strong rationale for the project being conducted.

With the development of electronic resources, conducting a search is achievable for the neophyte researcher. The novice needs to plan and allow time to understand the search process and achieve competency with the search process. With assistance from librarians, along with support from a respectable mentor, the novice researcher can manage database searches and create a literature review reflecting the evidence supporting a noteworthy research proposal or project.

Researchers must acknowledge when and where to request help. Anyone can accomplish an effective literature search. However, the key is determining which articles to include; which are not needed; and when an expert, such as a librarian, should be consulted. To complete a successful comprehensive literature review, developing collaborations with strategic mentors is paramount.

▶ The Research Idea: First Step

The first step in conducting a literature review is brainstorming about an idea or an area of interest with colleagues and mentors. The nurse's practice area is probably one of the most common sources for a research idea in the nursing field. Important issues in nursing provide abundant ideas for research. For example, the nursing shortage, the cost of health care, the quality of care for uninsured persons, and new delivery methods identified in federal legislative bills are all broad areas that may generate a study topic. Inspiration may also come from reading professional journals or the news media. A majority of current research endeavors tend to be done within peer-based teams whose members have common interests. This team work can lead to brainstorming discussions to strengthen the topic's foundation.

During a brainstorming session, every idea should be put on the table for consideration. Once a thorough list is developed, further development of the selected topics can be done by the group to clarify and cultivate the research and/or EBP idea.

In addition, articles in professional journals may end with the phrase, "additional research is needed to explore the nature of . . . ." Here is a snapshot of one such article: "Research on IV Ibuprofen and Acetaminophen Use Can Be Advanced Through a Large-Scale RCT Comparing These Medications With the Same Opioid" (Kwan & Sullivan, 2017, p. 131). In this systematic review example, areas within the existing study that could benefit from additional investigation are presented to encourage supplementary studies. Often, the conclusion of an article marks the starting point for other research ideas.

▶ The Research Question: Second Step

Most nurses have a hunch or curiosity about some aspect of nursing science or patient care. It is helpful to formulate that idea into a question that, if answered, would contribute to the field of nursing and/or health care. Each research or EBP project should initially answer the question, "So what?" In answering this question, the importance of the project is confirmed before time is wasted on ideas that do not have valid foundations. Formulation of a research question is covered in Chapters 1 and 6. For the purposes of this text, asking a simple question, such as a PICOT-based one, helps the novice researcher focus on topics and key concepts for conducting the literature search. Utilizing the PICOT format provides crucial components beneficial for conducting a successful literature search. For example, the student researcher may be curious about how long it takes a novice baccalaureate-prepared nurse to feel comfortable in a management position. A possible question could be, "What is the role transition time for baccalaureate-prepared nurse graduates in management positions in a small hospital?"

Reading is another very important source of research ideas. In the example provided earlier Kwan and Sullivan (2017) suggested the need for additional research related to the use of opioids, ibuprofen, and acetaminophen for surgical patients. Further work on data collection related to this topic, especially with the growing opioid crises, was suggested as an area needing additional investigation. This gap resulted from the work completed within this systematic review. Multiple questions could be developed to gain a more thorough understanding of how opioid reduction could be accomplished through the use of lower-risk pain management options. Of course, after undertaking further reading, the researcher may have different ideas. Thus, the research question must not be etched in stone. As additional information is acquired from the literature, the research project evolves.

Forming an initial question or medical query is a good place to start the literature-review search process. Without identifying the problem and the development of an initial question, the literature review could become both overwhelming and convoluted. This process of stating the initial idea and problem allows for commitment to a specific focus for the preliminary work. To start the literature review, it is important to distinguish between databases and search engines.

▶ Definition of Database

How does a database differ from a search engine? Regarding the latter, Google and Bing are examples of search engines, whereas Medical Literature Analysis and Retrieval System Online (MEDLINE) and Cumulative Index to Nursing and Allied Health Literature (CINAHL) are databases. A definition for *search engine* is "a computer program that searches documents, especially on the World Wide Web, for a specified word or words and provides a list of documents in which they are found" (Dictionary.com, 2018). Its job is to retrieve the information in a format that is accessible visually onscreen at an onsite library or in downloadable, readable (full-text) written format.

Bradley (2013) discusses, with regard to search engines, Boolean search strategies. Using at least two key words, the Boolean method utilizes the operatives AND, OR, and NOT. Another way is to add a plus sign (+) before search terms. By using this designation, the search engine concentrates the search on the designated word. A final idea for narrowing the search provided by a search engine is to place quotation marks around any phrase that is principal to the quest; this will usually find results with that exact phrase. Source material identified by search engines should be carefully considered for quality and accuracy. Some websites offer high-quality control, while others do not.

In contrast, a database is a work consisting of a structured file of information or a set of logically related data stored and retrieved using computer-based means; an example is PubMed MeSH. Per Merriam-Webster (2018), *database* is defined as "a usually large collection of data organized especially for rapid search and retrieval." A database is a storage location, like a library, where information is warehoused, cataloged, maintained, and updated systematically. Most, if not all, of the databases used within literature searches are available online. These sources include indexes, abstracts, encyclopedias, dictionaries, and other universal reference tools. Databases allow an individual to narrow the focus for the search using keywords, controlled vocabulary, titles, author names, years, languages, or combinations of these elements.

Two main types of databases are available—bibliographic and full text. Bibliographic databases give directions on where to find the information, whereas full-text databases contain the information itself. In other words, full-text databases contain the article itself in a downloadable format, such as portable document format (PDF) (LibGuides of the University Library Groningen, 2017). In recent years, more major databases, like those managed by EBSCO, have added an increasing number of full-text capabilities.

▶ Databases Useful in Nursing

The two most useful databases for nursing literature are PubMed (the public portal for the Medical Literature Analysis and Retrieval System Online [MEDLINE]) and the Cumulative Index to Nursing and Allied Health Literature (CINAHL) (BOX 7-2). MEDLINE provides literature related to medicine, nursing, and dentistry.

BOX 7-2 Databases Useful in Nursing

PubMed (Medical Literature Analysis and Retrieval System Online [MEDLINE])
MedLine Plus (patient education, both in English and Spanish, plus other languages)
Cumulative Index to Nursing and Allied Health Literature (CINAHL)
Nursing Reference Center (EBSCO)
Joanna Briggs Institute
Cochrane Library
ProQuest Dissertations and Theses Global
PsycINFO
PsychTESTS (EBSCO)
Google Scholar (good at finding grey literature, e.g., material not conventionally published)

The MEDLINE component of PubMed covers medically related articles for a period, 1946 to the present, with some older materials available (National Library of Medicine [NLM], 2017). The focus of information in MEDLINE is biomedical; however, this database also contains the citations that are provided in CINAHL. The CINAHL database delivers authoritative coverage of the literature related to nursing and allied health.

The PubMed database is generally considered the premier bibliographic database offering access to the North American biomedical literature. It stores and indexes more than 27 million citations and articles from thousands of full-text cataloged titles from MEDLINE and other life science journals dating back to the 1950s, and it is updated every workweek, Monday through Friday (NLM, 2017). In addition to medicine and nursing, it includes dental and veterinarian citations and can be accessed free of charge via the Internet. In other words, library privileges are not required; only access to the Internet is needed. Thus, this web-based resource is an excellent place to start a literature search. On the NLM's online site, individuals can also access ClinicalTrials.gov, MedlinePlus, ToxNet, and Digital Collections (NLM, 2017). A wide variety of services are available free of charge through the National Library of Medicine (NLM). It serves as an important reservoir for the healthcare data needed to advance medical research and EBP.

PubMed uses MeSH (Medical Subject Headings), a controlled vocabulary where information is cataloged according to specific words or subject headings as in a dictionary or thesaurus. It is arranged in both an alphabetic and a hierarchical format (NLM, 2017). Although most people start searches using fundamental words, this type of search does not yield the most comprehensive results. Instead, the dictionary for finding the words that most appropriately define or match the search term or concept in PubMed is the **Medical Subject Heading (MeSH)** guide. This feature is accessed via a link from the NLM/PubMed website, under the "More Resources" header. The MeSH home page (www.ncbi.nlm.nih.gov/mesh or www .nlm.nih.gov/mesh/) also allows individuals to access the "MeSH on Demand" link. Within this link, a person can submit text for which the NLM database identifies a list of MeSH terms relevant to the provided text (NLM, 2017). To be successful, individuals must provide well-defined sentences for the site to use. Once the MeSH database has provided a list of terms, the site offers a link to the corresponding

MeSH browser, which can be used to identify articles and documents for consideration (NLM, 2017).

How are MEDLINE and PubMed different? Per the NLM, PubMed citations come from (1) MEDLINE indexed journals, (2) journals and manuscripts deposited in PubMed Central (PMC), and (3) National Center for Bioinformatics Information (NCBI) Bookshelf. Both MEDLINE and other PubMed citations may have links to full-text articles or manuscripts in PMC, NCBI Bookshelf, and publishers' websites. If the users limit their PubMed search to MeSH controlled vocabulary or the MEDLINE subset, they will see only MEDLINE citations in their results.

Per our earlier focus on MeSH subject heading searches, how does a keyword search differ from it? For example, the terms "patient visitation" might be used to locate journal articles focusing on how nurses perceive open visitation in intensive care units. When searched as a simple keyword phrase, "patient visitation" returns 525 citations. If the Boolean operative AND is included (patient AND visitation), PubMed returns the same 525 citations. When the subject or controlled vocabulary term found in the MeSH database guide (thesaurus) was used ("visitors to patients"), 1,960 citations were located. In total, nine MeSH terms were suggested for inclusion in a search along with "patient visitation." Knowing how a database stores information is very important in conducting effective and relevant searches. Using dates, types of nursing units, or other strategies can narrow this search. The standard PubMed limiters recommended by the authors (Boswell, Real, and Wilkinson), are Abstract (under Text availability), Humans (under Species), and English (under Languages). For this specialized exercise, the authors also suggest nursing journals (under Journal Categories).

CINAHL is probably the most popular database used by nurses. It indexes over 5,000 journals, 770-plus of them full-text, and contains more than 5.5 million records going back to 1937 (EBSCO, 2018). CINAHL houses nursing publications, along with journals in the allied health fields related to physical therapy, occupational therapy, cardiopulmonary technology, emergency service, physician assistant health education, radiology technology, medical laboratory technology, medical records, surgical technology, and medical assistants, and selected journals related to biomedicine, consumer health, and librarianship health sciences (EBSCO, 2018).

CINAHL publications can be searched using the EBSCO*host* interface and are only available through a library. Many practical healthcare agencies, like hospitals and clinics, also find value in providing this resource to their staff members.

Just as in PubMed, records in CINAHL are indexed by subject headings or controlled vocabulary. Subject headings provide descriptors of the terms listed in the database. Searching by the terms or subjects yields results more relevant to the topic. Subject headings are viewable by clicking the CINAHL Headings button on the EBSCO*host* toolbar. To begin, the subject heading term should be entered in the "Find" field. Searches using this tool can also be done by using key words. The EBSCO*host* system matches articles with appropriate subject terms through the process of mapping.

A number of other databases are also useful in nursing practice, including:

- Cochrane Library: A regularly updated collection of evidence-based medicine (EBM) databases. These databases include systematic reviews of subjects, including economics, health interventions, controlled trials, and methodologies.
- PsycINFO: Includes journals from the social sciences.
- PsychTests (EBSCO).

🔼 THINK OUTSIDE THE BOX

Which databases do you normally use in your literature searches? Discuss the pros and cons of these tools.

▶ Basics of Searching

Any topic-focused review of published articles is only as good as what has been searched (see **BOX 7-3**). In other words, "the first requirement for writing a good literature review . . . is to do a good literature search" (Kellsey, 2005, p. 526). An effective place to start is to identify concepts from the research question/purpose statement that can be the focus of the search. An example is the research purpose statement offered by Cortez-Gann et al. (2017), "the purpose of this study was to identify the relationship of vital sign changes to signs and symptoms of blood product transfusion reactions in an effort to determine best practice for vital sign timing and frequency

---

BOX 7-3 Full-Text Databases Useful in Nursing

- Academic Search Premier (https://www.ebsco.com/products/research-databases /academic-search-premier): Designed for academic institutions; contains full-text scholarly publications; source—EBSCO*host* research database.
- AIDSinfo (https://aidsinfo.nih.gov): Federally approved HIV/AIDS research information for patients and healthcare providers.
- CINAHL (https://health.ebsco.com/products/the-cinahl-database).
- CINAHL Plus with Full Text (https://health.ebsco.com/products/cinahl-plus -with-full-text).
- EBSCO*host* (www.ebscohost.com/).
- The Cochrane Collaboration (www.cochrane.org): Evidence-based medicine systematic reviews.
- Health and Psychosocial Instruments (HaPI) (https://www.ebsco.com/products /research-databases/health-and-psychosocial-instruments-hapi): Evaluation and measurement instruments in health; available through Ovid Technologies.
- Journals@OVIDFullText (www.ovid.com/site/about/terms.jsp?top=42): The second generation of Ovid Full Text, which combines all the capabilities of Ovid Full Text Collections with several important features and functions. To access this link, you need a subscription through a university or library. The link provided allows you to see the terms and conditions for use of this site.
- PubMed/MEDLINE with Medical Subject Heading (MeSH) (www.ncbi.nlm.nih.gov /mesh): Medical Literature Analysis and Retrieval System Online (MEDLINE) is the U.S. NLM's premier bibliographic database that contains more than 16 million references to journal articles in life sciences, with a concentration on biomedicine.
- ProQuest Nursing Journals (www.proquest.com/products-services/pq_nursingahs _shtml.html): Designed to meet the needs of students and researchers at academic institutions; includes information on obstetrics, nursing, geriatric care, oncology, and more (ProQuest, 2015).

during blood product administration" (p. 89). The concepts "vital signs" and "blood product transfusion reactions" could be used as the search terms.

Successful searching takes planning and thought. According to Duncan and Holtslander (2012), individuals encounter the highest amount of frustration as a result of unsuccessful queries that result in the need for querying again. Using incorrect and incomplete terms can result in large, unmanageable search results, slowing down the process of finding useful articles. Search engines like Google, for example, can locate an enormous number of documents. The results can sometimes be overpowering. A clear search strategy is necessary to narrow the results to relevant, usable information. To develop an effective search strategy, it is important to identify the main concepts from the research question, or PICOT question, and/or topic and determine any synonyms for these terms. For the sample research purpose statement listed above, the concepts are "vital signs," "blood product transfusion reactions," and "blood product administration." Other alternate words include "blood transfusion-associated adverse reactions" (MeSH term) and "physiological vital sign changes" (MeSH term). Duncan and Holtslander (2012) offer strategies for lessening the number of search terms, including confirming concepts in one's textbook and using a thesaurus to locate other key words or subject headings identified in papers, plus nursing and other medical dictionaries. These tactics, along with the advanced search features in databases like CINAHL, can aid an individual in finding the articles and evidence needed to support a change in or validate a current practice.

The following steps outline the necessary actions of an electronic resource search. The researcher should consider the use of PubMed while following these steps:

■   Select a topic of interest and identify the concepts or search terms. Think in terms of controlled vocabularies or subject headings for databases when selecting the topic. Subject headings yield more precise results than keywords.

■   Access the PubMed website using an Internet browser: www.pubmed.gov.

■   Locate the MeSH database guide on the right-hand side of the PubMed homepage.

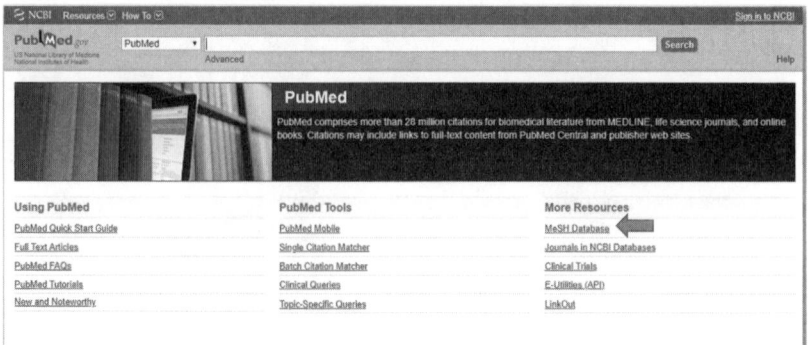

■ Type the search term in the MeSH search box.

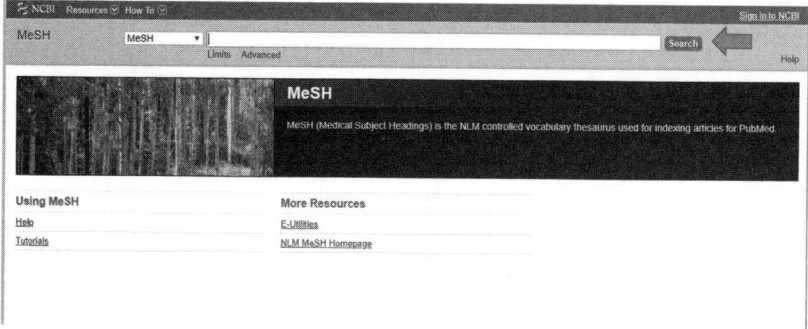

■ Select the subject heading from MeSH that best matches the search term and click "Add to search builder." Repeat this step for each term in your search.

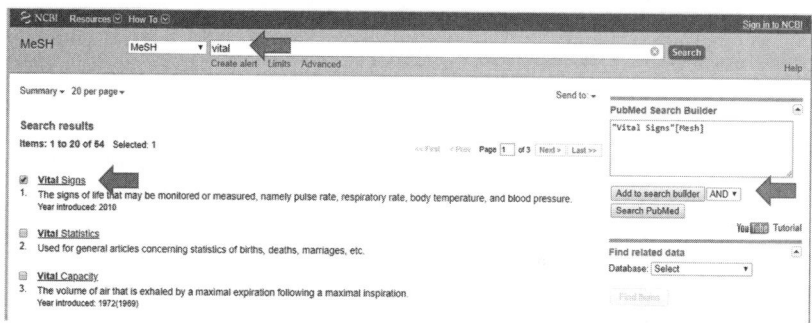

■ After adding additional terms, click "Seach PubMed" for the results list.

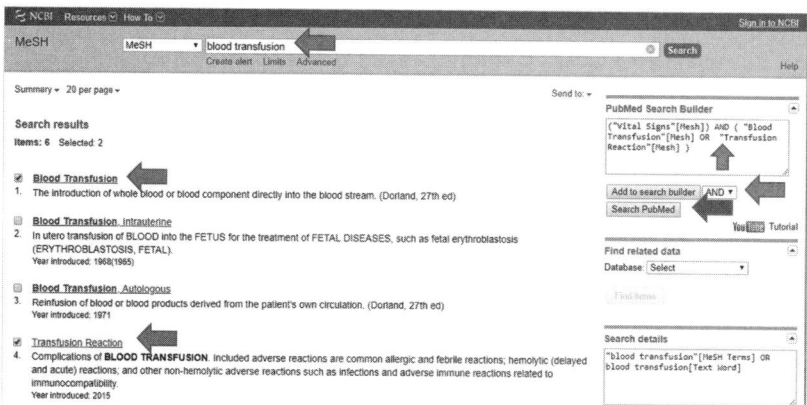

■ Results list example:

Choose limit options as appropriate by date, author, and title; this is a two-step process.

■ To combine search strategies, use "AND" or "OR" in the search box (must be uppercase). "AND" is more restrictive (reduces the number of citations); "OR" is less restrictive; that is, "AND is less, OR is more".

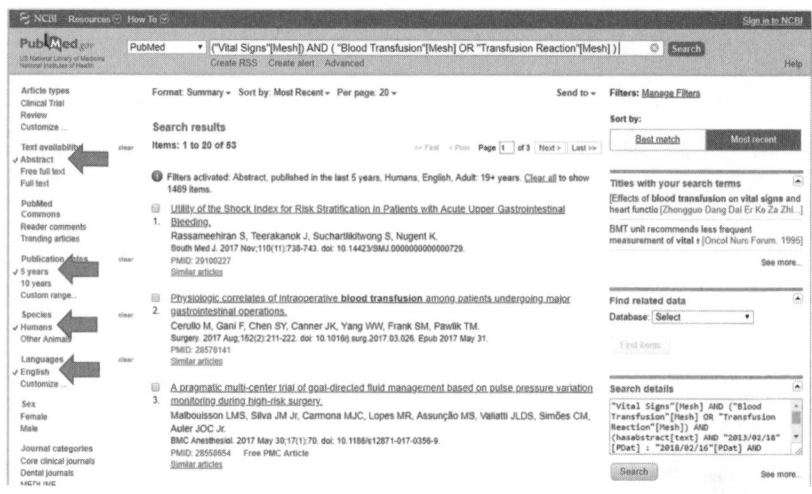

▶ Other Key Information

When searching for basic information, textbooks can sometimes be helpful and acceptable. A good textbook provides a foundation, framework, or gold standard by which other sources are measured. For example, when studying health disparities, the book containing the premier report is *Unequal Treatment: Confronting Racial and Ethnic Disparities in Health Care* (Smedley, Stith, & Nelson, 2003). It provides data sources, initial research findings, and suggested models attempting to explain some of the issues surrounding this problem. From reading this book, it is possible to identify the gaps in the literature and the authors of major articles describing the research in this area. Leedy and Ormrod (2012) recommend a very pertinent idea: Try to access primary sources of material. According to Gray, Grove, and Sutherland (2017), a primary source is "written by the person who originated or is responsible for generating the ideas published" (p. 122). Gray et al. (2017) also state that whenever material is extracted from one source to insert into another source, bias can be introduced. These interpretations and analyses of primary sources, even when care is given to ensuring accuracy, reflect a unique view of the material that may be contradictory to the original interpretation. Seeking out the primary material's discussion is imperative for getting an accurate picture originally gleaned from analyzing the information presented. This type of information can also be used as background for the research proposal. If the instructor(s) requires the proposal to include more recent information (e.g., not more than five years old), for example, then research journal articles should be used.

Also keep in mind that the more precise and focused the search, the fewer the number of resources that will be retrieved. The more general and broad the search, the larger the number of articles retrieved. The researcher should review the article's abstracts at the outset and determine if more or less information is needed. The search should then be modified based on how the materials match the research question.

▶ Evaluating the Literature

Evaluation means different things to different people and is sometimes a rather complex process. One way to label it is via the phrase "critiquing the literature." The term *evaluation* is used here because it is more representative of what takes place and does not seem as overwhelming. Novice researchers may view evaluation as an intimidating process because they have far less experience than the authors of the original works. This concern may not always be the case, of course. Many times, the reader has more clinical knowledge than some of the people writing the articles. It is necessary to build on the analytical skills that most nurses have and to draw from the practice experience. The good thing about nursing is that there is enough variety and specialization in practice and academia for every nurse to be able to offer something of value. Thus, it is important that beginning researchers be confident, knowing they have the skills necessary to raise questions about what is published; accessing and studying the available material on a topic is imperative.

The other side of the coin is also knowing when to stop researching and gathering and to initiate the next phases. Seeing repetition in search results is the signal to stop. When the material read and analyzed begins to demonstrate a repetitive pattern of material, accessing additional resources can cease. Additional searching may be needed later to confirm that no new information has been published since the initial cyclic pattern was found. The discussion section, where the authors talk about the limitations of the study, is a beneficial place to locate information for literature evaluation. The evaluation process involves reviewing components of the study and comparing it to other studies related topically. The driving force behind the evaluation is a need to determine whether the study supports the identified research question and whether it detects holes in the literature that support the knowledge gap identified by the beginning researcher or student.

Generally, the components of the study that should be reviewed include its (1) purpose, (2) sample size and selection, (3) design of the study (methods used), (4) data collection procedures, (5) analysis of the data, and (6) the author's (or authors') conclusion. The theoretical framework section is also important to review, although it is sometimes not included due to space restrictions imposed by the publisher. It remains an important part of the study, however, because it provides structure for conducting the study and explaining the results.

A discussion of the areas selected for evaluation follows. These areas correspond to the headings in **TABLE 7-1**.

Articles

When choosing articles from the literature, researchers should be aware of the author's credentials. It is important to identify where they work and how to contact an author if you have questions about her or his writings. An email address is often available; they may also have a profile on ResearchGate (www.researchgate.net) or LinkedIn (www.linkedin.com). In most cases, authors are available and willing to assist beginning researchers. The article usually provides brief background information on the author(s) that informs the reader about their credibility and expertise, as it relates to the topic. It is essential to document both the article's citation, plus the author's contact information. It may seem tedious, but it is time well spent comprehensively documenting this important information (how to locate the article, the author's name, the date of publication, title of the article, title of the work containing the article, the volume number, and page numbers). As a side note, the electronic resource Scopus can be used to determine a journal title's impact factor (Scopus, 2018).

Purpose

The purpose of the study explains why it is being done. It is distinct from the problem in that the problem addresses what the study is about (Nieswiadomy, 2018). This section is an appropriate component for the researcher to determine what he or she wants to do with the findings of the study. For example, if the study's focus is the problem of obesity in third-grade public school students, the purpose could be to determine if environmental factors, like the school and the age of the children, may contribute to food consumption choices. The findings could then be used to make changes in the school or to enhance healthy behaviors in the students while attending school. A study's purpose is usually located in its first few paragraphs.

TABLE 7-1 Gaps in the Literature

Article (Title, author, journal, publication date, contact information for author)	Purpose (Why study was conducted)	Sample (Number of participants, demographics, other characteristics, geographic location, sampling method)	Methods (Design, instruments or questionnaires, data collection, data analysis)	Major Findings (Results, statistical significance, conclusions)	Limitations (Factors that may complicate the interpretation of the findings)	Gaps (Suggestions for further study that support the research question)

Identifying the purpose may help in the later grouping of similar types of studies and also in organizing and composing the literature review itself.

Sample/Population

The sample is a representation of the entire population of interest. All persons in the world cannot be studied, so a representative sample is selected that may have characteristics similar to the general population being studied. For example, caregivers may be the population of interest. Because it is impossible to study all caregivers in the world, a sample with similar experiences could be chosen. To choose a manageable sample size, the sample may be narrowed to those caregivers who care for their spouses and live in a particular county of Texas.

The sample/population section of the study describes the study participants. The author describes demographic characteristics (e.g., age, gender, race, ethnicity, educational level, geographic location, income level) of the persons who will be studied. The description of the sample and how it was selected helps the researcher make statements about the generalizability of the study—that is, whether similar findings would be obtained in other locations under the same or similar conditions. How the sample was selected may affect study findings. If the participants were randomly selected using random tables or computer software, the findings are more likely to be generalizable to other similar subjects. In contrast, if the sample was selected based on who showed up at the announcement of the study (known as a convenience sample), it is less likely that the findings could be generalized to other groups.

This section can be documented by providing just a few statements, such as "persons 65 years of age and older caring for their 65-and-older spouses with Alzheimer's disease in their home in rural west Texas." Other examples of sample statements could be "a convenience sample of registered nurses working in home health agencies" or "a randomly selected sample of diabetics diagnosed within the last 6 months."

🔲 THINK OUTSIDE THE BOX

Select a topic. Discuss the specific steps you would use to conduct a literature review on that topic. Which words would you use to do the search, and why? Which databases would you use, and why?

Methods

The methods section of the study describes the strategy for how it is conducted. In quantitative research, the methods section includes (1) the inclusion criteria, explaining how the participants were selected; (2) the exclusion criteria, explaining why subjects were not selected; (3) the sample size and whether it was adequate; (4) the design; (5) the instruments or surveys used; (6) data collection procedures; and (7) data analysis (Portney & Watkins, 2018). Each of these components helps the reader to understand the thoughts and rationales used in the planning of the project.

The design describes whether the investigation was a descriptive, correlational, exploratory, or experimental study. (Research study designs are covered in Chapters 8 and 9.) When you read the article, especially the methods section, the emphasis should be on whether the techniques used for data collection were controlled for any outside conditions that could skew the study's findings and whether the methods affected the conclusion's accuracy. For example, if the study focuses on the relationship of weight to blood pressure, the researcher must have ensured that the weight scales and blood pressure machines were calibrated and functioning properly. The procedure for how this was done should also be described in the study. If the condition of the measuring instruments is not standardized, it will be impossible to know whether the findings were accurate. Thus, the methods section of the article should include a description of the conditions under which the weights and blood pressures were measured and the person taking the measurements. If surveys or questionnaires were used, the researcher should discuss how the reliability and validity of these instruments were determined when used with other subjects.

Put simply, the design identifies the number of subjects, the number of groups, the type of intervention, and the conditions under which the intervention was performed (Portney & Watkins, 2018). This section of the study helps the reader interpret the degree of accuracy or validity of the findings.

The analysis of the data describes the statistical tests that were used to test the research hypothesis. For example, if the study sought to determine the relationship between two variables, a correlational test would be done. If the study sought to determine the difference between two variables, a t-test would be used. The reader should note the type of testing and compare it with the testing done in other studies; he or she should also determine if the appropriate test was done to match the research hypothesis. In qualitative studies, the avenues used to control for biases must be listed to provide an understanding of how the researchers attempted to ensure unbiased management of the data collected.

Major Findings

The findings (or results) may overlap with the discussion section of the study, but it is most appropriate for the results to stand alone. The results section should be reported without the researcher's interpretation (Portney & Watkins, 2018). This section is a factual discussion that may be explained with tables and charts. It is important for the reader to determine whether the results match the purpose of the study and the research question. In addition, the reader should note any statistically significant results and the tests that were used. When the study discusses qualitative results, the reader should pay attention to how bias and control of the study were managed.

Limitations

The limitations of the study describe the elements that may have complicated its results. For example, suppose a study was conducted to measure improvement in test scores after an instructive video on avoiding needlesticks was presented to the participants. A pretest was given before the video was shown, and a posttest was given 1 week after the video presentation. If the scores were low on the posttest, a limitation could be that too much time had lapsed between the test, the instruction, and the posttest. Discussing this limitation of the study may suggest ways to improve the study if it is later replicated. Limitations may also help to identify gaps in the literature that could be considered in other studies.

Gaps in the Literature

As it relates to the review of the literature, this section is quite significant; however, it cannot be given due diligence unless all the other parts of the research study are examined first. The discussion and conclusion sections of the article are generally where most suggestions for future research are presented. Such suggestions for future research usually represent gaps in knowledge about the research topic. Perhaps a particular group suffers a worse outcome than other populations, relative to a particular disease condition. The gap in the literature might be that no studies have examined the nature of this problem.

The discussion and conclusion section is where authors most often compare their findings with other studies, offer alternative explanations, or offer support for existing practice (Portney & Watkins, 2018). This section is a reflection of the author(s)' interpretation and experience, biases, and interests relevant to the findings of the study. The authors discuss unanswered questions and point out gaps in the knowledge on the research topic.

The reader should peruse this section very carefully for knowledge gaps and unknowns about the research area, looking for information that justifies the research being proposed. This information could be holes related to unanswered questions regarding gender, age, ethnicity, characteristics of healthcare facilities, geographic locations, differences in disease outcomes, or any combination of variables that have not been examined. These aspects would represent gaps in the literature.

▶ Writing the Literature Review

The literature review is not a list of article summaries but a thorough synthesis of a topic that includes discussion of the available research and the evidence gathered, methodologies, strengths and weaknesses of findings, and gaps requiring more information. The approach should ultimately be to convince the reader that the information gleaned supports the need for the proposed study. Morgan-Rallis (2014) emphasizes the need to "stay on topic." When directly involved with the writing of the synthesis, it is easy to move in directions that are not consistent with the purpose for the document. Staying on track to ensure that the purpose is the outcome for the manuscript is fundamental. The format for writing the review may vary depending on its purpose. If the review is conducted for a class assignment, the student should follow the syllabus/grading criteria. If the review is part of a grant proposal, it is usually succinct and points out various themes, conceptual models, theories that explain the research question, and gaps in the literature that support the need for a grant.

Unfortunately, getting bogged down while actually writing the review is way too easy. The researcher usually reads numerous articles before settling on those used in the literature review. Each article included must clearly and concisely address the stated purpose for the manuscript and/or review. One handy tool of organization is an outline. Others have recommended the use of grids or matrices for organizing one's review of the articles or index cards for categorizing the materials read (McCabe, 2005; Polit & Beck, 2017). One way of developing headings for an outline is to mark notes on the articles or to use the variables identified for the study. After reading the articles chosen for the review, it is helpful to go back and write notes in the margins adjacent to pertinent information or to list on the article's first page the reasons why the article was chosen (e.g., good questionnaire, clearly written design, independent and dependent variables listed and defined, similarities to another study).

⬦ THINK OUTSIDE THE BOX

Access Cortez-Gann et al. (2017), "Blood Transfusion Vital Sign Frequency: What Does the Evidence Say?" *MedSurg Nursing, 26*(2), pp. 89–92. Examine which aspects from the article must be documented within the summary provided for a literature review.

Answering Key Questions

A good written review should answer basic questions. Listed here are questions developed from the information found in most published research studies based on the confluence of reading, teaching/training, conducting and critiquing research reviews, and information learned from courses in nursing, the humanities, social sciences, and library science:

- What was the primary focus of the articles (research question, purpose, objectives)?
- Did the articles represent a balanced mix of recent (less than 5 years from publication) and older ones?
- How were the studies designed (research questions, methodology, sample size, population characteristics, and conclusion)?
- Which studies did not support the research question?
- What were the studies' target populations (e.g., nurses in emergency departments, medical–surgical units, or operating rooms)?
- Which models or conceptual frameworks were used to explain the structure of the studies?
- What were the general findings and limitations in most of the studies?
- Which articles were the most similar in findings, design, or other features?
- Which gaps were identified in the articles?
- What was the overall conclusion for the literature review that supports the research question and need for your proposal?

An Outline for Writing the Review

Discussion of the preceding list of questions should be helpful in providing organization to the review. Organizing it requires thought and attention. One method for organizing the material is through the use of a well-constructed table. Tables help address key terms and concepts, research methods, and a summary of the research results (Morgan-Rallis, 2014).

Another useful tool is an outline. An outline provides further guidance for developing headings and completing the written review. Normally, an outline contains (1) the purpose, (2) a description of the search strategy, (3) the themes or categories of similar types of articles, (4) limitations, (5) gaps in what is known about

---

BOX 7-4 Outline for a Literature Review

1. Purpose of the review
2. Description of how the search was conducted
   a. Databases used
3. Key words and subject headings
4. Rationale or criteria for articles chosen in the review
   a. Articles 5 years old or less
   b. Classic articles or books
5. Themes of articles
   a. Similarities in articles that support the research question
      i. Purposes, designs, target populations, tools of measurement (e.g., questionnaires, methodologies)
      ii. General findings
   b. Conceptual framework, models, or theories that explain the research described in the articles
   c. Inconsistencies in articles
      i. Articles that do not provide positive support for the research question identified
6. Limitations
   a. Components identified by the authors of the articles that were limitations in the studies
7. Gaps in the articles
   a. Gaps identified by the authors of the articles
8. Discussion and conclusion
   a. Summary statement of how the articles support the proposal
   b. Identification of gaps perceived and how the proposal will meet the needs of some aspect of nursing practice

---

a research area, and (6) a discussion and conclusion. A more detailed description of an outline for organizing the writing of the review appears in **BOX 7-4**.

Other Writing Tips

When writing a class-assigned literature review, it is important to follow the syllabus, especially its grading criteria and course objectives. If a review is not drafted for a class assignment, give attention to what the audience, in your estimation, would find interesting to know about the topic. According to O'Neill (2015), the inclusion of a historical account and/or the topic's background helps the reader better understand the context of the information provided. The writer should ensure that persuasive arguments and articulated points are supported by the findings and succinctly communicated (O'Neill, 2015). The review's length, in terms of the number of pages, depends on its criteria and purpose. It is critical during the writing process to remain cognizant of the reference tools used. While several reference formats can be used, one that is frequently used within health care is American Psychological Association (APA) format (*Publication Manual of the American Psychological Association*, currently in its sixth edition). The framework for citing references provides assistance for grammar, font, margin, spacing, and document guidelines, along with how to format the citations and reference list for the different types of sources used.

Once the required style has been determined, paraphrase the crucial points of the articles and avoid using too many direct quotes. Lengthy writing does not necessarily mean comprehensive writing. The central point is the ability to synthesize the information while giving the reader what was promised in the writing's purpose. Staying on point, for example, answering the questions under consideration, keeps a document meaningful. Each paragraph and/or section provides a critical summary of how this material supports the purpose of the manuscript, project, or study. Using the summarization method brings the writer back to the idea of how each part connects to the document's intent.

▶ Linking the Literature Review to Evidence-Based Nursing Practice

EBP is an important issue in nursing today. Nurses need to know why they do what they do. Although many may support the idea of using intuition or gut feeling, the profession must provide logical explanations for the actions of real-world nurses based on scientific findings. The literature review provides the foundation for good research. Today's nurses must be well read to be able to make sound choices. The research presented in the literature review provides nurses with the needed background to make informed practice choices. The ability to study scientific literature analytically is a skill every nurse should develop. It is also an aptitude central to determining whether new information is to be incorporated into practice based on the strength of the evidence.

⏏ THINK OUTSIDE THE BOX

Explain how you would establish the credibility of information found on the Internet.

Summary Points

1. The literature review is the foundation of the research proposal.
2. An effective literature review begins with a thorough literature search, aided by a professional librarian.
3. The assistance of a professional librarian can enhance the relevance of a literature search and results, plus reduce the amount of time spent conducting it.
4. A subject heading–driven database search, for example, MeSH, yields more precise information than a keyword search.
5. The literature review identifies both the known and the unknown about the research topic.
6. The review should focus on original research studies dealing with the selected topic.
7. The literature review identifies gaps in the literature.
8. The gaps in the literature should support the research question.

> ⚑ **RED FLAGS**
>
> - Literature summaries should provide enough information about the different sources related to sample size, methodology, and results to allow for a clear understanding of the application of that information to the current project.
> - Within the literature review, the sources used should be predominantly *primary* sources, not *secondary* sources.
> - The current expectation is for references to be no more than 5 years ago, unless the article is a classic or a benchmark study.
> - For Internet-based sources, the credibility of the information must be reflected in the literature review; that is, does it come from a reputable source (for example, a *New York Times* health blog)?
> - Gaps in the literature review should be identified.

Multiple-Choice Questions

1. A literature review is:
   A. everything that is known about a subject.
   B. an analytical summary of research findings.
   C. all approved data on a research topic.
   D. a compilation of all positive results of research.

2. The purpose of the literature review is to:
   A. identify a problem that has not been resolved.
   B. clarify the importance of a research problem.
   C. identify gaps in the literature.
   D. all of the above.

3. The literature review should occur:
   A. near the end of the research process.
   B. shortly before the analysis of the problem.
   C. early in the research process.
   D. at none of these points.

4. When conducting a literature review, it is advisable to:
   A. seek most information from the Internet.
   B. gather all data from books.
   C. gather all data from journals.
   D. seek assistance from a librarian.

5. Evidence-based nursing literature provides the nurse with the ability to:
   A. choose only those practice activities based on evidence.
   B. describe and analyze published research results.
   C. use textbook information.
   D. solve all nursing issues.

6. A database differs from a search engine because:
   A. a database stores the information.
   B. a search engine takes you to the information.
   C. databases are specialized by area of knowledge.
   D. all of the above.

7. Which database is considered the premier bibliographic database for providing access to biomedical literature in North America?
    A. Google
    B. MEDLINE
    C. CINAHL
    D. Bing

8. It is appropriate to use keyword searches in which of the following contexts?
    A. Evidence-based medicine
    B. Ovid
    C. MEDLINE
    D. Evidence-based nursing

9. The purpose section of a research study usually:
    A. tells the geographic location of the study.
    B. tells why the study was done.
    C. reveals the study's methodology.
    D. tells what the study is about.

10. The gaps in the literature are:
    A. missing pieces in the knowledge of the research area.
    B. questions about the research that have not been explained.
    C. suggestions for future research made by the author.
    D. all of the above.

11. What is the main difference between a research article and a nonresearch article?
    A. A research article reports statistics on surveys, and a nonresearch article does not.
    B. A research article describes research by the original author.
    C. A nonresearch article describes the methods of how the study was conducted.
    D. A nonresearch article conducts analysis and statistical testing on the data presented in the article.

Discussion Questions

1. You are interested in researching smoking cessation and the literature discussing pharmacologic versus behavioral strategies. You have been told that the appropriate MeSH heading is "smoking cessation," but you want to use the MeSH database in PubMed to verify this term. You also know that you only want articles that meet the following criteria: English-language, have an abstract, no older than 5 years, exclusively from nursing journals, and are systematic reviews; thus, you limit your search by using the "Limits" functions found on the PubMed search screen. Execute your search, and examine the results. (This exercise was adapted from a practice case by Wilkinson and Real (2017), Texas Tech University Health Sciences Center.)

2. To gain a greater understanding of evidence-based nursing, conduct a search for published literature on how aspirin is used for prevention of myocardial infarction. Choose the CINAHL Plus with Full Text database produced by EBSCO*host*. Develop a search strategy for this topic. Review your results.

Suggested Readings

Ahern, N. R. (2005). Using the Internet to conduct research. *Nurse Researcher, 13*(2), 55–70.

Garrard, J. (2017). *Health sciences literature review made easy: The matrix method.* Burlington, MA: Jones & Bartlett Learning.

Lorenz, J. M., Beyea, S. C., & Slattery, M. J. (2009). *Evidence-based practice: A guide for nurses.* Marblehead, MA: HCPro.

Preston, J. (2015). Critiquing research. *Nursing Standard, Royal College of Nursing, Great Britain: 1987, 30*(14), 61–62.

References

Bolderston, A. (2008). Writing an effective literature review. *Journal of Medical Imaging and Radiation Sciences, 39*(2), 86–92.

Boswell, C., Real, T., & Wilkinson, C. *Searching PubMed and Other Evidence-Based Practice Resources* [PDF document]. Retrieved from https://ttuhsc.libguides.com/ld.php?content_id=43187997

Bradley, P. (2013). *Expert Internet searching.* London, UK: Facet Publishing.

CINAHL Information Systems. (2018). The CINAHL database. Birmingham, AL: EBSCO Industries. Retrieved from http://www.ebscohost.com/nursing/products/cinahl-databases/cinahl-complete

Cortez-Gann, J., Gilmore, K. D., Foley, K. W., Kennedy, M. B., McGee, T., & Kring, D. (2017). Blood transfusion vital sign frequency: What does the evidence say? *MEDSURG Nursing, 26*(2), 89–92.

Dictionary.com. (2018). Search engine. Retrieved from http://www.dictionary.com/browse/search-engine

Duncan, V., & Holtslander, L. (2012). Utilizing grounded theory to explore the information-seeking behavior of senior nursing students. *Journal of the Medical Library Association, 100*(1), 20–27.

EBSCO. (2018). *EBSCO Health.* Birmingham, AL: EBSCO Industries. Retrieved from https://health.ebsco.com/

Gray, J. R. (2017). Review of relevant literature. In J. R. Gray, S. K. Grove, & S. Sutherland (Eds.). *Burns and Grove's the practice of nursing research: Appraisal, synthesis, and generation of evidence* (8th ed., pp. 120–137). St. Louis, MO: Elsevier.

Gray, J. R., Grove, S. K., & Sutherland, S. (2017). *Burns and Grove's the practice of nursing research: Appraisal, synthesis, and generation of evidence* (8th ed.). St. Louis, MO: Elsevier.

Kellsey, C. (2005). Writing the literature review: Tips for academic librarians. *College Research Library News, 66*(7), 526–527.

Klein-Fedyshin, M. (2015). Translating evidence into practice at the end of life: Information needs, access, and usage of hospice and palliative nurses. *Journal of Hospice & Palliative Nursing, 17*(1), 24–30. doi:10.1097/NJH.0000000000000117

Kwan, T. M. & Sullivan, M. (2017). The use of intravenous ibuprofen and intravenous acetaminophen in surgical patient and the effect on opioid reduction. *MEDSURG Nursing, 26*(2), 124–142.

Leedy, P. D., & Ormrod, J. E. (2012). *Practical research: Planning and design* (10th ed.). Boston, MA: Pearson.

LibGuides of the University Library Groningen. (2017). Types of databases. Retrieved from https://libguides.rug.nl/c.php?g=470628&p=3283312

McCabe, T. F. (2005). How to conduct an effective literature search. *Nursing Standard, 20*(11), 41–47.

McGrath, J. M., & Brandon, D. (2014). Searching the literature is NOT for the faint of heart! *Advances in Neonatal Care, 14*(40), 229–231. doi:10.1097/ANC.0000000000000111

Merriam-Webster. (2018). Database. Retrieved from https://www.merriam-webster.com/dictionary/database

Morgan-Rallis, H. (2014). Guidelines for writing a literature review. Retrieved from http://www.duluth.umn.edu/~hrallis/guides/researching/litreview.html

National Library of Medicine. (2008). MeSH subject heading scope note. Retrieved from https://www.ncbi.nlm.nih.gov/mesh/?term=review+literature+as+topic

National Library of Medicine. (2017). Fact sheet: Medline®. Retrieved from http://www.nlm.nih.gov/pubs/factsheets/medline.html

Nieswiadomy, R. M. (2018). *Foundations in nursing research* (6th ed). New York, NY: Pearson.

O'Neill, J. (2015). Literature review guidelines. Retrieved from http://www.apa.org/pubs/journals /men/literature-review-guidelines.aspx

Oxford English Dictionary. (2013). Discursive. Oxford University Press.

Poe, S., & White, K. M. (Eds.). (2010). *Johns Hopkins nursing evidence-based practice: Implementation and translation.* Indianapolis, IN: Sigma Theta Tau.

Polit, D. F., & Beck, C. T. (2017). *Nursing research: Generating and assessing evidence for nursing practice* (10th ed.). Philadelphia, PA: Lippincott Williams & Wilkins.

Portney, L. G., & Watkins, M. P. (2018). *Foundations of clinical research: Applications to practice.* Philadelphia, PA: F.A. Davis.

ProQuest. (2015). Medline/Medline full text: Key facts. Retrieved from http://www.proquest.com/

Scopus. (2018). Elsevier: Scopus Support Center. Retrieved from www.scopus.com.

Smedley, B. D., Stith, A. Y., & Nelson, A. R. (2003). *Unequal treatment: Confronting racial and ethnic disparities in health care.* Washington, DC: National Academies Press.

Tarigan, L. H., Cifuentes, M., Quinn, M., & Kriebel, D. (2015). Prevention of needle-stick injuries in healthcare facilities: A meta-analysis. *Infection Control & Hospital Epidemiology, 36*(7), 823–829.

Taylor, D. (2012). The literature review: A few tips on conducting it. Retrieved from http://www .writing.utoronto.ca/advice/specific-types-of-writing/literature-review

Wilkinson, C. E., & Real, T. (2017). Searching PubMed and other Evidence-Based Medicine Resources: An OSCE Primer [PowerPoint Slides].

Worral, P. S., Levin, R. F., & Arsenault, D. C. (2009). Documenting an EBP project: Guidelines for what to include and why. *The Journal of the New York State Nurses' Association, 40*(2), 12–19.

CHAPTER 8

Quantitative Research Design

Sharon Cannon

CHAPTER OBJECTIVES

At the conclusion of this chapter, the learner will be able to:
1. List characteristics of quantitative designs.
2. Discuss descriptive designs.
3. Identify control for quantitative designs.
4. Compare experimental, nonexperimental, time-dimensional, and quasi-experimental designs.
5. Compare and contrast research design, quality improvement programs, and root cause analysis (RCA).
6. Select a quantitative design for research utilization in an evidence-based practice (EBP) clinical situation.

KEY TERMS

Comparative design
Control
Correlational design
Dependent variable
Descriptive design
Experimental design
Independent variable
Manipulation
Meta-analysis
Meta-synthesis
Nonequivalent control group

Nonexperimental design
Quality improvement (QI) project
Quantitative design
Quasi-experimental design
Randomization
Research design
Root cause analysis (RCA)
Secondary analysis
Sentinel events
Time-dimensional design

▶ Introduction

The most commonly used **research design** is a quantitative design. But precisely what is a quantitative design? This question, as well as the characteristics and types of designs for use in evidence-based practice (EBP) clinical situations, is discussed in this chapter.

Before exploring the characteristics of a study design, it is necessary to define quantitative research. Quantitative research is often identified with the traditional scientific method that gathers data objectively in an organized, systematic, controlled manner so that the findings can be generalized to other situations and/or populations (Brockopp & Hastings-Tolsma, 2003; Burns & Grove, 2009; Fain, 2009; Heavy, 2019; Polit & Beck, 2008). A design is a plan on how to proceed; thus, a quantitative research design can be defined as an objective, systematic plan or blueprint to gather data that has application to other situations and/or populations. **Quantitative design** may be (1) experimental, (2) nonexperimental, or (3) quasi-experimental. Studies utilizing an **experimental design** use treatment and control groups, those with a **nonexperimental design** generate questions for experimental design, and studies having a **quasi-experimental design** lack randomization or may not include a control group.

▶ Characteristics of Quantitative Research Design

The characteristics of quantitative design center on the "why," "where," "who," "what," "when," and "how" questions. The quantitative researcher must state why (purpose) the study is being done, where (setting) the study is being conducted (e.g., laboratory, hospital, or clinic), who (subject. e.g., animal or human) is being studied, what type of data is being collected, when the data are to be collected, and how (design) the data are to be collected.

Within the framework of these questions, quantitative research looks for cause and effect in an experiment. When considering potential causes and effects, different groups participating in the study are viewed in terms of being either treatment or control groups. **Control** is one of the most common and important characteristics of quantitative design. To understand the concept of control, it is necessary to understand variables. A variable can be a quality, characteristic, behavior, attribute, or property of a person, thing, or situation (Burns & Grove, 2009; Melnyk & Morrison-Beedy, 2012; Polit & Beck, 2008). The two types of variables found in quantitative research are dependent and independent variables. The **dependent variable** is the outcome caused or influenced by the independent variable; the **independent variable** is a treatment, intervention, or experiment. Consider the situation in which a nurse researcher studies the effect of patient teaching (independent variable) about wound care in an attempt to reduce the likelihood of wound infection (dependent variable) when the surgical patient is discharged from the hospital. In this example, the teaching is what affects the rate of wound infection.

Closely connected to the issue of control is **manipulation** of the independent variable. The researcher wants to make sure that the treatment is the only explanation for the outcome. In the previous example about wound care, the nurse researcher wants to ensure that the patient education on wound care delivered prior to discharge is the reason why the rate of wound infections in discharged surgical patients decreases. Control or manipulation in this situation would involve providing patient education to surgical patients who are not taking antibiotics when discharged from the hospital. Patients who are taking antibiotics would be least likely to develop a wound infection, and the use of antibiotics would be a variable that might skew the results.

Another important characteristic of quantitative research is randomization. **Randomization** is the assignment of subjects to a group so each subject has an equal opportunity of being selected to participate in the study. In the wound care example, the researcher might have two groups: The control group would include those subjects who did not receive any wound care education, whereas the experimental group would include those subjects who did receive patient education. Randomization would occur when the patients were assigned to either group in a way that each patient had an equal opportunity for inclusion in either group. This sampling could be done by selecting every third patient discharged to be a member of a group. Another way to randomize the sample might be to give each patient a number, draw the numbers out of a hat, and alternate assignment to the groups. Randomization helps to eliminate bias. For example, the nurse who thinks that only her patients should be in the treatment group would be biased; randomization of subjects would eliminate that possibility. Although randomization strengthens a study, be aware that not all studies can be randomized. Randomization can be costly and time consuming, and there may not be enough participants to randomize them effectively.

🔃 THINK OUTSIDE THE BOX

Which type of research design could be used in the following examples to provide the strongest methodology possible:

- What information has been used to determine the method of catheterizing a laboring mother?
- What information serves as the basis for the range of blood sugars used within elderly persons who are newly diagnosed with diabetes?
- What nursing model would be useful in a critical access type of agency?
- In the Cortez-Gann, Gilmore, Foley, Kennedy, McGee, & Kring (2017) article regarding blood transfusion vital sign frequency, what type of design was used?

In any quantitative research study, it is important to control the influence of extraneous variables, such as gender, age, and ethnicity. Randomization provides for internal validity of a study because the groups are equal at the beginning of the study. External validity is achieved when the outcome can be applied (generalized) to the target population; generalization helps strengthen the study results. In the wound care example, control of the extraneous variable could involve not providing patient education to pediatric patients but rather providing it only to adult patients.

Manipulation, control, and randomization are three essential characteristics of quantitative research design. These characteristics enable the researcher to be confident that the outcome is caused by the intervention and not by other variables and that it can be generalized to a target population. In the Cortez-Gann et al. (2017)

article, of 77,800 units of blood transfused, only 116 records were examined. Twelve variables determined inclusion in the study and limited the number of extraneous variables.

▶ Descriptive Design

Descriptive design examines the characteristics of just one sample population. According to Burns and Grove (2009), this type of research design may be used for theory development, practice problems, rationale for current practice, generating hypotheses, or clinical decision making based on what others are doing. Examples of descriptive design include comparative (looking at differences in two or more groups), time-dimensional (occurring over an extended period of time), cross-sectional (stages of development simultaneously), trends and events, and correlational (relationships) designs. A descriptive design delineates or explains the variables being studied and provides flexibility in examining a problem from many different angles. Be aware, however, that data obtained in quantitative, descriptive designs are limited to participant responses to things such as blood pressure equipment or scores on a survey. The two most commonly used types of descriptive designs are comparative and correlational.

The **comparative design** involves no manipulation or control of the independent variable, with the dependent variable being the only variable measured in two or more groups (Brink & Wood, 2001). This type of design can also be retrospective in nature. In the wound care example, a comparative design would assign patients with wounds to a group of surgical patients or to a group of patients with wounds resulting from trauma to compare the rates of postdischarge infections. The research question might be, "Is the rate of infection higher in trauma patients than in surgical patients?" The patients' past histories would then be examined for prior surgeries or trauma wounds. Cause and effect remain the focus of this design in that the two groups being compared for infection rates are identified according to the type of wound.

Perhaps the most widely used type of descriptive design is the correlational study. Simply stated, a **correlational design** examines the relationships between two or more variables within a situation without knowing the reason for the relationship. The researcher may use this design when there is uncertainty about whether the variables are related and, if so, how they are related. However, the researcher assumes that the variables are related and seeks to discover and explain that relationship. Correlational designs do not conclude that only one variable causes another because the independent variable cannot always be controlled (Polit & Beck, 2008).

Another aspect of a correlational design is that it is *ex post facto*, meaning "from after the fact" (Polit & Beck, 2006). For example, a study that compares a variable occurring in the past with a variable occurring currently would be characterized as using a retrospective correlational design. In other words, a study that looks at a variable after the fact is a retrospective study. For instance, the nurse researcher might conduct a chart review on all discharged surgical patients to determine if any patient education on wound care occurred prior to discharge from the hospital and then to check whether any of those patients were readmitted for a wound infection. The Cortez-Gann et al. (2017) study is another example of a retrospective descriptive design study.

Prospective correlational designs are usually considered stronger than retrospective designs because the researcher may be able to control or rule out explanations for some outcomes (Polit & Beck, 2008). These designs require the researcher to assume cause and effect and to implement the study under those assumptions.

Correlational designs may also be predictive in nature. In this type of study, one variable occurs prior to another variable—that is, the independent variable occurs prior to the dependent variable. In the wound care example, a predictive correlational study research statement might be, "The rate of wound infection will decrease 1 week postdischarge after the patient receives the wound care educational program in the outpatient clinic."

⬆ THINK OUTSIDE THE BOX

Explore the idea of control within a quantitative design methodology. Which aspects of the study design are important to consider and why? Did the Cortez-Gann et al. (2017) study have control for variables?

▶ Experimental Design

Experimental design looks for cause and effect (outcome). Obviously, a preceding cause must be present. A relationship between the cause and the outcome without any influencing variables to warrant the conclusion that a cause-and-effect relationship exists is also expected.

Several issues related to experimental design should be addressed before discussing the designs themselves. The first issue is that not all variables can be manipulated. In the wound care example, not every patient has a wound. A researcher cannot inflict a wound on all individuals to obtain a larger random sample.

Another issue is that of ethics. Consider the famous Tuskegee Syphilis Study (Centers for Disease Control and Prevention, n.d.), an experiment that was conducted over 40 years to examine the progress of syphilis in adult black males. Many of the subjects in this study were not even aware that they were participants. Also, even though an effective treatment for syphilis (penicillin) was available, not all subjects with syphilis in this study were given penicillin. To satisfy ethical concerns, some variables should not be manipulated.

Feasibility is another issue in experimental design. Some experiments may be too expensive, require cooperation from individuals from multiple key areas, require too much time, or not have enough subjects for participation. When considering the feasibility of a proposed study, careful attention should be given to what types of resources might be needed to conduct the research project.

In experimental design, another significant issue is the Hawthorne effect. Simply stated, the Hawthorne effect arises when the subjects know that they are part of the study and change their behavior accordingly; that is, the act of observing changes the observed subject's behavior. While it is not possible to prevent the Hawthorne effect from occurring, researchers must consider how to minimize the influence that attention has on the outcome of the study.

With these issues in mind, we now move to an examination of experimental design. The most classic experimental design is a pretest/posttest design. With this

Pretest/Posttest

$\quad$ R $\quad$ O_1 $\quad$ X_1 $\quad$ O_2

$\quad$ R $\quad$ O_1 $\quad$ X_2 $\quad$ O_2

Two-Group Posttest Only

$\quad$ R $\quad$ X_1 $\quad$ O_1

$\quad$ R $\quad$ X_2 $\quad$ O_1

Three Groups

$\quad$ R $\quad$ X_1 $\quad$ O_1

$\quad$ R $\quad$ X_2 $\quad$ O_1

$\quad$ R $\quad$ O_1

Four Groups

$\quad$ R $\quad$ O_1 $\quad$ X_1 $\quad$ O_2

$\quad$ R $\quad$ X_1 $\quad$ O_2

$\quad$ R $\quad$ O_1 $\quad$ X_2 $\quad$ O_2

$\quad$ R $\quad$ X_2 $\quad$ O_2

Note: O = outcome/measurement; R = random assignment; X = treatment/intervention.

FIGURE 8-1 Experimental design examples.

approach, subjects are assigned to one of two groups: a control (comparative) group that does not receive the treatment (intervention) or an experimental group that does receive the treatment. In the wound care example, patients would be assigned to a group that receives no specific wound care instructions (control group) or to the group that receives patient education regarding wound care (experimental group).

Another experimental design of considerable importance in the healthcare arena is the randomized controlled trial (RCT). The RCT is considered the true experiment. This design may involve two, three, or four groups. The tests used may involve both a pretest and posttest, a posttest only, or repeated measures (**FIGURE 8-1**).

▶ Nonexperimental Design

Some studies do not lend themselves to an experimental design; that is, manipulation of variables is not possible, nor is randomization controlled. Studies with this kind of nonexperimental design occur in the here and now and are observational rather than interventional in nature. Two types of nonexperimental designs used in EBP are secondary analysis and meta-analysis.

Secondary analysis follows the course implied by its name: It examines data obtained in another study and allows researchers to examine large and small data sets collected via different approaches. A secondary analysis asks new questions about data previously collected for another purpose. For example, a nurse researcher interested in the effects of patient education on decreased wound infection rates might examine one or several previously conducted studies. By analyzing a variable that had not been studied previously, such as the age of the patient, a secondary analysis might show a relationship to wound healing, especially for geriatric patients.

Meta-analysis also looks at previous studies and, as indicated by Bator, Taylor, and Catalano (2015), it is a way to rank similar study results. Brockopp and Hastings-Tolsma (2003) indicate that meta-analysis, through calculation of statistics, can help researchers establish the existence of bias and confounding variables in the cause-and-effect relationship identified in multiple studies. Polit and Beck (2006) explain that a data set is "the total collection of data for all sample members for analysis" (p. 642). The data set analysis carried out as part of a meta-analysis is similar to that performed for individual studies through statistical tests. The key facet of meta-analysis is the application of statistics to multiple studies looking at the same phenomenon (Burns & Grove, 2009). Stated another way, meta-analysis for quantitative designs is intended to connect the results from an independent project through the use of statistical method (Hopp & Rittenmeyer, 2012). Meta-analysis for quantitative designs focuses on statistical methods and is not to be confused with **meta-synthesis** of qualitative designs, which focuses on individual studies that are pooled.

Although secondary and meta-analyses are of particular importance for research utilization in EBP, caution should be taken when considering their findings. Not all studies focus on the same subject, and information may even be missing from some studies. Drawing conclusions or making generalizations in applying findings to specific populations should be done carefully because bias can result, especially in studies with small sample sizes. The researcher should keep in mind the adage that "one size does not fit all."

THINK OUTSIDE THE BOX

If you have elected to use a nonexperimental design, how can you strengthen the confidence in the research project's findings?

▶ Time-Dimensional Design

When establishing a research project, attention must always be given to the dimension of time. The determination of when and how long data are to be collected is an essential component to any research design, and this process is termed **time-dimensional design**. If data have already been collected, then the study is considered to utilize a retrospective design. An example of a retrospective design would be that of a chart review. Perhaps a new procedure has been implemented to decrease length of stay (LOS). The nurse might go to the medical records department and conduct a chart review for the average LOS for patients who did not receive the new procedure versus those who did receive it.

A second type of time-dimensional design comprises a cross-sectional design. The cross-sectional design measures only what is currently in existence; it does not examine anything that happened in the past or future. An example of this design could be a retrospective chart review of lung cancer patients for the past five years to discover how long they had smoked cigarettes. Many cross-sectional studies are retrospective in nature, but they all collect data at a specific point in time.

The third type of time-dimensional design is the longitudinal study. As is implied by the name, a study with a longitudinal design relies on data that are collected at various intervals over time. The times for data collection may be short or long depending on the rate of change. This design is useful to examine changes that occur over time and assist in determining causality (Polit & Beck, 2008). Longitudinal designs are considered stronger than cross-sectional study designs because longitudinal designs allow for the possibility that changes and trends might emerge. An example of a longitudinal study is that by Hanna, Weaver, Slaven, Fortenberry, and DiMeglio (2014), which was conducted over a period of 12 months. They examined emerging adults with type 1 diabetes at high school graduation and at 3, 6, 9, and 12 months later. However, longitudinal studies also face the extra danger of having subjects drop out over time, and they are generally more expensive to manage. For example, in the Hanna and colleagues (2014) study, three subjects withdrew, two died, and two did not complete the study.

Each of the time-dimensional designs has its own set of advantages and disadvantages that must be considered by the researcher. In addition, the strengths and weaknesses of each study design must be considered before the results of the studies are applied to practice.

▶ Quasi-Experimental Design

Given that randomization is often not possible in research studies, quasi-experimental design is the most frequently used quantitative research design. With this approach, the independent variable is still manipulated, but there is no randomization or control group. The purpose of quasi-experimental design is to examine causality, though it is acknowledged that this design is not as strong as the experimental design, which has a control group and randomization. Nevertheless, quasi-experimental design is considered stronger than descriptive design, and it is more practical when true experimental design is not possible.

Types of quasi-experimental design include (1) posttest only with nonequivalent groups, (2) one-group pretest/posttest, (3) untreated control group with pretest/posttest, (4) removal treatment and reversal treatment, (5) nonequivalent control group, and (6) time series. The two most commonly used designs—nonequivalent control group and time series—are discussed here.

The **nonequivalent control group** design (sometimes called a comparison group) compares two groups that are not randomized. The initial baseline measurement (O_1) is used to determine if the subjects assigned to groups are similar. A treatment/intervention (X) is applied, and then a second measurement (O_2) is performed to see if the outcome is a result of the treatment or intervention (**FIGURE 8-2**).

In the wound care example, all patients would be assigned to group 1 or group 2. A pretest assessment would be conducted. The intervention (patient education program) would then be implemented. Each group would then be tested to see if its members experienced a decreased infection rate (outcome). When using this type of study design, the nurse researcher should keep in mind potential confounding

Nonequivalent Control Group

$$O_1 \quad X \quad O_2$$

$$O_1 \quad O_2$$

Note: O_1 = baseline measurement; X = treatment/intervention; O_2 = outcome measurement.

Time Series (Simple)

$$O_1 \; O_2 \; O_3 \; X \; O_4 \; O_5 \; O_6$$

Note: O_1, O_2, O_3 = baseline measurements at various levels; X = treatment/intervention;

O_4, O_5, O_6 = outcome measures at various intervals.

FIGURE 8-2 Quasi-experimental design examples.

factors such as the Hawthorne effect as well as the threat of history. History, in this instance, refers to some other variable that might have occurred. In the wound care experiment, an example of the history variable might be the patients who received additional instruction by the doctor's office staff prior to undergoing surgery or again after the educational program was administered.

The second quasi-experimental design to be discussed is the time-series design. This type of study may be conducted over a long period, in which case it is also called a longitudinal study. With a time-series design, participants are not randomized, nor is a control group used. Data are collected at various intervals prior to the treatment as well as after the treatment (see Figure 8-2). Returning to the wound care example, in a time-series design, the first observation might be on days 2 and 3 postoperatively, with a subsequent observation being recorded on the day of discharge. The educational program would then be conducted. The next three measurements might be on days 5, 7, and 9 postoperatively.

A variable that should be considered as an alternative explanation for the outcome measurement within time-series studies is maturation. Maturation refers to change that occurs throughout the entire span of time that the experiment is conducted. It might be a result of the repetition of testing, which might influence the scores that follow. For instance, if the patients were tested about wound care knowledge prior to receiving the educational program, they might become aware of what was needed for wound care to prevent infection just because of the questions used to test their baseline knowledge.

Another area of concern with the time-series design is the potential for attrition of subjects. The study occurs over time, and subjects may drop out of the study for various reasons. As a result, the sample size may be too small when the study ends, causing the study's findings not to be generalizable to other situations or populations.

⧉ THINK OUTSIDE THE BOX

Discuss how you would use the ranking of research designs' strength in EBP.

The two quasi-experimental designs discussed here offer a practical approach when an experimental design is not possible. Nurse researchers should be alert to the possible threats of the quasi-experimental design that can lead to other reasons for the study's outcomes.

▶ Control

As indicated earlier in this text, control of variables is critical when the researcher is seeking to determine the extent of a cause-and-effect relationship for the treatment or intervention applied as part of a study. Randomization helps control extraneous variables, both internal and external, to a research project, especially when the study employs an experimental design.

In studies using nonexperimental and quasi-experimental designs that do not have randomization or control groups, using subjects who are similar helps control extraneous variables that can influence the outcome. As a result, history, maturation, and attrition threats must be considered when designing the research project to maintain control. Variables can be controlled through the establishment of specific inclusion and exclusion criteria for selection of subjects, timing of test intervals, use of scripts for data collectors, and the setting in which the study is conducted.

▶ Research Design, Quality Improvement Projects, and Root Cause Analysis

Care must be taken when designing quantitative research. Even though research and **quality improvement (QI) projects** or activities are focused on patient outcomes, they are different processes (Kring, 2008). QI results can provide direction for improving practice, but they are not necessarily considered true "scientific inquiry." For example, chart reviews may reveal a trend, but they do not inspire the same level of confidence as results produced from a quantitative retrospective research design. QI projects can and often do contribute additional evidence that may even give significance to previous findings. Nevertheless, research designs take a more rigorous approach toward producing results and have more significant implications for practice. Both research design and QI projects may have implications for EBP, however, and their relationship should be considered within the totality of quantitative research design.

Root cause analysis (RCA) began in 1949 when the U.S. military wanted to examine system and equipment failures. Other industries, such as the space, manufacturing, and automotive industries, then began to realize the importance of RCA (Dunn & Renner, 2012). Simply stated, RCA identifies whether a failure is due to system-related or human error. For instance, when a plane crashes, RCA determines whether there was a system or equipment error or pilot error. In health care, RCAs have been used to investigate adverse events or **sentinel events** since the Joint Commission mandated the use of RCAs in 1997 (Agency for Healthcare Research and Quality [AHRQ], 2012). RCAs have a significant impact in the design of research and QI projects to eliminate errors and provide safer health care to patients. Examples of errors can range from nurse staffing issues to incorrect dosage calculations and from amputations of the wrong limb to lack of appropriate policies and procedures. Research design and QI projects can provide evidence for RCA and thus improve patient safety.

▶ Evidence-Based Considerations

Using quantitative research design in EBP requires the nurse to be able to comprehend the various designs and understand both their benefits and their shortcomings. Whether the nurse is participating in research or is applying research findings in practice, the type of design is essential to guide clinical decision making. The concepts of randomization and control in quantitative research provide information about generalization of outcomes in experimental, nonexperimental, and quasi-experimental studies to current practice.

If a nurse wants to look at the relationship between vital sign frequency for blood transfusion and adverse reaction, a correlational design would be appropriate. In contrast, if a nurse wants to examine the effect of frequent vital signs reducing blood transfusion reactions, the appropriate quantitative design would be experimental or quasi-experimental. Use of a secondary analysis or meta-analysis is another way a nurse might use quantitative research to validate existing practice or the need to change practice.

Manipulation, control of variables, and randomization are essential components of quantitative research. Extraneous variables in the practice setting must be examined carefully so that the evidence obtained will be applicable to nursing practice. Thus, knowing whether the research design is experimental, quasi-experimental, or nonexperimental influences the strength and generalizability of a study's findings to the current practice being considered. This point is of particular significance when conducting a secondary analysis or meta-analysis of research for the purpose of making clinical decisions.

⚙ THINK OUTSIDE THE BOX

What could an RCA reveal about a patient who had the wrong leg amputated? What could be considered a system failure? What could be considered a personnel failure? What research design would be most appropriate to investigate this type of error?

Quantitative research design and QI projects are important when examining evidence to improve practice. Nurses need to make sure they fully understand the distinctions between QI and quantitative research designs, as well as how both are relevant in EBP.

Summary Points

1. Quantitative research is often identified as corresponding with the traditional scientific method, which gathers data objectively in an organized method to allow findings to be generalized to other situations and/or populations.
2. A quantitative research design is an objective, systematic plan to gather data.
3. Characteristics of quantitative designs center on "why," "where," "who," "what," "when," and "how" questions.
4. Quantitative research examines relationships for cause and effect in an experiment.
5. Manipulation of the independent variable, control of extraneous variables, and randomization are essential to quantitative research.
6. In comparative designs, there is no manipulation or control of the independent variable.
7. The most commonly used descriptive design is the correlational design, which examines relationships between two or more variables within a situation without knowing the reason why the relationship exists.
8. Correlational designs may be *ex post facto*, prospective, or predictive.
9. Experimental designs look for cause and effect (outcome).
10. Issues such as ethics, inability to manipulate all variables, feasibility, and the Hawthorne effect must be addressed when considering studies with experimental designs.
11. The most classic experimental design is the pretest/posttest design.
12. The RCT is considered to be a true experimental design.
13. Two types of nonexperimental designs are used in EBP: secondary analysis and meta-analysis. Both look at previously completed studies and create data sets from those earlier studies to be analyzed in a different approach.
14. Quasi-experimental designs are used most frequently because the independent variable can still be manipulated even when no randomization or control group is possible.
15. The two most commonly used quasi-experimental designs are the nonequivalent control group and time-series designs.
16. The nonequivalent control group design compares two groups whose members are not randomized.
17. The time-series design is not randomized, and there is no control group. Data are gathered at various intervals.
18. Control of threats such as history, maturation, and attrition is of prime importance in quantitative designs and is of significance when making clinical decisions based on outcomes from quantitative research.
19. Understanding the implications for utilization of quantitative research in EBP requires a working knowledge of quantitative design.
20. Quality improvement projects and quantitative research are important in confirming evidence for EBP.
21. RCA and QI are related to research design and EBP.

⚑ RED FLAGS

- For a study to be classified as an experimental (quantitative) design, the design must incorporate control, randomization, and an intervention.
- Experimental (quantitative) design is considered to be the strongest research design. Quasi-experimental (quantitative) design has less strength, and nonexperimental (quantitative) design has the least strength.
- When a small sample size is used for a quantitative study, the results of the study need to be examined closely for their generalizability to other populations.
- Prospective designs are stronger than retrospective design formats.
- Control of variables is critical when results are related to cause and effect.
- A comparative design does not involve any manipulation or control of the independent variable.
- Sentinel or adverse events require an RCA to improve.

Multiple-Choice Questions

1. Which of the following characteristics is not part of a quantitative research design?
   A. Randomization
   B. Manipulation
   C. Saturation
   D. Control

2. Which of the following is not an independent variable?
   A. Outcome
   B. Treatment
   C. Intervention
   D. Experiment

3. Quantitative research is often identified with which method of gathering data?
   A. Triangulation
   B. Saturation
   C. Ethnography
   D. Scientific method

4. Nonexperimental designs generate _____ for _____ designs.
   A. answers; quasi-experimental
   B. questions; experimental
   C. solutions; quantitative
   D. problems; experimental

5. Which of the following is one of the most common and important characteristics of a quantitative design?
   A. The dependent variable
   B. The independent variable
   C. Control
   D. The relationship

6. Manipulation of which variable is connected to control?
    A. Independent
    B. Dependent
    C. Extraneous
    D. Attribute

7. What does randomization help to eliminate?
    A. Confounding data
    B. Ethics
    C. Subjects
    D. Bias

8. Generalization can _____ a study.
    A. weaken
    B. strengthen
    C. shorten
    D. lengthen

9. A comparative design has:
    A. no manipulation and control of the dependent variable.
    B. only measurement of the dependent variable.
    C. no manipulation and control of the independent variable.
    D. both B and C.

10. A correlational study looks at the:
    A. cause of two or more variables.
    B. relationship of two or more variables.
    C. effect of two or more variables.
    D. both A and C.

11. Issues related to experimental design include:
    A. manipulation of all variables, ethics, and feasibility.
    B. the Hawthorne effect, ethics, and sample size.
    C. treatments, interventions, and no manipulation of variables.
    D. feasibility, the Hawthorne effect, and research questions.

12. An example of a randomized controlled trial (RCT) design is as follows (where R = randomization, O = measurement, and X = treatment):
    A. R O X O
    B. O X O
    C. O O X O O
    D. O O O X O O O

13. Meta-analysis is the examination of multiple studies through statistical analysis to establish:
    A. the nonexistence of bias.
    B. new data sets for analysis.
    C. the nonexistence of confounding variables.
    D. correlation of the variables.

14. A quasi-experimental design is one in which the:
    A. dependent variable is manipulated with randomization and a control group.
    B. independent variable is manipulated with randomization and a control group.
    C. independent variable is manipulated with no randomization and no control group.
    D. dependent variable is manipulated with no randomization and no control group.

15. The initial baseline measurement in a nonequivalent control group is used to determine if the subjects assigned to the group are:
    A. different.
    B. equal.
    C. bonded.
    D. similar.

16. Which of the following is the research design that collects data at various intervals?
    A. A long study
    B. A time-series study
    C. An experimental study
    D. A nonexperimental study

17. What is an area of concern in a time-series design?
    A. Randomization
    B. Control
    C. Manipulation
    D. Maturation

18. Some ways of controlling variables for nonexperimental or quasi-experimental designs are:
    A. timing of test intervals and the setting.
    B. randomization of subjects and control groups.
    C. flexible inclusion and exclusion criteria.
    D. control of history and maturation.

19. In EBP, a nurse using quantitative research for clinical decision making must be most knowledgeable about how:
    A. to calculate statistics.
    B. to write research reports.
    C. the study design applies to practice.
    D. to design a research study.

20. Using research in practice requires the nurse to be most aware of:
    A. limited funding.
    B. generalizability of the results to current practice.
    C. exclusion of subjects.
    D. the credentials of the researcher.

21.   Quality improvement (QI) projects are considered:
    A. the same as scientific inquiry.
    B. different from scientific inquiry.
    C. to focus on only patient satisfaction.
    D. a rigorous approach for research.

22.   Root cause analysis (RCA) had its origin in:
    A. the dental industry.
    B. mechanical engineering.
    C. military industry.
    D. business industry.

23.   In what year did the Joint Commission mandate RCAs?
    A. 1967
    B. 1977
    C. 1987
    D. 1997

Discussion Questions

1.   You are a nurse in a preoperative holding area in which all patients are classified as *nil per os* (NPO), meaning "nothing by mouth," after midnight to prevent possible aspiration. You wonder why that policy is necessary, and you and a surgical team want to design a research project to investigate the potential for providing at least some liquid nourishment to preoperative patients. The team decides to do a two-group, posttest only design.
    a. Using the previous example (all surgical patients being NPO after midnight), how would you and the surgical team conduct a meta-analysis?
    b. Using a nonequivalent control group design in the NPO scenario, explain how this design would be constructed.

2.   A medication error resulted in a sentinel event on your unit. How would you implement a root cause analysis (RCA) to investigate this event?

Suggested Readings

Bott, M., & Endacott, R. (2005). Clinical research: Quantitative data collection and analysis. *Intensive & Critical Care Nursing, 21*(3), 187–193.

Chulay, M. (2006). Good research ideas for clinicians. *AACN Advanced Critical Care, 17*(3), 253–265.

Freshwater, D. (2005). Integrating qualitative and quantitative research methods: Trend or foe? *Journal of Research in Nursing, 10*(3), 337–338.

Kinn, S., & Curzio, J. (2005). Integrating qualitative and quantitative research methods. *Journal of Research in Nursing, 10*(3), 317–336.

Onwuegbuzie, A., & Leech, N. (2005). Taking the "Q" out of research: Teaching research methodology courses without the divide between quantitative and qualitative paradigms. *Quality & Quantity, 39*(3), 267–295.

Walker, W. (2005). The strengths and weaknesses of research designs involving quantitative measures. *Journal of Research in Nursing, 10*(5), 571–573.

Yoder, L. (2005). Evidence-based practice: The time is now! *MedSurg Nursing, 14*(2), 91–92.

References

Agency for Healthcare Research and Quality (AHRQ). (2012). Patient safety primers: Root cause analysis. Retrieved from http://psnet.ahrq.gov/primer.aspx?primerID=10

Bator, S., Taylor, S., & Catalano, J. T. (2015). Nursing research and evidence based practice. In J. Catalano (Ed.), *Nursing now!: Today's issues, tomorrow's trends.* (7th ed., pp. 581–674). Philadelphia, PA: F.A. Davis.

Brink, P. J., & Wood, M. J. (2001). *Basic steps in planning nursing research from question to proposal* (5th ed.). Sudbury, MA: Jones and Bartlett.

Brockopp, D. Y., & Hastings-Tolsma, M. T. (2003). *Fundamentals of nursing research* (3rd ed.). Sudbury, MA: Jones and Bartlett.

Burns, N., & Grove, S. K. (2009). *The practice of nursing research: Appraisal, synthesis, and generation of evidence* (6th ed.). St. Louis, MO: Saunders Elsevier.

Centers for Disease Control and Prevention (CDC). (n.d.). The Tuskegee timeline. Retrieved from http://www.cdc.gov/tuskegee/timeline.htm

Cortez-Gann, J., Gilmore, K. D., Foley, K. W., Kennedy, M. B., McGee, T., & Kring, D. (2017, March–April). Blood transfusion vital sign frequency: What does the evidence say? *Medsurg Nursing, 26*(2), 89–92.

Dunn, E. J., & Renner, C. (2012). Root cause analysis: Faculty development [Presentation slides]. Retrieved from http://www.med.cornell.edu/risk-management/best_practices/RootCauseAnalysis.ppt

Fain, J. A. (2009). *Reading, understanding, and applying nursing research* (3rd ed.). Philadelphia, PA: F.A. Davis.

Hanna, K. M., Weaver, M. T., Slaven, J. E., Fortenberry, J. D., & DiMeglio, L. A. (2014). Diabetes-related quality of life and the demands and burdens of diabetes care among emerging adults with Type 1 diabetes in the year after graduation. *Research in Nursing and Health, 37*(5), 399–408.

Heavey, E. (2019). *Statistics for nursing: A practical approach.* Burlington, MA: Jones & Bartlett Learning.

Hopp, L., & Rittenmeyer, L. (2012). *Introduction to evidence-based practice: A practical guide for nursing.* Philadelphia, PA: F.A. Davis.

Kring, D. L. (2008). Research and quality improvement: Different processes, different evidence. *MedSurg Nursing, 17*(3), 162–169.

Melnyk, B. M., & Morrison-Beedy, D. M. (2012). *Intervention research: Designing, conducting, analyzing and funding.* New York, NY: Springer.

Polit, D. F., & Beck, C. T. (2006). *Essentials of nursing research methods, appraisal and utilization* (6th ed.). Philadelphia, PA: Lippincott Williams & Wilkins.

Polit, D. F., & Beck, C. T. (2008). *Nursing research: Generating and assessing evidence for nursing practice* (8th ed.). Philadelphia, PA: Wolters Kluwer/Lippincott Williams & Wilkins.

CHAPTER 9

Qualitative and Mixed Research Methods

JoAnn Long, Samara Silva, and Carol Boswell

CHAPTER OBJECTIVES

At the conclusion of this chapter, the learner will be able to:

1. Define qualitative and mixed methods research.
2. Describe the various qualitative research methodologies.
3. Describe the various mixed methods research methodologies.
4. Discuss analysis of qualitative and mixed method study data.
5. Discuss quality measures in mixed and qualitative research methods.
6. Contrast the goals and distinctive features of qualitative and mixed methods research.
7. Discuss the advantages of qualitative and mixed methods research.
8. Discuss issues of methodological rigor in qualitative and mixed methods research.

KEY TERMS

Action research	Mixed methods research
Bracketing	Nesting
Case study	Phenomenology
Content analysis	Purposeful sampling
Convergent validity	Qualitative research
Ethnography	Rigor
Grounded theory	Saturation
Meta-ethnography	

▶ Introduction

The expansion of nursing knowledge based on scientific findings is vital to advance and promote health, prevent disease, and enhance quality of life for those living with chronic conditions. Nursing knowledge flows from research and forms the basis for evidence-based practice (EBP). Nurses engaged in research play an important role in advancing worldwide health (Eckardt et al., 2017). Knowledge of qualitative and mixed methods, an integration of qualitative and quantitative research, is an important competency for nurses engaged in evidence-based care and is the focus of this chapter. Human beings are by nature complex. What drives human decision making and behavior is difficult to understand and measure. Understanding in depth the multifaceted nature of how people perceive what they have experienced is a challenging task. Qualitative research methods are based on the assumption that truth is fluid and offers an avenue for exploration of elements of humanity that are not best understood using quantitative research methods. Qualitative methods use narrative to understand meaning. Mixed methods research has a number of unique features and offers a joint and integrated approach to research, which values and draws on both objective numbers and subjective knowledge (Fabregues & Molina-Azorin, 2016). Mixed methods research blends the qualitative and quantitative perspectives and can profoundly enhance insight into the environment in which nurses practice, allowing for answers to research questions to be gathered from many perspectives (Ingham-Broomfield, 2016; Siddiqui & Fitzgerald, 2014).

This chapter presents an overview of qualitative research methods and mixed methods research. It provides a brief history of qualitative research in nursing; compares quantitative and qualitative research paradigms; presents an overview of the most commonly used qualitative designs in nursing research; discusses sampling, data collection, and data analysis and quality measures for both qualitative and mixed methods research; and guides the reader in the application to one's nursing practice.

▶ Qualitative Research

The word *qualitative* means that one is exploring the quality of something rather than the quantity, amount, intensity, or frequency. Examining the quality of something implies a level of subjectivity. Denzin and Lincoln (2011) note that the qualitative researcher considers the socially constructed nature of reality, the relationship between the research and the subject of the research, and the situational factors that shape inquiry. In other words, the social experience shapes the meaning of reality. Qualitative research generally aims for an in-depth understanding of the experiences of others (McCusker & Gunaydin, 2015).

Nursing has traditionally focused on the person as a whole. This holistic approach to the person lends itself well to qualitative methods. As a result, qualitative methods have become increasingly common in nursing research. Qualitative methods continue to gain recognition as being valuable to the science of nursing because these studies contribute to areas in which little research has been done, variables for quantitative research have yet to be defined, or the nature of the question itself is not amenable to numerical description. With the increased use of these methods, efforts to design qualitative methodologies that offer holistic understanding of persons while still offering reliability and validity are also improving.

▶ A Brief History of Qualitative Methods

Quantitative research methods are founded in the natural sciences with a positivist approach. Drawn primarily from the work of 20th-century philosophers, positivism asserts that only what can be verified and tested empirically through observation can be of cognitive value (Uebel, 2016). Simply stated, the positivist approach requires objectivity and neutrality to test theories and hypotheses logically. The underlying assumption is that truth is something that can be known and measured.

Alternatively, **qualitative research** methods are rooted in the disciplines of sociology, anthropology, and philosophy, with the underlying assumption that truth can only be approximated. In the early part of the 20th century, social scientists began to put structure to what had formerly been an unstructured process of qualitative research (Flick, 2009). Researchers at the Chicago School, in adopting and formalizing processes of qualitative social study, gave credibility to this new qualitative paradigm of research (Holloway & Wheeler, 2010). Qualitative research carefully investigates those aspects that are not quantifiable.

In the 1960s, qualitative research saw increased use when new qualitative approaches, such as grounded theory (Glaser & Strauss, 1967), were introduced. In the 1970s, it was increasingly common to see journals publishing qualitative research reports exclusively. The 1990s saw a steady growth in the number of textbooks and handbooks dedicated to the qualitative methodologies, and they enhanced the legitimacy of qualitative research in the applied and social sciences. Nurse researchers began adopting the qualitative paradigm to inform their practice. Today, well over 1,000 journals, many of them specific to nursing, are publishing only qualitative research. Reputable research journals worldwide routinely publish research drawn from both the quantitative and qualitative paradigms. Recent trends illustrate the growing appreciation of publishing synthesized findings from both qualitative and quantitative paradigms (Joanna Briggs Institute, 2015). Qualitative research may be considered a credible source of evidence and is now accepted as a viable method for discovering new perspectives.

▶ Comparing Qualitative, Quantitative, and Mixed Methods

It is not uncommon for both researchers and consumers of research to have strong opinions about the value of quantitative or qualitative methods. Individuals who favor quantitative methods may be skeptical about qualitative studies, citing limitations in reliability, validity, and structure. Researchers who favor qualitative methods may claim that quantitative studies are shallow or do not paint a complete and accurate picture of a phenomenon. A mixed methods approach integrates aspects of qualitative and quantitative research in a single study. In truth, each type of research has great scientific merit. The research question informs the type of research method selected.

A number of characteristics distinguish the qualitative research approach from the quantitative approach (Roller & Lavrakas, 2015). For example, qualitative research approaches phenomena from the "emic" perspective. That is, the viewpoint of the participant rather than the perspective of the researcher provides the source of meaning. Qualitative research also makes use of a holistic approach to the participant. The participant brings values and life experiences that affect his or her perspective on the phenomenon of interest. The holistic nature of nursing often demands more than what quantitative research alone can offer. Although quantitative methods often seek to minimize the impact of these values and experiences, qualitative methods embrace these individual differences. Qualitative research can help us to answer questions that can only be explained by the parties involved. Further, qualitative methods are inductive and interactive rather than deductive. Quantitative methods require that the researcher not deviate in the data collection process from one subject to another; qualitative methods allow the researcher the flexibility to adapt his or her inquiry as understanding of the phenomenon grows. For example, a case study on Felty's syndrome (Woolston & Connally, 2017) looked at how one patient struggled with the condition. Qualitative research on this medical problem brings to light the personal experience of what it is like to live with a particular condition and enables the researcher to understand the patient experience in more depth than would be possible with quantitative research methods alone (van den Berg & Struwig, 2017).

The consumer of research may also note that research participants are described differently based on the type of study. Quantitative researchers typically refer to the individual of interest in a study as a subject. Qualitative researchers may refer to the individual of interest in a study as an informant or a participant; however, the terminology for individuals participating in a study overlaps in quantitative and qualitative methods.

Qualitative and quantitative methods differ significantly in acceptable sample size. Sample sizes in qualitative studies are generally much smaller than in quantitative studies. Because the focus of the qualitative data is on the quality of the data collected, each participant is a source of a large volume of data. Thus, a smaller sample size is reasonable and common.

The differences between qualitative and quantitative methods are significant, but in many cases, combining both methods is a viable option for researchers. When quantitative and qualitative research methods are combined, a mixed methods design is the result. A researcher might choose to combine methods in order to supplement the data, validate the data, or determine in pilot studies the best approach to data collection with a larger group. Mixed methods are particularly well suited for cases when qualitative or quantitative data alone will not fully address the research question. Today, qualitative, quantitative, and mixed methods studies are acknowledged as valid sources in most nursing evidence hierarchies. Many questions in nursing require data generated from qualitative, quantitative, and mixed methods research for a comprehensive understanding of healthcare problems (Curry, Nembhard, & Bradley, 2009).

▶ Approaches to Qualitative Research

Many rich and varied designs are available from which to choose when planning a qualitative study (Smythe, 2012). The more commonly used designs are discussed here. Many qualitative designs share common features, particularly with regard to sampling strategies, data collection techniques, and data analysis.

Case Study

A **case study** is an in-depth examination of individuals or groups of people. A case study may be used when insight into a unique situation is needed (Rosenberg & Yates, 2007). For example, a researcher interested in parental decision making and the use of respite care in children receiving palliative care conducted a case study of families with seriously ill children receiving respite care (Ling, Payne, Connaire, & McCarron, 2016). The investigators followed nine families for a period of 2 years and conducted in-depth interviews with mothers and fathers caring for a child with a life-threatening condition. This type of study would be called a longitudinal (long-term) qualitative case study design. When a study is focused on the phenomenon and telling the participant's story, a case study approach is a realistic method to employ.

The researcher engaging in a case study is typically seeking to understand what is common about a case and what is unique about a case (Baxter & Jack, 2008). To fully understand commonalities and unique features of a case, the researcher is likely to explore case features such as:

- The specific nature of the case
- The historic background of the case
- The physical setting in which the case takes place
- Other contexts, including social, economic, political, legal, and aesthetic
- Other cases through which this case is recognized
- Informants through whom the case is known

A case study might include data such as temperatures or pain ratings (quantitative), along with data about the person's experience of pain and discomfort (qualitative). Together, such data paint a more complete picture of the disease experience.

Data analysis in case studies, as with other qualitative methods, involves **content analysis**, in which the researcher begins with observations made while reading the narrative data and looks for patterns and themes. During content analysis, more than one researcher independently reads the transcribed narrative and then compares observations with the other researcher(s) before reaching consensus on the final themes (Hagedoorn et al., 2017). For example, the researchers might identify the themes of "social isolation" and "mistrust and jealousy" in a case study of an adult male who has abused his spouse (Scott Tilley, Rugari, & Walker, 2008). As the research team endeavors to appreciate the theme more completely, the case takes on merit for understanding the unique nature of the experience.

Broad generalization is not entirely possible, but the readers or consumers of a case study should expect to be able to apply the findings from a case to their practice when the researcher has clearly delineated the case by defining the object of the study, identified patterns of data, and developed transferrable assertions about the case. Nurses should avoid applying findings from a case to their practice when the case is single or is a poor representation of a population or when a single case as a negative example is applied to general populations. For example, a single case about intractable pain that is poorly managed should not be used to guide policy. Conversely, several cases illustrating effective management of pain through the use of guided imagery might well be used to inform policy about optional use of guided imagery in a hospice agency.

Ethnography

Ethnography involves collection and analysis of data about unique groups. The ethnographer seeks to understand the culture of the group or to gain an understanding of the values, norms, and rules that characterize the group. For ethnography, groups of interest may be organizational, experiential, ethnic, and geographic. Ethnography is an excellent way to understand the norms of groups of interest to nursing. For example, outstanding ethnographies of organizations such as groups of patients or caregivers with specific illnesses (e.g., HIV and AIDS) and specific healthcare delivery settings (e.g., nursing homes, critical care units) are key to understanding the intricacies of the group.

Data collection for ethnography is usually accomplished through reading documents within the culture, conducting interviews, observation, embedding oneself within the specific group, or a combination of all these methods. Key informants or people who are most knowledgeable about the culture are usually a primary source of interview data.

The reader or consumer of studies based on this method might find practice applications if the ethnography informs one how to:

- Behave when with a certain group
- Approach a person within the group
- Recognize and respond to needs of a person within the group
- Appreciate group norms different from one's own culture

For example, a nurse might find ethnographic data of the experiential group of parents of children with cystic fibrosis (CF) helpful in the provision of care to a child with the disease. This ethnography might provide the nurse with insight about the needs of the parents, how the parents can access assistance within the community of parents of children with CF, and what experiences and feelings are common among the parents of children with CF. When researchers combine data from multiple ethnographic studies, they may use the term **meta-ethnography**. For example, when Purc-Stephenson, Jones, and Ferguson (2017) wanted to understand what it was like to find and sustain employment from the point of view of persons living with disabilities, they "synthesized" or combined findings from 19 different studies to answer their research question. Similarly, when researchers combine and/or reanalyze data from multiple quantitative studies that use experimental methods, they may use the terms *meta-analysis* or *systematic review* (Kwan & Sullivan, 2017; Cui et al., 2018).

Grounded Theory

Grounded theory is a general methodology for developing new theory that is inherent in data systematically gathered and analyzed (Denzin & Lincoln, 1998). Attributed largely to the work of Strauss and Glass in the 1960s, grounded theory has the explicit expectation of theory development and identification (Kenny & Fourie, 2014). Grounded theory is used when little to no research in the existing literature is available to guide practice and for which quantitative methods are not well suited (Ivey, 2017).

Data analysis in grounded theory is systematic and deliberate. The process begins with open coding, which involves categorizing the information and examining properties, dimensions, and visualization of the data (Mey & Dietrich, 2017; Strauss & Corbin, 1998). The next step is axial coding, in which the researcher identifies relationships between categories and subcategories. Selective coding, the final step in data analysis, is the integration of concepts around a core category and the filling in of categories in need of further development and refinement (Strauss & Corbin, 1998). **Saturation** is a concept of relevance in data analysis and data collection: It is a process in which the researcher continues data analysis until no new codes or categories emerge.

The final product of the grounded theory method is a theory that is established in data about the phenomenon of interest. The consumer of grounded theory research could expect to apply the model while developing interventions for a population. For example, reading a grounded theory about the attachment patterns of elderly adults might guide the nurse who is assisting family members in relocating their aging parent from a home environment to an assisted-living environment.

Narrative Inquiry

Narrative inquiry, sometimes known as storytelling, is a qualitative research method that seeks to understand the meaning that participants ascribe to their experiences. Telling the story of their experience, say, with illness or provision of health care, allows the participant to reflect on the experience from his or her own point of view to inform others about the experience. Meanings are derived by both the participant and the researcher. Narrations can come from patients, lay or professional care providers, parents, or other parties with stories that can serve to inform practice.

⬆ THINK OUTSIDE THE BOX

Carefully consider the idea of saturation. Discuss how you can determine that saturation has occurred within a research project.

Phenomenology

As the name implies, **phenomenology** is the study of events and trends considering a person's worldview and human perspective (Duckham & Schreiber, 2016). Phenomenology seeks to develop an understanding of lived experience, as described by participants. The firsthand report or description of one's experience of the phenomenon is central to understanding the phenomenon. The meaning one creates in the world is socially constructed and is rooted in the experiences of the person.

Data collection in phenomenology is done through unstructured interviews and inductive analysis. The guiding question in a phenomenological study typically centers on the essence, structure, or lived experience of a phenomenon. Data analysis occurs simultaneously with data collection. The researcher is identifying patterns and themes and developing new questions as data emerge. The reader or consumer of a phenomenological study can use the findings to understand the experiences of clients who are experiencing a similar event. For example, Leseyane, Mandende, Makgato, and Cekiso (2018) used phenomenology to understand the experience of dyslexic schoolchildren. Their in-depth look at the lived experience of learners with dyslexia helped to identify barriers to learning, the need for improved education of public schoolteachers, and increased awareness of the bullying and maltreatment experienced by children living with this condition.

Comparative Analysis

Qualitative comparative analysis (QCA) is used in the social sciences; however, it is a less well-known approach to the collection of narrative data in nursing that allows the researcher to compare elements of interest. Donnelly and Wiechula (2013) used QCA to explore the relationship between nursing education and the clinical placement experience of students. The researchers were interested in understanding how these choices influence the competence of graduate nurses. In QCA, principles of Boolean algebra, a deductive logical technique where variables are limited to two values, true or false (Dictionary.com, n.d.), and the construction of truth tables are used to analyze the data from a number of cases. The QCA method, while not used as widely as other qualitative research methods in nursing, is considered an innovative approach to nursing research that combines qualitative and quantitative data that may be particularly useful in small studies (Donnelly & Wiechula, 2013). The QCA method is an innovative research process to explore narrative data in interesting ways.

▶ Sampling Strategies in Qualitative Research

In contrast with quantitative research, which requires a careful sample plan that is designed before the study commences and seeks subjects representative of the larger population to which generalizations may be made, the sampling strategy in qualitative research is often an intraproject process that seeks to maximize variation of participants, saturation of data, and verification of data (Strauss & Corbin, 1998). Each of these components is discussed in detail in this chapter.

Researchers in qualitative studies often sample for variation. Even when a homogeneous sample is sought—for instance, patients with breast cancer—researchers often seek informants with slightly different experiences who can provide diverse perspectives. Sometimes also called criterion sampling, **purposeful sampling** is designed to select participants who are able to inform the researcher about elements of the phenomenon that remain poorly understood (Strauss & Corbin, 1998). With this sampling method, the researcher strives to identify individuals who reflect both sides of the issue to provide a complete picture of the situation under investigation.

Sample sizes are rarely decided upon before commencing a qualitative study. Rather, a reasonable sample size may be estimated based on similar studies. Qualitative researchers are often interested in understanding in depth what it is like to have a particular experience. Snowball sampling is a type of purposeful sampling and refers to one participant referring another person from among those he or she knows. Sampling is continued until data saturation is reached. The qualitative researcher knows that data saturation has been attained when no new themes or concepts arise or when redundancy of data is determined. Consumers of qualitative research may perceive that a small sample size in a qualitative study is a serious limitation of the study. In truth, sample sizes in qualitative studies are often expected to be small. Vast amounts of data are generated in a qualitative study, and analyses of these data from hundreds of participants may not be feasible or necessary. Given the longer time that researchers often spend with participants, data saturation may be reached with a small number of subjects. Depending on the study design, goal of the study, phenomenon of interest, and other factors, a reasonable sample size for a qualitative study might be as small as five or six participants, or it may be larger, with ten or more participants, depending on the nature of the research question and data saturation.

To verify data, qualitative researchers often seek out negative cases as they near completion of data collection. This process is similar to the notion of purposeful sampling, but the researcher seeks participants or cases in which the emerging theory or emerging interpretations of data can be challenged. Seeking negative cases is both a sampling strategy and a method of assuring rigor in qualitative research. Another approach used to verify data is respondent validation. Participants are provided a transcribed copy of their responses, asked to read through the data and analysis, and asked to provide feedback on the interpretation of their responses for correctness (Anderson, 2010).

▶ Approaches to Qualitative Data Collection

The most common approaches to data collection in qualitative studies are interviews and observations. Interviews may occur once, be done in a series, or be conducted in small focus groups. In general, interviews are not neutral in nature. The interviewer naturally introduces a variable into interviews by virtue of his or her race, class, ethnicity, gender, education, and experience. Structured interviews may follow a script of questions established prior to beginning data collection. Structured interviews allow little room for variation in response. The interviewer must remain neutral in the structured interview. The semistructured interview is commonly used in qualitative research. In a semistructured interview, the researcher uses a list of fairly broad questions with prompts. Rather than being an interested listener, the interviewer may engage in the conversation more than when in a structured interview. Qualitative data can be collected in a variety of ways, including audiotape, videotape, and written notes taken during the interview process (Agency for Healthcare Research and Quality [AHRQ], 2018b).

Interviews of groups, or focus groups, require a researcher who is experienced in the conduct of focus groups. The researcher must have access to a facility and group of people who fit the study criteria to hold a focus group (AHRQ, 2018b). Like individual interviews, group interviews can be structured or semistructured, and it is not unusual for small focus groups to take 1 to 2 hours to complete a guided discussion of predetermined questions (AHRQ, 2018a). Group interviews are not meant to replace individual interviews. They are an alternative way to collect data and should be conducted only when the question is appropriate or as a way to determine a direction for semistructured interview questions for individuals. For example, in a study investigating women veterans' preferences for intimate partner violence (IPV) screening, data were collected from 24 women during 5 focus groups (Iverson et al., 2014). The researchers performed content analysis of the focus group data by categorizing the narrative responses into themes describing participant attitudes and preferences (Iverson et al., 2014). Focus groups provide different ideas that build on each other to provide a clearer understanding of the situation being investigated.

Observation is an acceptable but less common method of data collection in qualitative research. Elements that may be observed include:

- Appearance
- Clothing
- Interactions
- Roles
- Exits
- Routines
- Rituals
- Temporal elements
- Organization
- Interpretations

Bracketing is a concept common to all qualitative methods, although all researchers may not describe using this process in their study. Bracketing is also known as phenomenological reduction. In bracketing, the researcher identifies his or her own personal biases and beliefs about the phenomenon and sets them aside in order to fully understand the experience of the informants. Through the use of bracketing, the potential negative impact of the researcher's preconceptions about the study are mitigated (Tufford & Newman, 2010). Bracketing typically commences during data collection and continues through the data analysis process. For example, researchers interested in the phenomenon of preconception health practices of women in abusive relationships would likely bracket by making a conscious decision to temporarily suspend their beliefs and attitudes about how women should plan for pregnancy and what they believe about the experience of being in an abusive relationship. They would make a decision to be open to what the participants had to say about this phenomenon without making prejudgments or assumptions about the phenomenon.

▶ Approaches to Qualitative Data Analysis

Qualitative data analysis is often a tedious and time-consuming process. With most qualitative methods, the data collection and data analysis processes are occurring simultaneously. As new data evolve, new questions emerge. This evolution of data collection is part of the reason for the lack of structure in interview guides. Although many qualitative researchers prefer to analyze data by hand, many commercial software programs, such as Atlas.ti and NVivo, are available to assist in the organization, coding, and analysis of data. Data collection to saturation implies a level of data analysis as data collection occurs.

From the brief descriptions of data analysis in the methods previously described, one can see that qualitative data analysis can be quite complex. While quantitative data analysis usually involves numbers and statistics, qualitative data analysis involves deep examination of large volumes of written data.

The qualitative research methods of grounded theory, phenomenology, and ethnography require specific steps in data analysis. Other qualitative methods have no specific "rules" for the analysis of data. In such cases, a researcher might simply state that content analysis was conducted. *Content analysis* is a generic term that is widely used to describe the process of data being analyzed and categories of data being created by experts.

▶ Methodological Rigor in Qualitative Research

Both qualitative and quantitative research methods require the researcher to strive for **rigor**, or the criteria for trustworthiness of data and interpretation of data. Some articles refer to the rigor of the research as the methodological integrity. The major methods for ensuring rigor are intricately linked with reliability and validity checks. Quantitative research seeks large representative samples to ensure accuracy, while qualitative data can find accuracy in the meaning of experiences in smaller numbers. Lincoln and Guba (1985) provided pioneering work in the area of qualitative research, particularly in the area of methodological rigor. The criteria frequently used to ensure qualitative rigor include (1) credibility, (2) transferability, (3) dependability, (4) confirmability, and (5) authenticity (Cope, 2014). A discussion follows on how each criterion can be achieved to establish the integrity of a study.

Credibility, or the truth value of data and data analysis, can be achieved in a proposed study through several methods. First, when possible, the data should be taken back to subjects to ensure accuracy. This review of the data provides participants an opportunity to clarify or deny the interpretation of the analysis. After data are coded, the coded data can be checked and confirmed with available participants. In addition, coded data can be independently reviewed and verified by experts in both the area of research and in the method used for the study to further support the quality of the data. These checks usually consist of validation of data, validation of findings, and checking of interpretations.

Transferability refers to the applicability of findings to other populations in different contexts. Often, this process is accomplished by providing a thorough, or thick, description of the sample, setting, and data in the report to allow the reader to determine the transferability of the study's findings to individuals and groups beyond those included in the original study. The researcher is telling a detailed story to provide the reader with the opportunity to determine if the findings can transfer to other settings (Amankwaa, 2016). The process requires that those aspects that can be effectively transferred are readily denoted for the readers to understand and consider. Therefore, the more thorough are the explanations, the more they are available for comparison and understanding.

Dependability in qualitative research can also be described as auditability. If other researchers can follow the investigator's decisions throughout the study and come to similar conclusions, the study is auditable (Lincoln & Guba, 1985). Thus, an audit trail also provides an element of rigor to any study. The audit trail documents the development of the project and provides an adequate amount of evidence for interested parties to reconstruct the process by which the investigators reached their conclusions (Morse, 1998). Audit trails can be documented in a variety of ways, including a diary of the research and the researcher's feelings and decision-making process. Documenting where the information was collected, how it was stored, and how it was analyzed provides a picture of the movement of information toward the final outcome of the study.

Confirmability represents freedom from bias, or neutrality (Amankwaa, 2016; Lincoln & Guba, 1985). It is important to analyze data in a way that keeps researcher biases, assumptions, and perspectives separate. These elements should be clearly identified early in the proposal process. Reviewing the analyzed data with informants or study participants and review by experts also serves to mitigate the effects of researcher bias and to understand different ways to analyze the data. This process can be referred to as analyst triangulation (Amankwaa, 2016).

Although many ways are available to establish the quality of qualitative data, researchers can select the appropriate criteria for the topic under investigation. It is suggested that researchers document their plan of validity to make the trustworthiness apparent to the reader. Having a predefined protocol at the start of the research that outlines the plan of establishing rigor can improve the quality of the quantitative study. However, it is not necessary for all of these criteria to be incorporated into each study project. Application of any research results to practice, whether qualitative or quantitative, must be considered in light of the study's reliability, validity, and generalizability or transferability. Qualitative researchers themselves may face a number of challenges as they approach qualitative research. Inherent in qualitative research is the recognition of differences in perception that create multiple realities. This concern about challenges is also true when interpreting qualitative findings; however, when reasonable methodological rigor is applied to qualitative methods, one can be assured regarding the authenticity of the results (Snelgrove, 2014). Care must be taken by the research team to clearly and effectively address and report how the results were determined.

▶ Understanding and Using Qualitative Study Results

Almost all areas within nursing lend themselves to qualitative study. Nursing practice should be guided by nursing theory that is solidly grounded in research data. Qualitative studies are often the first step in the development of a theoretical framework for a phenomenon that has not been fully explored and from which quantifiable research questions may emerge. Andrews and Waterman (2005) collected interview and observation data using the grounded theory approach in their study about how hospital-based staff members used vital signs and the Early Warning Score to predict physiological deterioration in clients. The authors reported that quantifiable evidence is the most effective means of referring patients to doctors and improving communication between professionals. The authors concluded that the Early Warning Score leads to successful referral of patients by providing an agreed-upon framework for assessment, increasing confidence in the use of medical language, and empowering nurses. After early qualitative studies, Early Warning Scoring systems have been further developed and tested quantitatively by nurses, resulting in decreased mortality and nursing empowerment in clinical care (Roney et al., 2015).

Qualitative research affords an opportunity to explore human issues that have previously been understood by way of assumption or simply not understood. For example, the high turnover and burnout rate of nursing staff have historically been assumed to be a function of long hours, physically strenuous work, and lack of power. The combined qualitative and quantitative studies of Cohen-Katz, Wiley, Capuano, Baker, and Shapiro (2004) and subsequently by Whitecombe, Cooper, and Palmer (2016) have illuminated the causes of nursing burnout and led to system-wide changes to help nurses manage stress and burnout. Their work resulted in a healthier, safer work environment.

Qualitative studies often offer immediate clinical applicability. These studies are sources of rich descriptions of a wide range of physical and psychosocial experiences of healthcare consumers. By gaining a deeper understanding of those experiences, nurses can counsel, plan interventions, and develop programs to meet the needs of clients in similar conditions.

A study exploring adapting qualitative research strategies to technology-savvy adolescents provides an example of how to determine which communication method was preferred by youth (Mason & Ide, 2014). A grounded theory methodology was used to explore how 23 adolescents were interviewed by email rather than traditional face-to-face interviews. Participants indicated email communication was slow and that they preferred instant messaging instead. The adolescents in this study preferred text-based communication, suggesting the need to modify the traditional qualitative approach of in-person interviews (Mason & Ide, 2014). Each step within the study was clearly presented to allow the readers to understand the path taken to arrive at the conclusions presented.

Qualitative research brings increased knowledge to the EBP of nursing. Qualitative research studies are typically listed as level 4 or 5 in nursing evidence hierarchies. Qualitative research methods are often used to develop theories and research questions needed to guide future quantitative studies. Qualitative studies can illuminate issues that are poorly or inaccurately understood. Finally, qualitative studies often offer immediate clinical applicability and can help to guide teaching and practice.

▶ Mixed Methods Research

Broadly defined, **mixed methods research** is a combination of quantitative and qualitative research methods and techniques for collecting and analyzing data that together make possible an increase in the understanding to be gained from the research data (Creswell et al., 2010). Mixed methods research originated in the social sciences and has expanded in use to nursing, medicine, and allied health disciplines and is well suited for a wide variety of research questions (AHRQ, 2013). This form of research is also referred to in the literature by several other names—multimethod, triangulated, and integrated designs. Mixed methods research is growing in use in the health sciences. A "best practices" guideline has been developed for use by healthcare professionals who are developing and evaluating mixed methods studies (Office of Behavioral and Social Sciences, 2011). The use of mixed methods requires a strong research team to effectively integrate both qualitative and quantitative into one research project; it has a number of features that are unique compared to a single method project, or monomethodology (Fabregues & Molina-Azorin, 2016).

Mixed methods research is often possible within the clinical arena. For example, nurses may believe that the dryness of quantitative research needs to be tempered with the "more personal" aspects of qualitative research. Within the realm of evidence-based nursing practice, a nurse might realize that the time spent in the surgical holding area causes increased stress to the patients. A study could collect physiological data related to stress, such as blood pressure and time in the surgical holding area, as well as observed signs of stress and emotional data (e.g., verbal comments about the experience while in the surgical holding area awaiting the surgical procedure). The conclusions resulting from the collection of both types of data would reveal each aspect of the individual's experiences while in the surgical holding area. This mixed methods study would provide needed data to facilitate the provision of evidence-based nursing practice within the institution.

Quality in Mixed Methods Research

Because mixed methods research has several unique features, a number of quality criteria are important to consider when using and evaluating this type of research (Fabregues & Molina-Azorin, 2016). Well-designed mixed methods research involves the collection and analysis of both quantitative and qualitative data; use of rigorous procedures; integration of data during collection, analysis, and discussion; and the use and framing of procedures that are situated within an identified theoretical model that allows for understanding an issue from more than one perspective (AHRQ, 2013).

Quantitative research, which is considered the foundational method, permits the researcher to make inferences only about the data that are being examined. These studies are not designed, however, to detect contextual nuances, which may produce a biased understanding of the variables being studied. By comparison, qualitative research spreads a much broader net, allowing for in-depth examination of elements of a phenomenon not considered when research is conducted using quantitative methods. Because both quantitative and qualitative methods have strengths and weaknesses, neither can perfectly establish the full truth about phenomena of interest to nursing (Polit & Beck, 2011). Joining methods is done to reduce the biases associated with one design alone, provide insight into the complexity of the problem under study, and introduce rigor into the study design (Creswell et al., 2010). This form of research entails more than just the combination of two or more methods in a single study. Multimethod (mixed methods) research implies the integration of both numbers and narrative, pragmatically offering enhanced results in terms of quality and span (Busetto, Luijkx, Calciolari, Gonzalez-Ortiz, & Vrijhoef, 2017; Shaw, Connelly, & Zecevic, 2010). An example of what is meant by multimethod research can be seen when a questionnaire includes both closed-ended questions (numbers) to provide quantitative data and open-ended questions (narrative) that require qualitative analysis. Simply stated, mixed methods design views both quantitative and qualitative research as useful and important, while avoiding the constraints that might hamper a study carried out using a single research methodology (Chow, Quine, & Li, 2010). Researchers must carefully consider each of the different pieces to determine the optimal method for addressing the research problem identified.

As the field of research has advanced, the use of mixed methods has sometimes been referred to as **action research** and as participatory research. It is seen as a research technique that may be useful in the implementation of EBP (Munten, van den Bogaard, Cox, Garretsen, & Bongers, 2010). This form of research may be employed to facilitate a change in strategy based on feedback about what is being observed in real time (Goodnough, 2008; Ponic, Reid, & Frisby, 2010). With the advancement of mixed methods research, attention must be given to the optimal avenue to get at the information being sought to address the identified problem and/or challenge. Action research is carried out in conjunction with participants while viewing the involvement of subjects as a collaboration in which participants are at the forefront (Cook, Atkin, & Wilcockson, 2018).

Components of Mixed Method Procedures

In using mixed method procedures, the researcher attempts to blend a combination of methods (qualitative and quantitative) that have complementary strong points while defusing the nonoverlapping weaknesses. Bliss (2001) has stated, "A common misconception about mixed method research is that it requires a blending of contradictory or competing research paradigms" (p. 331). This view is also supported by Johnson and Onwuegbuzie (2004): "Mixed methods research is an attempt to legitimate the use of multiple approaches in answering research questions, rather than restricting or constraining researchers' choices (i.e., it rejects dogmatism)" (p. 17). Allowing researchers to use multiple techniques to answer the questions posed provides clarity within the research project and allows for a synergistic use of data not possible by a single method alone (AHRQ, 2013).

Although quantitative and qualitative methods each have an established focus, the two are neither contradictory nor competing. Within the delivery of the methodology, the two research designs are frequently meshed within the sampling, data collection, and analysis aspects of the research project. Although these aspects are the current levels, the process does not restrict the versatility or variety of the potential combinations within the two methodologies. As Bliss (2001) has noted, "Mixed method research seems to offer an opportunity to deepen our insights, sharpen our thinking, develop sensitive methods, and accelerate our advances" (p. 331). By allowing the researcher to identify a combination of methods, this process merges the best of both worlds of research to address the identified healthcare problem in the optimal manner available to the profession. The primary restriction on the joining of the methodologies is the obstruction occurring through lack of vision and risk taking on the part of the researcher.

⬆ THINK OUTSIDE THE BOX

Carefully consider the idea of mixed methods studies. Which elements would need to be present to reflect effective use of quantitative methods in a qualitative research project? Explain your answer.

According to Creswell, Fetters, and Ivankova (2004), mixed methods (multimethod) research possesses the potential for rigor, methodological effectiveness, and investigation within the primary care setting. Mixed methods research techniques were used by the Agency for Healthcare Research and Quality (2013) to assess the complexity of the patient-centered medical home. Even though rigidity is not a problem within this kind of research, the aspects of each methodology employed must still be carefully considered and weighted by the researcher. All of the research designs have identified strengths and limitations. As a researcher tries to maximize the complementary points while modifying the limitations, certain concerns emerge that should be considered.

The ability to merge quantitative and qualitative data is one of the main advantages of using the mixed methods approach to research and may be referred to as triangulation. This principle states that the validity of the results from the use of various research approaches determines the appropriateness of the resulting outcomes of the analysis. A mixed methods design allows for the utilization of words, pictures, and narrative within the data collection process. Each of these qualitative aspects of the study augments the data provided via the statistical process. Numbers provide the precision, while the words, pictures, and narrative supply the textural aspects of the experience (Office of Behavioral and Social Sciences Research, 2011). Each part provides a view of the uniqueness of the experience being investigated.

As a result of having this intensity of data available for data analysis of the event, an extensive and more comprehensive array of research questions and/or hypotheses can be answered. Put simply, the researcher is not limited regarding the breadth of the questions to be searched within the study. Because both quantitative and qualitative aspects of the issue are being addressed through the mixed methods, the research team can draw from the different designs to develop the optimal research project to address the identified problem (AHRQ, 2013).

An example of how the use of mixed methodologies uncovers perceptions that might otherwise be missed is illustrated in the work published by Chen and Goodson (2009), who studied barriers to adopting genomics into public health education. On the one hand, qualitative data were collected from a small number ($n = 24$) of public health educators through personal interviews. Quantitative data, on the other hand, were collected using a large ($n = 1,607$) web-based survey method. The combined data gathered via the two methods highlighted barriers that extended beyond a lack of knowledge to more nuanced and complex issues of incompatibility of the individual's personal ethics and beliefs about genomics as factors in the adoption of genomics into public health education.

An additional strength visualized by the use of a mixed methodology for a research project relates to the enthusiasm of the evidence. The resulting power from the in-depth evidence comes from the triangulation (convergence and corroboration) of the results identified (Johnson, n.d.). Because the evidence is managed through several different processes, the truth of the results may be strengthened.

An additional strength associated with use of mixed methods strategies can be seen when complementary insights and perceptions arise that might have been missed if only one research methodology were employed. The use of both quantitative and qualitative methodologies allows the researcher to pull together a wider and deeper understanding about the identified research problem because it is considered from multiple viewpoints (AHRQ, 2013).

Mixed methods strategies are not without limitations, however. When both quantitative and qualitative methods are employed, the researcher must be well versed in both methodologies, especially if the two methods are managed concurrently. If the researcher does not feel competent to implement both methods, a research team may be required to complete the process effectively. The two methods should be combined carefully, preferably with a research team with complementary strengths in both quantitative and qualitative research methods. When this strategy is selected for implementation, care must be given to learning about the various methods and tactics to allow for the successful incorporation of the necessary approaches. Mixed methodology research can also be especially expensive to complete due to the use of teams, and it can result in additional time-consuming steps.

When an investigator elects to use this methodology, rationales for the decisions made must be documented and supported. These rationales need to be based on a thorough understanding of the relevant characteristics of both the quantitative and qualitative methodologies. Clear justification for the selection of a mixed methods approach to the research problem must be provided to ensure that the research community comprehends the reasons for the decisions. These rationales are most often cited in the introduction section of the study report, the study aims discussion, or the overview of the section on methods to be used. As a researcher initiates this discussion concerning the rationales, the priority of the data collection process must be one key aspect that is presented clearly and concisely. This dialogue addresses the question of whether the quantitative and qualitative data are both emphasized equally. Regardless of the direction a researcher elects to go with the prioritization of the data, understandable and succinct logic for the choice should be carefully and thoroughly documented within the project.

In two separate studies, Creswell and colleagues (Creswell et al., 2004; Creswell et al., 2009) have elaborated on the labor-intensive process needed for the involvement of multiple points of data collection and analysis. This process should not be seen as an easier way of arriving at results but rather as a process for obtaining richer and more thorough information about the phenomenon under investigation. Johnson and Onwuegbuzie (2004) contend that the fundamental piece driving this process should be the research question or identified problem. From the identified research problem, a researcher ought to be free to select those research methods that best address the research questions, thereby taking the best opportunity to obtain meaningful answers. If a single research design is considered the best option, then a researcher should utilize that design methodology. When the research problem is viewed as progressively complex, however, all avenues of research methodology should be contemplated to identify the best manner to gain a thorough understanding of the phenomenon successfully.

▶ Types of Mixed Method Strategies

A number of strategies are available for mixed methods research (Creswell, 2003). At least three aspects of the process of conceptualizing using both quantitative and qualitative methodologies need to be considered: implementation, prioritization, and integration. Each of these three aspects results in one of two subtypes of mixed methods models—within-stage or across-stage methods. Within-stage methods reflect the use of quantitative and qualitative approaches within one or more stages of the research process. An example of this method would be the inclusion of both open-ended questions and closed-ended questions on the same tool for administration at the same time. Across-stage mixed method approaches involve mixing the two research designs transversely between at least two of the stages within the research endeavor. Returning to the example given earlier concerning the surgical holding room, the use of physiological data collected while the individual is in the holding area, followed by development of a narrative regarding how the experience was perceived after the surgical process, is an example of the use of across-stage mixed methods. With this approach, the data are not collected at the same time; rather, data collection at each stage builds on data collection from the other stages.

A number of decisions must be made in mixed methods implementation (Creswell, 2003, 2009). In addressing the implementation question, the principal decision relates to whether the two methods—quantitative and qualitative—will be executed at the same time or sequentially. The research question aids in this choice.

Sometimes the information discovered within one of the methods is perceived as a valuable foundation for the gathering of the data within the following method. For example, to determine the extent of research used within an acute care facility, researchers could conduct focus groups with a select group of nurses to determine perceived barriers to the use of research. Based on the data collected via the focus groups, a questionnaire could be developed and given to all staff nurses to determine their level of agreement with the information identified by the focus group members. In this scenario, the qualitative data results and analysis are seen as critical forces determining the data to be collected within the quantitative piece of the project. When neither type of data is needed to drive the data collection, quantitative and qualitative data can be collected concurrently. The surgical holding area example could be considered from this viewpoint. If the nurse collected physiological data that included blood pressure levels, observations of stressed behaviors, and time in the surgical holding area, while also questioning the individual about his or her perceptions of being in the holding area, the data would be collected concurrently. The determination of the appropriateness of this implementation comes directly from the identified research problem and resulting research questions and hypothesis.

If the decision is to conduct both the quantitative and qualitative data collection aspects at the same time, the process tends to be used to confirm, cross-validate, or corroborate findings within a single study (Creswell, 2003). Even when the two methods are conducted simultaneously, the question concerning how the information will be delivered must still be answered. If one method is embedded into the other method, then the process is termed **nesting**, where the less predominant method is implanted in the other method.

An example of nesting would be the inclusion of open-ended questions at the conclusion of a previously validated quantitative tool. An advantage of using concurrent design for the mixed methods process is the shortened data collection time period. Because all of the data are collected at one phase, the expense and time allocation can be reduced.

Within the concurrent implementation of the methodology, each piece of data is weighted equally within the data analysis phase. That is, for concurrent implementation, neither quantitative nor qualitative data are awarded a higher priority relative to the other; each aspect is judged on its own merits. Within this approach to mixed methods research, data integration begins during the data collection phase and continues through the data analysis phase and into the data interpretation phase. The data are interconnected for the initiation of the research process. When concurrent processing is selected for the research project, the investigator must understand the conceptual issues associated with mixed methods research and be competent in both methodologies. This proficiency in both methods is imperative because the researcher must ensure that the protocols for the quantitative and qualitative processes are carried out appropriately at each juncture of the research process.

▶ Data Collection Procedures

In research methods of all types, the collection of data refers to information collected and organized by the researcher. Research data are collected in an effort to measure specific variables that are relevant to the study (Creswell, 2009; Macnee, 2004).

One often thinks first of data taking the form of numbers or statistics. Many preliminary steps must occur prior to the collection of such data in quantitative research. Polit and Beck (2008) describe the data collection plan in quantitative research as including the following steps:

- Determine the data that need to be gathered.
- Consider the type of measurement to be used for each variable.
- Identify the instruments available to capture each variable.
- Develop data collection forms/protocols.
- Collect and manage the data.

In mixed methods research, data collection may also take nonquantitative forms (AHRQ, 2013). Narratives, verbal feedback from focus groups, transcripts, and videotapes are examples of sources of nonquantitative data (Vogt, 2005). The purpose of qualitative data collection in mixed record research may vary. For example, qualitative data may be collected for the purpose of developing questions for a quantitative survey or instrument. This step assists in developing a more comprehensive understanding of the dimensions of a construct under study or in generating hypotheses.

The rationale for the data collection process used in mixed methods research studies should be stated clearly: Why and how did using one or more methods of collecting and integrating data contribute to the purpose of the study? The specific data that are collected by quantitative and qualitative methods and the priority and emphasis given to each type of data are determined by the researchers and driven by the research problem and goals of the study (Creswell et al., 2004). Johnson and Onwuegbuzie (2004) describe their mixed method process as having eight distinct steps:

- Determine the research question.
- Determine whether a mixed design is appropriate.
- Select the mixed methods or mixed model research design.
- Collect the data.
- Analyze the data.
- Interpret the data.
- Legitimate the data.
- Draw conclusions (if warranted), and write the final report.

Johnson and Onwuegbuzie's (2004) mixed methods process focuses on data collection. Data collection in multimethod studies is frequently carried out so that quantitative and qualitative components of the study are kept separate during the actual conduct of the study and are combined only later in the interpretation and reporting of results (Creswell et al., 2004; Polit & Beck, 2011). Careful thought concerning the timing and flow of the data collection process is required.

To illustrate this idea, consider the research reported by Long and colleagues (2013), in which quantitative methods were used to measure the differences among fruit, vegetable, and fat consumption in college students. Participants used digital pictures recorded on personal cell phones as a memory prompt prior to entering their diet information online and then crossed over to record their diet information online without the use of cell phone pictures for memory recall. Qualitative methods were employed to understand participant perceptions, satisfaction, and usability of personal cell phones for this purpose. In this study, the researchers identified statistical analysis and significance testing to evaluate the difference in diet recording with and without digital pictures for memory prompt. Focus group interviews and structured short answers were used to evaluate how participants felt about using personal cell phones for this purpose. In this study, both quantitative and qualitative mixed methods suggested the use of digital pictures of diet on cell phones as an acceptable and effective way to prompt short-term memory of what had been eaten (Long et al., 2013). Allowing the participants' voices to be heard within the process strengthened the outcomes found within the research project. A modified version of the study conducted by Long et al. (2013) was replicated by Doumit et al. (2015), who found comparable qualitative findings in focus groups with Lebanese youth.

▶ Data Analysis and Validation Procedures

How data are analyzed is inextricably tied to the type of information that has been collected. Quantitative data, at minimum, are to be counted and described. Inferential statistical analysis is applied depending on the type and level of data available to the researcher. Qualitative data analysis also takes multiple forms, but it generally involves the coding of narrative themes for depth of understanding. It is not surprising, therefore, that analysis of mixed methods research mirrors the variety seen in analyses of both quantitative and qualitative methodologies.

To illuminate this point, consider the subset of data analysis in the study conducted by Long and colleagues (2006), which compared the results from two quantitative measurements of fruit, vegetable, and fat intake for **convergent validity**. Quantitative data from a computer-based self-report and from a structured interview were compared statistically (triangulated) and determined to have a small to medium correlation (Long et al., 2006). This form of mixed methodology is generative. It assisted the researcher in determining the need for further development of the measurement methods used to determine fruit, vegetable, and fat consumption in an adolescent population. In the same study, the qualitative feedback obtained from observations of student enjoyment with using the web-based educational intervention and verbal feedback from focus groups was analyzed and coded thematically to capture observed variances among learners, raising new questions about the population and about how to best provide meaningful health education to this group.

In summary, both quantitative and qualitative research designs can be combined through the use of a mixed methods approach to data collection and analysis. The specific data collected by both methods and the emphasis given to each should be determined based on the research problem and the goals of the study. A research team whose members are experienced in the use of both types of methods is important to the success of mixed methods research. While each of the methods has its own strengths and weaknesses, mixed methods research offers the opportunity for a more complete investigation into the problem being studied (Creswell et al., 2004; Elliott, 2004; Ramprogus, 2005). Given the complexities and the nature of the problems of interest to nursing, mixed methods research holds promise for advancing evidence-based understanding that might lead to enhanced quality patient care.

▶ EBP Considerations

Problems of interest to nursing are characteristically complex in nature. Nurses in clinical practice need to know how to find, evaluate, and use research so that they can implement best practices at the bedside (Spruce, 2015). Understanding mixed methods research is important because it holds the potential for promoting methodologically sound studies that capture complexities that might otherwise be overlooked. According to Rolston-Blenman (2009), "Clinical stakeholders must participate in planning and championing the changes taking place. Staff must feel they have a voice in making decisions" (p. 21). Through the use of mixed methods (action research), the staff at the bedside can actively participate in different aspects of research, resulting in better management of the problems so identified. According to Myers and Meccariello (2006), "It's critical to help nurses understand how crucial their role is in the research process and how they can improve patient care by validating their own trial and error experiences" (p. 24). Each day, individuals must realize the importance of connecting the research process to key activities that occur within the workplace—one patient at a time. This permeation of the workplace with a critical thinking mindset allows for the deep consideration of multiple problems at the ground-zero level. Taking advantage of the strengths of qualitative and quantitative research design methods, while planning for ways to overcome the limitations of the research designs, allows the discipline of nursing to advance the body of knowledge toward clinical practice confirmed by evidence.

⬚ THINK OUTSIDE THE BOX

- Debate the benefits and restrictions involved in using a mixed methodology for a research project.
- How would you handle a PICOTS (population, intervention, comparison, outcome, time, and setting) question format when using a mixed methodology?
- How could you address, using both a quantitative method and a qualitative method, a clinical problem that you have confronted?
- Debate which types of rationales are necessary when a mixed methods approach is used.

▶ Conclusion

Qualitative research lends itself well to the study of complex human issues. Qualitative research is the study of the quality of something rather than the quantity, amount, or frequency of something. Subjectivity is an expected trait of a qualitative study. Qualitative and quantitative research methods differ in many ways. As described previously, qualitative studies approach phenomena from the emic perspective—the perspective of the participant provides the meaning rather than the perspective of the researcher. Qualitative methods are inductive, as opposed to the deductive approach of quantitative methods. Although quantitative methods seek to minimize differences among subjects, qualitative methods embrace differences among participants.

Sample size in qualitative research is often small compared with the requisite larger sample sizes in quantitative research.

Case studies, ethnography, grounded theory, and phenomenology are methods used within qualitative research to seek the essences of the situation being investigated. In data collection and analysis, saturation occurs when no new themes or codes emerge or the data analysis becomes redundant. The reliability and validity of qualitative research can be ensured by verifying credibility, transferability, dependability, confirmability, and authenticity of data.

Mixed methods design (called multimethod, triangulated, and integrated design) is an amalgamation of quantitative and qualitative research methods and techniques used to collect and analyze data. In mixed methods studies, two research patterns are regularly interlocked within the sampling, data collection, or analysis aspects of the project. The use of both methods permits the researcher to develop a wider and deeper understanding of the identified research problem as a result of the consideration of the problem from multiple viewpoints.

The fundamental force driving the use of mixed methods research continues to be the clear and concise identification of the research problem. The investigator must rigorously examine the issue of whether the two research designs should be conducted concurrently or sequentially.

🔼 THINK OUTSIDE THE BOX

- The table compares emic and etic research designs. Which other aspects can you identify that might be added to this table to further delineate the differences and similarities between these two research design methods?

Differences Between Quantitative And Qualitative Research Methods

	Point of View	Attachment to Participant	Process of Inquiry	Sample
Outsider view	Etic—analyzed without considering a person's role as a unit within a system	Seeks to minimize the differences among subjects	Deductive	Large sample size required
Insider view	Emic—analyzed with consideration of a person's role as a unit within a system	Embraces different perspectives of each participant	Inductive	Individuals; sample size is typical

- Discuss how sample sizes for qualitative, quantitative, and mixed methods research projects differ. How do researchers determine the optimal sample size for qualitative studies as opposed to quantitative studies?

■ Think for a moment about your current workplace. Identify one problem, process, or policy in your work area whose improvement by the healthcare team would favorably affect patient outcomes. Once you have identified a problem, list ideas about which quantitative data would assist you and your colleagues in solving the problem. Also consider those aspects of the issue in which your understanding would be enhanced through collection of qualitative data. How could you apply best practices to solve the problem you identified using aspects of both research methods? Now consider an unmet educational need of new staff members on your unit. How might an action research mixed methods approach assist you in understanding and meeting the changing educational needs of new staff members?

Triangulation allows the researcher to fully understand a phenomenon of interest through validation or supplementation of data. The term *triangulation* is used to describe the situation in which data are analyzed for the purpose of corroborating data from multiple methods. Justification for the ordering and prioritization of the different methods must be documented, with rationales being presented for each of the decisions made concerning the research process. During collection and analysis of data in mixed methods research, quantitative and qualitative data are often treated as independent components in the research design.

Summary Points

1. Qualitative research is the study of the quality of something rather than the quantity, amount, or frequency of something. Subjectivity is an expected trait of a qualitative study.
2. Qualitative research is conducted from the emic perspective; quantitative research is conducted from the etic perspective.
3. Sample size in qualitative research is often small compared with the requisite larger sample sizes in quantitative research.
4. The criteria for reliability and validity of a qualitative study include credibility, transferability, dependability, confirmability, and authenticity of data.
5. Mixed research methods—combinations of qualitative and quantitative methods—are used to supplement or validate data.
6. Saturation occurs in data collection or analysis when there is repetition or redundancy in the themes or patterns in the data.
7. Mixed methods design (called multimethod, triangulated, and integrated design) is an amalgamation of quantitative and qualitative research methods and techniques used to collect and analyze data.
8. In mixed methods studies, two research patterns are regularly interlocked within the sampling, data collection, or analysis aspects of the project.
9. The use of both methods permits the researcher to develop a wider and deeper understanding of the identified research problem as a result of the consideration of the problem from multiple viewpoints.
10. The fundamental force driving the use of mixed methods research continues to be the clear and concise identification of the research problem.

11. The criteria used when choosing the combination of methods for inclusion in a mixed methods study are related to implementation, prioritization, and integration needs.
12. Mixed methods research holds a number of unique features; a number of quality criteria are important to consider when using and evaluating this type of research.
13. The investigator must rigorously examine the issue of whether the two research designs should be conducted concurrently or sequentially.
14. Justification for the ordering and prioritization of the different methods must be documented, with rationales presented for each of the decisions made concerning the research process.
15. During collection and analysis of data in mixed methods research, quantitative and qualitative data are often treated as independent components in the research design.
16. The term *triangulation* is used to describe the situation in which data are analyzed for the purpose of corroborating data from multiple methods.

⚑ RED FLAGS

- Care must be given to explaining how different research methodologies are entwined as a single project.
- A lack of a rationale for using mixed methods is problematic.
- Any indication that quantitative and qualitative methods are competing with each other reflects lack of planning.
- When the rationale for weighting of the methods is not provided, then concerns must be raised about the results of the data analysis.
- The data collection process for each of the two research methodologies should be kept distinctive.
- If data collection methods are improperly conducted for the identified research methodology, then the validity of the results must be questioned.
- Attention must be given to the auditability of the data collected via a qualitative methodology.
- Within a qualitative research report, the reader should be able to pick out aspects that demonstrate credibility, transferability, dependability, confirmability, and authenticity of the research.
- Qualitative research designs use an inductive reasoning process.
- Patterns and/or themes coming from the data should be documented and supported by the discussion.
- Given that qualitative research deals with volumes of written data, the documentation of statistic results would cause concern when evaluating a project.

Multiple-Choice Questions

1. Qualitative data explores which of the following characteristics of a phenomenon?
   A. Frequency
   B. Quantity
   C. Quality
   D. Intensity

2. Which of the following best illustrates the emic perspective in research?
   A. Finding a quality of a phenomenon and looking for examples of the quality
   B. Taking an outsider's view of a phenomenon
   C. Exploring the way members of a group view themselves
   D. Validating perspectives about a group through discussion

3. Which of the following types of studies is considered qualitative research?
   A. Delphi technique
   B. Cross-sectional design
   C. Phenomenology
   D. Survey

4. Mixed methods research combines elements of which two methods?
   A. Quantitative and qualitative
   B. Transferability and trustworthiness
   C. Prospective and retrospective
   D. Phenomenology and ethnography

5. A researcher explores the phenomenon of how nurses make decisions about when to discuss end-of-life issues with clients. From this research, a model is developed to explain the decision-making process. Which type of research does this represent?
   A. Grounded theory
   B. Ethnography
   C. Phenomenology
   D. Case study

6. The extent to which a researcher can accurately and faithfully express the feelings and emotions of the study participants is a measure of which of the following concepts?
   A. Credibility
   B. Transferability
   C. Authenticity
   D. Dependability

7. A researcher conducts a study in which participants are asked to describe the lived experience of being a caregiver of a parent with Parkinson's disease. Which type of qualitative study does this represent?
   A. Constant comparison
   B. Ethnography
   C. Phenomenology
   D. Case study

8. Which of the following statements is true with regard to comparing qualitative and quantitative research methods?
   A. Qualitative studies seek to generalize findings.
   B. Qualitative studies don't require evidence of reliability and validity.
   C. Qualitative studies don't allow for the use of computerized data analysis.
   D. Qualitative research is often inductive in nature, whereas quantitative research is deductive in nature.

9. When writing a research project, the researcher describes in detail the audit trail used as conclusions about data were drawn. Which criterion for reliability and validity was met?
   A. Credibility
   B. Transferability
   C. Dependability
   D. Confirmability

10. When writing a research project, the researcher describes in detail the sample, setting, and data. Which criterion for reliability and validity was met?
   A. Credibility
   B. Transferability
   C. Dependability
   D. Confirmability

11. When writing a research project, the researcher describes in detail how biases, assumptions, and personal perspectives were identified and set aside, or bracketed. Which criterion for reliability and validity was met?
   A. Credibility
   B. Transferability
   C. Dependability
   D. Confirmability

12. The researcher collecting data notices that she is beginning to hear the same things repeatedly and that no new themes are emerging. The researcher recognizes that which of the following has occurred?
   A. Triangulation
   B. Saturation
   C. Quantizing
   D. Redundancy

13. Another term used within the literature for mixed methods design is:
   A. quantitative design.
   B. qualitative design.
   C. multimethod design.
   D. experimental design.

14. When a researcher endeavors to use mixed methods design to answer an identified research problem, the blending of the methods is based on:
   A. combining the methods to capitalize on their strong points while negating their flaws.
   B. combining the methods to blend both their strengths and their weaknesses.
   C. separating the strengths from the weaknesses within the different designs.
   D. separating the weaker method from the stronger method.

15. The research designs are merged within which sections of the report on the research project?
   A. Introduction, sampling, and problem identification
   B. Problem identification, data collection, and analysis
   C. Sampling, data collection, and analysis
   D. Introduction, data collection, and analysis

16. What is a primary reason the researcher might consider using mixed methods research?
    A. The need to examine a problem that calls for real-life and contextual understanding of multilevel perspectives
    B. Willingness to engage in the use of, and confidence in, one research method
    C. Willingness for risk taking
    D. Lack of confidence in qualitative methods

17. A nurse identifies individuals who seem to comply better with a treatment plan when several different teaching methods are used within the discharge planning process. In developing a mixed methods design for researching which educational methods work best, a question concerning the type of data to be collected is confronted. Which of the following groups of data collection methods represents a mixed methods format?
    A. Likert scale tool with a demographic component
    B. Observation of teaching sessions with videotaping
    C. Focus group discussion with audiotaping
    D. Likert scale tool with focus group discussion

18. The determination of the mixed methods design approach must address the meshing of the qualitative and quantitative methodologies through the use of which of the following criteria?
    A. Implementation, prioritization, and integration
    B. Implementation, analysis, and investigation
    C. Analysis, prioritization, and integration
    D. Collection, prioritization, and analysis

19. A researcher has elected to conduct a mixed methods research project. Within this project, the decision has been made to conduct the two types of data collection concurrently, with each type of data having equal weight within the analysis process. Based on these decisions, what must the researcher make sure is done for the reporting of the process?
    A. Establish a team to aid in the management of the study.
    B. Reevaluate the decision because quantitative research is the stronger method.
    C. Ensure that confidentiality is maintained within the process.
    D. Document the rationale for the decisions made within the process.

20. Triangulation in mixed methods research is utilized for the purposes of supporting _____ validity.
    A. criterion
    B. convergent
    C. construct
    D. variable

21. The data collected in mixed methods research and the emphasis given to each type of data should be determined by the _____ and goals of the study.
    A. source of funding
    B. preference of the research team
    C. research problem
    D. literature

22. Qualitative data analysis seeks _____ in understanding a phenomenon.
    A. rigor
    B. depth
    C. numbers
    D. statistical significance

23. A primary reason for using mixed research methodologies is the opportunity to _____ that might otherwise be overlooked.
    A. catch complexities
    B. define concepts
    C. describe new research problems
    D. uncover opportunities

24. In mixed methods research, how is the collection of quantitative and qualitative data often treated?
    A. Synchronously
    B. Stringently
    C. Independently
    D. Statistically

25. An advantage of using a mixed methods design for a research study is to:
    A. increase the biases associated with the use of two designs.
    B. provide insight into the complexity of the problem under study.
    C. impart generalizability to the findings of the study.
    D. decrease the impartiality associated with the use of one design.

26. Limitations related to the use of mixed method strategies include the:
    A. cost and additional time required.
    B. extensive and comprehensive research questions involved.
    C. vivacity of the evidence provided.
    D. complementary insights and perceptions provided.

27. What type of research provides a comprehensive understanding of healthcare problems?
    A. Mixed methods
    B. Qualitative
    C. Quantitative
    D. Case study

28. Qualitative data can be collected in which of the following methods?
    A. Audiotape
    B. Videotape
    C. Interview
    D. All of the above

29. A study that follows participants over a period of 2 years and conducts in-depth interviews would be a:
    A. cross-sectional study.
    B. quantitative study.
    C. case study.
    D. longitudinal qualitative case study.

Discussion Questions

1. You are the nurse manager of a perinatal care unit. You have read a phenomenology research report on the positive effects of music on the labor and delivery process for mothers. Consider the following: The study is one of many of this type with similar findings, there were five informants in the study, and the researcher did not provide a discussion of reliability and validity in the writeup. Will you use this study to support the practice of ensuring that all labor and delivery rooms are equipped to play music throughout the labor and delivery process? Support your answer.

2. You are the charge nurse on a medical–surgical floor. After reading several qualitative research reports on pet therapy, you approach your nurse manager about the possibility of implementing a pet therapy program on your floor. Your nurse manager states that no changes should be made based on qualitative research because the sample sizes are always too small. What is your best response?

3. You are reading a research report about a long-term care facility. The researcher describes in detail the demographics of the administrators, staff members, and clients. There is a lengthy discussion about how problems are solved in the facility, how various departments communicate, and how the facility values family involvement in client care. Which type of qualitative study does this represent? Support your answer.

4. A nurse on the labor and delivery unit wants to study the effects of having small children participate with the family in the delivery process on the bonding process between mother and child. For this study, the nurse has determined that a questionnaire will be mailed out to families who elect to have their toddlers in the delivery room during the delivery of a sibling. The questionnaire will include both open-ended questions and closed-ended (Likert-type) questions. Which aspects of the study should be considered to provide a rationale for selecting this mixed methods strategy?

5. A researcher working within a hospital striving to gain Magnet status wants to study the barriers to use of research at the bedside. For the design of this study, the individual is considering using a mixed methods format. Which pieces of the design should be considered as the researcher prepares the study?

6. A group of researchers has developed a new instrument to assess the degree of destruction noted within decubitus ulcers (pressure ulcers). As part of their study, the researchers are planning to compare the new instrument with instruments currently used within their acute care setting. Which components of the mixed methods strategies need to be considered carefully as the researchers develop the study design?

Suggested Readings

Bader, M. K., Palmer, S., Stalcup, C., & Shaver, T. (2002). Using a FOCUS-PDCA quality improvement model for applying the severe traumatic brain injury guidelines to practice: Process and outcomes. *Reflections on Nursing Leadership, 28*(2), 34–35.

Balas, E. A., & Boren, S. A. (2000). Managing clinical knowledge for health care improvements. In V. Schattauer, J. Bemmel, & A. T. McCray (Eds.), *Yearbook of medical informatics* (pp. 65–70). Stuttgart, Germany: Schattauer.

Borkan, J. M. (2004). Mixed methods studies: A foundation for primary care research [Editorial]. *Annals of Family Medicine, 2*(1), 4–6.

Classen, S., & Lopez, E. (2006). Mixed methods approach explaining process of an older driver safety systematic literature review. *Topics in Geriatric Rehabilitation, 22*(2), 99–112.

Doumit, R., Zeeni, N., Long, J., Kazandjian, C., Gharibeh, N., Karen, I., Song, H., & Boswell, C. (2015). Effects of recording food intake using cell phone camera pictures on energy intake and food choice. *Worldviews on Evidence-Based Nursing, 13*(3), 216–223 doi:10.1111/wvn.12123

Foss, C., & Ellefsen, B. (2002). The value of combining qualitative and quantitative approaches in nursing research by means of method triangulation. *Journal of Advanced Nursing, 40*(2), 242–248.

Freshwater, D. (2005). Integrating qualitative and quantitative research methods: Trend or foe? [Book review]. *Journal of Research in Nursing, 10*(3), 337–338.

Freshwater, D., Walsh, L., & Storey, L. (2002, February). Prison health care part 2: Developing leadership through clinical supervision. *Nursing Management, 8*(9), 16–20.

Grassley, J. S., & Nelms, T. P. (2008). The breast feeding conversation: A philosophic exploration of support. *Advances in Nursing Science, 31*(4), E55–E66.

Halcomb, E., & Andrew, S. (2005). Triangulation as a method for contemporary nursing research. *Nurse Researcher, 13*(2), 71–82.

Hanson, W. E., Creswell, J. W., Clark, V. L., Petska, K. S., & Creswell, J. D. (2005). Mixed methods research designs in counseling psychology. *Journal of Counseling Psychology, 52*(2), 224–235.

Happ, M. B. (2009). Mixed methods in gerontological research. *Research in Gerontological Nursing, 2*(2), 122–127.

Happ, M. B., Dabbs, A. D., Tate, J., Hricik, A., & Erlen, J. (2006, March/April). Exemplars of mixed methods data combination and analysis. *Nursing Research, 55*(2 Suppl.), S43–S49.

Harland, N., & Holey, E. (2011). Including open-ended questions in quantitative questionnaires—theory and practice. *International Journal of Therapy and Rehabilitation, 18*(9), 482–486.

Kinn, S., & Curzio, J. (2005). Integrating qualitative and quantitative research methods. *Journal of Research in Nursing, 10*(3), 317–336.

Kreutzer, J. S., Stejskal, T. M., Godwin, E. E., Powell, V. D., & Arango-Lasprilla, J. C. (2010). A mixed methods evaluation of the Brain Injury Family Intervention. *NeuroRehabilitation, 27*(1), 19–29.

Law, M., Stewart, D., Letts, L., Pollock, N., Bosch, J., & Westmoreland, M. (1998). *Guidelines for critical review of qualitative studies.* Retrieved from http://www.usc.edu/hsc/ebnet/res/Guidelines.pdf

Melnyk, B. M., & Fineout-Overholt, E. (2006, Second Quarter). Advancing knowledge through collaboration. *Reflections on Nursing Leadership, 32*(2), 1–5.

Melnyk, B. M., Fineout-Overholt, E., Stetler, C., & Allen, J. (2005). Outcomes and implementation strategies from the first U.S. evidence-based leadership summit. *Worldviews on Evidence-Based Nursing, 2*(3), 113–121.

Miller, S. I., & Fredericks, M. (2006). Mixed-methods and evaluation research: Trends and issues. *Qualitative Health Research, 16*(4), 567–579.

O'Neill, R. (2006). Advantages and disadvantages of qualitative and quantitative research methods. Retrieved from http://www.learnhigher.ac.uk/analysethis/main/quantitative1.html

Onwuegbuzie, A. J., & Leech, N. L. (2005). Taking the "Q" out of research: Teaching research methodology courses without the divide between quantitative and qualitative paradigms. *Quality & Quantity, 39*(3), 267–295.

Paton, B., Martin, S., McClunie-Trust, P., & Weir, N. (2004). Doing phenomenological research collaboratively. *Journal of Continuing Education in Nursing, 35*(4), 176–181.

Priest, H., Roberts, P., & Woods, L. (2002). An overview of three different approaches to the interpretation of qualitative data. Part 1: Theoretical issues. *Nurse Researcher, 10*(1), 30–42.

Rapport, F., & Wainwright, P. (2006). Phenomenology as a paradigm of movement. *Nursing Inquiry, 13*(3), 228–236.

Sale, J. E. M., Lohfeld, L. H., & Brazil, K. (2002). Revisiting the quantitative–qualitative debate: Implications for mixed-methods research. *Quality & Quantity, 36*(1), 43–53.

Schifferdecker, K. E., & Reed, V. A. (2009). Using mixed methods research in medical education: Basic guidelines for researchers. *Medical Education, 43*(7), 637–644.

Shih, F. J. (1998). Triangulation in nursing research: Issues of conceptual clarity and purpose. *Journal of Advanced Nursing, 28*(3), 631–641.

Silverstein, L. B., Auerbach, C. F., & Levant, R. R. (2006). Using qualitative research to strengthen clinical practice. *Professional Psychology: Research & Practice, 37*(4), 351–358.

Vishnevsky, T., & Beanlands, H. (2004). Qualitative research. *Nephrology Nursing Journal, 31*(2), 234–238.

Williamson, G. R. (2005). Illustrating triangulation in mixed-methods nursing research. *Nurse Researcher, 12*(4), 7–18.

References

Agency for Healthcare Quality and Research. (2013). Mixed-methods: Integrating quantitative and qualitative research methods and data collection and analysis while studying patient-centered medical home models. AHRQ Publication No: 13-0028-EF. Retrieved from https://pcmh.ahrq.gov/page/mixed-methods-integrating-quantitative-and-qualitative-data-collection-and-analysis-while

Agency for Healthcare Quality and Research. (2018a). Focus groups. Retrieved from https://www.ahrq.gov/professionals/quality-patient-safety/talkingquality/assess/collectionmethods.html

Agency for Healthcare Quality and Research. (2018b). Tools and other needs for quantitative and qualitative methods. Retrieved from https://www.ahrq.gov/professionals/quality-patient-safety/talkingquality/assess/tools.html.

Amankwaa, L. (2016). Creating protocols for trustworthiness in qualitative research. *Journal of Cultural Diversity, 23*(3), 121–127.

Anderson C. (2010). Presenting and evaluating qualitative research. *American Journal of Pharmacy Education, 74*(8), 141.

Andrews, T., & Waterman, H. (2005). Packaging: A grounded theory of how to report physiological deterioration effectively. *Journal of Advanced Nursing, 52*(5), 473–481. doi:10.1111/j.1365-2648.2005.03615.x

Baxter, P., & Jack, S. (2008). Qualitative case study methodology: Study design and implementation for novice researchers. *The Qualitative Report, 13*(4), 544–559.

Bliss, D. Z. (2001). Mixed or mixed up methods? *Nursing Research, 50*(6), 331.

Busetto, L., Luijkx, K., Calciolari, S., Gonzalez-Ortiz, L. G., Vrijhoef, H. J. M. (2017). The development, description and appraisal of an emergent multimethod research design to study workforce changes in integrated care interventions. *International Journal of Integrated Care, 17*(1). doi:10.5334/ijic.2510

Chen, L. S., & Goodson, P. (2009). Barriers to adopting genomics into public health education: A mixed methods study. *Genetics in Medicine, 11*(2), 104–110.

Chow, M. Y., Quine, S., & Li, M. (2010). The benefits of using a mixed methods approach—quantitative and qualitative—to identify client satisfaction and unmet needs in an HIV healthcare centre. *AIDS Care, 22*(4), 491–498.

Cohen-Katz, J., Wiley, S. D., Capuano, T., Baker, D. M., & Shapiro, S. (2004). The effects of mindfulness-based stress reduction on nurse stress and burnout: A quantitative and qualitative study. *Holistic Nursing Practice, 18*(6), 302–308.

Cook, T., Atkin, H., & Wilcockson, J. (2018). Participatory research into inclusive practice: Improving services for people with long term neurological conditions. Forum: *Qualitative Social Research, 19*(1), 117–142. doi:10.17169/fqs-19.1.2667

Cope, D. G. (2014). Methods and meanings: Credibility and trustworthiness of qualitative research. *Oncology Nursing Forum, 41*(1), 89–91.

Creswell, J. W. (2003). *Research design: Qualitative, quantitative, and mixed method approaches* (2nd ed.). Thousand Oaks, CA: Sage.

Creswell, J. W. (2009). *Research design: Qualitative, quantitative, and mixed methods approaches* (3rd ed.). Thousand Oaks, CA: Sage.

Creswell, J. W., Fetters, M. D., & Ivankova, N. V. (2004). Designing a mixed methods study in primary care. *Annals of Family Medicine, 2*(1), 7–12.

Creswell, J. W., Klassen, A. C., Plano Clark, V. L., & Klegg Smith, C. (2010). Best practices for mixed methods in the health sciences. Retrieved from http://obssr.od.nih.gov/scientific_areas/methodology/mixed_methods_research/pdf/Best_Practices_for_Mixed_Methods_Research.pdf

Cui, F., Sun, L., Xiong, J., Li, J., Zhao, Y., & Huang, X. (February, 2018). Therapeutic effects of percutaneous endoscopic gastrostomy on survival in patients with amyotrophic lateral sclerosis: A meta-analysis. *PLoS One, 13*(2). doi:10.1371/journal.pone.0192243.

Curry, L. A., Nembhard, I. M., Bradley, E. H. (2009). Qualitative and mixed methods provide unique contributions to outcomes research, *Circulation, 119*(10)1442–1452.

Denzin, N. K., & Lincoln, Y. S. (Eds.). (1998). *Collecting and interpreting qualitative materials.* Thousand Oaks, CA: Sage.

Denzin, N. K., & Lincoln, Y. S. (2011). *The SAGE handbook of qualitative research* (4th ed.). Thousand Oaks, CA: Sage.

Dictionary.com. (n.d.). Boolean algebra. Retrieved from http://dictionary.reference.com/browse/Boolean+algebra

Donnelly, F., & Wiechula, D. F. (2013). An example of qualitative comparative analysis in nursing research. *Nurse Researcher, 20*(6), 6–11.

Doumit, R., Zeeni, N., Long, J., Kazandjian, C., Gharibeh, N., Karen, I. Song, H. & Boswell, C. (2015). Effects of recording food intake using cell phone camera pictures on energy intake and food choice. *Worldviews on Evidence-Based Nursing, 13*(3), 216–223 doi:10.1111/wvn.12123

Duckham, B. C., & Schreiber, J. C. (2016). Bridging worldviews through phenomenology. *Social Work & Christianity, 43*(4), 55–67.

Eckardt, P., Culley, J. M., Corwin, E., Richmond, T., Dougherty, C., Pickler, R. H., Krause-Parello, C. A., Royer, C. F., Rainbow, J. G., & DeVon, H. A. (2017). National nursing science priorities: Creating a shared vision. *Nursing Outlook, 65*, 726–736.

Elliott, J. (2004). Multimethod approaches in educational research. *International Journal of Disability, Development and Education, 51*(2), 135–149.

Fabregues, S., & Molina-Azorin, J. R. (2016). Addressing quality in mixed methods research: A review and recommendations for a future agenda. *Quality and Quantity,* 51(6), 2847–2863, Retrieved from https://link.springer.com/article/10.1007/s11135-016-0449-4

Flick, U. (2009). *Introduction to qualitative research.* Thousand Oaks, CA: Sage.

Glaser, B. G., & Strauss, A. L. (1967). *The discovery of grounded theory: Strategies for qualitative research.* Chicago, IL: Aldine De Gruyter.

Goodnough, K. (2008). Moving science off the "back burner": Meaning making within an action research community of practice. *Journal of Science and Teacher Education, 19*(1), 15–39.

Hagedoorn, E. I., Paans, W., Jaarsma, T., Keers, J. C., van der Schans, C., & Luttik, M. L. (2017). Aspects of family caregiving as addressed in planned discussions between nurses, patients with chronic diseases and family caregivers: A qualitative content analysis. *BMC Nursing, 16*(37). doi:10.1186/s12912-017-0231-5

Holloway, I., & Wheeler, S. (2010). *Qualitative research in nursing and healthcare* (3rd ed.). Ames, IA: Wiley-Blackwell.

Ingham-Broomfield, R. (2016). A nurses' guide to mixed methods research. *Australian Journal of Advanced Nursing, 33*(4), 46–52.

Iverson, K. M., Huang, K., Wells, S., Wright, J. D., Gerber, M. R., & Wiltsey-Stirman, S. (2014). Women veterans' preferences for intimate partner violence screening and response procedures within the Veterans Health Administration. *Research in Nursing & Health, 37*(4), 302–311.

Ivey, J. (2017). Demystifying research: What is grounded theory? *Pediatric Nursing, 43*(6), 288–289.

Joanna Briggs Institute. (2015). Retrieved from www.Joannabriggs.org

Johnson, R. B. (n.d.). Mixed research: Mixed method and mixed model research. [Online lecture]. Retrieved from http://www.southalabama.edu/coe/bset/johnson/dr_johnson/lectures/lec14.htm

Johnson, R. B., & Onwuegbuzie, A. J. (2004). Mixed methods research: A research paradigm whose time has come. *Educational Researcher, 33*(7), 14–26.

Kenny, M., & Fourie, R. (2014). Tracing the history of grounded theory methodology: From formation to fragmentation. *The Qualitative Report, 19*(103), 1–9. Retrieved from https://nsuworks.nova.edu/cgi/viewcontent.cgi?article=1416&context=tqr

Kwan, T. M., & Sullivan, M. (2017). The use of intravenous ibuprofen and intravenous acetaminophen in surgical patients and the effect on opioid reduction, *MEDSURG Nursing, 26*(2), 124–142.

Leseyane, M., Mandende, P., Makgato, M., & Cekiso, M. (2018). Dyslexic learners' experiences with their peers and teachers in special and mainstream primary schools in North-West Province. *African Journal of Disability, 7*(0), 363. http://doi.org/10.4102/ajod.v7i0.363

Lincoln, Y. S., & Guba, E. G. (1985). *Naturalistic inquiry.* Beverly Hills, CA: Sage.

Ling, J., Payne, S., Connaire, K., & McCarron, M. (2016). Parental decision-making on utilisation of out-of-home respite in children's palliative care: Findings of qualitative case study research—a proposed new model. *Child: Care, Health & Development, 42*(1), 51–59. doi:10.1111/cch.12300

Long, J. D., Armstrong, M. L., Amos, E., Shriver, B., Roman-Shriver, C., Feng, D., . . . Blevins, M. W. (2006). Pilot using World Wide Web to prevent diabetes in adolescents. *Clinical Nursing Research, 15*(1), 67–79.

Long, J. D., Boswell, C., Rogers, T., Littlefield, L. A., Estep, G., Shriver, B., . . . Song, H. (2013). Effectiveness of cell phones and mypyramidtracker.gov to estimate fruit and vegetable intake. *Applied Nursing Research, 26*(1), 17–23.

Macnee, C. L. (2004). *Understanding nursing research: Reading and using research in practice.* Philadelphia, PA: Lippincott Williams & Wilkins.

Mason, D. M., & Ide, B. (2014). Adapting qualitative research strategies to technology savvy adolescents. *Nurse Researcher, 21*(5), 40–45.

McCusker, K. & Gunaydin, S. (2015). Research using qualitative, quantitative or mixed methods and choice based on the research, *Perfusion, 30*(7), 537–542.

Mey, G., & Dietrich, M. (2017). From text to image: Shaping a visual grounded theory methodology. *Historical Social Research, 42*(4), 280–300. doi:10.12759/hsr.42.2017.4.280-300

Morse, J. (1998). Designing funded qualitative research. In N. K. Denzin & Y. S. Lincoln (Eds.), *Strategies of qualitative inquiry* (pp. 56–85). Thousand Oaks, CA: Sage.

Munten, G., van den Bogaard, J., Cox, K., Garretsen, H., & Bongers, I. (2010). Implementation of evidence-based practice in nursing using action research: A review. *Worldviews on Evidence-Based Nursing, 7*(3), 135–157.

Myers, G., & Meccariello, M. (2006). From pet rock to rock-solid: Implementing unit-based research. *Nursing Management, 37*(1), 24–29.

Office of Behavioral and Social Sciences Research. (2011). Best practices for mixed methods research in the health sciences. Retrieved from http://obssr.od.nih.gov/mixed_methods_research/

Polit, D. F., & Beck, C. T. (2008). *Nursing research: Generating and assessing evidence for nursing practice* (8th ed.). Philadelphia, PA: Lippincott Williams & Wilkins.

Polit, D. F., & Beck, C. T. (2011). *Nursing research: Generating and assessing evidence for nursing practice* (9th ed.). Philadelphia, PA: Lippincott Williams & Wilkins.

Ponic, P., Reid, C., & Frisby, W. (2010). Cultivating the power of partnerships in feminist participatory action research in women's health. *Nursing Inquiry, 17*(4), 324–335.

Purc-Stephenson, R. J., Jones, S. K., & Ferguson, C. L. (2017). "Forget about the glass ceiling, I'm stuck in a glass box": A meta-ethnography of work participation for persons with physical disabilities. *Journal of Vocational Rehabilitation, 46*(1), 49–65. doi:10.3233/JVR-160842

Ramprogus, V. (2005). Triangulation. *Nurse Researcher, 12*(4), 4–6.

Roller, M. R., & Lavrakas, P. J. (2015). *Applied qualitative research design: A total quality research design.* New York, NY: Guilford Press.

Rolston-Blenman, B. (2009). Nurses roll up their sleeves at the bedside to improve patient care. *Nurse Leader, 7*(1), 20–25.

Roney, J., Maples, J., Whitley, Stunkard, K., Futrell, L., & Long, J. (2015). Modified Early Warning Score (MEWS): Evaluating the evidence for tool inclusion of sepsis screening criteria and impact on mortality and failure to rescue. *Journal of Clinical Nursing, 24*, 3–12.

Rosenberg, J. P., & Yates, P. M. (2007). Schematic representation of case study research designs. *Journal of Advanced Nursing, 60*(4), 447–452.

Scott Tilley, D., Rugari, S. M., & Walker, C. A. (2008). Development of violence in men who batter intimate partners: A case study. *The Journal of Theory Construction & Testing, 12*(1), 28–32.

Shaw, J. A., Connelly, D. M., & Zecevic, A. A. (2010). Pragmatism in practice: Mixed methods research in physiotherapy. *Physiotherapy Theory and Practice, 26*(8), 510–518.

Siddiqui, N., & Fitzgerald, J. A. (2014). Elaborated integration of qualitative and quantitative perspectives in mixed methods research: A profound enquiry into the nursing practice environment. *International Journal of Multiple Research Approaches, 8*(2), 137–147.

Smythe, L. (2012). Discerning which qualitative approach fits best. *New Zealand College of Midwives Journal, 46*, 5–12.

Snelgrove, S. R. (2014). Conducting qualitative longitudinal research using interpretive phenomenological analysis. *Nurse Researcher, 22*(1), 20–25.

Spruce, L. (2015). Back to basics: Implementing evidence-based practice. *AORN Journal, 101*(1), 106–112.

Strauss, A., & Corbin, J. (1998). *Basics of qualitative research: Techniques and procedures for developing grounded theory* (2nd ed.). Thousand Oaks, CA: Sage.

Tufford, L., & Newman, P. (2010). Bracketing in qualitative research. *Qualitative Social Work, 11*(1), 80–96.

Uebel, T. (2016, Spring). Vienna circle. In E. N. Zalta (Ed.). *The Stanford Encyclopedia of Philosophy*. Retrieved from https://plato.stanford.edu/archives/spr2016/entries/vienna-circle/

van den Berg, A., & Struwig, M. (2017). Guidelines for researchers using an adapted consensual qualitative research approach in management research. *The Electronic Journal of Business Research Methods, 15*(2), 109–115.

Vogt, W. P. (2005). *Dictionary of statistics and methodology: A nontechnical guide for the social sciences* (3rd ed.). Thousand Oaks, CA: Sage.

Whitcombe, A., Cooper, K., & Palmer, E. (2016). The relationship between organizational culture and the health and wellbeing of hospital nurses worldwide: A mixed methods systematic review protocol. *JBI Database System Review Implementation Reports, 14*(6), 103–116. doi:10.11124 /JBISRIR-2016-002650

Woolston, W. & Connelly, L. M. (2017). Felty's syndrome: A qualitative case study. *MEDSURG Nursing, 26*(2), 105–118.

CHAPTER 10

Population Management

Kathaleen C. Bloom, Julie A. Baker-Townsend, and Lucy B. Trice

CHAPTER OBJECTIVES

At the conclusion of this chapter, the learner will be able to:
1. Compare a population and a sample.
2. Discuss basic concepts related to sampling.
3. Contrast inclusion and exclusion criteria in the sampling process.
4. Distinguish between probability and nonprobability samples.
5. Identify types of sampling strategies used for qualitative and quantitative research.
6. Discuss approaches to determining sample size.
7. Evaluate populations and sampling plans found in research reports for their contribution to the strength of evidence for nursing practice.

KEY TERMS

Accessible population	Quota sampling
Cluster sampling	Random sampling
Convenience sampling	Representative sample
Exclusion criteria	Sample
External validity	Sampling error
Inclusion criteria	Simple random sampling
Internal validity	Snowball sampling
Nonprobability sampling	Stratified random sampling
Population	Systematic random sampling
Probability sampling	Target population
Purposive sampling	Theoretical sampling

▶ Introduction

We know that evidence-based practice (EBP) is about integrating the strongest research evidence with clinical expertise and patient needs (Melnyk & Fineout-Overholt, 2015). Now it is time to examine the research design decisions made in terms of sampling. Regardless of the topic of the research, every investigator must make decisions about which subjects will provide data to answer the research question. This process is done through the development of a sampling plan—a process that involves making choices about who or what to include in the sample, how to select the sample, and how many subjects to include in the sample for a study. The choices made in developing the sampling plan are critical in designing high-quality clinical studies to build evidence-based nursing practice. Careful appraisal of the sampling plan in a published research study is critical to determining both the quality of the evidence and the applicability of the findings to nursing practice.

A **population** is the entire set of elements that meet specified criteria. An element may be a person, a family, a community, a medical record, an event, a laboratory specimen, or even a laboratory animal. Often called the **target population**, this set encompasses every element in the world that met the sampling criteria, such as all pregnant adolescents, preterm infants, persons with diabetes, or children who are chronically ill. The **accessible population**, by comparison, is that portion of the target population that the investigator can reasonably reach. It might include pregnant adolescents enrolled in an alternative high school in the southeastern United States, persons with diabetes who are enrolled in diabetic education at a local hospital, or children with a chronic illness who are enrolled in a summer camp. The **sample**, drawn through a specified sampling strategy from the accessible population, consists of those elements from whom or about whom data are actually collected (**FIGURE 10-1**).

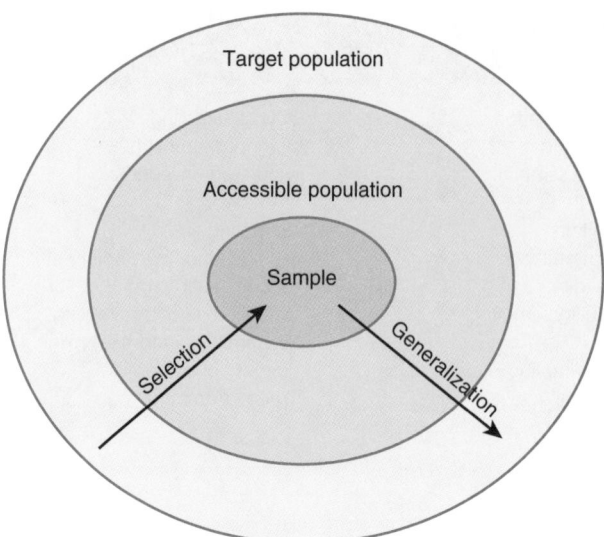

FIGURE 10-1 Relationships among target population, accessible population, and sample.

▶ Why Sample?

The purpose of sampling is to draw conclusions accurately about a population based on information from a subgroup of that population, called a sample. It is sometimes possible, even desirable, to obtain data from an entire population. For example, Antwi, Moriya, Simon, and Sommers (2015) performed a population-based study using a nationally representative database of more than 17 million emergency department (ED) visits to determine the effect of the Patient Protection and Affordable Care Act on ED visits by young adults ages 19 to 25 (the age group targeted by the law). The researchers found that ED visits decreased after the enactment of the law, indicating that young adults seemed to alter their healthcare visit pattern to reflect a more efficient use of medical care.

Researchers usually use samples rather than populations, however, for reasons of efficiency and cost-effectiveness. In most cases, it would be almost impossible, and generally impractical, to conduct a study on the entire population, even though this is the population to which the investigator would like to be able to generalize the conclusions. Sampling strategies, therefore, have been designed to select a subset of the population to represent the entire population.

The overarching concern in evaluating a sample in quantitative research is how well the sample represents the target population. A **representative sample** is one that looks like the target population in terms of important characteristics. Decisions with respect to sampling strategies are made in an effort to reduce sampling error. **Sampling error** is the difference between data obtained from the sample and data that would be obtained if the entire population were included in the study. Thus, to the extent that the sample from which data were collected possesses important characteristics of the accessible and target populations, the findings can be used to develop EBP with these populations.

The major concern in evaluating a sample in qualitative research is how well the sample represents the phenomenon of interest. In other words, the sample must be appropriate to provide information on the research problem. The data provided by the sample need to be both sufficient and relevant. For example, in a qualitative study of the experience of becoming a parent, researchers interviewed first-time mothers and fathers (Widarsson, Engström, Tydén, Lundberg, & Hammar, 2015). The researchers used focus groups and personal interviews during pregnancy. They found the men and women willing and eager to talk about their feelings and the realities of their anticipated parenthood. Another qualitative study used focus groups consisting of women veterans to determine their attitudes and preferences related to intimate partner violence (IPV) screening within the Veterans Health Administration (Iverson et al., 2014). Researchers found that women believed such screening was important. This screening was true both for women who had experienced IPV and those who had not.

Two key elements in evaluating quantitative research are issues related to the internal and external validity of the findings. **Internal validity** refers to the extent to which the results of the study present an accurate picture of the real world. In other words, did the independent variable make a difference in the outcome, or were other factors at work? The choice of a sampling strategy is designed to reduce sampling bias, one of the threats to internal validity. Sampling bias is evident when groups of people are either underrepresented or overrepresented in a sample. When assessing the sample in a study, the researcher should ask, "Did any characteristics of the sample influence the outcomes of the study?" Another threat to internal validity is a change in the world or within research participants themselves during the course of the study. Imagine, for example, the effects of the events on and after September 11, 2001; the 2015 terror attacks in Paris; or in the aftermath of the 2017 floods, fires, and acts of terror on emotional, mental, and physical health and how they might affect study outcomes.

External validity, in contrast, refers to issues with generalizability of the findings from the research beyond the sample and situation that were studied. In other words, to whom and under which circumstances could the findings from this study be applied? When assessing the sample in a study, the researcher should ask, "How well does this group reflect the population as a whole?"

Internal and external validity do not apply in the same way to qualitative research. In qualitative studies, the sample is evaluated as to whether it is representative of the phenomenon of interest rather than representative of the population as a whole. When assessing the sample in a qualitative study, the researcher should ask, "Did the sample chosen have the ability to talk about a phenomenon or an experience from the perspective of someone who was affected by it?"

▶ Whom to Sample?

The responsibility of the investigator is to specify the sampling criteria or the characteristics necessary to be part of the research sample. These criteria determine the target population. Sampling criteria may be very broad or very specific. These criteria are established to minimize bias or to control for irrelevant variability in the sample. Choosing a sample based on carefully selected criteria increases the strength of the evidence, thereby enhancing the ability to generalize the findings.

The researcher must make two different types of decisions—who should be considered for inclusion in the sample and who should be excluded from the sample. **Inclusion criteria** (sometimes called eligibility criteria) are characteristics that must be met to be considered for participation in the study. Here, the investigator specifies what the sample will look like and which characteristics all study participants will have in common.

Exclusion criteria are not the polar opposite of the inclusion criteria; rather, they are characteristics that, if present, would make persons ineligible to be in the sample, even though they might meet all of the inclusion criteria. These exclusions limit the representativeness of the sample and therefore the generalizability of the findings. As such, exclusion criteria should be specified after careful consideration. They should represent only those conditions or characteristics that might potentially make a difference in the outcome.

The specification of inclusion and exclusion criteria should not be taken lightly because of potential bias resulting in threats to internal validity and limitation of generalizability. Each criterion should be based on sound reasoning and be grounded in the goal of eliminating a potentially confounding effect on the outcome of the study. For example, in a study of predictors of diabetes-related quality of life in 17- to 19-year-olds in the last 6 months of high school, the researchers established the eligibility criteria to include having been diagnosed with diabetes mellitus type 1 for at least 1 year, having the ability to read and speak English, and living in a family unit with at least a parent or guardian (Hanna, Weaver, Slaven, Fotenberry, & DiMeglio, 2014). Individuals were eliminated if they had a significant psychiatric disorder or a secondary chronic illness that interfered with establishing independence (Hanna et al., 2014)

⬆ THINK OUTSIDE THE BOX

Discuss potential threats to generalizability when a study sets specific eligibility and exclusion criteria for the sample population.

▶ How to Sample?

Two categories of sampling strategies—probability and nonprobability sampling—are noted within the research process. **Probability sampling** employs specific strategies designed to yield an unbiased (i.e., representative) sample by giving each element the possibility of being selected. The elements, which are each potential members of a sample, are chosen at random (by chance). **Nonprobability sampling** does not include random selection of elements and therefore has a higher possibility of yielding a biased (i.e., nonrepresentative) sample. In this case, researchers use elements that are accessible and available. The researcher has no means for estimating the probability that an element will be included in the sample.

The researcher makes the choice of whether to use a probability or nonprobability strategy based on the problem under investigation and the purpose of the study. Quantitative studies can use either probability or nonprobability sampling strategies. All decisions made about sampling in quantitative studies are based on maximizing the representativeness of the sample. Qualitative studies, because of their very nature, employ nonprobability sampling strategies. All decisions made about sampling in qualitative studies are based on maximizing the representativeness of the phenomenon of interest.

⬆ THINK OUTSIDE THE BOX

Select an article. Based on the article's description of the sample, differentiate among the following terms: *target population, accessible population, representative sample, population,* and *sample.*

Probability Sampling Strategies

Probability sampling is the most well-respected type of sampling for quantitative studies because it is more likely to produce a representative sample. It is not the same thing as random assignment, however. Random assignment is the process of randomly placing subjects in an experimental study in different treatment groups. **Random sampling** involves processes in which each element of the population has an equal chance of being in the sample. Four probability sampling strategies are commonly used: (1) simple random, (2) stratified random, (3) cluster, and (4) systematic random.

Simple random sampling is a process in which the researcher defines the population, lists and consecutively numbers all elements of the population, and then randomly selects a sample from this list. The most simplistic method of simple random sampling is to put all the numbers in a hat or container and draw out the desired number of elements. Obviously, this technique would work only for a study with a very small number of elements. For larger lists, the researcher can assign a number to each element and then use a computer program to randomly select the number of elements desired for the sample.

The random selection of the sample may also be accomplished by using a table of random numbers (**TABLE 10-1**). With this strategy, the researcher begins at any point on the list of numbers and reads consecutive numbers in any direction, choosing those numbers that correspond to the numbered elements in the population until the desired sample size is reached. For example, if you have a list of 50 elements from which to choose a random sample of 15, each element would be numbered from 01 to 50. If you closed your eyes and pointed at the data in Table 10-1 and your finger ended up on the numeral 91254, deciding to go across the rows to the right, the first two-digit number would be 91 (91254), which is not in your range of possibilities. The next two-digit number would be 25 (91254); that element would be selected, as would 42 (91254 24090), and 40 (24090). The next two-digit number would be 90 (24090), which is not in your range, followed by 25 (25752), which you have already selected, then 75 (25752), which is not in your range. Thus, the next elements selected would be 24 (25752 42831), 28 (42831), and 31 (42831). This process would continue until 15 elements were selected. Simple random selection is not widely used because it is rather cumbersome and inefficient. Furthermore, it is rare to have the ability to list every element in the population.

Stratified random sampling is a variation on the simple random sampling technique. When the composition of a population with respect to some characteristic important to the study is known, the population is divided into two or more strata (groups) based on that characteristic. Simple random selection is then used to

TABLE 10-1 Excerpt from a Table of Random Numbers				
65321	41047	96423	34988	12015
16523	87651	54210	26792	46234
69874	42036	69723	45631	89063
34702	15423	91254	24090	25752
42831	74369	17961	59467	13265
95032	20348	62349	27478	72159

pick elements from each group. This selection strategy makes each group homogenous as far as the characteristic of interest is concerned. Examples of characteristics upon which stratification may be made include gender, age, ethnicity, occupation, education, and so forth. For example, Versnik Nowak et al. (2015) studied college students' use of complementary and alternative medicine in a sample stratified by grade level and preprofessional program; Suh, Ma, Dunaway, and Theall (2016) examined pregnancy intention and postpartum depression in a sample stratified by race. If desired, the researcher may use proportional sampling to ensure that the sample accurately reflects the composition of the population on the characteristic by which the population was stratified. If, for example, 60% of the known population is male, the researcher might want to randomly select 60 males and 40 females for a total sample of 100. Proportional sampling is not generally a wise choice if the strata are of extremely disproportionate sizes.

Cluster sampling, also called multistage sampling, is a probability sampling strategy in which not all the elements of the population need to be known. This strategy employs random selection of first larger sampling units (clusters), then successively smaller clusters, either by simple or stratified random selection techniques. It is a particularly efficient strategy when the population is large and spread out over a large geographic area. For example, in a comparison of emergency preparedness of the citizens of Oakland County, Michigan (population 1.2 million), 30 clusters (census blocks) were identified and 7 households in each cluster were interviewed (Nyaku et al., 2014). Interviewing the entire target population (all households in the county) would have been an impossible task. By identifying and selecting neighborhoods and then households within neighborhoods, however, researchers could conduct an overall assessment in a short period of time (3 days).

⚡ THINK OUTSIDE THE BOX

Why is the use of a sample randomly selected from a population a stronger sampling method than the use of a nonrandomized sample? Discuss the value of having the strongest sampling method possible for the research to be conducted.

Systematic random sampling is a probability sampling technique in which elements are randomly selected from the population at predetermined, fixed intervals. The researcher first determines the desired sample size and then decides on the sampling interval. If the researcher has a list of the elements in the population, the sampling interval is determined by dividing the total population by the desired sample size. Suppose the population includes 750 individuals and the sample size is 50; in this case, the sampling interval would be 15. The researcher selects the first element randomly and then selects every 15th element thereafter to obtain the 50 elements for the sample. If the list is exhausted before the sample size is reached, counting resumes at the top of the list. This technique produces a random sample in a more efficient manner than is possible with simple randomization. For example, in a study of the role of gender in mental health and delinquent behaviors, systematic random sampling was used to select adolescents detained in Connecticut juvenile detention centers (Grigorenko, Sullivan, & Chapman, 2015). Chart reviews were then used to gather data relevant to the research question.

Nonprobability Sampling Strategies

The second broad category of sampling strategies is nonprobability sampling. These techniques are less likely to produce samples that are representative of the population. Nonetheless, they are more widely used in many disciplines, including nursing, because such samples are generally easier to obtain. Commonly used nonprobability sampling strategies include (1) convenience sampling, (2) quota sampling, (3) purposive sampling, (4) snowball sampling, and (5) theoretic sampling.

Convenience sampling is the process of selecting elements to be in the sample simply because they are readily available. Also called accidental sampling, it is the simplest and potentially least representative of all the sampling strategies. It is also currently the most frequently used sampling strategy in nursing research studies. Hanna and colleagues (2014) used convenience sampling in their recruitment of adolescents, and Iverson and colleagues (2014) used convenience sampling in obtaining their sample of women veterans.

Quota sampling begins with the researcher identifying strata of the population and then determining the number of elements in each stratum necessary to represent the population proportionately. Actual selection of elements from each stratum is then accomplished in the same way as in convenience sampling. In a study of the impact of chronic migraine, quota sampling was used to recruit a sample from an Internet research panel that was broadly representative of the U.S. population (Adams et al., 2015).

Purposive sampling, also called judgmental sampling, is a sampling strategy in which participants are handpicked by the researcher, either because they are typical of the phenomenon of interest or because they are knowledgeable about the issues under investigation. This strategy is often used when the researcher desires a sample consisting of experts. Bray (2015) used this strategy to recruit 8 parents in her evaluation of their experiences of hope following their child's brain injury.

Snowball sampling, also known as network sampling, is a sampling strategy in which participants already in the study are asked to provide referrals to potential study subjects. Watson Campbell (2015) used purposive snowball sampling to recruit volunteers for her study of individuals who were discharged from a hospice program because of decertification. Tonsing (2015), in describing the recruitment of the 14 women in her study of South Asian women's experience of domestic violence, stated that participants were recruited primarily from social service agencies working with ethnic minorities. Since participants were asked to refer other women who had experienced domestic violence episodes, the sampling method depicted is one of snowball sampling.

Snowball sampling is a particularly good strategy to use when potential participants in the study are challenging to find, as might be the case, for example, with vegetarians, drug abusers, persons engaged in prostitution, people with a specific disability or rare condition, and homeless individuals.

⏀ THINK OUTSIDE THE BOX

Convenience sampling is the most commonly used sampling method. Which steps would you expect to see used within a study to strengthen the study in this type of sampling method?

Theoretical sampling is generally restricted to qualitative research methods, especially in conjunction with grounded theory. It is most analogous to the purposive sampling strategy. As the study unfolds and the interviews conducted with the first few participants are analyzed, conceptual categories and themes are identified. Subsequent decisions as to who will provide data and which data will be gathered are then based on who has already been sampled and which data have already been provided. Sampling and data collection continue until all the categories and themes are "saturated"—that is, no additional categories or themes are emerging, and no new facets of existing categories and themes are uncovered. Shimoinaba, O'Connor, Lee, and Kissane (2015) used theoretical sampling to select the 18 participants for a grounded theory exploration of the resilience of nurses working in palliative care and their own self-care.

▶ How Many to Sample?

Once the researcher has decided whom to sample and how the sampling will be done, it is time to make the decision about how many elements need to be in the sample. The question of sample size is a crucial one when the objective is the ability to generalize the findings to a larger population. The generally accepted recommendation is to sample as many elements as possible. It is wise to remember, however, that the validity of a study begins with the design. Even the largest of samples cannot make up for faulty design.

Quantitative Studies

Several factors must be considered when deciding about the desired sample size in quantitative studies, including factors related to (1) the population, (2) the study design, (3) measurement, and (4) practicability.

Population Factors

Population-related factors that influence required sample size include the homogeneity of the population; the expected rate of the phenomenon, event, or outcome being measured; and the anticipated attrition rate. In a population that is homogenous (i.e., in which sampling elements are very similar to one another), the required sample size is generally smaller than if the population were more heterogeneous. Similarly, if the phenomenon, event, or outcome occurs frequently, a smaller sample size is needed than if occurrences are infrequent.

In longitudinal studies, attrition may be a problem. When this phenomenon is anticipated, researchers often "overenroll" participants in the research. For example, if a study was expected to have an attrition rate of 20% (i.e., if 100 subjects were to begin the study, only 80 would complete it), then the researcher would enroll 125 participants to have the desired 100 at completion.

Design Factors

Design factors influencing sample size include the type of study, the number of variables, and the sampling strategy. Quantitative studies in general require larger sample sizes than do qualitative studies. Some differences also occur in relation to the quantitative designs themselves. First, a study that is more complex requires a larger sample size. For example, a study employing a longitudinal data collection plan needs to enroll increased numbers of participants at the beginning because of the increased possibility of losing subjects over the course of the study (sample attrition). Second, as the number of variables being measured increases, so does the needed sample size. Third, the sampling strategy itself can affect the required sample size. Stratified random sampling and quota sampling techniques, for example, allow the researcher to use smaller sample sizes than would be needed in studies employing simple random or convenience sampling because some of the representativeness is already built into the stratification procedure.

Measurement Factors

Measurement factors that influence sample size include the sensitivity of the research instruments and the effect that the process has on the outcome. Data collection instruments in which measurement error is minimal are said to be precise. The less precise the instrument, the larger the sample size might need to be. Because interval-level data are generally more precise, from a sample size perspective it is best to measure at that level if possible because a smaller sample size may be used.

Practical Factors

Practical factors such as cost and convenience also influence sample size. Although population factors, design factors, and measurement factors certainly affect the ideal sample size, practical factors like cost and convenience often prove most influential. When this is the case, adjustments in design and/or sampling strategies need to be made to strengthen the internal validity of the study.

Given these practical factors, how do researchers determine the sample size needed for a particular study? Some use the "rule of 30," which utilizes 30 subjects for each group or 30 subjects for each variable. This notion is based on the central limit theorem, which asserts that, in a randomly generated sample of 30 or more subjects, the mean of a characteristic approximates the population mean (Hinkle, Wiersma, & Jurs, 1988). It is essential to remember, however, that representativeness is more important than sample size. The "rule of 30" should therefore be considered the minimum acceptable sample size rather than the ideal.

The gold standard in determining sample size is power analysis, a statistical calculation of the number of subjects needed to accurately reject the null hypothesis (Jupiter, 2014). The actual calculation of sample size is beyond the scope of this text. The most commonly used significance level is 0.05, and the standard power is 0.80. The effect size is estimated based on pilot studies undertaken by the researcher or on reports in the literature drawn from previous studies on the same or similar problems. Performing the power analysis prior to conducting a study strengthens the study's credibility concerning the size of the sample utilized. For example, here is the description of the power analysis for a study of the impact of self-management strategies for individuals with long-term indwelling urinary catheters (Wilde et al., 2015): The power calculations employed a significance level of .05 and 80% power. With these levels set, the assessment revealed that a sample size of

220 (160 completers) would deliver appropriate power to distinguish an effect size at a medium effect sizes, which would identify a 15% to 30% difference between groups (Wilde et al., 2015).

Power analysis formulas are sometimes applied after the fact to determine the power of a test given the sample size and results obtained. Sometimes the formula is used on a post hoc basis to determine the optimal sample size. For example, in a study investigating the use of a postdelivery epidural saline bolus on time to full motor recovery in 46 parturients, the post hoc analysis revealed that a sample of 204 would have been necessary to show significance (Couture et al., 2016). Had this power analysis been done a priori, a larger sample size might have been employed, and the results would have been more meaningful.

Qualitative Studies

Qualitative studies generally employ relatively small, nonrandom samples. Because the aim of qualitative research is to describe and analyze the meanings and experiences of particular individuals or groups, large sample sizes are not generally appropriate or feasible in these scenarios. Instead, the sample size should be sufficient to provide enough information to answer the research question based on the notion of data saturation. Participants continue to be enrolled in a study until no new information is being uncovered; that is, redundancy occurs in all subsequent data collection encounters.

⬆ THINK OUTSIDE THE BOX

What would be the implications of the rule of 30 applied to qualitative research?

Redundancy may be achieved with a limited number of participants when the sample is homogenous. For this reason, it is not unusual to have very small sample sizes in phenomenological studies. For example, Fecher-Jones and Taylor (2015) had 11 participants in their study of patients who had laparoscopic colon resection and participated in an enhanced recovery program, and Bray (2015) interviewed eight parents of children with brain injuries in her evaluation of their experiences of hope. Sometimes a case study approach is used to examine concepts related to a specific, often rare, condition, such as Woolston's (2017) description of one patient's struggle with Felty's syndrome.

In contrast, for ethnographic or grounded theory studies in which the sample is usually more heterogeneous, larger sample sizes are generally the norm. For example, an ethnography approach was used with 21 adult tribal members who shared their perspectives on significant family health concerns (Martin, Yurkovich, & Anderson, 2016), 41 adults living with a long-term condition who supplied the data on which a grounded theory of mindfulness as a facilitator of transition was developed (Long, Briggs, Long, & Astin, 2016), and 24 women veterans who provided data with respect to screening for intimate partner violence (Iverson et al., 2014).

▶ Specific EBP Considerations

Evidence-based clinical decisions are essential for the practice of nursing. Melnyk and Fineout-Overholt (2015) have rightly asserted, "The goal of EBP is to use the highest quality of knowledge in providing care to produce the greatest impact on patients' health status and healthcare" (p. 75). It is imperative, therefore, to have the ability to critically examine the available research and to determine the strength of the evidence. Several guiding questions can help direct reading about and critiquing sampling plans. While these questions are similar in some respects in both quantitative and qualitative research, they differ in many other respects (**TABLE 10-2**).

Quantitative Evidence Critique

A well-written quantitative research report contains a detailed explanation of the sampling strategy (including sample size determination) and the inclusion and exclusion criteria, together with the rationale for their use. Richards, Ogata, and Cheng (2016), for example, provided the following description of the sampling plan in their discussion of measures of dog walking as an intervention to promote well-being. The power analysis calculation established a level of 19 dog owners needed for each of the two groups (intervention and control) (power = .80, when α = .05). To ensure a successful study, the researchers set a goal to recruit at least 21 dog owners per group for a total sample size of 42 to allow for dropouts from the study. The inclusion criterion was designated as dog owners age 18 years

TABLE 10-2 Guidelines for Critiquing the Sample for EBP	
Quantitative Research Studies	■ How and when was the desired sample size determined? ■ Was the sample size adequate to answer the research question? ■ What were the inclusion and exclusion criteria? ■ Was the sampling strategy one of probability or nonprobability? Was this strategy appropriate to the research question? ■ Is the sample for the study clearly described? ■ Are there potential biases in the sample selection or the sample itself that could influence the outcome of the study? ■ Is the sample representative of the target population? Is it representative of your own patients?
Qualitative Research Studies	■ Which sampling strategy was used to choose the participants? ■ Was the sample size adequate to answer the research question? ■ Is the sample for the study clearly described? ■ Is the sample representative of the phenomenon of interest?

or older who stated a minimum of dog walking periods in a typical week (<20 minutes per week). Participants were expected to utilize email regularly. Exclusion criteria encompassed known cardiac or pulmonary disease, joint instability, pregnancy, and known thyroid disease.

A well-written quantitative research report also thoroughly describes the demographic characteristics of the sample that actually participated in the study as including 49 initial individuals. Participants were middle age (M = 45.7 years, SD = 13.4), female (79.6%), and Caucasian (100%) with at least a 2-year college degree (Richards et al., 2016).

Descriptions such as these allow readers to determine the representativeness of the sample for their own population and establish the strength of the evidence for implementing the findings.

Qualitative Evidence Critique

A well-written qualitative research report also contains a detailed explanation of the sampling strategy and a description of the sample obtained. Moulin, Akre, Rodondi, Ambresin, and Suris (2015), for example, described the plan they used to recruit participants in their study of adolescents with medically unexplained symptoms (MUSs). Recruitment of participants was completed through the pediatric department (adolescent health, orthopedics, gastroenterology, and rheumatology clinics) of a university hospital located in Switzerland. Adolescents between the ages of 12 and 20 years and who spoke French fluently and had presented with MUS(s) for at least six months were eligible to participate along with their parents. A list of patients who met the inclusion criteria, along with their postal addresses, was provided by the designated clinics. The researchers sent out a letter to each adolescent and her or his parents describing the study aim with an invitation to contact the research team if they were interested in participating in a focus group session.

Evaluating the Evidence for Implementation

Once the sample characteristics and size have been critically analyzed, the next step in determining appropriateness for consideration for EBP is to establish whether this evidence, however good, is applicable in the local situation. For example, in a study of a smoking cessation intervention for pregnant women, Chertok and Archer (2015) employed an intervention using the five A's program (ask, advise, assess, assist, arrange) that was effective in decreasing smoking among pregnant women. Abroms and colleagues (2015) devised a mobile phone smoking cessation program (Quit4baby) in which encouraging and motivational messages were sent to participants via text messaging. The samples in both studies were primarily Caucasian, were married or living with a partner, and had at least a high school education.

A nurse who wanted to implement a smoking cessation program with a population that was primarily from ethnic minority groups would need to consider carefully whether the strategy designed by these researchers could be applied in the local setting. An alternative in this situation would be to examine the smoking cessation strategies employed in the studies conducted by Mahoney and colleagues (2014) and Nair, Patterson, Rodriguez, and Collins (2017), whose samples were predominantly from ethnic minorities, unmarried, and unemployed and had a high school education or less.

> ## 📦 THINK OUTSIDE THE BOX
>
> Specific EBP considerations: Identify the demographic characteristics of a sample that would be representative of the population with whom you are currently working in a clinical course.

Sampling Decisions for an Evidence-Based Project

After identifying the clinical question or problem on which to build an evidence-based project and deciding, based on the strength of the evidence, on an appropriate intervention or change in practice, a sampling decision must be made. Based on the information contained in this chapter, it should be clear that the best (i.e., the strongest) sampling technique would be a random assignment of patients to either the nursing intervention or the standard of care. If it were not possible to randomize the participants, then a nonrandom sampling plan would be appropriate if efforts to build in representativeness through matching or purposive sampling procedures were used.

▶ Conclusion

Although they are only one component in the overall research process, sampling decisions affect the internal validity and the external validity of a study. Critical analysis of the sampling strategy, the sample size, and the quality of the sample is essential in determining the relevance of the results of one study, or a group of studies, to EBP for nurses.

Summary Points

1. The population of interest is that group to whom the researcher wants to be able to characterize and generalize.
2. Sampling allows a researcher to draw conclusions about the research problem under investigation based on information from a portion of the population rather than from the whole population.
3. The researcher selects a sample from an accessible population that is representative of the target population to whom the findings may be generalized.
4. Probability sampling strategies employ random selection of elements of the population. Probability strategies include simple random, systematic random, stratified random, and cluster sampling.
5. Nonprobability sampling strategies employ nonrandom selection of elements of the population. Nonprobability strategies include convenience, quota, purposive, snowball, and theoretical sampling.
6. Sampling decisions in quantitative research are made based on the desire to have a representative sample. Sampling strategies include both probability and nonprobability strategies.

7. Sampling decisions in qualitative research are made based on the desire to obtain data that are representative of the phenomenon of interest. Sampling strategies are almost always nonprobability strategies.

8. Critiquing studies to determine their relevance for EBP involves evaluation of the sampling plan, sampling strategies, and sample size for their appropriateness to the research question and the research design.

⚑ RED FLAGS

- Randomization of a sample group strengthens a study. Bias within the sampling process is decreased by randomization.
- The appropriate sample size for a quantitative study is best established by performing a power analysis before the study gets under way.
- Convenience and snowball sampling methodologies are weak sampling methods owing to their higher potential for lack of generalizability and potential for bias.
- At the least, inclusion criteria should be documented for review within the research report. Both inclusion and exclusion criteria should be provided.
- Failure to utilize the rule of 30 can weaken a study.
- Inadequate or unclear description of the sampling strategy results in confusion when others attempt to understand the study's conclusions.
- Failure to use a sampling strategy that would produce a sample size appropriate for the particular research method leads to a limitation for the study.
- Attempts to generalize findings past the representativeness of the sample are inappropriate.
- Failure to acknowledge limitations resulting from sample size or sample selection decisions is problematic.

Multiple-Choice Questions

1. Which of the following types of studies would require the largest sample size?
    A. Correlational study
    B. Ethnography
    C. Grounded theory
    D. Phenomenology

2. A nurse researcher who is interested in studying the career paths of deans of nursing programs approached six deans whom she knew had been active in the American Association of Colleges of Nursing and asked them to participate in her study. This sampling strategy reflects:
    A. convenience sampling.
    B. network sampling.
    C. purposive sampling.
    D. inappropriate sampling.

3. Determination of appropriate sample size in qualitative research is based on the principles of:
    A. power analysis.
    B. the rule of 30.
    C. saturation and redundancy.
    D. convenience and access.

4. Which of the following samples is least likely to be representative of the overall population?
   A. Convenience
   B. Quota
   C. Random
   D. Stratified random

5. A total of 20 nursing students are randomly selected from a random sample of five nursing programs in one state. This is an example of what type of sampling?
   A. Simple random
   B. Cluster
   C. Convenience
   D. Purposive

6. A total of 20 nursing students are randomly selected from a random sample of five nursing programs in one state. Which of the following would be the largest of the groups?
   A. Accessible population
   B. Control group
   C. Sample
   D. Target population

7. A total of 20 nursing students are randomly selected from a random sample of five nursing programs in one state. Which of the following would be the largest of the identified groups?
   A. Accessible population
   B. Control group
   C. Sample
   D. Target population

Multiple Answer

8. A sample included 473 women: 106 had unplanned cesarean deliveries, 113 had planned cesarean deliveries, and 254 had vaginal deliveries. All of the women who had vaginal deliveries and the majority (79%) who had unplanned cesarean deliveries were recruited from childbirth education classes. The sample was predominantly white, and all subjects spoke English, had no major prenatal complications or underlying medical problems, and delivered healthy full-term infants. Which of the following represent sample characteristics? Choose all that apply.
   A. Type of delivery
   B. Predominantly white
   C. Spoke English
   D. Recruited from childbirth classes

9. A researcher's decisions related to sampling affect which of the following? Choose all that apply.
   A. Internal consistency
   B. Internal validity
   C. External validity
   D. Choice of target population

Short Answer

1. A sample included 473 women: 106 had unplanned cesarean deliveries, 113 had planned cesarean deliveries, and 254 had vaginal deliveries. All of the women who had vaginal deliveries and the majority (79%) who had unplanned cesarean deliveries were recruited from childbirth education classes. The sample was predominantly white, and all subjects spoke English, had no major prenatal complications or underlying medical problems, and delivered healthy full-term infants. What is the percentage of the women in the sample who had a cesarean section? If rounding is necessary, round to the nearest tenth.

Discussion Questions

1. You are a nurse working in the labor and delivery suite in an academic medical center. You are interested in nonpharmacologic pain management for your patients and would like to implement an evidence-based change project on your unit. Which particular sampling concerns will you examine in the research studies about nonpharmacologic pain management for laboring patients?
2. You are a BSN student enrolled in a research course. The instructor has given you the following problem statement: "Does music affect the perception of pain in patients who have undergone hip replacement?" Describe one probability sampling plan and one nonprobability sampling plan for answering this question.
3. Read the excerpt that follows from an article describing a study testing a self-management intervention for long-term indwelling catheters, and answer the following questions:
    *   What is the sampling strategy used?
    *   What were the inclusion and exclusion criteria?
    *   What are the sample characteristics?
    *   Is this sample representative?
    *   How could the sampling strategy be improved?

Participants consisted of community-dwelling individuals recruited in two distinct regions by two study sites: (a) a university in a large northeastern U.S. state and (b) a home care agency that conducts research in a large metropolitan area in the same state. For the university site, participants were recruited through nurses or physicians. . . . In the home care agency, their database was used to identify potential participants. . . . Screening for eligibility and interest in participation was conducted by phone. . . . Eligible participants were adults aged 18 and above. Inclusion criteria were as follows: (a) expect to use an indwelling urethral or suprapubic catheter for at least 1 year and will be in the study region for at least 4 months; (b) can complete study measurements alone or with the help of a caregiver; (c) speak English; and (d) have access to a telephone. . . . Individuals were excluded for terminal illness or cognitive impairments. Children under 18 were not included. . . . Ages ranged from 19 to 96 years (Mdn = 61). The range in duration of catheter use was 1–470 months

(39 years). Self-reported diagnoses involved spinal cord injury (40%), multiple sclerosis (23%), diabetes (12%), stroke (2%), prostate (10%), spina bifida (1%), neurogenic bladder not otherwise reported (8%), Parkinson's disease (2%), and others (3%). (Wilde et al., 2015, pp. 25, 28)

Suggested Readings

Cleary, M., Horsfall, J., & Hayter, M. (2014). Data collection and sampling in qualitative research: Does size matter? *Journal of Advanced Nursing, 70*(3), 473–475. http://dx.doi.org/10.1111 /jan.12163

Kandola, D., Banner, D., O'Keefe-McCarthy, S., & Jassal, D. (2014). Sampling methods in cardiovascular nursing research: An overview. *Canadian Journal of Cardiovascular Nursing, 24*(3), 15–18.

References

Abroms, L. C., Johnson, P. R., Heminger, C. L., Van Alstyne, J. M., Leavitt, L. E., Schindler-Ruwisch, J. M., & Bushar, J. A. (2015). Quit4baby: Results from a pilot test of a mobile smoking cessation program for pregnant women. *Journal of Medical Internet Research, 3*(1), e10. http://dx.doi .org/10.2196/mhealth.3846

Adams, A. M., Serrano, D., Buse, D. C., Reed, M. L., Marske, V., Fanning, K. M., & Lipton, R. B. (2015). The impact of chronic migraine: The Chronic Migraine Epidemiology and Outcomes (CaMEO) Study methods and baseline results. *Cephalalgia: An International Journal of Headache, 35*(7), 563–578. http://dx.doi.org/10.1177/0333102414552532

Antwi, Y. A., Moriya, A. S., Simon, K., & Sommers, B. D. (2015). Changes in emergency department use among young adults after the Patient Protection and Affordable Care Act's dependent coverage provision. *Annals of Emergency Medicine, 65*(6), 664–672. http://dx.doi.org/10.1016/j .annemergmed.2015.01.010

Bray, L. (2015). Parents' experiences of hope following a child's brain injury. *Nursing Children and Young People, 27*(7), 22–26. http://dx.doi.org/10.7748/ncyp.27.7.22.e618

Chertok, I. R., & Archer, S. H. (2015). Evaluation of a midwife- and nurse-delivered 5 A's prenatal smoking cessation program. *Journal of Midwifery & Women's Health, 60,* 175–181. http://dx.doi .org/10.1111/jmwh.12220

Couture, D., Osborne, L., Peterson, J. A., Clements, S. M., Sanders, A., Spring, J. A., & Spence, D. L. (2016). Effects of a 30-mL epidural normal saline bolus on time to full motor recovery in parturients who received patient-controlled epidural analgesia with 0.125% Bupivacaine with 2 μg/mL of fentanyl. *Journal of the American Association of Nurse Anesthetists, 84*(3), 159–165.

Fecher-Jones, I., & Taylor, C. (2015). Lived experience, enhanced recovery and laparoscopic colonic resection. *British Journal of Nursing, 24*(4), 223–228. http://dx.doi.org/10.12968/bjon .2015.24.4.223

Grigorenko, E. L., Sullivan, T., & Chapman, J. (2015). An investigation of gender differences in a representative sample of juveniles detained in Connecticut. *International Journal of Law and Psychiatry, 38,* 84–91. http://dx.doi.org/10.1016/j.ijlp.2015.01.011

Hanna, K. M., Weaver, J. E., Slaven, J., Fortenberry, D., & DiMeglio, L. A. (2014). Diabetes-related quality of life and the demands and burdens of diabetes care among emerging adults with type 1 diabetes in the year after high school graduation. *Research in Nursing & Health, 37,* 399–408. http://dx.doi.org/10.1002/nur.21620

Hinkle, D., Wiersma, W., & Jurs, S. (1988). *Applied statistics for the behavioral sciences* (2nd ed.). Boston, MA: Houghton-Mifflin.

Iverson, K. M., Huang, K., Wells, S. Y., Wright, J. D., Gerber, M. R., & Wiltsey-Stirman, S. (2014). Women veterans' preferences for intimate partner violence screening and response procedures within the Veterans Health Administration. *Research in Nursing & Health, 37,* 302–311. http:// dx.doi.org/10.1002/nur.21602

Jupiter, D. C. (2014). Counting your chickens before they're hatched: Power analysis. *Journal of Foot and Ankle Surgery, 53,* 519–520. http://dx.doi.org/10.1053/j.jfas.2014.05.001

Long, J., Briggs, M., Long, A., & Astin, F. (2016). Starting where I am: A grounded theory exploration of mindfulness as a facilitator of transition in living with a long-term condition. *Journal of Advanced Nursing, 72*(10), 2445–2456. http://dx.doi.org/10.1111/jan.12998

Mahoney, M. C., Erwin, D. O., Widman, C., Masucci Twarozek, A., Saad-Harfouche, F. G., Underwood, W., & Fox C. H. (2014). Formative evaluation of a practice-based smoking cessation program for diverse populations. *Health* Education & *Behavior, 41*(2), 186–196. http://dx.doi.org/10.1177/1090198113504415

Martin, D., Yurkovich, E., & Anderson, K. (2016). American Indians' family health concern on a northern plains reservation: "Diabetes runs rampant here." *Public Health Nursing, 33*(1), 73–81. http://dx.doi.org/10.1111/phn.12225

Melnyk, B. M., & Fineout-Overholt, E. (2015). *Evidence-based practice in nursing and health-care: A guide to best practice* (3rd ed.). Philadelphia, PA: Lippincott Williams & Wilkins.

Moulin, V., Akre, C., Rodondi, P.Y., Ambresin, A.E., & Suris, J.C. (2015). A qualitative study of adolescents with medically unexplained symptoms and their parents. Part 1: Experiences and impact on daily life. *Journal of Adolescence, 45,* 307–316. http://dx.doi.org/10.1016/j.adolescence .2015.10.01

Nair, U. S., Patterson, F., Rodriguez, D., & Collins, B. N. (2017). A telephone-based intervention to promote physical activity during smoking cessation: A randomized controlled proof-of-concept study. *Translational Behavioral Medicine, 7*(2), 138–147. http://dx.doi.org/10.1007/s13142-016 -0449-x

Nyaku, M. K., Wolkin, A. F., McFadden, J., Collins, J., Murti, M., Schnall, A., . . . Bayleyegn, T. M. (2014). Assessing radiation emergency preparedness planning by using community assessment for public health emergency response (CASPER) methodology. *Prehospital and Disaster Medicine, 29,* 262–269. http://dx.doi.org/10.1017/S1049023X14000491

Richards, E. A., Ogata, N., & Cheng, C. W. (2015). Evaluation of the dogs, physical activity, and walking (Dogs PAW) intervention: A randomized controlled trial. *Nursing Research, 65*(3), 191–201. http://dx.doi.org/10.1097/NNR.0000000000000155

Shimoinaba, K., O'Connor, M., Lee, S., & Kissane, D. (2015). Nurses' resilience and nurturance of the self. *International Journal of Palliative Nursing, 21*(10), 504–510. http://dx.doi.org/10.12968 /ijpn.2015.21.10.50

Suh, E. Y., Ma, P., Dunaway, L. F., & Theall, K. P. (2016). Pregnancy intention and post-partum depressive affect in Louisiana pregnancy risk assessment monitoring system. *Maternal and Child Health Journal, 20*(5), 1001–1013. http://dx.doi.org/10.1007/s10995-015-1885-9

Tonsing, J. C. (2015). Domestic violence: Intersection of culture, gender and context. *Journal of Immigrant and Minority Public Health, 18*(2), 442–446. http://dx.doi.org/10.1007/s10903 -015-0193-1

Versnik Nowak, A. L., DeGise, J., Daugherty, A., O'Keefe, R., Seward, S., Setty, S., & Tang, F. (2015). Prevalence and predictors of complementary and alternative medicine (CAM) use among Ivy League college students: Implications for student health services. *Journal of American College Health, 63*(6), 362–372. http://dx.doi.org/10.1080/07448481

Watson Campbell, R. (2015). Being discharged from hospice alive: The lived experience of patients and families. *Journal of Palliative Medicine, 18*(6), 495–499. http://dx.doi.org/10.1089 /jpm.2014.0228

Widarsson, M., Engström, G., Tydén, T., Lundberg, P., & Hammar, L. M. (2015). "Paddling upstream": Fathers' involvement during pregnancy as described by expectant fathers and mothers. *Journal of Clinical Nursing, 24*(7–8), 1059–1068. http://dx.doi.org/10.1111/jocn.12784

Wilde, M. H., McMahon, J. M., McDonald, M. V., Tang, W., Wang, W., Brasch, J., . . . Chen, D. G. (2015). Self-management intervention for long-term indwelling urinary catheter users: Randomized clinical trial. *Nursing Research, 64*(1), 24–34. http://dx.doi.org/10.1097/NNR .0000000000000071

Woolston, W. (2017). Felty's syndrome: A qualitative case study. *MEDSURG Nursing, 26*(2), 105–118.

CHAPTER 11
Data Collection

Carol Boswell

CHAPTER OBJECTIVES

At the conclusion of this chapter, the learner will be able to:
1. Contrast a researcher's decision to use accessible data versus new data.
2. Distinguish among various forms of data collection processes.
3. Discuss the use of Big Data sets within the management of data.

KEY TERMS

Accessible data	Metadata
Big Data sets	Novel data
Biophysiological data	Observation
Closed-ended questions	Open-ended questions
Data collection	Predictive analytics
Data mining	Primary data
Focus group	Questionnaire
Interview	Secondary data
In vitro	Systematic review
In vivo	Tests
Meta-analysis	

▶ Overview of Data Collection Methods and Sources

According to Merriam-Webster (2018), data is defined as "factual information (such as measurements or statistics) used as a basis for reasoning, discussion, or calculation" (para 1). Data occur in various style and can be acquired through diverse methodologies. **Data collection** is a prelude to all aspects of the research process. The data collection process drives the tool selection, aids in the determination of the research methodology, speaks to the questions about sampling, and drives the selection of the statistical/evaluation process for the study. As a result, the approach for collecting data effectively determines the boundaries for a project. As a researcher begins to conceptualize the implementation of a research project, the question of the appropriate facts required for addressing the PICOT (population, intervention, comparison, outcome, time) question(s), research question(s), research purpose(s), and/or hypothesis(es) becomes significant and crucial. Data collected for research requires objectivity and logical organization. The independence and organization of the data collection practice establishes the generalizability of a research project's resulting outcomes to a broader population. By painstakingly constructing the research project with the data that will focus on the question introduced within the study, each facet of the research process turns out to be progressively more suitable to assemble the information needed to answer the significant question.

The specification of the outcome for each phase of the data collection plan is mandatory. When all aspects and/or variables of the data required for the study are established prior to the initiation of the study, the selection of the appropriate data collection method can be addressed effectively as part of this specification. This process decreases the potential for unintentionally omitting a key component of the data. Data collection is fundamental to the entire process, resulting in the need to consider carefully the use of different types of data and/or processes when making decisions about data collection methods. The characteristics of the data that are needed to address the study topic must be indicated in the methods discussion to allow for the collection of the needed data to answer completely the question/questions being considered.

Before delving into a discussion of the functions of data collection sources and data collection tools/instruments, it is helpful to have an understanding of the definitions of selected concepts. The term *source* within the data collection process of research focuses on the processes used to collect the data. These sources can be any tool or instrument or any process, such as interviewing, observation, or focus groups, by which information can be accessed. The sources for data collection can be varied but require a connection with the participants. Data collection "tools and/or instruments" comprise the actual physical devices employed to collect the information that is under investigation. The use of a tool or instrument does not mandate a direct connection with the participants because these tools could be delivered by mail or through the Internet. Tools and instruments can be hard-copy collection forms such as tests and questionnaires, but they can also be tools that provide physiological data such as laboratory equipment, weight scales, and X-ray reports.

Several major methods of data collection are available for use:

- Tests
- Questionnaires
- Interviews
- Focus groups
- Observations
- Biophysiological data
- Systematic reviews
- Existing or secondary data
- Big Data sets

The data set identified by the researcher for any selected study can usually be accessed by one or more of these methods. Each of the collection methods does provide unique attention to the data being collected along with the process for getting the optimal level of participation within the data collection process.

According to Polit and Beck (2017), the researcher must try to determine which data will effectively address the question under investigation, describe the sample characteristics, establish methods for controlling extraneous variables, analyze impending biases, recognize subgroup effects, and check for manipulation of the data. Creswell (2014) reinforces this notion by identifying the data collection steps, including (1) establishing the boundaries for the study, (2) accumulating the data through the appropriate methodologies, and (3) clarifying the process for recording and managing the data collected. As a result, the researcher has the responsibility to understand the different formats of data collection, the strengths and weaknesses of the different methods, and the specific needs recognized for the topic under evaluation.

▶ Accessible Data Versus New Data

As the researcher begins the process of clarifying the data collection process, a key question arises concerning the type of information that will be used to satisfy the question being investigated. Two types of data can be identified—accessible (existing) or new (novel). The aspects of each of these data types need to be considered conscientiously as the researcher determines the data collection process.

Accessible data may also be called existing data; they provide an essential source for use in research endeavors. This information may be located in preexisting reports (e.g., hospital records, databases, narrative journaling documents, historic documents). They can also be used as the basis for a secondary analysis of the data gathered in a previous study or as records developed for some other reason, such as hospital patient records and national databases. The use of preexisting records, often called a retrospective chart/record review, is common in nursing research because these documents are an economical and convenient source of information.

Questions do arise with this form of data. The records' biases and areas that may not have been collected with the initial collection raise concerns because the data must be used "as is." Accessible data cannot be expanded or further clarified. Secondary analysis of data allows for the use of data collected for a prior project to test one or more different hypotheses and illuminate fresh relationships located within the data. Using preexisting data does eliminate the time-consuming and costly process of collecting the data before beginning the analysis process. The use of accessible (existing) data serves as the foundation for evidence-based practice (EBP). Meta-analyses, synthesis analyses, and meta-syntheses, which use obtainable research reports as their underlying database, integrate the material to provide the foundation for evidence-based protocol guidelines.

New or **novel data** comprise original information collected for a specific study. This type of data is unique to the question or questions under investigation. The researcher needs to determine judiciously each component of data needed for the particular question(s). Within the time sequence allocated for the research project, all of the various pieces of data must be collected. The data collection plan should address each aspect of the needed information so that, at some point during the process, it is all collected for use during the analysis process. It is helpful during the process to consult a statistician to ensure that the data will address the key questions being investigated.

Another way to classify data is either as primary data or secondary data. **Primary data**, or novel data, are data generated through the actual conducting of an original study. Primary data provide direct access to the actual process being reported. The information comes from the source without any additional interpretations or modifications. In contrast, **secondary data**, or accessible data, are pulled from existing data and documents (Management Study Guide, 2013). Secondary data are pieces of information interpreted by the alternative reviewer or investigator. Each reviewer tends to include his or her individualized analysis of the information as it applies to a given situation. Thus, additional biases from the further interpretation of the materials may be introduced. This process of using accessible or secondary data is termed **data mining**.

▶ Key Categories of Data for Nursing Studies

Within any research design, the data collection process must be matched to the stated study aims and/or purpose. The process must reflect the particular strategies implemented during the study. Many data sources are available for use, including secondary data from national surveys and other secondary data sources such as Medicaid, demographic indicators, nonclinical program data, clinical program data, public comments, informant groups, questionnaire/interview surveys, screenings, and epidemiology surveys. Researchers must contemplate carefully and thoroughly the various methods of data collection and the various sources of data, thereby ensuring they select the most appropriate options.

🔼 THINK OUTSIDE THE BOX

Use the following examples of research questions to select a data collection method and justify your selection:

- What information has been used to determine the use of 6-hour nil per os (NPO), or not by mouth, status prior to an outpatient surgical procedure versus a 12-hour NPO status level?
- What information serves as the basis for the range of blood sugars used within newly diagnosed adolescent diabetics?
- What information could be used to determine if 10-hour shifts would be better for nurses to reduce burnout?

Orcher (2005) identified two feasible incentives for using established instruments. Established tools are identified as validated tools based on the number of times that the tool has been used successfully while fostering a reliable body of research. By using a validated tool for a study, the results can be compared and contrasted to prior studies that used the tool. As tools are used in subsequent studies, the validity and reliability of the tools are further established for different populations. These enticements can have a philosophical influence on the characteristic of the research study results:

- Initially, time and energy should be expended to ensure that the data collected are appropriate for the study question(s).
- Efforts to determine the appropriate data collection process have an impact on the effectiveness of the methodology in capturing the total picture needed to address the research problem.
- Care should be given to identifying any confounding variables that could adversely affect the research outcomes.

▶ Significant Facets of Data Collection Schemes

As the investigator establishes the data collection methodology for a study, questions concerning the consistency of the data collected from each participant become of paramount importance. The basic idea is that the data should be collected in the same manner for each of the participants so that unique environmental, societal, and physical effects are diminished. One aspect affecting research projects is what has been labeled the Hawthorne effect. The original study was conducted at the Hawthorne Works to determine the effect of lighting on a worker's productivity (New World Encyclopedia, 2014). The Hawthorne effect refers to the susceptibility of some individuals to labor harder and/or function better when being observed, such as in a research study. As Cherry (2015) states, "Individuals may change their behavior due to the attention they are receiving from researchers rather than because of any manipulation of independent variables" (para. 1). Concerns related to the Hawthorne effect, for example, must be considered carefully to minimize the potential of participants modifying their behaviors because they are affected—either positively or negatively—by being included in a study. As studies of the Hawthorne effect have shown, the simple act of being selected to participate in a project can result in the modification of the behavior being evaluated. This effect is real. Researchers must carefully consider all aspects of the data collection process to diminish the likelihood that the resulting modifications will be so pronounced that the data collected are of little value.

Another important aspect within the data collection process is interrater reliability. In studies that employ more than one data collector, the goal is to ensure accuracy so that each of the data collectors accumulates the information in basically the same way. According to Melnyk and Fineout-Overholt (2017), it is critical to prepare data collectors to use the instrument planned for use in a study. This planning allows for interrater reliability, or consistency, in the paradigm that is being observed at least 90% of the time (Melnyk & Fineout-Overholt, 2017). If the 90% rate cannot be accomplished, the researcher and data collectors must establish a level of agreement for the specific project that considers the element of chance. Items that have to be considered carefully within this process are the need to use the same questions by each data collector, the ordering of the question delivery, and the acceptability of providing interpretations to the participants. If one data collector completes these items but another does not, the results could be affected.

Now let's turn our attention to the types of data collection methods. In the remainder of this chapter, we will discuss, for each method, an overview of the method expectations, strengths of the method, and limitations resulting from its use.

▶ # Test Methods

Overview

The use of **tests** within the research process is a fairly common methodology for ascertaining the explicit intelligence, talents, behaviors, or cognitive endeavor that is under investigation. Frequently, the terms *tool, instrument,* and *standardized test* are used interchangeably to describe this research method. These devices are used within research to appraise characteristics, aptitude, accomplishments, and performance. The use of self-reporting strategies when the goal is collection of vast amounts of research information appears to be an effective process. Directness and versatility are two key benefits associated with the use of tests (especially standardized tests) to discover the information that is sought within a research project.

The Educational Testing Service (ETS; 2015) Testlink Test Collection Database contains descriptions of more than 25,000 instruments, including research and unpublished instruments. By searching the ETS database for available tools, a researcher can determine the related material prior to downloading any test. Should a tool not have all of the material needed for inclusion in a study, the author or publisher contact information is provided to allow for direct engagement with the developer of the tool to determine the appropriateness of the tool for use in other studies. Another resource for locating possible tools is a review of the literature on a topic. As research articles are reviewed with the literature review process, tools used in prior studies can be identified and evaluated. Other research reports may also provide insight concerning tools that have been used in other research projects about an identified topic. A final place to look when attempting to locate a tool is the Internet. Due to the constant expansion of the Internet, entering key words related to evaluation tools into a search engine can provide potential instruments to consider.

When a tool cannot be located to address a particular topic, the following eight steps, identified by Orcher (2005, p. 121), for building an appropriate instrument can be used:

- Develop a plan.
- Have the plan reviewed.
- Revise the plan in light of the review.
- Write items based on the plan.
- Have the items reviewed.
- Revise the items in light of the review.
- Pilot-test the instrument.
- Revise the instrument in light of the pilot test.

Because an instrument is essential in addressing a topic, the development of a unique instrument can be a suitable alternative when the researcher cannot locate an appropriate one for data collection.

The strengths and weaknesses associated with using tests are provided in **TABLE 11-1.** These aspects related to this use of data collection need to be considered carefully and thoughtfully as tools, instruments, and standardized tests are contemplated.

⬡ THINK OUTSIDE THE BOX

Discuss the ethical aspects of using covert data collection methods.

TABLE 11-1 Strengths and Weakness of Test Methods	
Strengths	**Weaknesses**
■ Each potential participant is offered the same benefits for agreeing to participate in the study. ■ The equivalency of the measurement across research populations is another benefit from using this form of data collection. ■ Tests and assessments provide additional valid and reliable data because they tend to reduce the identification of perceptions and opinions. ■ Usability of the tool within multiple population samples certifies the effectiveness of that tool. ■ Availability of reference group data grows providing additional support for the tool and the data collected via use of that tool. ■ Tests can be dispensed within a group setting, thus saving time, expense, and energy. ■ Interrater reliability is improved since the instructions are given to the group rather than repeatedly for each individual. ■ An extensive assortment of tests is available. ■ The same instrument/tool can be used both prior to and after an intervention for comparison of the changes in the results between phases. ■ Use of a tool allows for a structured, organized process. ■ Data can be easily used within the statistical analysis.	■ Fees may be required to be paid for each individual taking the tests. ■ Standardized tests may have biases within the construction of the tool. ■ Tests do not lend themselves to open-ended and probing types of questions. ■ Plans must be made on how to manage incomplete test documents. ■ Instruments/tools may not have complete psychometric data. ■ With predeveloped tests, the tool may not evaluate the variables for a specific project effectively.

▶ Questionnaire Methods

Overview

When a questionnaire is the tool used for data collection, the data collection method is a survey process. A survey necessitates the querying of individuals through the use of some device that contains questions to be answered. A **questionnaire** is a data collection tool completed by a participant, where the researcher has the intent to discover what the individual thinks about a specific item. Questionnaires can be employed to gather information concerning knowledge, attitudes, beliefs, and feelings. A questionnaire, which is a self-reporting device, can be provided as a paper-and-pencil format, a telephone survey, or a structured document uploaded to or created on the Internet, for example, those generated through companies such as SurveyMonkey. As a result, the device can be administered in person, by mail, by telephone, or via the Internet.

According to Brink and Wood (2001), questionnaires limit the replies possible because they involve directed answers to prearranged questions. Several types of questions can be incorporated into the questionnaire format, including dichotomous (yes or no), multiple choice, cafeteria, rank order, forced-choice ratings, checklists, calendar, and visual analog (Polit & Beck, 2017). The researcher should consider the question format while assessing the applicability of different tools. In one example, Brennan and Parsons (2017) employed a verbal rating scale as a pain scoring tool. This tool uses a list of words describing pain progressing from less to more intense pain. Prior to using the tool, Brennan and Parsons (2017) had the validity, reliability, and appropriateness of the tool confirmed for use in a clinical setting.

Should a researcher elect to develop a tool specific for the topic under investigation, several facets of the instrument should be vigilantly contemplated in designing the questionnaire (**BOX 11-1**). Of course, the entire tool must address the research

---

BOX 11-1 Design Tenets for Questionnaires

- Ensure that the tool addresses the research purpose, objectives, goals, and questions.
- Carefully consider the target population to make the questionnaire easy for them to use.
- Use simple, familiar language without jargon and with correct grammar.
- Compose each question to be understandable and concise.
- Consider sequencing the questions from impersonal to personal, less sensitive to more sensitive, and broad to specific.
- Avoid using questions that hint at or direct responses, use double negatives, or embarrass the participant.
- Verify that each question addresses only a single topic.
- Structure the tool by beginning with questions that stimulate interest, and group questions by topics.
- Cautiously word questions dealing with painful situations.
- Incorporate into the question all information necessary to address the issue under investigation.
- Construct the tool with the questions in the same order for each testing session to provide consistency in delivery and data collection.
- Ascertain the necessary format to accumulate the appropriate information: open-ended questions, closed-ended questions, mutually exclusive and exhaustive response categories, or response categories for closed-ended questions (rating scales, ranking, semantic differential, checklists).
- Use various items and approaches to appraise conceptual ideas.
- Carefully consider the use of reverse wording on some of the questions to eliminate the possibility of a "response set."
- Determine the coding and/or weighting of the responses prior to the administration of the tool.
- Conduct a pilot test of the tool with a select group of the target population to confirm the applicability of the tool.

focus and be appropriate for the target population. These two features are fundamental to the process of developing the questions and the format for the tool. The language employed within the instrument must be free of jargon, use familiar words, and be easily understood by the potential participants. Each statement should be short and specific and address only one concept. Care must be given to the wording to prevent any leading of the participants toward a specific response.

According to Boswell (2010), "Good questions endeavor to scrutinize, evaluate, translate, illuminate, and reflect relationships about the multiple fragments of data assembled on any given topic" (para. 1). While neutral wording for each statement should be the goal, the use of active verbs in the statement is conducive to analysis, synthesis, and evaluation of the situation, thus resulting in an optimal response (Boswell, 2010). Careful thought must be given to each step in the development of questions to be used in any type of query. The questions must connect back to the PICOT questions, research question/hypothesis, or research purpose. While some demographic questions are frequently included, the primary questions should be developed to address the problem/challenge being answered by the project.

The type of questions (open-ended versus closed-ended) is one of the initial concerns to be addressed in terms of the format of the instrument. **Open-ended questions** leave the direction of the answer up to the individual participant. This type of questioning is more frequently used to assess qualitative types of issues and exploratory research. In contrast, **closed-ended questions** force a response because the researcher provides the answers. Closed-ended questions lend themselves to the collection of quantitative data and quantitative (confirmatory) research.

When developing closed-ended questions, the tool developer must ensure that the categories used for the answers are mutually exclusive and exhaustive. An example of a mutually exclusive category is the classification of years of service to an organization. The potential choices must not overlap because overlapping of categories would cause confusion. Therefore, the ranges would need to be stated as follows: "Years of service: Less than 3, 4–6, 7–9, 10–12."

For categories to be exhaustive, every possible option must be presented as a potential selection piece. In the ranges provided in the preceding example about years of service, individuals who had worked 13 or more years would not be provided with an option that they could select. Keep in mind, however, that the researcher may not want a certain range. In such a case, the researcher will need to provide a rationale for the exclusion. An example of when a lack of a specific range might be appropriate is when the researcher opens the year range to include every year possible.

The tool developer needs to carefully consider the information that is being sought through the use of the questionnaire. As that decision is confirmed, the tool should then address each and every potential aspect of the information being collected. For example, the types of response categories are an important consideration with closed-ended questionnaires. The instrument developer should consider several types of responses, including responses to rating scales, ranking, semantic differential, and checklists (**TABLE 11-2**). Ultimately, the type of information that is being collected should drive the choice of response categories used for the tool.

The concerns related to using questionnaires must be reviewed attentively and carefully to ensure that the best methods are used during data collection processes (**TABLE 11-3**).

TABLE 11-2 Types of Questionnaire Responses

Type of Response	Example of Response
Rating scales	On a scale from 0 to 10, with 10 being the most severe pain you can imagine and 0 being no pain at all, where does your current pain level fall? 0 1 2 3 4 5 6 7 8 9 10 No pain Most severe pain
Ranking	Nurses rank different things at different levels. The following is a list of items that many nurses value in the workplace. Please designate their order of significance to you by placing "1" beside the most significant, "2" beside the next most significant, and so on. _____ Salary _____ Competent peers _____ Effective workplace _____ Management workload _____ Opportunities to advance
Semantic differential	On each of the combinations provided, place an X to reflect how you see yourself function related to the two associated terms. Competent _ _ _ _ _ _ _ _ _ _ _ Incompetent Pleasant _ _ _ _ _ _ _ _ _ _ _ Unpleasant Responsible _ _ _ _ _ _ _ _ _ _ _ Irresponsible Successful _ _ _ _ _ _ _ _ _ _ _ Unsuccessful
Checklists	Please check all of the applicable characteristics you think a nurse should have in order to participate in EBP. _____ Critical thinking abilities _____ Energy _____ Knowledge about searching _____ Years of nursing experience _____ Desire for EBP

TABLE 11-3 Strengths and Weakness of Questionnaires

Strengths	Weaknesses
▪ Ability to access a larger sample in a group setting at minimum expense. ▪ A greater sense of anonymity. ▪ Time-sensitive for the participants. ▪ An enhanced quantity of data with an extensive variety of topics using a standard format. ▪ Opportunity to determine the validity and reliability of the tool.	▪ Must be short and to the point. ▪ Allows participants to be nonresponsive to selected items within the tool. ▪ Time-consuming nature of the data collection process. ▪ Time consuming because verbal responses are not preselected responses. ▪ Requires focused time to enter each piece of data manually.

▶ Interview Methods

Overview

Brink and Wood (2001) identified the key variation between a questionnaire and an **interview** as the presence of an individual to conduct the interview; this "personal touch" is the basic difference between the two data collection methods. Otherwise, the expectations and concerns about interview questions are the same as those that arise in the development of a questionnaire or survey.

Within this compilation design, the use of an interviewer to direct the questioning process requires that trust and rapport be developed between interviewer and interviewee. The interviewer has to be positive and supportive to engage the individual being queried. If the individual does not perceive the environment to be appropriate, the data collected may be skewed. Thus, the environment selected for the session is of paramount importance. Because the questions are presented by the interviewer, the ordering of the questions and the environment wherein the questions are presented should allow for openness from the interviewee and the increased depth of the resulting responses. If a room is too hot, too cold, too noisy, or too open, the participant may elect not to continue the interview or may be less open to engaging in dialogue. According to Bouffard and Little (2004), "Questions [in an interview] are generally open-ended and responses are documented in thorough, detailed notes or transcription" (p. 3).

Interview data collection can pull together information from both the quantitative and qualitative realms. When quantitative information is sought from the interview process, the questions are completed through the use of a structured format. Frequently, closed-ended questions are administered by means of a standardized test. Each question is asked in the same pattern or flow. The environment of the interview is controlled in an attempt to reduce the effect of confounding environmental variables.

If the purpose of the planned data collection is to seek qualitative information, the entire process can be managed in a less structured manner. Often, the questions used for this type of interview are geared more toward the open-ended type. When an informal conversational interview format is used, the process is impulsive and freely structured. An interviewer serves as a mediator who guides participants as they move between topics. To better facilitate the process, the interviewer should initiate the discussion with a subject matter that is significant but not problematic.

The flexibility of the interview process is perceived as both an advantage and a disadvantage for this data collection method. With the openness of the data collection process, the interviewer collects not only verbal data but also nonverbal data. By juxtaposing the nonverbal communication with the verbal statements, clarification related to the meanings of the comments and data is improved and facilitated. The disadvantage is related to the wealth of data that can be collected and then must be utilized or analyzed to determine the appropriateness of the material. The volume of data collected can make the data analysis process overwhelming and cumbersome.

An example of the use of interviews as the data collection method is presented in the study conducted by Woolston and Connelly (2017). Within this project, three interview sessions lasting a total of 150 minutes with observations were used to collect

TABLE 11-4 Strengths and Weaknesses of Interviews

Strengths	Weaknesses
■ Powerful and abundant information can be accumulated. ■ Ability through the use of communication to highlight issues that may be presenting during the session. ■ Ability to measure attitudes, probe feelings, pose follow-up questions, gather internal meanings and ways of thinking. ■ Control the depth of information amassed. ■ Allows collection of data without the requirement that the participants be able to read or write.	■ Expensive. ■ Time consuming. ■ Time-intensive interactions and close observation of the nonverbal communication. ■ Concerns about interrater reliability. ■ Bias can be introduced. ■ Potential for participants to say what they perceive is appropriate or socially desirable. ■ Analysis of open-ended, subjective data collected requires time and thought to ensure valid and reliable results supported by the information.

the information using semistructured interview questions. The researchers elected to audio-record and transcribe the interviews verbatim for use during the study. The study does speak to the setting of the environment for the interviews to ensure that the surroundings were conducive for the interview and observation processes.

Interviews have unique strengths and weaknesses that must be considered when determining if this data collection method is optimal for accumulating the data that is needed (**TABLE 11-4**).

▶ Focus Group Methods

Overview

Although focus groups share many of the characteristics discussed in relation to interviews, a **focus group** entails a type of "coordinated interview" in which approximately 6 to 12 homogeneous individuals are led in the discussion of a selected topic at the same time. According to Doody, Slevin, and Taggart (2013), "in essence, the focus group is a form of group interview where the aim is to understand the social dynamic and interaction between the participants through collecting verbal and observational data" (para 2). Each focus session tends to last approximately 1 to 3 hours. To facilitate the data collection process, the sessions typically are audio- or video-recorded for analysis at a later time.

The focus group leader should understand where the session should come together in regard to the data to be collected. This leader must ensure that the research topic is covered adequately during the discussion. The focus group leader's challenges are to persuade everyone to share in the dialogue, motivate conversation, channel the progression between the different topics, stay impartial, and endeavor not to interject any biases into the discussion while maintaining control of the discussion.

Many different features within the process need to be controlled and manipulated. The participants must understand that their opinions and experiences are important so that no answers are inappropriate within the context of the subject under investigation. Care concerning the setting for the focus group should address comfort, privacy, and convenience. Although the session is recorded in some manner, the focus group leader and researcher must ensure that the participants feel secure in the knowledge that the recording will be used only to pull out the information provided.

The researcher should also give thought and consideration to the membership of the group and members' educational background, job positions, and/or work environments. When these items are not taken into consideration, problems with feasibility, power, confidentiality, and integrity can develop. A homogeneous grouping with regard to gender, age, and socioeconomic status enhances the generalizability of the resulting data. Putting thought into the size and composition of each focus group is essential to maximize the effectiveness of the data collection process.

As the focus group is pulled together, the focus group leader should begin the session with a personal introduction concerning the research team members, purpose for the session, discussion about why the session is important, and what type of administrative support is in place. It is also important that the members of the focus group understand that any participation is completely voluntary on their part. For the session to be successful, members must feel comfortable in discussing their attitudes and opinions on the topic without fear of any type of repercussions. During the session, the focus group leader and/or research team member must make sure that distractions, such as background noises, are removed. Time must be allowed for the initial development of trust between the members of the focus group and the group leader. Without this trust, the information obtained can be biased and compromised.

When working with a group, the strengths of the process along with the weaknesses must be meticulously reviewed to account for all the members of the population being sought. Each focus group should demonstrate the population being sought for the study. As the focus group is convened, the group needs to include those individuals who are needed for the study (**TABLE 11-5**).

TABLE 11-5 Strengths and Weaknesses of Focus Groups

Strengths	Weaknesses
■ Same strengths identified for interviews can be listed for focus groups. See Table 11-4. ■ The moderator can probe the in-depth information for additional understanding of the phenomenon. ■ Each individual is allowed to react to other participants. ■ The group provides the complete picture, not one person having to answer all of the questions individually.	■ Moderators must be adept at conducting the process. ■ Expensive. ■ Extrovert personalities must be controlled to allow introvert personalities to participate.

▶ Observation Methods

Overview

According to Wood and Ross-Kerr (2011), **observation** requires the timely collection of descriptive, behavioral data which is particularly relevant to nursing since the researcher is observing behaviors. The entire process of observing individuals results in an interactive engagement. Frequently, what a person says and what a person does can be two different pieces of information. Observation allows for the confirmation of what is said by the viewing of specific behaviors and activities. It is a formulation of individualism, character preconceptions, and beliefs. Each individual assesses a situation based on his or her unique background and philosophy of life. As a result, the selectivity of this type of data collection must be highly patterned by the expectations of the study. Clarity related to the behavioral information under investigation is imperative.

LoBiondo-Wood and Haber (2014) specified four conditions needed for the use of observation as a data collection method:

- Observations undertaken are consistent with the study's specific objectives,
- A plan is standardized and systematic for the observing and recording of the data,
- All of the observations are checked and controlled, and
- Observations are related to scientific concepts and theories.

The complexity of the process requires attention to be given to the operationalization of the variables. The variables are frequently the behaviors being observed. Consequently, the individual characteristics and conditions (traits, symptoms, verbal communications, nonverbal conditions, activities, skills, or environmental aspects) should be clearly and distinctly documented for the integrity of the data collection process. Another issue that arises with this type of data collection process is whether the observer will be directed to try to provoke some behavior or action by the individuals being observed.

Both quantitative and qualitative observations can be used within this research effort. Because generalizability of the results is desired, a checklist of the behaviors and observations is frequently used to provide a structure for the analysis phase of the process. Put simply, quantitative observations require the standardization of those items to be counted or not counted. Likewise, clear directions related to the operational definitions of the selected behaviors must be given. When these behaviors are unmistakably defined, the observational sessions produce the quantitative data expected from the research process. The definition should include the "who," "what," "when," "where," "why," and "how" questions for the behavior on which data are to be collected within the study. As an example, if one piece of data that a researcher wants to collect is the number of times a person made eye contact during a lecture presentation, clarification is needed as to what duration of eye contact would be counted. In this case, the researcher might establish that each time the lecturer made eye contact with a student for at least 45 seconds, the contact would be counted. In contrast to quantitative observation, qualitative observation is investigative and open ended. The resulting information provides massive amounts of field notes to analyze.

Four diverse observer roles create a continuum of data collection with the observation methodology:

- *Complete participant.* The observer takes the role of member within the sample; the data are collected via a covert (hidden) process; the members of the group are not informed about the data collection process.
- *Participant-as-observer.* The observer continues to work from within the group but collects the data through an overt (informed) process; the members of the group are aware that the observer is taking on the dual roles of member of the group and spectator.
- *Observer-as-participant.* The observer does work from within the group but spends more time in the role of spectator instead of group member; data are collected in an overt manner.
- *Complete observer.* The observer is totally in the role of watcher; covert observations are used to collect the data.

For each data collection session, the researcher takes time to consider thoroughly which of these depths of observation is appropriate for the study population. Because some of the methods require covert (undercover) data collection, the researcher must also justify why this clandestine method is needed. In these situations, the question is raised about the necessity of collecting information without the individual's knowledge and the ethics of that undisclosed process. The researcher must diligently document the manner in which the individuals would be protected from harm.

On the other hand, when the participants know they are being watched, the researcher has to work to ensure that behaviors are not modified due to this knowledge (the Hawthorne effect). Frequently, the course of action used to ensure that individuals are behaving naturally is related to the length of time the observations are occurring. The researcher/observer may have to be immersed in this situation of being observed for a long period of time so that the participants become comfortable with his or her presence. As their comfort with the researcher's presence increases, the individuals return to their normal behaviors, allowing the observer to see the normalcy of the situation.

TABLE 11-6 Strengths and Weakness of Observation	
Strengths	**Weaknesses**
■ Highly detailed information from an external perspective. ■ Great depth of information can be obtained. ■ Activities that might otherwise be undetected in everyday life can be identified and discussed. ■ Can be used with any individual regardless of educational preparation. ■ Behaviors and attitudes can be evaluated and researched. ■ Individuals who may have weaker verbal skills can be evaluated and researched.	■ Time consuming. ■ Labor intensive. ■ Expensive. ■ Interrater reliability of the observers can be problematic. ■ Knowledge of the observers must be documented to ensure that data are complete. ■ Biases can be a major problem. ■ Acknowledgment of predispositions biases is critical.

As researchers contemplate using observation as their data collection method, they need to be careful about assessing the strengths and weaknesses associated with this method (**TABLE 11-6**).

▶ Secondary (Existing) Data Methods

Overview

The data collection process using secondary (existing) data builds on the information collected from another study. The use of secondary data takes the data compiled for another reason and applies it in a different manner. As a result, this method of reevaluating should be considered carefully. The researcher must explain which pieces of the primary data will be used in reassessment of the information. Within this process, the researcher reconsiders part of the information accumulated through some other manner in an attempt to address a follow-up question. Cortez-Gann and colleagues (2017) pulled data from medical records using a tool to get the needed information. Since patient records were being used, additional attention was needed to ensure that confidentiality of the records was protected. A tool was developed to protect the data that were needed. Only the study investigators collected the data so that confidentiality and correct management of the data were guaranteed.

According to Kitchin (n.d.), "data are commonly understood to be the raw material produced by abstracting the world into categories, measures, and other representational forms that constitute the building blocks from which information and knowledge are created" (p. 1). **Metadata** (Big Data) are data concerning data. The data sets become the foundation for the material to be investigated. Care must be given when using these large data sets to determine what type of algorithms can assist the investigator in accessing the scientific and objective data required to move any project forward in a positive manner. According to Metzler (2017), "big data is neither good nor bad inherently, it depends on the way it's used, by whom, and in service of what outcomes" (p. 8).

As individuals work with metadata sets, the practicality of the data management plan and the data-sharing plan is key. The determination of what data out of these enormous reservoirs of data are needed and how to access them is critical (Matteson, Sherrod, & Cetin, 2016). Using Big Data sets requires the investigators to consider carefully the **predictive analytics** for the process. According to Fenush and Barry (2017), predictive analytics is the "practice of extracting information from existing data sets to determine patterns and predict future outcomes and trends" (p. 27). Determining which data points will provide the patterns and predictions is paramount to the process. Careful consideration about what parts of the data set are needed becomes critical within the process. Data can become overwhelming when this initial processing is not done effectively. Another concern with using Big Data sets is the security surrounding the accessibility of the data sets. These data sets hold data points from many federal and state agencies. Accessing the data sets is strictly controlled. Thus, the researcher has to allow time within the planning for the project for gaining access to the data sets.

The data used for these secondary assessment projects might include, for example, documents, physical data, and/or archived research data. When documents are used, they could include personal documents, such as letters, diaries, or family pictures, and official documents, such as attendance records, budgets, annual reports, newspapers, yearbooks, minutes, or client records.

Using previous data files needs to be considered thoughtfully to ensure that the data collection method meets the expectations for the research purpose and/or hypothesis (**TABLE 11-7**).

TABLE 11-7 Strengths and Weakness of Secondary (Existing) Data Methods

Strengths	Weaknesses
■ Availability of existing records results.	■ Restrictiveness of the data sources to the resources currently existing.
■ Secondary data can be completed without any intrusion into peoples' lives.	■ Potential for the data to be out of date.
■ Extra time gained by using sources already assembled.	■ Difficulty in accessing certain documents.
■ Allows for exploration of alternative conclusions.	■ Controls in place to protect individual privacy.
■ Environmental aspects and historic perceptions can augment the interpretations.	■ Limitations resulting from the sample used in the initial data collection.
■ Entirety of the incident can be manipulated to reflect the identified trends.	■ Original sampling inclusion and exclusion criteria could negatively affect the secondary assessment.
■ Less expensive because the data are already collected.	■ Lack of open-ended or qualitative data related to the questions.
	■ Need to acknowledge the unavailability of certain types of data that were not collected during the initial study.
	■ Lack of initially collected information related to the topic.

▶ Biophysiological Methods

Overview

The final type of data collection method is the use of biophysiological indicators to organize the data sought for the research activity. The research community views biophysiological measures as objective data. Researchers may use the **biophysiological data** collection process either alone or in combination with other methods.

This method of data collection necessitates the use of specialized equipment to establish the physical and/or biological condition of the subjects. Two types of biophysiological methods are possible:

- **In vivo** Requires the use of some apparatus to evaluate one or more features of a participant. Examples of the types of items evaluated include blood pressure measurements, electrocardiograms, temperatures, muscular activity, and respiratory rates and rhythms.

- **In vitro** Requires the extraction of physiological materials from the participants, frequently via a laboratory analysis. Examples of the types of in vitro items include bacterial counts and identifications, tissue biopsies, glucose levels, and cholesterol levels.

Hanna, Weaver, Slaven, Fortenberry, and DiMeglio (2014) document the use of glycemic control (HbA1C), which requires the extraction of a small amount of blood to determine glycemic levels, and thus is an example of the use of in vitro data. Within the article, they discuss the levels that they used to control for bias.

This type of data collection process is frequently used with experimental and quasi-experimental research designs. Typically, the data are used to advance the implementation of specific nursing actions. Research projects gathering biophysiological data tend to be more structured and controlled.

When collecting specimens, the strengths and weaknesses of this data collection process take on a different level of importance. Specialized equipment is frequently needed, so concerns about data collection are heightened to protect the individual along with the specimen (**TABLE 11-8**).

TABLE 11-8 Strengths and Weakness of Biophysiological Methods

Strengths	Weaknesses
■ Objectivity, precision, and sensitivity of the information. ■ Increased independence from bias and subjectivity. ■ This type of data viewed as having a greater level of respect.	■ Cost of obtaining the measurements and calibrating the instruments. ■ Requires specialized knowledge and training to be able to gather the data accurately. ■ Additional research assistants may be required to perform the testing processes. ■ Escalating costs. ■ Time commitments. ■ Concerns related to interrater reliability. ■ Reluctance of the accessible population to participate.

▶ Systematic Analysis

With the increasing focus on EBP, systematic reviews and meta-analysis reviews are becoming common in the literature. These different forms of pulling the evidence together provide a clean synthesis of current knowledge about a topic. The Institute of Medicine (2011) defines a **systematic review** as a process of identifying, selecting, assessing, and synthesizing the findings from similar but individualized studies. This process of data collection allows for the clarification of what is known and not known about an identified topic. Robertson-Malt (2014) notes the international standard for systematic reviews is the Preferred Reporting Items for Systematic Reviews and Meta-Analyses (PRISMA). This document maintains that it is vital and fundamental for PRISMA to record the material in plain and transparent language. The PRISMA statement holds six items to be essential:

> unique records identified by the searches, records excluded after preliminary screening, records retrieved in full text, records or studies excluded after assessment of the full text, studies meeting the eligibility criteria for the review, and studies contributing to the main outcome. (Robertson-Malt, 2014, p. 49)

Within the data collection process and within EBP, another method utilized is **meta-analysis**. According to materials developed by Northern Arizona University (2001), a meta-analysis is the process of merging the outcomes from multiple studies related to one primary topic. The strength of each set of conclusions is determined to provide an overall view of the evidence available on the identified topic. The methods used within the various studies, along with the quantification of the findings from the studies, are condensed into a summary document related to the topic under investigation. The effect size within a meta-analysis seeks to establish the relevance of the tests, treatments, and methods used in the research studies under consideration. These documents are then used to provide the context for the next steps in the research process and the determination of the reliability of the evidence related to that topic.

The Institute of Medicine (2011) developed what it calls Standards for Systematic Reviews to provide direction to individuals for completing a systematic review using an effective and manageable approach. Hemingway and Brereton (2009) identified five aspects that demonstrate a high-quality systematic review. To generate an effective review, all relevant published and unpublished evidence should be included within the document. Porritt, Gomersall, and Lockwood (2014) strongly endorse the idea that the study selection process is the vital stage within the review process. Determining which types of studies will be included is critical to the overall success of the review. After all the evidence is compiled, inclusion criteria defining which pieces of evidence are to be included in the review must be determined. It is not possible to include everything, so care must be given to the determination of the inclusion criteria to allow for effective evidence to be included. After the selection of the evidence to be included in the review, each piece and report must be assessed for the quality of that evidence in relation to the goal of the review. As the appraisals are completed on each of the studies, incorporation of the results into an unbiased report of those findings is imperative. Porritt and colleagues (2014) identified the different types of bias to consider, including selection, performance, detection, and attrition biases. Following the synthesizing of the results, an interpretation of the findings in a balanced and impartial summary is the culmination of the review. Effective consideration of any flaws in the evidence must be noted within a high-quality systematic review.

Systematic reviews must be completed with a peer-reviewed protocol to allow for replication of the review as needed. Hemingway and Brereton (2009) stated that, individually, "each article may offer little insight into the problem at hand; the hope is that, when taken together within a systematic review, a clearer (and more consistent) picture will emerge" (p. 2). The process for completing a review requires that each member of the review team assess each of the selected articles/documents carefully utilizing the agreed-upon criteria. To conduct an effective systematic review, five steps should be followed. The first step within the process is the formation of a suitable and fitting review question. Within the healthcare question, attention to the principal objective, along with the phenomena of interest, is critical. Once the question is clearly worded, a search of the literature and other sources of evidence is initiated. Because systematic reviews need to be unbiased, the search for evidence must be accomplished in any venue where the evidence for that topic could be located. It is essential that each and every view of the topic is included in the search. The third component within the review process is an assessment of the studies. Specific documents are selected to be included in the review according to the inclusion criteria. From this point, the researcher performs a critical appraisal of each document to determine the strength of the evidence based on the methodological quality of that study. Some questions that can be used to drive the appraisal of each document are:

- Is the subject defined adequately to allow the development of the review?
- How thorough was the search for studies and evidence?
- Did the inclusion criteria provide a clear and concise description to be used that allowed for the fair application of the criteria?
- Is the review conducted as a blind or independent review to decrease biases?
- How was missing information managed within the review?
- Do the included studies and documents reflect similar effects? If not, why?
- Did the review speak to the idea of robustness of the process?
- Were the recommendations supported by the strength of the quality of the evidence? (Hemingway & Brereton, 2009)

Once the overview of the documents is determined, the combining of the findings is integrated carefully and thoughtfully into the review. Care and attention to the depth and quality of the review must be established. Two types of systematic reviews used in the research field are meta-synthesis and meta-analysis. A meta-synthesis is a review that focuses primarily on qualitative data. A meta-analysis utilizes quantitative data to address a clinical effectiveness problem. The process for either type of analysis includes the same questions listed earlier. The difference between these two reviews is the types of studies and evidence considered within the review. The analysis is directed by the research method used in the different documents included in the review.

▶ Achievement of the Data Collection Strategy

Each of the data collection strategies profiled in this chapter has both benefits and limitations. The researcher must carefully consider the PICOT question, research purpose, research question/hypothesis, research design, sampling method, cost considerations, and time restrictions as he or she identifies the appropriate data collection plan. According to Bouffard and Little (2004), "Using multiple methods to assess the same outcomes [e.g., using surveys and document review to assess program management] provides a richer, more detailed picture" (p. 5). Although it certainly adds to the richness of the results, the use of multiple methods of data collection also increases the resources (cost, personnel, and tools) required to carry out the project.

Each researcher must consider carefully the many different strategies available for accessing the information needed to address the identified research problem. In singling out the appropriate data collection process, justification for those choices needs to be documented. Because each method has its own set of strengths and limitations, the primary objective for the researcher is to substantiate the rationale for the choices made to dispatch the research challenge.

In determining the strategy, the objectives of the project, along with the type of data required, should be taken into account during the decision-making process. If the strategy for a research or evidence-based project has been determined to be the use of a tool, several aspects must be considered. The selection of a tool, the questions that need to be developed, and the method for implementing the tool and the questions must all be contemplated. In addition, the environment of the data collection process is just as important as the individual questions to be addressed. Within the environment, the participants must be made to feel secure with the process, or the resulting data could be compromised.

▶ EBP Considerations

Within the realm of EBP, the focus is more on the idea of outcome measures. According to Melnyk and Fineout-Overholt (2017), the usefulness of outcomes measurement is affected by changes within the characteristics of the data, the reliability of the data collection method, the ability of the researcher to collect the needed data effectively, and the scheduling of data collection times and places. The principal issues for data collection, as viewed from the EBP perspective, are the quality of the process and the content of the data collected. Each choice made by a researcher concerning the data to be collected, the method or methods to be used, and the environment used to collect the data must be founded on reliable, sensible judgments. The rationales for these decisions can make or break the study by determining the validity and reliability of the results produced by the study. If the decisions are not supported by appropriate thought processes and planning, then the entire inquiry is in jeopardy.

Researchers need not select the strongest data collection methods possible, but they must select the optimal strategies for getting the data needed to answer the questions asked and provide an appropriate justification for each of those decisions.

The key is to make a decision and justify the selection with sound reasoning and a sound decision-making process. The entire research or evidence-based process rests on the quality of the data. The data form the foundation on which the results, recommendations, and outcomes of a study are based; the merit of the data becomes the underpinning for the research or evidence-based conclusions. The researcher must provide a sound rationale and strong support for the decisions made concerning the data collection process.

Summary Points

1. Data come in many varieties, and data collection is achieved through numerous methodologies.
2. Data collection sources are items or strategies for accumulating the information desired.
3. Data collection tools are the tangible devices used to collect the data.
4. The major methods of data collection are tests, questionnaires, interviews, focus groups, observations, secondary (existing) data, and biophysiological data.
5. Attention must be given to the information that actually exists and the information that is accessible. These two types of data may not be the same.
6. The basic objective in research is to collect the data in the same manner for each of the participants so that unique environmental, societal, and physical dimensions are diminished.
7. Interrater reliability is vital when more than one data collector is used to gather evidence.
8. Tests are used to ascertain the specific knowledge, talents, behaviors, and/or cognitive capabilities under investigation.
9. A questionnaire/survey is a data collection tool that is completed by a participant and allows the researcher to discover what the individual thinks about a specific item.
10. When interviews are used as the data collection process, establishing trust and rapport between interviewer and interviewee is essential.
11. Environmental aspects of the study setting must be taken into account when planning to conduct interviews and/or focus groups.
12. Observation allows for the confirmation of what is said by viewing the participant's specific behaviors and activities.
13. Several ethical issues need to be considered carefully as the method of observation is determined.
14. A data collection process that uses secondary (existing) data builds on the information collected from another study or document.
15. Systematic reviews are key components within the documentation of evidence.
16. A systematic review is a process of identifying, selecting, assessing, and synthesizing the findings from similar but individualized studies.

Multiple-Choice Questions

1. Which of the following processes is not a major method of data collection?
   A. Observations
   B. Open-ended questions
   C. Secondary (existing) data
   D. Tests

2. When considering the different data collection schemes, researchers must be careful to contemplate the presence of the Hawthorne effect. The Hawthorne effect is defined as a process in which the:
   A. participant does not modify his or her behavior to meet the expectations of the study.
   B. researcher modifies his or her behavior because of conducting the study.
   C. researcher modifies the participants' behavior based on the data collected.
   D. participant modifies his or her behavior as a result of engagement in the study.

3. Which of the following is/are tenet(s) to follow when designing a questionnaire?
   A. Use a variety of items and approaches to appraise conceptual ideas.
   B. Ensure that each question addresses the entire scope of the topic.
   C. Use simple but appropriate jargon for the designated topics.
   D. Both A and B.

4. Which of the following is a method of data collection?
   A. Experimental
   B. Grounded theory
   C. Observation
   D. Cross-sectional

5. A researcher should word questions carefully when developing questions for an instrument to:
   A. provide hints about the response.
   B. use jargon as needed.
   C. use single-topic questions.
   D. use cultural aspects to provide context.

6. Open-ended questions provide primarily _____ data.
   A. confirmatory
   B. exhaustive
   C. qualitative
   D. quantitative

7. Which of the following statements is true concerning observation?
   A. Clear directions related to the operational definitions of the selected behavior must be determined.
   B. Ethical considerations are a minor concern within this method of data collection.
   C. Observation data collection strategies result in manageable amounts of field notes to analyze.
   D. Within observational sessions, the observer is always known to the participant.

8. When creating a questionnaire, it is essential to do each of the following except:
   A. be concise and reasonably brief.
   B. code and weight the responses prior to the administration of the tool.
   C. conduct a pilot test of the tool with a select group of the target population.
   D. use double-negative questions regularly within the tool.

9. A researcher decides to use observation as the data collection method for a study. To collect the needed data effectively from college-age students, the researcher enrolls in a selected college course to observe and collect data about the behaviors of the students in the course. The researcher is using which observation role?
   A. Complete participant
   B. Participant-as-observer
   C. Observer-as-participant
   D. Complete observer

10. Which of the following terms best describes data compiled for another reason and applied in a different manner?
    A. Primary data
    B. Secondary data
    C. Novice data
    D. Experimental data

11. Which of the following biophysiological tests is an example of in vivo data?
    A. Complete blood count
    B. Urinalysis
    C. Respiratory rate
    D. Bacterial count

12. A systematic review considers:
    A. reports about clinical standards.
    B. research and other documents that address the topic being reviewed.
    C. only opinion documents that address a topic of interest.
    D. only quantitative research reports.

Discussion Questions

1. A researcher begins to develop the demographic section for use within a project. The three questions developed are the following:
   a. How many years have you been practicing professional nursing?
      - 0–5 years
      - 5–10 years
      - 10–15 years
      - More than 15 years
   b. What is your highest level of nursing degree?
      - ADN
      - BSN
      - MSN
      - Doctorate
   c. I have never been identified in a legal case.
      - Yes
      - No

   Which problems are present within these three questions that need to be corrected?

2. A researcher initially planned to use covert data collection techniques (observing a class of teenagers via a one-way mirror) for a research project designed to determine the aggressive behaviors of boys and girls. Neither the parents nor the students were to be informed about the research project because no intervention was planned. Which other observational role might the researcher use to make the data collection process an overt one?

3. A researcher has decided to conduct a structured interview with nursing students concerning their perceptions of what tasks constitute the provision of spiritual care within an acute care setting. Write three open-ended questions and three closed-ended questions related to this idea.

Suggested Readings

Ahern, N. R. (2005). Using the Internet to conduct research. *Nurse Researcher, 13*(2), 55–70.

Colling, J. (2004, June). Coding, analysis, and dissemination of study results. *Urology Nursing, 24*(3), 215–216.

Duffy, M. E. (2005). Systematic reviews: Their role and contribution to evidence-based practice. *Clinical Nurse Specialist, 19*(1), 15–17.

Halcomb, E., & Andrew, S. (2005). Triangulation as a method for contemporary nursing research. *Nurse Researcher, 13*(2), 71–82.

Happ, M. B., Dabbs, A. D., Tate, J., Hricik, A., & Erlen, J. (2006). Exemplars of mixed methods data combination and analysis. *Nursing Research, 55*(2), S43–S49.

Holopainen, A., Hakulinen-Viitanen, T., & Tossavainen, K. (2008). Systematic review: A method for nursing research. *Nurse Researcher, 16*(1), 72–83.

Institute of Medicine. (2011). *Standards for systematic reviews: Report at a glance.* Retrieved from http://iom.edu/Reports/2011/Finding-What-Works-in-Health-Care-Standards-for-Systematic-Reviews/Standards.aspx

Kuipers, P., & Hartley, S. (2006). A process for the systematic review of community-based rehabilitation evaluation reports: Formulating evidence for policy and practice. *International Journal of Rehabilitation Research, 29*(1), 27–30.

Priest, H., Roberts, P., & Woods, L. (2002). An overview of three different approaches to the interpretation of qualitative data. Part 1: Theoretical issues. *Nurse Researcher, 10*(1), 30–42.

Vishnevsky, T., & Beanlands, H. (2004). Qualitative research. *Nephrology Nursing Journal, 31*(2), 234–238.

Examples of Data Collection

Focus Groups/Interviews

Wood, E. B., Hutchinson, M. K., Kahwa, E., Hewitt, H., & Waldron, D. (2011). Jamaican adolescent girls with other male sexual partners. *Journal of Nursing Scholarship, 43*(4), 396–404.

Interviews

Adhiambo Onyango, M., & Mott, S. (2011). The nexus between bride-wealth, family curse, and spontaneous abortion among southern Sudanese women. *Journal of Nursing Scholarship, 43*(4), 376–384.

Questionnaires

Palese, A., Tomietto, M., Suhonen, R., Efstathiou, G., Tsangari, H., Merkouris, A., ... Papastavrou, E. (2011). Surgical patient satisfaction as an outcome of nurses' caring behaviors: A descriptive and correlational study in six European countries. *Journal of Nursing Scholarship, 43*(4), 341–350.

Secondary Data Analysis

Nantsupawat, A., Srisuphan, W., Kunaviktikul, W., Wichaikhum, O. A., Aungsuroch, Y., & Aiken, L. H. (2011). Impact of nurse work environment and staffing on hospital nurse and quality of care in Thailand. *Journal of Nursing Scholarship, 43*(4), 426–432.

References

Boswell, C. (2010). Questioning students to develop critical thinking. In L. Caputi (Ed.), *Teaching nursing: The art and science* (2nd ed., vol. 2, pp. 423–453). Glen Ellyn, IL: College of DuPage Press.

Bouffard, S., & Little, P. M. D. (2004). Detangling data collection: Methods for gathering data. *Harvard Family Research Project, 5*, 1–6. Retrieved from http://www.hfrp.org/publications-resources /browse-our-publications/detangling-data-collection-methods-for-gathering-data

Brennan, C. & Parsons, G. (2017). Enhanced recovery in orthopedics: A prospective audit of an enhanced recovery program for patients undergoing hip or knee arthroplasty. *MEDSURG Nursing, 26*(2), 99–104.

Brink, P. J., & Wood, M. J. (2001). *Basic steps in planning nursing research: From question to proposal* (5th ed.). Sudbury, MA: Jones and Bartlett.

Cherry, K. (2015). What is the Hawthorne effect? Retrieved from http://psychology.about.com/od /hindex/g/def_hawthorn.htm

Cortez-Gann, J., Gilmore, K. D., Foley, K. Q., Kennedy, M. B., McGee, T., & Kring, D. (2017). Blood transfusion vital sign frequency: What does the evidence say? *MEDSURG Nursing, 26*(2), 89–92.

Creswell, J. W. (2014). *Research design: Qualitative, quantitative, and mixed method approaches* (4th ed.). Thousand Oaks, CA: Sage.

Doody, O., Slevin, E., & Taggart, L. (2013) Focus group interviews in nursing research: Part 1. *British Journal of Nursing, 22*(1), 16–19. doi:10.12968/bjon.2013.22.1.16

Educational Testing Services. (2015). *Testlink test collection database.* Retrieved from http://www .ets.org/test_link/find_tests/

Fenush, J., & Barry, R. M. (2017). Predictive analytics empower nurses: Quality care requires robust staff scheduling tools. *American Nurse Today, 12*(11), 26–28.

Hanna, K. M, Weaver, M. T., Slaven, J. E., Fortenberry, J. D., & DiMeglio, L. A. (2014). Diabetes-related quality of life and the demands and burdens of diabetes care among emerging adults with type 1 diabetes in the year after high school graduation. *Research in Nursing & Health, 37*, 399–408. doi:10.1002/nur.21620

Hemingway, P., & Brereton, N. (2009). What is a systematic review? *Hayward Medical Communications.* Retrieved from http://www.whatisseries.co.uk

Institute of Medicine. (2011). *Finding what works in health care: Standards for systematic reviews.* Retrieved from http://iom.edu/Reports/2011/Finding-What-Works-in-Health-Care-Standards-for-Systematic -Reviews.aspx

Kitchin, (n.d.). Conceptualising data. Retrieved from https://www.sagepub.com/sites/default/files /upm-binaries/63923_Kitchin_CH1.pdf

LoBiondo-Wood, G., & Haber, J. (2014). *Nursing research: Methods, critical appraisal, and evidence-based practice* (8th ed.). St. Louis, MO: Mosby.

Management Study Guide. (2013). Secondary data. Retrieved from http://managementstudyguide .com/secondary_data.htm

Matteson, S. M., Sherrod, S. E., & Cetin, S. C. (2016). Collection, storage, protection, and sharing issues with large-scale data sets. *Sage: Research methods cases,* London, England: SAGE Publication Ltd. doi: http://dx.doi.org/10.4135/9781473999053

Melnyk, B. M., & Fineout-Overholt, E. (2017). *Evidence-based practice in nursing and healthcare: A guide to best practice.* Philadelphia, PA: Lippincott Williams & Wilkins.

Merriam-Webster. (2018). Data. Retrieved from https://www.merriam-webster.com/dictionary/data

Metzler, K. (2017). Putting Big Data to good use. Retrieved from https://campus.sagepub.com/blog /putting-big-data-to-good-use

New World Encyclopedia. (2014). Hawthorne effect. Retrieved from http://www.newworldencyclopedia .org/entry/Hawthorne_effect

Northern Arizona University. (2001). Module 2: Methods of data collection: Chapter 2 [Online lesson]. Retrieved from http://www.prm.nau.edu/prm447/methods_of_data_collection_lesson.htm

Orcher, L. T. (2005). *Conducting research: Social and behavioral science methods.* Glendale, CA: Pyrczak.

Polit, D. F., & Beck, C. T. (2017). *Nursing research: Generating and assessing evidence for nursing practice* (10th ed.). Philadelphia, PA: Lippincott Williams & Wilkins.

Porritt, K., Gomersall, J., & Lockwood, C. (2014). Study selection and critical appraisal: The steps following the literature search in a systematic review. *American Journal of Nursing, 114*(6), 47–52.

Robertson-Malt, S. (2014). Presenting and interpreting findings: The steps following data synthesis in a systematic review. *American Journal of Nursing, 114*(8), 49–54.

Wood, M. J., & Ross-Kerr, J. C. (2011). *Basic steps in planning nursing research: From question to proposal* (7th ed.). Sudbury, MA: Jones and Bartlett.

Woolston, W., & Connelly, L. M. (2017). Felty's syndrome: A qualitative case study. *MEDSURG Nursing 26*(2), 105–118.

CHAPTER 12

Reliability, Validity, and Trustworthiness

James Eldridge

CHAPTER OBJECTIVES

At the conclusion of this chapter, the learner will be able to:
1. Identify the need for reliability and validity of instruments used in evidence-based practice (EBP).
2. Define reliability and validity.
3. Discuss how reliability and validity affect outcome measures and conclusions of evidence-based research.
4. Develop reliability and validity coefficients for appropriate data.
5. Interpret reliability and validity coefficients of instruments used in EBP.
6. Describe sensitivity and specificity as related to data analysis.
7. Interpret receiver operand characteristics (ROCs) to describe validity.

KEY TERMS

Accuracy
Concurrent validity
Consistency
Construct validity
Content-related validity
Correlation coefficient
Criterion-related validity
Cross-validation
Equivalency reliability
Interclass reliability
Intraclass reliability

Objectivity
Observed score
Predictive validity
Receiver operand characteristics (ROCs)
Reliability
Sensitivity
Specificity
Stability
Standard error of measurement (SEM)
Trustworthiness
Validity

▶ Introduction

The foundation of good research and of good decision making in evidence-based practice (EBP) is the **trustworthiness** of the data used to make decisions. When data cannot be trusted, an informed decision cannot be made. Trustworthiness of the data can only be as good as the instruments or tests used to collect the data. Regardless of the specialization of the healthcare provider, nurses make daily decisions on the diagnosis and treatment of a patient based on the results from different tests to which the patient is subjected. To ensure that the healthcare provider makes the proper diagnosis and gives the proper treatment, the nurse must first be sure that the test results used to make the decisions are trustworthy and correct.

Working in an EBP setting requires the nurse to have the best data available to aid in the decision-making process. How can an individual make a decision if the results being used as the foundation of that process cannot be trusted? Put simply, a person cannot make a decision unless the results are trustworthy and correct.

This chapter presents five concepts to help the nurse determine whether the data upon which decisions are based are trustworthy: reliability, validity, accuracy, sensitivity, and specificity. Each defines a portion of the trustworthiness of the data collection instruments, which in turn defines the trustworthiness of the data, ensuring a proper diagnosis or treatment.

Reliability and validity are the most important qualities in the decision-making process.

- Reliability = the instrument consistently measures the same thing.
- Validity = the instrument measures what it is intended to measure.

If either of these qualities is lacking in the data, the nurse cannot make an informed decision and therefore is more likely to make an incorrect decision. An incorrect decision in the medical field can have catastrophic consequences for the patient. Thus, one can see why reliability and validity are so important. What do these concepts mean? What would happen if the same test was run on a person several times but the results were different each time? In the case of varying results, a decision becomes ambiguous because the results are unclear.

Reliability is defined as the consistency or repeatability of test results. Other descriptors used to indicate reliability include *consistency, repeatability, objectivity, dependability,* and *precision.* Accuracy is a function of reliability: The better the reliability, the more accurate the results. Conversely, the poorer the reliability, the more inaccurate are the results, which increases the chance of making an incorrect decision. Accuracy is also affected by the sensitivity and specificity of the test. **Sensitivity** can be defined as how often a test measures a "true" positive result, while **specificity** determines the capability of the test for determining "true" negative results. The greater the sensitivity and specificity are for a test, the more accurate the test results. The concepts of sensitivity and specificity are discussed in more detail later in this chapter.

Validity is defined as the degree to which the results are truthful. It depends on the reliability and relevance of the test in question (**FIGURE 12-1**). Relevance is simply the degree of the relationship between the test and its objective, meaning that the test reflects what was reported to be tested.

An example of relevance is the measurement of the height of a patient. A nurse uses a stadiometer (a ruler used to measure vertical distance) to establish a patient's

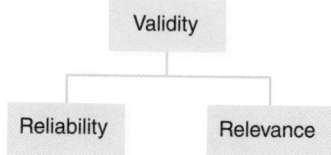

FIGURE 12-1 Relationship of validity to reliability and relevance.

height. Is the stadiometer a relevant height measurement device? Height is the vertical distance from the floor to the top of an individual's head, and a stadiometer measures vertical distance from the floor to any point above the floor; thus, the stadiometer is a relevant measure of height.

Validity cannot exist without reliability and relevance, but reliability and relevance can exist independently of validity. **FIGURE 12-2A** depicts the case in which there is a high degree of reliability and a low degree of relevance. In this representation, even when reliability is high, validity is low due to the lack of relevance. This figure shows that, under the most reliable test, a low degree of relevance decreases the validity of the test.

FIGURE 12-2B depicts the situation in which there is a high degree of relevance and a low degree of reliability. In this representation, even when relevance is high, validity is low due to the lack of reliability. Even when a nurse uses what might be considered the most relevant test for the situation, if the instrument has a low degree of reliability, it will also have a low degree of validity.

FIGURE 12-2C shows the desired capacity for an instrument—to have both a high degree of reliability and a high degree of relevance, thereby creating a high degree of validity. Whereas the other examples show that a test can be reliable but not relevant, or relevant but not reliable, a valid test will always have some degree of reliability and relevance. When validity is absent, the results of the testing are not truthful, and making an informed or evidence-based decision is impossible. However, when validity is present, a nurse can be assured that the decision is based on truthful evidence.

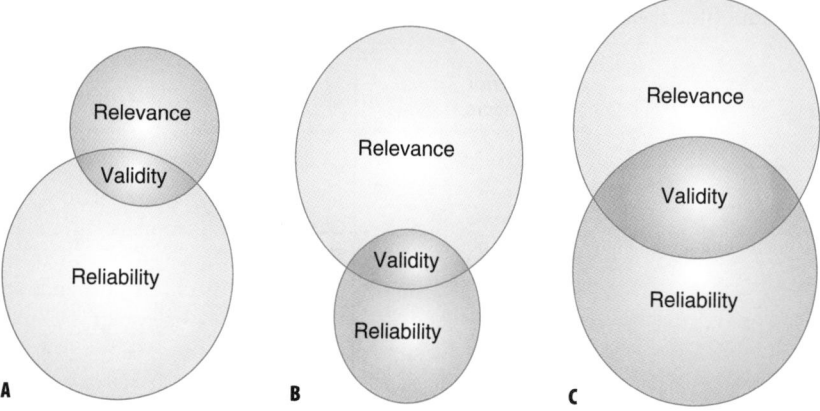

FIGURE 12-2 Relationship among reliability, relevance, and validity.

▶ Reliability as a Concept

As previously described, reliability focuses on the repeatability or consistency of data. To understand the theoretical constructs of reliability, one must understand the concept of the observed score. By definition, the observed score is the score that is seen; stated in other terms, the observed score is the actual score printed on the readout of an instrument.

An example of an observed score is the measurement of a patient's blood pressure. The systolic and diastolic pressures are determined based on the aneroid dial or digital liquid crystal display (LCD) readings associated with the first sound (systolic) and the last sound (diastolic) heard in the brachial artery. If the first sound occurs at a reading of 130 mmHg, this sound is the systolic observed score. If the last sound occurs at 85 mmHg, this sound is the diastolic observed score. These observed scores for blood pressure are not the true blood pressure scores for the patient because those scores ultimately depend on factors such as the amount of error incorporated in the type of sphygmomanometer, the quality of the stethoscope, the quality of hearing of the person taking the blood pressure, the experience of the person taking the measurements, and placement of the cuff over the artery.

A second example that may help in understanding the reliability of an observed score is the measure of quality improvement of a specific program. For instance, consider a hospital that wants to determine whether a specific pain management protocol helped reduce hospital days for patients. It used a pain scale that patients completed every 6 hours, and patient discharge was determined by the patient achieving an observed score of 3 on a 10-point pain scale. In this case, the scale would need very little error because a change of 1 point on the scale might determine the discharge or premature discharge of a patient. If the scale had a high error rate—for example, 2 points of error—and the patient scored a 3 on the scale, then it would not be possible to know if the score was a 3, as high as 5, or as low as 1. The scale number may be affected by the time of day the question was asked, the way the question was asked, the type of pharmaceuticals the patient is receiving, the patient's language skills, the patient's tolerance, and the severity of the initial injury causing the pain.

Each of these nuances can add or subtract error from the true score, which increases the variability between the observed score and the true score. This variability can be described as the error score, thereby defining the observed score as the sum of the true score and the error score. As shown in **FIGURE 12-3**, any error

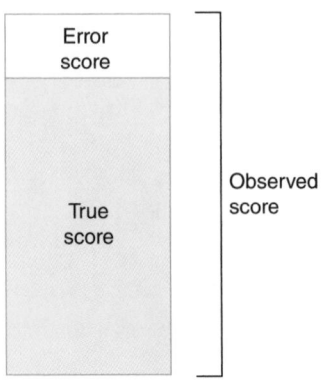

FIGURE 12-3 Observed score, true score, and error score.

$$\text{Reliability} = \frac{S^2 \text{ true}}{S^2 \text{ observed}} = \frac{S^2 \text{ observed} - S^2 \text{ error}}{S^2 \text{ observed}}$$

FIGURE 12-4 Theoretical calculation of reliability.

within the measurement decreases the degree to which the observed score reflects the true score. Note that the net effect of an error score can be positive or negative, depending on the nature of the error.

The true score exists only in theory because all data collected are observed score data. A nurse can think of the true score as the perfect score of a test—that is, a score without any error and void of any misinterpretation. Of course, the world is not perfect and therefore neither are any data that might be collected. Thus, a true score exists and never changes for a given period of time; changes occur only in the error score, which then determines the observed score.

Reliability is the degree to which the observed score of a measure reflects the true score of that measure. Therefore, reliability could theoretically be calculated as the proportion of observed score variance that consists of true score variance (**FIGURE 12-4**). In this equation, if no error exists, then the observed score variance and the true score variance are equal, and the reliability coefficient is 1.0. Conversely, when the observed score variance and the error score variance are equal, the reliability coefficient is 0. Thus, reliability always falls within the range of 0–1.0, with perfect reliability equaling 1.0 and no reliability equaling 0. For research purposes, high reliability measures are desired if at all possible. The general rule is that reliability coefficients greater than 0.80 are considered to be high. Note that if the reliability coefficient is calculated to be greater than 1 (e.g., 1.15), a calculation error has been made because the range of reliability is always between 0 and 1.0.

🔲 THINK OUTSIDE THE BOX

In Cortez-Gann et al. (2017), the authors suggest that vital sign frequency during blood transfusions is highly individualized and subjective among patients. Discuss how the subjectivity and individualization affects the elements of trustworthiness as related to making decisions about the data collected on pain scales. Where might error(s) occur within the measurement of vital signs?

▶ Forms of Reliability

Although the purpose of the theoretic concept of reliability is to determine the relationship between the true and observed scores of a measurement, practical use of this concept allows a nurse to determine the relationship only between two or more observed scores. The relationship between these observed scores allows an individual to estimate reliability and to determine a range for the true score. The outcome of the calculation of the relationship between two or more observed scores is known as the correlation coefficient. The **correlation coefficient** is the practical calculation of the theoretic expression of the proportion of observed score variance that consists of true score variance, as described previously.

Given this basic understanding of reliability as a concept, it is now time to learn about the forms of reliability. Reliability can be described as either interclass reliability or intraclass reliability. The most basic description of **interclass reliability** is the reliability between two and only two variables or trials, whereas **intraclass reliability** is the reliability between more than two variables or trials. The limiting factor that separates the two forms of reliability is the number of variables or trials that can be used in the calculation of the correlation coefficient. The number of variables also determines which statistical equation is used to develop the correlation coefficient. Each of these considerations has its place in EBP depending on the number of variables a nurse uses to calculate the reliability coefficient.

Interclass Reliability

Interclass reliability is the reliability between two measures that are presented in the data as either variables or trials. There are four types of interclass reliability:

- Consistency
- Stability
- Equivalency
- Internal consistency

Each of these reliability coefficients is developed using a Pearson Product Moment (PPM) correlation. Most statistical packages or spreadsheet software can calculate PPM correlations; therefore, the actual equation is not included in this text. Although each interclass reliability coefficient uses the same formula, the calculated reliability coefficient is defined by the type of variables to be compared and the methods used for interpretation of the results. This concept becomes more evident as the types of interclass reliability are further defined.

Consistency

One type of interclass reliability to report is the consistency of a measure. **Consistency** simply describes the degree to which you can expect to get the same results when measuring a variable more than once on a single day. Consistency reliability is sometimes described as test–retest reliability because it compares two trials of a single measure. An example of testing for consistency would be running two tests on a single blood sample from each subject to measure hemoglobin using a single hemoglobin analyzer. The question is whether the results from the hemoglobin analyzer are consistent within a single day.

In **TABLE 12-1**, the subjects' hemoglobin from a single sample of blood was measured twice, and the reliability coefficient was calculated to be 0.996. This coefficient simply means that 99.6% of the observed score variance is true score variance. Because the reliability coefficient is close to 1.0, the reliability of the instrument is high. The initial question with this data was whether or not the machine was consistent. The results demonstrate that it was consistent, with a consistency reliability coefficient of $r_{xx'} = 0.996$.

TABLE 12-1 Consistency and Stability of the Ac·T diff Analyzer		
Subject Number	**Test 1 (g/dL)**	**Test 2 (g/dL)**
1	14.10	14.00
2	12.20	12.10
3	11.90	11.90
4	14.50	14.40
5	13.80	13.90
6	13.20	13.10
7	13.50	13.60
8	14.00	14.10
9	11.10	11.00
10	9.60	9.90

$r = 0.996$

Stability

When results of trials or tests are collected over 2 or more days, consistency becomes **stability**. Suppose we take the same data from Table 12-1, this time imagining that the samples were tested over a 2-day period. The question now becomes whether a blood sample is stable over a 2-day period. Notice that the results remain constant because nothing has changed except the theoretical timing of the tests. The reliability coefficient is still 0.996, but this time a nurse would interpret the samples as being stable over a 2-day period, with a stability reliability coefficient of $r_{xx'} = 0.996$.

Both consistency and stability have their place in EBP. In the current example of hemoglobin testing, the consistency of the measures is described by determining that, for any time during a single day, the data would be repeatable. A nurse can expect the same results as long as no other factors have occurred in the interim, such as acute onset of anemia. In other words, the nurse is sure that the hemoglobin analyzer gives the same measure of hemoglobin for the same sample within the same day. Notice that nowhere in this example of consistency do we assume that the measurement gives the correct amount of hemoglobin, only that it indicates the presence of the same amount of hemoglobin. To determine if this is the correct amount of hemoglobin, the relevance and the validity of the instrument would have to be known.

When discussing this example in terms of stability, the key determination relates to the length of time that the blood samples remain stable. Hemoglobin analyzers usually have instructions that indicate the time frame for running samples before differing results would be seen. In most instances, the time frame is 24 hours. A question might arise concerning how the manufacturer determined this time frame. The answer simply is that the manufacturer developed a stability coefficient using the same techniques described previously.

Again, notice that nowhere in the example of stability is there any mention of the correctness of the amount of hemoglobin over a 24-hour period; the only consideration is that it is the same amount of hemoglobin measured for a 24-hour period. To determine whether this is the correct amount of hemoglobin over the 24-hour period, the relevance and the validity of the instrument and the measures would need to be determined.

Equivalency

Another type of interclass reliability to report is equivalency. This kind of reliability allows a person to report whether one type of test is equivalent to another. Equivalency reliability is calculated in the same manner as the consistency and stability coefficients described previously, except that a PPM correlation between two forms of a single test is calculated rather than a single variable over two trials.

An example of testing for equivalency reliability would be comparing two methods of blood pressure measurement to determine if they are equivalent. In this case, the question is whether the systolic blood pressure results determined by an automatic blood pressure cuff are equivalent to those recorded from manual blood pressure measures using a stethoscope and sphygmomanometer.

As shown in TABLE 12-2, subjects' systolic pressure was measured once with an automatic cuff and once using manual methods. The reliability coefficient was calculated to be 0.959. This coefficient simply means that 95.9% of the observed score variance consists of true score variance. The reliability coefficient is close to 1.0, which reflects the fact that the reliability between the instruments is high. The initial question with these data was whether automatic cuff readings are equivalent to manual readings of systolic blood pressure. A person can now report that the two methods are equivalent, with an equivalency reliability coefficient of $r_{xx'} = 0.959$. These results indicate that either an automatic cuff or manual methods are acceptable for measuring systolic blood pressure because they are equivalent. No matter which method is used, a nurse can expect to get similar measures from a single individual. Notice again that there is no mention of the correctness of the data, only the similarity of the data. To determine if the blood pressure measures are correct, the relevance and the validity of the measures would need to be determined.

In Cortez-Gann et al. (2017), the authors did a retrospective analysis of vital signs such as blood pressure, heart rate, and body temperature to determine if a reaction to a blood transfusion occurred. Specifically, they wanted to determine if these variables changed over time and thus could be used to determine if the patient was having a reaction to the transfusion. In the previous example of equivalency between manual and automatic blood pressure consistency, does it matter how blood pressure was measured in Cortez-Gann et al. (2017)?

TABLE 12-2 Equivalency of Automatic Versus Manual Systolic Pressure Readings

Subject	Automatic Cuff Systolic (mmHg)	Manual Method Number Systolic (mmHg)
1	150.00	155.00
2	130.00	128.00
3	125.00	129.00
4	124.00	120.00
5	122.00	125.00
6	148.00	144.00
7	133.00	135.00
8	146.00	143.00
9	117.00	120.00
10	121.00	120.00

$r = 0.959$

Internal Consistency

The final type of interclass reliability discussed here is the internal consistency of written tests. Internal consistency reliability is sometimes described as split-halves reliability because it entails comparing two halves of a written test. To calculate the internal consistency of a written instrument, the instrument responses are divided into two equal halves. The sum of each half is calculated to make the comparison.

The simplest means for dividing a test in half is to compare the sum of the odd-numbered question responses with the sum of the even-numbered question responses. If possible, the questions should be matched between each half, based on their content and difficulty. Another possible method is to make the a priori assumption that both halves are equal because the questions were placed in a random order during the development of the written test. As with the other types of interclass reliability, the PPM correlation is used to develop the reliability coefficient.

Data for a 10-item pain questionnaire are presented in TABLE 12-3 to demonstrate the principle of internal consistency. Each item of the pain questionnaire is scored from 0 (strongly disagree) to 5 (strongly agree). The questionnaire is then divided into

TABLE 12-3 Internal Consistency of a 10-Item Pain Questionnaire

Subject	Odd-Numbered Item Scores	Even-Numbered Item Scores
1	25.00	21.00
2	18.00	14.00
3	16.00	18.00
4	12.00	14.00
5	10.00	10.00
6	18.00	19.00
7	15.00	18.00
8	12.00	9.00
9	14.00	15.00
10	17.00	13.00

$r = 0.761$

odd and even scores, with the sum of the scores for the odd-numbered items and the sum of the scores for the even-numbered items presented in the table. The question under consideration is whether this questionnaire has internal consistency. As with the previous types of reliability, the reliability coefficient is reported; here, it is 0.761. This coefficient simply means that 76.1% of the observed score variance consists of true score variance. Notice that the internal consistency is lower than in previous examples. The fact that the reliability coefficient is lower does not mean that the questionnaire is not reliable—just that it is less reliable than it could be.

🔲 THINK OUTSIDE THE BOX

Look around your clinical setting. Which tools or instruments are present, and how are they typically used for data collection? Do they include surveys of employees, patients, and/or consumers? Are the tools or instruments used appropriately? In Brennan and Parsons (2017), how would you determine the internal consistency of the audit form described in the reading?

The initial question for these data was whether the pain questionnaire was internally consistent. We can now report that it has some internal consistency, with

$$r_{xx'} = \frac{k \times r_{xx'}}{1 + r_{xx'}(k-1)}$$

FIGURE 12-5 Spearman–Brown prophecy formula.

a reliability coefficient of $r_{xx'} = 0.761$, but at least some error is present in the questionnaire. In other words, the questionnaire is not perfectly consistent internally, so the results from using the questionnaire will not be an accurate reflection of the true score. This finding does not mean that this questionnaire should not be used; rather, it means that a person needs to be careful in the interpretation and use of the results of the questionnaire. When using written item tests, individuals can actually estimate how reliability will change as a result of adding items to the questionnaire. To estimate a new reliability for a written questionnaire with added items, the Spearman–Brown prophecy formula (**FIGURE 12-5**) can be used.

Where $r_{kk'}$ is the new reliability coefficient, $r_{xx'}$ is the original reliability coefficient, and k is the total number of items on the new questionnaire divided by the number of items on the original questionnaire, the Spearman–Brown prophecy formula can be determined. In the example given in Table 12-3, the reliability coefficient was 0.761. To calculate the reliability of the questionnaire if 10 questions were added, you would solve for $r_{kk'}$ using the information shown in **FIGURE 12-6**.

The original reliability coefficient is 0.760, and the number of total items on the new questionnaire divided by the total items on the original test is 2. Notice that by increasing the number of items on the questionnaire to 20, the new reliability coefficient for the questionnaire becomes 0.864. This coefficient is higher than the original value. Thus, adding items to the questionnaire improves this tool's internal consistency and strengthens the interpretation of its results. As discussed earlier, as reliability and relevance increase, so does validity. If the questionnaire being used has a high degree of relevance, the addition of more questions to the questionnaire (assuming they are relevant) would increase the reliability of the questionnaire, thereby improving the validity of its results.

In Hanna, Weaver, Slaven, Fortenberry, and DiMeglio (2014), Cronbach's alpha coefficients were provided for both instruments used within the study. The diabetes-related quality of life (DQOL) tool demonstrated Cronbach's alpha coefficient scores on the subscales of 0.84, 0.83, and 0.90 during T1 and 0.85, 0.84, and 0.90 during T2. For the second tool, the Emerging Adult Diabetes Management Self-Report, the Cronbach's alpha coefficient was 0.81 at T1 and 0.85 at T2. Each of these scores is close to the 1.0 level, which implies a high internal consistency. As was stated earlier, a common interpretation of the reliability coefficient scores reflects that any level greater than 0.80 is considered to be high. All eight of these Cronbach's alpha coefficient scores exceed this level. The article does discuss the covariates for the depressive symptoms as measure by the Beck Depression Inventory (BDI-II). In-depth discussion related to the internal consistency was not provided within the article. The discussion centered on providing the statistical levels found for the different tools.

$$r_{xx'} = \frac{2 \times 0.761}{1 + 0.0761(2-1)}$$

FIGURE 12-6 Example of the Spearman–Brown prophecy formula.

$$r_{xx'} = \frac{MS_{between} - MS_{within}}{MS_{between}}$$

FIGURE 12-7 Intraclass reliability coefficient using ANOVA (Example 1).

Intraclass Reliability

Now that we have an understanding of interclass reliability, it is time to move on to intraclass reliability. As discussed earlier, the basic difference between interclass reliability and intraclass reliability is the number of variables that can be analyzed. Interclass reliability testing allows for the reliability analysis of only two variables, whereas intraclass reliability testing allows a researcher to develop a reliability coefficient for more than two variables.

Suppose we wanted to measure the reliability of three different pain scales. One of the scales requires only 2 minutes for completion, the second scale requires 10 minutes for completion, and the third scale requires 30 minutes for completion. The nurse would prefer to use either the 2-minute or 10-minute scale for efficiency, but the 30-minute scale is currently being used. Although the data could be analyzed using three PPM correlations to determine the equivalency reliability coefficients for these tools, this kind of analysis would miss a very important portion of the error: In the PPM interclass analysis, the statistic estimates only the error between the items, but it ignores the error within the item that reflects the differences in individuals taking the test.

In contrast, the intraclass reliability coefficient uses analysis of variance (ANOVA) to determine not only the error between the tests but also the error within the tests. Using ANOVA allows for construction of a better estimate of the overall reliability of the scales and the errors that reduce the observed score variance, which is the true score variance. Thus, whereas PPM analysis allows for only a two-dimensional view of reliability, ANOVA supports a three-dimensional view of reliability. Notice that the basic terms of reliability remain the same. In the current example, a nurse is still estimating the equivalency of the scales, but now an error that might exist within each individual scale is included.

FIGURE 12-7 shows the equation used in determining a reliability coefficient using ANOVA. In this equation, a reliability coefficient is developed using the mean square between scales and the mean square within scale data from the ANOVA table.

TABLE 12-4 presents data for the example of the three pain scales. These ANOVA data include the between-cells mean square of 2908.233 and the within-cells mean square of 35.100. As shown in FIGURE 12-8, the reliability coefficient is determined by substituting the numbers represented in the table into the ANOVA equation for reliability (Figure 12-7).

In this example, the equivalency reliability is 0.988 for the three scales. We can now state that the 2-minute pain scale is equivalent to the 10-minute pain scale and the 30-minute pain scale. The evidence for replacing the longer 30-minute test with the more efficient 2-minute test is now documented because the tests are equivalent. The same ANOVA reliability equation can be used to determine consistency, stability, and equivalency, depending on the intended use of the data.

Objectivity

An area of intraclass reliability that is often overlooked is the measure of objectivity. Objectivity is the reliability of scores assigned by judges, multiple observers,

TABLE 12-4	Intraclass Reliability Using ANOVA			
	Scale			
Subject Number	2-Minute Scale	10-Minute Scale	30-Minute Scale	
1	15.00	35.00	60.00	
2	12.00	30.00	51.00	
3	9.00	22.00	40.00	
4	10.00	25.00	42.00	
5	11.00	19.00	43.00	
6	14.00	31.00	45.00	
7	6.00	20.00	38.00	
8	3.00	15.00	33.00	
9	12.00	22.00	45.00	
10	11.00	21.00	45.00	
Source of Variation	SSq	DF	MSq	F
Between cells	5816.467	2	2908.233	82.86
Within cells	947.700	27	35.100	
Total	6764.167	29		

Note: DF = degrees of freedom; F = *F*-distribution; MSq = mean square; SSq = sum of squares.

$$r_{xx'} = \frac{2908.233 - 35.10}{2908.233} = 0.988$$

FIGURE 12-8 Intraclass reliability coefficient using ANOVA (Example 2).

$$SEM = s \sqrt{1 - r_{xx'}}$$

FIGURE 12-9 Standard error of measurement.

or reviewers. In theory, if three individuals see the same performance, they should score the performance based on the merits of the performance, and their scores should not be affected by internal biases that each may possess. When no bias is evident, the scores should be similar among the judges.

A good example of objectivity (or lack of objectivity) comes from the 2002 Winter Olympics figure skating competition, in which three judges rated the performance of the Canadian skating pair. Two of the judges assigned scores of 9.9 and 9.8 for the pair's performance, but a third judge scored the pair at 7.8. If no biases were associated with the scoring method, then the third judge should have been expected to score the performance in the 9.8 range.

Objectivity also has relevance for EBP. The Apgar score—a tool for assessing the health of newborn infants—offers an example of objectivity in healthcare practice. If three medical professionals are in the delivery room, the Apgar scores each assigns to the newborn should be equivalent. This factor can be tested using the same ANOVA techniques described in the previously given pain scale example, albeit with scores for each observer, rather than each scale, being used. A researcher could determine if the Apgar scores are objective. If they are not, the researcher could meet with the observers to determine where differences occurred.

By now, it should be clear that the same formula (either PPM or ANOVA, depending on the number of trials) is used to determine the reliability of any measure. The only difference in the results relates to the interpretation based on the intended use of the data.

Accuracy

Another item that is important when determining the intraclass reliability of a test is the test's **accuracy**. The measure of the accuracy of a test is known as the **standard error of measurement (SEM)**. The SEM reflects the fluctuation of the observed score attributable to the error score. Computing the SEM allows a researcher to determine confidence intervals for the observed score based on the standard deviation of the test and its reliability. The relationship between the true score and the observed score was discussed earlier in this chapter. The SEM allows a researcher to provide a range for which the true score is present.

The equation shown in **FIGURE 12-9** is used to calculate the SEM. Notice that, in this equation, the reliability coefficient of the test and the standard deviation of the sample are used.

The SEM can be determined for any of the prior examples. For the example in Table 12-1, the standard deviation of the sample is 1.496, and the reliability coefficient is 0.996. Using the equation in Figure 12-9, we can compute the SEM as $\pm$ 0.0946 mg/dL (**FIGURE 12-10**).

$$SEM = 1.496 \sqrt{1 - 0.996}$$
$$= \pm 0.0946 \text{ mg/dL}$$

FIGURE 12-10 SEM for consistency of a hemoglobin analyzer.

🔼 THINK OUTSIDE THE BOX

On most clinical units, many different tools are regularly used, such as thermometers, glucometers, sphygmomanometers, and weight scales. Are these tools accurate? How can you be sure that they are reliable and valid for what they are being used to evaluate? Are they valid and reliable tools?

In a normal distribution, 68% of the sample scores fall between ± 1 standard deviation of the mean. Thus, for this example, we have 68% confidence that the hemoglobin scores will fall between ± 0.0946 mg/dL of the measured score. If a ± 2 standard deviation from the mean is used, a 95% confidence interval for the scores is expected. To find the SEM for ± 2 standard deviations from the mean, we multiply the SEM by 2 (the number of standard deviation units). In our example, we have 95% confidence that the true hemoglobin score will fall between ± 0.1892 mg/dL of the measured score. If a blood sample is run in the analyzer and the hemoglobin level is found to be 14.0 mg/dL, we would therefore have 95% confidence that the true score is between 13.1080 mg/dL and 14.1892 mg/dL. Notice that, as the standard deviation increases for a set of scores, the SEM increases. Also, as the reliability of a set of scores decreases, the SEM increases. To proclaim a tool as giving an accurate measure, test scores need a relatively low standard deviation and a high reliability coefficient.

Up to this point, we have examined accuracy as it relates to continuous data. But what happens when a test uses nominal data—how do we determine its accuracy? In the case of nominal data, we use the χ^2 (chi-square) statistic and its corresponding phi coefficient as a measure of accuracy. Think of the phi coefficient as a correlation or reliability coefficient for nominal data. A χ^2 statistic and its corresponding phi coefficient would most likely be used when you are trying to determine whether a new test is equivalent to a "gold standard" test. All of the same rules apply just as they have in the previous discussion of reliability for continuous data; however, now you are simply determining the accuracy of the new test based on its pass-or-fail performance compared to the gold standard test.

Be aware that reliability and accuracy can be sensitive to situational changes; although a test is reliable in one situation or within one group, it may not always be reliable when the situation or group changes. This consideration is especially important concerning written items. Factors that can affect reliability and accuracy include the following:

- *Fatigue.* Fatigue for the person taking the test or collecting the data can decrease reliability.
- *Practice.* The more practiced a person becomes at taking a test or in collecting data, the more reliability is improved.
- *Timing.* The more time that passes between test administrations, the more the reliability of the test decreases.
- *Homogeneity of the testing conditions.* The more homogeneous the testing conditions (e.g., same room, same time taken to collect data, same time of day), the better the reliability.
- *Level of difficulty.* The more difficult a test or data collection procedure, the lower the reliability.

- *Precision.* The more precise the measurement (e.g., 0.01 versus 0.001 decimal), the better the accuracy.
- *Environment.* Environmental changes such as ambient pressure or temperature variations can decrease reliability.

The more control maintained over these factors, the better the reliability and accuracy of the resulting data. Accuracy and reliability improve the decision-making process in EBP.

Receiver Operand Characteristics (ROCs) and Accuracy

Historically, the use of the x^2 statistic determines accuracy when discussing nominal data; however, newer statistical methods such as receiver operand characteristics (ROCs) curves are being implemented in the field of nursing to determine accuracy of test results (Zou, O'Malley, & Mauri, 2007). ROC analyses were first developed for the armed services during World War II as a method for determining the accuracy of radar signals. More recently, this statistical method is being adapted to the medical field for defining the accuracy of diagnostic tests. ROC analysis determines the sensitivity and specificity (accuracy) of a diagnostic test to predict a specific outcome of disease the test is reported to measure. Most of the time, ROC analysis uses dichotomous variables much like a $2 \times 2\,x^2$ statistic; however, the analysis can also be used when an ordinal grading system is available for determining disease severity. The most basic form of ROC analysis uses a 2×2 method for determining accuracy of positive and negative results from a specific diagnostic test compared to whether or not the patient actually possesses the disease. TABLE 12-5 represents the conceptual nature of a dichotomous diagnostic test comparing the positive and negative test results to the actual disease state of a patient (nondiseased or diseased).

In Table 12-5, a perfectly accurate test would indicate only true negative results and true positive results; however, as discussed previously, some inherent measurement error is always possible with diagnostic tests. The ROC analysis allows the medical provider a means to quantify this error and determine in which area of the figure the error is greatest. Unlike the SEM, which gives the researcher a global characterization of the measurement error, ROC analysis allows the researcher to determine the sensitivity (rate of true positive results) and the specificity (rate of true negative results) for any diagnostic test.

Calculations for sensitivity and specificity are fairly simple to develop. The researcher needs to know the rates or number of individuals within each of the four

TABLE 12-5 Conceptual Nature of a Dichotomous Test

Test State	Disease State	
	No Disease	Disease
Negative test result	True negative	False negative
Positive test result	False positive	True positive

TABLE 12-6 Variables for Calculating Sensitivity and Specificity

| Test | Disease State | | Total |
	No Disease	Disease	
Negative	TN	FN	TN + FN
Positive	FP	TP	FP + TP
Total	TN + FP	FN + TP	*n*

Note: FN = false negative; FP = false positive; TN = true negative; TP = true positive.

groups (true negative, false negative, true positive, and false positive). **TABLE 12-6** simplifies the variables necessary to calculate sensitivity and specificity.

In Table 12-6, TN represents the number of individuals who do not have the disease and have negative test results on the diagnostic test (true negatives). FP represents the number of individuals who do not have the disease but have positive results on the diagnostic test (false positives). FN represents the number of individuals who have the disease but have negative test results on the diagnostic test (false negatives). TP represents the number of individuals who have the disease and have positive results on the diagnostic test (true positives). To calculate sensitivity (the probability of the test to predict true positive scores correctly), the formula used is TP/(TP + FN). To calculate specificity (the probability of the test to predict true negative scores correctly), the formula used is TN/(TN + FP). We could discuss many reasons why ROC analyses might be used, but one of the most common reasons is to determine if a less invasive and less expensive diagnostic test will provide as good or better results when compared to the gold standard diagnostic test for a given disease.

For an example of calculating sensitivity and specificity of a diagnostic test, let's assume a new diagnostic test was developed for assessing the presence of carpal tunnel syndrome. The test uses a tactile response of the index fingers by touching the fingers with a thin monofilament line while conducting a modified Phalen's test (MPT) for carpal tunnel syndrome. The response from the patient is simply yes, he or she feels the thread (positive MPT), or no, he or she does not feel the thread (negative MPT). Previously each patient was diagnosed for the presence (positive electrodiagnostic neural conduction study [EDS]) or absence (negative EDS) of carpal tunnel syndrome via an EDS. The data for the test are provided in **TABLE 12-7**.

To determine the sensitivity of the modified Phalen's test, the equation would be: sensitivity = 39/46, where 39 represents the number of individuals who reported a positive MPT and a positive EDS score, and 46 represents the total positive EDS scores. The sensitivity of the modified Phalen's test is 0.848, or 84.8% probability of predicting true positive tests. To determine the specificity of the modified Phalen's test, the equation would be: specificity = 20/21 , where 20 represents the number of individuals who reported a positive MPT and a negative EDS score, and

TABLE 12-7 Sensitivity and Specificity of the Modified Phalen's Test

Neg	Negative EDS	Positive EDS	Total
Negative MPT	20	7	27
Positive MPT	1	39	39
Total	21	46	66

Note: EDS = electrodiagnostic neural conduction study; MPT = modified Phalen's test.

21 represents the total negative EDS scores. The specificity of the modified Phalen's test is 0.952, or 95.2% probability of predicting true negative tests. The conclusion from these data is that the modified Phalen's test can accurately predict both true positive and true negative tests.

The philosophical discussion that occurs when using ROC analysis in the healthcare field is what should be considered acceptable values for sensitivity, specificity, and overall accuracy. Acceptable values often depend on the severity of the disease state. If the disease is life threatening, then sensitivity values should be above 85%, while specificity values may be somewhat lower. If the disease or diagnosis is mundane, then sensitivity values may be lower, but specificity values should be higher. The overall accuracy of a test should still follow the general rules of reliability and exceed 80%.

▶ Validity

To this point in the chapter, the knowledge necessary to understand the reliability and accuracy of the data collected has been provided. The fact that a test has accuracy and reliability does not mean that the test is valid, however. A valid test is defined as a test that truthfully measures what it purports to measure. Validity can be classified as either logical or statistical in nature. Logical validity requires inference and understanding of the subject being measured. Statistical validity uses statistical formulas to compare the test in question with a specific criterion or known valid measure. In EBP, validity is further delineated into three types: content-related validity, criterion-related validity, and construct-related validity. Depending on the measure, either one type or several types of validity can be used to determine if a measure is valid.

Content-Related Validity

Content-related validity is based on the logical thought process and interpretation of the measure. Many people refer to this quality as face or logical validity. The American Psychological Association (APA, 1985) defines content-related validity as "demonstrating the degree to which the sample of items, tasks, or questions on a test is representative of some defined content" (p. 10). A humorous restating of this concept is the cliché, "If it looks like a duck and quacks like a duck, then it must be a duck." A valid test using content-related validity should logically measure the content being reported.

Consider the pain scale example introduced earlier in this chapter. Content-related validity would assume that if the scale logically asks questions concerning the specific nature and degree of pain for a patient, then it must be measuring the pain of the individual. Another example arises with the stadiometer: If the stadiometer is a ruler, and a ruler measures distance, then it must logically be able to measure height. Both of these examples show the use of a logical thought process to validate the measure as a truthful representation of what the instrument purports to measure.

The fact that a test has content validity does not always mean that the test is valid. Other nuances may add error to the test and negate the test's content validity. Consider the practice of measuring blood pressure at the arm, which is an accepted, valid method for measuring blood pressure. But what happens when the person obtaining the measurement is inexperienced or does not place the cuff in the proper position? The result will be an invalid measurement owing to the use of an improper measurement procedure. Any deviations in measurement procedures decrease the reliability of the test, thereby invalidating the data collected with the instrument.

The criteria for content-related validity can be traced back to the process used in developing the test, the interpretation of the results, and a well-defined protocol for collection of the data. In developing content-related validity, the researcher needs to be aware of extraneous factors that can affect the outcome of the test and render the test invalid. Whenever content-related validity for an instrument is relied upon, a set of strict guidelines concerning the use and collection methods of the instrument need to be in place to ensure that the validity of the instrument is not rendered useless by these factors.

Criterion-Related Validity

Criterion-related validity is based on a comparison between the test being used and some known criterion. According to the APA (1985), criterion-related validity involves "demonstrating test scores are systematically related to one or more known criteria" (p. 11). Criterion-related validity is the statistical validity identified earlier in this chapter. (Terms such as *statistical validity* and *correlational validity* are sometimes used as synonyms for *criterion-related validity*.) The same statistical technique used to determine reliability (i.e., PPM) is used to develop a validity coefficient.

Consider the following example: measurement of oxygen saturation of arterial blood in patients. The criterion for arterial saturation would be blood gas analysis from an arterial line; however, this type of measurement brings the risk of complications and should not be used during a routine office visit. An alternative method for measuring oxygen saturation is via an infrared monitoring device that attaches to the fingertip. The infrared monitor is minimally invasive, can be used with the general population without risk, and is supposedly valid for estimating arterial oxygen saturation. To verify that the alternative method of infrared monitoring is valid, a researcher would identify a small sample of patients, subject those patients to both tests, and compare their actual blood gas results with the infrared monitoring scores. The PPM would be calculated to quantify the comparison, which would be between the alternative test to be used and the known criterion. The results would have a validity coefficient associated with the infrared monitoring model instead of a reliability coefficient. Interpretation would be done in the same manner used to interpret the reliability coefficient.

Criterion-related validity can be subdivided into concurrent validity and predictive validity, based on the time between the collection of data using the alternative method test to be validated and the criterion measurement. Concurrent validity can use the PPM statistic for validity coefficient development. With predictive validity, however, the researcher is not limited to using the PPM correlation; a linear or logistic regression can be used to develop a validity coefficient. Concurrent validity coefficients are developed simultaneously for the criterion and the alternative method test, whereas predictive validity is not limited by time.

The arterial blood oxygen saturation testing described previously is an example of concurrent validity. In this example, both criterion and alternative method measures are collected at the same time to develop the validity coefficient.

The criterion in predictive validity can be measured years after the collection of alternative method test data. Testing for the occurrence of heart disease is an example of predictive validity. A patient's total cholesterol, high-density lipoprotein (HDL) cholesterol, and low-density lipoprotein (LDL) cholesterol levels, along with other measures, are used to predict the future occurrence of atherosclerosis. Atherosclerosis—the criterion in this example—does not occur until later in life, whereas the lipid profiles, which are the alternative method test, are collected years earlier. In the predictive validity example, if a PPM correlation is used, the validity coefficient might be low because the criterion measure is a nominal value. In this case, a researcher might use logistic regression techniques to predict the probability of occurrence and develop the validity coefficient from the probability of occurrence rather than simply from the dichotomous variable (i.e., either a person does or does not have heart disease). A good point to remember is that whenever the criterion is a continuous variable, there is a better chance of having a high validity coefficient due to the possibility of improved true score variance and lower error score variance.

When a dichotomous or nominal variable is used as the criterion, a researcher should expect to have a lower validity coefficient due to a decline in true score variance and an increase in error score variance. An example of this mystery is presented in **TABLE 12-8**.

⭐ THINK OUTSIDE THE BOX

Discuss how you could make sure that each person who collects data as part of a research project does the collection in the same manner to ensure reliability of the study results.

In this example, the criterion measure of atherosclerosis is presented both as a dichotomous variable and as a probability of occurrence based on a logistic regression formula. The alternative test for the validity coefficient is the total cholesterol levels of the subjects collected when they were 40 years of age. Notice that when a continuous variable is used as the criterion in this example, the validity coefficient is 10% higher compared with use of a dichotomous criterion. When using dichotomous variables as measures of validity, a researcher can expect to have lower validity coefficients than when using continuous variables. This decline in the validity coefficient reflects the lack of variability within the dichotomous measure—the

	TABLE 12-8 Effects of Variable Scale on Validity Coefficient		
Subject Number	**Heart Disease (Yes or No)**	**Probability of Heart Disease**	**Total Cholesterol Level**
1	0	40%	145
2	1	75%	200
3	1	89%	225
4	0	45%	170
5	0	30%	160
6	1	65%	195
7	0	40%	165
8	1	85%	250
9	1	88%	300
10	0	50%	180

Heart disease and total cholesterol $r = 0.777$

Probability of heart disease and total cholesterol $r = 0.879$

lack of variability decreases the effectiveness of determining the true score of the measure. If the true score measure is decreased, then the error score measure is increased, which also affects reliability.

Cross-validation techniques are often used to develop a validity coefficient from a predictive validity criterion. Cross-validation simply implies that the researcher uses one group of subjects to develop the regression equation to predict the criterion and then gathers data from a second separate but similar group to develop the actual validity coefficient. Cross-validation techniques are generally used in developing new prediction models for a criterion.

ROC Analysis for Determining the Criterion-Related Validity of Diagnostic Exams

Because predictive analysis as a subsidiary of criterion-related validity compares an alternative method test to a criterion measurement for developing a validity coefficient, one can logically infer that ROC analysis may be used not only to describe the accuracy of a diagnostic test but also as a measure of the validity of a diagnostic test. When using ROC analysis for validation of testing, the evidence-based practitioner can develop an inherent validity coefficient that quantifies the predictive quality of the alternative test to predict the presence or absence of the disease. An inherent validity coefficient quantifies the ability of the alternative diagnostic test to identify true positive and true negative results. The inherent validity coefficient is calculated using the following equation:

Validity Coefficient = (True positive tests + True negative tests)/n

In the case of the modified Phalen's test from Table 12-7, the inherent validity is $(20 + 39)/66 = 0.893$, or 89.3% probability of correctly identifying true positive and true negative disease states (Bilkis et al., 2012).

Construct Validity

The most abstract of validity procedures is construct validity. **Construct validity** refers to the concept of "focusing on test scores that are associated with a psychological characteristic" (APA, 1985, p. 9). In practice, construct validity attempts to develop validity for measures that exist in theory but are unobservable.

The best example of this type of validity in EBP is the measure of pain perceived by a patient. Although we know pain exists, direct measurement of pain is somewhat convoluted and is affected by the psychological traits, tolerance levels, and perceptions of the patient. The tool most commonly used to measure pain today is the analog pain scale, which measures pain on a one-dimensional scale of 1 to 10. To develop a more precise pain scale that measures several dimensions of pain and has a high validity coefficient, constructs must be developed that can measure these traits associated with pain. Thus, we can think of construct validity as the combination of content validity and statistical validity to develop a validity coefficient for an abstract variable such as pain.

To develop construct validity of a variable, the variable must first be defined as specifically as possible. The researcher would then need to identify all of the constructs associated with the variable and to define them as specifically as possible. These definitions would prove helpful in developing the measurement scales and tools to quantify the variable. In the case of the pain example, pain might be defined as the degree to which a physical symptom causes discomfort at greater than normal levels for a patient. In using this definition, the constructs associated with this variable need to be identified and defined. Notice in the definition of pain that the term *degree* is used, which assumes that some type of quantifiable scale with specific unit differences is available to quantify the intensity and severity of the variable. Also, the term *discomfort* is used in the definition, which assumes that some type of non-well-being exists. In this case, intensity is one construct, severity is another construct, and discomfort is the final construct that needs to be defined and measured.

To start the process of developing a pain scale, think about the physical pain that you have experienced previously in relation to the constructs of intensity, severity, and discomfort. If your experience with pain is limited, you might seek the help of others who have more experience with pain or investigate current publications in pain research to help you with the definition and development of these constructs. For the current example, assume the definitions for your constructs are as follows:

- Intensity is the degree of pain.
- Severity is the degree of debilitation associated with pain.
- Discomfort is the degree of the measure associated with the patient's pain tolerance.

In this example, it is assumed that these three constructs are measurable and part of the content that defines the overall construct of pain.

Once you have defined the constructs, you need to determine the type of scale that can be used to measure each one. For intensity, you might decide to use a scale of 0 to 10, where 0 is defined as the absence of pain and 10 is defined as the most excruciating pain imaginable. For severity, you might have to develop a scale using terms that reflect a decline in functional capacity associated with debilitation. For discomfort, you might use a scale that reflects the type of pain, such as sharp, dull, or throbbing.

After developing the scales for the constructs that are included in the measurement of pain, you must determine how each scale should be weighted to reflect the absolute construct of pain. Again, you might want to rely on personal experience when developing your construct weights; alternatively, you might wish to seek expert opinions or explore previous research to help in developing your weighting system.

When you have accomplished this last step, you have a measure that logically measures pain (content validity). You are ready to test the merits of the measure by applying it to comparable groups to determine the statistical validity of the measure. In using statistical validation measures, you are attempting to prove the following hypothesis: Those individuals with diseases that are not associated with pain should score low on the new pain scale, and those individuals with diseases or disorders associated with a high level of pain should score high on the new pain scale. By combining the logical validation of the pain scale with the statistical interpretation of the pain scale, you have developed construct validity for a measure of pain. As you become more comfortable with the process of developing construct validity for abstract or unobservable measures, you will find that the greater the number of definable constructs, the greater the validity gained by the measure.

▶ Conclusion

This chapter focused on two key principles that determine trustworthiness of research data: reliability and validity. Whereas reliability and relevance can exist independently of each other, validity cannot exist without the presence of both reliability and relevance.

The two basic statistical techniques used to determine reliability and validity are the PPM correlation and the ANOVA test. As with most techniques, the selection of which to use is based on the number of variables being compared. When there are only two variables, a researcher would use PPM; when more than two variables are being compared, the ANOVA technique would be used. Both techniques generate a coefficient between an absolute value of 0 and 1.0, and the presence of a coefficient greater than 1.0 signifies an error in the calculations.

The interpretation of the coefficient is the only change that should occur regardless of the technique used. In the case of reliability, the coefficient can be used to interpret the consistency, stability, equivalency, or objectivity of the measure depending on which aspects were used to determine the estimate. A researcher can also use the reliability coefficient in conjunction with the standard deviation of the sample to determine the accuracy of the measure using the SEM equation. With reliability and accuracy determined, a nurse can be sure that comparable measures are similar and can be interpreted as consistent, stable, equivalent, or objective within a defined range of error. In the case of validity, these techniques can be used to develop a validity coefficient for concurrent validity or predictive validity based on the time between the collection using the alternative method test, or a validity coefficient for construct validity to improve the interpretation of the measure beyond simple content validation.

Summary Points

1. Trustworthiness of study data is only as good as the instruments or tests used to collect the data.
2. Reliability and validity are the most important concepts in the decision-making process when designing research studies.
3. Reliability is the determination that an instrument consistently measures the same thing.
4. Validity is the determination that an instrument measures what it is supposed to measure.
5. Validity cannot exist without reliability and relevance.
6. Reliability and relevance can exist independently of validity.
7. The correlation coefficient is the degree (positive or negative) of the relationship between the variables.
8. Interclass reliability is the consistency between two measures that are presented in the data as either variables or trials.
9. The three types of interclass reliability are consistency, equivalency, and internal consistency.
10. Intraclass reliability allows for the development of a reliability coefficient for more than two variables.
11. Within intraclass reliability, objectivity and accuracy need to be considered.
12. The three types of validity are content-related validity, criterion-related validity, and construct-related validity.
13. Content-related validity is the level at which a sample of items, tasks, or questions represent the defined content.
14. Criterion-related validity reflects the demonstration that test scores are systematically related to one or more identified measures.
15. Criterion-related validity is subdivided into concurrent validity and predictive validity.
16. Construct-related validity concentrates on the test scores that are associated with a psychological characteristic.
17. A receiver operand characteristics (ROC) analysis can be used for determining the criterion-related validity of diagnostic exams.

⚑ RED FLAGS

- If reliability and validity are missing from the data, an informed decision concerning the trustworthiness of the results of a research study cannot be made.
- If validity is documented in a study without any indication of reliability and relevance, concerns about the trustworthiness of the results should be raised.
- If a tool is documented as being used within a study, the report should provide information concerning the validity and reliability indices for the tool.

Multiple-Choice Questions

1. When making good decisions in evidence-based practice, the _____ of the data is necessary.
   A. confirmability
   B. trustworthiness
   C. independence
   D. timing

2. Reliability is defined as the case in which an instrument measures:
   A. the same thing consistently.
   B. what it is supposed to measure.
   C. demographic data.
   D. the same sample consistently.

3. Reliability and relevance may exist:
   A. with dependence on validity.
   B. only independently of validity.
   C. independently of validity.
   D. none of the above.

4. A valid test will _____ have some degree of reliability and relevance.
   A. never
   B. sometimes
   C. frequently
   D. always

5. When measuring blood pressure, the actual score is the:
   A. observed score on the instrument.
   B. estimated score determined by the nurse.
   C. perfect score without error.
   D. first sound heard by the nurse.

6. Reliability coefficients greater than _____ are considered to be high.
   A. 0.50
   B. 0.60
   C. 0.70
   D. 0.80

7. As an example of consistency and stability in EBP, when a urinalysis is done four times in a 24-hour period, the urine sample needs to be the _____ amount.
   A. correct
   B. same
   C. smallest
   D. largest

8. Dividing scores on a pain questionnaire (with 0–5 items) into odd-numbered and even-numbered scores is a mechanism that can be used to determine:
   A. external consistency.
   B. relevance.
   C. internal consistency.
   D. validity.

9. A research study was developed to consider the assessment of skin color. Nurses on a medical–surgical unit were asked to record their judgments of the skin color from four pictures of individuals with differing skin tones. This process is an example of which area of reliability measurement?
   A. Accuracy
   B. Objectivity
   C. Feasibility
   D. Equivalency

10. Which test is used to establish the measurement of the accuracy related to reliability?
    A. ANOVA
    B. Standard error of measure (SEM)
    C. Pearson Product Moment (PPM) correlation
    D. Reliability coefficient

11. To establish a test as an accurate measurement of reliability, the test scores need a relatively _____ standard deviation and a _____ reliability coefficient.
    A. high; high
    B. low; low
    C. low; high
    D. high; low

12. Factors that can affect the reliability, objectivity, and accuracy of a tool or test include:
    A. practice, timing, and environment.
    B. fatigue, subjects, and environment.
    C. precision, homogeneity of the test conditions, and the researcher.
    D. sequencing, practice, and level of ease.

13. Validity can be classified as:
    A. universal.
    B. concise.
    C. general.
    D. logical.

14. A criterion for content-related validity determination is:
    A. the inclusion of extraneous variables.
    B. establishment of brief guidelines for using the tool.
    C. a well-defined protocol for data collection.
    D. the clarification of nuances that might add errors.

15. A researcher was comparing alternative methods for establishing a child's core body temperature for a study. The testing included the measurement of anal, oral, and aural temperatures. This example reflects which type of validity determination?
    A. Construct-related validity
    B. Criterion-related validity
    C. Content-related validity
    D. Predictive validity

16. A study presented the results from the development of a new tool. This tool was established to measure the level of anxiety perceived by children. Which type of validity would this study need to document for the tool?
    A. Content-related validity
    B. Criterion-related validity
    C. Construct-related validity
    D. Concurrent validity

Discussion Questions

Use the following data to answer questions 1–5 below.

Patient Number	Oral Temperature (°F)	Temperature (°F)
1	98.6	98.7
2	99.4	99.3
3	101.2	101.3
4	98.6	98.6
5	100.5	100.7
6	99.7	99.4
7	101.0	101.1
8	98.4	98.6
9	102.9	102.5
10	103.1	102.9

Patient Number	Oral Temperature (°F)	Tympanic Temperature (°F)
1	98.6	98.7
2	99.4	99.3
3	101.2	101.3
4	98.6	98.6
5	100.5	100.7
6	99.7	99.4
7	101.0	101.1
8	98.4	98.6
9	102.9	102.5
10	103.1	102.9

1. Is tympanic temperature a similar measure of oral temperature?
2. Which type of reliability coefficient have you developed with these data?
3. What is the accuracy of tympanic temperature?
4. Is tympanic temperature a valid measure of patient temperature based on the information provided in the second half of the table?
5. Use the example of the pain scale provided in the chapter to define and develop five additional constructs that might be used to measure pain.

Suggested Readings

Baumgartner, T., & Jackson, A. J. (1999). *Measurement for evaluation in physical education and exercise science* (6th ed.). Dubuque, IA: McGraw-Hill.

Brennan, C., & Parsons, G. (2017). Enhanced recovery in orthopedics: A prospective audit of an enhanced recovery program for patients undergoing hip or knee arthroplasty. *MEDSURG Nursing, 26*(2), 99–104.

Cortez-Gann, J., Gilmore, K. D., Foley, K. Q., Kennedy, M. B., McGee, T., & Kring, D. (2017). Blood transfusion vital sign frequency: What does the evidence say? *MEDSURG Nursing, 26*(2), 89–92.

Cunningham, G. K. (1986). *Educational and psychological measurement.* New York, NY: Macmillan.

Glass, G. V., & Hopkins, K. D. (1996). *Statistical methods in education and psychology* (3rd ed.). Englewood Cliffs, NJ: Prentice Hall.

Golafshani, N. (2003). Understanding reliability and validity in qualitative research. *Qualitative Report, 8*(4), 597–607.

Kwan, T. M., & Sullivan, M. (2017). The use of intravenous ibuprofen and intravenous acetaminophen in surgical patients and the effect on opioid reduction. *MEDSURG Nursing, 26*(2), 124–131.

MedicalBiostatistics.com. (n.d.). Sensitivity-specificity, Bayes' rule and predictivities. Retrieved from http://www.medicalbiostatistics.com/Sensitivity-specificity.pdf

Morrow, J. R., Jackson, A. W., Disch, J. G., & Mood, D. P. (2000). *Measurement and evaluation in human performance* (2nd ed.). Champaign, IL: Human Kinetics.

Thomas, J., & Nelson, J. (2005). *Research methods in physical activity* (5th ed.). Champaign, IL: Human Kinetics.

References

American Psychological Association (APA). (1985). *Standards for educational and psychological testing*. Washington, DC: Author.

Bilkis, S., Loveman, D. M., Eldridge, J. A., Ali, S. A., Kadir, A., & McConathy, W. (2012). Modified Phalen's test as an aid in diagnosing carpal tunnel syndrome. *Arthritis Care & Research, 64*(2), 287–289. doi:10.1002/acr.20664

Brennan, C., & Parsons, G. (2017). Enhanced recovery in orthopedics: A prospective audit of an enhanced recovery program for patients undergoing hip or knee arthroplasty. *MEDSURG Nursing, 26*(2), 99–104.

Cortez-Gann, J., Gilmore, K. D., Foley, K. Q., Kennedy, M. B., McGee, T., & Kring, D. (2017). Blood transfusion vital sign frequency: What does the evidence say? *MEDSURG Nursing, 26*(2), 89–92.

Hanna, K. M., Weaver, M. T., Slaven, J. E., Fortenberry, J. D., & DiMeglio, L. A. (2014). Diabetes-related quality of life and the demands and burdens of diabetes care among emerging adults with type 1 diabetes in the year after high school graduation. *Research in Nursing & Health, 37*, 339–408. doi:10.1002/nur.21620

Zou, K. H., O'Malley, A. J., & Mauri, L. (2007). Receiver-operating characteristic analysis for evaluating diagnostic tests and predictive models. *Circulation, 115*(5), 654–657.

CHAPTER 13

Data Analysis

James Eldridge

CHAPTER OBJECTIVES

At the conclusion of this chapter, the learner will be able to:
1. Identify the types of statistics available for analyses in evidence-based practice.
2. Define quantitative analysis, qualitative analysis, and quality assurance.
3. Discuss how research questions define the type of statistics to be used in evidence-based practice research.
4. Choose a data analysis plan and the proper statistics for different research questions raised in evidence-based practice.
5. Interpret data analyses and conclusions from the data analyses.
6. Discuss how quality assurance affects evidence-based practice.

KEY TERMS

Analysis of variance (ANOVA)
Central tendency
Chi-square (χ^2)
Interval scale
Magnitude
Mean
Median
Mode
Nominal scale
Ordinal scale

Qualitative analysis
Quality assurance
Quality improvement
Quantitative analysis
Ratio scale
Statistical Package for the Social Sciences (SPSS)
t-test
Variability

▶ Introduction

This text methodically explains how to move from the formulation of the hypothesis to the data collection stage of a research project. Data collection in evidence-based practice (EBP) might be considered the easiest part of the whole research experience. The researcher has already formed the hypothesis, developed

301

the data collection methods and instruments, and determined the subject pool characteristics.

Once the EBP researcher has completed data collection, it is time for the researcher to compile and interpret the data to explain them in a meaningful context. This compilation and interpretation phase is completed using either quantitative data analysis or qualitative data analysis techniques. **Quantitative analysis** is defined as the numeric representation and manipulation of observations using statistical techniques for the express purpose of describing and explaining the outcomes of research as they pertain to the hypothesis. In other words, quantitative analysis uses numerical values to explain the outcomes of a research project. In contrast, **qualitative analysis** techniques use logical deductions to decipher gathered data dealing with the human element and do not rely on numerical values or mathematical models to explain the results. In other words, qualitative analysis uses words and phrases to explain the outcomes of a research project. Do not confuse qualitative analysis with **quality improvement**, which is a measure of change over time and may use both quantitative and qualitative analyses to develop results and conclusions.

An example of the contrast between quantitative and qualitative analyses would be a research project involving the study of a specific treatment for the reduction of pressure-induced bedsores during convalescent care. To determine if the treatment was effective, data would be collected to compare two groups of individuals who were bedridden. One group would receive the treatment, while the other group would not receive the treatment. Using a scale, such as the Braden Scale, that quantified the number and size of bedsores, the researcher would collect numerical data to determine if differences were apparent between the treatment group and the no treatment group. This custom is a classic example of quantitative analysis. Using the same group of subjects, the researcher could also observe the patients' movement characteristics, attitude, and facial expressions during pretreatment and posttreatment phases. The nursing staff could chronicle the patients' improvement using a written journal. This process would be an example of qualitative analysis.

In the example using quantitative analysis techniques, the researcher could report significant differences between the end treatment values of the treatment and no treatment groups. For example, a significant difference between the mean posttreatment occurrences of pressure ulcers of the treatment group compared to those of the no treatment group might be the result from the treatment. In the qualitative analysis example, the researcher would state the results in a different way. For example, the treatment group exhibited more positional changes during bed rest, with an observed decline in localized long-term pressure points in a single area of the body, skin blood flow changes, rashes, and blisters; furthermore, the patients had a better attitude and were less likely to complain to the nurse while undergoing the posttest procedures.

Notice that in the qualitative analysis example, no mention of statistical differences occurs. Only a description of the observed differences and changes is included. The only time a researcher can report a significant difference is when he or she has used quantitative analysis techniques to interpret the data. In this chapter, the learner will discover when and how to use these two techniques in the reporting and explanation of a project's results.

▶ Quantitative Analysis

Measurement Scales

As described previously, quantitative analysis requires the use of numeric data to describe and interpret the results. It is often referred to as statistical analysis; however, statistical analysis is a subunit of quantitative analysis. Before a researcher can understand the nuances of quantitative analysis, he or she must first understand the types of numeric data that are available for analysis. Numeric data are classified into four measurement scales: (1) nominal, (2) ordinal, (3) interval, and (4) ratio. These four scales are listed here in hierarchical order, with the nominal scale being the least precise measurement scale and the ratio scale being the most precise measurement scale in describing results.

The **nominal scale** is the simplest of the measurement scales because it is used for identification or categorization purposes only. This level of measurement lacks numeric order, magnitude, or size. Examples of nominal scales include race, gender, and patient identification number. A scale for race might collect data in the following way: Anglo equals 1, African American equals 2, Hispanic equals 3, and other race equals 4. In this scale, the number assigned to each race is indicative of group identification only, with no other assumption of magnitude, order, or size. The reason that we use the numerical scale rather than the word terms for race is because most statistical analysis packages have a difficult time interpreting word terms, especially when capitalization and misspellings occur.

The second measurement scale in the hierarchy is the **ordinal scale**. This scale is more precise in measuring items compared to the nominal scale. It incorporates order or ranking yet lacks magnitude and size. A researcher using an ordinal scale is unable to make direct comparisons between ranks because he or she does not know whether the difference between a ranking of 1 and 2 is very small or very large. The only known aspect is that a ranking of 1 is greater or better than a ranking of 2. A medical example of an ordinal scale is the transplant recipient list for a donor heart. A transplant recipient is given a number that identifies his or her order on the list based on symptoms, severity, cross-matching/typing, and time of request. When a donor heart becomes available, the person ranked highest on the list who meets the criteria of proper cross-matching/typing, being symptomatic, with the highest level of illness severity, and the longest time on the donor list receives the heart. Potentially, two patients with the same symptoms, severity, and cross-matching/typing might be separated in the order only by the time (sometimes a few seconds) at which they were placed on the list. Thus, the different aspects have no magnitude or set units of measure between each numeric value. This example illustrates how an ordinal scale represents order but lacks magnitude and size. For both nominal and ordinal scales, mathematical calculations have no meaning because the scales are unable to represent the magnitude and size of the variable.

The final two scales of measurement in the hierarchy are considered continuous scales because each incorporates order and magnitude within its description. Continuous scales allow for mathematical calculations to give the results meaning. Researchers can truly describe significant differences because each number in the scale represents a unique place of order within the scale, and there is equal distance between it and the number directly above and below it in the order.

The third scale of measurement is the **interval scale**. This scale is more precise than the nominal and ordinal scales because it incorporates both order and magnitude within the description; at the same time, it lacks a defined size or, for want of a better term, an "absolute" zero point. An example of the interval scale is the Fahrenheit temperature scale. The degrees in the Fahrenheit scale are ordered from high to low. Each degree within the scale has an equal distance from the next degree; however, the point taken as zero in the scale is arbitrary. Using the term *arbitrary zero* in a scale means that the zero point is not defining a complete lack of quantity; rather, it just serves as a starting point for the measurement. In the Fahrenheit scale, the point chosen as zero is arbitrary because you can actually have a score that is below zero. This same consideration also applies when using the Celsius scale for temperature.

The final and most precise scale in the hierarchy is the **ratio scale**. This scale combines the attributes of the interval scale with the addition of an absolute zero point. The best example of a ratio scale is weight, whether measured in pounds or kilograms. The weight scale has order: 1 pound weighs less than 2 pounds. It has magnitude, and the difference between 1 pound and 2 pounds is the same as the difference between 2 pounds and 3 pounds. Finally, it has an absolute zero point because 0 pounds means there is a complete absence of weight.

Multiple levels of measurement can be identified in the article by Hanna, Weaver, Slaven, Fortenberry, and DiMeglio (2014). The glycemia control (HbA1c) represents an interval level of measurement. The diabetes-related quality of life tool, emerging adult diabetes management self-report, and independent functioning and decision making in daily and nondaily diabetes management checklist provide examples of ordinal levels of measurement. The final grouping of data collected for the Hanna et al. article describes living independently from parents, which represents the nominal level of measurement.

This section of the chapter has opened with the description of the measurement scales because the measurement scale used determines the type of statistical analysis performed. It is important to understand that the more precise a scale, the more stable the statistic is to calculate the outcome. Consider the measure of pain. When determining pain, a physician might use a nominal pain scale that implies only the absence or presence of pain (1 = pain, 0 = no pain), or a physician could use the ratio analog pain scale that implies degrees of pain. If the physician used a nominal scale, no differences between the groups (treatment versus no treatment) could be identified because all the patients in both groups still exhibited pain at the end of the study. In the analog pain example, however, the physician used a ratio scale so that the degree of pain could be measured. Although none of the patients completely lacked pain, it is clear that the group receiving the treatment had a lower degree of pain at the end of the study when compared with the no treatment group. Remember, precision not only adds reliability and validity to the study; it also enhances the statistical power of the results.

🔲 THINK OUTSIDE THE BOX

Review the article by Cortez-Gann and colleagues (2017) and determine what types of scales were used to collect the data.

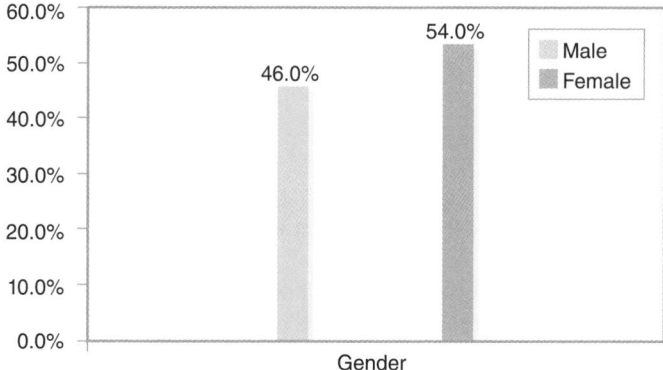

FIGURE 13-1 Descriptive presentation of a nominal scale.

Descriptive Statistics: Nominal and Ordinal Data

The first step and lowest order of any quantitative analysis is the description of the data in numeric terms. As described earlier, the measurement scale used for each item on an instrument determines how the data are presented in a descriptive form. Reporting of data for instrument items that use a nominal or ordinal scale usually takes the form of frequencies or percentages of the response for the item. For example, demographic data for a sample might be reported using variables such as gender, race, marital status, or educational status. Data of this type are presented in the form of percentages, such as the percentage of males and females in the sample (**FIGURE 13-1**).

Novice researchers often make the mistake of reporting nominal or ordinal data in the form of means; this is absolutely incorrect. Nominal and ordinal data have no **magnitude**, size, or measures of central tendency; therefore, a mean and standard deviation are meaningless with these data.

Interval and Ratio Data

Central Tendency

Central tendency is a way to allow the researcher to show the audience how the scores are distributed around a central point. Central tendencies are described in three ways: the mean, the median, and the mode.

The **mean**, or average, of a set of scores is determined by the sum of the scores divided by the total number of scores. An example of the provision of the mean scores can be seen in the Hanna and colleagues (2014) article. Within the first table provided in the article (p. 403), each of the mean scores for the different variables is provided in a column designated with the letter M. Consider also the example of taking a patient's systolic blood pressure five times. The systolic scores are 125, 130, 122, 128, and 130 mmHg. Notice that these scores are ratio scale data because an absolute zero point (meaning no pressure or the absence of any pressure might be measured) is possible. The calculation of the mean of these scores is shown in **FIGURE 13-2**. The average (mean) for the systolic pressure scores is 127 mmHg. Notice that 127 mmHg does not appear in the set of original scores. Rarely does the mean actually equal one of the scores in the observed list; rather, it represents a best estimate of the central point of all the measured scores. Measurement error

$$\text{Mean} = \frac{\Sigma x}{n} \text{ where } X \text{ is the observed score and } n \text{ is the number of scores}$$

$$= \frac{\Sigma 125,130,122,128, \text{ and } 130}{5}$$

$$= \frac{635}{5}$$

$$= 127$$

FIGURE 13-2 Mathematical representation of the mean.

is inherent in all instruments. The mean allows a researcher to develop a central point within the data, incorporating the error within the measure. The process and rationale for doing so are explained in more detail in the discussion of the standard deviation that appears later in this chapter.

The median is the second measure of central tendency. The **median** is the middle score of a set of data. It represents the 50th percentile; thus, it allows the researcher to show the exact point at which half of the scores fall above the median and half of the scores fall below the median. In the previous systolic pressure example, the median of the scores 125, 130, 122, 128, and 130 is 128 mmHg. Notice that in these readings, the score of 128 is the second to the last score. If the median is the middle number, then how can 128 be the median score? A specific point needs to be made when determining the median. The data should always be ordered from lowest to highest when determining the median. In this case, the data for the systolic pressure example should be ordered as follows: 122, 125, 128, 130, 130. When determining the median, all the scores are included; even the duplications stand within the listing of the scores.

The final measure of central tendency is the mode. The **mode** is the most frequently observed score within a variable's data. In the previous example, the systolic pressure of 130 mmHg is the mode of the data because it occurs twice, while all other scores appear only once. Whereas the mean is the most stable measure of central tendency (meaning it represents the absolute possible middle score), the mode is the least stable measure of central tendency (meaning it represents only the most frequently occurring score). As a researcher increases the number of observations of a variable, the chances are that the mean, median, and mode will be more representative or equal to each other.

Variability

A second issue when describing interval and ratio data is the variability of the data. **Variability** describes how the data vary between each score and from the mean. Two types of variability that the EBP researcher might report are the range of the data and the variance or standard deviation of the data.

The range of the data is calculated by subtracting the lowest score for the variable from the highest score for the variable. In the previous example involving systolic blood pressures, the range of the data is from 130 to 122 mmHg, or 8 mmHg. This calculation simply means that the highest score and lowest score vary by only 8 mmHg. When reporting this range, the reader can infer that, because the mean of the data was 127 mmHg and the range was 8 mmHg, then the scores ranged from 123 to 131. In such a case, the reader of the report must assume that the variability was uniform. This rating reflects that the scores varied from the mean evenly: In other words, the upper scores varied 4 mmHg from the mean, and the lower scores varied 4 mmHg

$$\sqrt{\dfrac{\sum x^2 - \dfrac{(\sum x)^2}{n}}{n-1}}$$ where X is the observed score and n is the number of scores

FIGURE 13-3 Mathematical representation of standard deviation.

from the mean. With the aforementioned assumption, the reader infers some error because the actual scores ranged from 122 to 130 mmHg. When reporting the range of 8 mmHg and the mean of 127 mmHg, however, the range was 123 to 131 mmHg.

One other point to remember is that the range is unstable if the data being used include numerous outliers, either above the mean or below the mean. Again, using the systolic pressure example, assume that the data were 125, 130, 122, 128, and 160 mmHg. The mean for these data is 133 mmHg (approximately 6 mmHg higher than the mean found in the first example), and the range is 38 mmHg. Notice that the inclusion of a single high value increased the range by 30 mmHg. Also notice that, when interpreting the data, the reader would assume falsely that with a mean of 133 mmHg, the data would range from 114 to 152 mmHg. In this case, the description of the data is lacking because the outlier of 160 mmHg negatively affects the description.

The second measure of variability in describing data is the standard deviation, which is the square root of variance. Variance is the measure of the spread of scores around the mean based on the squared deviations of the observed scores from the mean of the data. The concept of a standard deviation allows a researcher to develop a description of the scores' variability from the mean based on a normal distribution. The standard deviation, which can be determined using the formula in **FIGURE 13-3**, provides the ability to describe the data based on a normal distribution and the percentage of the normal distribution expected to occur between each standard deviation unit.

As shown in **FIGURE 13-4**, the researcher can describe the pattern of the data more fully by using both the mean and the standard deviation. The standard deviation can be interpreted as meaning that the reader of the data can expect 68.26% of the observed scores to fall ± 1 standard deviation from the mean. Conversely, the reader can expect less than two-tenths of 1% of the scores to fall ± 1 standard deviation from the mean. In presenting both the mean and the standard deviation, a researcher describes the data in terms of a normal distribution, allowing the reader of the results to get a mental picture of how the scores compare to the normal distribution. For example, Hanna and colleagues (2014) provide each of the standard deviation calculations along with the range of scores for the different variables noted within their study (p. 403).

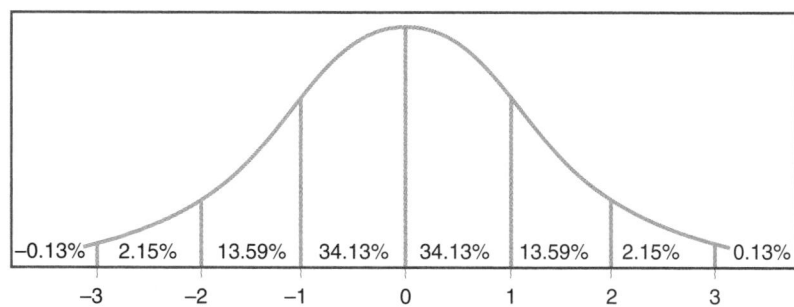

FIGURE 13-4 The normal distribution.

🔲 THINK OUTSIDE THE BOX

Discuss how statistics can be used in an evidence-based practice and/or quality improvement project.

Consider the systolic pressure example once again. With scores of 122, 125, 128, 130, and 130 mmHg, the mean is 127 mmHg, with a standard deviation of 3.46 mmHg. When data are presented in this form, the reader can visualize that 68.26% of the scores fell between 123.54 and 130.46 mmHg. The reader can also determine from the mean and the standard deviation that less than 0.26% of the scores were less than 116.62 mmHg or greater than 137.38 mmHg. In looking at the data described in this manner, the reader begins to understand that most of the scores from this sample were within the normal range for systolic blood pressure.

This type of analytical presentation emphasizes the verbal descriptions that are made when describing the sample demographics. ("The sample when beginning the study had normal systolic blood pressures.") Some people might shy away from reporting the mean and the standard deviation in their research reports because of math phobia. This fear is unwarranted because most statistical software packages make the process of computing these values very simple. In the current world of research, most researchers utilize a statistics software package, such as the **Statistical Package for the Social Sciences (SPSS)**, to complete all the calculations for the data collected.

From this point forward in this chapter, all data analysis is described for the learner. To finish the lesson on the mean and standard deviation, the learner is asked to determine the mean and standard deviation of a set of scores for hemoglobin content (**TABLE 13-1**). In this example, all the scores need to be totaled and divided by 10.

TABLE 13-1 Hemoglobin Scores

Patient ID	Hemoglobin
1	14.10
2	12.20
3	11.90
4	14.50
5	13.80
6	13.20
7	13.50
8	14.00
9	11.10
10	9.60

TABLE 13-2 Differences Between Dependent and Independent Variables	
Independent Variable	**Dependent Variable**
Cause	Effect
Manipulated	The consequence
Measured	Outcome
Predicted to	Predicted from
Predictor	Criterion
X	*y*

Inferential Statistics

Once a researcher has described the study subjects through descriptive analysis, it is time to quantitatively analyze and present the data for the results. To accomplish this task, a researcher must understand not only the scales of measurement but also the type of variable. Research design typically includes two types of variables—the dependent variable and the independent variable. The dependent variable is the criterion that determines the entire purpose of the research. The independent variable is the variable that affects the change in, or is related to, the dependent variable. A dependent variable can be categorized as the outcome variable or the effect variable, while the independent variable is categorized as the manipulated variable or the cause variable. **TABLE 13-2** lists other differences between the dependent and independent variables.

An example of a statement using an independent variable and a dependent variable would involve a researcher attempting to determine if there is a difference between use of a statin drug and use of niacin alone in reducing cholesterol level. The dependent variable in this case is cholesterol level (the outcome measured in mg/dL); the independent variable is the type of treatment (statin or niacin). Determining which variable is the dependent variable and which is the independent variable is only the first step, however, in identifying the statistic to use for data analysis. The second step is to determine the scale of measurement for both the dependent variable and the independent variable. The scale of measurement for each of these variables then determines the proper statistic for analysis of the data. General guidelines for choosing the proper statistic based on the measurement scale of the dependent and independent variables are presented in **TABLE 13-3**.

Chi-Square

Whenever the dependent variable is scaled nominally, the chi-square statistic is typically used for its analysis. The **chi-square (X^2)** value suggests whether an association exists between nominally scaled variables.

TABLE 13-3 Statistical Choice for Measurement Scales of Dependent and Independent Variables

Independent Variable	Dependent Variable	Statistical Test
1 nominal	1 nominal	Chi-square
1 nominal (2 groups)	1 continuous	t-test
1 nominal (2 groups)	1 continuous	One-way ANOVA
2 nominal	1 continuous	Two-way ANOVA

Note: ANOVA = analysis of variance.

An example of a research design that warrants a chi-square analysis would be the case in which a researcher wants to know if there are differences between men and women in undergoing annual checkups (yes or no). The dependent variable for these data is whether the person underwent an annual checkup, while the independent variable is gender. With the use of a statistical software package, the chi-square value can be calculated quite easily. Once the calculation is completed, the determination of any difference between men and women in terms of whether they underwent an annual checkup could be made by reviewing the chi-square statistic and the significance of the test. Generally, most research studies seek to find statistical differences at the $p < 0.05$ level. Anything greater than 0.05 is considered not significant.

At this time, it is important to point out that, in data analysis, the results are either significant or not significant. Statistical significance does not "prove" anything. When a statistical significant result is determined, the understanding is that the independent variable has an impact on the dependent variable but does not prove that something will occur. The p value does not impose magnitude. Therefore, even if the results have a significance of 0.0001, this finding does not mean that the results are "extremely" significant—just that they are significant.

t-Test

Now that we have described the analysis of a nominally scaled dependent variable, it is time to learn how to determine which test to use for a continuous scaled dependent variable. Review Table 13-3 to refresh your memory. The number of nominal variables and levels within the nominal variables for the independent variable determines which statistic (t-test or analysis of variance [ANOVA]) should be used.

If the independent variable has one nominal variable with two groups (e.g., gender), the researcher would use a **t-test** to determine statistical differences between the groups. Two types of *t*-tests can be calculated—the independent *t*-test and the dependent *t*-test. An independent *t*-test is used when a single continuous dependent variable is being compared, while a dependent *t*-test allows a researcher to compare two continuous variables as long as the variables are related.

An example of a dependent *t*-test is a comparison of the pretreatment and posttreatment cholesterol levels of a group of individuals receiving a statin drug as single-agent therapy. Interpretation of the *t*-test statistic is the same for both variables; the nuance is a function of the number of dependent variables and whether they are related.

The independent *t*-test statistic determines if a difference is present in a single dependent variable between the two groups. An example of a research design that warrants an independent *t*-test analysis would be a researcher who wants to know if there are differences between men and women in terms of their hemoglobin content. The dependent variable for these data is hemoglobin content, which is a ratio-scaled continuous variable; the independent variable is gender. Data are provided in **TABLE 13-4** to assist in determining the answer to this question.

Once the results are input and statistics are calculated using a statistical software package, the determination of the difference between men and women in hemoglobin levels could be identified by assessing the significance of the test. Again, remember that most research studies seek to find statistical differences at the $p < 0.05$ level.

🔁 THINK OUTSIDE THE BOX

Describe the different numerical values used in the clinical setting. Discuss which level of measurements each of those types of values represents (i.e., blood pressure readings, fasting blood sugar, weights). Differentiate among the different measurement scales that you use on a daily basis. Does this understanding change the way you think about the values that you use when delivering care?

ANOVA

The final statistical analysis to be discussed for interpreting data is the **analysis of variance (ANOVA)**. As described previously in the *t*-test section, the number of nominal variables and levels within the nominal variables for the independent variable determine which statistic (*t*-test or ANOVA) should be used. If the independent variable has one nominal variable with more than two groups (e.g., race), an ANOVA test would be used to determine statistical differences.

Two types of ANOVA can be calculated: the one-way ANOVA and the two-way ANOVA. The one-way ANOVA is used when a research study is comparing a single nominal independent variable. The two-way ANOVA allows the researcher to compare two nominal independent variables. An example of a two-way ANOVA would involve comparing men and women (one independent variable) by trial (pretreatment versus posttreatment; the second independent variable) in terms of their

TABLE 13-4 Quantitative Analysis: Data for *t*-Test Analysis		
Patient ID	**Gender**	**Hemoglobin**
1	Male	14.10
2	Female	12.20
3	Male	11.90
4	Female	14.50
5	Female	13.80
6	Female	13.20
7	Male	13.50
8	Male	14.00
9	Male	11.10
10	Female	9.60

cholesterol levels. This example would be considered a 2 × 2 design, which is used in many clinical trials.

Interpretation of the ANOVA statistic is the same for both variables; the nuance relates to the number of independent variables. The one-way ANOVA statistic determines whether a difference is present in a single dependent variable among the several groups within a single independent variable.

An example of a research design that warrants an ANOVA analysis would be used by a researcher who wants to know if there are differences among people of various ethnicities in terms of their hemoglobin content. The dependent variable for these data is hemoglobin content, which is a ratio-scaled continuous variable, while the independent variable is ethnicity (white, African American, or Hispanic). Data are provided in **TABLE 13-5** to assist in answering this question. Notice that in the data entry for race, the variables are dummy coded (1 = white, 2 = Hispanic, and 3 = African American). These variables are treated as nominal scale variables. To determine if a difference among people of these races in terms of their hemoglobin levels is present, the significance of the test would need to be calculated using a statistical software package. Again, remember that most research studies seek to find statistical differences at the $p < 0.05$ level.

A final note about ANOVA techniques: When completing either a one-way ANOVA or a two-way ANOVA, the statistical program requires the ANOVA to be

TABLE 13-5 ANOVA Model		
Patient ID	**Race**	**Hemoglobin**
212	1	8.119
172	2	16.029
183	2	14.569
152	2	17.624
153	2	15.242
154	2	19.942
182	2	16.111
186	2	14.230
213	3	16.951
237	1	12.400
105	1	12.350
106	1	12.106
107	1	11.811
149	1	12.972
150	1	13.930
151	1	12.038
181	2	13.703
227	2	16.433
228	2	13.446
128	2	14.953

(continues)

TABLE 13-5 ANOVA Model		*(continued)*
Patient ID	Race	Hemoglobin
129	2	12.624
130	2	13.169
142	2	14.987
159	2	12.596
170	3	15.996
171	3	11.476
179	1	11.233
187	1	12.253
222	1	14.090
173	1	14.060

defined as a one-tailed or two-tailed test. Defining the number of tails simply means that the researcher must determine whether the differences among the data are expected to occur in a single direction on the normal curve or in both directions on the normal curve. A single-tailed test suggests that the expected differences for all groups will occur in a single direction, either above the mean (an increase) or below the mean (decrease). A two-tailed test assumes that group differences are expected to change in a bidirectional manner, where one group may have a decrease from the mean while another group may have an increase from the mean. An example of a single-tailed test would be the measurement of body temperature with the onset of a disease. The researcher might expect that body temperature will increase from the normal temperature of 98.6°F only with the onset of a disease, so the ANOVA in this study will be a single-tailed test.

An example of a two-tailed test would be the measurement of body weight among a dieting group and a control group. The researcher might expect that body weight will decrease in the dieting group, whereas it will increase with the control group, so the ANOVA will be a two-tailed test.

Repeated Measures ANOVA

A final type of ANOVA not only looks at differences between groups but also differences between times. This type of analysis is known as a repeated ANOVA. Repeated ANOVA in EBP not only can describe endpoint differences but can also describe differences in the change among variables over time. Repeated ANOVA is specifically important in developing quality improvement measures where numerous time points of data may be collected to determine if a quality metric is improving.

An example of a research design that warrants a repeated ANOVA analysis would be similar to the pressure-induced bedsore study described previously. In this example, rather than determining only the treatment effect, the nurse practitioner could also determine if time influenced individuals who were bedridden. The study design would be similar so that one group would receive the treatment, while the other group would not receive the treatment; however, in this study, data would be collected each week. Using the same group of subjects, the researcher could observe how bedsore numbers, size, and pain level increased over time to determine if changes in the timing of treatment implementation might improve the treatment's effect.

Reporting the Results of Quantitative Analysis

The final step in the quantitative analysis of data is disseminating the results in an intelligible form. Put simply, a researcher must thoroughly describe the sample using the descriptive analysis techniques. Once the sample is described, each inferential statistic needs to be described within the results. The a priori probability value (usually $p < 0.05$) must be stated. Finally, the statistical tests need to be reported, including what their probability is and whether these results are significant. These analyses allow a researcher to develop the discussion by comparing the results of the study with the findings from other research and inferring whether these results have substantial implications for practice.

▶ Qualitative Analysis

The second major form of analysis that an EBP researcher may perform is a qualitative analysis. As described previously, qualitative analysis incorporates observation and language to develop an in-depth description of the results. Whereas quantitative analysis describes results and outcomes based on numeric data, inferential statistics, and sample size, qualitative analysis relies on the observational method of the researchers and their ability to describe the in-depth intricacies of the observations to explain outcomes and develop theories for the research. The final outcome of most qualitative analyses is not based on significant differences from the numeric data; rather, it consists of a refined conceptual framework of the research that is improved through logical reasoning.

Another way to think about the difference between quantitative and qualitative analysis is to frame it in the terms of the reasoning process. Quantitative analysis uses the deductive reasoning process—that is, a top-down method of analysis. With this approach, the researcher begins with a theory on a topic, then narrows the scope to one or more hypotheses, and finally homes in on conformational results collected from a specific sample. In contrast, qualitative analysis most often uses the inductive reasoning process—a bottom-up analysis that goes in the opposite direction of the deductive process. With this approach, the researcher starts with observations of a specific pattern and, from those observations, develops hypotheses and theories.

Once these theories are developed, the quantitative method can be used to test those theories and generalize the results to a population. The final outcome of a qualitative analysis is often not a set of specific results but rather a set of specific questions or hypotheses in need of quantitative analysis.

Two types of qualitative analysis apply to the EBP provider—the case study and the program evaluation. Each of these types of analysis occurs at some time during a nurse's professional practice. Each has commonalities and distinct characteristics that are based in the foundation of observation. The major skills that all EBP researchers must possess to ensure well-derived products from qualitative analyses are good language skills and keen observational techniques.

Notice that observation is the key element in all qualitative analyses. As a result, most qualitative research plans focus on small groups of individuals to develop the conceptual framework that encompasses the final deductions, unlike quantitative analyses that use large samples to derive the results. For example, Woolston and Connelly (2017) used content analysis and member checking for the audio-recorded/transcribed interviews data; care and thought were given to the determination of specific themes. Also, comparison data are minimal because qualitative analysis, although not constrained by the assessment of significant differences, lacks the distinct comparable traits that are inherent in the use of quantitative analysis.

The Case Study

The case study is the most commonly practiced type of qualitative analysis occurring in EBP research. Case studies are individualized and personal. Many of the case studies gleaned from EBP eventually lead to larger quantitative analysis trials. In developing a case study, the researcher's initial response is to assume that all aspects of the case are important and to take a broad overview of the topic to explain the outcomes.

In any qualitative analysis, focus on the conceptual framework determines the success or failure of the end product. The conceptual framework explains the dimensions of the study, the key factors, the variables, and the relationship among different variables. The EBP researcher must focus on and define the conceptual framework prior to implementing a case study. Effective preparation and focus can help eliminate unnecessary observations and shorten the time for completion of the study.

To develop a conceptual framework for a case study (or any other qualitative analysis), the EBP nurse must be well-versed in the area of study and thoroughly familiar with research previously conducted on the topic (i.e., the literature). The conceptual framework often starts as a new observation that piques the curiosity of a researcher. In the process of becoming interested, the researcher begins to focus his or her observations, collecting data through a written journal or diary of the observations, and then attempts to develop a coherent framework that explains the novel observations. In nursing practice, patient files may be reviewed and described to develop the conceptual framework for the analysis.

Once a conceptual framework sets the boundaries of the analysis, the research questions must be developed. This is done in the same manner as in any research—through review of the literature and comparison of the case with the previous findings of other research. Case studies, like program evaluations, must be described in depth to improve the impact of their findings. A lack of depth in such descriptions may lead subsequent reviewers of the research to discard it as being poorly substantiated.

Once the conceptual framework is completed and the research questions are defined, it is time to develop the means to explain the observations in the context of the questions. A researcher should focus on and include only those material observations that are relevant. Inclusion of minutiae and irrelevant observations in the report of a study tends to detract from the impact of the overall analysis. The relevant findings should be described in detail, and previous research should be used, when available, to help derive the conclusions. The end product of the effective completion of this process is often the identification of questions needing further study. In Woolston and Connelly (2017), the authors used case study techniques to examine Felty's syndrome. Review the article in detail. Notice the questions that were asked, and then compare the presentation of the results to a quantitative study such as the Cortez-Gann et al. (2017) study discussed in Chapter 12.

The Program Evaluation

Program evaluation is another method of qualitative analysis that the EBP researcher may use to evaluate a specific program rather than an individual case. Program evaluation allows the EBP researcher to observe the workings of a specific program rather than a single case and to develop explanations for the success or failure of the program.

Like the case study, program evaluation needs a well-defined conceptual framework through which to judge success or failure. The program evaluator often asks the program participants to complete a self-study exercise listing the items that each participant perceives as important to the successful implementation of the program. The evaluator then reviews the self-study and compares it with previously successful programs that incorporated the same conceptual framework. The researcher may also review characteristics of the site where the program implementation occurs to determine if site-specific barriers are present that might potentially hamper the successful implementation of the program.

The end product of a program evaluation should include well-defined areas of success within the program and identification of all observed barriers in the program that might increase the likelihood of failure. The final product of a program evaluation should include well-founded conclusions that will improve the likelihood of successful implementation of the program. Often, the end product either helps strengthen the implementation of the program or determines that, in the present state and site reference, the program needs to be reconceptualized.

▶ Quality Assurance

Quality assurance analysis is becoming one of the most important analyses required of the EBP researcher in the healthcare setting. Patients, insurance companies, and regulatory agencies demand that programs, hospitals, and clinics provide ever-increasing evidence of the quality of the health care available to the public. Quality assurance analysis is not a recognizable single technique for analyzing data; instead, it is the process that allows the EBP researchers to guide them in developing the necessary outcome measures that will provide the evidence of quality health care.

Quality assurance analyses may include using both quantitative and qualitative statistical techniques. These statistical techniques define the degree to which quality exists in the healthcare services provided to the patient or the community. The ultimate outcome of a quality assurance analysis is to help the EBP researcher determine strengths and weaknesses associated with the healthcare service and allow for the development of quality improvement practices that may improve the likelihood of desired health outcomes or improve the process of efficiently delivering the healthcare service. The Institute of Medicine (2010) defines healthcare quality as being effective, safe, patient-centered, timely, efficient, and equitable. Two specific elements expected from measuring healthcare quality are the assessment of the effects of the healthcare service on improved health status and the assessment of the degree to which the healthcare services adhere to evidence-based practices and processes as defined by current scientific research, professional body consensus statements, and/or patient preferences.

The ultimate goal of quality assurance is to provide feedback to the EBP researcher for the development of quality improvement initiatives. Thus, the EBP researcher must carefully define the desired measures of quality. To aid in the development of a quality assurance measure, the EBP researcher must first determine if the measure will assess outcomes or processes associated with health care. Advantages and disadvantages to both types of quality measures must be considered. Process measures are easily benchmarked, tend to use readily accessible data, require smaller sample sizes, take less time to accumulate the data, and can provide clear feedback to the provider; however, process measures must have well-defined criteria for patient inclusion and may be difficult to summarize due to lack of available comprehensive data. Outcome measures use easily defined populations; tend to be more specific; produce clearer results concerning patient survival, health changes, and well-being; and can be compared across conditions. However, outcome measures require much larger sample sizes, tend to be more labor intensive, and require collection of data beyond that which is collected for clinical or billing purposes. In addition, feedback generally cannot be interpreted for changes in processes. Once the type of measurement is defined as an outcome measure or a process measure, the EBP researcher can then decide which of the six measurable characteristics of quality (efficacy, efficiency, safety, timeliness, equity, and/or patient-centeredness) will be incorporated into the measure. Finally, the EBP researcher must ensure that the defined measure has adequate validity and reliability. Well-defined and well-developed quality assurance measures result in effective treatments and policies, thereby improving healthcare services and healthcare delivery.

▶ Conclusion

Data analysis is one of the most stressful aspects of the research process because of the complexity of the endeavor. Table 13-3 is designed to help address some of the confusion related to which tests to use. Care must be taken to select the appropriate data analysis test, thereby ensuring the broad applicability of the study's findings. For quantitative data, focusing on the level of measurements for the different variables is of paramount importance. Consideration of the appropriate central tendency measurement becomes important when determining which statistical test to use. For most researchers, the statistical tests are calculated using statistical software. The researcher must then make sense of the results that are provided.

Summary Points

1. Quantitative analysis uses numeric values to explain the outcome of a research project.
2. Qualitative analysis uses words or phrases to explain the outcomes of a research project.
3. Nominal scales use only group identification or categories to organize data.
4. Ordinal scales use ranking to organize data.
5. Interval scales have an arbitrary zero point.
6. Ratio scales have an absolute zero point.
7. Measures of central tendency include the mean, median, and mode.
8. Variability of the data describes how data vary between each score and from the mean.
9. The standard deviation statistic provides the ability to describe data based on a normal distribution and the percentage of the normal distribution expected to occur between each standard deviation unit.
10. A chi-square test is used to analyze data when the dependent variable is scaled nominally to determine if an association exists between the variables.
11. A *t*-test is used to analyze data that include one nominal variable with two groups.
12. ANOVA is used to analyze data that include one nominal variable with more than two groups.
13. Case studies often lead to larger quantitative analysis trials.
14. Quality assurance is a means of assessing the outcomes and processes of health care in terms of efficacy, efficiency, safety, timeliness, equity, and patient-centeredness.

⚑ RED FLAGS

- Means are not calculated for nominal data.
- Large standard deviations imply a wide range within the individual scores. This result suggests there is greater variability and less consistency within the resulting data.
- Outliers within the data set can skew the results of analysis of those data.
- If the data consist of a nominal level of measurement for the variable, the chi-square (χ^2) statistic is the statistical test of choice.
- Chi-square (χ^2) tests reflect association between variables.

Multiple-Choice Questions

1. Which statistic is often used for nominally scaled variables?
   A. *t*-test
   B. ANOVA
   C. Chi-square
   D. Pearson Product Moment

2. What level of measurement is most often associated with categorical data such as gender?
   A. Nominal
   B. Ordinal
   C. Interval
   D. Ratio

3. What inferential procedure is used in Cortez-Gann et al. (2017) to determine differences in blood pressure measures across time?
   A. Chi-square
   B. *t*-test
   C. Repeated measures ANOVA
   D. Factor analysis

4. Inferential statistics are used to decide if differences among treatment groups are due to the:
   A. significance.
   B. dependent variable.
   C. confounding variable.
   D. independent variable.

5. Selection of the appropriate statistical technique is based on:
   A. the research question.
   B. the level of measurement of the independent variable(s).
   C. the level of measurement of the dependent variable(s).
   D. all of the above.

6. What do statistically significant findings imply?
   A. The results are very important.
   B. The results are not very important.
   C. The results are likely due to chance differences among groups.
   D. The results are likely due to real differences among groups.

7. A researcher investigated the relationship between vitamin C supplements (none, 500 mg, 1,000 mg) and workers (office, outdoor) in terms of the frequency of colds. Which of the following is (are) the dependent variable(s)?
   A. Colds
   B. Vitamin C
   C. Colds and workers
   D. Vitamin C and workers

8. Which of the following is an inferential statistic?
   A. Mode
   B. *t*-test
   C. Standard deviation
   D. Range

9. Which statistical test has a dependent variable that is nominal in nature?
   A. Chi-square
   B. *t*-test
   C. ANOVA
   D. Two-way ANOVA

10. What is standard deviation?
    A. The square of the mean deviation
    B. The square of the variance
    C. The square root of the variance
    D. The square root of the sum of squares

11. The *t*-test is used to:
    A. adjust for initial differences within the groups.
    B. estimate the error of prediction.
    C. test whether two groups differ significantly.
    D. test whether more than two groups differ significantly.

12. Use of a one-tailed versus a two-tailed test of significance of the difference between two samples is determined by:
    A. whether there is expected overlap between the error curves of the two sample distributions.
    B. whether the difference is expected to be in one direction only.
    C. the size of the samples relative to population size.
    D. whether the subjects were matched or chosen randomly.

Discussion Questions

1. A nurse has decided to research the following PICOT topic: "Adult clients who are admitted to the cardiac unit with congestive heart failure are more likely to develop nosocomial infections than other cardiac clients admitted to the cardiac unit." A quantitative research design is planned for this project. From the PICOT topic, determine the variables, the levels of measurement of each variable, and the statistical test to be used.

2. When comparing the Cortez-Gann et al. (2017) presentation of results to the results presented by Woolston and Connelly (2017), what are differences in the verbiage used that show one is quantitative and one is qualitative research?

3. A research project is intended to analyze preintervention and postintervention cholesterol levels for a group of high school students participating in an after-school athletic program. Which type of statistical test could be used for this study and why?

Suggested Readings

American Psychological Association (APA). (2001). *Standards for educational and psychological testing* (5th ed., pp. 8–9). Washington, DC: Author.

Baumgartner, T., & Jackson, A. J. (1999). *Measurement for evaluation in physical education and exercise science* (6th ed., pp. 57–109). Dubuque, IA: McGraw-Hill.

Colling, J. (2004). Coding, analysis, and dissemination of study results. *Urology Nursing, 24*(3), 215–216.

Cortez-Gann, J., Gilmore, K. D., Foley, K. Q., Kennedy, M. B., McGee, T., & Kring, D. (2017). Blood transfusion vital sign frequency: What does the evidence say? *MEDSURG Nursing, 26*(2), 89–92.

Cunningham, G. K. (1986). *Educational and psychological measurement.* New York, NY: Macmillan.

Glass, G. V., & Hopkins, K. D. (1996). *Statistical methods in education and psychology* (3rd ed., pp. 31–77). Englewood Cliffs, NJ: Prentice Hall.

Happ, M. B., Dabbs, A. D., Tate, J., Hricik, A., & Erlen, J. (2006). Exemplars of mixed methods data combination and analysis. *Nursing Research, 55*(2), S43–S49.

Institute of Medicine. (2010). *The future of nursing: Leading change, advancing health.* Washington, DC: National Academies Press.

Magee, T., Lee, S., Giuliano, K., & Munro, B. (2006). Generating new knowledge from existing data: The use of large data sets for nursing research. *Nursing Research, 55*(2S), S50–S56.

Morrow, J. R., Jackson, A. W., Disch, J. G., & Mood, D. P. (2000). *Measurement and evaluation in human performance* (2nd ed., pp. 65–70). Champaign, IL: Human Kinetics.

Owen, S., & Froman, R. (2005). Focus on research methods. Why carve up your continuous data? *Research in Nursing & Health, 28*(6), 496–503.

Priest, H., Roberts, P., & Woods, L. (2002). An overview of three different approaches to the interpretation of qualitative data. Part 1: Theoretical Issues. *Nurse Researcher, 10*(1), 30–42.

Rubin, H. R., Pronovost, P., & Diette, G. B. (2001). The advantages and disadvantages of process-based measures of health care quality. *International Journal for Quality in Health Care, 13*(6), 469–474.

Seibers, R. (2002). Data in abstracts of research articles: Are they consistent with those reported in the article? *British Journal of Biomedical Science, 59*(2), 67–68.

Thomas, J., & Nelson J. (2005). *Research methods in physical activity* (5th ed., pp. 110–212). Champaign, IL: Human Kinetics.

Woolston, W., & Connelly, L. M. (2017). Felty's syndrome: A qualitative case study. *MEDSURG Nursing, 26*(2), 105–109.

References

Cortez-Gann, J., Gilmore, K. D., Foley, K. Q., Kennedy, M. B., McGee, T., & Kring, D. (2017). Blood transfusion vital sign frequency: What does the evidence say? *MEDSURG Nursing, 26*(2), 89–92.

Hanna, K. M., Weaver, M. T., Slaven, J. E., Fortenberry, J. D., & DiMeglio, L. A. (2014). Diabetes-related quality of life and the demands and burdens of diabetes care among emerging adults with type 1 diabetes in the year after high school graduation. *Research in Nursing & Health, 37*, 399–408. doi:10.1002/nur.21620

Institute of Medicine (IOM). (2010). *The future of nursing: Leading change, advancing health.* Washington, DC: National Academies Press.

Woolston, W., & Connelly, L. M. (2017). Felty's syndrome: A qualitative case study. *MEDSURG Nursing, 26*(2), 105–109.

CHAPTER 14

The Research Critique Process and the Evidence-Based Appraisal Process

Carol Boswell and Sharon Cannon

CHAPTER OBJECTIVES

At the conclusion of this chapter, the learner will be able to:
1. Provide a rationale for completing a research critique.
2. Itemize the essential components in a research critique.
3. Analyze the evidence-based appraisal.
4. Evaluate evidence needed for clinical decision making.
5. Utilize evidence-based practice (EBP) guidelines to manage holistic nursing practice.

KEY TERMS

Critique	Qualitative research
Hypothesis	Quantitative research

▶ Rationale for Doing a Research Critique

When an important question in nursing practice has been identified, the immediate consequence is often itself a question: What's in the literature? What does the current evidence say about the question being considered? A common assumption made by most people is that the printed words are absolute or true. This assumption is even more commonplace when the literature is a researched study. Regrettably, not all published research and/or evidence is scientifically sound. As a result, it is important that a nurse be able to appraise a report.

According to Gray, Grove, and Sutherland (2017), in the 1940s and 1950s, generated critiques from nursing research were poorly constructed. As a result, nursing research was limited until the 1980s and 1990s. All studies have some imperfections that can raise concerns regarding the conducting of research. The basic concept of research management is that the researcher makes decisions about the research plan and justifies those decisions. According to Glasofer (2014), the quality for any study must be founded on the reduction of biases during the research planning and implementation along with the minimizing of outside factors on the results obtained. If the researcher has done a good job with the justifications, then the strength of the results is supported. When poor justifications for the research decisions are evident, the strength of the results must be questioned. As a result of this realization, scrutiny focusing on the limitations and strengths of studies is now commonplace. This shift from criticism to analysis provides a more positive approach to examining the usefulness of the scientific data generated. Mick (2017) states that, "healthcare organizations and leaders are under pressure to improve outcomes by creating structure/culture/environment in which exploration of critical inquiry and the available body of evidence is [sic] an integral part of daily nursing practice" (p. 28). Nurses must contemplate and evaluate studies critically, particularly research studies, to determine the appropriate application to practice. Melnyk and Fineout-Overholt (2015) support this sentiment in relation to research and evidence-based practice (EBP). In EBP, research provides the evidence that guides clinical practice in making decisions about the care nurses provide.

According to Polit and Beck (2017), a research critique is a mechanism to provide feedback for improvement. They suggest that nurses who can critically review a study make valuable contributions to the body of nursing knowledge. Individuals conducting critiques need to be aware of biases that they could insert into their review. Care needs to be given when looking at sources to determine the effectiveness of the material for practice so that changes in practice are based on material that has minimal biases within the review of the material. Mick (2017) addresses the importance of individuals and groups of professionals being able to raise questions about their practice as a result of conducting clinical inquiry to advance practice changes through research utilization and experiential learning.

⬡ THINK OUTSIDE THE BOX

Look critically at the evidence required of nurses today. How could you start the process of gaining confidence in doing research critiques? What are some of the reasons for doing research critiques?

Finally, considering a rationale for a research critique can be found in the definition of the word *critique* offered by Merriam-Webster (2018) "a careful judgment in which you give your opinion about the good and bad parts of something (such as a piece of writing or a work of art)" (for English language learners). If a person considers nursing as both an art and a science, then a critical review of nursing research can be viewed as a work of art. Studies withstanding the test of time through careful exploration of findings and implementation allow nurses to practice the art and science of the profession. Each nurse is asked to scrutinize habitually and consistently how and what he or she is doing in light of the evidence to guarantee that the care provided is contemporary. By examining articles for positive and negative items, gaps and consistencies can be determined. Research is a significant aspect of EBP; therefore, this chapter discusses the research critique first.

▶ Elements of a Research Critique

Before considering the elements of a research critique, let's discuss the types of critiques. Gray, Grove, and Sutherland (2017) have identified eight times when critiques, ranging from student critiques to critiques of research proposals, are used to advance nursing:

- Students learn to critique in their nursing education programs.
- Practicing nurses analyze studies for evidence on which to base the care provided.
- Educators approach critiques from the aspect of improving instruction.
- Nurse researchers focus on building a program of research emphasizing the review of studies in one specific area.
- Presenting research at meetings, conferences, and workshops allows participants to critique studies verbally.
- Several nursing journals publish critiques of published articles, with the authors of the original article subsequently responding to concerns raised with the critique. These types of critiques often take the form of letters to the editor.
- An article submitted for publication in a peer-reviewed journal undergoes a review by peers who assess the quality of the study.
- Requests for funding for research studies from agencies such as the National Institute of Nursing Research (NINR) are subjected to scrutiny.

Critiques are essential to EBP and are expressed in the various forms just discussed. Regardless of the type of critique, each critique includes certain elements. Brink and Wood (2001) have suggested that the rationale for a research critique is to ascertain whether the conclusions are serviceable within the setting in which you are functioning. Some general questions can be associated with the elements of a critique.

Study Purpose

The first element of a research critique generally involves determining the purpose of a study. Questions to be asked concerning the purpose of the research process include the following:

- Is the purpose understandable?
- Is it appropriate to your practice?
- Is a need for the study clearly stated?
- Will the study improve nursing practice and add to the body of nursing knowledge?

In the Cortez-Gann et al. (2017) article, these questions would be assessed by reading the untitled introduction along with the purpose section provided in the paper. Answers to these questions guide the critique. If the responses are negative, then the notion of applying the study to practice is questionable. The purpose section should clearly and effectively present the importance of the need to complete this study on this topic. When the goal of the study is not evident with the initial information, the article may be overlooked as not being connected to the material being sought. This determination is based on that key, preliminary clarification of the "why" statement. The reasons for the study must be unmistakably declared within the first few paragraphs of the article.

Research Design

A second element involves the design of the research. In the Cortez-Gann and colleagues (2017) article, this material is found in the section labeled "Methods." Another example of the design element can be reviewed from the section labeled "Methods and Design" within the Woolston and Connelly (2017) article. When looking at the design elements for the qualitative study, the specifics are not as clearly denoted. Questions to ask about these elements include the following:

- Is there a framework/theory to guide the study?
- If there is no framework/theory, are you able to identify how data will be evaluated?
- Do the authors provide a clear discussion of how data will be collected and maintained?
- Who will be studied?
- What is the plan for conducting the study?
- Are the research plan decisions adequately justified?

Each question provides a nuance related to the different components of a study. Constructing the different components for a research study with the rationales for the decisions made along with the generating of the research project is a multifaceted and intricate enterprise. Adequate planning is important to allow the use of the best evidence for incorporation in nursing practice. An effectively considered design allows for assurance that the evidence has practicality. The research design can be likened to a set of instructions allowing the builder to put together the pieces of a puzzle resulting in a usable product. The determination of the rationales as to how and why decisions within the research process were made is imperative to the successful development of a sound and reasonable research application. The justification for the decisions made provides the foundation for users of the research to determine the reasonableness of the results and outcomes recommended.

Literature Review

Another element to consider is whether the literature review focuses on the problem presented. The literature review should speak to the gaps and consistencies found within the evidence. This material is found throughout the Woolston and Connelly (2017) article; Cortez-Gann and colleagues (2017) present the literature within the untitled introduction. A resourceful and constructive literature review provides clarity about what has been done and what continues to be needed.

Questions to ask about the literature review include the following:

- Is the literature review thorough and detailed?
- Is the literature review current—that is, has the literature been published within the last 5 years?
- Are there benchmark publications?
- Are the majority of sources primary or secondary?
- Is the literature review well organized, and does it include an introduction and a summary?
- Does the literature review include a section for a model/theory?

🔄 THINK OUTSIDE THE BOX

Which aspects of a research article do you perceive as important, and why? Which aspects of the article seem to be the hardest to locate, and why?

A thorough literature review allows for assessment of the credibility of the present study. Of major importance in beginning a research study is the need to ask, "What has been written about the problem?" The literature review provides the foundation for the study's significance and relationship to practice. Benchmark publications are valuable because they serve as the foundation for the ongoing investigation on the topic of interest. Publications that have been deemed as underpinning and supporting of the ongoing work are paramount to successful progression to the next level of knowledge concerning a topic of interest.

Research Question/Hypothesis

The next element of a research critique is the research question(s) or **hypothesis** (or hypotheses). This element of the critique is of extreme importance because it should reflect the purpose of the study. Within the Cortez-Gann and colleague (2017) article, this material is denoted as the purpose statement and it comes at the end of the introduction. Research questions in EBP are the "who," "what," "when," "where," "why," and "how" guiding the nursing care provided to patients. Thus, it is essential to assess the following issues:

- Is the research question clearly stated?
- Does it match the purpose of the study?
- Are the decisions made about the research question adequately justified?
- Is there a theory/framework/model discussed that establishes a relationship with the question?

Within the Woolston and Connelly (2017) article, these questions are noted in the purpose statement, which follows the introduction section. A study can contain a hypothesis rather than a research question. In some studies, the research purpose may be the only statement provided. Whether it is a research purpose, research question, and/or hypothesis, it is important that the connection to the study purpose is evident. The expectation that the study purpose is evident in all aspects of the development of the study is crucial. Polit and Beck (2017) characterize a hypothesis as the statement of the anticipated relationship between the variables under investigation. Simply put, a hypothesis may predict, propose, suppose, explain, or test a quality, property, or characteristic of people, things, or settings. People often talk about or discuss "hypothetical situations." A hypothesis proposes a solution. Questions to ask about a hypothesis and/or research questions include the following:

- Are the independent and dependent variables described?
- Is the hypothesis clearly stated?
- Does the hypothesis reflect the purpose of the study?
- Are the decisions made regarding the hypothesis adequately justified?
- Is there a theory/framework/model discussed that establishes a relationship with the hypothesis?

The establishment of the research question or hypothesis is paramount to the focus of the study. Each aspect of the wording within the questions or hypotheses needs to be clear and concise to allow for the effective concentration of the research endeavor. The PICOT (population, intervention, comparison, outcome, time) statement should play a part toward the development of the research question or hypothesis. The PICOT process drives the literature review and can evolve into the research question or hypothesis, based on the outcomes of the literature review. From the gaps and consistencies identified during the literature review within the EBP process, the research question/hypothesis can be structured to advance the body of knowledge concerning the topic under investigation toward the next level.

Study Sample

Another element of the research critique focuses on the sample. Sampling questions address the different aspects of the population. Within the Cortez-Gann and colleagues (2017) article, the sampling process is described in the first paragraph within the methods section of the article. Each aspect within the clarification of the sampling design should be supported by rationales within the dissemination of the study. Questions regarding the sample should include the following:

- Who is identified as the target population?
- How were the subjects chosen (e.g., randomly, conveniently)?
- Who is included (e.g., males, females, children, adults)?
- Who is excluded (e.g., elderly, pregnant women, minorities)?
- How large is the sample?
- Are the decisions made regarding the sampling plan adequately justified?
- Were ethical considerations clearly addressed within the sampling process?

In the Woolston and Connelly (2017) article, these questions can be answered by initially reading the section labeled "Sample Selection." Answers to these questions can help the nurse decide if decisions about patients and clinical problems are practical for his or her unique setting. By looking at these aspects of the sampling plan, generalization to a population can be supported. Clarification of the sample population must be denoted. Each aspect of the sampling process should be described carefully and thoroughly within the discussion of the project.

Data Collection

Data collection embraces many aspects that are critical to the success of the research study. Essential to the critique is a description of how the data were collected. Within both of the articles by Cortez-Gann and colleagues (2017) and by Woolston and Connelly (2017), the data collection aspects are integrated into the methods sections. Questions about this element include the following:

- What steps were taken to collect the data?
- How often were data collected and for how long?
- Which instruments or tools were used?
- Who designed the tools?
- Are the tools valid and reliable?
- Are the tools adequately described so that readers can understand what the scores mean?
- Were data analysis procedures appropriate?
- Are the plans for data collection and analysis decisions adequately justified?
- Were ethical considerations adequately addressed within the data collection process?

Justification for the data collection processes should be evident within the discussion of the data. Data collection gives information about the research question or hypothesis. Quantitative data, for example, are often collected by a survey mechanism that provides a score for analysis. In such a case, a clear understanding of how and where the data were collected, the description of the instrument (tool) that was used, and how the results were statistically analyzed is essential. In contrast, the data collected for a qualitative study are presented in narrative format. Qualitative data utilize collection methods that must include a discussion of how potential biases were addressed.

Study Results

Clear discussion of the results from a study is essential. Results must be placed within the context of where and when they were collected. Within the Cortez-Gann and colleagues (2017) article, this material is found in the two sections labeled "Results" and "Nursing Implications." A critique should provide the results of the study. Questions about results include the following:

- Is the research question answered or is the hypothesis supported?
- Were limitations listed and explained?
- Can generalizations to a wider population be made?
- Did the results support what was reported in the literature?
- Were there any unexpected findings?
- Did the outcomes affirm the theory used as the basis of the study?

⚙ THINK OUTSIDE THE BOX

Frequently, the theoretical foundation for a study seems to be omitted in research articles due to page restrictions imposed by the journal. Debate the importance of including the theoretical foundation for a study in the report of the study's findings.

In the Woolston and Connelly (2017) article, these questions would be assessed by reading the sections entitled analysis and trustworthiness.

The elements of the critique summarize the study, including what was found and how the findings might be applied to similar situations. The summary of the findings needs to be presented carefully to allow for generalization to other settings and populations. Care must be given to this aspect within the report of the study outcomes to provide an understanding for where and how the results can be used within the practical world of health care.

Study Recommendations

The final element of the research critique is the section presenting the author's recommendations. The author understands what the study means and is responsible for providing guidance about where the next steps should be directed. In the Cortez-Gann and colleagues (2017) article, this material is found in the nursing implications and limitation sections. With the in-depth work pivotal to the study completion, avenues that were identified but not addressed and/or unexpected outcomes are key areas that should be recommended for further study. Questions for this element include the following:

- Are suggestions for further use in practice included?
- Is there an identified need for further research?
- Could you make a change in your practice based on the results of this study?
- What are the benefits to using the information learned?

In the Woolston and Connelly (2017) article, these questions would also be assessed by reading the "Findings/Discussion" and "Nursing Implications" sections.

The necessary elements of a research critique can be organized as answers to a series of questions. Utilizing a logical format for reporting the decisions made as the study was planned, along with the results that were obtained, provides a foundation for moving healthcare research forward. This process of carefully and thoroughly considering all aspects within a reported study demonstrates accountability for advancing health care and patient safety. Those questions then form the basis for the process of conducting a research critique. As the individual investigates the quality of a study, these questions can provide a beginning place for the critique. A validated study should successfully address the majority of these questions in a positive and constructive manner. The purpose of reporting the results of a study is to allow colleagues to assess the outcomes carefully to identify ways to improve patient care.

▶ Process for Conducting a Research Critique

The word **critique** can be defined as "an article or essay criticizing a literary or other work; detailed evaluation; review, a criticism or critical comment on some problem, subject, etc., the art or practice of criticism to review or analyze critically" (Dictionary.com, 2018). Although *research critique* is the term frequently used, several other terms—such as critical *analysis, review, evaluation,* and *appraisal*—can also be associated with the process. Any of these terms can be and are used to describe the method for assessing a published research article.

To gain a true understanding and appreciation of the process of a research critique, one must recognize the expectations for conducting the process. As the definition implies, it is undertaken to allow individuals to examine a research endeavor carefully and thoroughly. The outcome is not anticipated to be a negative grilling of the project to identify all of its shortcomings. Wood and Ross-Kerr (2011) affirm this point by instructing individuals to decide if what is presented in a manuscript addresses the issue and/or challenge being investigated through the EBP process. The materials should be practical and applicable to your individual practice setting and the patient situation.

Studies should be examined for their merits, limitations, implications, and consequences. Each and every report should be assessed with an analytical eye toward each distinct setting. The resulting critique should be objective, presenting both strengths and challenges. Any review should have a goal of providing constructive recommendations related to how the study might be improved, along with where the results and/or outcomes could be used within health care. It is envisioned as a review or analysis of the research undertaking. Both the strengths and challenges within the process of conducting the research study are judiciously examined to verify that the ending results can truly be generalized to the target population.

🔁 THINK OUTSIDE THE BOX

If nurses do not value research, their engagement with the critique process and their participation in research studies are decreased. Identify steps and incentives that might be used to get you and your peers involved in doing research critiques or research projects.

By completing a successful research critique, a reviewer becomes aware of both the strengths and the deficiencies of the research project. As a result of identifying these concerns, the assessor can efficiently assimilate the outcome into practice based on this in-depth knowledge of the study findings. Thus, the incorporation of the results into nursing practice is based on an understanding of the comprehensiveness of the study.

Every study has limitations because researchers must inevitably make multiple methodological judgments that influence the significance, integrity, and value of the resulting research outcomes (San Jose State University, 2005). No study utilizing humans is ever perfectly conducted, and even nonhuman studies frequently have limitations and weaknesses. It is true that research conducted on laboratory animals can be controlled with greater success than projects in which humans are the subjects. Put simply, when working with laboratory animals, the variables can be manipulated. If the same project were envisioned using human subjects, however, the ethical ramifications could be increased because manipulation of the variables for human subjects might result in damage. Thus, the ethical nuances of human research must be considered when the results are proposed for incorporation into practice.

Another factor—the austere style of journal articles—also triggers some concerns. The amount of space allocated to articles within journals is prescribed by the companies that publish those journals. As a result of these restrictions regarding page length and word count limits, key elements within the research process must be presented succinctly. Depth of discussion about the basic research principles must therefore be limited or even omitted. Unfortunately, discussions of the operational definitions for key variables; models, plans, and systems; and conceptual or theoretical frameworks are often omitted due to space restrictions. Classic research studies include a description of the theory and/or framework and concepts underlying the study, but many other studies use a model, plan, or system for the research.

🔼 THINK OUTSIDE THE BOX

Look at some research articles. Can you identify any discussions in these articles related to patient preferences that are part of EBP? Discuss your thoughts about your findings.

Another facet of the process that discourages nurses from participating in research critiques is the unknown terminology. Statistical aspects are quite daunting to countless practicing nurses. The definitions used within research to discuss sampling, variables, hypotheses, and quantitative and qualitative methods are typically foreign to the practicing nurse. Although many of these terms, such as *independent, dependent, convenience*, and *variable*, are common, they take on new meanings within a research project. This specificity of the terms within research leads to conflict and misunderstanding for novice evaluators of research. In the future, nurses will be increasingly confronted with the expectation that they will center their practice on evidence. Chipps, Nash, Busk, and Vermillion (2017) acknowledged that "inquiry and science are fundamental to raising the bar in nursing practice, improving the patient experience, and enhancing patient outcomes" (p. 29). By becoming familiar with reading and analyzing research and technical reports, nurses will be able to utilize innovative results to advance health care. Nurses must become proficient at reading and understanding research reports to incorporate their findings into EBP. They need to take a deep breath now and plunge into the critiquing process.

The most valuable advice for developing expertise in this process is to continue doing research critiques because practice does diminish the confusion and overwhelming nature of the process. Chipps and colleagues (2017) assert that, "nurses who are becoming familiar with searching the literature to find answers to clinical questions are no longer satisfied with the 'this is the way we've always done it' approach" (p. 30). By reading research articles, nurses become progressively more accustomed to the format and terminology. Evidence-based nursing practice mandates that nurses begin to construct a knowledge base by the "steady diet" approach—specifically, by digesting at least one research report each week. By accepting the ultimatum to become comfortable with research reports, nurses will find that the different aspects of the report become more familiar, even commonplace, and therefore less threatening. Not all nurses will strive to carry out research activities, but it is vital that all nurses become comfortable with the employment of research results to enhance the discipline of nursing and ultimately enrich nursing care.

Initially, some general areas of the research study must be considered. The author(s) of the study need(s) to be evaluated. Precisely who is completing the research, including the persons' job titles and qualifications to conduct the project, needs to be carefully contemplated. After the author information is pondered, an assessment of the study title provides valuable information. The title of the project should provide a clear, concise description of the project. It should stimulate a prompt perception of the fundamental nature of the paper or article.

At this point, the abstract is examined to further clarify the focus for the research endeavor. The abstract should condense the main points from the research project. A quick read of the abstract and discussion sections should provide valuable insight into the complexity of the study and its applicability to a unique practice setting.

Four key aspects should be carefully addressed when initiating a research critique:

- Recognizing the purpose and problem while determining if the design and methodology are consistent with the study intent
- Verifying that the methodology is utilized appropriately
- Determining that the outcomes and conclusions are credible and confirmed by the findings
- Reflecting on the report's overall quality, strengths, and challenges, and whether they contribute to the knowledge base and offer suggestions for improvement

Research critiques can take many different paths. The principal idea is to make sure that, regardless of the tool or process used, each aspect of the research process is carefully examined for appropriateness. An example of the research critique process should involve the following steps:

- Read the entire study carefully and with purpose.
- Examine the organization and presentation of the different components for logical flow.
- Identify any term you don't understand by seeking clarification as to its meaning.
- Highlight and examine each step of the research process.
- Identify the strengths and challenges without bias.
- Consider modifications for future studies.
- Determine how well the study followed the expectations for an ideal study.

TABLE 14-1 provides an example of a critique worksheet. Some worksheets provide areas for comments while others may have checkboxes to complete. Any format that addresses the different areas that need to be included in a critique can be used to help the individual develop confidence in completing a review of a scholarly article.

These guidelines are fairly general, but they do provide a place to start. A careful, general reading of the entire study must be the beginning point for any critique. The examiner initially should read the complete research report to gain an awareness of the study and its contribution to knowledge improvement. A second reading of the document allows the focus to be directed toward the questions appropriate to each stage of the critiquing process. A photocopy of the article may facilitate the research critique process because areas can be highlighted, questions can be added in the margin, and key points can be circled. For individuals just beginning the process of critiquing articles, notetaking and making comments in the margin allow for the questions to be placed correctly within the article.

As the reader begins this initial review of the research project, he or she develops a feel for the organization of the article, along with the manner of presentation for the entire research process. At this point, the examiner becomes aware of the complexity of the identified material. To become somewhat relaxed

TABLE 14-1 Critique Worksheet

Areas for Consideration	Comment Concerning Completeness of the Information Provided
Title of the study	
Author credentials	
Purpose of the study	
Timeliness of literature used	
Literature review addressed each of the variables	
Theory and/or framework, concepts, and the relationship to nursing	
Research question or hypothesis	
Dependent and independent variables listed	
Definitions given	
Tools and their reliability and validity information (quantitative)	
Data collection methods and triangulation of process (qualitative)	
Sample description	
Study ethics description (i.e., institutional review board [IRB] information)	
Data collection procedures	
Data analysis	
Results, recommendations, and implications for practice	

with the content, he or she should expect to read the article several times. Each time the article is read, the examiner comes to terms with a different aspect of the article. Frequently, an initial question relates to the researcher's ability to verbalize the process in a manner that nurses can understand and be able to use in practice. The reader may also find that some of the initial questions raised in the introductory section are answered in other sections within the article. After this general overview of the article, a more critical examination of the document can then be completed.

Each aspect within a research article is examined to identify areas of concerns and assets (**TABLE 14-2**). The evaluator can benefit from taking the time to highlight each of the steps of the research process, spotlighting the hypothesis (or hypotheses), literature review, sample, ethical considerations, and research design. During this focused examination, any limitations identified by the researchers should be noted. Another area to recognize explicitly is the operational definitions, which reflect the standards used within the research project to clarify the specific variables. After noting the operational definition for each variable, a reviewer should not have many additional terms that require explanation. The evaluator should define any term that continues to be unfamiliar to enable him or her to better understand the entire process. Every reader should develop a habit of looking up unfamiliar terms instead of skipping over them, which simply keeps those terms unfamiliar. The objective of critiquing any research report is to become familiar with the language and procedures used regularly within the scheme.

At this point in the research critique, the reviewer attempts to identify the strengths and limitations of the research process described in the report. The reviewer should be aware that the limitations so identified might actually be a consequence of the lack of space allowed within the documentation of the research endeavor rather than representing an intended omission of the aspect. All journal articles have space limitations, which can result in some items being cut because of space considerations rather than because they were lacking in the study.

One major challenge for novice research readers is the evaluation of statistics. In considering this aspect of any research process, the key point is to ask for help. To better understand the material presented in articles, reviewers could either find someone to provide help in this area or obtain an introductory book about statistics to aid in the assessment of the statistical data. Nurses who practice evidence-based nursing are not expected to become statisticians. Nurses are expected, however, to acknowledge their limitations and seek help from statisticians and others as needed to improve their evaluation of research results for incorporation into everyday nursing practice.

One way to take advantage of the expertise of peers and colleagues is through establishing a journal club. The journal club members can select a different article on a regular basis. The group then completes the review or critique. By joining a group to complete the work, each participant grows in her or his own knowledge and confidence to be able to complete a review individually.

As nurses are asked to become involved with the critiquing of research articles for EBP, several formidable factors emerge and must be confronted. Internet sites can be searched to identify resources for developing research critiques geared toward EBP.

TABLE 14-2 Rules for an Ideal Study

Areas for Consideration	Comments Concerning Completeness of the Information Provided
Research problem	■ Significance of problem noted ■ Clarification of aim of study ■ Practicality of study ■ Clarity, significance, and documentation
Review of literature	■ Organization of literature ■ Progression toward study question through previous research reports ■ Rationale and direction for the study presented
Conceptual framework and/or theory of the study	■ Clear link between conceptual framework and/or theory and research question and/or purpose ■ Any maps and models logically presented
Research questions or hypotheses	■ Expressed appropriately and clearly ■ Logically related to the research purpose or aim and framework and/or theory
Variables	■ Concepts identified within the framework and/or theory used ■ Variables operationally defined ■ Conceptual definition consistent with operational definition of each variable
Research design	■ Design appears appropriate ■ Clearly defined protocol for conducting research project ■ Any treatment closely scrutinized to guarantee consistency ■ Threats to internal validity minimized ■ Logically connected to the sampling method and statistics used
Sampling method	■ Method appropriate to result in representative sample ■ Biases identified ■ Human rights protected ■ Setting described and appropriate for target population
Measurements	■ Instruments sufficient for measuring the study variables ■ Instrument validity and reliability levels ■ Instrument scoring techniques clearly described
Data collection	■ Techniques for using observation clearly described ■ Methods for recording measures clearly described ■ Interrater reliability described when appropriate ■ Process clearly, consistently, and ethically described
Data analysis	■ Procedures suitable for the type of data collected ■ Analysis procedures clearly portrayed ■ Outcomes offered in a comprehensible way

Data from San Jose State University. (2005). Reading and critiquing research. Retrieved from http://www.sjsu.edu/upload /course/course_969/Reading_and_CritiquingResearch.ppt

▶ Critically Assessing Knowledge for Clinical Decision Making

The various aspects of EBP are of fundamental importance in considering the assessment of knowledge related to clinical decision making. According to Shingler-Nace and Gonzalez (2017), "it's essential for healthcare professionals to understand and apply strong research to every aspect of healthcare, not only the clinical domains" (p. 44). As nurses, the evidence required to steer a competent and effective practice does not occur after reviewing a single independent study. Changes within best practices are based on a sound foundation of evidence, not just the results from a single study. Gray, Bliss, and Klem (2015) provide an example of a level of evidence ranking system along with a taxonomy for strength of recommendation for treatment (SORT) statement. While the level of evidence ranking mirrors most other ranking tools, the SORT statement provides clear guidance on how to use the level of evidence ranking to determine the level of recommendation. Within this discussion, the idea moves from the strength of the evidence to the level of recommendation related to implementing the results into day-to-day practice. The practicing nurse comes to the research critique process with a foundation of clinical experience. Thus, the critique of the research endeavor is tempered by this clinical expertise. Yoder (2005) suggests, "Clinical decisions require that one use a problem-solving approach to clinical practice that integrates a systematic search for and critical appraisal of the relevant evidence to answer the clinical questions" (p. 91). Every nurse has been taught a problem-solving methodology. During the review of research, it becomes essential for nurses to utilize this critical thinking framework, which has already been incorporated into practice, to validate and conceptualize the research critique process. The idea behind a research critique is to provide a systematic process for critically appraising research projects. Within this process, nurses must become comfortable with looking at all aspects of the various studies to assess any strengths and limitations that might be apparent. Carefully considering these different aspects of the report facilitates critical thinking concerning the results reported and the applicability of those results to the workplace.

One aspect of paramount importance to be considered within any research critique is the determination of the sampling process. According to Pajares (2007), "the key word in sampling is representative" (Section VI.E.4). Determining the appropriateness of the sampling method is critical in any study appraisal. Whatever sampling method is used, the rationale and limitations related to this methodology must be discussed meticulously. While all aspects of the research decision-making process are important, the inclusion of an effective sample (representative of the population) is critical.

Evaluating Quantitative Research Evidence

Quantitative research reports tend to be slightly easier to critique because of the concreteness of the quantitative research design. The various aspects of quantitative research reports document the expectations for all the various elements of the article—that is, the introduction, literature review, hypothesis (or hypotheses), sampling, research design, statistical testing, and discussion. Although each of these areas includes considerable levels and components, the clarity of the descriptions of these aspects is more distinct than in qualitative methodologies.

According to Carter (2006), critiquing quantitative research reports should address four basic areas: comprehension, comparison, analysis, and evaluation. Each of these four levels of review adds a different dimension to the resulting scrutiny. Comprehension and comparison provide the overall appraisal of the report. Analysis then takes the investigation of the report to the level of reflecting on the continuity among the different parts (Carter, 2006). At this point of assessing the report, the principal concern is whether the hypothesis flows into decisions made about the sample and whether that sample is appropriately managed by the research design. The final aspect of the review carefully considers the meaning and significance of the study process for implementation into nursing practice. The focus is to determine whether the findings, implications, and recommendations presented in the study report are truly supported and presented.

A key aspect of this review process unique to the quantitative research appraisal is the use of a conceptual or theoretical framework (Pajares, 2007). Although it can be provided in any of the research methodologies, this framework is essential in all quantitative research endeavors. Having said this, within printed articles documenting quantitative research, the discussion of the conceptual/theoretical framework is frequently omitted to satisfy the journal's page length requirements. Of course, the omission could also reflect the researcher's failure to include a conceptual/theoretical framework as part of the study design. The total omission of this framework would be a marked limitation within a quantitative research methodology. When a lack of theoretical foundation for a study is determined (yet the study outcomes appear to be applicable to your setting), sending a query to the author(s) about the issue may be helpful to determine the status of the theoretical foundation.

Evaluating Qualitative Research Evidence

When evaluating **qualitative research** efforts, the examination of the entire process assumes a slightly different perspective from that employed with a quantitative research undertaking. Assessment of the clarity of the purpose and statement of the phenomenon remains consistent with that of any other methodology critique. These components must be presented up front. From that point on, the specificity of the qualitative design must be considered. Broad research questions, instead of hypotheses, are employed within this type of research design. The literature review may follow the data collection process rather than driving the research attempt from its inception. A framework may or may not be clearly presented as part of the study report. Qualitative research reviews must consider carefully the researcher–participant relationship because this aspect is a critical component of the data collection process. Ethical considerations also play significant roles in determining the appropriateness of this methodology.

Carter (2006) has detailed five standards to keep in mind when conducting a qualitative research critique. First, the research report must present a comprehensible depiction of the research environment, data collection process, sampling process, and the researcher's thought process. A second standard relates to the importance of congruence among the methodological aspects. According to Carter (2006), the method section must have objectivity and accuracy related to the documentation, process, ethical considerations, and audit-ability. The third standard is the analytical preciseness: The researcher's thoughts and decisions related to the data should be evident in the report. The fourth standard stresses the importance of addressing the theoretical connectedness presented within the report. The fifth standard suggests that the relevance (value of the study) needs to be apparent within the documentation of the research project. Appropriate examination of each of these facets within a research report should yield a strong, valid depiction of the research project.

The data collection aspect of the study is a crucial component of the presentation of qualitative research projects. The reader must be walked through the entire process, from identification of the participants to the management of the data collected from them. The congruence of these data with the research purpose, question, and tradition needs to be assessed. The researcher is obliged to discuss how the field engagements and observations ought to build trust and ensure validity of the data collected. Another aspect that should be identifiable within the report is the ongoing and concurrent nature of data collection and analysis. Because data collection and analysis occur in tandem in qualitative research, the codes used as categories and the process utilized to determine data saturation must be discussed explicitly in the report. The research report should also address triangulation, peer review of the research process, articulation of researcher biases, member checking, and external audit by expert consultants.

A final aspect that must be noted within qualitative research reports is the sampling data. Because the sample population in such studies is usually small and focused, a description of this population is critical for allowing the reader to determine if the study findings are generalizable to other populations.

Qualitative research often employs additional terminology that must be defined and clarified, which can cause further confusion and frustration. As a result, the critique of qualitative research tends to be an area that is best entered into after learning how to conduct critiques of quantitative research. Put simply, qualitative research tends to be less structured than quantitative research.

Evaluating Mixed Methods Evidence

Mixed methods research embraces both quantitative and qualitative design aspects. According to Creswell (2003), the mixed methods approach takes advantage of the strengths of both quantitative and qualitative research by employing sequential, concurrent, and transformative strategies of inquiry. As a critique of a mixed methods research study is undertaken, the reader must therefore consider the presentation of both methodologies within the discussion. A unique aspect of a mixed methods research critique is the expectation of a stated rationale for the use of this method.

The quantitative and qualitative data in a mixed methods research report are frequently presented separately, which allows the reader to concentrate on one type of data prior to considering the other type. Within mixed methods research, one type of research design usually drives the second research design process. The reporting of the data and results must reflect this research progression of data collection. The discussion section should integrate the two types of data, thereby strengthening the study's findings. When a transformative study design is employed, this section should address the advancement of the agenda for change or reform that has developed as a result of the research.

▶ Employing EBP Guidelines: Instruments for Holistic Practice

EBP requires that multiple related articles be correlated to provide a sum of evidence rather than a single data set. Kowalski (2017) challenges nurses to analyze published research, practice improvement initiatives, and evidence-based reviews. Contradictory evidence must be reconciled through the evaluation and association of data from multiple quality research projects. Of course, this process of reconciling contradictory evidence and multiple research discussions generates additional questions that need to be investigated at some point. According to the Oncology Nursing Society (2005), the EBP process comprises six steps:

- Identify the problem.
- Find the evidence.
- Critique the merit, feasibility, and utility of the evidence.
- Summarize the evidence.
- Apply the ideas to practice.
- Evaluate the results.

🔲 THINK OUTSIDE THE BOX

Can you think of any data other than research that can be used as evidence for nursing practice? Identify data that nurses provide in their practice.

Each of these steps, with the exception of the application to practice (Step 5), can be visualized within the research critique process. Research critiques require the identification of the problem; an examination of the literature review; a critique of the merits, feasibility, and use of the research process; summarization of the research process; consideration of the applicability of the research results to practice; and evaluation of the results.

▶ The Evidence-Based Appraisal

Evidence comes from many different sources. The first part of this chapter examined the research critique process, which is part of EBP. Now let's examine other important elements for nurses to use in their nursing practice. According to Vincent, Hastings-Tolsma, Gephart, and Alfonzo (2015), "many clinical decisions are undergirded by value judgments, tradition or habits, and a mixture of evidence from a variety of sources that may or may not include robust research" (p. 48). By including evidence-based appraisals, the inconsistencies identified by the challenge of assessing evidence can be managed in an increasingly positive and beneficial manner. Asserting the strength of each component of evidence used to support a healthcare practice should be a penetrating and significant expectation from each healthcare discipline. By carefully and thoroughly considering the biases and implications from research projects, quality improvement activities, and EBP investigations, the optimal health care can be determined and implemented. Melnyk, Gallagher-Ford, Long, and Fineout-Overholt

(2014) employ three strategies for integrating EBP competencies into health practices: "(1) Promote a culture and context or environment that supports EBP, (2) establish EBP performance expectations for all nurse leaders and clinicians, and (3) sustain EBP activities and culture" (p. 13). As an assessment is done on EBP projects, these three strategies should be considered and supported. As the health community becomes increasingly comfortable with EBP integration, the health practices provided will further move toward being based on the best evidence available.

Expert Opinion

When no definitive data are available, nurses often turn to experts with knowledge needed about a specific aspect of nursing care. A body of thought exists that implies that expert opinion is not valuable. When no valid answers or data are available, however, expert opinion is considered a viable alternative. Expert opinion may be expressed in books, conferences, forums, reports, or even from expert clinicians in practice. Most often, textbooks and expert clinicians are the only valid resources when scientific data are not readily available.

Hopp and Rittenmeyer (2012) suggest the use of the term *local data*. This type of data may be internal to an organization, such as patient/employee satisfaction surveys, audits, or employee performance evaluations. Of particular interest to local data is quality improvement (QI)/quality assurance (QA). Hospitals and clinics accredited by the Joint Commission and other accreditation agencies compile QI/QA data. These data are often reported to national agencies, which allows comparisons between a local hospital clinic and other agencies of like size and function. For example, the Agency for Healthcare Research and Quality (AHRQ) looks at access to care, costs, and patient outcomes. The Area Health Resource Files (AHRF) examines data specific to a county. The Hospital Consumer Assessment of Healthcare Providers and Systems (HCAHPS) is a national survey of patients about the quality of hospital care they receive (Mason, Leavitt, & Chaffee, 2012). The Joint Commission is particularly interested in sentinel events. Sentinel events may be medication errors, wrong-site surgery, suicide, operative and postoperative complications, or even nurse staffing issues (Sorbello, 2008). Sentinel events require healthcare organizations to conduct a root cause analysis, which is a structured process for examining why an adverse event occurred. A plan is then developed to ensure that the event does not occur again.

Each of the items discussed in this section demonstrates a variety of ways to obtain data that may not be the result of scientific research. Kowalski (2017) postulates: "EBP drives best nursing practice through evidence and strengthens autonomy when clinical nurses play a role in making practice decisions" (p. 14). The evidence-based appraisal is necessary to provide nurses with knowledge to improve their nursing practice through expert opinion and internal data. The evidence-based appraisal is an important aspect in the daily practice of nurses, whether it applies to patient/nurse satisfaction, cost, or patient safety. Kowalski (2017) further states that, "the triplet of clinical issues, emerging innovations, and constant generation of evidence-based publications necessitates the evolution of nursing practice" (p. 15). Each nurse must accept and engage in the critical review and analysis of the evidence being submitted for implementation into practice. Ineffective work needs to be identified and removed, while stellar work needs to be moved into the practice arena with increasing frequency and effectiveness.

Summary Points

1. Critiques of research are essential to EBP and allow nurses to practice the art and science of the profession.
2. Nine types of critiques were presented for consideration.
3. The necessary elements in a research critique can be compiled in a series of questions for the process of critiquing research.
4. Critiques should be balanced, identifying both strengths and limitations in the study report examined.
5. Journal articles have restrictions on page limits and word limits, which sometimes result in information being omitted from an article.
6. Jargon in research reports often deters nurses from doing research critiques.
7. The critical appraisal of research is a skill to be developed through repeated practice.
8. General areas of the research study include author qualifications, study purpose, study design, sample, research methodology, outcomes, limitations and strengths of the research, and recommendations.
9. Nurses in EBP do not need to be statisticians, but they do need to be comfortable asking for help when evaluating the statistical analysis portion of a research report.
10. Quantitative research studies are concrete in nature and should include a theoretical framework.
11. Qualitative research studies contain broad research questions and are unstructured.
12. Mixed methods research embraces both quantitative and qualitative aspects of study design.
13. Research critiques should consider the applicability of the research results to practice.
14. Evidence-based appraisals may include evidence from sources other than research.

⚑ RED FLAGS

- A critique is not a negative process; rather, it should entail a careful examination of all aspects of the research process.
- A research critique should identify gaps within the study's research process.
- Future research possibilities should be identified as part of the original study and the critique of that study.
- Recommendations for advancement of the nursing profession should be documented in transformative research.
- For EBP, multiple related articles need to provide a sum of evidence rather than a single data set.
- Evidence-based appraisals are critical to patient safety and quality of patient care.

Multiple-Choice Questions

1. Nurses must critically assess research studies to:
    A. understand that all research is scientifically sound.
    B. determine the applicability of their findings to practice.
    C. know that all studies are perfect.
    D. identify a negative approach to research utilization.

2. Of the nine types of critiques, which of the following are considered essential to EBP?
    A. Student, practicing nurse, and peer review critiques
    B. Abstracts, presentations, and email critiques
    C. Program of research, letters to the editors, and lay-journal critiques
    D. National Institute of Nursing Research, educator groups, and newspaper critiques

3. The purpose of a study applies to EBP when it:
    A. adds to the body of nursing knowledge.
    B. is complete and requires multiple readings.
    C. is relevant to the authors.
    D. is hard to find in the literature.

4. A hypothesis may be described by which of the following terms?
    A. Results, introduces, criticizes, reviews
    B. Findings, improvements, collections, sets
    C. Studies, plans, appreciates, concerns
    D. Proposes, predicts, supposes, tests

5. An essential component of a critique is a description of how the data were collected. Which of the following statements provides the best data collection description?
    A. Data collection was timely and used a tool developed by the researcher.
    B. Multiple tools were used to collect the data.
    C. The data was collected at 2-week intervals using a pretest/posttest procedure.
    D. The score for the tool is easily understood and needs little description.

6. Results of the study should include:
    A. unexpected findings.
    B. unanswered questions.
    C. pictures of subjects.
    D. endorsements of peers.

7. A research study recommendation should include:
    A. no further need for research.
    B. no benefits for use in practice.
    C. ways to change practice based on results.
    D. ways to avoid using the results in other studies.

8. What is the definition of a research critique understood to imply?
    A. Analytical examination or commentary of a research report
    B. A negative assessment related to the weaknesses of a research report
    C. An analytical evaluation of the literature review
    D. A positive assessment of the research design

9. Although many aspects are discussed within a research critique, the basic aspects that the critique is attempting to identify are:
    A. hypothesis (or hypotheses) and literature review.
    B. strengths and limitations.
    C. research design and sampling methodology.
    D. shortcomings and critical problems.

10. Evidence-based nursing practice requires that nurses initiate a pattern to facilitate effective utilization of research results. The best method for improving a nurse's ability to incorporate research results into practice is:
    A. planning a monthly session to complete a literature review.
    B. completing a critique of a single research project.
    C. assessing at least one research report on a weekly basis.
    D. reviewing abstracts from selected research projects.

11. Several basic guidelines can be used to make the research critiquing procedure less threatening. Which of the following reflects the utilization of these guidelines?
    A. The nurse reads the entire discussion section carefully to gain an overview of the research report.
    B. The nurse identifies shortcomings that are unfamiliar to clarify the limitations within the study.
    C. The nurse reads the entire study meticulously to acquire a general understanding of the research report.
    D. The nurse identifies modifications for the selected research report.

12. Quantitative research design tends to be easier to critique due to the:
    A. length of the research reports.
    B. incorporation of triangulation into the process.
    C. use of convenient sampling methodology.
    D. concreteness of the research design.

13. When attempting to critique a qualitative research endeavor, what must individuals be able to do?
    A. Easily identify the hypothesis (or hypotheses).
    B. Carefully assess the data collection and management processes.
    C. Quickly determine the conceptual framework utilized.
    D. Understand the statistical results.

14. One unique aspect present in reports of mixed methods research projects is a(n):
    A. rationale for the utilization of the method.
    B. clear delineation of the sampling method.
    C. in-depth discussion of the methodology.
    D. list of the strengths and limitations.

15. What do sentinel events require?
    A. The nurse to be fired
    B. The hospital to ignore it
    C. A root cause analysis
    D. The doctor to be present

Discussion Questions

1. You and your peers, as staff nurses, have found a research article that has the potential to change the way you practice. List questions about the report elements that could guide your critique of the study. Take the article and determine what sections within the article would be reviewed to address the questions raised.
2. Select an article on a research topic for your practice area and complete the critique worksheet in Table 14-1. After completing the critique of the article, give the article a "level of evidence" rating and a "strength of evidence" score. Would you change your practice based on the information in this article?
3. You are a manager on a medical–surgical acute care unit. Your facility is moving toward an EBP format. Each unit has been charged with establishing a process for involving the staff nurses in this transformation. You have decided to implement a journal club for staff nurses to review and critique research articles for potential inclusion in evidence-based policies. What would you set as the ground rules for the implementation of this journal club activity?

Suggested Readings

Daggett, L., Harbaugh, B. L., & Collum, L. A. (2005). A worksheet for critiquing quantitative nursing research. *Nurse Educator, 30*(6), 255–258.

Riley, J. (2002). Understanding research articles. *Tar Heel Nurse, 64*(3), 15.

Scherzer, R., Shaffer, K. M., Maceyko, K., & Webb, J. (2015). Journal club for prelicensure nursing students. *Nurse Educator, 40*(5), 224–226.

Valente, S. (2003). Critical analysis of research papers. *Journal for Nurses in Staff Development, 196*(3), 130–142.

References

Brink, P. J., & Wood, M. J. (2001). *Basic steps in planning nursing research: From question to proposal* (5th ed.). Sudbury, MA: Jones and Bartlett.

Carter, K. (2006). *How to critique research.* Retrieved from http://www.runet.edu/~kcarter/Course Info/nurs442/chapter12.htm

Chipps, E., Nash, M., Buck, J., & Vermillion, B. (2017, April). Demystifying nursing research at the bedside. *Nursing Management, 48*(4), 26–35. doi:10.1097/01.NUMA.0000514063.45819.c1

Cortez-Gann, J., Gilmore, K. D., Foley, K. W., Kennedy, M. B., McGee, T., & Kring, D. (2017). Blood transfusion vital sign frequency: What does the evidence say? *MEDSURG Nursing, 26*(2), 89–92.

Creswell, J. W. (2003). *Research design: Qualitative, quantitative, and mixed methods approaches* (2nd ed.). Thousand Oaks, CA: Sage.

Dictionary.com. (2018). Critique. Retrieved from http://dictionary.reference.com/browse/critique

Glasofer, A. (2014). Searching with critical appraisal tools. *Nursing Critical Care, 9*(2), 18–22. doi:10.1087/01.CCN.0000444001.15811.a2

Gray, M., Bliss, D., & Klem, M. L. (2015). Methods, levels of evidence, strength of recommendations for treatment statements for evidence-based practice cards: A new beginning. *Journal of Wound, Ostomy, and Continence Nursing, 42*(1), 16–18. doi:10.1097/WON.0000000000000104

Gray, J. R., Grove, K. S., & Sutherland, S. (2017) *Burns & Grove's The practice of nursing research: Appraisal, synthesis, and generation of evidence* (8th ed.). St. Louis, MO: Saunders Elsevier.

Hopp, L., & Rittenmeyer, L. (2012). *Introduction to evidence-based practice: A practical guide for nursing.* Philadelphia, PA: F. A. Davis.

Kowalski, M. O. (2017, February). Strategies to heighten EBP engagement. *Nursing Management, 48*(2), 13–15. doi:10.1097/01.NUMA.0000511928.43882.55

Mason, D. J., Leavitt, J. K., & Chaffee, M. W. (2012). *Policy & politics in nursing and health care* (6th ed.). St. Louis, MO: Elsevier Saunders.

Melnyk, B. M., & Fineout-Overholt, E. (2015). *Evidence-based practice in nursing and health-care: A guide to best practice* (3rd ed.). Philadelphia, PA: Lippincott Williams & Wilkins.

Melnyk, B. M., Gallagher-Ford, L., Long, L. E., & Fineout-Overholt, E. (2014). The establishment of evidence-based practice competencies for practicing registered nurses and advanced practice nurses in real-world clinical settings: Proficiencies to improve healthcare quality, reliability, patient outcomes, and costs. *Worldview on Evidence-Based Nursing, 11*(1), 5–15. doi:10.1111/WBN.12021

Merriam-Webster. (2018). Critique. Retrieved from https://www.merriam-webster.com/dictionary/critique

Mick, J. (2017). Funneling evidence into practice. *Nurse Management, 48*(7), 27–34. doi:10.1097/NUMA.0000520719/70926.79

Oncology Nursing Society. (2005). *Evidence-based process.* Retrieved from http://onsopcontent.ons.org/toolkits/evidence/Process/index.shtml

Pajares, F. (2007). The elements of a proposal. Retrieved from http://www.des.emory.edu/mfp/proposal.html

Polit, D. F., & Beck, C. T. (2017). *Nursing research: Generating and assessing evidence for nursing practice* (10th ed.). Philadelphia, PA: Lippincott Williams & Wilkins.

San Jose State University. (2005). *Reading and critiquing research.* Retrieved from http://www.sjsu.edu/upload/course/course_969/Reading_and_CritiquingResearch.ppt

Shingler-Nace, A., & Gonzalez, J. Z. (2017). A pathway to EBP evidence-based nursing management. *Nursing2017, 47*(2), 43–46. doi:10.1097/01.NURS.0000510744.55090.9e

Sorbello, B. C. (2008). Responding to a sentinel event. *American Nurse Today, 3*(10), 30–32. Retrieved from http://www.americannursetoday.com/assets/0/434/436/440/5426/5428/5442/5446/5b587e3d-6b56-4558-b2f7-05ab3738549b.pdf

Vincent, D., Hastings-Tolsma, M., Gephart, S., & Alfonzo, P. M. (2015). Nurse practitioner clinical decision-making and evidence-based practice. *The Nurse Practitioner, 40*(8), 47–54. doi:10.1097/01.NPR.0000463783.42721.ef

Wood, M. J., & Ross-Kerr, J. C. (2011). *Basic steps in planning nursing research: From question to proposal* (7th ed.). Sudbury, MA: Jones and Bartlett.

Woolston, W., & Connelly, L. M. (2017). Felty's syndrome: A qualitative case study. *MEDSURG Nursing, 26*(2), 105–118.

Yoder, L. H. (2005). Evidence-based practice: The time is now! *MEDSURG Nursing, 14*(2), 91–92.

CHAPTER 15

Translational Research, Improvement Science, and Evaluation Research with Practical Applications

Carol Boswell

CHAPTER OBJECTIVES

At the conclusion of this chapter, the learner will be able to:
1. Discuss the use of translational research, improvement science, intervention research, and evaluation research principles within the process of systematic decision making.
2. Construct a basic logic model for an identified project of individual choice.

KEY TERMS

Applied research
Basic research
Executive summary
Impact
Intervention research
Logic model

Outcomes
Outputs
Patient-oriented research
Population-based research
Translational research

▶ Introduction

Investigators must grapple with many diverse concepts, ideas, and challenges as they carefully and thoughtfully consider the intention and purpose of systematic decision making. Chipps, Nash, Buck, and Vermillion (2017) stated, "Inquiry and science are fundamental to raising the bar in nursing practice, improving the patient experience, and enhancing patient outcomes" (p. 29). Evidence-based practice (EBP), research, and quality improvement are all aspects that play a part in the development of critical decision making and the validation of successful and competent healthcare practices. These processes take distinct alternatives centered on the outcomes desired. Full experimental, basic research can be the process required to get to the results being sought when rigid quantitative research methods are needed, such as with random controlled trials. At other times, a quality improvement exercise is the way to gain the information essential for the advancement of quality practice. With each clustering of questions, the type and depth of evidence needed must be sensibly and consciously considered. According to O'Brien (1998), individuals within the focus of structured inquiry are embracing the phrase, "If you want it done right, you may as well do it yourself." This idea, while interesting, does not hold with the current health environment of interprofessional engagement. The inclusion of strategic individuals to respond to the questions and challenges identified requires different individuals to appreciate the multifaceted nature of systematic decision making. Interprofessional education and engagement has become increasingly important to move critical questions and inquiries forward with a full team of professionals to consider multiple viewpoints. Within the idea of interprofessional research engagement, the inclusion of patients and stakeholders into the team with the researchers has become a resounding expectation for advancing healthcare knowledge. Each and every member affected by the patient challenge must be given a voice in the solutions to be considered within the research and/or investigation for best practices.

▶ Translational Research

Wethington (2018) describes **translational research** as a systematic process of moving basic researching findings into the practical application resulting in the enhancement of health and well-being for individuals. The idea of moving basic research from laboratory facilities to the frontline to aid in the day-to-day care of patients is critical for the healthcare community. The National Institutes of Health (NIH) embraced the idea of translational research in 2006 with the formation of centers to manage the process, and with the unveiling of the Clinical and Translational Science Award (CTSA) program (Rubio et al., 2010). This program supports the development of a national system of medical research organizations designated as hubs that strive to operate collectively using translational research methods to move treatments to patients quickly (National Center for the Advancing of Translational Sciences, 2018). While translational research has been discussed since 2006, it continues to be complicated and obscure. Rubio and colleagues (2010) define translational research as fostering a long-term ambition of assimilating basic research, patient-oriented research, and population-based research using multiple routes with involvement from a variety of disciplines to improve the health of the public. Within the process of implementing translational research, diverse components are integrated to focus the attention of the decision-making process on the patient and populations.

Several types of research methodologies can be incorporated into this delivery idea. **Patient-oriented research** strives to provide knowledge advancement through the use of inclusion of groups of patients or healthy individuals to determine the patients' perceptions related to health care. When employing patient-oriented research, the patient and stakeholders are embraced from the beginning. They are not just the subjects but serve as part of the research team, from preplanning to dissemination. For this methodology, the patient is at the center for the entire process. Each aspect within the study focuses on the manner in which the patient will be impacted. From a different focus, **population-based research** seeks to mesh epidemiology, social and behavioral sciences, public health, quality evaluation, and cost-effectiveness into the research process to allow for a holistic outcome when answering critical questions. While the population of individuals is important within the study, the holistic nature of the research is a driving force. Another trend with inquisitive thinking is the development and utilization of **intervention research**. According to the Division of Services and Intervention Research (DSIR) (2018) within the National Institute of Mental Health, intervention research seeks to determine the efficacy of pharmacologic, psychosocial, somatic, rehabilitative, and combined interventions related to mental and behavior disorders throughout the life span. Fraser and Galinsky (2010) defined it as "the systematic study of purposive change strategies" (p. 325). Within intervention research, the clarification of the intervention is critical. Until the intervention is explicitly defined, the research cannot move forward. The problem tends to be examined from multiple fronts instead of from a single vantage point. **Basic research** embraces the research conducted within a laboratory setting to advance the knowledge on a topic for the sake of knowledge, without any focus on clinical practice at that point. Basic research is a foundation for the examination of questions. The process does not have to be linked to a group of people or a situation. It is research to discover information. All research that is not basic research is placed into the category of applied research. **Applied research** encompasses translational research, patient-oriented research, population-based research, and any other research that strives to utilize research results in a practical application.

Translational research has two areas of focus. The initial area relates to basic research. During this phase of investigation, the preclinical studies along with human trials are used to establish the foundation for further development of the information. The second focus within translational research strives to move the outcomes determined through basic research to actual adoption at the bedside, or frontline of health care, as examples of best practices for the community. The process of moving the basic research to the frontline includes nurses at all levels. As basic research is completed, the frontline nurse takes on the challenge of implementing the process with patients in unique settings. As new medications, procedures, and equipment are developed and studied using basic research strategies, the frontline nurse becomes the tool for implementing those innovations into clinical practice in an operational and methodical manner. With the assimilation of each new skill and/or instrument, the translational aspect of research becomes significant. The process for making it serviceable in the clinical setting requires the proficiency of the nurse working in cooperation with the patient for the optimum outcome. Each component of the process is crucial and imperative. The first phase provides the foundation of evidence on which to structure the best practices for the day-to-day delivery of health care. The central and noteworthy consequences from the totality of the translational research process address the "cost-effectiveness of prevention and treatment strategies" (Rubio et al., 2010, p. 472). By embracing a focus toward prevention and treatment that is cost-effective, the ultimate outcome is improved health for the public.

When reading about translational research, the initial stage that incorporates the basic research and patient-oriented research is identified as T1. This process undertakes the challenge of moving new knowledge and understanding about disease processes identified within the laboratory setting into new areas. Those unique areas include the diagnosis, treatment, and prevention of the disease progression within patients. The timely movement of identified strategies for the management of diseases is needed within the healthcare arena to support the prevention and aid in the supervision of the disease within individuals.

The second phase (T2) assimilates the identified results from laboratory research into the practical management at the bedside. This transformation of results from the clinical, laboratory setting into the judicious guidance of healthcare delivery allows for the up-to-date harnessing of knowledge to advance health care. Woolf (2008) notes that this process supports the involvement of disciplines that utilize clinical epidemiology, evidence synthesis, communication theory, behavioral science, public policy, finances, organizational theory, system redesign, and informatics. Each of these different applications requires that the investigator carefully considers the implications within the human world of change and conflict. The uniqueness of the individual patient comes into the picture as the laboratory results are moved into the practical world.

Action research is a term, identified with patient-oriented research, that integrates the ideas of best practices, patient inclusion, inclusion into practice, and EBP. Action research is the process of integrating concerned and involved individuals into a sequence of ascertaining a problem or trigger, determining a method for investigating the situation, and scrutinizing the outcomes. Action research is the practical application of systematic inquiry that reflects the evolution of solutions toward the bedside and/or frontline of health care for quality management of disease processes.

Within the process of translational research, basic research, population-based research, and patient-oriented research play a part toward the goal of moving research outcomes to frontline implementation for the advancement of disease prevention and management. Basic research and population-based research are not totally translational in nature (see **FIGURE 15-1**). As a result, these two types of research do not reside completely within the realm of translational research. On the

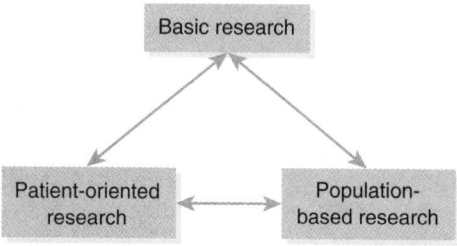

FIGURE 15-1 Translational research.

other hand, patient-oriented research essentially tackles those areas and issues foundational for utilization in the clinical setting, which eventually impact health care (Rubio et al., 2010). All aspects of patient-oriented research support and advance the concept of translational research.

▶ Improvement Science

In 2003, the idea for *improvement science* was introduced. Its beginning resulted from work initiated by Don Berwick, who sought to challenge health care to embrace the idea of continuous improvement as a foundation for the health community (Improvement Science, 2010). The term *improvement* was defined as the collective efficiency when system changes were viewed within uncertain situations (Improvement Science, 2017). The general question related to the process of improving the work to be done. Improvement science moved this definition to the point of viewing uncertainty related to systems changes in the direction of using the shared learning to advance the knowledge (Improvement Science, 2017). Thus, the general question associated with improvement sciences speaks to the manner in which the improvement will work within the healthcare environment. Maximizing the learning to improve healthcare provision is the foundation resulting from improvement science. Systems thinking and statistical thinking components are essential within the implementation of improvement science research. The process of improvement sciences moves from knowledge-based change (improvement) to knowledge about change (improvement science). Improvement science strongly embraces the plan–do–study–act (PDSA) process developed in association with quality improvement efforts (Institute for Healthcare Improvement, n.d.). Within this process, a team approach is embraced enthusiastically and passionately. Having the right people working to improve care delivery by accelerating improvements is paramount within this process. According to Perla, Provost, and Parry (2013), the seven propositions of the science of improvement:

- Are grounded in testing and learning cycles
- Are philosophically founded on conceptualistic pragmatism
- Adopt an amalgamation of psychology and logic
- Respect the perspectives of justification and discovery
- Stipulate the inclusion of operational definitions
- Utilize Shewhart's theory of cause systems, which is a process of control charts used to present statistical process control and link with systems thinking (Wilcox, 2003)
- Enlighten by systems theory

By using these seven assumptions related to improvement science, the healthcare community has embarked on a process to address core operating principles in an attempt to redesign a healthcare system to meet the growing demands for improved care, lower costs, and safer health care for the population. Change is not easy. Stavor, Zedreck-Gonzalez, and Hoffmann (2017) stated that healthcare organizations must strive to use the optimal evidence within the provision of care to promote healthy outcomes for patient populations. With the mounting pressure to transform healthcare delivery, healthcare providers must use every opportunity to uncover innovative ways to meet the challenges presented within the healthcare environment.

▶ Logic Modeling

With the advancement of translational research, the innovative application of planning, implementation, and evaluation has been advocated and sponsored. The Centers for Disease Control and Prevention (CDC) (2018) lists several variations to the term *logic model*, such as *road map*, *theory of change*, *program action*, *model of change*, *conceptual map*, and *outcome map*. One decisive concept incorporated within the movement toward best practice and EBP has been the logic modeling process. Different terms may be used for this process, such as *program theory*, *logical framework*, *theory of change*, or *program matrix*. A **logic model** is a step-by-step road map for getting to the desired result. According to Erwin and colleagues (2015), logic models "help identify underlying assumptions, focus on the processes and systems of change, and clarify desired outcomes" (p. 1). According to the CDC (2018), the number of columns used within the tool is not as critical as the categorization of the activities and the outcomes. These two sections hold the foundation for the successful implementation of the process. **TABLE 15-1** lists the multiple definitions

TABLE 15-1 Definitions for Logic Modeling

Source	Definition
University of Wisconsin–Extension (2003, section 1, p. 2)	■ Simplified picture of the projected program ■ Logical relationships found within the process ■ Program theory of action that reflects the different activities within the project ■ Denotes the underlying rationales for the activities selected to advance the project ■ Provides core for planning, implementation, management, communication, and evaluation of the project
California Living 2.0 (2009, p. 1)	■ Process used to create a graphic picture for how you think your work will lead to a collective vision for your community ■ Shows relationships among resources, strategies, and changes
Innovation Network, Inc. (n.d., p. 2)	■ Commonly used tool to clarify and depict a program within an organization ■ Logical framework ■ Theory of change ■ Program matrix
W. K. Kellogg Foundation (2004, p. III)	■ Define a picture of how your organization does its work— the theory and assumptions underlying the program ■ Links outcomes with program activities ■ Facilitates thinking, planning, and communications about program objectives and actual accomplishments
Centers for Disease Control and Prevention (2018, p. 1)	■ Instrumental in explicitly stating assumptions ■ Clarity about main strategies, activities, and intended outcomes

Inputs →	Outputs →		Outcomes–Impact		
Resources	Activities	Participation	Outcomes	Outcomes	Outcomes
What we invest	What we do	Whom we reach	Short-term	Long-term	Impact
(To achieve this set of activities, the following resources are needed.)	(To address the identified challenge, the following activities will be conducted.)	(To be successful at addressing this challenge, the following individuals should be engaged.)	(Once the activities are completed, the following short-term [1–3 years] outcomes will be realized.)	(Once the activities are completed, the following long-term [4–6 years] outcomes will be achieved.)	(Once the activities are completed, the following impact [7–10 years] outcomes will be achieved.)

FIGURE 15-2 Logic model template.

Data from University of Wisconsin-Extension. (2003). Enhancing program performance with logic models. Retrieved from http://www.uwex.edu/ces/lmcourse; W. K. Kellogg Foundation. (2004). *Logic model development guide*. Battle Creek, MI: Author. Retrieved from http://www.wkkf.org/knowledge-center/resources/2006/02/WK-Kellogg-Foundation-Logic-Model-Development-Guide

provided for this process. Each of the definitions speaks to the idea that the logic model is utilized to advance a project in a focused, organized manner. Whether the modeling is used for a research endeavor, quality improvement project, or EBP venture, the aspects included within the model help to pull the needed components together to provide a clear and concise visual of the steps within the planned activity. **FIGURE 15-2** provides a simple version of a logic model framework.

Erwin and colleagues (2015) discuss the benefit of using a logic model to depict graphically the activities within the project along with the processes that lead to the outcomes attained. Each aspect builds on the previous components to provide a template for planning, implementation, and evaluation. Becker (2017) notes the importance of using the logic model as an action-oriented tool for program planning, implementation, quality improvement, and evaluation. The model encourages the connection of strategies to the results. It also advocates timely and knowledgeable communication regarding the project and/or task. The sequencing of events related to the resources needed for a project, activities involved in a project, and the changes and/or benefits resulting from a project should be depicted within the tool. According to the W. K. Kellogg Foundation (2004), the declaration of the resources and activities reflects the planned work, while the **outputs, outcomes**, and **impact** demonstrate the intended results. Each aspect endorses and promotes the next step.

Three categories of logic modeling are available for agencies to use (W. K. Kellogg Foundation, 2004). Each of the unique types emphasizes discrete strengths. The theory approach model spotlights change theory that influences the designing and planning of a program. This model strives to provide a vivid justification for the development of a new program. Its intent is to make a case for the program through the use of the different components found within the model. This model type is frequently utilized by grant funders and individuals involved with grants. A second category is the outcome approach model. This type is also utilized early in the planning phase but grapples with the connections between the resources and the activities. Within this model, short-term (1–3 years), long-term (4–6 years), and impact (7–10 years) outcomes are provided for the set of activities. This category is most effective when designing effective evaluations. The third type of logic modeling is called activities approach modeling. This modeling process concentrates on the implementation strategies needed to accomplish the project. This model is used for program supervision and administration.

The initial step in this process of establishing a logic model is the analysis of the challenge identified or the problem. The Pell Institute (2010) lists several key steps for creating a logic model, including the following:

- Assemble a self-motivated and energetic team.
- Disseminate strategic and significant details before the initial meeting.
- Clarify a process for keeping effective annotations.
- Establish a timetable for managing progress within the process.
- Determine a method for staying on topic to ensure the momentum for the project.

The University of Wisconsin–Extension (2003) identifies six questions to use during this process of problem/challenge analysis:

- What is the problem?
- Why is this a problem? (What causes the problem?)
- For whom (individual, households, group, community, society in general) does this problem exist?
- Who is involved in the problem?
- Who has a stake in the problem? (Who cares whether it is resolved or not?)
- What do existing research and experience say? What do we know about the problem? (p. 10)

Each of these questions provides essential information as the problem/challenge is conceptualized. Frontline nurses are asked to implement innovative strategies to advance healthcare delivery, and these questions are key to ensuring that the process is organized and timely. By using a tool such as the logic model, implementation of change within a clinical setting can be accomplished successfully. Significant progress, such as introducing a new instrument (e.g., an intravenous pump), can be organized and managed to ensure that the optimum result can be reached through the use of the new information. While this tool can be time consuming, it is crucial for the management of large projects addressing multiple sites and components. By addressing these questions, the focus for the project can be distinctly established and presented.

Once the problem is determined clearly, a goal for the project can be formulated. The problem statements can also be classified as issue statements or situations. The problem statement usually addresses the ideas of who, what, why, where, when, and how. These components are also used in the PICOT (population, intervention, comparison, outcome, time) and/or hypothesis statements. The problem statement and goal should be narrow in focus, while objectives used within the process can reflect the scope of the project. Each component should drive the subsequent aspects within the model. The goal statements should address the intended results and target populations in general terms.

The following steps within the framework are driven by if-then statements. Regarding resources, certain means and/or assets are needed to activate the project.

Resources identify currently available assets and opportunities. Resources can also be viewed as inputs or program investments. Some of the common areas of resources are people, budgetary items, space, technology, equipment, and materials. From this idea of common areas of resources, the framework moves to the idea of *if* these means and/or assets are used, *then* specific activities can be utilized to advance the project. Thus, activities that support and utilize the resources are listed within the plan. The determination of activities is not the to-do list, but it should include the processes, strategies, methods, and/or action steps. The to-do list is provided within an action plan tool.

In relation to the activities, the statement is depicted: *If* the activities are successful, *then* certain outputs such as products or services will be completed. These outputs should be measurable, perceptible, and ensuing from the activities. The outputs reflect the deliverables, units of services, or products resulting from the project. Usually within the outputs, quantity is addressed, but quality is not.

Once the outputs are determined, the outcome declaration demonstrates: *If* the deliverables are obtained, *then* the participants will be rewarded with certain benefits. The outcomes are the results, effects, and/or objectives for the project. Outcomes should be measurable and reflect the change that occurs from the project process. Outcomes can reflect who or what will undergo the expected change. The focus can embrace the individual (client-focused), family/community, systemic, or organizational level. Olney and Barnes (2006) include within the individual level a focus toward cognitive, affective, skills, and quality-of-care outcomes. At the community level of the outcomes, environmental and social aspects need to be carefully considered and included as appropriate (Olney & Barnes, 2006).

The final aspect within the model is the impact. The statement that depicts the process is: *If* the benefits are achieved, *then* the resulting change to the organization, community, or system can be expected. The output, outcome, and impact aspects manifest the intended results of the project. The outcomes and impact fall into three categories. Outcomes can be viewed as short-term (1–3 years) and intermediate (4–6 years) results, while the impact (7–10 years) is understood to represent the long-term results. The W. K. Kellogg Foundation (2004) utilized the acronym SMART for the outcomes and impact statements: SMART represents *s*pecific, *m*easurable, *a*ction-oriented, *r*ealistic, and *t*imed. When short-term outcomes, long-term outcomes, and impact statements are developed, these five aspects should be integrated into the record. Short-term outcomes address the individual, while the long-term outcomes and impact statements tackle the idea of the community and/or populations. Both the short-term and long-term outcomes endeavor to change "attitudes, behaviors, knowledge, skills, status, or level of functioning expected to result from program activities" (W. K. Kellogg Foundation, 2004, p. 18). Impacts work to affect organization-, community-, or system-level modifications.

With some formats of the logic model, assumptions and external factors are provided. Assumptions consider how and why the change activities will work with the identified community or population. The assumptions are often viewed in a box directly below the input and output sections of the model to reflect the link between the sections. External factors are viewed as rationales, existing policy environments, risk factors, successful strategies, and other factors that can affect the outcomes and impacts recognized for the project.

Logic models are becoming an integral part within grants, research, quality improvement, and EBP projects. The models allow for concise and organized planning, implementation, communication, and evaluation to provide an effective decision-making path for projects. For each and every project that necessitates multiple applications, the utilization of a logic model framework endeavors to organize and structure the process for success. By using this type of framework on large projects, each component needed within the implementation can be planned and controlled. One example of using this type of framework on a large project would be when an acute care setting is planning a move into a new construction area. The many different aspects that must be planned and organized to allow for a successful, smooth transition can be laid out within a logic model. According to Milstein and Chapel (2018), the advantages for using a logic model within the process are that it:

- Incorporates planning, implementation, and evaluation
- Counteracts discrepancies concerning activities and effects
- Has an impact on the influence of partnerships
- Enriches accountability for the stakeholders

The logic model provides a framework for addressing clearly and distinctly the different components required for effective and efficient planning, implementation, and evaluation. With all the elements in one tool, the entire process moves with one voice toward success. Each member of the team can easily and productively identify the components needed within each phase of a project. Evaluation becomes increasingly operational because the objectives and activities are organized within the framework. Strategic planning for the next steps can be openly developed on the foundation provided within the logic model management.

🔄 THINK OUTSIDE THE BOX

A new catheter kit is being introduced within the acute care setting. Try to complete an action plan for this change from one type of catheter kit to the new one.

▶ Action Plans

Once the logic model is carefully constructed, it can be used to formulate the action plan for the day-to-day management of the project. The action plan (**FIGURE 15-3**) specifies the means to obtain concrete measurements of the objectives or outcomes. According to Sajdyk and colleagues (2015), "teams of experienced investigators with a wide variety of expertise are now critical for developing and maintaining a successful, productive research program" (p. 40). Action plans provide the structure needed by these teams to pull the different aspects of the projects together in an organized, progressive manner. Community Tool Box (2018) calls the action plan a heroic process for keeping the project moving forward in a realistic manner. The action plan takes the form of the to-do list for the logic model. At this level of development, the clearly worded objectives are supported by measurable indicators, target levels, and time frames. Also within the process, the key individuals who are responsible for each level are denoted. By thoroughly and painstakingly completing this level of clarity, the progression toward the goal is visibly noted. According to Community Tool Box (2018), an effective action plan should be complete, clear, and current. Community Tool Box (2018) recommends the idea of the 80/20 rule: Productive

Target Completion Date	Action Step	Accountable Person(s)	Assigned Person(s)	Actual Completion Date

FIGURE 15-3   Action plan worksheet.

endeavors are 80% follow-up on planned activities with the additional 20% of the effort contributing to the effective planning of the project. Pulling the activities from the logic model helps to determine the step-by-step process needed to advance the project. Taking the time and energy to plan in an organized manner allows for successful management of the project. Carefully and thoroughly considering the different aspects of the program and putting the results into an action plan enables:

- The development of credibility for the organization, group, or project
- The group to be sure that all aspects are addressed
- Improved understanding of the magnitude of the organization's potential
- Efficiency related to time, energy, and resources
- Accountability for the project being considered and implemented

The action plan should be viewed as a working document. Leedy and Ormrod (2013) suggest that breaking down full projects into manageable pieces allows for several beneficial outcomes. By dissecting the project into small activities, the ordering of the activities can be determined. For projects of small to moderate size, the use of an action plan provides the structure needed to move the project forward. As frontline nurses look to institute a quality improvement plan, the use of a planning tool ensures that each of the steps is in place and that all aspects are carefully and thoroughly considered. A project development team can be functional for mentoring other team members by providing a single point for accessing resources, responding to requests, breaking down institutional barriers, and managing the data accumulated (Sajdyk et al., 2015). For example, one medical–surgical unit elected to use the action plan format when the decision was made to convert from routine checking to hourly rounding on patients. For each of the different aspects used in the conversion to hourly rounding, specific target completion time periods, action steps, the accountable individual, and assigned personnel were laid out on an action plan worksheet. By establishing this plan, the process over the following months was organized and calculated. When the manager for the unit changed during the implementation of the quality improvement project, the plan provided structure and organization for the new manager to use.

In addition, small successes as each activity is completed can be acknowledged. The division of the project into a series of actions provides the opportunity to establish multiple target dates to strive toward instead of just one huge hurdle to confront. Self-confidence can be developed when the project is viewed by the group as moving forward. The communication of the completion of the smaller tasks toward the larger goal reflects the evolution toward the goal.

While attempting to be as clear and complete as possible with the initial design, changes and situations may develop requiring a change within the action plan. The columns used in an action plan (Figure 15-3) need to address the key areas identified within the unique project. Each column and element provides the structure for the advancement of the project by providing support and enhancement of the group's mission and goal. The action plan can also be used to present opportunities for communication across the group. Communication of the successes and challenges is paramount for the progression of the project. A final benefit of the use of an action plan relates to its ability to keep the project on track. Columns are provided for a time line and accountability so that the supervision of the project becomes visible and to the point.

⬛ THINK OUTSIDE THE BOX

What types of projects in your facility could benefit from completing an action plan?

Executive Summary

Another strategic tool used within project management is the **executive summary**. According to Berry (2018), the executive summary serves as a succinct starter to a business plan. An executive summary is provided to showcase critical details for individuals such as grant funders and agency management teams to use for the initiation of a discussion concerning the viability of an EBP, research, or quality improvement project. It serves as a pitch to allow a project to be considered for implementation. An executive summary provides a beginning discussion when healthcare agencies consider projects for implementation because it is usually restricted to one to two pages in length. The high points of the project along with the purpose and problem being solved are carefully presented. These aspects provide a review group with the foundational information needed to consider a project thoughtfully for support.

▶ Conclusion

EBP, research, and quality improvement must be organized and directed appropriately to facilitate the success of the process. Care must be given to the creation or selection of tools and processes that can be used to advance the achievements of the selected challenges. Translational research, with two components of basic and applied research processes, is established to move knowledge from the laboratory to the bedside. Improvement science, intervention research, and evaluation research are strategies that can be used to move a project into the workplace. Movement of the results from research projects, EBP activities, and quality improvement ventures is critical to advancing health care toward improved patient care and safety. By moving the results of the different projects to actual implementation for the patients, quality and best practice become standards in the practice arena. Tools such as logic modeling, action plans, and executive plans are crucial and strategic instruments to advance the science of nursing and health care. These tools can be used to support and coordinate the different venues within the decision-making process. According to Mick (2017), "learning how to better link dollars to outcomes to portray a return on investment that demonstrates how EBP contributes to an organization's project margin may justify additional investment in time and resources" (p. 29). By using each tool and resource available, the evidence becomes second nature in the practice sites.

Summary Points

1. EBP, research, and quality improvement are all aspects that play a part in the development of critical decision making and the validation of successful and competent healthcare practices.
2. The inclusion of strategic individuals to respond to the questions and challenges identified requires the different people to appreciate the multifaceted nature of systematic decision making.
3. Translational research has two areas of focus. The initial area relates to basic research. The second focus strives to move the outcomes determined through basic research to actual adoption at the bedside or on the frontline as examples of best practices for the community.
4. Within the process of translational research, basic research, population-based research, and patient-oriented research each play a part toward the goal of moving research outcomes to bedside and/or frontline implementation for the advancement of disease prevention and management.
5. Intervention research serves to encourage innovative applications to facilitate a purposive change strategy related to a variety of community and institutional settings.
6. Each aspect of a logic model builds on the previous components to provide a template for planning, implementation, and evaluation.
7. Three categories of logic modeling are available for agencies to use—theory approach model, outcome approach model, and activities approach model.
8. The outputs reflect the deliverables, units of services, or products resulting from the project. Usually within the outputs, quantity is addressed but quality is not.
9. The outcomes are the results, impacts, and/or objectives for the project. Outcomes should be measurable and reflect the change that occurs from the project process.
10. Logic models are becoming an integral part as a means for grants, research, quality improvement, and EBP projects.
11. Once the logic model is carefully constructed, it can be used to formulate the action plan for the day-to-day management of the project. The action plan specifies the means to obtain concrete measurements of the objectives and/ or outcomes.

12. Improvement science moved the process of improving health care from the position of viewing vagueness as it is associated to changing systems forward toward the focus of applying shared learning for the enhancement of knowledge.

⚑ RED FLAGS

- Each aspect within a logic model should build on the prior pieces. No part stands alone.
- Within any decision-making process, attention to the entire process should be evident within the materials provided.

Multiple-Choice Questions

1. Translational research strives to use a decision-making process to:
   A. move the results from the bench to the bedside.
   B. identify selected topics for research.
   C. restrict who can complete research to individuals understanding the entire process.
   D. focus only on the use of basic research.

2. The focus of attention for the implementation of translational research is on:
   A. patients only.
   B. populations only.
   C. patients and populations.
   D. patients, animals, and populations.

3. The type of research conducted in a laboratory setting to advance the understanding of knowledge is:
   A. translational research.
   B. patient-oriented research.
   C. population-based research.
   D. basic research.

4. What are the two areas of focus for translational research?
   A. Basic research and moving the outcomes to the best practices
   B. Basic research and patient-oriented research
   C. Cost-effectiveness and communication
   D. Understanding prevention and treatment options

5. Terms used for logic modeling are:
   A. basic research, patient-oriented research, and program theory.
   B. program theory, logical framework, and action plan.
   C. logical framework, theory of change, and program matrix.
   D. theory of change, action plan, and program matrix.

6. The logic modeling approach that underscores the use of change theory to transform the design and plan for a program reflects which approach?
   A. Theory approach
   B. Outcome approach

    C. Activities approach
    D. Action plan approach

7. The logic modeling approach that concentrates on the implementation strategies to transform the program reflects which approach?
    A. Theory approach
    B. Outcome approach
    C. Activities approach
    D. Action plan approach

8. The preliminary action taken for logic model development is:
    A. determining the challenge or problem.
    B. setting up the resources and activities to be done.
    C. clarifying the impact of the process.
    D. developing the action plan.

9. The outputs as used within a logic model depict the:
    A. action plan.
    B. translational research.
    C. deliverables and/or units of services.
    D. activities.

10. What do impact statements within a logic model tend to address?
    A. Individuals
    B. Clients
    C. Action plan statements
    D. Communities

Discussion Questions

1. A medical–surgical unit at your hospital wants to change from using a team nursing model to a primary care nursing model. The unit director asks the group to develop a logic model tool to show the problem, goal, resources, activities, and short-term goals involved in making this type of change. You are one of the staff members charged with preparing these aspects for the logic model. Discuss the details of the logic model you prepared. Items to consider when completing this request include the following: The initial step in this process of establishing a logic model is the analysis of the challenge identified or the problem. Once the problem is determined clearly, a goal for the project can be worded. The problem statements can also be classified as issue statements or situations. Usually the problem statement addresses the ideas of who, what, why, where, when, and how. The problem statement and goal should be narrow in focus, while objectives used within the process can reflect the scope of the project. From the activities, the statement is depicted: *If* the activities are successful, *then* certain outputs such as products or services will be completed. These outputs should be measurable, perceptible, and ensuing from the activities. Once the outputs are determined, the outcome declaration demonstrates the following: *If* the deliverables are obtained, *then* the participants will be rewarded with certain benefits. The outcomes are the results, impacts, and/or objectives for the project. Outcomes should be measurable and reflect the change that occurs from the project process. Outcomes can be viewed as short-term (1–3 years).

2. Using the SMART acronym, change the following outcome and impact statements to include the needed information.

Outcome statement: Registered nurses will enjoy 12-hour shifts.

Impact statement: Having 12-hour shifts will improve the retention rate of registered nurses.

Items to consider when completing this request: W. K. Kellogg Foundation (2004) utilized the acronym SMART for the outcomes and impact statements. SMART represents *s*pecific, *m*easurable, *a*ction-oriented, *r*ealistic, and *t*imed.

Suggested Readings

Dillon, K. A., Barga, K. N., & Goodin, H. J. (2012). Use of the logic model framework to develop and implement a preceptor recognition program. *Journal for Nurses in Staff Development, 28*(1), 36–40.

Glasgow, L., Adams, E., Joshi, S., Curry, L., Schmitt, C. L. Rogers, T., Willett, J., & Van Hersh, D. (2017). Using a theory of change to guide grant monitoring and grantmaking. *Journal of Public Health Management & Practice, 23*(2), 126–130. doi:10.1097/PHH.0000000000000421

Grill, J. (n.d.). Good and bad examples of an executive summary. Retrieved from http://www.business-plans-guide.com/executive-summary-example.html

Kowalszyk, D. (2018). Basic research and applied research: Definitions and differences. Retrieved from https://study.com/academy/lesson/basic-research-and-applied-research-definitions-and-differences.html

Leach, H. J., Covington, K. R., Pergolotti, M., Sharp, J., Maynard, B., Eagan, J., & Beasley, J. (2018). Translating research to practice using a team-based approach to cancer rehabilitation: A physical therapy and exercise-based cancer rehabilitation program reduces fatigue and improves aerobic capacity. *Rehabilitation Oncology, 36*(1), 1–8. doi:10.1097/01.REO.0000000000000123

Olney, C. A., & Barnes, S. (2006a). *Collecting and analyzing evaluation data.* Seattle, WA: National Network of Libraries of Medicine Outreach Evaluation Resource Center.

Olney, C. A., & Barnes, S. (2006b). *Getting started with community-based outreach.* Seattle, WA: National Network of Libraries of Medicine Outreach Evaluation Resource Center.

W. K. Kellogg Foundation. (2004). Logic model development guide. Battle Creek, MI: Author. Retrieved from http://www.wkkf.org/knowledge-center/resources/2006/02/WK-Kellogg-Foundation-Logic-Model-Development-Guide

References

Becker, K. L. (2017). Dance your heart out: A community's approach to addressing cardiovascular health by using a logic model. *Family and Community Health, 40*(3), 212–220. doi:10.1097/FCH.0000000000000153

Berry, T. (2018). How to write an executive summary. Retrieved from https://articles.bplans.com/writing-an-executive-summary/

California Living 2.0. (2009). Logic modeling & frequently asked questions. Building Healthy Communities: The California Endowment. Retrieved from http://www.calendow.org/healthy communities/pdfs/EvaluationLogicModeling_FAQs_9_11_09.pdf

Centers for Disease Control and Prevention. (2018). Logic models. Retrieved from https://cdc.gov/eval/logicmodels/index.htm

Chipps, E., Nash, M., Buck, J., & Vermillion, B. (2017, April). Demystifying nursing research at the bedside. *Nursing Management, 48*(4), 29–35. doi:10.1097/01.NUMA.0000514063.45819.c1

Community Tool Box. (2018). Section 5: Developing an action plan. Retrieved from http://ctb.ku.edu/en/table-of-contents/structure/strategic-planning/develop-action-plans/main

Division of Services and Intervention Research. (2018). Overview. Retrieved from https://www.nimh.nih.gov/about/organization/dsir/index.shtml

Erwin, P. C., McNeely, C. S., Grubaugh, J. H., Valentine, J., Miller, M. D., & Buchanan, M. (2015). A logic model for evaluating the academic health department. *Journal of Public Health Management Practice, 22*(2), 182–189. doi:10.1097/PHH.0000000000000236

Fraser, M. W., & Galinsky, M. J. (2010). Steps in intervention research: Designing and developing social programs. *Research on Social Work Practice, 20*(5), 325–466. doi:10.1177/1049731509358424

Improvement Science. (2010). Defining improvement science: A means to a beginning. Retrieved from http://improvementscience.org/?p=263

Improvement Science. (2017). Becoming science: Science of becoming. Retrieved from http://improvementscience.org/becoming-science-science-of-becoming/

Innovation Network, Inc. (n.d.). Logic model workbook. Washington, DC: Author. Retrieved from http://www.innonet.org/client_docs/File/logic_model_workbook.pdf

Institute for Healthcare Improvement. (n.d.). Science of improvement: How to improve. Retrieved from http://www.ihi.org/resources/Pages/HowtoImprove/ScienceofImprovementHowtoImprove.aspx

Leedy, P. D., & Ormrod, J. E. (2013). *Practical research: Planning and design* (10th ed.). Boston, MA: Pearson.

Mick. J. (2017). Funneling evidence into practice. *Nurse Management, 48*(7), 27–34. doi:10.1097/NUMA.0000520719/70926.79

Milstein, B., & Chapel, T. (2018). Section 1. Developing a logic model or theory of change. Retrieved from https://ctb.ju.edu/en/table-of-contents.overview/models-for-community-health-and-development/logic-model-development/main

National Center for Advancing Translational Sciences. (2018). About the CTSA program. Retrieved from https://ncats.nih.gov/ctsa/about

O'Brien, R. (1998). An overview of the methodological approach of action research. Retrieved from http://www.web.ca/robrien/papers/arfinal.html

Olney, C. A., & Barnes, S. (2006). *Including evaluation in outreach project planning.* Seattle, WA: National Network of Libraries of Medicine Outreach Evaluation Resource Center.

Pell Institute. (2010). How to create a logic model. Retrieved from http://toolkit.pellinstitute.org/evaluation-guide/plan-budget/use-a-log

Perla, R. J., Provost, L. P., & Parry, G. J. (2013). Seven propositions of the science of improvement: Exploring foundations. *Quality Management in Health Care, 22*(3), 170–186. doi:10.1097/QMH.0b013e31829a6a15

Rubio, D. M., Schoenbaum, E. E., Lee, L. S., Schteingart, D. E., Marantz, P. R., Anderson, K.E., . . . Esposito, K. (2010). Defining translational research: Implications for training. *Academic Medicine, 85*(3), 470–475.

Sajdyk, T. J., Sors, T. G., Hunt, J. D., Murray, M. E., Doford, M. E., Shekhar, A., & Denne, S. C. (2015). Project development teams: A novel mechanism for accelerating translational research. *Academic Medicine, 90*(1), 40–46. doi:10.1097/ACM.0000000000000528

Stavor, D. C., Zedreck-Gonzales, J., & Hoffmann, R. L. (2017). Improving the use of evidence-based practice and research utilization through the identification of barriers to implementation in a critical access hospital. *JONA, 47*(1), 56–61. doi:10.1097/NNA.0000000000000437

University of Wisconsin–Extension. (2003). Enhancing program performance with logic models. Retrieved from http://www.uwex.edu/ces/lmcourse

Wethington, E. (2018). What is translational research? Retrieved from http://evidencebasedliving.human.cornell.edu/2010/08/18/what-is-translational-research/

Wilcox, M. (2003). The philosophy of Shewhart's theory of prediction. Modified version of the author's presentation to the Proceedings of the 9th Research Seminar Deming Scholar's Program, Fordham University, New York.

W. K. Kellogg Foundation. (2004). *Logic model development guide.* Battle Creek, MI: Author. Retrieved from http://www.wkkf.org/knowledge-center/resources/2006/02/WK-Kellogg-Foundation-Logic-Model-Development-Guide

Woolf, S. H. (2008). Commentary: The meaning of translational research and why it matters. *Journal of the American Medical Association, 299*(2), 211–213.

CHAPTER 16

Application of Evidence-Based Nursing Practice with Research

Sharon Cannon and Carol Boswell

CHAPTER OBJECTIVES

At the conclusion of this chapter, the learner will be able to:

1. Synthesize key components from evidence-based nursing practice and research utilization to drive the provision of quality nursing care.
2. Demonstrate proficiency in one component of evidence-based practice (EBP) using the principles of the research process and evidence-based appraisal.

KEY TERMS

Evidence-based practice (EBP)
Integrative review
Meta-analysis

Research utilization
Systematic review

▶ Introduction

Evidence-based practice (EBP) is defined as a process of utilizing confirmed evidence (research and quality improvement), decision making, and nursing expertise to guide the delivery of holistic patient care. The recent need for and acceptance of EBP is apparent in the literature. Cost-effective, high-quality care based on evidence is essential today. Results of a 2006 survey conducted by Sigma Theta Tau International (STTI, 2006) suggest that a majority of the nurses surveyed needed evidence on a weekly basis to guide practice. Approximately 90% of the participants indicated a moderate to high level of confidence in EBP. However, a more recent U.S. study on EBP competencies by Melnyk et al. (2018) indicates that, for the most part, nurses do not believe they are capable of meeting EBP competencies. While the premise is that EBP is a driving force for the use of scientific data in the decision-making process in providing nursing care, nurses do not feel competent in EBP. In addition, Finkelman and Kenner (2009) recommend nurses be actively engaged with patient safety issues and concerned about quality research. They also stated that nurses must participate in the evaluation of nursing care because it is connected to safety and quality (Finkelman & Kenner, 2009). Their pronouncement is a direct result of the Institute of Medicine's imperative to ensure patient safety. Nurses' involvement in gathering evidence to support safe, quality nursing care is essential for the future growth of the profession and, most important, to the patients receiving the care they deserve.

As the United States moves forward with the implementation of the recommendations from the Institute of Medicine (1999) and the requirements included in the Patient Protection and Affordable Care Act (PPACA), attention to how best to address these recommendations and requirements is vital. EBP is a problem-solving process that mandates the use of current evidence to ensure safe and appropriate health care for patients. Melnyk (2012) states that the "ultimate purpose of EBP is to improve healthcare quality and patient outcomes and reduce hospital costs" (p. 130). Seger (2018) differentiates between EBP, research, and quality improvement (QI) through a model that determines when to use EBP, research, or QI. Of use in any model is the current emphasis on big data. Marr (2015) suggests that big data is and will continue to change health care. Combining the ideas of research and quality improvement to address areas of concern within healthcare delivery allows for optimal use of the information currently available. Care must be given to the incorporation of scientific inquiry concepts as a mainstay for nurses. Bator, Taylor, and Catalano (2015) state, "It takes approximately 20 years to fully embed research findings into facility-wide client care" (p. 582). They further indicate that EBP is a compelling movement for today's nursing issues. Nurses should and must be willing to challenge the status quo as health care moves forward to address the problems and opportunities facing them. Nurses are the underpinning for addressing clinically relevant questions and solving problems systematically and efficiently.

Understanding the research process is the first step in using evidence in everyday nursing practice. It is also important to have some historical background knowledge about research in nursing (as provided in this text) to better comprehend the research process. According to Gawlinski and Miller (2011), "research is one of the most powerful tools for advancing the science of nursing and improving the quality of patient care and outcomes" (p. 190). Examples of EBP have been given elsewhere in this textbook to demonstrate how EBP is applied in specific components of the research process.

Difficulty in analyzing the evidence has been identified as a major obstacle to **research utilization**. The modern-day nurse can use this text in the analysis of research findings, with their subsequent application to nursing care. This text is designed to "pull the pieces together" by suggesting a practical approach for research utilization in evidence-based nursing practice. EBP and research utilization must become common for the frontline staff nurse. Only when it develops into a practical and everyday part of health care will evidence truly become a mainstay of healthcare practice.

EBP and research are interconnected. As a dilemma is acknowledged, a PICOT (population, intervention, comparison, outcome, time) statement should be created. This PICOT statement propels the literature review. Each element in the PICOT statement provides strategic words to limit the search for applicable articles. Gaps and consistencies within the literature need to be determined to provide the pathway to the next phase of the process. These gaps and consistencies direct the process toward either a research study or a quality improvement project. If the evidence reveals that a policy, procedure, or protocol needs to be scrutinized, a quality improvement process is recommended for that purpose. If the gaps and consistencies indicate that supplementary research is needed to find an answer for the recognized problem, a full research project would need to be designed and executed.

If a research project is the trajectory, the principal process for conducting a thorough project needs to be ascertained. As a research venture is considered, the methodology for best addressing the challenge needs to be selected. Certain steps are generally followed when performing quantitative or qualitative research.

▶ Process for EBP

According to Myers and Meccariello (2006), "Outdated practices are barriers to decreased length of stay, favorable patient outcomes, and lowered costs" (p. 24). To move evidence-based nursing practice forward, a realistic approach for allowing frontline nurses to engage in the process must be determined and used. At each stage of providing holistic care, nurses have to be confident in asking the questions and seeking the best practices to advance the provision of effective nursing care. Nurses must seek the best evidence to make sure that the care provided represents the optimal health care available for the specified treatment plan. By determining a functional method for documenting an EBP search, nurses can then gain confidence in the overall process of conducting and implementing EBP.

⛁ THINK OUTSIDE THE BOX

Prior to a surgical procedure, patients are instructed not to take anything by mouth (NPO) after midnight on the preceding day. Due to surgical schedules, some patients may have to go as long as 10–12 hours without any liquids.

- Based on the evidence, what time limit is the best choice to manage this health challenge for the patient scheduled to have a surgical procedure?
- List PICOT questions that could be generated from this scenario.
- Which ethical considerations would need to be addressed prior to conducting a research study on this topic?
- How would you incorporate patient preferences into EBP?

The process for EBP determination is different from the process for research utilization. Research assessment involves completing a research critique. The research utilization process involves carefully examining a distinct study to determine the strengths and limitations assumed within that one study and deciding whether to apply its findings to nursing practice. Research utilization becomes a key aspect within the overall process of EBP, but it is only one piece of the EBP puzzle. For a nurse to be able to utilize EBP effectively, it is clear that he or she must be able to perform research critiques. The idea that nurses need to be able to use research, while acknowledging that not everyone has to be able to conduct research, is imperative. To facilitate implementation of EBP, frontline nurses need to understand how to recognize those elements of a particular research process that either strengthen or limit the use of its results.

Armed with this understanding of the applicability of the research results to practice, a nurse can then determine which study results might be used to sustain best practices in EBP. To make this determination, nurses clearly need to appreciate the intricacies of the research process. Frontline nurses should be able to identify the justifications that a researcher provides for selecting a specific method of sampling, data collection, research design, and data analysis. If a researcher has a valid explanation for the choices employed within a study, the results can be assigned a higher value and incorporated into practice. Having begun the work with research critiques, the nurse can then move to the next step of development to use those skills within the EBP process.

Melnyk and Fineout-Overholt (2015) suggest that the process of EBP involves five critical steps:

- Raise the urgent clinical question using a format that includes the key aspects of the issue.
- Assemble the most appropriate evidence that addresses the issue identified.
- Evaluate the evidence critically to determine its validity, relevance, and applicability.
- Assimilate the evidence into clinical practice.
- Assess the changes resulting from the use of the best evidence.

Each of these steps must be finished conscientiously to come to a conclusion about the best practices for a nursing setting. If an EBP process does not include all five steps, the result does not take into consideration all of the available evidence related to the clinical question.

Many models for EBP are currently being evaluated and modified, and TABLE 16-1 summarizes the key points quickly and easily for evidence consideration. This tabular format allows the reader to pull the needed aspects from any group of articles to reflect the current knowledge available regarding the topic under consideration. Within this format, the initial step is to refine the question confronting the nurse. Careful time and attention should be given to clarifying the five aspects driving the EBP question. As discussed previously, the question should consider the following aspects of the research issue (PICOT):

P   Population of interest (required aspect)

I   Intervention of interest (required aspect)

C   Comparison of interest (recommended aspect)

O   Outcome of interest (required aspect)

T   Time (recommended aspect)

TABLE 16-1 Format for Documenting Aspects of EBP

Questions to Consider Within the EBP Process

P (Population of Interest): _____

I (Intervention of Interest): _____

C (Comparison of Interest): _____

O (Outcome of Interest): _____

T (Time): _____

Articles (Level of Evidence/ Evaluation of Strength of the Evidence)	Who Is Involved (Sample Size, Sampling Method, Population)	What Occurred (Qualitative, Quantitative)	Where Completed (Type of Agency, State, Country)	When (Year Research Done)	Why (Research Question)	How (Data Collection, Tool Used with Validity and Reliability, Statistical Tests, Qualitative Control)	Consistencies (How It Addresses the PICOT Question, How Similar to Other Studies Reviewed)	Gaps (How It Does Not Address the PICOT Question, What Did the Researchers State Still Needed to Be Studied)

Summary of Findings

Application of Findings to EBP That Validates or Changes Policies and Procedures

⬆ THINK OUTSIDE THE BOX

In recent years, more parents have begun seeking alternative birthing options. Some individuals elect to deliver at home due to the burden placed on them by rising healthcare costs. Others make this decision based on a desire to have a more natural birthing process. When complications occur during the birthing process, however, the baby may have to be admitted to an acute care setting. For newborn infants, the standard initial treatment process includes erythromycin eye ointment, application of triple dye onto the umbilical cord, and a vitamin K injection. If the parents voice concerns about these procedures, which steps would a nurse need to take to provide evidence-based information to alleviate their fears?

- List PICOT questions that could be generated from this scenario.
- Which ethical considerations would need to be addressed prior to conducting a research study on this topic?
- Which key words would be used in a literature search to locate evidence related to this EBP question?
- Which type of research project could be developed to further study this concern?
- How would you incorporate patient preferences into EBP?

The development of a clear and concise clinical question is vital because the question guides the comprehensive EBP and/or research process. Once the question is clarified, the nurse needs to work with a librarian to establish strategic words and terms to employ in accomplishing the literature review. Using appropriate terms for the diverse search engines improves the search results and ensures the appropriate materials are located for the subsequent analysis of the best practices. As Melnyk (2003) has stated, "Evidence-based practice is a problem-solving approach to clinical decision making that incorporates a search for the best and latest evidence, clinical expertise, and assessment, and patient preference and values within a context of caring" (p. 149). Concerns are being raised at this time as to what are "best practices." Proehl and Hoyt (2012) contend that the term *best practices* is an indistinct phrase that could indicate that the practice is founded on data but not necessarily research. The data on which best practices are constructed tend to be based on data utilized by respected and highly valued organizations and/or practitioners.

Malloch and Porter-O'Grady (2010) have classified investigations of practices as meta-analyses, systematic reviews, or integrative reviews. The combining of these different study types identified through the literature review and search engine inquiry process provides the foundation for determining whether there is a need to change practice patterns. **Meta-analysis** incorporates a statistical technique to determine the rigorousness of the findings from multiple studies dealing with a focused question. A **systematic review** summarizes all quantitative evidence found through the literature search that is correlated to an identifiable research or clinical issue, employing a rigorous format to ensure completeness of the assessment. An **integrative review** also summarizes prior research studies on a selected topic but, in addition, draws conclusions from the summary concerning the studies examined.

Evidence can be evaluated using two different formats. One method is to use the levels of evidence. The levels of evidence are based on the research method design. If an article or information is not research, the classification of that data into the levels of evidence becomes complex. To determine the level of evidence, the available literature is ranked. For example, level 1 evidence (meta-analysis) is considered to be the highest-level, most important evidence that can be gathered. While level 1 evidence is the most desirable, the researcher should not toss out evidence classified as being at the other levels. Sometimes the only evidence that is available is a case study (level 5). A case study can still provide evidence for clinical decision-making purposes, even if it is not the strongest form of support. The depth of the justification for using this level of evidence provided by the researcher aids in the determination of the value of the results documented.

The second method for classifying evidence is based on the perceived strength of the evidence. Evaluating the strength of evidence classification involves looking into the risks and benefits of using the information for the client population. Healthcare agencies tend to focus more on this aspect of a procedure than on what type of research design was used. Risks and benefits can allow increased bias to be used in the determination of the level. Once the level of evidence is established, the researcher needs to evaluate the strength of the evidence. A simple rating system for this aspect of evidence can be used. Depending on the study, the evidence may be very strong or insufficient. The rating tool provides the researcher with a means for further discriminating which studies have significance for the project being considered.

The form provided in Table 16-1 allows for either a systematic review or an integrative review. Once the PICOT question has been determined and the literature review is completed, each of the identified studies is carefully assessed. For each article (citation, level of evidence, and evaluation of strength of the evidence), who is involved (sample size, sampling method, population), what occurred (qualitative, quantitative, level of evidence), where completed (type of agency, state, country), when (year research was done), why (research question), and how (data collection, validity and reliability of any tool used, statistical tests, qualitative control [trustworthiness, confirmability, transferability]) are determined and documented. As these aspects of a research critique are completed on the different studies, consistencies (how the study addresses the PICOT question, how similar it is to other studies reviewed) and gaps (how the study does not address the PICOT question, what the researchers stated still needs to be studied) within the different studies begin to surface. The identification of consistencies within the various studies may either support the proposed changes in practice or confirm that best practices are currently being used. The detection of gaps within the studies suggests the need for further or more in-depth research into the topic under consideration. The idea of identifying consistencies and gaps within the different articles and research reports also incorporates the concept of similarities and omissions that may be present.

During the EBP process, as a clinical problem is identified, individuals are directed to develop that problem concern into a PICOT format. The PICOT question

⬧ THINK OUTSIDE THE BOX

EBP should cause members of the nursing profession to query their normal activities. A simple skill such as catheterizing an individual can result in an EBP question such as, "How much urine should a nurse drain off the bladder at one time following a catheterization of a client?"

- List PICOT questions that could be generated from this scenario.
- Which ethical considerations would need to be addressed prior to conducting a research study on this topic?
- Which key words would be used in a literature search to locate evidence related to this EBP question?
- Which type of research project could be developed to further study this concern?
- How would you incorporate patient preferences into EBP?

drives the EBP literature search and the subsequent review of the literature discovered. Following the completion of the literature review, the PICOT question can evolve into a research question/hypothesis or a quality improvement focus. The gaps and consistencies found within the review process help to clarify the question to be used for the research or quality improvement process. From the literature review, the focus for the management of the problem is confirmed. When consistencies are identified in the literature, the nurse can elect to repeat the research concentration to strengthen the evidence related to the clinical challenge. Conversely, when gaps in the literature are recognized, additional research projects will be needed to address the gaps found. The third potential outcome is that the literature review might result in either a confirmation or a change in the agency's policies and procedures. In such a case, a quality initiative project may be needed to validate the practices, although further research might not be necessary.

Thus, within an EBP-focused endeavor, the outcomes could be either research projects (to replicate prior work or to address gaps) or quality initiatives (to validate clinical practice). Should the outcome lead to a research study, the research must be conducted in compliance with sound research design. By comparison, for quality initiative projects, any of the many quality initiative models—for example, Six Sigma, plan–do–check–act (PDCA), define–measure–analyze–improve–control (DMAIC), Lean, and root cause analysis—can be utilized. The development of these models has been largely driven by manufacturing businesses, with the models subsequently being adapted to many quality improvement efforts and used in the healthcare arena to improve performance. Some methodologies, such as Six Sigma, rely heavily on statistics and research as their underpinnings. The Lean philosophy relies on standardization to improve both the process and the organization from a consumer approach.

Associations established from the results of the various studies need to be collected to add strength to the rationale for making any changes in policies and procedures related to the selected clinical question. If several studies produce equivalent results, then nursing practice should embrace the behavior as supported by evidence. Conversely, if multiple studies reflect a gap in knowledge related to the selected clinical question, then further research should be directed toward the identified segment of nursing practice. According to Pravikoff, Tanner, and Pierce (2005), "The finding that a lack of value for research in practice was the most frequently selected barrier to the use of research in practice is of greatest concern" (p. 48). When practicing nurses cannot or do not use research results to strengthen and sustain holistic nursing practice, the implementation of EBP at the bedside or on the frontline falls short of its potential.

After completing the grid portion of Table 16-1, time must be allocated to summarizing the findings. The nurse should pay careful attention to, and consider carefully, the meaning ensuing from the consistencies and gaps identified. This painstaking contemplation of the discovered omissions and similarities serves to narrow the focus of the next steps within the process. By taking the time and energy to summarize and synthesize the information collected, the nurse becomes well versed in the current state of the clinical problem. Obtaining this clearer viewpoint related to the clinical problem allows the nurse to make an informed decision about what is needed next in dealing with this challenge.

The final section of Table 16-1 relates to the application aspect of EBP-related research. After completing each of the prior steps, the nurse has a basis for making recommendations for maintaining or changing a policy or procedure. The time taken to complete this exercise allows for any recommendations to be based on sound, factual data. The suggestions can then be supported effectively by a wealth of tested research endeavors. At this point, the nurse would take this review of the evidence and combine it with the decision-making method employed, personal expertise, and holistic client focus to drive sound, quality nursing care.

⚄ THINK OUTSIDE THE BOX

Frequently, an insulin drip protocol seeks to maintain a serum blood sugar level between 70 and 110 mg/dL. At one healthcare agency, a pilot research project revealed that the mean blood sugar for patients dismissed from a cardiac intensive care unit after 3 months was 148 mg/dL. The nurses questioned the protocol ranges as a result of this pilot study result.

- List PICOT questions that could be generated from this scenario.
- Which ethical considerations would need to be addressed prior to conducting a research study on this topic?
- Which key words would be used in a literature search to locate evidence related to this EBP question?
- Which type of research project could be developed to further study this concern?
- How would you incorporate patient preferences into EBP?

▶ Conclusion

According to Yoder (2005), "Both EBP and QI [quality improvement] initiatives require ongoing evaluation of the practice environment, the appropriate use of data collection and evaluation, and the dissemination of the information learned through the excellent communication process both from the top down and the bottom up" (p. 92). A variety of resources are available to help the nurse in strengthening the healthcare organization's EBP foundations and activities. The current healthcare community requires nurses and other healthcare providers to be diligent in the determination and provision of holistic health care. Whitmer, Auer, Beerman, and Weishaupt (2011) clearly identified that the utilization of a core group of individuals knowledgeable about EBP generates a foundation for the advancement of EBP within an organization. These champions for EBP must be given the time, educational opportunities, and resources to be able to conduct EBP inquiries effectively. The different treatments and plans of care put forth for clients must be based on factual, tested data. Each nurse must take responsibility for ensuring that the care provided is based on firm, accurate research data. These research data are then used to provide individualized health care to clients based on factual data, patient preferences, and nursing expertise.

A major emphasis on safety in healthcare requires today's nurse to access data. One such big data source is through the cognitive power of IBM's supercomputer named Watson (Clark, 2017). For example, IBM's Watson has been used to fight cancer and diabetes. Watson can help nurses access a literature review when considering an EBP, research, or QI project. Translating evidence into practice can require the use of big data. Brown and Chapa (2018) and Marr (2015) recommend differing approaches as "one approach does not fit all."

Vaidya, Zimmerman, and Bean (2018) identify 10 safety issues for 2018: (1) sharing data among electronic health records, (2) hand hygiene, (3) nurse–patient ratios, (4) drug and medical supply shortages, (5) quality reporting, (6) resurgent diseases, (7) mergers and acquisitions, (8) physician burnout, (9) antibiotic resistance, and the (10) opioid epidemic. Healthcare providers such as nurses need evidence to provide positive patient outcomes in all these issues. Evidence-based nursing practice must examine research and QI project results to apply evidence for safe, effective nursing care.

Another future aspect to consider will be the use of artificial intelligence, such as robots, to collect data and assist nurses in providing care. Thus, intervention research will need to provide evidence for the application of care through the use of robotics.

It is truly an exciting time and certainly a challenge for nurses to seek innovative approaches to nursing care. Using evidence for individualized, safe patient care for the 10 projected safety issues mentioned above can be accomplished through the use of big data and research through robotics.

🔁 THINK OUTSIDE THE BOX

Gather at least three of your peers and form a journal club. Select a topic of your choice and identify a PICOT question. Conduct an integrative review for the selected topic. What conclusions can you draw from the review? How will this new understanding change your practice?

Summary Points

1. EBP is the process of utilizing confirmed evidence (research and quality improvement), decision making, and nursing expertise to guide the delivery of holistic patient care.
2. Understanding the research process is the first step in using evidence in everyday nursing practice.
3. To move evidence-based nursing practice forward, a realistic approach for allowing frontline nurses to engage in the research process must be determined and used.
4. The process for research utilization carefully examines a distinct study to determine the strengths and limitations assumed within that one study.
5. Armed with an understanding of the applicability of the results to practice, a nurse can determine which studies can be used to sustain best practices in EBP.
6. The development of a clear and concise clinical question is of paramount importance because this question directs the entire research process.
7. Meta-analysis uses a statistical technique to determine the rigorousness of the findings from multiple studies conducted to answer a focused question.
8. A systematic review summarizes all quantitative evidence found in a literature search that is correlated to an identifiable research or clinical issue, employing a rigorous format to ensure completeness of the assessment.
9. An integrative review summarizes prior research studies on a selected topic but, in addition, draws conclusions from the summary concerning the studies examined.
10. For each article (citation, level of evidence, and evaluation of strength of the evidence), the who involved (sample size, sampling method, population), what occurred (qualitative, quantitative), where completed (type of agency, state, country), when (year research was done), why (research question), and how (data collection, validity and reliability of tools used, statistical analysis, qualitative control) are determined and documented as part of the evaluation process.
11. The identification of consistencies (how the research addresses the PICOT question; how similar the research is to other studies reviewed) within the various studies evaluated may either support potential changes in practice or confirm that best practices are currently being used.
12. The detection of gaps (how the research does not address the PICOT question; what the researchers stated still needs to be studied) within the studies evaluated suggests the need for further or more in-depth research endeavors on the topic under consideration.
13. Obtaining a clearer viewpoint related to the clinical problem allows the nurse to make an informed decision about what is needed next in this challenge.
14. Quality improvement activities are designed to incorporate research into the healthcare environment from a consumer approach.

Case Scenario 1

A Hispanic woman presents to the emergency room complaining of epigastric pain in atypical form, nausea, diaphoresis, and neck pain. The initial assessment reveals a 60-year-old, Hispanic female with a history of diabetes and hypertension. The client reports being a smoker with a family history of cardiac problems. She is 5 feet, 3 inches tall and weighs 185 pounds. She is a homemaker with no outside employment. For the most part, she reports a sedentary lifestyle and denies alcohol consumption.

The emergency department (ED) physician orders an electrocardiogram (ECG) and cardiac panel to rule out an acute myocardial infarction. Other tests ordered include a chest X-ray, urinalysis, and standard chemistry (complete blood count [CBC], troponins, creatinine protein). The tests reveal elevated troponin and ECG changes with an elevation in the ST segment. The client is diagnosed with a full-blown myocardial infarction. The ED physician mobilizes the cath lab team and orders a cardiology consultation. The client is transported to the cath lab for an angiogram, which reveals two blocked cardiac vessels.

After a double angioplasty is performed, the client is transferred to the cardiac care unit (CCU). After she arrives in the CCU, the nursing staff member assesses the client and determines that the angioplasty versus manual compression was completed with Perclose. The use of this closure for angioplasty has been a topic of debate in the CCU.

As a result of this case and others, members of the nursing staff elect to engage in an EBP activity to determine if the policies and procedures currently used on the unit reflect the best practices for this type of client and medical treatment plan. The PICOT question shown in **TABLE 16-2** was identified, and the EBP process was initiated.

As can be seen from the case study analysis in Table 16-2, there are gaps in the literature—specifically, a lack of actual research projects on the use of Perclose versus manual pressure. All of the literature reviewed consisted of case studies with reference to recommendations from the manufacturer of Perclose. However, the case study illustrates how EBP and research can lead to specific actions to improve nursing care, thereby improving patient outcomes.

Summary of Findings

Perclose can reduce length of stay and improve outcomes. Proper use of Perclose and consideration of prophylactic antibiotic therapy should be implemented. All of the reviewed articles were case studies; no quantitative research was found, and no nurse-directed research was located. The length of time before infections were identified ranged from 3 days to 4 weeks. Use of sterile technique during the procedure is paramount.

TABLE 16-2 Documenting Aspects of EBP: Use of Perclose for Angioplasty

Questions to Consider Within EBP

P (Population of Interest): Hispanic Adult 50 Years Old or Older

I (Intervention of Interest): Perclose Usage for Percutaneous Arterial Closure

C (Comparison of Interest): Manual Pressure

O (Outcome of Interest): Decreased Length of Stay, Decreased Hematoma, Decreased Discomfort, Decreased Infection Rate

T (Time): Within 2 Weeks from Discharge from Hospital

Articles (Level of Evidence/Evaluation of Strength of the Evidence)	Who Is Involved (Sample Size, Sampling Method, Population)	What Occurred (Qualitative, Quantitative)	Where Completed (Type of Agency, State, Country)	When (Year Research Done)	Why (Research Question)	How (Data Collection, Tool Used with Validity and Reliability, Statistical Tests, Qualitative Control)	Consistencies (How It Addresses the PICOT Question, How Similar to Other Studies Reviewed)	Gaps (How It Does Not Address the PICOT Question, What Did the Researchers State Still Needed to Be Studied)
Geary, K., Landers, J. T., Fiore, W., & Riggs, P. (2002). Management of infected femoral closure devises. *Cardiovascular Surgery, 10*(2), 161–163. Level of evidence: 5 Strength of evidence: B	4 males, 1 female, age range 63–73, purposive sampling	Qualitative, case study	New York, acute care unit, outpatient general hospital	2002	Examined Perclose	Case study; no indication of prophylactic antibiotic use, *Staphylococcus* infection	Population correct for age; all had infections, suture placement, antibiotics	Little research; recommendations came from manufacturer; no indications of ethnicity or manual pressure

(continues)

TABLE 16-2 Documenting Aspects of EBP: Use of Perclose for Angioplasty

(continued)

Articles (Level of Evidence/Evaluation of Strength of the Evidence)	Who Is Involved (Sample Size, Sampling Method, Population)	What Occurred (Qualitative, Quantitative)	Where Completed (Type of Agency, State, Country)	When (Year Research Done)	Why (Research Question)	How (Data Collection, Tool Used with Validity and Reliability, Statistical Tests, Qualitative Control)	Consistencies (How It Addresses the PICOT Question, How Similar to Other Studies Reviewed)	Gaps (How It Does Not Address the PICOT Question, What Did the Researchers State Still Needed to Be Studied)
Heck, D. V., Muldowney, S., & McPherson, S. H. (2002). Infectious complications of Perclose for closure of femoral artery puncture. *Journal of Vascular and Interventional Radiology*, 13(4), 430–431. Level of evidence: 5 Strength of evidence: B	2 females, 1 male, age range 40–76, purposive sampling	Qualitative, case study	Three different institutions	2002	No specific question documented; report of cases, 3 days postop	Case studies	Age range exceeds PICOT range; 2 cases had staphylococcal infection, one from bacterial source; concerns about suture placement	Neither manual pressure nor ethnicity noted in this study; refers to published trials
Tiesenhausen, K., Tomka, M., Allmayer, T., Baumann, A., Hessinger, M., Portugaller, H., & Mahler, E. (2004). Femoral artery infection associated with a percutaneous arterial suture device. *VASA: European Journal for Vascular Medicine*, 33(2), 83–85. Level of evidence: 5 Strength of evidence B	77-year-old male, purposive sampling	Qualitative, case study	Austria	2004	No specific questions documented; single case	Add to data; infection identified 4 weeks post-hospitalization; seen in ED prior to final admission to hospital with sepsis; Perclose carries risk of femoral artery infections	Age complies with PICOT; sterile field must be maintained	Neither manual pressure nor ethnicity noted in this study; refers to research

Citation	Sampling	Design	Setting	Year	Purpose / Variables	Specific Details	Comments
Dumont, C. J. (2007). Blood pressure and risks of vascular complications after percutaneous coronary intervention. *Dimensions of Critical Care Nursing, 26*(3), 121–127. Level of evidence: 4 Strength of evidence: B	Convenience sampling, 150 subjects, mean age 62.4, 45% women, 92% white	Case-matched control design	South Atlantic state, tertiary care teaching facility	2006	Determine which variables are significant individual predictors of vascular complications post-PCI—(1) 0 comorbidities: (2) physician-sensitive procedural factors (hemostasis method [Perclose compared with manual compression for hemostasis]), and (3) nurse-sensitive procedural factors	Specific details not provided; data collected—body mass index, comorbidity, physician-sensitive procedurals, and nurse-sensitive procedural factors	Mean age within PICOT level; use of Perclose compared to manual pressure included; outcomes of interest addressed Ethnicity not addressed
Lasic, Z., Nikolsky, E., Kesanakurthy, S., & Dangas, G. (2005). Vascular closure devices: A review of their use after invasive procedures. *American Journal of Cardiovascular Drugs, 5*(3), 185–200. Level of evidence: 5 Strength of evidence: B	Not a research article, so no sampling done	In-depth review of vascular closure devices	Not a research article	2005	Meta-analysis data related to complications and success rates; research reports discussed within the summary of the different closure devices	Not a research article	Outcomes related to Perclose usage provided Not a research article, so no sampling done

Summary of Findings

Perclose can reduce length of stay and improve outcomes. Proper use of Perclose and consideration of prophylactic antibiotic therapy should be implemented. All of the reviewed articles were case studies; no quantitative research was found, and no nurse-directed research was located. The length of time before infections were identified ranged from 3 days to 4 weeks. Use of sterile technique during the procedure is paramount.

Application of Findings to EBP That Validates or Changes Policies and Procedure

(Which policies and procedures does this information directly address and why?)

- All articles suggest prophylactic antibiotic use and strict adherence to the manufacturer's recommendations for ensuring a sterile surgical site.
- Emergency departments should review their policies concerning the assessment of postangioplasty clients who present with vague symptoms because the infection may be masked until it develops into a sepsis-type infection even as late as 4 weeks postprocedure.

Application of Findings to EBP That Validates or Changes Policies and Procedures

Which policies and procedures does this information directly address and why?

■ All articles suggest prophylactic antibiotic use and strict adherence to the manufacturer's recommendations for ensuring a sterile surgical site.

■ Emergency departments should review their policies concerning the assessment of postangioplasty clients who present with vague symptoms because the infection may be masked until it develops into a sepsis-type infection even as late as 4 weeks postprocedure.

■ Patient education should be addressed within policies to ensure that clients are taught to maintain a clean site at the incision area, to complete all antibiotic treatment ordered, and to report vague symptoms reflective of infections even up to 4 weeks postprocedure.

Case Scenario 2

A school nurse wanted to determine if the placement of alcohol hand sanitizers within the elementary school buildings would decrease the incidence of illnesses. Illnesses for this project were based upon children's absentee patterns. The school nurse has to consider carefully the cost and instructional process that would be required as a result of the placement of these hand sanitizer units.

The case study analysis in **TABLE 16-3** reflects that research has not been adequately carried out within the elementary school population. Research is available for acute care settings and other healthcare settings but not successfully within this setting. A foundation is established that the use of hand sanitizers is effective for the management of illnesses. Gaps are evident within this case study. A foundation for the use of hand sanitizers can be established with the understanding that application to this setting would need to be verified.

Critical Thinking Exercise

Multiple ideas related to potential clinical questions are provided for your consideration here. Select one of these situations to use in working through the process outlined in Table 16-1. The situations are presented briefly in the following list. Take the chosen idea and develop a PICOT question to best meet the needs at a selected healthcare agency of your choice.

1. One possible clinical question relates to whether a relationship between adequate pain control and length of stay in a community hospital setting could be determined.

2. Another clinical situation for investigation involves the determination of any relationship between glucose control during the operative period and length of stay in an acute care setting.

3. An alternative clinical circumstance relates to the effect of a one-on-one diabetic education course on the patient's HbA1C level.

TABLE 16-3 Documenting Aspects of EBP: Hand washing in Elementary Schools

Questions to Consider Within the EBP

P (Population of Interest):

I (Intervention of Interest):

C (Comparison of Interest):

O (Outcome of Interest):

T (Time):

Articles (Level of Evidence/Evaluation of Strength of the Evidence)	Who Is Involved (Sample Size, Sampling Method, Population)	What Occurred (Qualitative, Quantitative)	Where Completed (Type of Agency, State, Country)	When (Year Research Done)	Why (Research Question)	How (Data Collection, Tool Used with Validity and Reliability, Statistical Tests, Qualitative Control)	Consistencies (How It Addresses the PICOT Question, How Similar to Other Studies Reviewed)	Gaps (How It Does Not Address the PICOT Question, What Did the Researchers State Still Needed to Be Studied)
Vessey, J. A., Sherwood, J. J., Warner, D., & Clark, D. (2007). Comparing hand washing to hand sanitizers in reducing elementary school students' absenteeism. *Pediatric Nursing, 33*(4), 368–372. Level of evidence: 3 Strength of evidence: B	Sample size—Part I: 383; Part II: 13; sampling method—Part I: randomized cross-over, Part II: Convenient; Population—Part I: 2nd graders and 3rd graders, Part II: teachers, school nurses, and office personnel	Randomized cross-over design; mixed methods	Elementary schools in Butte, Montana	Not stated; published in 2008	Compare the efficacy of a hand sanitizer to standard hand washing in reducing illness and subsequent absenteeism in school-age children	Part 1: Data collected—absentee rates, two groups: cohort 1/phase 2—hand washing, cohort 2/phase 1—hand sanitizer; cohort switched in second phase; Part 2: focus group, no tools were used, so no validity and reliability; Statistical test for Part 1: t-test; Control for Part 2: audit trail, audio-taped	Population correct for age; intervention and comparison included in this article	The outcome was not directly associated with this one; article looked at absenteeism

(continues)

TABLE 16-3 Documenting Aspects of EBP: Hand washing in Elementary Schools

(continued)

Articles (Level of Evidence/Evaluation of Strength of the Evidence)	Who Is Involved (Sample Size, Sampling Method, Population)	What Occurred (Qualitative, Quantitative)	Where Completed (Type of Agency, State, Country)	When (Year Research Done)	Why (Research Question)	How (Data Collection, Tool Used with Validity and Reliability, Statistical Tests, Qualitative Control)	Consistencies (How It Addresses the PICOT Question, How Similar to Other Studies Reviewed)	Gaps (How It Does Not Address the PICOT Question, What Did the Researchers State Still Needed to Be Studied)
Foster, K. M., & Clark, A. P. (2008). Increasing hand hygiene compliance: A mystery? *Clinical Nurse Specialist*, 22(6), 263–267. Level of evidence: 1 Strength of evidence: B	6 articles; topic—hand hygiene compliance strategies	Meta-analysis	Literature review	Published 2008	The purpose of this article is to investigate some of the evidence-based strategies for increasing hand hygiene compliance, focusing on system-wide solutions to see if they might offer insight to the CNs and other organizational leaders	Articles were reviewed for study design/procedures, sample size/population, findings, and conclusions	Intervention and comparison aspects were present in the articles	Population and outcome not addressed
Fuller, C., Savage, J., Besser, S., Hayward, A., Cookson, B., Cooper, B., & Stone, S. (2011). "The dirty hand in the latex glove": A study of hand hygiene compliance when gloves are worn. *Infection Control and Hospital Epidemiology*, 32(12), 1194–1199. Level of evidence: 5 Strength of evidence: B	*n* = 56 Healthcare workers in medical or care of the elderly ward and ICUs	Observational study	15 hospitals across England and Wales	October 2006 to November 2009	Carried out a study of glove use and associated hand hygiene behaviors	Observed hand hygiene and glove usage during 249 1-hour sessions Tool: hand hygiene observation tool, rigorously standardized and validated; Statistical tests: proportions of moments and adjusted odds ratios used	Intervention, comparison, and outcome aspects addressed	Age group not addressed by this article

| Haessler, S., Connelly, N. R., Kanter, G., Fitzgerald, J., Scales, M. E., Golubchik, A., Albert, M., & Gibson, C. (2010). A surgical site infection cluster: The process and outcome of an investigation—The impact of an alcohol-based surgical antisepsis product and human behavior. *Anesthesia Analgesia, 110*(4), 1044-1048. Level of evidence:4 Level of Strength: B | Sampling—convenience sampling; Sample size—77; Population—patients having an SSI according to National Healthcare Safety Network SSI criteria | Quality improvement methodology | Academic tertiary care medical and level 1 trauma center in New England | 2007 | The process by which quality improvement methodology was used to investigate and manage the surgical site infection cluster | Specific details not provided; data collected—body mass index, comorbitity, physician-sensitive procedurals, and nurse-sensitive procedural factors | Outcome addressed | Age, intervention, and comparison not addressed |

Summary of Findings

The use of hand sanitizer can affect the number of illnesses reported by individuals. Research reports directed toward the use of these care items within an elementary school-age population are not effectively documented at this time.

Application of Findings to EBP That Validates or Changes Policies and Procedure

(Which policies and procedures does this information directly address and why?)

Policies within an elementary school setting that might need to be reviewed include:

- Instructions to provide to children regarding the proper way to use hand sanitizer systems
- Infection control measures that can be started
- Effective hand washing procedures

Note: CNS = clinical nurse specialist; ICUs = intensive care units; SSI = surgical site infection.

4. When a medication error occurs, the value of full disclosure to patients and/or family members in building trust and restoring confidence, as opposed to nondisclosure, with a look at the impact on perceived quality of care, could be investigated.
5. An additional idea involves determining whether the length of time and frequency of visits to patients' rooms by nursing staff members affect the number of calls and the perception of quality of care by the patient and/or family members.
6. Maternal/child nurses understand that certain treatments (prophylactic eye treatments, vitamin K injections, phenylketonuria [PKU] tests) are provided for all newborn children. What happens to children born outside an acute care setting (e.g., home births)? What rationales do we have to support these treatments?
7. Childhood immunization is a state-directed process that applies to all school-age children. Certain immunizations (measles–mumps–rubella [MMR], polio, diphtheria–pertussis–tetanus [DPT]) are designated at key times prior to and during the school-age years. What is happening with the growing number of homeschooled children? Are they receiving these immunizations? What happens when these children come into acute care settings without having received the expected childhood immunization series?

Suggested Readings

Brody, A. A., Barnes, K., Ruble, C., & Sakowski, J. (2012). Evidence-based practice councils: Potential path to staff nurse empowerment and leadership growth. *Journal of Nursing Administration, 42*(1), 28–33.

Clark, J. (2017). Is Watson the best medicine? The impact of big data analysis on healthcare. https://www.ibm.com/blogs/internet-of-things/iot-and-healthcare

Coopey, M., & Clancy, C. M. (2006). Translating research into evidence-based nursing practice and evaluating effectiveness. *Journal of Nursing Care Quality, 21*(3), 195–202.

Marchiondo, K. (2006). Planning and implementing an evidence-based project. *Nurse Educator, 31*(1), 4–6.

Newhouse, R. P. (2006). Examining the support for evidence-based nursing practice. *Journal of Nursing Administration, 36*(7–8), 337–340.

References

Bator, S., Taylor, S., & Catalano, J. T. (2015). Nursing research and evidence-based practice. In J. Catalano (Ed.), *Nursing now! Today's issues, tomorrow's trends* (7th ed., pp. 581–674). Philadelphia, PA: F.A. Davis.

Brown, M. M., & Chapa, D. W. (2018, May). One approach does not fit all: Methods for translating evidence into practice. *Voice of Nursing Leadership, 16*(3), 4–6.

Dumont, C. J. (2007). Blood pressure and risks of vascular complications after percutaneous coronary intervention. *Dimensions of Critical Care Nursing, 26*(3), 121–127.

Finkelman, A., & Kenner, C. (2009). *Teaching IOM: Implications of the IOM reports for nursing education* (2nd ed.). Silver Spring, MD: American Nurses Association.

Foster, K. M., & Clark, A. P. (2008). Increasing hand hygiene compliance: A mystery? *Clinical Nurse Specialist, 22*(6), 263–267.

Fuller, C., Savage, J., Besser, S., Hayward, A., Cookson, B., Cooper, B., & Stone, S. (2011). "The dirty hand in the latex glove": A study of hand hygiene compliance when gloves are worn. *Infection Control and Hospital Epidemiology, 32*(12), 1194–1199.

Gawlinski, A., & Miller, P. S. (2011). Advancing nursing research through a mentorship program for staff nurses. *AACN Advanced Critical Care, 22*(3), 190–200.

Geary, K., Landers, J. T., Fiore, W., & Riggs, P. (2002). Management of infected femoral closure devices. *Cardiovascular Surgery, 10*(2), 161–163.

Haessler, S., Connelly, N. R., Kanter, G., Fitzgerald, J., Scales, M. E., Golubchik, A., Albert, M., & Gibson, C. (2010). A surgical site infection cluster: The process and outcome of an investigation— The impact of an alcohol-based surgical antisepsis product and human behavior. *Anesthesia Analgesia, 110*(4), 1044–1048.

Heck, D. V., Muldowney, S., & McPherson, S. H. (2002). Infectious complications of Perclose for closure of femoral artery punctures. *Journal of Vascular and Interventional Radiology, 13*(4), 430–431.

Institute of Medicine. (1999). *To err is human: Building a safer health system and the future of nursing.* Washington, DC: National Academy Press.

Lasic, Z., Nikolsky, E., Kesanakurthy, S., & Dangas, G. (2005). Vascular closure devices: A review of their use after invasive procedures. *American Journal of Cardiovascular Drugs, 5*(3), 185–200.

Malloch, K., & Porter-O'Grady, T. (2010). *Introduction to evidence-based practice in nursing and health care* (2nd ed.). Sudbury, MA: Jones and Bartlett.

Marr, B. (2015, April 21). How big data is changing healthcare. *Forbes/Tech.* Retrieved from https://www.forbes.com/sites/bernardmarr/2015/04/21/how-big-data-is-changing-healthcare

Melnyk, B. M. (2003). Finding and appraising systematic reviews of clinical interventions: Critical skills for evidence-based practice. *Journal of Pediatric Nursing, 29*(2), 125, 147–149.

Melnyk, B. M. (2012). Achieving a high-reliability organization through implementation of the ARCC model for systemwide sustainability of evidence-based practice. *Nursing Administration Quarterly, 36*(2), 127–135.

Melnyk, B. M., & Fineout-Overholt, E. (2015). *Evidence-based practice in nursing and healthcare: A guide to best practice* (3rd ed.). Philadelphia, PA: Wolters Kluwer.

Melnyk, B. M., Gallagher-Ford, L., Zellefrow, C., Tucker, S., Thomas, B., Sinnott, L. T., & Tan, A. (2018, February). The first U.S. study on nurses' evidence-based practice comprehensive indicate major deficits that threaten healthcare quality, safety and patient outcomes. *Worldviews Evidence Based Nursing, 15*(1), 16–25. doi:10.111/WVN0

Myers, G., & Meccariello, M. (2006). From pet rock to rock-solid: Implementing unit-based research. *Nursing Management, 37*(1), 24–29.

Pravikoff, D. S., Tanner, A. B., & Pierce, S. T. (2005). Readiness of U.S. nurses for evidence-based practice. *American Journal of Nursing, 105*(9), 40–51.

Proehl, J. A., & Hoyt, K. S. (2012). Evidence versus standard versus best practice: Show me the data! *Advanced Emergency Nursing Journal, 34*(1), 1–2.

Seger, B. M. (2018). Evidence-based practice, research and quality improvement: Using three initiatives to foster high-quality care. *Voice of Nursing Leadership, 16*(3), May 2018.

Tiesenhausen, K., Tomka, M., Allmayer, T., Baumann, A., Hessinger, M., Portugaller, H., & Mahler, E. (2004). Femoral artery infection associated with a percutaneous arterial suture device. *VASA: European Journal for Vascular Medicine, 33*(2), 83–85.

Vaidya, A., Zimmerman, B., & Bean, M. (2018). 10 top patient safety issues for 2018. Retrieved from https://www.beckershospitalreview.com/10-top-patient-safety-issues-for-2018.html

Vessey, J. A., Sherwood, J. J., Warner, D., & Clark, D. (2007). Comparing hand washing to hand sanitizers in reducing elementary school students' absenteeism. *Pediatric Nursing, 33*(4), 368–372.

Whitmer, K., Auer, C., Beerman, L., & Weishaupt, L. (2011). Launching evidence-based nursing practice. *Journal for Nurses in Staff Development, 27*(2), E5–E7.

Yoder, L. (2005). Evidence-based practice: The time is now! *Medsurg Nursing, 14*(2), 91–92.

Glossary

A

Accessible data Data that can be linked into for use within a research study.

Accessible population Individuals and/or groups accessible for a specific participation study, frequently a nonrandom division of the target population.

Accuracy The correctness of the information used within the process.

Action research Applied research that is attentive to the resolution of nursing personnel's identified challenges.

Analysis of variance (ANOVA) Parametric statistical test used to determine the statistical differences between the means among two or more groups; computed as either one-way or two-way. *Also called* F-test.

Annotated bibliography A listing that summarizes the research and published information related to a given topic; presents a concise and succinct synopsis of the knowledge known on a topic.

Applied research Research that concentrates on resolving functional questions to supply reasonably direct solutions.

Associative hypothesis A hypothesis stated in a way that indicates that the variables exist side by side and that a change in one variable is caused by a change in another variable.

Autonomy The state of being free from influence; the ability to make informed decisions.

B

Basic research Research designed to generate elemental knowledge and theoretic agreement about crucial human and foundational innate processes.

Beneficence Maximizing possible benefits while minimizing potential harm to individuals involved within the conducting of a research project.

Best practice Nursing action that produces the most desirable patient outcome, as determined through scientific data.

Bias Any pressure that generates an alteration in the outcomes of an inquiry.

Big Data sets The investigation and use of data sets that deal with an excessive quantity of data, an extensive diversity of data categories, and the swiftness by which the data should be processed.

Biophysiological data Objective data that use a specialized piece of equipment to establish the physical and/or biological condition of the subjects.

Bracketing Categorizing or classifying collectively; incorporating or eliminating through the use of established specialized limitations.

Bundling Multiple identified interventions that, taken together, enhance the clinical outcomes.

C

Case-controlled Describes a type of project pattern used in epidemiology in which two groups with varying outcomes are recognized and contrasted in relation to differing contributory characteristics.

Case report The documentation of the aspects identified with a situation such as a case study.

Case series Several case studies that have resulted in similar outcomes.

Case study A qualitative research method that concentrates on supplying a comprehensive description and scrutiny of an identified case situation.

Categorical variable A variable that diverges in type or kind but that has distinct values instead of values spaced along a continuum.

Causal hypothesis A hypothesis stated in a way that indicates that one variable causes or brings about a change in another variable or variables.

Central tendency Statistical quality associated with quantitative data that can be classified in three ways: the mean, median, or mode.

Chi-square (χ^2) Statistical test employed to establish if an association recognized in a contingency table is statistically significant.

Clinical decision making The course of action by which a person resolves who needs what and when it is needed.

Clinical research Research calculated to produce knowledge to direct nursing practice.

Closed-ended question A question that is set up to force specific responses through the options provided within the question.

Cluster sampling A method of sampling in which a sizable group is divided into consecutive subsampling of smaller units; a style of sampling in which groups are randomly selected.

Code of ethics Underlying ethical assumptions that are recognized by a discipline or organization to direct researchers; management of the research related to the safe handling of human subjects.

Comparative design A design that does not entail any manipulation or control of the independent variable such that the dependent variable is the only variable measured in two or more groups.

Comparison group A group of participants whose results related to a dependent variable classification are used as a foundation for appraising the results of the grouping of designated significance; phrase employed in place of "control group" for studies not applying an exact experimental plan.

Complex hypothesis A statement that specifies the relationships among more than two variables.

Conceptual definition Characterization of the identified word, variable, or activity from the dictionary-specific explanation of the term.

Concurrently Occurring at the same time (data or processes).

Concurrent validity Verification that is based on the correlation between the calculated scores and criterion scores acquired at the same time.

Confidence interval A range of numbers assessed from the sample that has a specific likelihood or probability of containing the population limitation.

Confidentiality Protection of study participants that results in the individuals' identities not being linked to the information they provided, meaning that the information can be provided only in the aggregate; not revealing the data collected from study participants to any person except the researcher and designated staff members.

Confounding variable A type of extraneous variable that is not controlled for; it regularly fluctuates with the independent variable and affects the dependent variable.

Consensus Coming to a common understanding about the topic; reaching an agreed upon resolution or understanding.

Consistency The extent to which the equivalent outcome can be anticipated when measuring a variable more than a single time.

Construct validity The degree to which a higher-order concept is characterized in a specific inquiry.

Content analysis The practice of categorizing and combining qualitative results to establish the materializing premises and perceptions.

Content-related validity The extent to which the details in a tool effectively characterize the totality of the content that needs to be included.

Contingency table A table that places data in cells produced by the juncture of two or more categorical variables.

Continuous variable A term that can take on a wide range of values, such as from 0 to 100 or larger.

Control The procedure for managing the extraneous influences that could affect the dependent variable.

Control group A group of participants in an experiment who provide the baseline for the study, in contrast to the treatment group. Members of the control group do not receive the experimental treatment.

Convenience sampling The process of selecting individuals to be in the sample who are accessible and/or who volunteer. *Also called* accidental sampling.

Convergent validity A type of construct validity.

Correlational design Any of a variety of nonexperimental research designs in which the primary independent variable of interest is a quantitative variable.

Correlation coefficient The outcome of the calculation of the relationship between two or more observed scores.

Covert Covered up, hidden. Covert data are collected without the subject knowing about the collection of the information.

Criterion The yardstick or benchmark used for predicting the accuracy of test scores.

Criterion-related validity Based on the comparison of the tests being used with some known criterion.

Critique An impartial, analytic, and reasonable appraisal of a research report.

Cross-validation A method for triangulating qualitative data by confirming the results through some other process.

Cumulative Index to Nursing and Allied Health Literature (CINAHL) A database supplying reliable reporting of the literature associated with nursing and allied health.

D

Database An organized body of related information arranged for speed of access and retrieval.

Data collection The compilation and assembling of information related to concepts and variables in a reputable manner that facilitates answers for PICOT (population, intervention, comparison, outcome, and time) questions, research questions, and hypotheses leading to establishing outcomes.

Data mining The process of investigating and analyzing sizeable databases with the expectation of creating fresh evidence.

Demographic variable Characteristic of the subjects in the study.

Deontology Ethical theory connected with duties and rights; intrinsic nature or "rightness" of an action itself.

Dependent variable The outcome variable that is alleged to be influenced by one or more independent variables; the presumed outcome of the study.

Descriptive design A research study whose foremost intention is providing the truthful depiction of the distinctiveness of persons, situations, or groups and/or an accurate explanation or representation of the condition of a state of affairs or phenomenon.

Dichotomous variable A characteristic that can be measured only in the sense that it is present or not present; often assigned a number for identification purposes rather than to represent a quantity.

Directional hypothesis A statement that predicts the path or direction that the relationship between variables will take.

Discrete variable A term that can take on only a finite number of values, usually restricted to whole numbers.

Discursive prose Summary of material provided in a manner organized by themes or identified trends, not as a summary of different reports.

E

Editorials Statements of the opinions of an owner, manager, or the like. Weight of the evidence is based on the perceived biases associated with the thoughts and statements.

Effect size The expected strength of the relationship between the research variables; used in the calculation of desired sample size through power analysis.

Eligibility criteria The conditions employed by a researcher to indicate the detailed characteristics of the target population that are used to select participants for a study.

Emic term The point of view provided by the individuals directly involved in a situation.

Empiric Established by inspection, experiment, or practice (data and/or results).

Equivalency reliability A measure of reliability that is calculated in the same manner as the consistency and stability coefficients; however, instead of a single variable over two trials, the test is between two forms of a single test.

Ethical theories A collection of ideology and philosophy of right behavior; a system of moral principles and ideals.

Ethics The main beliefs, ideology, and guidelines that facilitate the maintenance of an issue that people and/or professionals appreciate and respect.

Ethnography A type of qualitative research that conscientiously illustrates the customs of a grouping of individuals.

Evidence Foundation on which beliefs and proofs are established; a pathway to clear and organized proof on a given topic.

Evidence-based practice (EBP) A process of utilizing confirmed evidence (research and quality improvement), decision making, and nursing expertise to guide the delivery of holistic patient care.

Exclusion criteria Characteristics that, if present, would make persons ineligible for participation in a study, even if they meet all of the other inclusion criteria.

Executive summary A concise document that condenses a lengthier proposal in a manner that readers can quickly become familiar with key information without having to read the entire long document.

Experimental design Research in which the independent variable is manipulated, a control group is established, and randomized selection of the participants is employed to select who does and does not receive the treatment or intervention.

Expert opinion Information provided by an individual who is viewed as an authority, based on a set of criteria related to information applicable and/or significant to a designated problem or situation.

External validity The degree to which the analysis outcomes can be generalized to a specific group of persons, settings, times, outcomes, and treatment variations.

Extraneous variable A variable that confuses the association between the independent and dependent variables; for this reason, it needs to be restricted either within the research design or through statistical procedures.

F

Fidelity Demonstration of loyalty and defense for a person, cause, or belief.

Focus group A small group of people assembled to participate in a moderator-facilitated discussion geared toward the designated topic being researched.

Forensic science The study of evidence; the process of utilizing data to formulate judgments and decisions.

Formative evaluation An appraisal conducted to improve the evaluation process.

Framework The conceptual foundation of a study; sometimes classified as a theoretic framework, for projects centered on a theory, and as a conceptual framework, for projects with a connection to a definite conceptual model.

G

Generalizability The extent to which findings from a study can be extended from a sample of a population to the population at large.

Grounded theory A general methodology for developing new theory that is based on data that are systematically gathered and analyzed.

H

Hawthorne effect A change in a dependent variable that occurs as a result of the participants' recognition that they are engaged in a study.

Honesty Integrity, truthfulness, and straightforwardness.

Hospital Care Quality Information from the Consumer Perspective (HCAHPS) Nationwide, standardized, publicly reported appraisal of patients' perceptions of healthcare delivery.

Human experimentation Medical testing performed on human beings with the expectation of gaining new knowledge to improve a situation or manage a health-related problem.

Hypothesis A prediction or educated guess about the relationships among variables; the recognized proclamation of the researcher's prediction of the affiliation that exists among the variables under investigation.

I

Ideas Thoughts, convictions, and/or principles based on a potential or actual existing foundation, considered to be individual work.

Impact The consequence or influence resulting from the use of a logic model.

Inclusion criteria Characteristics that must be met to be considered for participation in a study. *Also called* eligibility criteria.

Independent variable The variable in experimental research that is established as the cause or influence on the dependent variable; it may be identified as the manipulated (treatment) variable.

Informed consent The decision of an individual to participate in a research study based on an understanding of the project's purpose, procedures, risks, benefits, alternative procedures, and limits of confidentiality.

Institutional review board (IRB) Individuals representing an institution who assemble to evaluate the ethical considerations related to proposed and ongoing research studies.

Instrument A tool that a researcher uses to accumulate information.

Integrative review Summarization of prior research studies on a selected topic with a summation provided as a conclusion.

Interclass reliability The reliability between two measures that are presented in the data as either variables or trials.

Internal validity The capacity to conclude that a contributory affiliation exists between two or more variables.

Interval scale Scale of measurement used in statistical analysis that incorporates both order and magnitude within the description but lacks a defined zero point.

Intervention The experimental treatment or manipulation employed during a research endeavor.

Intervention research Studies where the researchers coordinate a structured change to ascertain the consequences of the changes on a physical capacity or skill.

Interview A data collection technique in which an interviewer poses questions to the interviewee.

Intraclass reliability A type of reliability that allows a person to develop a reliability coefficient for more than one variable.

In vitro Requiring the extraction of physiologic materials from a participant in a research study, frequently via a laboratory analysis.

In vivo Requiring the use of some apparatus to evaluate one or more elements of a participant in a research study.

J

Justice The standard of decent rightness; agreement with truth, fact, or sensible intention.

L

Literature review A rigorous examination of research related to a topic of interest that is documented to categorize a research problem or as the beginning of a research use project.

Logic model A plan that denotes how an intervention produces distinct consequences using four aspects in a linear cycle: inputs, activities, outputs, and outcomes.

Longitudinal design A study design in which information is accumulated at various times for use in comparisons.

M

Magnitude The degree of size of a result or outcome.

Manipulation An intervention or treatment initiated in an experimental or quasi-experimental study to assess the independent variable's impact on the dependent variable.

Mean The mathematical average of a data set.

Median The 50th percentile.

Medical Literature Analysis and Retrieval System Online (MEDLINE) The leading bibliographic database for retrieval of North American biomedical literature.

Medical subject heading (MeSH) A glossary for finding the terms that correctly identify or agree with the search terms or concepts in the MEDLINE database; the controlled vocabulary for MEDLINE.

Meta-analysis A process of quantitatively comparing the results from multiple research studies on a selected subject.

Meta-ethnography An explanatory qualitative research method advanced by Noblit and Hare which blends ethnographic research findings with the field of education.

Meta-synthesis The process for analyzing information to determine a conclusion from the facts.

Metadata A data set to depicts and organize evidence about previous data.

Mixed methods research A type of study in which a researcher uses qualitative research methodology for one phase of the study and quantitative research methodology for another phase of the study. *Also called* multimethod research.

Mode The most frequently occurring number in a data set.

Morality What a person believes to be right and wrong; it is shaped by what a person has been taught within society and his or her own culture.

N

National Center for Nursing Research (NCNR) A division within the National Institutes of Health that directs research efforts within the profession of nursing.

National Institute of Nursing Research (NINR) A division of the National Institutes of Health that focuses on funding nursing research projects and conducting studies to advance the profession of nursing.

National Institutes of Health (NIH) Biomedical research facility that oversees federally funded research projects directed toward health care.

Nesting A collection of comparable ideas and processes related to the management of research projects.

Nominal scale A level of measurement that applies symbols, such as numbers, to describe, categorize, or recognize people or objects.

Nondirectional hypothesis A statement that predicts a relationship between variables but not the path or direction of that relationship.

Nonequivalent control group A research sampling method where random selection is not used to determine the membership of the control group.

Nonexperimental design A research study in which data are collected without introducing any treatment, and no random assignment of participants to groups occurs.

Nonmaleficence A bioethics principle directed toward the expectation of not inflicting intentional harm when dealing with individuals.

Nonprobability sampling A sampling strategy that does not include random selection of elements.

Nonsignificant results The outcome of a statistical test demonstrating that the connection between variables could have transpired as a consequence of chance, at the designated level of significance.

Novel data New data collected as part of a research study.

Null hypothesis A prediction or educated guess that no relationship exists between the designated variables.

O

Objectivity The degree to which two researchers working independently would reach comparable findings or conclusions.

Observation Inconspicuous surveillance of people as they engage in everyday activities.

Observed score The actual score seen and/or printed by the instrument or tool.

Obstacle Something that resists and/or hampers the forward progress of or reroutes movement in a certain way or path.

Open-ended questions Questions that permit the respondent to answer without any restrictions or barriers.

Operational definition The characterization of a concept or variable in terms of the operations or procedures by which it is to be measured for a specific research endeavor.

Opinions Attitudes and viewpoints that do not rest on adequate foundations to be viewed as completely without biases and represent a person's beliefs, judgments, and/or values concerning a designated subject.

Ordinal scale A rank-order level of measurement.

Outcomes Results that proceed from an accomplishment or achievement; effects; consequences.

Outputs The work or practice of delivering a result.

P

Patient-oriented research Studies carried out with human subjects where a researcher openly interrelates with the participants.

Phenomenology A type of qualitative research in which the researcher endeavors to comprehend how individuals experience a phenomenon.

PICOT An abbreviation for patient population of interest, intervention of interest, comparison of interest, outcome of interest, and time: the five components of an evidence-based question.

Population The complete group of individuals (or objects) possessing various characteristics to which a researcher wants to generalize the sample results. *Also called* universe population; target population.

Population-based research Studies incorporating epidemiology, social and behavioral sciences, public health, quality evaluation, and cost-effectiveness.

Predictive analytics A type of enhanced analytics where both novel and historical facts to predict and/or project actions, behaviors, and tendencies.

Predictive validity A characteristic based on the time between the collection of the alternative method tests to be validated and the criterion measured. It does not limit the researcher to using the Pearson Product Moment (PPM) to develop a validity coefficient because a linear or logistic regression can also be used.

Primary data Information and/or data collected and/or observed directly from the project.

Primary sources Firsthand testimony to facts, findings, or events; reporting of the research results structured by the individual who conducted the study.

Probability sampling A sampling strategy using some form of random selection of elements.

Problem statement A declaration of the research problem, occasionally verbalized in the form of a research question.

PubMed unrestricted search engine used to access predominantly the MEDLINE database of references and abstracts related to life sciences and biomedical topics.

Purposeful sampling Selecting sample participants in a meaningful and direct way to ensure the representation within the sample members.

Purposive sampling A nonprobability sampling process in which the researcher chooses study participants based on personal decisions about which individuals would be most representative of the general population. *Also called* judgmental sampling.

Quantitative analysis The numeric representation and manipulation of observations using statistical techniques for the express purpose of describing and explaining the outcomes of research as they pertain to the hypothesis.

Quantitative design The scrutinizing of a phenomenon that contributes to the collection of meticulous measurement and quantification while using a painstaking and manipulative strategy.

Quantitative research Systematic, empirical investigation of observable activities using statistical measures to reach a conclusion.

Quasi-experimental design An experimental research design in which individuals are not randomly assigned to groups; rather, the researcher manipulates the independent variable and implements specific controls to augment the internal validity of the outcome.

Questionnaire A self-report data collection tool completed by research participants.

Quota sampling A nonrandom selection of participants by which the researcher identifies specific properties and/or characteristics that are used to establish the sample and determine the sample size for the groups to increase their representativeness.

Q

Qualitative analysis Examination and investigation using subjective reasoning established on nonquantifiable data.

Qualitative research The analysis of phenomena, characteristically in a comprehensive and holistic manner, through the compilation of abundant narrative notes based on an adaptable research model.

Qualitative research question A question that poses a query about a selected practice, concern, or phenomenon to be investigated.

Quality assurance An orderly practice of examining a product or service to determine if it meets precise requirements.

Quality improvement A process utilized to investigate a policy, procedure, or protocol to determine if it addresses an aspect identified through an evidence-based practice process and works to validate current practice.

Quality improvement (QI) project A project intended to increase the effectiveness of the activities and processes used within a setting.

R

Randomization A selection system that creates assignments in a manner that augments the probability that the comparison groups will be equivalent on all extraneous variables.

Random sampling Selection of a sample so that every member of a population has an equal possibility of being included in the sample.

Random selection Picking a group of individuals from a population where every member of the population has an equal chance of being included in the sample.

Range The variation between the uppermost and lowest numbers in a data set.

Ranking The arranging of responses into ascending or descending sequence.

Ratio scale A level of measurement that has a true zero position while also having the characteristics of the nominal (labeling), ordinal (rank ordering), and interval (equal distance) scales.

Receiver operand characteristics (ROCs) A graphical chart illustrating the functioning of data points.

Reference librarian An information professional educated and qualified in library and information science, particularly in the area of the collection of specialized or technical information or materials.

Reliability The extent to which a tool measures the attribute it is intended to evaluate; a measure of consistency.

Representative sample A sample that bears a resemblance to the target population.

Research A methodical examination that uses regimented techniques to resolve questions or decipher dilemmas.

Research articles Published manuscripts describing the results of research projects.

Research design The inclusive design for addressing a research question that incorporates the outline, plan, or strategy used to enhance the integrity of the study.

Researcher bias An intentional or unintentional manipulation of a study so that it achieves results consistent with what the researcher intends to uncover.

Research hypothesis A testable statement that predicts the relationship between two or more variables in a population of interest.

Research process Methodical process of conducting exploration and examination of an identified question.

Research question A statement of the particular inquiry the researcher desires to resolve through a research endeavor.

Research utilization The application of selected facets of a scientific analysis through a process unconnected to the fundamental research.

Respect The process of showing honor or appreciation; motivation to demonstrate thoughtfulness or gratitude.

Response rate The proportion of individuals in a sample who participate in a research project.

Retrospective research The analysis of existing data to address the question to be answered.

Rigor Firmness or precision.

Root cause analysis (RCA) An approach for recognizing aspects involved in understanding what affected the development of a harmful outcome in order to detect behaviors and/or actions useful in preventing the recurrence of similar harmful outcomes.

S

Sample A division of a population chosen to participate in a study.

Sample size The number of individuals included in a sample; denoted by n.

Sampling The practice of extracting a designated group from a population.

Sampling bias Misrepresentations that occur when a sample is not representative of the target population from which the group was extracted.

Sampling error The variation between a sample statistic and a population parameter.

Sampling interval The total number within the target population divided by the preferred sample size; denoted by k.

Sampling plan The plan for selection of the study participants proposed prior to the beginning of the study; it specifies the eligibility criteria; the sample selection process; and, in the case of quantitative studies, the number of subjects to be used.

Saturation In qualitative research, the point at which sufficient data have been accumulated for all new data to produce redundant information.

Scientific misconduct Deeds designed to deliberately and consciously influence the veracity and/or truthfulness of scientific research.

Search engine A web-based tool providing access to needed data. It takes a person to the information and helps to retrieve the information in a format that is accessible visually on screen or in downloadable written/readable format.

Secondary analysis Analyzes of data initially accumulated by various persons for a purpose other than the present research.

Secondary data Data initially accumulated by various persons for a purpose other than the present research.

Secondary source Second-hand explanation of proceedings or facts; explanation of a study or studies organized by someone other than the primary researcher.

Sensitivity Frequency that a test will measure a "true" positive result when calculated.

Sentinel events Unanticipated episodes resulting in a death or grave physical or psychological injury or the risk thereof.

Simple hypothesis A statement that specifies the relationship between two variables.

Simple random sampling A population group extracted by a formula in which each member of the population has an equivalent possibility of being chosen.

Snowball sampling A type of sampling in which every research contributor is asked to recommend additional prospective research participants. *Also called* network sampling.

Specificity Determination of the capability of a test to establish a "true" negative result.

Stability The determination of the results from trials and/or tests over a set time period that extends beyond 48 hours.

Standard error of measurement (SEM) A statistic that reflects the fluctuation of the observed score due to the error score.

Statistical Package for the Social Sciences (SPSS) A computer program used for statistical analysis; the initial program was made available in 1968.

Statistical significance A mathematical expression demonstrating that it is improbable that the results achieved in an examination of sample data would have been produced by luck at a particular level of probability.

Stratified random sampling A random selection of study participants from two or more levels of the population.

Subject A person who supplies information in a study. This term is predominantly used in quantitative research studies.

Systematic random sampling The selection of research study participants such that each kth individual (or facet) in a sampling frame is selected.

Systematic review A literature review directed by a research question that strives to recognize, evaluate, and integrate relevant research evidence.

T

Target population The total population to whom the research outcomes are to be generalized.

Teleology The use of final intention or design as a method of explaining phenomena within an ethical situation.

Tests Devices used to determine the selected intelligence, talents, behaviors, health status, or cognitive endeavor that is under investigation.

Theoretical sampling The qualitative research process of selecting new study participants based on emerging findings from previous data collection and analysis; followed until the point of data saturation.

Theory A rationalization that challenges how a phenomenon functions and why it functions as it does; a generalization or series of generalizations employed methodically to clarify certain phenomena.

Time-dimensional analysis A research tactic employing the investigation into the implications of patterns of change, growth, or trends across time.

Translational research Using both basic and applied research findings to ensure that best practices are incorporated within a population.

Trustworthiness An expression used in the appraisal of qualitative data; it is measured based on the decisive factors of credibility, transferability, dependability, and confirmability.

t-test Statistical method used to determine the differences between the means of two groups.

V

Validity The extent to which a research tool measures what it is proposed to measure.

Variable A characteristic of a person or entity that fluctuates.

Variability The amount of inconsistency identified within a data set.

Veracity Accuracy; truthfulness.

Vulnerable subjects Distinct groups of individuals whose rights require particular protection because of their inability to grant informed consent or because their state of affairs consigns them to higher-than-average risk of adverse effects from a proposed treatment or intervention.

Index

Note: Page numbers followed by *b*, *f*, and *t* indicate material in boxes, figures, and tables respectively.

A

a priori probability value, 315
AACN Evidence Rating System. *See* American Association of Critical-Care Nurses Evidence Rating System
absolute zero point, 304–305
abstract, critique of, 333
ACA. *See* Affordable Care Act
academia, 70
Academic Search Premier database, 153*b*
access, use of research, 23–24
accessible data *vs.* new data, 245–246
accessible population, 224, 224*f*
accidental sampling, 230
accountability of researcher, 330
Accountable Care Organizations (ACOs), 66
accuracy, 284–288
    chi-square statistic measuring, 285
    as function of reliability, 272
    relationship to validity, 288
    ROC testing, 286–288
    standard error/measurement, 294
    as test for trustworthiness, 272
ACOs. *See* Accountable Care Organizations
across-stage mixed method, 205
Act of Congress, 70
action plans, 356–358, 357*f*
action research, 202, 209, 350
activities approach models, 354, 359
acute care facility, 206
acute settings, quality improvement, 85–86
adverse events, 181
aesthetic knowledge, 46
Affordable Care Act (ACA), 3, 33, 66, 366
    quality improvement, 85–86
African American males, 96
Agency for Healthcare Research and Quality (AHRQ), 66
    evidence grading methods, 47–52, 49*f*, 50*f*
    expert opinion for evidence-based appraisal, 341

    need for research, 8
    nursing research priorities, 127
    RCA, 181
    tool for evaluating evidence, 49*f*, 50*f*, 51
AGREE collaboration. *See* Appraisal of Guidelines Research and Evaluation collaboration
AHRF. *See* Area Health Resource File
AHRQ. *See* Agency for Healthcare Research and Quality
AIDSinfo database, 153*b*
alternative explanations, 45
alternative measure test, 289–294
American Association of Critical-Care Nurses (AACN), 127
American Association of Critical-Care Nurses (AACN) Evidence Rating System, 50
American Nurses Association (ANA), 92
    Code of Ethics for Nurses, 93, 97–98
    nursing-sensitive indicators, 84
    position statement on research, 64
American Nurses Foundation, 127
American Nursing Foundation, 62
ANA. *See* American Nurses Association
analysis of variance (ANOVA), 313*t*, 319
    appropriate use, 311
    inferential statistics, 315
    intraclass reliability, 282, 282*f*, 283*t*, 294
    one-tailed test, 312, 314
    one-way ANOVA, 310*t*, 311–312
    two-tailed test, 312, 314
    two-way ANOVA, 310*t*, 311–312
analytical preciseness, 339
animals, ethics of research, 111
annotated bibliography, 142
annual reports, 259
anonymity
    of questionnaire method, 252*t*
    of subjects in EBP projects, 109
    of subjects in qualitative research, 106
ANOVA. *See* analysis of variance
AORN. *See* Association of periOperative Registered Nurses

Apgar scores, 284
application of research to practice, 348
applied research, 349, 358
    basic research *vs.*, 69–70
appraisal. *See* research critique
Appraisal of Guidelines Research and
    Evaluation (AGREE) collaboration, 51
appropriateness
    of data, 51, 235, 253
    of patient care, 21
    of research design, 206, 333
    of results of research, 204
    of sample size, method, strategy, 337
arbitrary zero, 304
Area Health Resource File (AHRF), 341
arterial blood oxygen saturation, 290
articles
    austere style in journals, 331–332, 342
    differentiation of research from
        nonresearch, 146–147, 146*b*
    evaluation, 158–162
"A's program (Ask, Advise, Assess, Assist,
    Arrange), 235
assistance, for researcher, 126
assisted suicide, 101
associate degree nurses, 65*b*
Association of periOperative Registered
    Nurses (AORN), 48, 127
associative hypothesis, 134
assumptions of logic model, 355
attendance records, 259
attitudes, 23
attrition
    of nursing staff, 145
    of research participants, 179–180
audit trail, 199
auditability, 199
authors
    credentials, 145
    evaluation, 332
    order of recognition, 110
    viewpoint, 145
autonomy, 93, 104
availability
    of facilities and equipment and feasibility of
        problem, 125–126
    of subjects and feasibility of research
        problem, 125
average (mean), 305–306, 306*f*
axial coding, 195

B

baccalaureate degree nurses, 65*b*
background questions, 13

BARRIERS to Research Utilization Scale, 72
basic research, 349
    vs. applied research, 69–70
    appropriateness, 349
    as aspect of translational research, 349–350,
        350*f*, 358
    definition, 69
basic science, 70
bedsores, 302
beliefs, 23
Belmont Report, The (NIH), 94, 98, 103
bench research, 69
bench science, 70
benchmark publications, 327
benchmarking, 44
beneficence, 93–94
benefits, 371
Bernard, Claude, 95
best available research evidence, 69
best practices
    action research, 350
    adoption of outcomes as, 349, 359
    analysis, 368
    definition, 68–69
    determination of applicability of research,
        367–368, 371
    as goal of nursing, 367
    implementation, 359
    research as basis of, 40, 337
    validation, 39, 68–69, 371
bias
    addressing in report of research, 329
    confirmability as freedom from, 199
    determination of level of evidence, 371
    in EBP projects, 109
    of expert opinion, 45
    freedom from in biophysiological
        data, 260*t*
    in literature, 157
    meta-analysis revealing, 177
    in nonexperimental design, 177
    of observation, 46
    in patient records, 245
    in qualitative research, 106
    in quantitative research, 106
    in research critique, 324
    in sampling process, 173, 225
bibliographic database, 150
Big Data sets, 259
Bill of Rights for Community-Based
        Research Partners (Cartwright &
        Hickman), 111
biophysiological data, 244, 260
blood pressure measurement
    calculation of central tendency,
        305–306, 306*f*

as indicator of stress, 201
reliability testing, 278
validity testing, 289
variability, 306–308
bracketing, 198
Braden Scale, 109, 302
brainstorming research ideas, 148–149
budgets, 259
bundling, 65

C

cafeteria questions, 250
calendar questions, 250
Carnegie Foundation reports, 4, 9
case-controlled, 51
case reports, 45
case scenarios
handwashing in elementary schools, 380, 381t–383t
incorporation of EBP into bedside nursing, 72
use of perclose for angioplasty, 376, 377t–479t
case series, 45
case study
as evidence for clinical decisions, 45, 371
qualitative analysis, 315–316
qualitative research, 193
categorical variable, 131
causal hypothesis, 134
causality, 178
cause-effect relationship
assumed in prospective correlational designs, 174–175
focus of comparative design, 174–175
focus of experimental design, 175–176
focus of quantitative design, 172
need for control to determine, 180
CDC. See Centers for Disease Control and Prevention
Centers for Disease Control and Prevention (CDC), 96, 175
Centers for Medicare and Medicaid Services (CMS), 66
central limit theorem, 232
central tendency, 305–306
Certificate of Confidentiality, 101
CF. See cystic fibrosis
change theory, 353
checklists, 250, 252t
chi-square statistic, 285, 309–310
chi-square test, 309–310

children
study on parent presence during procedures, 131
as subjects of research, 104
cholesterol
relationship to heart disease, 290
treatment, 309
CINAHL database. See Cumulative Index to Nursing and Allied Health Literature database
CIOMS. See Council for International Organizations of Medical Sciences
class qualities of evidence, 44
classification of evidence pyramid, 52
client involvement, 11f, 12
client records, 259
Clinical and Translational Science Award (CTSA), 348
clinical decision making, 36, 174, 337–339
mixed methods evidence, 339
qualitative research evidence, 338–339
quantitative research evidence, 337–338
clinical decisions, 2
clinical expertise, 47
clinical focus, 11t, 12
clinical outcomes, 61–62
clinical pathways, 65
clinical problem, 371, 373
clinical program data, 246
identification, 246
clinical questions
determination of type/evaluation of evidence sought, 47
development of, 368, 370
formation, 13–14, 14b–16b, 17–18
PICOT characteristics, 371–372
problem-solving approach to answering, 337
steps in answering, 368
closed-ended questions
collection of quantitative data/confirmatory research, 251
disadvantages, 253
in interviews, 253
in mixed method research, 202, 205
cluster sampling, 229
CMS. See Centers for Medicare and Medicaid Services
Cochrane Collaboration, 49
Cochrane Library, 152
code of ethics, 93, 97–98
Code of Ethics for Nurses (ANA), 93, 97–98
Code of Federal Regulation, Protection of Human Subjects Rule, 98
coding, 194–195, 208
coercion, 103

collaboration, 21, 148
collective case study, 193
communication, 20
communication strategies, 20
community-based care facility, 111
community settings, quality improvement, 86
Community Tool Box, 356
comparative analysis, qualitative research methods, 196
comparative design, 174, 183
comparison group design, 178
comparison of interest, 17
compelled disclosure, 101
complete observer role, 257
complete participation observer role, 257
complex hypothesis, 134
conceptual definition of variables, 134
conceptual framework, 315–317, 338
concurrent validity, 290, 294
concurrent validity coefficient, 290
confidence intervals, 284–285
confidentiality, 99
    in EBP projects, 108, 109
    in focus group methodology, 255
    HIPAA's effect on, 107
    protection, 98–101
    of subjects in EBP projects, 109
    of subjects in qualitative research, 106
confidentiality covenants, 101
confirmability, 199
conflict of interest, 110
confounding variables
    extraneous variables as, 130
    identification, 177
    for interviews, 253
    meta-analysis revealing, 177
consensus, 46, 51, 69
consent, 94, 97
consistency
    confirmation of best practice, 372
    definition, 276, 277t
    within discussion of evidence, 44
    internal consistency, 279–281, 280t
    reliability based on, 272, 279
    support for quality of evidence, 44
    as type of interclass reliability, 279
construct-related validity, 289–290, 294
construct validity, 292–293
content analysis, 193, 197–198
content-related validity, 289–290, 294
continuous data, 285
    validity coefficient, 290
continuous dependent variables, 311
continuous performance improvement (CPI), 20
continuous scaled dependent variable, 311

continuous scales, 303
continuous variable, 131
control
    as characteristic of quantitative research, 172
    lacking in comparative design, 174, 183
    means of establishing in nonexperimental and quasiexperimental designs, 180
    of threats, 180
    of variables, 183
control group
    in experimental designs, 176
    lacking in quasi-experimental design, 172, 178
    in quantitative research design, 172–173
controlled vocabularies, 154
convenience sampling, 160, 230, 328
convergent validity, 208
cooperation, 126, 175
correctness of data, 278
correlation coefficient, 276, 294
correlational design, 174, 181
correlational test, 161
correlational validity, 289
cost
    of biophysiological data collection, 260t
    consideration in data collection plan, 263
    generation of evidence to reduce, 20
    of longitudinal studies, 178
    of research facilities and equipment, 125–126
    of research projects, 125
cost-effectiveness of prevention and treatment, 349–350
Council for International Organizations of Medical Sciences (CIOMS), 94
    vulnerability, 94
cowpox vaccination, 95
CPI. *See* continuous performance improvement
credibility, 199, 210
credit for research, 110
criterion-related validity
    concurrent and predictive validity, 290, 294
    definition, 289, 294
    development of validity coefficient, 289
    ROC determining, 289, 294
    use in EBP, 292
criterion sampling, 196
critical decision-making, 348, 359
critical thinking, 5, 209, 337
critique, 324, 330, 342
critique of literature, 326–327
critique worksheet, 334t
critiquing sampling in research, 234, 234t
cross-section design, 174, 177–178

cross-validation techniques, 291
Crossing the Quality Chasm: A New Health System for the 21st Century (IOM), 82
CTSA. *See* Clinical and Translational Science Award
Cumulative Index to Nursing and Allied Health Literature (CINAHL) database, 45, 150–152, 153*b*, 154
curriculum vitae (CV), 99
cystic fibrosis (CF), 194

D

data
    accessible *vs.* new, 245–246
    biophysiological, 260
    case studies, 193
    central tendency, 305–306, 306*f*
    continuous data, 285
    demographic variable, 130
    of ethnographic studies, 194
    examination in secondary analysis, 177
    inclusion in literature reviews, 145
    interval and ratio data, 305–308
    key categories for nursing studies, 246–247
    in mixed method research, 203–204
    observed, true, and error score, 274, 274*f*, 275
    premature destruction, 105
    primary, 246
    secondary, 245–246, 258–259
    types of numeric data, 303, 305*f*
    variability, 306–308
data analysis, 301–319
    case studies, 193
    credibility (truth value), 199
    difficulty as obstacle to research use, 366
    for EBP projects, 109
    ethics, 105–106
    grounded theory, 194–195
    interviews, 253
    in mixed method research, 205–206
    observational data, 257
    phenomenology, 195–196
    procedures, 208
    qualitative analysis, 302, 315–316
    qualitative research, 198
    quality assurance, 317–318
    quantitative analysis
        descriptive statistics, 305
        inferential statistics, 309–315
        interval and ratio data, 305–308
        measurement scales, 303–304

reporting results of, 315
    quantitative research, 210
data collection, 243–265
    accessible *vs.* new data, 245–246
    achievement of the strategy, 263
    approaches in quantitative research, 198
    critique process, 329, 338–339
    EBP considerations, 263–264
    EBP projects, 107–110
    ethics, 105–106, 108–109
    ethnographic studies, 194
    evaluation of qualitative methods, 338–339
    implementation, 244
    key categories of data for nursing studies, 246–247
    overview of methods and sources, 243–245
    phenomenology, 195–196
    procedures for in mixed method research, 206–208
    quantitative research, 207, 256, 265
    research, 243–245
    self-reporting strategies, 248
    significant facets of scheme, 247
    steps in process, 245
    tools/instruments for, 244–245, 263
    use *of* scripts *for* control of variables, 180
data collection methods
    biophysiological data, 244, 260
    focus groups, 244, 254–255
    interview, 244, 253–254
    observation, 244, 256–258
    questionnaire, 244, 249–252
    secondary (existing) data, 244, 258–259
    selection, 244, 263
    systematic analysis, 244, 261–262
    tests, 244, 248–249
    types, 244
data collection process, 206–208
data integration, 206
data interpretation, 206
data mining, 246
data saturation, 196–197, 233
data security, 106
data set, 177
data sources, 246
data verification, 196
database
    definition of, 150
    search engine *vs.*, 150
    types, 150
decision-making process
    as aspect of EBP, 12, 272
    aspects, 348
    assignment of evidence, 40*f*, 41

decision-making process *(Continued)*
  attention to entire process in materials provided, 360
  critical and systematic decision making, 348, 359
  critically assessing knowledge, 337–339
  descriptive design, 174
  EBP and use of scientific data, 366
  elements of EBP, 6, 7*f*, 11*f*, 12
  foundation, 7
deductive reasoning process, 315
define-measure-analyze-improve-control (DMAIC) model, 372
demographic characteristics of samples, 235
demographic indicators, 246
demographic variables, 130
dependability, 199, 272
dependent *t*-test, 310–311
dependent variable, 309*t*
  choice appropriate scale of measurement, 309–310, 310*t*
  in comparative design, 174
  definition, 130, 172, 309
  independent variables *vs.*, 309, 309*t*
  for study of children during procedures, 134
  for weight maintenance study, 128
descriptive design, 174–175
descriptive ethics, 93
descriptive statistics, 305
design factors, 231–232
diabetes, 224
diabetes-related quality of life (DQOL) tool, 128, 281
diagnostic tests
  ROC testing for accuracy, 286–288
  validity tests, 288–293
diaries, 259
dichotomous diagnostic test, 286, 287*t*
dichotomous variable
  about, 131
  ROC tests, 286
  validity coefficient, 290
Dictionary.com, 150, 196, 330
directional hypothesis, 133
discrete variable, 131
discursive prose, 143
distributive justice, 94
DMAIC. *See* define-measure-analyze-improve-control
documentation
  case reports, 45
  conclusions in literature for review, 145
  current knowledge, 142
  of data collection strategy, 263, 265
  definition, 25

EBP searches, 367
  ethical aspects, 112
  format, 369*t*
  functional method for, 367
  problem statement, 127
  qualitative research, 199
  sample/population, 160
  steps in systematic review, 265
  validity and reliability of tools, 295
  validity of findings, 295
Donabedian model, 80
DQOL tool. *See* diabetes-related quality of life tool

E

Early Warning Score, 200
EBP. *See* evidence-based practice
EBSCOhost databases, 152
editorials, 45
education, barrier to research utilization, 22–23
Educational Testing Service (ETS), 248
effective decision-making, 356
electrodiagnostic neural conduction study, 287
electronic library, 148
electronic medical records (EMR), 20
eligibility criteria, 226
empiric knowledge, 46
EMR. *See* electronic medical records
environment, 286. *See also* setting of data collection
epidemiology surveys, 246
equipment
  availability for research, 125–126
  needed for biophysiological data collection, 260
equity, 94, 97
equivalency, as type of interclass reliability, 278, 279*t*
equivalency reliability, 278
error score, 274–275, 274*f*
error score variance, 290
ethical codes, 92
ethical knowledge, 46
ethical theories, 92–94
  values theories, 93–94
ethics, 91–113
  CIOMS guidelines, 103
  Code of Ethics for Nurses, 93
  considerations for experimental design, 175
  data collection and analysis, 105–106
  definition, 92

EBP and ethical implications, 107–110
  emerging issues, 110–111
  of experimental research, 175, 331
  external pressures, 106–107
  historical overview, 95–97
  ICN Code of Ethics for Nurses, 97
  institutional review board, 98
  issues in quantitative and qualitative
    research, 106
  normative and descriptive, 93
  principles relative to nursing, 93
  publication of research/EBP, 110
  recruitment and informed consent,
    103–104
  research ethics, 97–98
  researchable question development,
    102–103
  researchable topic development, 100–102
  theories, 92–94
ethnography
  data analysis, 194
  data collection, 194
ETS. *See* Educational Testing Service
evaluation
  effective decision-making, 356
  evidence for implementation, 235, 371
  gaps in literature, 159*t*, 162
  limitations, 161
  logic modeling process, 352–356, 352*t*,
    353*f*, 359–360
  major findings, 161
  methods of study, 160–161
  mixed method research, 339, 342
  outcome approach model for designing,
    353, 359
  qualitative research, 338–339, 342
  quantitative research, 337–338, 342
  sample/population, 160, 224
  validity of finding, 225
evidence, 31–54
  alternative styles of, 45
  case studies, 45
  classification method, 371
  consensus, 46
  difficulty of analysis, 366
  discovery of significant, 19–20
  evaluation, 235, 371
  expert opinion, 45
  factors for consideration, 45
  forms, 12
  foundations for EBP, 35–41, 37*f*, 38*f*, 40*f*
  grading methods, 47–52, 49*f*, 50*f*
  ideas, 45
  importance of generating, 19–21
  observation, 46
  opinions, 45

qualities of, 41–47
reconciliation of contradictions, 340
searching and writing, 141–165
sound, 44
evidence-based appraisal, 340–341
"Evidence-Based Care Sheets," 45
evidence-based clinical decision making, 36
evidence-based decision making model, 12
evidence-based guidelines for critique, 340
evidence-based practice (EBP), 31, 224, 373
  application with research, 365–366
  as aspect of critical decision making,
    348, 359
  aspects, 368
  clinical applications, 3
  clinical questions posed, 13–18
  components, 7, 7*f*
  consideration for quantitative research
    design, 135, 181, 234–236
  considerations for mixed method
    research, 209
  critical skill required, 9
  data collection consideration, 263
  decision-making process, 6–7, 7*f*, 11*t*,
    12, 272
  definitions, 2, 10–13, 11*t*, 13*f*, 365, 370
  development, 2, 20
  elements, 6, 11
  emergence, 65
  and ethical implications, 107–110
  evolution, 61–67, 63*f*, 64*b*, 65*b*
  examples of, 366
  format for documenting aspects of, 369*t*
  foundations for, 35–41, 37*f*, 38*f*, 40*f*
  goal, 135, 234
  holistic patient care, 6, 12
  impact of research, 20–21
  impact on practice, 20–21
  implementation of evidence, 34, 135
  instruments for holistic practice, 340
  level of confidence in, 366
  linking literature view to, 165
  literature on, 92
  nurses' role in process, 3, 22–23
  nursing confirmation, 6, 7*f*
  nursing expertise, 6, 7*f*
  obstacles to use of research, 21–24, 72
  optimization, 67
  outcomes, 32–33
  process, 2–3, 367–373
  purpose, 366
  qualitative analysis methods used, 315–316
  reasoning, 3–7, 7*f*
  vs. research and quality improvement, 82,
    82*t*–83*t*
  research interconnectedness, 2–25, 367

evidence-based practice (EBP) *(Continued)*
   research utilization, 18, 19*b*
   role of research, 324–325
   steps for, 368
   types of validity associated with, 288
   use of nonexperimental design, 177
evidence-based practice determination, 367
evidence-based practice projects
   definition, 367
   development, 107–109
   ethics, 107–110
   issues in, 109–110
   sampling decisions, 236
evidence-based practice questions, 108
evidence-based project, sampling decisions
   for, 236
evidence-based proposals, 142
evidence-based protocol guidelines, 245
evidence grading methods, 47–52, 49*f*, 50*f*
evidential material, 45
ex post facto correlation design, 174
executive summary, 358
exclusion criteria, 180, 226
exhaustive answers on questionnaires, 251
existing data, 245–246
existing data collection method, 258–259
experimental design
   collection of biophysiological data, 260
   focus and types, 175–176
   use of treatment and control groups, 172
experimental group, 173, 176
expert opinion, 45, 51, 341
expertise of researcher, 126
external factors of logic model, 355
external pressures, 106–107
external validity, 173, 226
extraneous variables
   about, 130
   content-related validity testing, 289
   control of, 173–174, 180–181
eye contact, 256

F

fabrication of results, 106
face validity, 288
facilities, availability for research, 125–126
Fahrenheit scale, 304
falsification of results, 106
FAME level of evidence. *See* Feasibility,
      Appropriateness, Meaningfulness,
      Effectiveness level of evidence
family pictures, 259

fatigue, 285
Feasibility, Appropriateness, Meaningfulness,
      Effectiveness (FAME) level of
      evidence, 51
feasibility of research problem, 125–126,
      175, 255
federal regulations, 103
Felty's syndrome, 129
fidelity, 93
financial incentives, 103
findings, evaluation, 161
focus group leader, 255
focus groups
   data collection method, 208, 244,
      254–255
   interviews, 197
   overview of, 254–255
   as source of data, 244
   strength of, 255*t*
   use in mixed methods, 206
forced-choice ratings, 250
foreground questions, 13
forensic science, 44
foundation of practice for EBP, 9, 11*t*
framework, 338
   of nursing care, 68
   for structuring research problems, 37
freedom of choice, 103
frequency of results, 44
frontline nurses, 354, 367
full-text database, 150, 153*b*
funding
   acknowledgement of sources, 110
   effect on ethics, 107
   priorities of NINR, 123–124, 124*b*
   for research, 70, 123

G

gaps in literature, 159*t*, 162, 367, 372–373
generalizability
   external validity, 226
   implementation of results considering, 200
   nurses' knowledge of, 181
   sample criteria affecting, 226
goal statement, 354
gold standard tests, 285, 287
grading methods, 47–52, 49*f*, 50*f*
grant funders, 353, 358
grant proposal, 162
grounded theory, 200–201
   Andrews and Waterman's use of, 200
   data analysis, 194–195

introduction into nursing practice, 195
sample size, 231
group interviews, 197
group norms, 194

H

HAPI database. *See* Health and Psychosocial
Instruments database
Harvey Cushing/John Hay Whitney Medical
Library, 51
Hawthorne effect
data collection process, 247, 265
experimental design, 175
nonequivalent control group design, 179
observation methods, 257
HCAHPS. *See* Hospital Consumer Assessment
of Healthcare Providers and Systems,
Hospital Care Quality Information
from the Consumer Perspective
Health and Psychosocial Instruments (HAPI)
database, 153*b*
Health and Wellness Resource Center
database, 153*b*
health care, 3–4
quality improvement in, 85
Health Insurance Portability and Accountability
Act (HIPAA), 23, 97, 107
*Health Professions Education: A Bridge to
Quality* (IOM), 20
Health Research Extension Act of 1985, 62
Health Resources and Services Administration
(HRSA), 4
quality improvement, 86
Health Sciences: A Sage Full-Text Collection,
153*b*
healthcare agencies, 371
healthcare community, 81, 374
healthcare costs
barriers to reduction, 367
EBP's goal of reduction, 366
effects of clinical pathways, 65
generation of evidence to reduce, 20
research studies, 66
healthcare quality, 318
healthcare settings, 71
heart disease, 290
Helene Fuld Health Trust, 127
hemoglobin analyzer, 276–277, 284*f*
hemoglobin scores, 308, 308*t*
hexamethonium research, 96
HHS. *See* U.S. Department of Health and
Human Services

hierarchy of levels of evidence, 48, 49*f*
HIPAA. *See* Health Insurance Portability and
Accountability Act
history, threat of, 179, 180
holistic approach, 192, 349
holistic patient care
as aspect of EBP, 365
elements of EBP, 6, 11
evaluation, 340
instrument, 340
homogeneity
focus group members, 255
reliability and accuracy impacts, 285
sampled population, 196
of testing conditions, 285
honesty
data analysis, 105
qualitative research, 106
Hospital Care Quality Information
from the Consumer Perspective
(HCAHPS), 80
Hospital Consumer Assessment of
Healthcare Providers and Systems
(HCAHPS), 341
HRSA. *See* Health Resources and Services
Administration
human drug testing, 96
human experimentation, 92, 93
human participant
attrition, 179–180
checking of coded data, 199
ethical issues, 331
Hawthorne effect, 175, 179, 247, 257, 265
informed consent, 103–104
protection of rights, 93
recruitment, 103–104
rights, 97
voluntary consent requirement, 97
vulnerability, 94, 100, 103
hypotheses
appropriateness for qualitative
research, 133
and qualitative studies, 133
testing nature of relationships, 132–134
types, 133–134
hypothesis
components, 354
consideration in data collection plan, 263
critique process, 327–328
definition, 327
determination of timing of mixed
methods, 206
framing, 372
mixed method research as means of
answering, 206

hypothesis *(Continued)*
  as result of qualitative analysis, 315–316
  use *of* descriptive design in
    generation, 174

I

ICN. *See* International Council of Nurses
ICN Code of Ethics for Nurses, 97
ideas, 45
"if-then" statements, 354
impact, 353, 355–356
implementation of research
  activities approach models, 354
  choice of research methods, 202
  logic modeling process, 352–356, 352*t*,
    353*f*, 359–360
  obstacles to, 21–24, 72
  translational research, 348
implementation science, 8
improvement science, 351
in vitro biophysiological methods, 260
in vivo biophysiological methods, 260
inclusion criteria, 180, 226
independent *t*-test, 310–311
independent variables, 309*t*
  child anxiety in procedures example, 130
  choice appropriate scale of measurement,
    309–310, 310*t*
  control of in correlation design, 175
  definition, 134, 172, 309
  dependent variable *vs.*, 309, 309*t*
  lack of control of in comparative
    design, 174
  manipulation of, 172–174, 178, 183
  weight maintenance example, 128
individual characteristics of evidence, 44
inducements to participation, 103
inductive analysis, 195
inductive reasoning process, 315
inferential statistical analysis, 309
  analysis of variance (ANOVA), 311–315
  application, 208
  chi-square, 309–310
  chi-square statistic, 285
  t-test, 161, 310–311
informant groups, 246
information, research-tested and confirmed, 2
informed consent, 94, 97, 99, 103
  HIPAA's effect on, 107
  in quantitative research, 106
  subjects for research, 99, 103–104
  use of proxy, 111
informed decision, 94, 99, 272

infrared monitoring of blood oxygen levels, 289
inherent validity coefficient, 292
input, 355
Institute of Medicine (IOM)
  Committee on the Responsible Conduct of
    Research, 100
  *Crossing the Quality Chasm: A New Health
    System for the 21st Century*, 82
  focus on patient safety, 366
  on future of nursing, 4
  *Health Professions Education: A Bridge to
    Quality*, 20
  Health Professions Education Summit, 32
  *Keeping Patients Safe: Transforming the
    Work Environment of Nurses*, 66
  *Nursing and Nursing Education: Public
    Policy and Private Actions*, 62
  quality assurance, 79, 318
  quality improvement, 79, 318
  Standards for Systematic Reviews, 261
  *To Err is Human: Building a Safer Health
    System*, 66, 82
institutional review board (IRB), 98
  approval of multisite research projects, 104
  approval of research with animals, 111
  policy associated with HIPAA, 107
  publication without approval, 110
instructional design, 70
insurance groups, 85
integration, 205
integrative reviews, 370–371
integrity, 255
interclass reliability, 276
  ANOVA, 282, 282*f*, 283*t*
  consistency, 276, 277*t*
  definition, 276, 294
  equivalency, 278, 279*t*
  internal consistency, 279–281, 280*t*
  intraclass reliability *vs.*, 276
  stability, 277–278
interest of researcher, 126
intermediate outcome, 355
internal consistency, 279–281, 280*t*
internal validity, 225
International Council of Nurses (ICN), 92
  Code of Ethics for Nurses, 97
International Ethics Guidelines for Biomedical
    Research Involving Human Subjects
    (CIOMS), 103
Internet, survey methods, 248
interpretations, 199
interrater reliability
  in data collection process, 247, 265
  for observation methods of data
    collection, 258*t*
  for tests, 258*t*

interval data
central tendency, 305–308, 306*f*
variability, 306–308
interval scales, 304, 319
intervention, depiction of in clinical
questions, 17
intervention research, 349
interviewer, 197, 253–254
interviews, 197
as method of data collection, 244, 253–254
overview of, 253–254
as qualitative method of data collection,
195, 197
strength of, 254*t*
intimate partner violence (IPV), 129
screening, 197
intraclass reliability, 276, 282–288, 283*t*, 284*f*,
286*t*–287*t*
accuracy, 284–288
objectivity, 282–284
receiver operand characteristics (ROC),
286–288
IOM. *See* Institute of Medicine
IPV. *See* intimate partner violence
IRB. *See* institutional review board
issue statements, 354

J

jargon, 342
JBI. *See* Joanna Briggs Institute
Joanna Briggs Institute (JBI), 51
Johns Hopkins School of Medicine, 96
Joint Commission, 341
journal club participation, 72, 335
journals
austere style of articles, 331–332, 342
in CINAHL database, 152
publication of research, 109–110
report of qualitative and quantitative
research, 191
as source of research ideas, 149
Journals@OVIDFullText database, 153*b*
judgmental sampling, 230
justice
as principle of ethics relevant to nursing,
93, 94
in quantitative research, 106

K

*Keeping Patients Safe: Transforming the Work
Environment of Nurses* (IOM), 66

key informants, 194
"knowledge-focused trigger," 13

L

labor-intensive process, 205
Lean philosophy, 372
Leapfrog Group, 80–81
learning research, 22
length of stay (LOS), 177, 367
letters, 259
Level 1 evidence (meta-analysis), 371
level of difficulty, 285
level of evidence, 47–48, 51–52, 371
in EBP, 366
librarians, 147–148, 370
limitations
research, 331
secondary (existing) data collection
method, 259*t*
of study, 161
linear regression, 290
literature
critique of, 326–327
on EBP, 92
identification of gaps and consistencies,
367, 372–373
as source of definition of variables, 134
as source of researchable problems,
122–123
literature review, 141–165
aspects included, 143
brainstorming research ideas, 148–149
critique process, 326–327, 338
definition, 142
evaluation of, 158–162
formula for commencement, 145
formulation of research questions, 149–150
identification of gaps and consistencies,
367, 372–373
identification of researchable problems,
122–124
linking to EBP, 165
purpose, 142–144
search engine and databases searches,
149–150
using PICOT statement, 37, 371
writing, 162–165
local data, 341
logic model, 352
logic modeling process, 352–356, 352*t*, 353*f*,
359–360
logical framework, 352, 352*t*, 353*f*, 354–355
logical validity, 288, 293

logistic regression, 290
long-term outcome, 355
longitudinal studies, 178, 231
LOS. *See* length of stay

M

magnitude, 305
maleficence, 96
manipulation of variables
    as component of research design, 178
    descriptive design, 174
    ethical issues, 331
    of independent variable, 172
    lacking in comparative design, 183
    predictive correlational design, 175
    quasi-experimental design, 183
master's degree nurses, 65*b*
maturation, 179–180
mean (average), 305–306, 306*f*
measurement error, 305–306
measurement factors, 232
measurement scales
    appropriate choice for project, 309–310, 310*t*
    interval scale, 304
    nominal scale, 303–304, 305*f*
    ordinal scale, 303
    of quantitative analysis, 303–304
    ratio scale, 304
measures of central tendency
    mean, 305–306, 306*f*
    median, 306
    mode, 306
    most appropriate measure, 319
median, 306
Medicaid, 66, 80, 85, 246
Medical Literature Analysis and Retrieval
        System Online (MEDLINE) database,
        150–152, 153*b*
Medical Subject Heading (MeSH), 151, 153*b*
Medicare, 66, 80, 85
medication errors, 108
MEDLINE database. *See* Medical Literature
        Analysis and Retrieval System Online
        database
Melnyk, B. M., 324, 340
Merriam-Webster's Learner's Dictionary, 324
MeSH. *See* Medical Subject Heading
meta-analysis
    appropriate use, 245, 262, 370
    definition, 261, 370
    establishment of bias and confounding
        variables, 177
    as Level 1 evidence, 371

metadata, 258
meta-ethnography, 194
meta-synthesis of research, 51, 177, 245, 262
methodological rigor, 199–200
methodology, selection of, 48
methods of grading evidence, 47–52, 49*f*, 50*f*
minutes, 259
mixed method research, 201–205
    approach, 190
    components, 203–205
    data analysis and validation
        procedures, 208
    data collection procedures, 206–208
    EBP considerations, 209
    evaluation, 339, 342
    lack of classification, 49
    lack of rationale, 204–205
    limitations, 204
mixed method strategies, types of, 205–206
mode, 306
models
    defined, 68
    logic modeling process, 352–356, 352*t*,
        353*f*, 359–360
    of nursing care, 68
    theory approach model, 353, 359
modified Phalen's test, 287, 288*t*, 292
moral, 92
moral philosophy, 93
morality, 92, 93
multifaceted care, 9
multifaceted interventions, 72
multiple-choice questions, 250
multisite research, 104
multistage sampling, 229
multivariate hypotheses, 134
mutually exclusive answers on
        questionnaires, 251

N

narrative inquiry, 195
National Center for Nursing Research
        (NCNR), 62
National Commission for the Protection of
        Human Subjects of Biomedical and
        Behavioral Research, 97
National Database of Nursing Quality
        Indicators (NDNQI), 84
National Institute of Nursing Research
        (NINR), 62, 123–124, 126, 325
National Institutes of Health (NIH)
    Belmont Report, The, 94, 98, 103
    nursing research, 62

Nursing Research Study Section, 62
Revitalization Act of 1993, 62
translational research, 348
National League for Nursing (NLN), 70
National Library of Medicine (NLM),
151–152, 153*b*
MeSH database, 142
National Quality Forum (NQF), 80
National Quality Strategy, 84
Nazi experiments, 96
NCNR. *See* National Center for Nursing
Research
NDNQI. *See* National Database of Nursing
Quality Indicators
need assessment, 7–19
nesting, 206
network sampling, 230
neutrality, 199
new data, accessible data *vs.*, 245–246
newspapers, 259
Nightingale, Florence
evolution from, 61–67
Notes on Matters Affecting the Health,
Efficiency and Hospital Administration
of the British Army, 62
polar-area diagram, 62, 63*f*
work on sanitation, 61
NIH. *See* National Institutes of Health
NIH Revitalization Act of 1993, 62
NINR. *See* National Institute of Nursing
Research
NLM. *See* National Library of Medicine
NLN. *See* National League for Nursing
nominal data, 285
descriptive statistics, 305, 305*f*
ROC and accuracy, 286–288
tests for predictive validity, 290
nominal scales, 303–304, 319
descriptive presentation of, 305*f*
nominally scaled dependent variable,
310, 310*t*
nominally scaled independent variable,
310, 310*t,*
nonclinical program data, 246
nondirectional hypothesis, 133
nonequivalent control group, 178, 179*f*
nonequivalent control group design, 178
nonexperimental design, 172, 176–177
nonmaleficence, 93, 94
nonprobability sampling, 227
strategies, 230–231
nonrandom sampling, 236
nonrepresentative sample, 227
nonresearch article, 146–147
nonverbal data, 253
normal distribution, 285, 307, 307*f*

normative ethics, 93
Northern Arizona University, 261
Notes on Matters Affecting the Health,
Efficiency and Hospital Administration
of the British Army (Nightingale), 62
NQF. *See* National Quality Forum
null hypothesis, 133
numerical data
interval scale, 304
nominal data, 285–288
nominal scale, 303–304
ordinal scale, 303
ratio scale, 304
Nuremberg Code of 1946, 97
nurse researcher
ethics, 98
qualification, 93
nurses, 366
EBP process, role in, 3, 21–24
frontline, 367
implementation of evidence, 34
implementation of innovations, 349
participation in research critique process,
332, 337, 367–368
research process, role in, 111, 209
nursing
evidence-based profession, 36
focus, 192
history of, 61–67, 63*f,* 64*b,* 65*b*
moral obligation, 106
overarching principle for practice, 1–3
research as tool for advancement, 366
Nursing and Nursing Education: Public Policy
and Private Actions (IOM), 62
nursing care, 32
nursing confirmation
as aspect of EBP, 12
elements of EBP, 6, 7*f*
nursing education research, 70
nursing expertise, 6, 7*f*
nursing homes, 111
nursing practice, 20–21
nursing research
applied research methods, 69–70
ethics, 92–112
history of, 61–67, 63*f,* 64*b,* 65*b*
key categories of data, 246–247
priorities, 124*b,* 126–127
qualitative methods used in, 192
researchable question development,
102–103
researchable topic development, 100–102
sources, 70–71
useful databases, 150–152, 153*b*
Nursing Research journal, 62
Nursing Research Study Section, 62

nursing-sensitive indicators, 84
Nursing Studies Index (Henderson), 62
nursing theory, 200

O

Obama, Barack, 3
obesity study, 127–128
objectivity
    definition, 282–284
    reliability based on, 272
observation
    conditions needed for use, 256
    definition, 46
    as key element in qualitative analysis, 316
    as method of data collection, 51, 197, 208,
        244, 256–258
    role of observers, 257
observed score, 274, 274*f*
observed score variance, 274–275
observer-as-participant role, 257
obstacles/barriers to using research, 21–24
    beliefs/attitudes, 23
    education, 22–23
    support/resources, 23–24
official documents, 259
Oncology Nursing Society (ONS)
    EBP process steps, 340
    evidence grading methods, 48
    Putting Evidence into Practice (PEP)
        schema, 48
one-group pretest/posttest design, 178
one-tailed test, 312, 314
one-way ANOVA, 310*t*, 310–311
100,000 Lives Campaign, 66
ONS. *See* Oncology Nursing Society
open coding, 194
open-ended questions
    assessment of qualitative issues, 251
    disadvantages, 253
    in interviews, 253
    in mixed method research, 206
operational definitions, 332, 335
    of variables, 134
opinions, 45
ordinal data, descriptive statistics, 305
ordinal grading system, 286
ordinal scales, 303, 319
organizations, 21
outcome approach model, 353, 359
outcomes, 353
    action plans, 356–358, 357*f*
    of EBP, 32–33
    of interest, 17

logic modeling process, 352–356, 352*t*,
    353*f*, 359–360
measures, 318
patient, 125, 366
research, 8
short- and long-term, 355
translational research, 349–350
outcomes-based practices, 65–66
outliers, 307
outline for literature review, 163–164, 164*b*
output, 353, 355, 359

P

pain questionnaire, 279
pain scales
    construct-related validity, 292
    content-related validity, 288–289
    intraclass reliability, 282
    types, 304
parental consent, 104
participant-as-observer role, 257
participatory research, 202
patient-centered care, 66
Patient-Centered Outcomes Research Institute
    (PCORI), 66
patient-oriented research, 348–351, 350*f*
patient outcomes, 125, 366
patient preferences, 32, 318
Patient Protection and Affordable Care Act
    (PPACA), 3, 366
patient safety, 66, 181, 366
patient satisfaction, 20
PCORI. *See* Patient-Centered Outcomes
    Research Institute
PDCA cycle. *See* plan–do–check–act cycle
PDSA. *See* Plan-Do-Study-Act
Pearson Product Moment (PPM)
    development of reliability coefficient,
        282, 293
    development of validity coefficient,
        289–290, 293
peer referees, 109
peer review, 262
peer-reviewed manuscripts, 109
Pell Institute, 354
PEP schema. *See* Putting Evidence into
    Practice schema
persistence of result, 44
personal knowledge, 47
persuasiveness, 145
phenomenological reduction, 198
phenomenology, 195–196, 198
phenomenon of interest, 192, 195, 197, 225

phi coefficient, 285
PICOT (population, intervention,
    comparison, outcome, time)
    advantages for quantitative research, 129
    aspects of research issue, 371
    components, 354
    consideration in data collection plan, 263
    data collection procedure answering, 244
    determination in literature research, 144
    development of EBP questions, 108
    development of hypotheses, 327–328
    development of researchable questions,
        327, 371
    foreground questions, 14, 14b–16b
    literature review characterized by,
        142–143, 367
    problem statement component, 129–131
    question development, 371
    questions, 17–18
    research critique, 371
    statement, 37, 367
    translational research, 354
    used for literature searches, 149, 372
plagiarism, 106
plan-do-study-act (PDSA), 351
plan–do–check–act (PDCA) cycle, 20, 372
planning activity, 326, 352, 352t
policies, 36, 367
Polit, D. F., 324, 327
population
    definition of, 224
    evaluation of, 160
    factors, 231
    in quantitative research, 129
    target vs. accessible, 224
population-based research, 349–350, 350f
positivist approach, 191
posttest only with nonequivalent groups
    design, 178
power analysis, 233
PPACA. See Patient Protection and Affordable
    Care Act
PPM. See Pearson Product Moment
practical application
    action plans, 356–358, 357f
    logic modeling process, 352–356, 352t,
        353f, 359–360
    translational research, 348–351, 359
practical factors, 232–233
practicality, 259
practice
    relationship to research and theory,
        67–70
    reliability and accuracy impacts, 285
practice problems, 174
pretest/posttest experimental design, 175

precision, 272, 286
predictive analytics, 259
predictive analysis, 291
predictive correlational design, 175
predictive validity, 291, 294
Preferred Reporting Items for Systematic
    Reviews and Meta-Analyses
    (PRISMA), 261
pressure ulcers, 109, 302
primary data, 246
primary material, 157
priorities, 205
prioritization, 211
PRISMA. See Preferred Reporting Items
    for Systematic Reviews and
    Meta-Analyses
privacy
    HIPAA's effect on, 107
    of human subject, 105, 107
probability sampling, 227
probability value, 315
problem/challenge analysis, 354
problem-focused trigger, 14
problem identification, 37
problem-solving process, 366
problem statement, 127
    components, 129–131
    format, 132t
    translational research, 354
    writing process, 131, 132t
procedure, 37, 367
process measures, 318
process of EBP, 367–373
professional body consensus
    statements, 318
program evaluation, 317
program theory (matrix), 352
programs, 70
proportional sampling, 229
ProQuest Nursing Journal database, 153b
prospective correlational designs, 175, 183
Protection of Human Subjects Rule, Code of
    Federal Regulation, 97
protocols
    data analysis establishing, 245
    quality improvement process investigating,
        38–39, 367
    proxy, 111
PsycINFO database, 151b, 152
public comments, 246
Public Health Service, U.S., 97
publications
    benchmark, 327
    of research, 109–110
PubMed, 144, 150–155
purpose of study, 158–160, 325–326

purposeful sampling, 197
purposive sampling, 230
Putting Evidence into Practice (PEP)
    schema, 48

Q

QA. *See* quality assurance
QA/QI initiatives. *See* Quality Assurance/
    Quality Improvement initiatives
QCA. *See* qualitative comparative analysis
QI. *See* quality improvement
qualitative analysis, 302, 319
    approaches, 198
    case study, 316–317
    deductive reasoning process, 315
    definition, 302
    inductive reasoning process, 315
    program evaluation, 317
    quantitative analysis *vs.*, 302
qualitative comparative analysis (QCA), 196
qualitative data analysis, approaches to, 198
qualitative data collection, approaches to,
    197–198
qualitative evidence critique, 235
qualitative questions, 18
qualitative research, 35, 189–212
    about, 190, 338
    approach, 192–196
    avoidance of moral/ethical questions, 122
    characteristics, 191
    consumers of, 196
    critique process, 342
    data analysis, 198, 208
    data collection, 207, 256
    ethical issues, 106
    evaluation, 338–339
    focus, 126, 133
    level of evidence, 48, 49*f*
    methodological rigor, 199–200
    mixed method research, 201–205
    number of subjects needed, 125
    research question, 128
    sampling decisions, 236
    sampling strategies, 196–197
    understanding and using results, 200–201
qualitative research methods, 190
    basic assumption, 191
    characteristics, 191
    data collection, 197–198
    documentation, 200
    ethnographic studies, 194
    grounded theory, 194–195
    history, 191

narrative inquiry, 195
quantitative research design *vs.*, 191–192
qualitative research report, description of
    sampling strategy/sample, 235
qualitative studies, 233
    hypotheses and, 133
quality
    overview of, 79–87
    quality improvement. *See* quality
        improvement
quality assurance (QA), 79, 84
    analysis, 317–318
Quality Assurance/Quality Improvement
    (QA/QI) initiatives, 66–67, 341
quality health practices, 8
quality improvement (QI), 3, 35, 79, 107, 302,
    348, 358–359
    action, 39
    application of
        acute settings, 85–86
        community settings, 86
    flow sheet, 38, 38*f*
    history of, 79–80
    process, 39
        EBP's role in, 365–366
        investigation of policy, procedure,
            protocol, 38–39
    project
        development, 372
        goals, 367
    outcomes management of, 35
    research design *vs.*, 180–181
    purpose of, 81
    vs. research and EBP, 82, 82*t*–83*t*
    settings, 85–86
    sources of, 82, 82*t*–83*t*
    thrusts of, 81
Quality Improvement/Quality Assurance
    (QI/QA) data, 341
quality initiative models, 372, 373
quality initiative project, 372
quality nursing care, 1, 3, 5
quality of care, 9, 10*t*
quantitative analysis, 319
    central tendency, 319
    definition, 302
    descriptive statistics, 305
    inferential statistics, 309–310
        analysis of variance (ANOVA),
            311–315
        chi-square, 309–310
        t-test, 310–311, 312*t*
    interval and ratio data
        central tendency, 305–306
        variability, 306–308
    measurement scales, 303–304

qualitative analysis *vs.*, 302
    reporting results of, 315
quantitative design, 172
quantitative evidence critique, 234–235
quantitative questions, 18
quantitative research, 35
    avoidance of moral/ethical questions, 122
    clarity of variables, 122
    correspondence with scientific method, 172
    critique process, 342
    data analysis, 208
    data collection methods, 207, 256, 265
    definition, 172
    definition of variable, 134
    evaluation, 337–338
    level of evidence, 48, 49*f*
    methods section of report, 160–161
    mixed method research, 201–205
    problem-statement components, 129–131
    vs. qualitative research methods, 191–192
    quality improvement projects *vs.*, 180–181
    report, 234–235
    research question, 127–128
    systematic review, 371
quantitative research design, 171–183
    characteristics, 172–174
    control, 180
    descriptive design, 174–175
    EBP considerations, 181
    experimental design, 175–176, 176*f*
    nonexperimental design, 176–177
    quality improvement projects and RCA,
        180–181
    quasi-experimental design, 178–180, 179*f*
    time-dimensional design, 177–178
    types, 172
quantitative studies
    design factors, 231–232
    measurement factors, 232
    population factors, 231
    practical factors, 2–233
quasi-experimental design
    collection of biophysiological data, 260
    overview, 178–180, 179*f*
    strength of evidence produced, 183
questionnaire/interview surveys, 246
    design tenets for, 250, 250*b*
    internal consistency, 379–381, 380*t*
    as method of data collection, 244, 249–252
    for mixed method research, 202, 206
    overview of, 249–251
    strength of, 252*t*
    types of responses, 251, 252*t*
questions
    to ask in research critique process, 326,
        327–328

closed-ended, 251, 253
closed-ended questions, 202
determination of type of evidence sought, 47
development of EBP questions, 108
development of questionnaires, 251
development of researchable questions,
    102–103, 263, 316
    examination through basic research, 349
    interviews, 253
    open-ended questions, 205–206, 251,
        253, 256
    as result of qualitative analysis, 316
    systematic reviews, 262
    use during problem/challenge analysis, 354
quota sampling, 230

R

random assignment, 227
random sampling, 160, 227–228
randomization
    as characteristic of quantitative research, 173
    control of variables through, 180
    quasi-experimental design lacking, 172,
        178–179
randomized control trial (RCT), 25, 176, 176*f*
range of data, 306
rank-order questions, 250
ranking, 251, 252*t*
rating scales, 251, 252*t*
rating tool, 371
ratio data
    central tendency, 305–306
    variability, 306–308
ratio-scaled continuous variable, 311
ratio scales, 304, 319
rationales for research method, 204–205
RCA. *See* root cause analysis
RCT. *See* randomized control trial
reality, 190
reasoning in EBP, 3–7, 7*f*
receiver operand characteristics (ROC), 286
    determining accuracy, 286–288, 294
    determining criterion-related validity of
        diagnostic exams, 291–292, 294
    SEM compared to, 286
recommendations, 330, 373
recruitment, 103–104
red flags
    application of EBP with research, 376
    data analysis, 319
    data collection, 265
    ethics, 112
    evidence overview, 54

red flags *(Continued)*
  literature review, 165
  mixed research, 183, 212
  qualitative research, 212
  quality improvement, 87
  quantitative research, 183
  reliability, validity, and trustworthiness, 295
  research, connections with EBP, 25
  research critique process, 342
  research overview, 72
  research terms and planning, 136
  sampling, 237
  translational research and practical
    applications, 360
redundancy, 196, 199–200, 233
reference librarian, 148
regulations for research, 99
reimbursement, Medicare/Medicaid, 66
relevance
  definition, 272
  relationship to validity and reliability, 272,
    273*f*, 294–295
  saturation as aspect, 195
reliability, 272
  as a concept, 274–275
  criteria for qualitative research, 200
  of data collection tools, 246, 265
  definition, 272, 294
  forms of
    interclass reliability, 276–281
    intraclass reliability, 281–288, 283*t*,
      286*t*–288*t*
  hemoglobin analyzer, 276–277
  implementation of results considering, 200
  quality assurance, 319
  questionnaires/surveys, 105
  relationship to validity and relevance, 272,
    272*f*, 288, 294–295
  reliance on in decision-making
    process, 294
  as test for trustworthiness, 272, 295
  theoretical calculation, 275, 275*f*
  as type of interclass reliability, 276
reliability check, 199–200
reliability coefficient
  calculation, 276
  development, 294
  uses, 294
removal treatment design, 178
repeatability, 274
reporting results
  publication, 109
  of qualitative analysis, 315
  of quantitative analysis, 315
representative sample, 225, 227

research, 366
  application in EBP, 8, 21, 365–384
  as aspect of critical decision making,
    348, 359
  assessing need for research in practice area,
    7–19
  basic *vs.* applied, 69–70
  current focus, 62
  data collection, 243–265
  definition, 6, 67
  documentation of projects, 25
  vs. EBP and quality improvement, 82,
    82*t*–83*t*
  EBP interconnectedness, 2–25, 367
  emerging ethical issues, 110–111
  environment for ethical research, 98–102
  ethics, 97–98
  evidence, importance of generating,
    19–21
  flowchart, 37, 37*f*
  forms of evidence, 12
  generally, 1–3
  historical perspective, 61–67, 63*f*, 64*b*, 65*b*
  impact on EBP, 20–21
  implementation science, 8
  learning, 22
  as means of quality care improvement, 348
  models and frameworks, 68
  need for quality nursing care, 1–3
  nurses' role, 22–23
  obstacles to use, 21–24
  outcomes, 8
  overview, 61–73
  posing forceful clinical question, 13–18
  priorities, 4
  publication of results, 109–110
  reasoning in EBP, 3–7, 7*f*
  relationship to theory and practice, 67–70
  relationship with EBP, 37, 37*f*
  requirements for review, 97
  researchable question development,
    102–103
  researchable topic development, 100–102
  responsibility to use research, 24
  sources, 70–71
  steps in process, 41
  theory and practice, 67–70
  as tool for advancing nursing, 366
  translational, 8
  validation of best practices, 68–69
research articles, 146–147, 146*b*
research course, 22
research critique, 323–342
  aspects of, 371
  considerations, 334*t*, 336*t*, 342

critically assessing knowledge for clinical
  decision making, 337–339
determination of sampling process,
  328, 337
EBP guidelines for reconciliation of
  contradictions, 340
elements, 325–330, 367–368
  data collection, 329
  literature review, 326–327
  purpose, 325–326
  recommendations, 330
  research design, 326
  research question/hypothesis, 327–328
  results, 329–330
  sampling, 328
mixed methods research, 339, 342
nurses' participation, 332, 367–368
nurses' role in, 332
process for conducting, 330–336
purpose, 330, 342
qualitative research, 338–339, 342
quantitative research, 337–338, 342
rationale, 323–325
rules for an ideal study, 336t
steps, 333
types, 325, 342
worksheet, 334t
research design
  about, 172
  consideration in data collection plan, 263
  critique process, 326
  quality improvement projects and RCA,
    180–181
  selection, 367
Research Factor Questionnaire, 72
research hypothesis, 133
research idea sources, 148–149
research librarian, 148
research management, 324
research methodologies, 35
research problem, 122–136
  about, 127
  defining variable, 134
  determination of significance, 124–125
  determination of timing of mixed methods
    of research, 206
  EBP considerations, 135
  factors determining researchability, 122
  feasibility, 125–126
  hypotheses, 132–134
  identifying, 122–124
  nursing research priorities, 126–127
  problem significance, 124–125
  problem statement, 122, 127
  research questions, 127–121, 132t

sources, 122
statement, 129–131, 132t
research process, 18
  definition of variable, 134
  literature review's role in, 144
  understanding for implementation, 366
research project
  gaps and consistencies in literature
    directing, 367
  limitations, 161
  methods, 160–161
  reporting results, 109, 315
  sample/population, 160
research purpose, 244, 263
research question, 127–131, 263
  critique process, 327–328
  data collection procedure answering, 244
  determination of timing of mixed methods
    of research, 206
  development, 102–103, 317–318, 372
  within EBP, 135, 328
  mixed method research as means of
    answering, 205–206
  problem statement
    components of, 129–131
    writing, 131, 132t
  as starting point for literature search,
    149–150
  as starting point for qualitative research,
    338
research report. *See also* research critique
  elements of, 325–330
  rules for an ideal study, 336t
research use, obstacles to, 366
research utilization, 9, 37
  as aspect of EBP, 18, 19b, 366
  definition of, 366
  EBP determination *vs.*, 368
  process, 368
researchable question development, 102–103
researchable topic development, 100–102
researcher
  data collection and analysis, 105–106
  expertise, 126
  interaction in qualitative research, 106
  interest and feasibility of problem, 126
  need for assistance, 126
  risk of researching certain topics, 101–102
  selection of data collection method, 263
  specification of sample criteria, 226
  topic development, 100–102
resources, 23–24, 353, 353f, 354–355
responsibility, 24
results of study, critique, 329–330
retrospective chart/record review, 245

retrospective correlational design, 175
retrospective design, 177–178, 183
retrospective study, 174
reversal treatment design, 178
review of research, 97
Revitalization Act of 1993, 62
rightness, 100
rights of human subjects, 97
rigor, 199–200, 202–203, 370
risks, 371
Robert Wood Johnson Foundation (RWJF)
    reports, 4
ROC. *See* receiver operand characteristics
root cause analysis (RCA), 181–181, 334t
"rule of 30," 232
RWJF reports. *See* Robert Wood Johnson
    Foundation reports

S

safety engineered devices (SEDs), 145
sample, 224
    decisions for EBP, 236
    evaluation of, 160, 225–226
    guidelines for critiquing, 234, 234t
    inclusion and exclusion criteria, 226
    purpose for use, 225
    relationship to population, 225f
sample size
    attrition, 179
    design factors, 231–232
    determining, 233
    evaluation, 160
    measurement factors, 232
    population factors, 231
    practical factors, 232–233
    in qualitative research, 196–197, 210
    qualitative *vs.* quantitative, 196, 210
    in quantitative research, 210, 234–235
sampling, 224–237
    critique process, 328, 337, 338
    methods, 230
    probability sampling strategies, 227–229
    purpose, 225
    strategies in qualitative research, 196–197
    whom to sample, 226–227
sampling bias, 225
sampling decisions for evidence-based
        project, 236
sampling error, 225
sampling plan, 224
San Jose State University, 331
sanitation reform, 61–62
saturation, 195

SBAR. *See* situation, background, assessment,
    recommendation
scientific ethics, 93
scientific inquiry concept, 366
scientific method, 172
scientific misconduct, 105–106
scientific validity, 102
screenings, 246
search engine, 150, 370
search process, literature
    assistance with, 370–371
    basics, 153–156
    differentiation of research from
        nonresearch articles, 146–147
    with search engines and databases, 150
    textbooks as sources, 157
searching, basics of, 153–156
secondary analysis, 176–177, 245
secondary data, 244–245, 258–259
selective coding, 195
self-confidence, 358
self-reporting strategies for data collection,
    248
self-study exercise, 317
SEM. *See* standard error of measurement
semantic differential response, 251, 252t
semi-structured interview, 197
sense of humor, 126
sensitivity
    acceptable values, 288
    definition, 272
    ROC tests, 287, 288t
    as test for trustworthiness, 272
    variables for, 287t
sentinel events, 181, 341
setting of data collection, 180, 255
short-term outcome, 355
Sigma Theta Tau International (STTI), 127, 365
significance of research problem, 124–125, 127
significance of results, 315
simple hypothesis, 134
simple random sampling, 228
situation, background, assessment,
    recommendation (SBAR), 20
Six Sigma, 20, 372
smallpox vaccination, ethics of research, 95
SMART for impact statements, 355
snowball sampling, 230
social experience, 190
social issues, 123
sound evidence, 44
sources of data, 244
Spearman-Brown prophecy formula, 281, 281f
specificity
    acceptable values, 288
    definition, 272

ROC tests, 287, 288*t*
  as test for trustworthiness, 272
  variables for, 287*t*
split-halves reliability, 279
SPSS. *See* Statistical Package for the Social
    Sciences
stability, 277–278
  outliers effect on, 307
stability coefficient, 278
stadiometer, 272
stakeholder, 124, 209
standard deviation, 319
  as measure of variability, 307, 307*f*
  use in SEM calculation, 294
standard error of measurement (SEM), 284,
    284*f*
  calculation, 294
  intraclass reliability and accuracy, 285–286
  ROC compared to, 286
standardized test, 253
Standards for Systematic Reviews (IOM), 261
standards implementation, 39
statistical difference, 310–312
Statistical Package for the Social Sciences
    (SPSS), 308
statistical software packages, 308, 310–312
statistical technique, 370
statistical validity, 289–291
  content-related validity, 292
  criterion-related validity, 289–291
  definition, 289
  pain scales, 293
  ROC analysis, 292
statistics
  application to multiple studies, 177, 332
  nurses' difficulty in evaluation, 335
steady diet approach, 332
storytelling, 195
stratified random sampling, 228–229
strength
  biophysiological data collection method,
    260*t*
  of evidence, 371–372
  focus groups, 255*t*
  interviews, 254*t*
  observation methods, 258
  questionnaires, 252*t*
  secondary (existing) data collection
    method, 259*t*
  tests, 249*t*
strength of recommendation for treatment
    (SORT) statement, 337
structured interviews, 197
STTI. *See* Sigma Theta Tau International
study recommendations, 330
study results, 329–330

subject heading search, 152
SUNY Downstate Medical Center, 52
support, 23–24
supporting information, 44
surgical holding area example, 206
SurveyMonkey, 250
synthesis analysis, 245
syphilis, research study, 96, 175
systematic analysis, 261–262
systematic decision making, 348, 359
systematic random sampling, 229
systematic review
  definition, 261, 370
  documentation of evidence, 265
  as investigation of practices, 370
  method of data collection, 244
  process, 261–262
  standards, 261
systolic pressure scores, 305

T

T1 research phase, 350
T2 research phase, 350
t-test, 161, 310–311, 312*t*, 319
table of random numbers, 228, 228*t*
target population, 224
TCAB. *See* transforming care at the bedside
technologies, 70
technology-savvy adolescents, 201
telephone survey, 250
temperature scale, 304
tenure, 107
test intervals, 180
testing of nominal data, 285
Testlink Test Collection Database (ETS), 248
tests
  definition of valid test, 288
  as method of data collection, 244,
    248–249
  ROC testing for accuracy, 286–288
  as test for trustworthiness, 272
textbooks, 157
thalidomide, 96
theoretical framework, 200, 338
theoretical sampling, 231
theory
  complexity and functionality of, 21
  definition, 67
  development, 174
  models and frameworks, 68
  relationship to research and practice, 67–70
theory approach model, 353, 359
theory of change, 352, 352*t*

time
as component of research design, 177
consideration in data collection plan, 263
consideration of information of clinical
questions, 17–18
required for biophysiological data
collection, 260*t*
required for observation methods of data
collection, 257
time constraints, 125, 175
time-dimensional design, 174, 177–178
time-series design, 178
timing, 285
title of study, 332
"to-do" list, 355, 356
*To Err Is Human: Building a Safer Health
System* (IOM), 66, 82
tools
preparation, 263, 265
test of consistency, 281
topic development, 100–102
transferability, 199–200, 210
transformative study design, 339, 342
transforming care at the bedside (TCAB), 20
translational research, 8, 348–351, 359
transplant recipient list, 303
treatment groups, 173
trends and events, 174
triangulation, 203–204, 211
TRIP database. *See* Turning Research Into
Practice database
true score, 274–275, 274*f*
true score variance, 275, 276, 278, 280,
282, 290
trustworthiness
of data, 272, 294, 295
of data analysis, 105–106
dependence on credibility of researcher,
100, 105–106
of focus group leader, 255
of qualitative research, 199–200
truth value of data, 199
Turning Research Into Practice (TRIP)
database, 51
Tuskegee Syphilis Study, 96, 175
2 × 2 design, 312
two-tailed test, 312, 314
two-way ANOVA, 310*t*, 311–312

U

*Unequal Treatment: Confronting Racial and
Ethnic Disparities in Health Care*
(Smedley, Stith, & Nelson), 157

United States Preventive Services Task Force
(USPSTF), 49, 49*f*, 50*f*, 52
University of Wisconsin-Extension, 352*t*, 354
untreated control group with pretest/posttest
design, 178
U.S. Department of Health and Human
Services (HHS)
Certificate of Confidentiality, 101
Code of Federal Regulations, 98
participant recruitment, 103–104
scientific misconduct, 105
U.S. Office of the Surgeon General, Division
of Nursing, 62
usefulness, 100, 110
USPSTF. *See* United States Preventive Services
Task Force

V

vaccination method, 95
valid consent, 103
validation of data, 199
validation of finding, 199
validation procedures, 208
validity, 288–293
coefficient, 291*t*
concurrent validity, 294
construct-related validity, 288–289, 292, 294
content-related validity, 288–289, 292, 294
criteria for qualitative research, 200
criterion-related validity, 289–292, 294
of data collection tools, 246, 265
definition, 272, 288, 294
implementation of results considering,
203–204
inherent validity coefficient, 292
logical, 288
quality assurance, 319
questionnaires/surveys, 252*t*
receiver operand characteristics (ROC),
291–292
relationship to reliability and accuracy, 288
relationship to reliability and relevance,
272, 273*f*, 294–295
reliance on in decision-making process, 294
statistical, 288–293
as test for trustworthiness, 272, 295
validity check, 199
validity coefficient
cross-validation techniques developing, 291
developing for criterion-related validity, 291
effects of variable scale, 291*t*
ROC developing, 291–292
use, 294

value neutral, 106
values theories, 93–94
variability, 306–308, 319
variables
 about, 122
 calculating sensitivity and specificity,
  286–287, 287t
 conceptional and operational
  definition, 134
 control in comparative design, 174
 control in research, 180
 control of extraneous variables, 174
 definition, 129–130
 explanation in descriptive design, 174
 independent and dependent, 127, 134–135,
  172, 309, 309t
 manipulation of independent variable,
  172–174
 in observation method of data
  collection, 256
 in predictive correlational design, 175
 in quantitative research, 134
 relationship investigated in correlation
  design, 175
 types of, 130
variance, 282, 306–307
veracity principle, 93
verification, 196
video recording, 105
visual analogue questions, 250
voluntary consent requirement, 97
vulnerability
 definition, 94
 effect of research, 100
 effect on recruitment of subjects, 103
vulnerable populations, 103
vulnerable subjects, 94
 protection of rights, 100
 recruitment and informed consent, 103

W. K. Kellogg Foundation, 127, 352t,
 353, 355
weight loss example, 128
weight scale, 304
within-stage methods, 205
wound care example, 172–176, 178–179
writing process
 about evidence, 141–165
 problem statement, 131, 132t
written instrument, internal consistency, 279

x^2 statistic, testing when both independent
 and dependent variable are nominal,
 309–310

Y

yearbooks, 259